BEFORE WE WERE

MONIQUE MEDVED

To the forgotten dreamer within you who found these pages—
They told you to "be realistic," but your wild heart was never meant for
ordinary. Dream louder, laugh till it hurts, and chase the life that makes your
pulse race, not just the one that pays the bills.

————

And to my mum, who waited fifteen years to hold this book in her hands. Thank
you for never letting that little dreamer inside me give up.

A NOTE TO READERS

This novel contains themes and content that may be distressing to some readers. These elements are integral to the story and are approached with care, but reader discretion is advised.

Sensitive Content Includes:
- Childhood trauma and domestic abuse (Chapters 15, 32, 51)
- Substance abuse and addiction (Chapters 30, 74)
- Sexual assault and its emotional aftermath (Chapter 25)
- Grief and loss of a parent (Chapter 1 & throughout)
- Verbal and physical altercations (Chapter 66)
- Open door intimate scenes (Chapters 48, 52, 57)
- Mental health struggles, including anxiety and depression (throughout)

If you find these subjects triggering, please prioritize your well-being and proceed with caution. The author has endeavored to address these themes with sensitivity and authenticity.

WELCOME TO EDEN MIXTAPE

Music has always been the heartbeat of my creative process. This playlist has been my lifeline through endless drafts, 4AM writing sessions, and moments of pure creative magic. Each song has fingerprints all over Eden's story. Though most tracks weren't playing on radios in the 2000s when our characters were living their lives, somehow they captured exactly what I needed to feel.

PROLOGUE

THERE ARE MOMENTS THAT ATOMIZE A PERSON—SCATTERING THEM SO wide that gathering the pieces seems like capturing starlight with bare hands.

Seconds. That's all it takes.

One choice. One cosmic blink, and certainty dissolves into smoke.

Time doesn't just break—it fractures completely.

Before stands forever separated from after, the boundary marked not by a gentle line but by a jagged barrier of broken glass and scattered memories.

When death arrives, it brings no patience for bargaining. It watches the raw, animal desperation of someone seeing their future burn. Death only laughs—cold and ancient—reminding that each heartbeat was merely borrowed, asking with cruel interest: *What did you do with my generous loan?*

It's where the realization hits you: life isn't possessed but temporarily held, like a library book with its due date written in vanishing ink. No one belongs to another forever. The universe simply allows brief custody, its permission already fading as it's granted.

These are the moments that transform. That demolish and reconstruct something entirely different—something permanently marked by the knowledge that everything changes between inhale and exhale.

Seconds. That's all it takes.

Blink.

Gone.

Only darkness remains, with echoes of words forever unspoken.

1

CHAPTER 1
THE SUMMER BEFORE SEVENTEEN
NORA

June 2006
15 years old

BREATHE.

Just breathe.

My fingers dig into my palms as I remind myself to do the one thing that should come naturally to anyone alive. But right now, my lungs feel like they're filled with cement, each breath a battle I'm losing.

Human?

My reflection in the window stares back, hollow-eyed and foreign.

Sure.

Functioning?

A bitter laugh threatens to escape.

Barely.

Who am I kidding? I'm a disaster. The panic attack I've been suppressing all morning claws at my chest, like a wild animal trying to break free. The room I've been stuck in for the last two and a half hours shrinks with each passing minute, the walls inching closer like a slowly tightening fist.

Condolences float around me like static, blending with the endless clinking of teacups. Each clink sends shards of sound through my skull, splintering what's left of my composure. The sound will haunt my dreams, I'm sure of it – the musical notes of mourning, the symphony of loss.

I need to get out of here.

Time has warped since the funeral this morning. Somehow, two hours feel like two lifetimes, while last week – the last time I heard Dad's laugh – passed in the blink of an eye. The only reason I know what day it is?

It's the day before my sixteenth birthday.

And now, it's also the day I said goodbye to dad forever.

Hugs come at me like waves, each one threatening to pull me under. The scent of perfume, aftershave, and sympathy surrounds me, a suffocating cloud of forced affection. The walls creep closer, the air growing thinner with each "I'm so sorry for your loss."

After two days of pretending I'm okay, I feel like a helium balloon cut loose from its string, floating away into nothingness.

Detached. Untethered. Lost.

Is this how every moment will feel now?

Trapped and numb?

My face aches from wearing this mask of composure, from murmuring polite thanks to people whose names blur together in my grief-addled mind.

It's not fine. Nothing about this is fine.

I'm in purgatory.

The living room of our small Boston home has become a sea of mourners, black-clad figures packed shoulder-to-shoulder like a murder of crows. Dad would've cracked a joke about it – something about penguins at a funeral. I can almost hear his laugh, the way his eyes would crinkle at the corners. The ghost of that sound makes my chest ache.

People get weird at funerals, hovering between awkward sympathy and desperate attempts at comfort. I just wish they'd say less. A simple nod would be better than the endless echoes of empty words reminding me he's gone.

Half the people here, I don't even know.

And I don't care to.

My eyes find Mom across the room, drawn to her like a compass finding north. Despite her puffy eyes and the exhaustion etched in the lines around her mouth, she's poised – a picture of quiet strength. Her black dress wraps around her like armor, elegant yet protective. She's beautiful, even in grief. Her dark hair is pinned back, soft curls falling loose in a way that looks effortless, but I know it took her three tries to get right this morning. I watched her hands shake as she fixed it, over and over, like getting her hair perfect could somehow make this day bearable.

I wish I could be like that.

Instead, I cling to the edges of the room, pressing my back against the cool wall, hoping no one sees me, talks to me, or—God forbid—tries to hug me again. Each embrace feels like sandpaper against my raw nerves.

By Mom's side is Lydia Sullivan, Dad's *"other wife"* as he used to joke. His voice echoes in my memory: *"Some men fear their wives having best friends. Me? I got a two-for-one deal with my family."* She's been a permanent fixture in our lives since Mom and Dad met.

Katherine Holt and Lydia Murphy were a packaged deal, inseparable from the start. Dad had known what he was signing up for when he proposed.

Since Dad's passing, Lydia has been an anchor. She's handled every-thing—the endless phone calls, funeral arrangements, even making sure we eat. It drives Mom crazy, this fierce efficiency born of love, but Lydia doesn't expect gratitude. She loved Dad like a brother, their bond forged through years of shared holidays and inside jokes.

When Mom called to tell her the news, Lydia was on the first flight from New York. She hasn't left Mom's side since, just like when they were teenagers.

For that, I'm grateful.

My gaze shifts to Ollie, my brother, hovering near the kitchen island. Ollie turns eighteen at the end of this year but somehow today he looks like an old soul and a kid at the same time. Most days, I'm the responsible one, while Ollie plays the part of a kid trapped in a growing athlete's body.

But now? Now he wields charm and humor like armor, each joke a shield against the pain I see flickering behind his eyes. He's been like that for as long as I can remember—quick with a laugh, never filtering his thoughts. The words tumble out of him like they can't wait to be heard, but never with cruelty. His humor brings light, even when it's self-deprecating.

It's his way of making everything seem okay, of holding our world together with duct tape and punchlines. But behind that easy smile, he feels everything with an intensity that scares me. He feels it all at once, and even now, on this impossible day, he's trying to make others laugh. I worry about him as much as he worries about me.

Dad was his hero, his compass, and losing him at seventeen is a wound Ollie won't talk about, maybe because he thinks it'll break me to see him break.

But I can handle it.

I can handle anything but this suffocating silence between us.

He's been carrying more weight than any teenager should. His broad shoulders, usually relaxed and confident, now bear the invisible burden of being the *"man of the house"*—a phrase I heard some well-meaning relative whisper earlier, making me want to scream.

Beside him stands Jake Sullivan. He and Ollie grew up like brothers, thick as thieves, always giving me grief for not being fast or strong enough to keep up with them.

Jake's head snaps up from his hushed conversation with Ollie, and our eyes meet across the room. He smiles, soft and boyish, his sapphire-blue eyes and sun-kissed chestnut hair catching the afternoon light in a way that shouldn't feel possible right now. For a moment, I see the ten-year-old boy who used to chase fireflies with me in the Sullivan's backyard.

But that was before.

Before everything changed.

I want to smile back, to give him some sign that I'm still me, still here. But the ache in my chest has become a permanent resident. It's been there for over a week, like a thorn lodged deep, impossible to ignore. Smiling only seems to make it worse. This morning at the cemetery plays on a loop in my mind, the raw pain tightening its grip around my heart.

"David Wells wasn't just a father or husband; he was a beacon of light," Lydia had said at the funeral, her voice steady but threaded with grief. Her words echo in my mind, cutting through the fog of numbness I've been hiding behind.

It's impossible to accept how quickly life can flip, how one moment you're arguing about curfew, and the next, the person you thought would always be there to argue with is just... gone.

No warning. No goodbye.

Just emptiness where his laughter used to be.

A sharp pang shoots through me, and suddenly, the room feels like it's closing in, the walls pulsing with each heartbeat.

Breathe, Nora.

Just breathe.

My heart races, a runaway train threatening to jump its tracks. It's the same every time the tears threaten to come—this wild panic, this desperate need to escape.

Get out. Now.

Run. Hide.

Jake's face flickers with concern, his eyes following me as I move. There's history in that look, years of shared summers and secret hideouts, of understanding without words. But I can't bear his kindness right now. I can't bear anyone's. I turn toward the hallway, away from the suffocating crowd and their endless condolences.

And those goddamn clinking teacups that won't stop their mournful symphony.

This isn't a nightmare. It's worse than that.

One I can't run from.

No one's entered the spare living room since I found Dad there eight days ago. Yet now, my feet move toward it, pulled by a force I can't fight against.

I take a jagged breath and slide open the glass doors, the smooth metal cool against my palm. The sound of the party—because that's what funeral receptions become, somehow—fades to a distant hum.

This was Dad's sanctuary. His library. His refuge. Shelves of books stretch across the room like embracing arms, interrupted only by carefully curated photographs. It should feel warm, alive with memories—but nothing makes a space emptier than the absence of the person who gave it life. The air is heavy with what's missing, thick with the ghost of his presence.

Dad was an English lecturer, the kind of man who could find poetry in a grocery list. Books weren't just his passion; they were his love language. He passed that love on to me early.

Sundays were our sacred ritual: just Dad and me, lost in stories that spanned from Siddhartha to Nicholas Sparks. He never judged my teenage romance phase, just smiled and said, *"Every great story is a love story at its heart, Leni."*

Those quiet afternoons, sharing passages and possibilities, are what I'll miss most. Dad was my greatest cheerleader, the only one who ever truly believed I could make it as a writer. That dream feels further away now than ever before.

The hush of the room wraps around me as the door slides shut, muffling the sounds of forced normalcy outside. The photos on the walls catch my eye, each one a snapshot of a life I took for granted. My fingertips graze the frames like I'm reading braille, trying to decode the stories behind each frozen moment.

There's Mom in Paris, caught mid-laugh with a chocolate-smeared croissant in front of the Eiffel Tower on their honeymoon. Her hair was longer then, wild and free like her smile. Ollie beams from another frame, his first football uniform hanging loose on his lanky thirteen-year-old frame. And there—my heart catches—I am at six, gap-toothed and glowing, clutching my first poetry competition certificate. Dad helped me write that poem—a simple ode to the sun and moon, to light and darkness, to the dance of day and night.

"Sometimes the simplest truths are the most profound, Len," he'd said, helping me practice my reading. Now the memory of his voice feels like a punch to the gut.

Then there's the last summer at the Sullivan lake house, one of the rare photos where Dad allowed himself to be captured instead of playing photographer. He was always behind the camera, preserving our moments while staying safely removed from them.

"Remember, my little love," he'd said, his voice carrying across the water as I sat on the dock with him, "life is just an accumulation of micro-moments. If we're not present for them, we'll miss the beauty of a moment we'll never get back."

His words echo now, bittersweet and sharp as broken glass. He was right—when a moment's gone, it's gone forever. Memories don't stay neatly contained; they ebb and flow like tides, dragging you into seas of either joy or sorrow. Loss sharpens their edges, turns even the happiest memories into weapons that cut when you least expect it. The moments we lose hurt because they remind us how precious they were to begin with.

My throat tightens, tears pricking my eyes, but I blink them back.

My gaze drifts to the floor—the exact spot where I found him. My feet are rooted, frozen in place. And just like that, I'm back there again.

Eight days ago.

My voice calling his name as I walked through the door, receiving only silence in return. The casual push of the spare living room door revealing what my mind still struggles to process.

Dad on the floor, unnaturally still. Time suspends as my brain frantically tries to make sense of the scene—this can't be happening—but my body understands immediately. My knees buckle. My lungs forget how to draw breath. My hand reaches for my phone while some distant part of me is already screaming.

I don't remember dialing 911, just fragments of my own voice—broken, desperate—explaining what I've found. The operator's calm instructions seem to come from another universe while I kneel beside him, touching his hand, still warm but wrong.

Behind me, Mom appears in the doorway. Her gasp slices through the room before morphing into a sound I'll never forget—not quite a scream, not quite a sob, but something primal that echoes the exact shattering I feel inside.

Ollie arrives next, summoned by the commotion. He crumples to the floor, whispering prayers to a God he never believed in before this moment.

The paramedics burst in—a blur of uniforms and equipment. Hands on my shoulders pull me back. "Let us try to save him," a voice says, but something in their tone tells me they already know.

My body trembles as I watch them work, going through motions that seem increasingly futile with each passing second. I stand there, holding Mom up as she shakes against me, both of us suspended between hope and the terrible truth my body already knows.

He's gone.

The memory releases me and I'm back in the present, staring at that same spot, now empty but somehow still the center of a universe that collapsed eight days and eight centuries ago.

I shake myself from the memory, trying to claw my way back to the present. The late afternoon sun filters through the library's shutters, painting streaks of gold across Dad's desk. Summer has arrived, its warmth usually a promise of freedom and laughter. But not this year. This year, it feels like a cruel joke.

The counselors Mom forced me to see said grief comes in stages, as if it's a process you can check off like a to-do list for heartbreak. Five neat little boxes to tick: denial, anger, bargaining, depression and acceptance. But they don't tell you how these stages crash into each other like waves, how you can feel all of them at once until you're drowning.

They said I'm strong, resilient, and a survivor.

What they don't understand is that surviving isn't a choice.

It's instinct.

Like breathing when your lungs are on fire or clawing at the surface when you're drowning. It doesn't feel brave. It feels relentless.

Because finding Dad will go down as one of the worst days of my life. But the hardest?

That was twelve days ago.

The day something inside me shattered beyond repair. The day I became a ghost inside my own body.

The irony doesn't escape me—I was already mourning one death when another came to claim what little remained of me. Dad never knew about those darkest hours, about what happened that night.

How could he? I became an expert at smiling through fractured places, at carrying wounds no one could see.

The weight of untold truths clings to me like a second skin—dark and suffocating. Secrets are their own kind of grief—slow, corrosive, isolating. They carve you up piece by piece until you're not sure who's left. They leave you stranded in a loneliness no one else can see.

Now I stand in the doorway of two separate hells. One I can share— the public grief of a daughter who found her father—and one I carry alone, a private devastation no one suspects lies beneath.

But still, you move forward. Because you have to.

Tomorrow will come, indifferent and unyielding. Life will go on, dragging you with it whether you're ready or not.

It won't be the same.

It'll never be the same.

But it will go on.

And somehow, so will I.

CHAPTER 2
DON'T FORGET THE CURLY FRIES

NORA

June 2007

PRESENT DAY

"Is there anything else?" the waiter asks, his voice gentle, like he can sense the empty chair at our table. Maybe he recognizes us. Or maybe he just sees what everyone else does—a family with a missing piece.

The Roadhouse Diner used to be our pit stop, our tradition, our marker that summer had officially begun. Dad discovered this place before Ollie and I existed, dragging Mom here on their first road trip to Lake Eden. The curly fries became our ritual—extra mustard on the side because Dad swore they weren't the same without it, his eyes crinkling at the corners as he dunked each perfectly spiraled fry.

But today, none of us mention the fries.

Two years.

That's how long it's been since we've made this drive, since everything changed. Walking back into this life feels like trying to wear a coat that doesn't fit anymore—the sleeves too short, the shoulders too tight, everything slightly wrong in ways I can't fix.

We don't need menus here. After years of visits, our orders live in muscle memory. But even though I know what I want, nothing about this moment feels familiar.

Everything is quieter. Heavier.

The waiter stands there, his notepad in hand, freckled face open and kind. He can't be much older than sixteen, probably a summer hire who doesn't understand why we're all holding our breath. His eyes flit between Ollie, Mom, and me, searching for someone to take charge.

My chest tightens, but I force my voice steady. "You know what? Let's add the curly fries. A double serving."

"And mustard. On the side," Ollie chimes in, his tone artificially bright, like he's trying to patch a hole in the universe with cheerfulness alone.

"Forgot our manners, did we?" Mom says, her eyebrow lifting as she gives Ollie a look that's so achingly normal it hurts.

"Please, good sir," Ollie adds with an exaggerated flourish, handing back the menus we never opened. For a moment, he sounds exactly like Dad, and I watch Mom's fingers tighten around her glass.

The waiter grins, oblivious to our private pain. "Great choice. Can't go wrong with the curly fries." He jots down our order and disappears, leaving us in the kind of silence that feels too big for this small booth.

Mom sits across from Ollie and me, her lemonade leaving condensation rings on the table. She's trying to hold it together, and for the most part, she's succeeding. But I know better. I've heard her crying late at night, muffled sobs that seep through the walls like ghost stories. I've caught her brushing away tears when some old show she and Dad used to watch comes on TV, her hand moving so quickly you'd miss it if you weren't looking.

I lost my father, but she lost her best friend. Her soulmate. The love of her life. I can't even imagine what that kind of pain feels like. Not yet.

And still, she's Mom of the Year.

She juggles her job as head of Pediatrics at Boston General with the precision of a surgeon and the grace of a dancer. She's at every one of Ollie's football games, channeling Dad's enthusiasm into her cheers. She still gets croissants with me on Sunday mornings at our favorite bakery, just like she and Dad used to. She's Wonder Woman, and I don't know how she does it.

People say I look like her, though I've got more of Dad's spirit. Our similarities paint an obvious picture—the same oval face, the same habit of tucking hair behind our ears when we're nervous. But the differences tell their own story. Mom's hair is lighter, with honey highlights that catch the light; mine is rich chocolate brown, like Dad's was. Her eyes are deep brown, while mine are Dad's straightforward green. Mom's petite frame carries a natural elegance, while I inherited Dad's athletic build— not that I've ever used it for anything remotely athletic. That's Ollie's department.

"Have you talked to the boys yet?" Mom asks, breaking the silence as she sets her glass down, leaving another perfect ring on the table.

Ollie doesn't look up from his phone, thumb scrolling mindlessly. "Texted Nate earlier. Told him we'd be there by three. Haven't heard back."

Of course, Nate hasn't responded.

His name pulls at something in my chest, a string I can't stop tugging even though I know it'll only unravel me more. It's stupid, really. I know nothing will ever happen between us, but there's a gravity I can't escape. In Nate's eyes, I'll always be "little Leni", the nickname Dad gave me when I was small enough to ride on his shoulders.

I've spent years trying to prove I'm more than that, more than just the kid sister of the group. Whether it was climbing the highest tree or sneaking out past curfew, I was always trying to keep up, to be seen. Nate always had to save me. And he was always annoyed about it.

Even now, just the thought of him makes my pulse quicken, a betrayal of every promise I've made to myself. After what happened last year—the silence, the unanswered messages, the empty chair at Dad's funeral—I should be over him. I should be angry.

But I'm not.

And I hate that.

"Have you spoken to Jake, Nora?" Mom asks, studying me with that knowing look that makes me feel transparent.

"He messaged me this morning. Wished us a safe trip."

"I heard he's been offered a scholarship to Duke," Mom says, her lips curving into that proud smile she always saves for the Sullivan boys. "And made captain of the swim team, too."

"That kid was a fish in a past life," Ollie pipes up, rolling his eyes. "I mean he's got an ego the size of a whale, so it fits."

"Says the guy who refers to himself as the GOAT," I shoot back, smirking.

"My ego is perfectly under control, thank you very much," Ollie retorts, puffing out his chest.

"Well, your head begs to differ."

"My head is symmetrical and scientifically proven to be the perfect size," he argues with mock seriousness.

Mom shakes her head, but I catch the ghost of a smile. "Well, anyway, Jake's worked hard for it. Lydia and Scott will be thrilled that at least one of them is going to college." She pauses, wincing slightly at her own words.

I glance at her but stay quiet. She's not wrong, though. The Sullivan family story reads like a tale of two worlds. Ollie and I grew up in a home where laughter echoed through every room, where security came from more than just a bank account. Mom and Dad, both proudly middle-class, poured their hearts into jobs they loved without letting work over-shadow family. Sunday dinners, chaotic game nights, and bedtime *"I love yous"* were our constants—our foundations.

The Sullivans lived a different reality. Sure, Nate and Jake had the kind of life that teenage dreams are made of—shiny cars, MTV-worthy parties, and a house that belonged in architectural magazines. But beneath that glossy surface, I'd seen the fractures. Without Lydia's grounding presence, those boys might have become exactly what everyone expected—entitled trust fund kids wearing designer labels like armor.

But they didn't. They became something else entirely.

Scott Sullivan's empire stretched back generations, old money that whispered of privilege and power. I'd be lying if I said I hadn't wondered, at least once, what it would be like to grow up without watching your parents check price tags or calculate monthly budgets. But mostly, I was grateful for our life. Dad taught us hard work builds character, and that lesson stuck.

Jake, though—he was different. Even with privilege cushioning his fall, he earned everything that mattered. The Duke scholarship wasn't bought; it was won through countless pre-dawn practices and late-night training sessions. Jake didn't just swim; he became the water itself, moving through it like he'd found his true element. Watching him glide through a pool was like witnessing poetry in motion, every stroke purposeful, every turn precise.

My phone buzzes and Jake's messages light up my screen like small beacons of normalcy.

Jake
How far are you guys?

Me
About 28 minutes out.

The instant response makes me smile, a rare genuine one these days.

Jake
That is oddly specific.

Me
Well, now it's 27 minutes and 47 seconds.

Jake
I'll be seeing you in 27 minutes and 33 seconds then :)

Jake's messages always have this effect. His boundless Labrador-like enthusiasm is infectious, even through a screen.

Me
You better get ready to get your ass handed to you in UNO comps this year.

Jake
HA! You are dreaming, sunshine. I will be the only one doing the ass-kicking. Yours truly, the (reigning) heavyweight UNO champion of the world.

Jake
Drive safe. See you soon x

As we wind through town toward the lake, the transition from seaside to lakeside unfolds like a familiar story. The salt air gradually gives way to the earthy perfume of redwood trees embracing the lake. This aroma, rich and grounding, whispers of home and belonging. I roll down the window, letting the humid air wash over my face, the familiarity of it cleansing something deep inside me—a yearning I've carried since last summer without knowing it.

The long driveway appears ahead, concealed from the street like a secret passage. The house and its lakefront backdrop wait five hundred miles away, hidden from view until that final turn. Despite the deep sense of rightness that comes with returning, an undercurrent of unease reminds me how much has shifted. The lake house stands solid and unchanged, but everything else feels different.

The second Ollie kills the engine, the front door flies open and Lydia bursts out, already barrelling down the stairs toward us with the kind of energy that makes exhaustion look like a foreign concept.

"Oh, my God! You're finally here!" She reaches for Mom's door before we can unbuckle. "I've been watching for you since breakfast!"

"Oh God, Lydia, my neck. Hold on will you. Let me get out of—"

"I'm just so happy to see you all!"

I watch these two women reunite and something in my chest loosens. Their friendship exists outside of time, untouched by distance or circumstance. It's the kind of bond that makes you believe in permanence—the way Mom has Lydia, and Lydia has Mom, constant as the tides.

Some friendships stand immovable against time's current. Like the one I share with the blue-eyed boy standing at the top of the porch steps, his smile catching the light like the sun on water. Jake's presence has always been a constant, especially when everything else spins off axis.

This summer stretches before me like a blank page.

It's a new chapter because, this summer, things will be different.

I will be different.

The girl who left Eden two years ago died with her father. It's time to discover who she's become—and maybe find a way to make peace with the boy who never showed up to say goodbye.

CHAPTER 3
BUSTED
NATE

"Nate, where the fuck are you?" Jay's voice grates against my already frayed nerves, each word like sandpaper on raw skin.

"I'm about ten minutes out." My jaw clenches tight enough to crack teeth, the muscle twitching beneath my skin like a live wire.

"Hurry the fuck up, man. They're waiting and these people don't like waiting." The panic in his voice feeds the rage simmering beneath my skin, a pot about to boil over.

"Jay, relax." The words come out low, dangerous—a rattlesnake's warning before the strike.

"Relax? I'll relax when I'm dead, Nate. Which is going to be in about two minutes if you're not here."

"I'm hanging up now."

I end the call with enough force to crack my screen, watching as notifications flood the display like vultures circling prey. Missed calls, texts, demands piling up like bodies in a mass grave. Another buzz cuts through the silence—Jake, adding his voice to the chorus of people who think they own a piece of me.

> **Jake**
> Seriously, where the fuck are you?

> **Jake**
> Mom wants you home NOW.

> **Jake**
> Stop being a dick and reply to her calls.

17

I ignore it, letting it join the dozen other unopened messages from him, Mom, and Farrah. Farrah's name on my phone screen feels like a bad taste I can't wash out. I still don't know why I've let her cling to me for this long.

The morning started with me hauling ass out of the house, escaping Mom's endless nagging about the Wells coming back this summer. She's been hammering on about it for days like it's some impending apocalypse, and just the thought of sharing space with them all summer makes my skin crawl.

Last time I saw the Wells family was nearly two years ago. The memory hits like a sucker punch. I was a fucking wreck when David died, and the guilt of blowing off his funeral still eats at me like acid in my gut. They're probably all still pissed about it, but showing up wasted and ready to explode would have been worse. At least, that's the lie I keep feeding myself to get through each day.

The truth sits heavier, a weight pressing against my lungs: I couldn't handle it.

Couldn't stomach a world without David, the one person who saw past my bullshit and still gave a damn.

Couldn't bear seeing Nora broken when I was already shattered beyond repair.

The Mustang roars to life under my hands, the engine's growl matching the chaos in my head as I point it toward the other side of Lake Eden. Today, my thoughts are a war zone, memories exploding like land mines with every breath. The human mind is a torture chamber, stuck on replay, obsessing over every failure, every promise broken like bones that never set right.

I try to steady myself because that's what everyone expects—good old Nate, always in control, always holding it together. But with everything I'm walking into, the tension builds like a sealed pressure cooker about to blow. Memories of two summers ago flood in, sharp as broken glass and twice as dangerous. I crank the radio, desperate to drown out the chaos, and fucking *"Save Me"* by Remo starts playing. I laugh, but it's a sound that would make devils flinch. The universe really knows how to twist the knife.

The bait shop looms ahead, its peeling Tack and Bait sign swaying in the humid breeze like a hangman's noose. Jay's already outside, a nervous shadow pacing the warped boards of the porch. His fingers drum against his thigh in a frantic rhythm that matches my pulse.

"About fucking time," he snaps as I kill the engine, but the fear in his eyes undermines the bite in his words.

We push past aisles of fishing gear, hooks glinting like tiny daggers in the dim light. The air is thick enough to choke on—a toxic cocktail of saltwater, mildew, and something darker. A tank bubbles in the corner, bait fish swimming endless circles, waiting for death. Felix, another lost soul caught in this web, cracks open the back room door. The hinges cry out like they're warning us to run. Inside, six of Monty's crew crowd around a plastic table that's one breath away from collapse, playing poker with the kind of stakes that end in blood.

The door snaps shut behind us with the finality of a coffin lid.

"Well, well, look what the country club dragged in." Monty's voice slithers through the stale air, each word dripping with a disdain that makes my skin crawl. He's all sharp edges and bad endings—a late twenties psycho with a body count inked on his arm like notches on a bedpost. Cross him and you're either out cold or becoming his next tattoo.

He pops a beer with his teeth and spits the cap at my feet. The metallic ping against the concrete floor echoes like a warning shot. "You rich fuckers think the world's got nothing better to do than wait on you, huh, Preppy?"

The rage in my chest coils tighter. "Family emergency," I lie through clenched teeth, tasting copper where I've bitten the inside of my cheek.

A smirk twists his lips as he stands, looming close enough for me to catch the stale stench of beer and weed and something darker—something that smells like violence waiting to happen.

"Family? Must be nice having one. Never knew mine. Didn't have a daddy to spoon-feed me gold and grease my path to the Ivy League."

His eyes glint with the kind of madness that's earned him every one of those body-count tattoos. The room crystallizes into sharp focus. Something dark inside me smiles at the odds: just Jay and me against his gang of six. The kind of math that ends in hospital visits.

"Are we gonna wax poetic about my so-called privileged childhood or your daddy issues, or are you gonna take the money?" My voice cuts through the thick tension like a blade, each word dripping with contempt. Part of me wants him to snap, to give me an excuse to paint these walls red.

He laughs, the sound low and menacing as a growling beast. "You got some balls on you, Preppy. Showing up late, making us wait, and now pushing me to hurry?" His eyes catch the fluorescent light like broken glass. "You're playing with fire."

The room holds its breath. Even the ceiling fan seems to slow its lazy spin. I feel Jay trembling beside me, his fear a tangible thing in the heavy air.

The attack comes faster than my anger-dulled reflexes can track. Monty's hand wraps around my throat like a python, squeezing until black spots dance at the edges of my vision. The rough concrete wall slams against my back, but I barely feel it. Part of me welcomes the pain, craves it even.

"Don't you fuck with me or my time again, you ungrateful little shit. Got it?" His breath hits my face, hot and sour with beer.

I stay silent—not from fear, but because the darkness inside me is enjoying this too much. Some sick part of me wants him to squeeze harder, to give me an excuse to unleash the hurricane building in my chest.

"Whoa, whoa, hey, Monty." Jay's voice wavers like a candle in the wind. "He screwed up, but he's got the cash. It won't happen again."

Monty's eyes narrow, shooting Jay a look that could strip paint from walls. Jay shrinks back, but his mouth keeps running, desperation making him brave or stupid—probably both.

"We'll be early next time," Jay stammers, words tumbling out like dice on a rigged table.

The grip on my throat loosens just enough for me to drag in a ragged breath. The room spins back into focus, sharp and mean as a knife's edge.

"Where's the fucking money, kid?" The word 'kid' comes out like poison.

I fish out an envelope from my back pocket, movements deliberately slow. Every eye in the room tracks my hand like sharks scenting blood. "It's all there—$1,500." Each word scrapes past my bruised throat.

"You owe me another grand by the end of the week for wasting my fucking time." His voice drops lower, a promise of violence wrapped in velvet.

"Felix," Monty barks, jerking his chin at me like I'm garbage to be taken out. "Hand him his shit."

Felix, looking young enough to still believe in redemption, passes over the stash with trembling fingers. I grab it, the weight of bad decisions heavy in my palm.

"And Preppy," Monty calls out as we turn to leave, his tone mocking but promising blood, "don't pull that shit again. Not even thirty seconds late next time, or I won't be this nice."

The muggy summer air hits like a slap when we stumble outside, reality crashing back in waves. My throat throbs in time with my pulse, a rhythm of rage and adrenaline.

20

"Are you out of your fucking mind?" Jay explodes the moment we're clear of the shop, his voice cracking like thin ice. He runs shaking hands through his hair, leaving it standing up like a startled cat. "What the fuck, Nate? Are you trying to get yourself killed?"

I stride toward the Mustang, the rage still singing in my veins, drowning out his words. The stash burns in my pocket like a guilty secret.

"Shut up and get in the car," I snap, my patience a frayed wire sparking dangerously. "I don't have time for this."

"I don't know what's got you so messed up lately, but you need to sort your shit out." Jay jogs to keep up, his finger trembling as he points back at the shop. "That was too fucking close. Like, funeral close."

"You looking for a medal for the world's best friend or something?" The words come out sharp enough to draw blood, but underneath them lurks the acid taste of guilt. Jay's the closest thing to a real friend I've got, and here I am, treating him like everyone else treats him—like he's disposable.

"You're being a bigger dick than usual, you know that?" Fear makes him brave, makes him say what others won't.

I know, and it's not the first time I've heard that today.

"Do you need a ride or not?" I slip into the driver's seat, tossing the stash into the console.

"For fuck's sake," Jay mutters, slamming the car door hard enough to rattle teeth. "What's going on with you?"

"I don't pry into your life, so don't pry into mine." My voice comes out arctic, warning him off.

"Yeah, well, your 'not' friend just saved your ass back there." The 'not' drips with sarcasm.

"I had it handled." I reply dryly, the ignition roaring to life like an angry beast.

"Handled? Looked more like you were about to hand over your ass to that fucking psycho. Willingly." Jay slumps in his seat, the adrenaline crash hitting him hard.

A silent question hangs between us like a noose: what if I had let go? What if I had let Monty finish what my own self-destruction started?

We drive through Eden's south side in silence heavy as death itself. These streets tell their own stories—broken windows, peeling paint, dreams dying slow in the summer heat. Jay's life, marked by hard knocks and savage breaks, sits in stark contrast to my gilded cage up north. I pull up to his place, a rundown dump that makes the bait shop look somewhat classy. The screen door hangs crooked on its hinges, like everything else in his world—slightly broken but still hanging on.

"Thanks for the ride," Jay mutters as he reaches for the door handle. His shoulders slump with exhaustion, or maybe it's just the weight of everything else he carries.

"How's your mom?" The question slips out before I can stop it, betraying more care than I want to show. Behind the walls of their house, I can almost smell the lingering ghosts of her latest binge.

He smirks, a flash of the smart-ass kid still alive beneath the scars. "Thought we weren't prying?"

Something in my chest loosens slightly, and the corner of my mouth twitches upward despite myself. "She's hanging in there. Better, I guess. You know how it is."

And I do know —his mom, a perpetual disaster, loves him in her own fractured way. She battles her demons and loses to heroin's sweet promises more often than not, leaving Jay to pick up the pieces. Just like I picked up my own mother's pieces after dad's rages, though our broken pieces came from different kinds of battles.

"Take care, Jay." The words carry more meaning than I'll ever admit. In another life, in another Eden, we might have been real brothers instead of just broken boys holding each other's secrets. He cracks a smile that makes him look his age for once—seventeen, and somehow still undefeated despite everything.

"You're still a dick." There's affection buried in the insult, like a flower growing through concrete.

"And you're still the pain in my ass I can't shake," I call after him.

Without turning back, Jay sticks his middle finger in the air, waves it like a victory flag, and I can't help but laugh.

I linger until he's safely inside, watching the screen door swing shut behind him. The laugh fades as quickly as it came, replaced by a familiar heaviness. Some people you can't save, no matter how much you want to. Sometimes all you can do is watch them burn and hope they rise from their own ashes.

My phone buzzes again, the screen lighting up with my mother's name like an accusation. The brief moment of lightness with Jay evaporates, reality crashing back in. Time to face the music at home, where the Wells family waits like an approaching storm I can't outrun.

Pulling into my driveway, dread hits me like a physical blow. The familiar Jeep wedged between the luxury cars stands out like a wound, and my heart slams against my ribs in recognition. My breathing grows shallow, thoughts spiraling into chaos as reality crashes in. The bruises

22

from Monty's grip throb in time with my pulse, a reminder of the violence I just walked away from. Now I'm walking into a different kind of danger altogether.

My phone lights up again with another barrage of texts, each one stoking the rage already burning in my chest.

Farrah
Why are you not answering my calls?

Less than thirty seconds later...

Farrah
Babe, I miss you.

Farrah
Come over so I can show you just how much.

I scoff and chuck my phone onto the passenger seat like it's contaminated.

Not today, Farrah.

Not when I need my head clear, or as clear as it can be with the chaos already screaming inside it. I can't deal with her manufactured drama or anyone else's bullshit until I've dulled these razor edges of anxiety and silenced the demon that's been gnawing on my brain like a starved rat.

It's nearly five, and I haven't returned any calls or texts all day. The moment I step inside, the cold war at home will resume—nothing said aloud in front of guests, all the family drama saved for behind closed doors like the good little actors we are. The Wells family's presence turns our usual dysfunction into a command performance.

Taking a deep breath, the first real one of the day, I pocket the stash and force myself toward the front door. With each step, the laughter and conversations inside amplify like a crescendo of impending doom, squeezing my chest tighter. The bruises from Monty's grip ache with every breath, but they're nothing compared to the pain I know is waiting inside.

Let's fucking do this.

Then, a familiar voice cuts through the rest, pulling tighter on my already taut nerves like a violin string about to snap. I'm almost at the door when it swings open.

"I'll be right there, just need to grab my—" Her words halt with a sharp intake of breath that mirrors my own.

23

Before I even process it, my body reacts on pure instinct, lunging forward to catch her as she stumbles on the step.

She's safe in my arms, and suddenly the world begins to spin when she looks up at me.

Time warps as I hold her, everything slowing to a crawl like honey dripping from a spoon. The adrenaline that was surging through my veins from Monty's threats shifts into a different kind of heat, spreading wherever our bodies connect. She's different now, changed in ways that make my throat go dry and my pulse spike.

Holding her feels like revisiting an old favorite book; the cover's altered, the pages more worn, but the words inside still grip you with the same fierce intensity. Her hair, scented like honey and summer winds and tossed into a messy knot, hints at the beautiful chaos I know defines her. Gone is the awkward girl in baggy clothes. She's... stunning.

Christ. Stop it.

The crop top she wears exposes her lower back, my arms cradling her waist, skin against skin, igniting unwanted, dangerous desires that threaten to consume what's left of my self-control. I can't pull my eyes away from hers—those emerald depths still blaze with the wild spirit I remember, promising secrets and depths I'm aching to explore but damn well know I shouldn't.

"You missed a step," I say, a slight grin managing to break through, muscle memory of catching her like this a hundred times before making my hands remember places they shouldn't.

"Wouldn't be the first time," she replies, her smile disarming every defense I've built, gripping me for a second too long. I notice her catch her breath. I hope it's from my hold and not the stumble, then immediately hate myself for hoping.

"Guess some things never change," she adds, and the double meaning in her words hits like a punch to the gut, reminding me of everything I've broken between us.

We steady ourselves, though every cell in my body protests as she straightens up, and I do the same. Then something hits the porch with a clatter that sounds like a gunshot in the charged silence.

Shit.

Before I can move, she bends down, and I force my gaze away from the curves her movement reveals, focusing instead on the small bags of weed she's now holding in hands that once knew every callus on mine. Disappointment flickers across her face—a look that cuts deeper than any blade.

Thank fuck it's just the weed and not the pills.

24

Footsteps approach, and tension mounts like a storm about to break as my mom's voice carries from inside. "Nate? Is that you?"

I'm screwed.

So fucking screwed.

"You finally decided to come home, did you?" Mom's voice slices through the tension like a knife.

Nora presses against me, her proximity sending chaotic signals through my brain like fireworks. I yearn to touch her, to trace the lines of who she's become, but she leans back against me, holding out the bag of weed for me to take. Our hands brush as I take it, her warmth penetrating every fiber of my being like a brand. My eyes drift traitorously to the heart-shaped birthmark just above her lower back, visible beneath her crop top. She's grown up in more ways than one, and each way is another nail in my coffin.

"Nate was just helping me with my bags," Nora covers smoothly, her lie as practiced as my own. The ease of her deception triggers a memory of us covering for each other countless times before, back when we were partners in crime instead of whatever the hell we are now.

"Oh, good. Nate, can you get the rest of Nora's stuff to her room and help Kat too, please?"

"Sure," I manage, a half-smile playing on my lips as I stash the weed back in my pocket, trying to ignore how her presence has already dismantled every wall I've spent years building.

Mom heads back inside, her voice trailing like smoke. "Kat, let's open that Rosé while we cook," she calls back, leaving us alone in a silence that feels like a loaded gun.

"Listen—" I start, but Nora strides past me like I'm nothing but air, dismissive of the moment we just shared, of the electricity still crackling between us.

She grabs a bag from the backseat, and I pick up the other, watching her movements like a man memorizing his own execution. My gut sinks as I realize she's pissed, and this new Nora's anger feels dangerous as a hurricane on the horizon.

"You're just going to ignore me?" The irritation in my voice weighs heavy as chains, and I try to catch her eye, desperate for some sign of the girl I used to know. I shouldn't be irritated—I've got no right—but I am.

"Learned from the best," she fires back, her sass catching me completely off guard, sharp as a blade between ribs. There's something thrillingly different about her now, and damn if I don't find myself drawn to it. She's always been fiercely independent, but this version of

Nora seems to have no use for me. Can't say I blame her, but it doesn't quench my craving for her attention one bit.

"Are you going to rat me out?" I probe, genuinely curious as we retrace our steps, each one feeling like walking deeper into quicksand. The question hangs between us, loaded with two years of silence and suspicion.

"What am I, five?" There's a new edge to her that I can't help but admire—confident, bold, lethal. She never hesitated to call me out on my bullshit, even as kids, but now her words carry weight like ammunition.

She halts suddenly, almost causing me to bump into her again, and the near contact sends electricity racing down my spine. Her piercing gaze locks on mine, stirring a flutter of unease in my gut that feels like falling. I'm on edge, unsure of what's coming next but certain it'll leave a mark.

"You know there are better things to spend your money on, right?" Her voice drops low, private—a reminder of conversations we used to have when she was the only one who could talk sense into me.

"I already have enough Rolexes."

What. The. Fuck. Nate?

The words come out before I can stop them, dripping with the kind of privileged arrogance I hate in others. I want to snatch them back the moment they leave my mouth.

Her eye roll is monumental, like watching someone dismiss your entire existence, and she spins away, continuing forward with the grace of someone who knows exactly how to wound.

"Look, I just don't need you causing issues with my mom or Jake. It's nothing, really. I sometimes just need to—"

She pauses again, her shoulders rigid as steel. Before she even turns, I sense the anger radiating from her like heat from a fire.

"You know, I'm trying really hard to see things from your perspective, but I can't quite jam my head that far up my ass." Her words are a soft hiss as she steps closer, invading my space until all I can smell is her honey-sweet perfume mixed with summer air. "Don't worry, Nate, your little secret? It's safe with me."

The pat on my chest feels like a brand, her smug smirk a promise of warfare to come. If I thought I was screwed before, now I'm certain I'm standing at the edge of my own personal hell.

"Besides," she adds, voice honey-sweet but laced with venom, "I think you can create enough chaos in your life without any help from me." She snatches the bag from my grasp and strides into the house, every step a declaration of independence, screaming that she's not just capable of tearing me apart, but also perfectly willing to leave me bleeding in her wake.

We're just twelve minutes into day one of summer together, and I'm already drowning in the undertow of everything she is now—fierce, fearless, and absolutely fucking dangerous to every wall I've built. The realization hits me like a knockout punch, this summer isn't just going to be long; it's going to be the death of every defense I've ever had.

My throat still burns from Monty's grip, but it's nothing compared to the ache Nora's presence leaves behind. She's always had that power—to make physical pain feel like a fucking paper cut compared to what she does to me just by existing. And now she's here, breathing this same air, carrying all our history like a weapon she knows exactly how to use.

Standing in the shadow of our broken past, watching her disappear into the house that holds too many memories of us, I realize I'm not just screwed—I'm standing on the edge of an abyss I've spent two years trying to convince myself I didn't want to fall into.

Fuck my life indeed.

The summer already feels like a minefield, and Lenora Wells isn't just another explosive to dodge—she's the one with her finger on the detonator, and something tells me she remembers exactly where all my weak spots are.

The worst part?

Part of me wants her to press that button.

CHAPTER 4
YOU'RE ONLY SIXTEEN ONCE
NORA

I WISH I COULD CLAIM I RECOVERED GRACEFULLY AFTER NEARLY FACE-planting into the pavement. In some perfect world, I would've flashed a radiant smile and maintained my composure while those piercing hazel eyes studied me. But any pretense of dignity evaporated the moment his arms encircled my waist, fitting there as naturally as if they belonged. My breath caught—a momentary lapse that probably starved my brain of oxygen long enough to short-circuit my common sense.

The world around me blurred into meaningless shapes the second our eyes met. Time stood stilled, and I found myself mapping the land-scape of his face like it was territory both familiar and foreign—his deep mahogany hair shot through with threads of caramel and auburn, catching sunlight in a way that transformed him into something almost mythical. The strong cut of his jaw and those impossible lashes only added to the illusion. If not for that fleeting half-smile that curved his lips as he steadied me, I might have mistaken the intensity in his gaze for anger.

Seeing Nate for the first time in over a year unleashed a flood of memories I'd fought to lock away in the darkest corners of my mind. The image I'd preserved of him now felt like a mirage, something that shim-mered and shifted the closer I tried to examine it. Time has this cruel way of fooling you—making you believe nothing has changed until suddenly everything does. It reshapes people, sometimes into better versions of themselves, sometimes into strangers wearing familiar faces.

Standing before him now left me unmoored, experiencing the vertigo you get when you lock eyes with someone from your past only to realize you've both become different people, traveling separate paths. Even though he stood right there, looking at me the way he always had, the Nate I once knew felt like a ghost. Or maybe he was still there, hiding beneath layers, concealing himself from truly being seen.

But I've always seen Nate Sullivan, always.

Nate had always been that bright-eyed kid who shot up in height early, bypassing the awkward teenage phase entirely and landing straight in heartthrob territory—an annoyingly smooth transition that still irritates me. He can make torn jeans and a simple dark grey t-shirt look like haute couture, as if he just stepped off a Paris runway. Now he's even taller, his already imposing six-foot-four frame somehow stretching further skyward. The lean build from high school remains, but everything about him seems more defined—his shoulders broader, his presence more commanding. There's a new edge to his aura too, something darker and more guarded, as if he's carrying secrets he's determined to keep buried.

Being this close to him scrambles my thoughts. The intoxicating blend of tobacco, leather, and bergamot that clings to him makes it impossible to think straight.

He's been talking since our collision on the front porch, but my traitorous eyes keep drifting to the solid plane of his chest, only to snap back up when I catch his knowing, sideways grin—the one that tells me he knows exactly why I haven't heard a word he's said.

Stupid grin. Stupid piercing eyes. Stupid perfect face.

No, we're not doing this.

Never again.

Wait—what did he just ask?

Shit.

One moment with Nate is all it takes to unravel years of carefully constructed defenses. A single look, one ghost of a smile, and suddenly I'm that seven-year-old girl again, helplessly drawn to a boy who's always been just out of reach.

When our eyes meet, something electric crackles between us—a bone-deep recognition that thunders through my body. For a heartbeat, wrapped in his arms, I forget everything: where I am, what happened, even the anger I've harbored against him for so long.

Damn you, Nate.

The solid warmth of his body, his overwhelming proximity, the way his eyes hold mine as if I'm the only person in his universe—it's too much, too intense, too everything.

Reality crashed back when I spotted the bag of weed he was trying and failing to hide. Maybe I don't know him anymore. Reality has a way of shattering illusions, leaving nothing but sharp edges and uncomfortable truths.

Standing in my bedroom—the one where I've spent every summer since I was four—memories assault me from every corner. This space, with its sun-drenched layout and that old rocking chair still nestled in the corner, feels like a time capsule of my past. I've devoured countless books in that chair, lost in stories while summer light painted patterns across the pages. The expansive windows frame the lake vista perfectly. This room is mine because, as the only girl, I was given this sanctuary.

The Sullivans could have sold this house years ago, upgraded to something grander, more polished. But this place—with its worn edges and imperfect charm—has something money can't buy: it feels loved, lived in, real. It's my favorite spot in the world. The walls remain that same soft off-white they've always been, unchanged even after Lydia's redecorating phase. Every photo on the mantle stays exactly where it's always been, holding my memories in place.

Bones, my battle-scarred stuffed toy from Dad—a gift after I broke my ankle the summer I turned twelve—watches me from the bed, his button eyes somehow managing to look judgmental.

"Don't look at me like that, Bones."

Great, now I'm talking to a stuffed animal out loud.

"Talking to stuffed animals again, are we?" Jake's voice cuts through my reverie, warm and familiar.

"I think Bones is mad I left him behind," I reply, nodding toward the toy.

Jake's laugh feels like sunshine breaking through clouds, instantly lifting the heaviness from the room. "He probably just missed you. Give him time," he suggests, his presence as comforting as always.

He leans against the doorframe with that easy grace of his, and I can't help but notice how much he's changed too. The gym selfies he's been sending don't do justice to the athlete he's become. His shoulders have broadened, muscles defined by countless hours in the pool. Even at rest, his stance radiates quiet confidence. His sun-bronzed skin tells stories of early morning practices and dedication that's finally paying off.

"All settled in?" he asks, his eyes meeting mine with that grounding steadiness that's so uniquely Jake.

"I guess you could say that," I respond, gesturing to my half-hearted unpacking attempt.

He settles onto the bed, immediately making himself at home in a way that feels right, natural. His fingers find Bones' floppy ears, fidgeting with them as he speaks.

"So, tell me everything I missed."

"What do you mean? You know everything," I say, genuinely puzzled. We've stayed connected—texts, calls, those ridiculous gym selfies.

"I think you're the one who needs to do the catching up. Duke?" I prod, watching color rise in his cheeks.

He brushes the back of his neck, that endearing humility surfacing whenever someone mentions his achievements. "Uh yeah, it's pretty cool, I guess..."

I can't help but laugh, playfully smacking his chest. Getting into Duke's swim program has been his dream since forever. Everyone who knows Jake knows this.

"Ow!" He rubs the spot where my hand connected, though we both know I barely fazed him. "What was that for?"

I slap his chest again, harder this time. "For being ridiculous. I'm trying to knock some sense into you."

"You don't get it," he sighs, still playing with Bones' ears. "The guys at Duke swim at an Olympic pace. Everything's so cutthroat." A shadow crosses his face. "I'm not even sure I'll be able to stay on the team next year."

Another slap, this one meaning business.

"Ow, fuck! Shit, Nora."

"You, Jacob Sullivan, are not a quitter. And you don't back down from jocks in pretentious speedos."

"I have to wear those pretentious speedos too, you know," he points out. "What's that say about me?"

"You're an idiot." I ruffle his sun-bleached hair, lighter now from endless hours of training. "I don't care how fast those jackasses are, they're not you. You've been working toward this your whole life, Jake. It's yours for the taking."

His laugh starts small but grows into that full-bodied sound I've missed so much. "Did you just call them jackasses?"

We dissolve into laughter, and the familiar warmth of our friendship wraps around me like a favorite blanket. God, I've missed this—missed him.

He stands suddenly, squaring his shoulders with mock solemnity. "Clear your schedule for tomorrow morning," he announces, mischief dancing in his eyes.

"I've been here fifteen minutes. What plans could I possibly have made?"

"True. Well, tomorrow morning is just about us." His excitement proves contagious.

"Should I be worried?"

He grips my shoulders, meeting my eyes with playful intensity. "You should be excited." Heading for the door, he adds, "Oh, and heads up—five-thirty-five wake-up call."

"That's oddly specific," I smirk.

"We'll grab the bikes from the shed and hit the road," he says, his smile heavy with nostalgia. "Just like old times." He throws in a wink as he exits.

"Is that early really necessary?" I call after him.

"Nora, we have to seize the day!" His voice echoes down the hallway, arms raised dramatically. "Sunrise is at six. We've got a lot to catch up on this summer."

Something in my chest tightens. This place, these people—it physically hurts how much I've missed it all.

THE AROMA OF LYDIA'S FAMOUS REUNION DINNER PULLS ME FROM WHAT was supposed to be a quick nap but somehow stretched into a two-hour slumber. Checking my phone, I head downstairs to find Ollie and Jake sprawled across the couch, thumbs dancing across their screens while the moms transform the kitchen into something worthy of a cooking show.

"Well, if it isn't Sleeping Beauty," Ollie teases as I wander in.

I answer with an eye roll that says everything it needs to.

"Need a hand with anything?" I offer, stepping into the kitchen's controlled chaos.

"We're all set, sweetie." Lydia's words tumble out in one breath. "Did you sleep okay? Was the bed comfy? I bought new pillows—tell me if they're not good, we'll get new ones tomorrow."

"Perfect sleep. Perfect bed. Perfect pillows, Lydia."

"Okay, good." She finally breathes, shoulders relaxing. "But if you need anything—"

"Lydia, the Hilton doesn't offer service like yours."

"Oh, hush." She playfully snaps a tea towel at Mom, who responds with a mock scowl. Their easy friendship warms something inside me—a reminder of how lucky Mom is to have someone like Lydia in her life. "I just want you all to feel at home. This place is as much yours as it is ours."

Jake appears beside me, draping an arm across my shoulders. "So, when's dinner ready, Queens?" He swipes a potato from the counter.

Lydia swats his hand. "Ow! Jesus, what's with the women in my life and slapping me today?"

I jab him in the ribs, earning that troublemaker grin that makes me stick out my tongue—childish but genuine.

"It'll be ready once you set the table, like I've asked three times already."

"Mom, I was entertaining our guests. His royal highness here is high maintenance," Jake protests.

"Me? That's rich coming from you," Ollie calls from his couch fortress.

"Well, can you season this salad?" Lydia asks, but Ollie intercepts, grabbing the bowl. "I've got it."

"The last time you 'got it', you nearly poisoned us all," Jake reminds him.

"One time! And the internet swore those were the best dumplings."

"You never learn to trust the internet."

"God, you boys."

We settle into our usual spots around the dining table, the empty chairs more noticeable than ever—one permanently vacant, its absence a physical ache in the room.

"Is Nate joining us?" Mom asks, placing the salad before me.

Jake, already shoveling food onto his plate, mumbles, "I wouldn't count on it."

Lydia taps her glass with a fork, ever the matriarch. "Before we eat, I just want to say something."

Lydia squeezes Mom's hand, her eyes bright. "I'm just so grateful you made it here this summer. This place feels more like home when you're all here."

"I second that, Mama Bear," Jake adds, throwing me a wink before nodding at Ollie. "That includes you too, shithead," he says with a playful jab.

Ollie responds by mock-headlocking him, planting a theatrical kiss on his temple. "Don't go soft on me now."

"We missed being here," Mom adds warmly, her gaze sweeping the table like she's memorizing each face.

"All right, enough sap. Can we eat? I'm dying here," Ollie declares.

"Wait," Lydia says, her eyes lighting up with sudden excitement. "I can't believe I almost forgot! We need to start planning for your birthdays!"

Jake groans dramatically but can't hide his smile. "Mom, can't this wait until tomorrow? Or at least till after we eat?"

"Well, sorry for being excited," Lydia continues, undeterred. "God, I can't believe my baby boy is turning eighteen and Nora you'll be seventeen." She looks at us like we're still the kids who used to blow out candles together, chocolate frosting smeared across our faces.

She looks to mom who can't help but laugh at her best friend. "Kat, when did our babies stop being babies?"

My stomach knots at the mention of my birthday, an instant heaviness settling into my chest. The date looms in my mind like a shadow—June thirteenth. One year since we lowered Dad into the ground. One day after Jake's birthday, one day before mine. The universe's cruel joke, sandwiching the anniversary of the worst day of my life between two celebrations.

"We'll do something special this year." Lydia continues.

"Especially for Jake," Ollie chimes in. "Finally legal... well, for some things."

"Like voting," Mom adds pointedly.

"Yeah, exactly what I meant," Ollie says with a smirk, earning him a warning look from Mom.

"What do you think, Nora?" Lydia asks, her enthusiasm refusing to be dampened.

Everyone's looking at me now, waiting. I force my face into something resembling normalcy, swallowing past the thickness in my throat. "Whatever you plan will be great, Lydia. You always make it special."

What I don't say is: How do I blow out candles and make wishes when the biggest wish—to have Dad back, to hear his laugh one more time, to feel his arms around me—will never come true?

How do I smile when all I want to do is scream at the unfairness that he's gone and somehow the world keeps spinning, birthdays keep coming, as if nothing has changed?

"I vote for something low-key this year," Jake says, his eyes finding mine across the table. Sometimes I think he can read my thoughts. The gentle understanding in his gaze nearly breaks me.

"We can do low-key." Lydia claps her hands together.

Growing up close in age with the Sullivan boys meant we were always attached at the hip. Nate was the eldest, a year older than Ollie who is now nineteen. Jake a year younger than Ol and then little old me, the youngest of them all. Dad used to joke that they had planned it that way—one Sullivan, one Wells, perfectly spaced out like stepping stones.

"Speaking of time flying," Mom interjects gently, her eyes lingering on me a beat too long. She sees it—the struggle, the way I'm barely holding it together. "Maybe we should let the food get eaten before it gets cold?"

"Mom, you read my mind." Ollie says, stabbing a fork into a potato before shoving it into his mouth.

The conversation shifts, but my mind remains stuck on the date, circling it like a shark around prey. Three hundred and sixty-five days. That's how long it's been since we gathered in black instead of summer colors. Looking across the table at the people I've loved my whole life, I feel like an actress in a play.

Smiling. Nodding. Pretending that celebrating my birthday won't feel like dancing on his grave.

"Damn Lyds, I missed your cooking," Ollie says before immediately looking at Mom apologetically. "I mean, I love your cooking too Mom."

"Sure," mom says with a playful eye roll.

This time, everyone laughs, and the moment passes. But the knot in my stomach remains, tight and insistent, a physical manifestation of the dread building for that day. The first anniversary of goodbye.

We're all finding ourselves in our own conversations, when footsteps thunder down the stairs. Nate rushes past the dining room without a glance our way.

"Excuse me, where are you off to?" Lydia's voice carries a particular mom-tone that usually stops kids in their tracks.

"Out," Nate snaps back.

"We have guests, Nate," she reminds him, gentler now.

"They'll be here tomorrow, won't they?" The door slams behind him, leaving a heavy silence in his wake.

"Told you not to get your hopes up," Jake murmurs, earning a sharp look from Lydia.

The chatter eventually resumes, but there's a new tension threading through it. After dinner, we fall into our old routine—adults cook, kids clean, a rule Mom's enforced since we could reach the sink. The familiar rhythm of it feels like stepping back in time.

It's Jake who brings up the party Nate disappeared to, casually suggesting we all drop by. My stomach knots itself. After this morning's awkward encounter, the last thing I want is another round with Nate, especially not at a party. Ollie's enthusiasm doesn't help, but I opt for the safety of a book and early bedtime.

"You sure you don't want to come? It's your first night back, and it could be fun." Jake leans against my door frame, that boyish charm of his in full effect—dimples and all.

"As tempting as that sounds," I gesture to my comfy clothes, "someone sentenced me to an ungodly wake-up call tomorrow. I need all the sleep I can get."

His laugh fills the room like summer light. "It'll be worth it, I promise," he says, eyes sparking with barely contained excitement.

"Go have fun. I'll see you at the crack of dawn," I say, settling the matter.

"Okay, but if you change your mind—"

"Jake, I'm good," I cut him off gently, softening it with a smile. "My book and I have a date."

"Fine, guess I do need you rested for tomorrow." He steps forward, wrapping me in a hug that smells like clean laundry and something uniquely Jake. "Missed you, Nor."

"Missed you, too."

"Sweet dreams."

"Always."

The house settles into silence after they leave. I'm alone with my laptop, staring at a cursor that blinks like an accusation. I've been trying to write—anything, something. But the words have been stuck since the funeral. Writing used to be my escape, my dream, a passion Dad helped nurture. Now the blank screen feels like staring into an abyss. My attempts at creativity are interrupted by Lydia's soft knock.

"You didn't want to join the boys?" she asks, voice gentle as she appears in the doorway.

"Not really in a party mood this summer," I reply, the words trailing off as unwanted memories threaten to surface.

Lydia settles beside me on the bed, brushing a stray hair from my face with maternal tenderness. "Nora, honey, you're only sixteen once. After everything you've been through, it's okay to just be a teenager again. Your dad would want you to keep living, to experience life," she encourages, her voice soft but sure.

"I still have nightmares about it," I admit, my eyes fixed on the mockingly empty screen.

"Come here." Lydia opens her arms, and as I lean into her embrace, it feels like being wrapped in pure warmth. "He may be gone physically, but he'll always be here." She taps my head, then my heart. We share a moment of understanding before she stands, her gaze falling on the outfit I'd tossed across the rocking chair earlier.

"I think you should wear that tonight," she suggests, her tone light but encouraging.

"The boys have already left, and it's late—"

"It's only 9:30. Your ride is waiting downstairs," she counters, presenting the outfit with a hopeful smile.

"Go enjoy your last couple of weeks being sixteen," she insists, laying the clothes on my bed. At the door, she adds with a conspiratorial wink, "Just don't do anything your mother and I wouldn't. And definitely don't tell her I said that."

Standing in my room, I hover between two versions of myself—the one who crawls into bed with a book, and the one who takes a chance tonight. The past will always be there, but maybe I don't have to live in its shadow forever. I want to feel something other than this numbness that's become my constant companion this past year.

I smooth down my denim skirt—definitely shorter than my usual comfort zone—and try to ignore how exposed I feel in this top. A jacket would defeat the purpose, but the evening air reminds me exactly how much skin I'm showing. Standing here, I seriously question my sanity.

I should be in pajamas, not whatever this is. I head for the stairs anyway.

"Have fun!" Lydia calls from the kitchen.

"Be safe, Nora!" Mom adds.

"I will!" I shout back, my voice projecting more confidence than I feel.

Closing the front door behind me, I walk down to where Jake leans against his Range Rover, arms crossed, muscles defined under his shirt. His gaze catches on me as I approach, surprise and something else flickering across his face.

"Well, shit. You look..." His eyes sweep over me again, admiration clear in his expression. He grabs my arm, spinning me in a playful twirl, his grin widening. "Amazing."

I laugh, uncertain how to handle his scrutiny. "You're being weird," I deflect.

He grins, stepping back but keeping hold of my hands. "Well, that's not unlike me, now is it?"

"You came back," I state, more observation than question.

"For you, always," he replies, that signature boyish grin lighting up his features.

Jake's reliability has never been in question. I remember one summer when my attempt to impress the boys ended with me falling from a tree, resulting in three fractures and a bruised ego. While Nate carried me home, it was Jake who stayed in with me all summer, making sure I didn't feel like I'd ruined everything.

It turned out to be one of my favorite summers—just Jake and me, endless UNO games, movie marathons, and heated debates over which Harry Potter book reigned supreme.

"Shall we?" he asks, opening the passenger door with an exaggerated flourish.

"Why, thank you," I reply with a smirk, sliding into the seat.

Jake leans against the door frame, watching me with a soft expression. "What?" I ask, puzzled by his stare.

"Nothing, I'm just... happy. Happy you're here again."

"Me too."

He walks around to the driver's side and gets in, starting the car. "So, whose house party is this?" I ask as we pull away.

"Farrah Olsen's. Her parents are away until next week. She's invited practically everyone in town for an official opening weekend party."

We pull into a driveway that leads to what could easily be featured in Architectural Digest. A marble fountain dances in the center of the circular drive, casting ethereal reflections under the evening lights— probably worth more than my entire house in Boston. Music pulses from inside, and clusters of people filter through the grand front doors, their laughter and chatter melding with the unmistakable sound of privilege.

Stepping into this scene feels like entering another world. The Sullivans have money, sure, but they've never flaunted their wealth like this.

"Farrah's been living in this palace alone?"

"Well, she has a whole entourage that caters to her every whim. Nate sometimes stays over too," Jake replies casually, oblivious to how that detail twists something sharp inside me. It doesn't take a genius to piece together that Farrah is Nate's latest distraction.

"So, Farrah and Nate?" I venture, aiming for indifference and probably missing by a mile.

"They're together, sort of. Been on and off more times than I can count." His voice stays neutral.

"This place is absurd," I comment, desperate to change the subject as we step through the grand entrance.

Jake laughs, agreeing it's excessive for a summer home they barely use. "Her dad's some big-shot Wall Street investor, and I think her mom's an interior designer or something."

That explains the imported marble floors and the pristine everything —so untouched it practically screams wealth and careful curation.

Jake turns to me, sliding his arm around my shoulders protectively. "You ready?"

I nod, though I'm not entirely sure what I'm ready for. My heart races beneath my ribs, and something must show on my face because Jake gives me a gentle squeeze.

"Come on," he grins, offering his arm. "Time to show you off."

I link my arm through his, letting him guide me inside. Each step feels like moving closer to something inevitable, my pulse a symphony of anticipation and dread.

CHAPTER 5
SPECKS WITH COLOSSAL PROBLEMS
NATE

"THERE'S OUR BOY!" CHRISTIAN BELLOWS AS I STRIDE INTO THE PARTY. THE bass thrums through the floorboards, matching my racing pulse. This is the last fucking place I want to be, yet here I am, weaving through a crowd that's slapping my back like I'm some sort of hometown hero.

"About fucking time you showed." An arm hooks around my neck, pulling me into a headlock that's more aggressive than friendly. "You got it, yeah?"

"Yeah," I mutter, handing over the small bags of weed and pills. The weight of them leaving my pocket doesn't lighten the burden I carry.

"Now it's a fucking party!" Christian shouts, igniting a chorus of cheers around us.

Drink. I desperately need a drink.

The anger and anxiety I've been carrying lately weigh me down like a brick. The panic attacks aren't new, but their frequency is becoming suffocating. The weed and pills are my crutch, dulling the chaos inside just enough so I can stand to be in places like this, surrounded by people who feel more like cardboard cutouts than actual humans.

Then there's Nora.

She's been haunting my thoughts more than I'm willing to admit, and it's not just because of our awkward encounter earlier. It's been over a year since we last spoke, but she's lived rent-free in my mind for years. Every thought of her is tangled with anxiety and guilt. I shouldn't care that she's here—I knew she would be. Yet within fifteen minutes of sharing the same air as her, my composure is completely shot to shit.

Her eyes carried a depth of pain that mirrored my own, an infinite cosmos of unspoken words. She used to burn with fire, and now she's cloaked in ice, but beneath it, the embers still smolder. Life has hardened her, a feeling I know all too well.

Everything feels different because it is.

We're different people now. Life has turned us into strangers wearing familiar faces. Part of me thinks it's better, safer, to keep my distance. But being close to her this morning stirred something I thought I'd buried. Four fucking minutes in her presence made me feel more than I have in the past year.

My sanity is hanging by a thread.

Navigating this house is second nature—I know exactly where Farrah's dad stashes the good scotch. Even on a normal day, this lake house feels suffocating, steeped in too many memories of a past that's long gone. Add a crowd into the mix, including one girl who can barely stand the sight of me, and it's like being caged while the air is thick with unresolved tension.

I lean over the bar, pouring four-hundred-dollar scotch into a plastic cup. There's something poetically tragic about that. I down it quickly, then pour another. The liquid burns, but it's not enough to cauterize the wounds I'm trying to ignore.

"Nate! What the fuck?" Farrah's slurred shout cuts through the music. She's drunk, eyes glassy, barely keeping herself upright. "Why haven't you been answering my calls?"

Despite her disheveled state, she looks immaculate—not a hair out of place.

Perfect.

Fake.

The touch I once craved now feels hollow, like touching a mannequin instead of skin.

"Been busy," I mutter, my patience wearing thin.

"Busy doing what?"

"Busy, Farrah," I snap back. She leans in for a kiss—it's rough and desperate, tasting of vodka and neediness.

"I missed you, baby. You seem on edge," she murmurs against my lips, her arms tightening around my neck. "Let me help you relax." Her eyes lock onto mine, fierce and trying too hard. She licks her lips, a clear play for seduction that feels more mechanical than passionate.

"Farrah—" I start, but she's already sliding her hands down my jeans. The frustration I feel isn't the kind that leads anywhere pleasurable.

I grab her hand firmly. "No."

She reels back, confusion and hurt flooding her eyes.

"No? What is going on with you? You don't reply to my texts, you ignore my calls, now you don't even want to fuck me?" Her voice rises, drawing stares like moths to a flame.

"You're right, I don't want to fuck you, so drop it," I growl, shrugging off her hand and taking another swig of scotch.

She scoffs. "Well, that wasn't a few days ago."

My mind reels back to that dismal three-day bender—David's death anniversary and the last disastrous encounter with Scott, whom I can't bring myself to call Dad anymore. Farrah was the perfect distraction then. Farrah, booze, and pills: a destructive cycle I'm not proud of.

"I need some air," I mutter, snatching the scotch bottle from the bar and making for the pool area before anyone can follow me with their empty fucking small talk.

The night air slaps my face—a blessed relief from the suffocating heat of bodies packed inside. I collapse onto a deck chair, muscles aching with a fatigue that has nothing to do with physical exertion. Uncapping the bottle, I take a long pull, welcoming the burn as it scorches down my throat. Better to feel something, even if it's pain. My fingers work automatically, rolling a joint with practiced precision. The first hit fills my lungs, and I exhale slowly, watching the smoke twist and curl into the darkness above. There's poetry in that smoke—how it appears substantial then dissipates into nothing. Like everything else in this godforsaken life.

Years of constructing elaborate fictions. Years of lying, distracting, deflecting. It's fucking exhausting, but I've grown accustomed to the weight of the lies I carry. They've become part of my skeletal structure—remove them and I might collapse entirely.

All I want—all I've ever wanted—is to feel weightless.

Free.

But self-pity is a luxury I abandoned years ago, leaving nothing but hollow echoes where emotions used to live. Sometimes I wonder if I even remember how to feel anything real anymore.

The moon hangs overhead like a silent witness to everything we are and aren't. Funny how we're just these insignificant specks with our colossal problems while that rock has watched empires rise and fall. There's a strange comfort in that cosmic perspective—knowing we're all just trying to navigate this chaotic existence, brief flashes in an endless narrative that everyone forgets. Everyone except that cold, dead rock floating above us all.

Images of Nora infiltrate my thoughts like persistent ghosts.

Why now? Why tonight?

She's always had this hold over me, even when we were kids. It's as if part of me is perpetually searching for her in my darkest moments—her eyes, her voice, the way she moves through space like she was born to command it. But I forfeited any right to her, even in my thoughts, when I din't show up for her, for Ollie. The hurt and suspicion that clouded her face earlier today cut deeper than I expected.

Deeper than I deserve to feel.

I scan the sea of strangers around the pool, all too wasted to remember their own names, let alone mine.

Thank fucking god.

I stub out the joint and light a cigarette instead, drifting toward the pool's edge where the water fractures the party lights into disjointed patterns. The conversations washing over me are shallow, slurred echoes of the same pretentious bullshit I've navigated my entire life—people chasing money, status, or some illusion they'll never catch no matter how fast they run.

My moment of solitude doesn't last.

Of course it doesn't.

Nothing good ever does.

Farrah appears flanked by Shay and Harlow like some discount version of a royal entourage. Before I can escape, she situates herself onto my lap without invitation, her perfume invading my senses—too sweet, too manufactured, nothing like the natural scent of—

No. Not going there.

It figures why they're all friends—cut from the same designer cloth, sharing the same cultivated tastes and remarkable tolerance for Farrah's casual cruelty. The weight of her on my lap feels wrong. Everything about this night feels wrong.

"Baby, you look so tired. Are you sure you don't want me to help you relax a little?" Her hands wander across my chest, her touch lingering longer than I want. When her fingers edge lower, I snap, grabbing her wrists. The motion is gentle but firm—a warning.

"I'm good right here," I say, my voice sharp enough to slice through steel.

Instead of taking the hint, she drapes herself over my body, claiming me in a possessive display that makes my skin crawl.

"We heard you nearly got shot by your dealer today," Shay drones on, her voice as dull as her personality. She and her twin sister have morphed into robotic clones, perfectly crafted by Farrah to follow her every whim.

"You need to find a new hobby," I growl, irritation boiling over. I'm on

43

the verge of exploding, surrounded by whispers and accusations I don't need.

My attention snaps to a nearby conversation, where Christian and his crew are eyeing someone new.

"Who's the new girl hanging off Jake's arm?" Christian leers, his voice carrying over the music. Farrah blocks my view, but I strain to see past her.

"Must be a new out-of-towner. Fuck, she's nice to look at," another voice chimes in. "He's one lucky son of a bitch."

A sickening feeling coils in my gut before I even see her—Nora. I feel her presence like a shift in the atmosphere, a gravitational pull that's impossible to resist.

"I'd like to get between tho—"

"You won't finish that sentence if you know what's good for you," I snap, my voice low and deadly.

I turn, and there she is.

Nora moves through the crowd with an effortless grace that draws every eye in the room. Her skirt clings to her curves, Chuck Taylors stark against the white hemline, crop top revealing a strip of golden skin that makes my fingers itch to touch. Her hair flows over her shoulders in waves I remember running my hands through in dreams. Despite her casual confidence, her eyes remain distant, guarded like she's wearing invisible armor.

I've watched her draw attention effortlessly all her life, a force of nature that can't be contained. But the truth hits hard—I'm not the guy she once knew. I'm damaged goods, fractured by life's harsh trials, while she remains untouched by the darkness that consumes me.

"Who is she?" Farrah presses, her curiosity laced with venom.

"No one," I lie.

"If she's no one, why are you getting so defensive over her?"

"I'm not in the mood for interrogations tonight, Farrah."

"It's a fucking question, Nate."

"And I'm done answering questions," I growl, shoving her hands away. A surge of claustrophobia washes over me. Nora shouldn't be here. Jake should never have brought her. I can't be near her, yet I can't leave now that she's here.

"Are you fucking her?" Farrah's voice slices through the tension.

"What?" I snap, incredulous.

"You heard me. Are you—"

"No. She's not—it's not like—" I cut myself off, realizing this isn't a conversation I want to have with anyone, especially not Farrah.

"Well, she looks like a sl—"

I'm in her face before she can finish, my finger pointed sharply. "Choose your words wisely, Farrah. Very fucking wisely."

She leans in, her face inches from mine, her breath hitching as if she might kiss me.

Instead, she whispers, "Looks like your little damsel just made a new friend."

I follow her gaze, and my stomach drops. Nora's no longer with Jake; she's laughing with Connor fucking James. Of all the people at this fucking party, it had to be him. I loathe him on a good day, but seeing him with Nora—watching her smile at him—that's enough to make me want to tear every limb from his body. Or maybe it's just the sting of seeing him hold her attention—attention I desperately want, that's driving me insane.

"I need a drink." I don't glance back at Farrah as I head straight for Ollie, who's sprawled on a sofa looking far too comfortable with a girl clinging to his side.

"Natey boy!" Ollie slurs his greeting, words swimming in alcohol. He's plastered, but I'm not one to judge.

"Your sister's here," I snap, cutting through his drunken haze.

"I know. Jake said he was going back to get her." Concern flickers across Ollie's face as he sits up. "Where is she? Is she all right?"

Yeah, well, he's done a pretty shitty job of that.

"Have you seen him?"

"Nah man, sorry. Oh, this is Vanessa, by the way." He gestures to the brunette beside him.

"Ol, Nora shouldn't be here." My reply is terse, focus already shifting.

"It's good that she's finally out. Let her have tonight, okay?"

No. Not okay.

"If you see Jake, tell him I'm looking for him."

"I think he's over there with Kelsie Timmins," Vanessa chimes in, pointing toward my brother who's propped against the kitchen island, chatting up a blonde who seems utterly enamored.

I storm toward the kitchen, and Jake catches my glare, quickly dismissing his company. He straightens, preparing for the confrontation he knows is coming.

"What did I do now?" he asks, tone-deaf.

"You brought her here?"

"If by 'her' you're referring to Nora, then yes."

"Why?" My voice is a mix of disbelief and anger.

Jake scoffs. "Why not, Nate? Jesus. Why should she be cooped up at home with our moms?"

His casual dismissal of my concerns grates on me. These people are toxic and she doesn't need to be dragged into this.

Or maybe it's me—I'm the toxic one, and I don't want her caught up in my mess.

"Take her home."

"What's your problem?"

"Are you being serious right now? You brought her here. Then you left her, and now she's over there with that fucking dropkick."

"Okay? So she's talking to Connor. Big deal, they're not—"

I cut him off. "Take her home."

"If she wants to leave, I'll take her home. Until then, why don't you go smoke another joint and relax while the rest of us enjoy ourselves?" His smug tone is like a slap in the face. To add insult to injury, he brushes past me, patting my shoulder condescendingly.

Little fucker.

I scan the chaotic mess of a party again, searching for Nora through the haze of smoke and bodies. The room spins slightly with each pulse of music, reminding me how fucked up everything has gotten since she walked back into my life.

"Nate, you gotta try this, man!" A guy named Tyler thrusts a baggie at me, his smile too wide, pupils blown. "It's primo stuff, man, just like acid."

I stare down at the tiny, potent promise of escape in his hand. The urge to snatch it, to let the chemical bliss wash away everything—her face, her laugh, her everything—is almost overwhelming. But then I remember her eyes, wide and clear, looking right through me earlier today.

"I'm good." My voice barely cuts through the bass as I back away, hands shoved deep in my pockets to keep them from betraying me. Tyler shrugs and turns back to his eager audience.

Every step through the crowd is fueled by a mix of dread and antici-pation. I should walk away, let her enjoy her night without me looming over her like some dark cloud. But I can't. Every instinct screams at me to find her, to make sure she's okay.

And then I see her, across the room, smiling up at Connor. The sight of his hand casually touching her arm, ignites a wildfire in my chest. I want to tear him away from her, to shout that she's off limits. But she's not mine to claim, and that realization is a cold knife twisting in my gut.

Why am I even here?

I'm just the fucked-up guy with too many demons, watching from the sidelines while she lights up the room. But even as I debate turning around and leaving, my feet carry me closer to her, each step heavier than the last.

She's the kind of beautiful that stops you in your tracks. And I'm the kind of disaster that should keep walking. But here I am, standing at the edge of the precipice, looking down at the one person who's ever made me want to jump.

I just hope to hell I don't drag her down with me.

CHAPTER 6
VODKA, LIME AND OLD FLAMES
NORA

"Wow." The word escapes me in a breath as I take in the chaos before us. Jake runs a hand through his tousled chestnut hair, his eyes following mine as we scan the room.

"Yeah, I guess I forgot to mention it gets a little wild with these people." He catches my stunned expression and grasps both of my hands, his touch grounding me in the mayhem. "We can bail if you want?"

"No, it's okay," I manage, though my heart pounds against my ribs like a trapped bird.

I'd braced myself for the typical markers of wealth—marble floors, soaring chandeliers, artwork worth more than my college tuition.

But this? This is a collision of worlds: old money meets frat house chaos. Farrah's guest list seems to include half the town's population, transforming the mansion's vast foyer and sunken living area into a writhing sea of bodies.

The air is thick with perfume, sweat, and spilled drinks. Bass thunders from the DJ booth near the pool, vibrating through my bones. Couples tangle in shadowed corners while a girl in a gossamer dress twirls through the crowd, lost in her own private dance.

Eden isn't just a place—it's *the* place in the summertime. But this isn't your average college party; it's an elitist playground where old-money families have interwoven their lives for generations. The last time I attended one of these parties, invisibility became my shield. Tonight, I'm hoping for the same superpower.

Jake's arm threads through mine as we navigate the crowd, his presence an anchor in the chaos. "Thirsty?" he asks.

My eyes betray me, drifting to Nate by the pool. A tall blonde—Farrah, I assume—clings to him, her dress barely more than a whisper against her skin. The sight twists something deep in my chest. "Actually, a drink sounds good," I say, hoping the tremor in my voice isn't as obvious as it feels.

"Vodka or beer?"

"Surprise me," I respond with a smile that doesn't quite reach my eyes. If I'm going to survive tonight, I need something to dull these sharp edges.

"You good to wait here a sec?" Jake's tone is light, but his eyes search mine with concern.

"Sure." The thought of diving into that sea of bodies makes my anxiety spike higher than it already is.

"All right, I'll be right back. Don't get into trouble while I'm gone," he says before heading for the bar.

I watch as Jake weaves through the crowd, his confident stride and easy smile drawing attention like a magnet. When did he become Eden's most eligible bachelor? Sure, his swimmer's build explains the lingering glances, but I run on black coffee and cynicism these days—I'm immune to that all-American charm.

My gaze drifts back to Farrah and Nate. Her delicate features and glossy lips seem ready for a photoshoot, one arm draped possessively around his neck while the other holds a champagne flute. While Nate looks simultaneously bored and tense as she whispers in his ear. When he catches my eye, I quickly look away, still rattled by our intense encounter this morning.

Jake returns with two drinks. "Vodka, lime, and soda for the lady."

"You're drinking?" I ask, surprised.

"Vodka, lime, and soda—minus the vodka. Got to keep this body in top form." He winks, nodding toward Ollie, who's working his charm on a pretty brunette. "And I've got to get you and that mess home safely."

Jake can read my distraction. "You sure you're okay?"

"Yeah." I force a smile, but my eyes betray me as they notice Nate and Farrah's absence. Anxiety coils in my stomach like a spring. I take a long sip of my drink; it burns a path down my throat.

Do people actually enjoy this?

"Whoa, easy tiger. I already have one Wells sibling I'm babysitting tonight," Jake teases.

"Ollie's the only one who needs babysitting," I retort with a smirk that masks the chaos beneath. Truth is, I'm barely holding it together—the anxiety is suffocating, and seeing Nate makes my skin feel too tight for my body.

"There are a few people I want to say hi to. Want to come?" Jake offers.

"No, you go," I say, the thought of small talk sending fresh waves of unease through me. *Stay invisible*, I remind myself.

"Are you sure? I could introduce you."

"No, it's fine, really. Go. I'll find you later." Another reassuring smile. I can always find a quiet corner to hide in until he's ready to leave.

"Okay, I'll come find you in a bit. Try to have some fun, yeah?" he says, playfully tapping my nose like when we were kids.

I watch Jake move through the crowd with enviable ease, unaffected by the whispers and glances that follow him. Meanwhile, I'm dodging spilled drinks and overeager partiers, feeling like a fish swimming upstream.

The party pulses with increasing intensity as more bodies pour in, until the mansion seems to breathe with their collective energy. Tables once decorated with family photos now host drinking games and lines of white powder. The music pounds through my bones, making thought itself difficult.

I keep my head down, trying to navigate the chaos, when I collide with what feels like a brick wall.

"Shit, sorry," I mutter.

"Holy shit, is that you, Lenora Wells?" A husky voice cuts through the noise, and I look up into Connor James's face.

Connor James—Ivy League royalty personified. Since I last saw him, the boy has evolved into something more dangerous: sharp jawline, carefully disheveled hair, shirt unbuttoned just enough to hint at a sculpted torso. His charm still radiates like a gravitational field.

"Connor. Hey," I say, the words feeling artificial on my tongue.

"Damn, Wells. You aged up nicely."

I force a smile, swallowing my discomfort. "Thanks. You, uh, same." I gesture vaguely at his torso, earning a laugh that sounds practiced.

"I didn't expect to see you here."

"That makes two of us," I murmur.

"Sullivan let you out on your own for once, huh?" The comment stings with its implications.

"I'm here with Jake."

"Oh yeah? Where is the little guy?" His condescension hasn't changed since I last knew him.

"He's around."

"And he's left you out here all alone?"

"Are you under the impression I can't fend for myself?"

"No, I didn't mean—uh." He runs his fingers through his hair, flustered. "I just meant—"

"I'm pulling your leg. Relax."

He flashes that practiced smile again. "You're pretty funny. And pretty in general, too."

I suppress an eye roll and pretend to sip my drink.

"You do not look like you're enjoying that."

"Does anyone actually enjoy drinking?" My rhetorical question draws another calculated laugh.

"What are you, sixteen going on sixty?"

"May as well be." My eyes continue scanning the crowd for a specific face.

"Do you want to go somewhere quieter?" he suggests, leaning closer.

"Go somewhere?"

"It's just really loud in here, and I don't want to be yelling all night."

"What makes you think I want to talk to you all night?"

"I take it back, you're very funny." He leans in, beer breath washing over me.

"I think I'll get another drink."

"Please, let me. I'll get you something that tastes less like ass and is actually enjoyable." He winks and vanishes into the crowd before I can protest.

The social overwhelm hits its peak, and I decide it's time to find Jake. Maybe I should take him up on his offer and get out of here. But as I turn to search for him, fate proves its cruel sense of humor—Nate appears before me, his presence both magnetic and suffocating.

And boy does he looked pissed to see me.

His arms trap me for the second time today, but this encounter crackles with a different energy. He plants his palms against the wall on either side of me, his muscled forearms flexing as he leans in. I'm caged between his broad shoulders and the cold wall at my back, close enough to catch the faint scent of his cologne.

The space between us shrinks to nothing but charged air. His eyes blaze with anger, clearly unhappy to see me here. His body is coiled tension, jaw clenched tight, the strong column of his neck betraying a pulse that hammers as rapidly as my own. I could count each dark eyelash if I wanted to, we're that close—close enough that I feel the heat radiating from him, see the smallest flecks of color in his irises as they narrow on mine.

"What are you doing here?"

"Hi to you too," I retort, my irritation rising to match his.

"You shouldn't be here." His voice is razor-sharp.

I scoff, "You should stick to sparkling water; it might lighten your mood."

He takes a small step back, his eyes rake over me, leaving burn marks in their wake. "What the actual fuck are you wearing?" he sneers, his gaze glassy and hollow—any warmth from this morning has evaporated, replaced by drug-induced fog and simmering rage.

Oh, now he wants to pick a fight?

I pull away from his hold, squaring my shoulders. "Clothing," I say flatly.

"That glorified washcloth is not clothing. You look ridiculous," he mocks, pulling out a cigarette and lighting it with deliberate slowness, while completely disregarding the fact that we're indoors.

Is he for real right now?

I fight the urge to shrink beneath his criticism, to cover the parts of myself he's made me doubt. Instead, his sneer ignites something defiant in me.

"Well, good to know your eyes are working," I snap back, plastering on a sweet smile. "Connor seems to like it."

"He likes it because he can see your tits and is probably picturing his face between them," Nate retorts, exhaling smoke like venom.

In one fluid motion, I snatch the cigarette from his lips and drop it in my untouched drink. "Very vivid image you're painting, Nate. Almost sounds like you've pictured it yourself."

He crowds me against a table I hadn't noticed, caging me with his arms once again. His dark hair falls in his eyes but can't hide his dilated pupils or bloodshot whites. I force my expression neutral, even as my heart races at our proximity.

Without warning or taking his eyes off me, he shrugs off his button-up and thrusts it at me. "Put it on."

"I'm good, thanks," I say coolly.

"Why are you being so fucking difficult?" His breath is mint and spice, tinged with weed—an intoxicating combination that does nothing to calm my nerves.

"It seems you're the one with a problem here, Nate." I shove his shirt back at him and pat his chest lightly. Our faces inches apart, tension crackling between us.

Connor's voice cuts through the moment. "Sullivan, stop bothering my date." He drapes an arm around my shoulders, radiating smug satisfaction while holding two beer bottles.

I don't look at Nate, but I feel the fury rolling off him in waves.

Nate's control snaps. "She's not your date."

"I think Nora is old enough now to not need a babysitter," Connor counters smoothly, then turns to me with a conspiratorial glance. "Besides, we have some catching up to do, right?"

"We do," I affirm, tasting victory.

Nate looks ready to explode. I twist the knife deeper, nodding toward Farrah at the bar. "I think your girlfriend is waiting for you."

I get rid of the beer bottles and take Connor's hand. "Come on, let's dance Connor."

We leave Nate to stew in his anger as we join the pulsing crowd on the dance floor. Bodies press close, the air thick with sweat and bass. Connor pulls me into his rhythm, hands finding my hips. "He looked like he was about to pop a blood vessel," he chuckles.

"Connor, just dance," I cut him off, not interested in dissecting Nate's reactions.

"Damn, Wells, you're not the shy little girl anymore. Kind of sexy," he murmurs appreciatively.

I turn, pressing my back against him, arms threading behind his neck as I lose myself to the music. Across the room, Nate's gaze burns into us. If looks could kill, we'd both be ash.

Connor's hands grow bolder, his breath hot on my neck, pushing past my comfort zone and I start to panic.

"I, uhh… I need to use the bathroom," I blurt, needing escape.

"I can come?" he offers, half-joking.

"To help with what exactly?"

"Well, there are a few things I can think of," he smirks.

"I'm good," I state firmly, pulling away before he can respond.

I weave through the crowd, past a coffee table where lines of cocaine disappear amid cheers. I don't know where I'm going; I just need space.

Door after door yields no bathroom, until Jake's voice catches me. "There you are." His arm finds it's way around my shoulders.

"Why is it so hard to find a bathroom in this place? Shouldn't there be like twelve on this floor?" I deflect, trying to lighten my mood.

Jake laughs and leads me around the corner to a line of drunk teenagers waiting for the bathroom.

"So when did you become such a ladies' man?" I tease.

"Shut up." He nudges me, blushing. "Hang on, are you implying that I'm hot?"

"In my eyes, you'll forever be the kid who ate purple crayons."

"I was testing if they actually tasted like grapes," he protests, "and you promised that would be our secret."

I mime zipping my lips, but our levity fades as Jake sobers. "So, Nate's pissed off because I brought you here."

"I'm aware," I reply, masking frustration with a tight smile. "Is there anything that doesn't piss him off these days?"

Jake straightens, tension visible. "It's Nate's world, we're all just living in it," he says, sarcasm barely masking truth.

"Well, in the real world, not everything revolves around what ticks your brother off," I counter.

"Welcome to what my life has been like for the past two years," he agrees with a hollow laugh. "I'm going to check on Ollie. You okay now?"

I nod. "Make sure Ollie doesn't propose or do something stupid."

Jake salutes before disappearing into the crowd.

When I finally make it to the front of the cue, I feel relief. Closing the door behind me, feels like shutting out the entire world. Silence descends like a blessing, and I release a breath, letting the quiet wash over me like cool water.

Breathe.

Just breathe.

CHAPTER 7
CONNOR JAMES
NATE

THE BASS POUNDS THROUGH THE FLOORBOARDS, BUT CAN'T DROWN OUT the roaring in my ears as Connor's fingers trace paths across Nora's body. Each touch is a match strike against my skin. My jaw clenches as bile rises in my throat watching him stake his claim. The jealousy burns close, a wildfire spreading through my chest with nowhere to fucking go.

I should be past this.

Should be immune to the way she still pulls at something deep in my chest. But watching Connor touch her with such casual possession makes my blood surge hot and deadly, obliterating what little high I had left.

Keep telling yourself that, Nate.

I grab another drink and a bottle of water, shoving my way outside where the night air clings to my skin like a second shadow. Finding a quiet spot away from the party's relentless heartbeat, I collapse onto a weathered bench. The weight of every bad choice I've made settles over me like a burial shroud. I'm the reason we're strangers now, why this gulf between us only grows wider with each passing day. Regret sits like stone in my chest as I wonder how to fix something that might be beyond repair.

The click of my lighter briefly illuminates the darkness. I inhale deep, hold the smoke until my lungs burn, then exhale through my nose. The nicotine barely touches the edge of my tension. Having her close is torture, but her absence is its own special kind of hell. This summer already feels like a lifetime too long. I'll spend it chain-smoking and drinking, trying to numb the parts of me that still yearn for her.

The air shifts and I know she's here before I see her. Nora emerges onto the patio, her breathing measured as she leans against a pillar. Like gravity, I find myself moving toward her despite every instinct screaming to maintain distance. I rest my elbows on the railing beside her.

"You should reconsider who you spend your time with."

She turns, arms crossed. "Does that include you?"

My lips curl into a smirk.

There she is.

"Just looking out for you."

"And why are you all of a sudden acknowledging my existence now?" The challenge in her voice makes my pulse skip.

I can't tell her I never stopped being aware of her. That she's been a constant hum under my skin since we were kids. The pull ebbed during freshman year but never truly faded. She's always there, a persistent rhythm in my chest that I can't shake.

"Why are you looking at me like that?" I ask, trying to decode the mystery in her eyes.

"I'm just trying to figure out which Nate I'm getting now. The considerate one or the arrogant one."

"I just thought you'd have standards when it comes to company," I bite out, fury and frustration tangling in my throat.

"That's rich coming from you. I thought you had taste." She nods toward Farrah downing another shot. "Guess we were both wrong."

Silence stretches between us, thick with unspoken words. She takes another long drink.

"You need to slow down," I say, concern bleeding through my anger.

She leans against the railing, and I force myself to meet her gaze. Even in the dim light, she's devastating—all forest-green eyes and quiet defiance. It's like playing with matches in a room full of gasoline.

"Are you keeping tabs on me now?"

I ignore her question, holding out the water bottle. "Drink it."

She accepts with an eye roll, taking slow sips. "You don't need to babysit me, Nate. I'm not five anymore."

"I'm not trying to babysit you, I just—" The words tangle in my throat. "My mom would kill me if she knew I let you get wasted and hang out with that dickwad."

"Well, Nate," she steps closer, confidence radiating from her like heat, "I'm not your problem or a chore you need to handle, so you don't need to worry about me."

I study her, thrown off balance by her certainty. Her eyes catch me, pulling me in like they always have. "I don't see you as either of those things."

The music fades to white noise as we lock eyes. Having her this close soothes an ache I've been carrying so long I forgot it was there.

"Whatever. I'm not here to play whatever twisted games you're pushing. We can just go back to ignoring each other." She turns to leave, but instinct makes me reach for her arm.

She flinches.

The reaction hits me like a physical blow. Fear flashes across her face as she wraps her arms around herself, staring at the floor.

I release her immediately, stepping back to give her space. When she finally looks up, the sadness in her eyes makes my jaw clench with guilt. There's something else there too, but she looks away before I can name it.

Connor's arrival shatters the moment.

"Got that drink you asked for," he says with a smug grin that makes my fists itch, balancing two cups in his hands. My jaw tightens as he drapes an arm around her shoulders.

"Farrah's been looking for you, man," he adds, nodding toward the bar where she's shooting daggers at me.

Without breaking eye contact, I step forward and pluck one of the drinks from Connor's hand. His smile falters as I tilt my head back and drain the entire drink in one continuous gulp, the liquor burning a path down my throat. I crush the empty cup back into his palm before gesturing at the water bottle in Nora's hand.

"Drink more water," I manage through clenched teeth before turning to head inside.

"He's insane. I'd watch myself with that one." Connor's chuckle follows me, and it takes everything I have not to show him what real insanity looks like. But Nora doesn't need to see that side of me, not here, not now.

I bite my tongue and keep walking.

Fucking progress.

Weaving through the crowded house, my thoughts as dense as the press of bodies, I wonder how I let her get under my skin again. Unease gnaws at me knowing she's out there with Connor. I need to find Jake— he brought her here, maybe she'll listen to him. But first, I need to find Christian.

Just one more hit to get through this night.

"Where's the weed?"

"Sure you don't want to try something a little stronger?"

Yes.

"No. Where's the weed?"

"It's not like Nate Sullivan to turn down a—"

"Give me a fucking joint. I'm not asking again."

"Jesus, chill man." Christian hands me a joint, annoyance flickering in his eyes. I snatch it and storm out, hoping to find Nora alone, Connor nowhere in sight. But the patio is empty. Panic claws at my chest— Connor is bad news, and if that son of a bitch touches her...

The backyard reveals nothing but typical party chaos. They couldn't have gone back inside; I'd have felt her presence. There's only one other place he'd take her to be alone.

Farrah's voice cuts through my thoughts like a rusty blade. "Nate! Are you going to ignore me the entire night?"

"Have you seen my brother?"

"Are you serious right now?"

"Have you seen him or not?"

"Oh, so I have to answer all your questions, but you get to ignore mine?"

"Fine," I snap, turning to face her. "Yes, I'm ignoring you. No, I don't want to fuck you. Yes, I'm preoccupied. No, I don't want to discuss it. Now, have you seen my brother?"

Her anger is almost tangible. "I actually cannot believe you."

"I'm going for a walk."

"I'll come with—"

"No," I cut her off sharply. "I need to be alone."

Her sneer is immediate. "Alone? Alone with that little—"

I whirl around, voice dropping to a dangerous whisper. "Don't."

"What's your obsession with her?"

A bitter laugh escapes me. If only she knew.

"Go do a few more lines, Farrah."

"Fuck you. You're one to talk, asshole."

She's not wrong. But at least I'm honest about it.

I storm toward the beach, party noise fading into the rhythm of waves. In the distance, I spot Nora, her posture heavy with whatever weight she's carrying.

I freeze.

Let her go, Nate. She doesn't need you fucking up her life more than you already have.

I've repeated that a hundred times, yet I still can't walk away.

Then I see Connor following her, something predatory in his easy stride. My stomach turns.

I move without thinking, staying hidden but drawn forward by something I can't fight. Nora's voice drifts over, soft and placating, followed by Connor's darker tones and a laugh that chills my blood. I see them clearly now.

Nora tries to step back, but Connor's hand snakes around her waist, pulling her close. Her body goes rigid, panic in her eyes, then his lips press against hers.

I snap.

And all I see is red.

CHAPTER 8
BREATHE IN, BREATHE OUT
NORA

I TAKE ANOTHER SIP OF WATER, COURTESY OF NATE EARLIER. THE COOL liquid does little to wash away the bitter taste of being caught between Connor and Nate's egos.

"So, what's the story with you and Sullivan?" Connor's curiosity has an edge to it, predatory almost. "He's been glaring holes into my back all night. Looks about ready to go for my throat."

"There's no story. He's just... being Nate." My voice wavers just enough to betray me, and I curse my inability to lie convincingly.

Connor's smirk deepens as he closes the distance between us. "Here's to bad decisions then." The way he tips back his beer feels like a countdown to something I desperately want to avoid.

"Actually, I'm feeling a bit dizzy. Need some fresh air." The excuse sounds weak even to my ears.

"You're already outside," he laughs, the sound laced with something that makes my skin crawl.

"It's too loud here," I stumble back, seeking escape. "I'm just going to—"

I don't finish. Instead, I flee into the darkness, each step away from Connor easing the vice grip around my lungs. The party's chaos fades behind me as I make my way to the shoreline, where my heels sink into cool, wet sand. I slip off my shoes, letting the damp grains soothe my feet.

The ocean stretches before me, a vast darkness under a star-scattered sky. My chest aches with longing for simpler comforts: worn pajamas, a soft blanket, the familiar comfort of my favorite movies. I close my eyes, breathe in the salty air and listen as the waves create their endless rhythm.

"Hey, Dad," I whisper to the moon, its gentle light a poor substitute for his presence. "I miss you. I'm sorry it's been a while." The words feel foolish, yet they're the only bridge I have to him now. Grief is relentless. It comes in waves and the one person who could help me navigate these feelings is the very one who is gone.

Footsteps interrupt my solitude. Before I can react, unfamiliar hands wrap around me. The scent is wrong—not the one that means safety. My heart pounds against my ribs as Connor pulls me closer.

"Who are you talking to out here all by yourself?" His breath reeks of alcohol, hot against my neck.

"Connor, you're drunk." I struggle against his grip, but he only tightens his hold when I turn to face him. His fingers digging into my waist.

"Come on, Nora. You've made me chase you, save you, all night." His words slither between us as he edges closer.

"I didn't ask you to do either," I snap, pushing against his chest, but he's immovable.

"But I still did." His grin turns predatory, misinterpreting my fear for coyness.

"We should go back to the party." Desperation edges into my voice.

"Or we could go to my place."

My stomach lurches. "I'm good."

"Fine, we could do it here." The dangerous edge in his tone makes my blood run cold. "You like playing hard to get, don't you?"

"I'm not playing. Let me go, Connor." Terror roots me to the spot as his grip tightens further.

"Or what?" His lips brush my ear, sending revulsion through me.

This can't be happening.

Not again.

I need to fight, to scream, but panic throttles every instinct.

"Connor, seriously get off me. Now." My shove against his chest only makes him press closer, his lips trailing down my neck as tears blur my vision.

"I bet you taste so fucking good, Nora. His whispered words make me shudder before his mouth crashes onto mine.

A familiar, husky voice cuts through the night like a blade. "You have three seconds to get away from her."

Nate appears, his expression murderous, body coiled with fury. Relief floods through me, tangled with fresh fear.

"Fuck off, Sullivan," Connor hisses, his hold loosening slightly.

"Get your fucking hands off of her, or you won't have any left to fuck yourself with." Nate's voice drops to a deadly whisper. "I'm not going to tell you again."

"Is that a threat?"

"Did it sound like a compliment?"

"Nora and I were just get—"

Nate's fist connects with Connor's face before he can finish. "Time's up."

The impact sends him stumbling backward, blood trickling from his split lip. Nate advances, each punch precise and brutal.

"What the fuck is wrong with you?" Connor clutches his jaw, trying to defend himself.

"I warned you." Nate grabs Connor's shirt, pulling him close. "But then again people like you never fucking listen."

Another punch lands with a sickening crunch. Connor collapses, groaning.

"Nate!" My voice breaks through his rage. He freezes, fist raised, chest heaving.

Jake and Ollie appear, pulling Nate back. His eyes never leave Connor, who struggles to his feet, face bloodied.

"This isn't over, Sullivan," Connor spits.

"Stay away from her." Nate's voice carries a deadly promise.

Connor glares at me. "Bitch."

Nate lunges, but Jake and Ollie hold him back. "He's not worth it, man," Ollie pleads.

"You're gonna pay for this, Sullivan!" Connor shouts as he retreats.

"Try me, asshole." Nate spits back.

My legs threaten to give way as the adrenaline ebbs. I wrap my arms around myself. How did I get caught in the middle of this chaos?

"Nate," I call softly. He stands apart, back turned, blood staining his shirt from his split lip and knuckles. A bruise blooms under his eye—I hadn't noticed Connor landing a hit.

"I fucking told you to take her home," he snaps at Jake, his voice sharp with fury. His bloodshot eyes carry a wild edge I've never seen before.

This is all too much.

My chest constricts suddenly, lungs forgetting how to fill. The air turns thick, impossible to swallow.

"Hey Nora, are you all right?" Ollie's concern draws attention to my trembling form. Suddenly I'm on my knees, the cool sand against my skin is all I can feel until someone gathers my hair back.

"How much did she drink?" Nate's voice comes from behind me, sharp with worry.

"She wasn't really drinking," Jake answers.

"Connor was feeding her drinks all night. This is exactly why I told you to take her home."

The world tilts beneath me as I search for focus. Everything—the sand, the party's distant thrum, Nate's gentle touch in my hair—blends into a disorienting blur.

This was a mistake. The idea of losing myself in the crowd's anonymity seems stupid now.

"Hey." Nate's voice softens as he kneels beside me, his hand making soothing circles on my back. "Take a few deep breaths. Can you do that?"

I nod, closing my eyes against the dizziness.

"Good." His hand continues making circles on my back. It's not working because each breath seems to fuel the panic until tears slide down my cheeks. There's a crowd of people that's now gathered on the beach watching.

"Hey, don't worry about them." Nate shifts, moving in front of me, blocking out the curious onlookers with his broad shoulders. He cups my face gently with one hand, thumb brushing away a tear. His eyes lock onto mine, steady and grounding—now he's all I can see. The world narrows to just his face, his concerned expression, the slight furrow between his brows.

"You're okay. You're safe."

You're safe.

The words echo through me—I hadn't felt safe in so long. I focus on his face through my tears, trying to steady my breathing. The intensity in his gaze holds me there, anchoring me to the present moment instead of the panic.

He scoops up some sand, pouring it into my palm. "Feel that?"

I nod.

"Good. Feel the sand and take a few more slow breaths. In and out..." he demonstrates, his chest rising and falling in a rhythm I try to match. "In and out..."

My body gradually relaxes as I follow his lead, my fingers curling around the sand, its grittiness oddly comforting against my skin. I wonder where he learned this technique, how he knew exactly what to do when I was spiraling.

63

"Get her some water and meet me at the car," he tells Jake and Ollie. Turning back to me, he asks, "Can you walk?"

I want to say yes, but my legs feel like water. "I... I think—"

He lifts me into his arms effortlessly. My head spins from the combination of anxiety and his familiar scent as I rest against his neck, arms circling him.

"I can... I can walk," I protest weakly.

"Nora," his eyes meet mine, a ghost of a smile in his voice, "shut up and let me help you."

So I do, letting him carry me to the car through the neighbor's yard, avoiding the chaos of the party. His arms hold me securely, the scent of spearmint and whiskey more intoxicating than any drink. When he sets me down by the car, the silence between us fills with unspoken words.

"You weren't drinking?" Confusion and concern color his voice.

"I hardly finished the one I had." The memory of that night last year right before dad died stops me cold. "I just want to go home."

His expression tightens.

"Why did you—?" I begin, but I already know he won't answer fully.

"Because he deserved it," he says shortly, jaw set in that familiar, protective line.

It's not the whole truth, but with Nate, it rarely is. His guarded nature serves as both shield and fortress—keeping everyone at arm's length while somehow remaining close to me. Despite our distance, despite the changes, he still sees me as something to protect rather than an equal.

His dark eyes pull me in like gravity, making my heart race. He's different now, but what draws me to him—what both repels and attracts—remains as powerful as ever.

"Thank you," I mutter, barely above a whisper.

Nate opens his mouth to respond, but Jake interrupts with my water. "It was impossible to find a bottle of water in that place."

"Thanks," I manage, steadying my voice. To Nate, I just smile a half-heartedly.

Something in his gaze softens momentarily before vanishing. He opens the car door, his movements careful. "Get some rest," he murmurs as I slide into the seat.

He steps back, lighting a cigarette. The flame briefly illuminates the tension in his features before he exhales slowly, smoke curling around him.

"Drink more water. And Jake, make sure she takes an aspirin before bed," he adds roughly, then walks away.

I watch his retreating form, marked by the cigarette's glow until he disappears. In that moment, despite everything, I see him clearly. Nate might hide behind indifference, might play the detached protector, but his actions reveal deeper truths he won't—or can't—acknowledge.

Nate can pretend he doesn't care, that he doesn't need anyone. But I see him. I always have.

And maybe that's why he keeps his distance.

Because being seen is Nate's greatest fear, and his greatest need.

CHAPTER 9
LAST SUMMER
NORA

June 2006
15 years old

THE SUN STREAMING THROUGH THE CURTAINS CASTS A HONEYED GLOW across the spare lounge room. The walls feel like they're closing in until Jake appears, shutting the door behind him with a quiet click that somehow grounds me. His presence has always been my anchor, especially now when everything else feels like it's drifting away.

"It's a dumb question but I'm going to ask it anyway, how are you holding up?" His voice carries a gentle concern that makes my chest ache.

"I'm surviving." The lie sounds hollow even to me.

He laughs softly, seeing right through me as always. "Still a terrible liar." His elbow bumps mine, the casual touch anchoring me to the present.

"I am as good as anyone can be, considering." The words catch in my throat.

Instead of pressing further like everyone else has today, Jake moves to examine a photo on the mantle. It's from last summer on the family boat —me at fourteen, Ollie and Jake at sixteen, and Nate, freshly eighteen. We're all sun-kissed and laughing, unaware that these moments would become precious memories far too soon.

"He wanted to be here," Jake murmurs, his voice strained as he mentions his brother. "Nate's just been... busy with school and football."

The lie hangs between us. I know the truth—I overheard Lydia telling Mom about Nate's spiral. Skipped classes. Missed practices. Lost scholarship. The golden boy who was supposed to carry on the family legacy at Stanford, derailing instead. It hurts to think about how much he's changed, but right now, I can't let myself sink into that particular grief. Today's pain is enough.

Jake sets the photo down and crosses to me, his warm hand finding mine. The touch feels as natural as breathing.

"I'm here for you, always. You know that, right?"

His turquoise eyes, deep as the ocean and just as constant, hold mine. There's something about Jake that creates a pocket of calm in any situation, since we were kids. I lean into him, breathing in the familiar mix of a spicy-sweet blend of cinnamon that clings to his skin.

"We should probably head back out," I mumble against his shirt. "Ollie's probably feeling lost out there."

Jake catches my tears with his sleeve, unconcerned about the makeup staining the white fabric. "You're going to be okay, Nora. I promise." He extends his pinky, the childhood gesture hitting me right in the heart.

"Swear?"

"A pinky promise is legally binding, I'm pretty sure," he jokes, pulling me close again. His lips brush my hair. "No matter what, you'll always make your dad proud."

The day bleeds into night, leaving behind a house full of emptiness and too many casseroles. Mom and Lydia are asleep on the couch as *Footloose* credits roll silently across the TV screen. I kiss Mom's forehead, my chest tight with love and worry. The clock reads 11:34 PM—marking the clear divide between my life with Dad and without.

A polaroid on the fridge stops me in my tracks—the last photo of Mom and Dad together, taken with the camera Dad gave me for my fifteenth birthday. They're smiling, unaware it would be their final picture. My fingers trace Dad's face through the tears. How is it possible to still have tears left?

When I make it back to my room, Jake's there by the window, funeral suit disheveled in a way that somehow makes him look more put-together. His sleeves are rolled up, collar loose, hair a mess from running his hands through it all day.

"Didn't think anyone was still up," I whisper.

He turns, leaning against the windowsill. "Had to escape Ollie's *Grand Theft Auto* rampage. Kid was about to demolish the controller."

The silence between us feels comfortable, weighted with understanding. Jake moves to sit beside me, close enough our shoulders touch.

"I feel like I'm barely hanging on," I admit, the water bottle crinkling in my grip.

"Well that's understandable." His arm slides around my shoulders, solid and warm. "Nor, you're not alone in this."

"Could you stay?" The words slip out before I can stop them. "Just for tonight?"

Without hesitation, he nods, pulling off his dress shirt. I try not to stare at the lean muscle underneath—when did Jake start looking like that?—as he tugs on the hoodie I'd taken from the lake house last summer.

"So you're the hoodie thief," he teases.

"Borrowed," I correct, my cheeks warming. "And it's mine now."

We settle into bed like we've done a hundred times before, during backyard campouts and storm-scared nights. Jake tucks me against his chest, his heartbeat steady against my back.

"Hey Jake," I whisper into the darkness.

All I get is a drowsy "Mmm," his voice thick with sleep.

"Happy birthday for yesterday."

There's a pause, followed by a sharp intake of breath. "Oh fuck, Nor." His body tenses behind me. "It's 12 AM, it's..." He trails off as realization dawns on him.

My sixteenth birthday.

Jake's arm tightens around me. "Shit, I'm so sorry. With everything happening, I didn't..." His voice cracks. "I should have remembered."

"Don't say it, please." I fight back tears but it's useless because they're already flowing, dampening the pillow beneath my cheek.

Jake shifts, propping himself up on one elbow. In the dim light, I can see the guilt written across his face.

Birthdays going forward will forever be tainted by this day.

Jake settles back down, pulling the blanket higher around us both. "I'll be here in the morning when you wake up, promise." He whispers, his breath warm against my ear. His pinky finds mine beneath the covers, linking together like when we were kids.

"Thank you." The words come out fragile, barely there.

I stare at the moonlight painting shadows across my floor, thinking about how grief moves like waves, pulling at the shore of memory. No one knew Dad was sick—not until the tumor made itself known too late. Time is cruel that way, slipping through our fingers while we're busy making plans.

I'm scared to close my eyes, because when I wake up tomorrow, I'll have to face the truth all over again—he's really gone. My sixteenth birthday, and he won't be there with his goofy dad-dance and off-key singing.

Sweet sixteen.

There will be nothing sweet about birthdays going forward, just another day to count the ways he's missing, another milestone that turns the knife of his absence. From now on, every candle I blow out will just be a reminder of the wish that can never come true.

Jake's breathing eventually steadies behind me, but his grip remains protective, as if he could somehow shield me from tomorrow.

As sleep claims me, I let myself drift into dreams where time stands still, where laughter echoes across summer lakes, and Dad is forever calling us home for one more sunset.

CHAPTER 10
NEVER DRINKING AGAIN
NORA

PRESENT DAY

I LOOK LIKE A DISASTER. FEEL LIKE ONE, TOO. MY HEAD'S POUNDING LIKE A drumline, and my body feels like it's been steamrolled. The reflection staring back at me is a stranger. The echoes of last night crash into me—the sharp snap of flesh hitting flesh, the dark fury in Nate's eyes, the blood. Seeing him like that, consumed by darkness, was like peering into a chasm ready to swallow us whole. Part of me was pissed he treated me like some damsel in distress, but a bigger part was grateful he stepped in before Connor could go further.

Connor.

My chest tightens at the memory. That suffocating paralysis when he grabbed me returns full force—his touch burning my skin, his breath hiss by my ear. Those predatory eyes stripped away my sense of safety, leaving an indelible mark. The room shrinks around me, my breathing shallow and ragged. I'm caught in a web of panic, each thought tangling tighter.

Breathe, Nora.

You're okay. He can't hurt you.

But the words feel hollow. Connor's presence lingers in every shadow, woven into my nightmares. Yet despite this rocky summer kick-off, I refuse to let him steal what's left of it because I've survived worse.

Passing Nate's room with the door wide open, his bed remains untouched. The thought of him out there somewhere, maybe with

Farrah, his bloodied hand still messed up, twists my stomach. He made it clear it wasn't my concern but that only makes it worse.

"Well, well, look who decided to grace us with her presence," Ollie quips, his smirk wide and annoying. Before I can react, Jake smacks him upside the head.

"What was that for?" Ollie rubs his head, scowling.

Jake grins, all charm. "Because you snore so fucking loud and kept me up for half the night. Seriously, someone from Argentina could probably hear how loud you snore." He hands me a glass of orange juice, his eyes searching mine. "How'd you sleep?"

"Pretty good," I lie, forcing down a sip.

The nightmares are relentless, but who's counting?

"Good," Jake nods, then suddenly says, "We're leaving in five minutes."

"Five—" I start, but Lydia sweeps in, her presence filling the room with maternal energy.

"Oh good, you're all up. How was last night?" Her keen eyes scan us, reading between unspoken lines.

"It was—" Jake begins.

"Utterly boring," Ollie interrupts, earning a sharp glance. "For real, if I knew it was going to be that lame, I'd have stayed in bed and caught up on my beauty sleep."

"Beauty sleep?" Jake scoffs. "It's gonna take more than sleep to fix what's going on with your face, sunshine."

Lydia waves off their banter. "Well, I'm just glad everyone's in one piece. And Nate? Is he home?"

Jake's expression tightens. "He stayed at Farrah's. They're hitting the beach today he said."

The idea of Nate with Farrah constricts something in my chest.

I shouldn't care. But sometimes the truth cuts deeper than lies. Expecting everything to snap back to normal was pure fantasy.

Jake leans in close, his voice low and tinged with excitement. "You now have three minutes to get ready. Got a big day planned."

I arch an eyebrow. "Why the mystery?"

His grin is infectious, a sly smile that promises adventure. "It's no fun without a little mystery. Two minutes now."

"What am I getting myself into?"

"Today is the official start of our summer." His expression feigns innocence, but anticipation sparkles in his eyes. "No hang-ups, no dramas."

My lips curve despite themselves. Leave it to Jake to flip the script. "Alright, alright. I'm going."

71

Lydia catches our exchange. "Where are you two off to?"

"We're heading out," Jake responds casually.

"What!? You're both ditching me too?" Ollie's head snaps up from the second bowl of cereal he poured himself.

"Sorry man. I'll make it up to you when I get back."

"Jake, before you go—" Lydia starts, and his shoulders slump slightly. "Could you swing by Antonio's garage later? My car needs picking up around one. I asked your brother, but—"

"I've got it," Jake jumps in and Lydia's face brightens with relief.

"I can drop you off, Lyds. Seeing as no one else seems to want to hang with me."

"Ohh, Buck, you know I'll always hang with you." Lydia kisses Ollie's head and his cheek fluster like they have ever since he was a kid.

Jake's mystery morning starts off at the one place he knew I couldn't wait to visit. Stepping into Gracie's Bookstore feels like coming home. The air is thick with aged paper and polished wood, each creaky floorboard a familiar friend. Towering shelves whisper stories beneath flickering vintage lamps that cast everything in honey-gold. The massive emerald armchair still beckons from its corner, beside Alfie's perpetually cluttered mahogany desk.

Jake trails behind me, his fingers brushing against book spines as we walk. "Still smells exactly the same," he murmurs.

I know exactly what he means. This place exists outside of time, somehow both ancient and eternally new.

A new face greets us from behind the counter—older, laid-back in a worn white tee and plaid shirt, sorting through a stack of leather-bound classics. His movements are careful, reverent almost, as he handles each volume. He looks up at the sound of the bell, warm brown eyes crinkling at the corners.

"Hi there, I'm Nick. Can I help you find anything?"

There's something endearing about his enthusiasm, and the way his hands gesture toward the special collection section. Jake and I exchange a knowing look—we've spent countless hours in that very corner.

"Is that Miss Lenora Wells?" Alfie's warm voice cuts through my thoughts, drawing an instant smile.

"Alfie!" The hug feels like sanctuary, but as I step back, change writes itself across his features. Silver threads his once-dark hair, and those kind eyes behind round spectacles seem dimmer, though they still sparkle with gentle humor. The slight tremor in his hands stirs worry in my chest—perhaps why he's hired help.

"How's my favorite customer?" Alfie asks, voice soft with memory. His eyes drift to Jake. "And her faithful reading companion, of course."

"You say that to all your customers," I tease, trying to ignore the way my chest tightens at the familiar exchange.

"Only the ones I actually like," he winks, then softens. "I heard about your father, Nora. I'm terribly sorry. He was a fine man."

The sympathy in his eyes is genuine but stirs carefully managed grief.

Nick clears his throat gently, a welcome interruption. "Uncle Alfie has been telling me stories about you two practically living here every summer," he says, gesturing between Jake and me. "Something about a secret reading club in the back corner?"

A surprised laugh escapes me. "The Midnight Readers Society," I confirm, catching Jake's eye. "Though it was hardly midnight. More like closing time."

"And hardly secret," Alfie adds with a knowing smile. "Not with all the candy wrappers you left behind."

"That was entirely Jake's fault," I protest, the memory warming me from the inside out.

Alfie's eyes twinkle. "I see you've met my nephew, Nick. He'll be with us through the summer. Hopefully longer." His tone carries a weight of expectation.

Nick gives a noncommittal shrug, but there's a hint of fondness in his expression. "We'll see, Uncle. Still got some things to figure out."

Alfie turns to Jake, who's been quietly observing our exchange with that half-smile of his. "And you, young man, better be taking good care of Nora here."

"I try, sir," Jake responds, his tone light but his eyes serious. "But she can be a handful."

The familiar warmth of the bookstore, the presence of people who care, it wraps around me like well-worn pages. Here, the weight lifts, if only briefly. Nick's presence adds something new to the familiar scene, like a fresh chapter in a beloved book.

"What's caught your eye lately?" Alfie asks, genuinely curious as always. He settles into his chair, a sign that we're in for one of his famous book talks.

"*The Fault in Our Stars*," I respond, continuing without prompting. "I like the books without fairy-tale endings." I take a look around the store, admiring my surroundings. "They're nice reminders of how temporary all this really is."

His smile illuminates the room. "That's quite a mature insight. Come, let me show you some limited editions we just got in."

I follow Alfie down one of the aisles and that vintage book scent wraps around me, making me feel more at home than anywhere else.

"It's really good to see you, Alfie," I manage, voice catching.

"Well, you were missed last summer," he replies, patting my shoulder. His eyes hold a mix of sadness and understanding. "I've had my share of losses too. Lost my Gracie years back. But she's still here. In every story, every book I touch."

"Do you believe in soulmates, Alfie?" The question slips out without a second thought.

He smiles wistfully. "I do. But soulmates aren't just lovers. They're friends, family. The connections that shape us, help us heal. Gracie reminded me of that often."

We spend the morning trading stories with Nick, soaking in Alfie's casual wisdom.

"Remember when Alfie claimed he hung out with Stephen King?" Jake grins.

Nick's eyes widen. "You never told me that, Uncle."

Alfie laughs. "Well, 'met' might be stretching it. Saw him at a signing. Makes for a better story though, doesn't it?"

As we browse the aisles later, Jake pulls out a battered edition of *The Secret Garden*.

"Remember that summer we tried making our own secret garden with Ollie and Nate?" he asks, nostalgia coloring his voice.

I laugh. "Yeah, until Mrs. Lowell's dog literally shat all over it."

He flips through pages, golden-chestnut hair falling just right across his forehead, those ridiculous eyelashes making him look like an indie film lead. "You were quite the hit at the party last night," I tease.

"What do you mean?"

"I mean, every girl there was practically gawking at you."

He laughs genuinely. "Gawking, really? Who uses that word?"

"Just calling it like I see it."

He leans close, mock-serious. "Someone's keeping a pretty close eye on me."

I roll my eyes, fighting a smile. "Just an observation."

"Is that jealousy I detect?"

"Jealous? Of what?"

"You said it, not me," he smirks.

His teasing infuriates and comforts me in that uniquely Jake way, proof some things never change.

Stepping into the bright street with my new book pressing against my chest feels like an anchor.

"So, where to?" I ask, already knowing.

"You know where."

"Corrigan's?"

"Bingo. If we hurry, we'll beat the rush for Cinnabons."

His hand finds mine, and suddenly we're running-laughing down the sidewalk, grief falling away like shed layers. In these moments with Jake, I'm just Nora again.

The bakery envelops us in warmth and spice. Jake orders our usual, and we claim our spot by the window, sunlight pooling on worn wood.

"I've been thinking," he starts, fidgeting with a napkin. "We should make a summer list."

"A summer list?"

"Yeah, all the things we want to do. Things we want to revisit." His voice carries determination, a promise to reclaim joy after everything that's changed.

"I love that."

He grabs a pen. "Sixteen things each. One for every summer. And the seventeenth? We'll keep secret until we do it."

"Deal."

We write and laugh until we lose track of time. Jake's phone interrupts the fun and his face falls while checking it. "Ah, shit. Mom's car."

"Go," I urge, masking disappointment. "I'll stay and read."

"You sure?"

"Positive. See you at home."

He ruffles my hair before dashing out, that familiar gesture sending warmth through me. Alone with my list, the pen feels heavy, but my heart is lighter.

This summer, despite everything, we'd make it count.

Before I can escape into my book, two figures approach. The girl catches my attention immediately—vibrant orange and pink outfit flowing perfectly, long black hair framing striking features. Her companion rocks a retro yellow bomber covered in patches, platinum buzz cut stark against deep skin, carrying quiet confidence.

"Oh, my God, hey!" The girl's voice carries. "You're Nora, right? From the party?"

I nod cautiously. "Yeah. How did you—?"

"Everyone there knows who you are now."

Great. So much for staying invisible.

"I'm Camilla," she beams, claiming the seat across from me. "And this is Marcus."

Marcus nods, grinning as he takes Jake's vacant spot. "Just an FYI, Camilla has no filter or personal boundaries. But it's nice to meet you."

I smile despite myself. "Likewise. I think."

His laugh is warm. "Well, you definitely made the night interesting."

"Glad someone enjoyed the show."

"So, what's your plan for tonight?" Camilla asks, radiating energy.

"Tonight?"

Is this stranger I met less than twenty seconds ago really asking what my plans are tonight?

"Yeah, there's going to be a bonfire at East End Beach. You should come."

Yes, yes, she is.

"Do you always invite strangers to things?"

"Told you, no filter or personal boundaries," Marcus whispers, nudging my arm.

"Only the interesting ones," Camilla grins, a confident sparkle in her eyes. "We'll pick you up on our way through. It'll be fun."

I hesitate, my fingers unconsciously tracing the edge of the summer list peeking out from my notebook. The whole point was to push myself beyond these comfortable walls I've built. To say yes when every instinct screams no. The paper might as well be glowing, challenging me directly.

"Uhh, yeah," I finally manage, swallowing down the anxiety rising in my throat. "Yeah sure, why not?" The words feel foreign on my tongue, but somehow right.

Camilla claps excitedly, her bracelets jingling with the movement. "It's settled. Give me your phone so you can text me your address."

She punches in her digits and hands me back the phone.

"I think this is the start of a really amazing friendship, girlfriend."

"We'll see you tonight at seven!" Camilla yells as she walks toward the front door.

As they leave, I glance at my blank seventeenth item. Maybe it's a placeholder for unexpected adventures. This summer might just be one for the books after all.

CHAPTER 11
YOU SHOULD SEE THE OTHER GUY
NATE

Watching Nora get into the car with Jake twists something deep in my gut. I can't take her home myself—not in my state—but knowing he's the one taking care of her drives a thorn deeper into my side. She hasn't been here a full day and she's already wreaking havoc in my head.

The party rages on around me, everyone too caught up in their own worlds to notice what just went down. Lines of white powder disappear up noses, couples lose themselves in dark corners, and I need a minute alone. In the bathroom, I lean over the sink, examining Connor's blood on my knuckles. At least that bastard got what he deserved.

The vanity's cold marble grounds me as I take a few steadying breaths. I pull out my phone and dial Jay's number. He picks up on the second ring.

"What's wrong?" Jay grunts, his voice rough with sleep.

"Who shit in your corn flakes?"

"Newsflash, asshole, you don't call unless something's wrong. Unless you've suddenly developed a taste for pleasant chitchat."

"Fuck off," I say, but there's no real heat behind it.

"You called me, remember."

"I need a ride. Can you come get me?"

"Where are you?"

That's one thing about Jay—he never asks too many questions. As much of a dick as I've been lately, he's one of the few who's had my back these past couple years. I know he'll answer whenever I call, even though I don't deserve that kind of loyalty.

I text him the address, and ten minutes later, the familiar roar of his black Camaro pulls up. I crush out my cigarette and head toward the car. Besides drugs, cars are our common ground. I helped him restore this piece of shit he bought, and somehow, we managed to turn it into something I'm actually proud to be seen in.

"Who the fuck lives here? Bill Gates?" Jay peers at the mansion, whistling low.

"Let's go."

"Where to?"

"You know where. I need to unwind."

His eyes catch on my poorly bandaged hand, swollen and likely broken, though whatever I took earlier is numbing the pain. "What happened to your hand?"

"Nothing. Just drive."

"Are you sure you don't wan—"

"Drive, Jay."

I close my eyes and lean back, letting the seat cradle my throbbing head. Jay mutters something under his breath, but I'm too exhausted to care. I want to get as far from this party and these people as possible. There's only one place that lets me escape.

A couple winters back when everything at home went to hell—Mom and Scott's screaming matches that could wake the dead—I needed out. My late-night wanderings led me to South End, where I met Jay and others seeking the same escape. These people weren't friends but acquaintances who never probed too deep. That's how I found myself at the Quarters, a sort of halfway house for the lost.

The dim room greets us with its familiar mix of ragged couches and a coffee table scattered with baggies—white powder, pills, my old friends.

But tonight, something new catches my eye: capsules and vibrant blotter paper.

"It's like LSD," Jay says casually, watching my reaction.

The urge to grab it, to feel the tab dissolve on my tongue or snort the contents straight into my bloodstream is almost unbearable. Instead, I reach for an oxy. As it hits my tongue, my muscles start to unwind. I shut my eyes, picturing the pill's journey, imagining it dissolving into nothing, seeping into my veins, slowing the relentless pace of everything.

The bass pulses through me, owning my heartbeat, dragging lights into long, haunting streaks across my vision. The music cages me, wrapping around my bones like barbed wire.

"You're gonna be so fucked up," a girl laughs, her voice grating against my ears.

"Isn't that the point?" I snap back. "To fade into oblivion?" The words come out sharper than intended, but she just smirks—that calculating kind of smile I've seen too many times before.

"You're Nate Sullivan, right?" she asks, like she hasn't already figured me out.

I despise small talk; silence is rare currency here. "Depends who's asking."

Her smile sharpens, predatory—the universal look of someone who thinks they're about to get fucked. After everything that happened tonight with Nora, all I want is to be left alone.

Time warps around me as the high kicks in. The bathroom becomes my sanctuary when the room starts spinning too fast. A girl snorting lines off the bathtub scrambles past me as I stumble in. I slam the door, gulping down air that tastes like cheap perfume and desperation.

My reflection tells the story—bloodshot eyes, pupils blown wide. Heat builds inside my skull, my chest vibrating with each thundering bass note.

Maybe both.

But fuck, it feels good.

Too good.

Scarily good.

This feeling, right here, is the slippery slope everyone warns about.

I slide down against the cold tile wall, letting the chaos fade into white noise. Time stretches and I'm not sure if minutes or hours have passed. My pulse pounds against my temples, drowning out the music. The world outside this small sanctuary carries on, unaware or uncaring of the storm brewing inside me. Exhaustion claims me there on the grimy bathroom floor, and I drift into uneasy dreams of emerald eyes.

THE HANGOVER HITS LIKE A FUCKING FREIGHT TRAIN TODAY. IT'S currently 5 PM and I have this fucking headache hasn't left me alone since I woke up.

I suppose I deserve it.

Every pothole in Jay's path is agony, each jolt a hammer to my skull. I should focus on keeping my stomach contents down, but my mind's stuck on replay—on last night.

Nora looked petrified. Of me.

That image of her backing away, eyes wide and trembling is seared into my brain. I became the villain in her story, the guy she never thought I'd be. She wasn't just scared of Connor sprawled on the ground, she was terrified of me, the monster I'd become.

I wanted to tell her, to scream that it wasn't really me, that I snapped seeing how that asshole handled her. But what's the use? She saw what she saw. There's no talking my way out of that.

Seeing myself through her eyes—through the lens of fear and profound disappointment—that's a special kind of hell. One I have no idea how to escape from.

The front door's creak echoes through the silent house, sounding almost accusatory. Inside, stillness grips me—the uneasy quiet that feels like walking into a scene you weren't meant to witness. Then the smell hits me—apple pie.

Kat's apple pie.

I find her in the kitchen, back turned, rolling out dough with practiced precision. The sight of her, so content and focused, nearly drives me to retreat but my feet won't move. She turns, probably sensing my presence, and her face lights up with that old, comforting smile.

"Nate, you're back." But as her eyes truly meet mine, her smile fades to concern when she sees I'm wearing the same clothes from last night. Only now, my t-shirt is painted red in places.

"Yeah," I mumble, hands diving into my pockets. "Where is everyone?"

She studies me, that maternal worry etched deep. "Your mom is at the country club for a volunteer meeting, Ollie went to the beach, and Jake and Nora spent the morning out."

Nora's name twists something inside me. I nod, feigning indifference and failing miserably. I wonder if Kat knows about what happened last night.

"Nate..." she starts, eyes fixed on my busted hand. "What happened?"

My fucking hand.

"Rough night," I say, which isn't entirely a lie.

Kat steps closer, commanding, "Sit," in a tone that brooks no argument. So, I do, feeling more like a kid than a twenty-year-old.

She tends to my cuts with gentle hands but sharp eyes that dare me to break.

Does she know how many times her daughter has done this for me when we were kids?

"Want to tell me what's really going on?"

I swallow hard. "It's nothing, Kat. Just boys being boys."

"Mhm." Her skepticism is thick. "I've known you your whole life. I know when you're bottling things up. And I'd bet it's more than just last night."

I wince, not from the antiseptic but because she's right. She's always been. "It's complicated," I admit, my voice barely a whisper.

Kat finishes with my cut but doesn't pull back. Instead, she takes my hand in hers, anchoring me to the moment. "Most things are. But you don't have to keep everything bottled up. I know I'm probably the last person you want to spill everything to, but just know that if you ever do, I'm here. Now take your shirt off so we can hide the evidence from your mom."

I look down at the blood-stained shirt that's also covered in dirt, probably from the dusty couch I slept on last night. Kat takes the shirt and when she does, I notice her staring at old scars across my body.

"Football," I lie. "It's a rough sport."

The lump in my throat swells, and I look away to hide the storm of emotions inside me.

"Kat, I know I haven't been around much. I'm sorry for that. I've just... been dealing with a lot and it shouldn't be an excuse but—"

She stays quiet, her thumb softly caressing the back of my hand. It's a simple touch, but it makes me feel less adrift. "Stop. We've all got our demons, Nate," she murmurs. "But you've got people who love you that you can lean on."

I nod, unable to speak, and finally, she releases my hand. She turns back to her pie dough, giving me space to breathe. I think about walking out, escaping this gentle scrutiny, but I stay. Maybe it's her unpushy kindness, or maybe I can't stand the thought of being alone right now.

"How's Nora?" The question slips out before I can stop it.

Kat pauses, then faces me again. There's a weight in her gaze that tightens my chest because I know what she's about to tell me has nothing to do with what happened last night.

"Honestly, she's like you in a lot of ways. She's been struggling but won't talk about it," she admits. "After everything that happened with David... and there were issues at school."

"What issues?" My voice sharpens with concern.

Kat hesitates. "She kept it to herself mostly. I tried to get her to talk, to see someone. But in the end, I didn't push. She withdrew from her friends, stopped going out. Seems like she's trying to handle too much on her own."

A storm of anger and guilt churns inside me—anger at whoever hurt her, and guilt for being so caught up in my own mess that I missed her suffering.

"You've always been there for her," Kat says softly. "Just be there for her now."

Not enough.

I stare at the table. "I should've been there more. Especially after..."

The words fade, choked by grief—after her dad died, after everything crumbled.

"You're fighting your own battles, Nate. You can't be everything for everyone all the time." Her voice is gentle but firm. "But I've seen how you care for her. The only other person who loved her as much as her dad was you."

The mention of David hits me hard, dragging me back to the last time I saw him. He'd joked about welcoming me as his son-in-law, and those words had made me feel like maybe I could be someone worthy.

The screech of the front door cuts through our moment. Mom's voice carries from the entryway—sharp and tinged with that familiar edge of concern. She's chirping while talking to Jake; she always is. I steel myself as they enter the kitchen.

The shift happens instantly when her eyes land on me. "Nate," she snaps, zeroing in on my battered face. "Where the hell were you last night? Do you have any idea how worried we were?"

I open my mouth, but Kat steps in before I can stammer out a lie. "Lydia," she interjects, her tone firm yet soothing. "He's back now, that's what matters."

Mom's gaze flicks between us. I watch her wrestle with her anger before she finally sighs. "Fine," she says, though it's clearly not. "Can you at least tell me where you were?"

"Crashed at a friend's," I mumble, the lie bitter on my tongue.

"Jake said you were staying at Farrah's?"

Fuck.

"Farrah's a friend, Mom."

Her frown deepens, probing for more, but she lets it drop—for now. "And why aren't you wearing a shirt?"

"He was helping me with the pie, got flour all over himself," Kat covers smoothly, shielding my stained shirt from view as I try to hide my fucked-up hand.

Mom's skepticism fills the air, but she shakes her head and mutters something about boys and their secrets as she exits. Once she and Kat start discussing their day, Jake, who quietly snuck in while Mom went off at me, nods toward the backyard.

"You should see something," he says, voice grave. He leads the way outside, closing the door with a soft click that seals off any chance of being overheard. Pulling out his phone, his expression grim, he adds, "Someone caught your freak-out on camera last night."

My stomach drops.

Jake presses play, and there it is in stark clarity—my fists flying, uncontrolled and brutal. But it's Nora's face that guts me—her eyes wide with fear, body recoiling from the monster I'd become.

"Turn it off," I choke out.

Jake stops the video but keeps his phone raised, gaze heavy with unspoken questions.

What can I say?

That I lost my mind seeing another guy touch her? That I've become everything I promised myself I'd never be?

The silence stretches between us like a widening gulf, filled with the echoes of what I've done. I shake my head, nausea crawling up my throat. Jake lets me escape without argument, and I'm silently grateful for that small mercy.

Back in my room, I slam the door, the silence of the house weighing down on me like a physical force. Nora's terrified face haunts me, her voice echoing in my head on a relentless loop. There's no escape from it.

I sink into my bed, letting the familiar chords of *"With Arms Wide Open"* fill my ears. It's not just the lyrics that speak to me, but the way each note seems to stretch and bend, echoing the tumult inside. Scott Stapp's voice cuts through the chaos of my thoughts, raw and gritty. Every line about change and redemption hits too close to home.

As the guitar riffs swell, I feel a momentary reprieve from the relentless replay of last night's events. The chords climb and fall like my chest as I try to breathe through the tightness gripping me. It's a small escape, a moment where the weight seems just a bit lighter. The forgotten vodka bottle on the floor beside my bed tempts me. It's been there for ages, untouched, but today it feels like the only answer. I grab it and take a swig, the liquid burning down my throat—a welcome pain compared to the turmoil in my head. Yesterday's hangover still lingers, and as much as I want to numb this overwhelming guilt until I can't feel the edges so sharply, I set the bottle down.

This is fucking pathetic.

A soft knock cuts through the music, yanking me back to reality. Her voice filters through the door, tentative but sure.

"Nate? Can I come in?"

Shit.

My whole body tenses up like I've been hit with a live wire. Just her voice and I'm already a goddamn mess. I shove the bottle under my bed and sit on the edge, gripping the sheets till they might tear. Like that's gonna stop me from doing something stupid the second she walks in.

"Yeah." It comes out rougher than I meant.

She steps almost hesitantly inside, and her attempt at a casual smile doesn't reach her eyes.

Fuck me.

The way she smells hits me like a sucker punch—lavender and something that's just... her. My mouth goes dry and my brain short-circuits.

God, I need to get a grip.

"I wanted to check on you after—" Her gaze drops to my bandaged hand.

"You shouldn't have been at that party," I growl, hating myself even as the words come out. But I need the wall. Need something between us before I do something we'll both regret.

Her smile vanishes and she takes a step closer, crossing her arms across her chest. "Seriously? We're doing this again?"

I don't move, my skin's too tight and it feels like I might explode if I get near her. "That party wasn't for you."

"Why are you acting like this?"

"Because you saw what happens at parties like that. Guys like Connor —they're fuckboys. They don't care about girls like you." My chest tightens with every word, this mess of anger and fear and this other thing I refuse to name churning inside me. "He cares about one thing, and he almost got it last night."

Her posture stiffens, chin lifting in that way that drives me crazy, that makes me want to—fuck. Don't go there.

"I didn't need your help."

"Are you fucking kidding me?" The words tear out of me, raw and desperate. My hands ache to grab her shoulders, to make her get it. "What would you have done if I hadn't stepped in?"

Her eyes flash, and Christ, she's beautiful when she's pissed.

"I can handle myself, Nate. I'm not a fragile thing that needs protecting."

"That's not what I'm—"

"Then what are you trying to say? Because all you have been is a total asshole for no reason since the moment I got here."

She's furious, and some sick part of me loves it. The way her cheeks flush, the way her chest rises and falls faster. It's proof she still feels something around me. At least anger's better than nothing.

My silence is enough for her to turn around and head for the door. No way in hell am I letting her walk out like this.

Before I can think better of it, I'm up, slamming the door shut, trapping us in this too-small room. Her perfume's everywhere now, making my head spin. She gasps, this tiny sound that shoots straight through me, making my heart hammer against my ribs. I'm too close.

Way too fucking close.

Close enough to see the gold flecks in her eyes, close enough that if I shifted even an inch, we'd be—

"Maybe," I say, my voice dropping low, every muscle in my body straining with the effort not to touch her, "I am an asshole. But I'd never touch you without your permission."

The words hang between us, loaded with everything I'm not saying. My eyes drop to her lips, and holy shit, I have to ball my hands into fists to keep from doing something monumentally stupid.

She shifts, her back against the door, her body so close I swear I can feel her heartbeat matching mine. "I need to get ready."

"For what?" It comes out like gravel.

"The bonfire tonight."

"Why the hell are you going to a bonfire after what happened last night?" Jealousy rips through me, ugly and hot. The thought of her around those guys again makes me want to put my fist through a wall.

She laughs, but it's hollow. "Why are you asking questions you don't want answers to?"

I move closer, my body no longer taking orders from my brain. I can feel the heat coming off her skin, and it's making me lose my mind. "Because I like to know things."

Her head leans back against the door, her throat exposed, and Jesus Christ, the things I want to do. My hands twitch at my sides, itching to slide up her arms, to tangle in her hair.

"I want to try and enjoy myself this summer, Nate. Can I do that, or do I need to start getting permission slips signed off for everything?"

Her defiance hits me like a kick to the chest. "You think being with strangers will make you feel normal?"

"Would you prefer me miserable and locked up all summer?" Her voice softens, something vulnerable breaking through, and it wrecks me.

We're breathing the same air now.

"Why can't we just talk, like we used to?"

The question tears me open. My hand moves before I can stop it, hovering near her, not touching her, but fuck, I want to.

"Because things aren't like they used to be."

Because you exist in a world where I can't have you.

Because every time you look at me like that, I'm one second away from completely losing it.

85

She looks at me like I've slapped her, and it kills me. "So you're just going to keep shutting me out?"

A knock on the doorframe interrupts us, and I step back like I've been burned, my heart still trying to pound its way out of my chest.

"We're heading out," Mom announces. "Are you two all good?"

"Yeah," Nora forces a smile, but her eyes stay locked with mine, this electric current still running between us. "We're fine."

They leave, and Nora's eyes meet mine one last time.

That look—hurt, confusion, and something else that mirrors the ache in my gut—nearly breaks my resolve. I don't stop her as she walks out, though every muscle in my body screams to follow her, to pull her back.

I just stand there, like a coward, listening to her footsteps fade, breathing in what's left of her. The room feels too empty now. The silence she leaves behind echoes with all the shit I couldn't say, with all the ways I wanted to reach for her but didn't.

CHAPTER 12
STICKS AND STONES MAY
BREAK MY BONES
NATE

April, 1994
7 years old

I SQUEEZE MY TOY CAR REALLY TIGHT, MY HANDS ARE SWEATY AGAINST THE
plastic. Tomorrow's my birthday, but I don't feel happy like I should.
Instead, my tummy feels funny and I'm scared because Daddy is yelling
in the living room. He's never been this loud before. There's a big crash
that makes me jump and hide under my blanket.

I peek through the little space where my door isn't closed all the way.
Mommy looks really scared; her face all scrunched up weird.

Then Daddy hits Mommy, and she falls down crying.

My heart goes *boom-boom-boom* so fast it hurts. Jake's still sleeping in
his room far away because he's just a baby, and I'm glad he can't hear all
the scary noises.

I want to run out there and tell him to stop, like how superheroes do
in my cartoons, but I'm too scared. Daddy doesn't look like my Daddy
anymore—his face is all red and mean, and he's acting like the bad guys
on TV.

"You want to lie to me again, Lydia? How fucking dare you. After
everything I've done for you." Daddy's words are super loud and angry.

"Scott, please. I'm sorry. I wasn't thinking clearly. It shouldn't happen
but it did." Mommy talks really quiet, like when I'm sick and she tells me
stories to help me sleep.

"You're right, you weren't fucking thinking. But then again, you never do." Something else goes crash—it sounds like when I accidentally broke Mommy's favorite glass cup last summer.

"You will be sorry, Lydia, believe me. You will be."

WHEN MORNING COMES, MOMMY WAKES ME UP WITH A BIG SMILE THAT looks weird and wrong. She helps me put on my Superman shirt, because it's my favorite. She keeps talking about how fun the party will be, but her eyes are all red and puffy like when she cries. There's a dark spot on her face that she tried to hide with her makeup stuff, but I can still see it.

"Mommy, you're sad."

"No, honey, I'm not sad. How can I be sad when it's my beautiful boy's seventh birthday today?" A tear falls down her face even though she's trying to smile.

"I don't like it when Daddy gets loud," I whisper, holding my car even tighter. Mommy kneels in front of me, and I can smell her flowery perfume that she always wears.

"Honey, listen to me, okay? Sometimes grown-ups have arguments, but they figure things out eventually. Today's your special day, so let's try to think about happy things, all right? Can you do that for me?"

I nod because I want to make Mommy happy, but my chest feels funny and empty.

The doorbell keeps ringing, and lots of kids from my class come in. Justin comes with his big smile, already talking about games we can play. Then Ollie shows up with a huge present, but Nora is the one that makes me feel a little better. She runs right to me and gives me the biggest hug ever.

"Happy Birthday, Natey!" She shows me a picture she drew. "I made this for you."

It's all of us being superheroes. I'm flying with big wings because I told her once that I wish I could fly like birds do. Ollie has super big muscles, Jake can run super fast with lightning around his feet, and Nora can touch stuff and make it pretty with flowers and colors. My face gets all warm looking at it. It's my favorite present ever!

"I love it," I say, my voice getting stuck in my throat a little. "I'm going to stick it on my wall in my room."

Her smile makes everything feel brighter, like when the sun comes out after it rains.

"Hey, Nate! Let's play Seven Minutes in Heaven because you're seven!" Justin says, super excited. We don't know what that means, but big kids play it, so we want to try.

Me and Nora end up in the dark closet together. I can smell the laundry soap Mommy uses and feel Nora sitting close to me. I can't see her because it's dark but my tummy feels all fluttery, like there are butterflies inside.

"Nate?" Nora whispers. "Why do you look sad?"

"I'm not sad," I lie, but my voice sounds wobbly.

"Liar, liar, pants on fire," she says, but not in a mean way. She says it nice, like when Mommy tells me everything will be okay.

"When Mommy or Daddy is sad, they give each other a kiss to feel better." Then Nora leans in and gives me a quick kiss on my lips. "Did it make it better?"

My heart does a funny jump, and I feel dizzy like when I spin around too much. "Yeah, I think so."

The door opens super fast, and the light hurts my eyes. "Time's up, lovebirds!" Justin yells and runs away laughing. Nora stands up and holds out her hand.

"Come on, Nate, I got you." Her hand feels warm and safe in mine.

In those seven minutes, Nora didn't just give me my first kiss—she made everything better. I think she took a piece of my heart. But I was okay with it because it was Nora.

CHAPTER 13
BITCHES AND BONFIRES
NORA

PRESENT DAY

I TRAIL BEHIND CAMILLA AND MARCUS, MY SANDALS CRUNCHING SOFTLY against the path as we approach the bonfire's inviting glow. The crisp night air carries notes of sea salt and burning driftwood, mingling with bursts of laughter that rise above the rhythmic crash of waves. It should feel peaceful but my stomach remains knotted with anxiety.

Camilla catches my eye, her smile warm and reassuring. "You okay?"

"Yeah," I say, aiming for confidence I don't quite feel. "I'm gonna look for Jake and Ollie real quick."

"We'll meet you by the fire." As I turn away, Camilla catches my hand. "If anything goes sideways, come find me, okay?"

I nod, touched by her protectiveness after knowing me less than a day. But as I weave through the crowd, my heart plummets. Connor is here, a smirk playing across his features despite the fresh bruise where Nate's fist connected. His eyes lock onto mine, predatory, and each step he takes in my direction sends ice through my veins. I stand frozen, the festivities blurring around me as he closes in.

"I need to have a word with you," he says, voice low and menacing.

Before I can respond, salvation arrives in the form of a girl with flawless caramel skin and expressive brown eyes. Her long dark hair cascades in waves down her back as she steps between us with practiced grace. Dismissing Connor with a glance, she grabs my hand.

"You came!" she exclaims, her voice rich with both warmth and steel as she steers me away from him.

Relief floods through me once we're clear. "Thanks for the save," I manage, my voice lighter than it has felt all evening.

"No problem," she replies, her smirk blooming into a genuine smile. "I've had my fill of dealing with guys like him. Egotistical jackoffs seem to be everywhere."

I raise an eyebrow, intrigued. "I see you're already acquainted with Eden's local wildlife."

"Well, I'm from London. We have our share of pompous jerks too. But trust me, they're universal." She pauses. "I'm Mia, by the way."

"I'm Nora." Despite her polished appearance, there's something immediately approachable about her.

She opens her mouth to speak, but I cut her off preemptively, bracing for questions about last night's drama.

Instead, she asks, "Oh, I was wondering if you knew Lydia Sullivan?"

My features soften with surprise. "Uh, yeah. She's a family friend. We spend every summer with the Sullivans at their lake house." Guilt washes over me for assuming the worst. "Sorry, I thought you were about to ask if I was the girl from the—"

"I try to stay out of drama," Mia interrupts kindly. "But you know how it is around here."

"Small town, big ears."

She gives me a sympathetic look. "People who thrive on gossip usually don't have much else going for them. Don't let it get to you."

If only it were that simple. "I wish I could erase last night from everyone's memory. Including my own," I admit quietly.

"Well, for what it's worth, I'm sorry you had to deal with Connor at all. He's notorious."

"That he is," I say, feeling unexpectedly at ease with her. "Thanks for stepping in though. I wasn't up for it tonight."

"Anytime," she says with a reassuring smile. "I've only been back in town a few weeks myself. My family just returned from India after two years. It's been quite the adjustment."

"India?" My interest piques. "That must have been amazing."

"It was," she confirms, eyes sparkling with memory. "But it's nice to be back. I missed the beach... and a bit of normalcy."

Before she can elaborate, Camilla and Marcus weave through the crowd toward us. "There you are!" Camilla calls out. "We were starting to wonder if you'd ditched us. Did you find Jake and your brother?"

"No, but guys, this is Mia," I say.

She offers them a warm smile. "Nice to meet you both."

Marcus cocks his head. "Do I detect an East London accent?" His attempt at British pronunciation makes Mia laugh.

"Fresh off the plane," she replies with a playful eye roll that has Camilla chuckling.

"Well, welcome to our little slice of chaos," Camilla says, linking her arm through mine as we head toward the fire.

Ollie materializes beside us, his presence as bold as his personality. "There's my little sis," he announces, throwing an arm around me. His eyes catch on Mia, and I practically see him falling in real time. "You good, Nor?"

"Yes, Ol, I'm fine. You can go now," I say, trying to dismiss him gently.

"Hang on, let me say hello to your friends properly," he insists, turning on the charm as he greets everyone, his attention lingering on Mia. Jake appears beside me, chuckling quietly at his friend's obvious interest.

"Wanna join us for volleyball?" Ollie asks Mia. "You can be on my team." He winks, aiming for smooth.

"Sure," she responds with a confident grin, their chemistry instantly apparent.

Jake steps up, volleyball tucked under one arm. "Nor, you should join us too."

I hesitate. "I'm all thumbs and toes."

"Come on," he pleads with those puppy dog eyes that nearly break my resolve.

Camilla quickly interjects, "I've claimed Nora tonight. You get to keep her every day, tonight it's my turn."

"Next time, promise," I say, grateful for the save.

Jake gives me a playful wink and a quick kiss on the temple. "Fine. Stay out of trouble," he teases before jogging off with Ollie and Mia.

Watching them go, I'm struck by how much Jake has changed from the shy, awkward boy I once knew. He's grown into himself, drawing others naturally while never failing to circle back to me with reassuring smiles.

Camilla nudges me, eyes gleaming. "That boy has a serious case of puppy love for you, girlfriend."

I laugh despite the flutter in my chest. "Jake? No, he doesn't."

"Oh, please," Marcus joins in. "It's as obvious as a giraffe in a flock of sheep. Has there ever been anything between you two?"

My thoughts drift to summers past. "No, nothing like that. He's been my best friend since we were kids. Not to mention he's like a brother to me."

"Really?" Camilla presses.

"Yeah," I affirm.

"Does the little golden retriever know that?" She nods toward Jake as he spikes the ball, celebrating the point.

"I'm steering clear of the Sullivan boys—and all boys—this summer."

"Oh girl, good luck with that," Marcus says, gesturing at me with a flourish. "You're a force, sweetie, not to mention an absolute stunner. If I didn't swing the other way, I'd totally shoot my shot with you."

His compliment, though sweet, makes me squirm. I've always seen myself as average, preferring to blend into the background. Even as my body has changed over the past year, I shy away from attention. Complications are exactly what I'm trying to avoid.

The night deepens, shadows dancing across the sand as the volleyball game continues. Jake's athletic grace draws admiring glances he seems oblivious to, though he keeps checking on me with little looks that make Camilla's earlier words echo in my mind.

Is it really that obvious to everyone?

I head to the makeshift beach bar to grab a bottle of water, and it takes less than sixty seconds to be cornered by another hellhound.

"You're brave showing your face tonight." Farrah's voice drops my stomach to my feet. She stands with arms crossed, flashy rings catching firelight like warning signals.

All I wanted was a bottle of water and a drama free night. Was that too much to ask for?

"What can I say? I love the beach," I reply, hoping my sarcasm masks my nerves.

"Especially after your little stunt last night," she snaps. "Where's Nate?"

"He's not here," I say, keeping it short as her smile turns saccharine.

"Kind of pathetic this damsel act you pull around him."

The air constricts around us. "We're just friends," I say firmly. "You have nothing to worry about."

"You think you're a threat?" she smirks, continuing, "That's cute."

Camilla sweeps in before Farrah can continue, and I exhale silently in relief.

"Hey, peroxide Barbie, turn around and walk away," Camilla says, looping her arm through mine.

Farrah's eyes flash as her minions appear beside her, tension crackling.

How do I keep landing in these situations?

Farrah's lips curl. "I admire you Camilla. Not everyone can pull off the bargain bin chic look as well as you do."

Camilla's grip tightens slightly, but her voice stays cool. "Sweetheart, my headband costs more than your hooker earrings do. And Farrah, if you're going to insult me, at least do it right."

"Jesus, Camilla, you should really come with a warning label," Jake laughs as he appears with Ollie and Mia, diffusing the tension.

Farrah's smirk falters and she turns away, clearly frustrated.

As we walk off, Camilla leans close. "Farrah's just salty 'cause Nate blew up at her last night. Big drama, but who knows the full story with those two and their fucked up situationship."

"They fought? Over what?"

She gives me a knowing look. "She's probably pissed because Nate's been avoiding her, or maybe because he played hero to you at the party."

"It wasn't like that. He just—" I trail off, unsure how to explain. The Nate who protected me felt like my Nate, the one I grew up with. I push that thought aside. He's not my anything anymore.

"What's even their deal? Why hang on to whatever they have?"

Camilla shrugs, watching the flames. "I mean, you know him better than I do. But Nate's not the type to play by anyone's rules, especially not Farrah's."

True.

"Wait, have you guys ever...?" Her question hangs.

"What, Nate and me? No. No way."

"Just asking. I mean from what I saw last night..." She studies the fire thoughtfully. "It was like the moon watching the sun."

Her words leave me speechless. I hadn't realized anyone could see the currents between us amid the shit show that was happening.

The longer I linger, the more displaced I feel, fighting the urge to pull my shirt down or wrap my arms around myself. I scan the crowd for Jake before turning to Camilla. "Hey, I think I'm going to bail."

"Don't leave because of that witch. Seriously, fuck her," she says fiercely. After being abandoned by a supposed friend when things got tough, her loyalty moves me deeply.

"I appreciate it, but I'm not feeling it anymore. I'll see you around." I give her a grateful look. "Call me tomorrow and we'll grab brunch or something, yeah?"

"Sure. Thanks, though. Really."

"For what?" She shrugs it off.

"For having my back."

"It's you and me now. Plus Marcus, too."

Jake jogs up, slightly winded. "You're leaving? I'll come with you if you want."

I shake my head. "Stay, have fun. I'm just tired, and honestly, I'll be out like a light. Plus, someone needs to keep an eye on Ollie." I nod toward where he and Mia share a blanket, lost in conversation.

"He's got it bad, huh?" Jake chuckles.

"He's a goner. And it took him what? A whole two days?"

He looks torn but hands over the keys. "Just text me when you get home, okay?"

"I will," I promise, turning away as the sounds of celebration fade behind me.

The gravel crunches under my tires as I pull into the driveway, killing the engine. The dark, silent house stands in sharp contrast to the bonfire's energy. The empty driveway is strange—everyone's usually home by now. I'm desperate to shed the night's drama like an unwanted skin.

"Hello?" My voice echoes through the quiet house, met only with heavy silence that sends unease crawling up my spine.

The faint sound of music grows clearer as I move toward the back-yard. Oasis' *"I'm Outta Time"* floats through the air, tugging at something deep inside me. Following the sound leads me to the pool.

And there's Nate, half-submerged and floating with his back to me, unaware of my presence. Moonlight traces the water streaming down his muscular shoulders, highlighting how much he's changed—more mature, more everything. My heart pounds as I struggle against a flood of emotions.

Goddammit. Why does he have to look so good?

I've spent years trying to convince myself my feelings for him were just a childhood crush meant to fade. But here he is, magnetic as ever, effortlessly pulling those old feelings to the surface.

He turns slightly, his eyes meeting mine. My breath catches, cheeks burning. His hair clings wet to his forehead, his expression softer than I've seen in ages. For a moment, everything else disappears—just us, the night air thick with memories, and music that feels like it's playing only for us.

I swallow hard, aiming for casual. "I didn't realize anyone was home."

His lopsided grin makes my heart stutter. "Everyone's still out."

"I didn't mean to interrupt."

"It's your house too now," he says, leaning back against the pool's edge, gaze steady on mine. The way he looks at me, like I'm the only person in his world, sends shivers down my spine.

"You're home early."

It wasn't a question but demanded an answer.

"Wasn't feeling it tonight."

I feel that familiar pull toward him, impossible to ignore now. Years of pretending I didn't care crumble away, leaving me with the raw truth: I don't think this feeling toward him ever went away.

Not for a second.

CHAPTER 14
LATE NIGHT SWIMS
NATE

OPTING OUT OF THE BONFIRE TONIGHT WAS PROBABLY ONE OF THE FEW good decisions I've made lately. The thought of pretending everything is fine feels like a sick joke. Instead, I play chauffeur, driving Mom and Kat to a bar before peeling off with some bullshit excuse about other plans. Mom doesn't push it. Guess that's what happens when you start to ghost your own life—people stop asking questions, either scared of the answers or just done giving a fuck altogether.

At least she's got one son who has his act together.

When I get back home, the silence slams into me harder than expected. The place is empty, the kind of quiet that amplifies every thought bouncing around in my skull.

Being left alone with my thoughts?

Dangerous territory.

I feel that old, familiar itch start to creep up, the one that screams for a hit to numb it all, or maybe something stronger. I head straight for the kitchen, reaching for the whiskey on the top shelf—the one Mom thinks she's hidden.

Tonight, it's a booze over anything harder. The crystal bottle catches the kitchen light as I pull it down, and my reflection fragments across its surface—distorted, broken, fitting. Drinking solo has turned into one of my pathetic hobbies lately. No need to let anyone see how deep I've really sunk.

I'm about to pour when I spot the mess the boys left behind. Cans, bottles, wrappers—like they think a maid's going to materialize and clean up after them. I set the bottle down with a sigh that echoes in the empty kitchen.

"Fucking kids," I mutter to the silence.

Mom has got enough shit to deal with without coming home to this mess. I grab a trash bag and start cleaning up, my movements automatic yet cautious, thanks to my fractured hand. If I keep busy, maybe I won't have to think about all the other shit that's gone down recently.

Something catches my eye as I pass the living room.

Nora's makeshift workstation is a disaster, papers and notebooks everywhere, just like she always leaves it when she's lost in her writing. A ghost of a smile tugs at my lips—same old Nora. I'm not trying to snoop, but as I move past, my hip catches the table, sending everything flying.

"Shit," I curse, dropping to my knees to gather up the mess. That's when I see it—a thick application form lying on the floor.

In bold letters: **McMillion and Sons UK - Writing Scholarship.**

So she is writing again. The realization does something weird to my chest. I start reading before I realize what I'm doing. Seeing that application twists something inside me. Pride, because she's getting back to what she loves, what she's brilliant at. But then it hits me like a sucker punch—she's actually doing something with her talent, while I'm just here, wasting away.

I toss the papers back on the table when my phone buzzes—missed calls from Farrah, texts from the boys about the bonfire, a couple from Jay. I ignore them all. Tonight I just need the quiet, even if it's the last thing I want.

The cleaning distraction lasts all of twenty minutes. My fractured hand throbs—a steady reminder of recent mistakes. I need something more to clear my head, something other than booze or pills.

Lately, the only thing that's been helping is the late-night swims. As soon as I step outside, the cool air brushes against my skin—a stark contrast to the day's heat and my own inner turmoil. The pool water gleams under the moonlight, still and inviting, as if ready to absorb all the shit weighing me down.

I slip into the water, and the immediate chill jolts through me, snapping me out of my spiraling thoughts. Each stroke is deliberate, each kick pushing away the noise in my head. The water cradles me, almost forgiving, offering a brief escape. With every lap, the tightness in my chest loosens, the simmering anger dissipates. Time becomes fluid until I'm floating on my back, gazing up at the stars.

I let myself sink until the water muffles everything but my heartbeat.

When my lungs start to burn, I push up, breaking the surface with a gasp. That's when I see her—a silhouette in the doorway I'd know anywhere.

The sight of her hits harder than the need for air.

I'm suddenly hyper aware of every inch between us. The music drifts through the speakers—Oasis, one of her favorites—and for a second, I'm thrown back to summers ago when this pool was our sanctuary, not some kind of battleground.

My chest tightens, the burn not from the swim but from the piercing intensity of her eyes on me. How can she look at me like that—like I still mean something to her—after all my fuck-ups?

Her eyes hold a mix of concern and something unspoken—a depth that scares the shit out of me because I don't know if I deserve it. The guilt gnaws at me, sharp and heavy, because if anyone knows the worst parts of me, it's Nora. Yet here she is, her presence a silent question I'm not sure I have the right to answer. I watch her swallow hard, like she's been caught in the act.

"I didn't know anyone was home," she murmurs, voice barely carrying over the gentle splash of water.

"Everyone's still out."

She nods, a hint of relief in her expression. "I didn't mean to interrupt."

"It's your house too now," I say, trying to ignore how the moonlight catches in her hair. "You're back early."

"Wasn't feeling it tonight," she admits, her eyes shadowed with something that looks a lot like sadness.

"Why not?"

"Why do you care?" she fires back, her tone sharper than expected.

I can't help but smirk as she tries to pretend like she's not affected by me just as much as I am by her. "I told you I like to know things."

"I told you not to waste your time."

She steps closer to the pool, slipping off her shoes to dangle her feet in the water. The dim pool lights cast shadows across her face, revealing the troubled look in her eyes.

Nora has a tell when she's upset—she can't meet your gaze, and she seems to shrink into herself.

I fucking hate it.

I push off the edge toward her, each stroke mirroring my mind's struggle for clarity. The cool water parts for me like the last of my restraint giving way. With every inch closer, I cross invisible boundaries that once seemed sacred, venturing into territory that feels both forbidden and inevitable.

"Do I make you nervous, Nora?"

The words rip out of me, rougher than I meant, but fuck it. I watch her fingers dig into the pool's edge like she needs something to hold onto. The water between us pulses, each tiny ripple drawing me closer like a tide answering the moon's irresistible call. So damn close but still out of reach, kinda like she's always been.

"No," she says, and I catch it—that little crack in her voice. Trying to sound sure but I hear what she's hiding. "You're not my type." Her eyes do that thing where they skate away from mine.

I can't help the grin that spreads across my face.

She's so full of shit. Playing this game where she pretends she's got walls I can't touch. She thinks all that armor she's built keeps me out, but her body's selling her out big time. That pulse hammering at her throat, the way her skin flushes pink when I get close—her body doesn't lie like her mouth does.

She feels me. Every-fucking-where.

"I never said I was," I whisper, moving in closer, the space between us disappearing. "But I think you're lying." My voice drops low, the way that used to make her shiver. I plant my hands on either side of her legs, trapping her between my arms. The concrete digs into my palms but I barely notice. She's so close now I can feel the heat coming off her skin, mixing with the water droplets on my chest. We're close enough that each breath we take feels borrowed from the other.

"You're dreaming," she fires back, a sweet venom in her smile.

She's been weaving through my fucking dreams for years. And what irks me now, despite all the shit between us, is I still want her in ways I shouldn't.

"You know how I know you're full of shit? Your lips say one thing, but your eyes," I lean closer, her breath hitching, "they tell me something else entirely."

There's a charged silence, our energy speaking volumes more than words ever could.

"Wow. I knew you were an asshole but an arrogant one too?" she challenges.

I laugh, real and raw. "You're confusing arrogance for confidence. I'm confident you're full of shit."

"You still know how to get on my nerves." She flicks water at my face.

"You're welcome." I laugh again, the sound genuine, echoing around us.

She shakes her head, moving to get up from the pool edge. "Goodnight, Nate."

She's retreating to the house, every instinct screaming at me to shut up, but I don't. "I didn't like the way he touched you." The words tumble out, harsh and raw.

She pauses, turning, shock flitting across her face.

"I'm not sorry I beat the shit out of him," I cut in before she can speak, my voice laden with a gravity I seldom let show. "But I am sorry he touched you. I don't want you to think... I didn't want you to see me like that."

She stares at me blankly.

"And thanks for not ratting me out about the weed," I add after a heavy silence, my voice dropping to a murmur. It feels dumb, trivial even, but it's all I can voice.

She gives me a faint smile. "Guess we're even."

"Goodnight, Leni." The nickname slips out, a ghost of past closeness.

Her eyes widen, a flash of something vulnerable.

"Night, Nate." She glances back, a lingering look, then disappears inside.

I watch her go, a gnawing loss settling in. Maybe she's just another loss—another ghost in a long line of things I can't hold onto.

THE CLOCK HITS MIDNIGHT, AND I'M BACK TO BEING TWELVE YEARS OLD, sitting on these same stairs, listening for Mom's key in the lock. Jake would be asleep upstairs, trusting his big brother to keep watch. Some habits are carved too deep to break, like making sure there's aspirin by her bed before she gets home or knowing exactly how to guide her up the stairs without waking the whole house.

Eventually, the front door creaks open. Kat's laughter filters through the hall, along with Mom's slurred words.

"Shh, the kids are asleep." Kat's whisper carries down the hallway.

They stumble past the lounge room, supporting each other in their drunken state.

"Oh, Nate, are you still up?" Kat whispers, half-laughing.

"Natey is always up. He never sleeps, right, honey?" Mom's laugh has that brittle edge I know too well—the one that means she's trying to joke away the guilt.

I get up from the couch, moving on autopilot to support her weight. Jake used to ask why I always waited up, but he stopped questioning it around the same time he stopped waiting with me.

"I'll take it from here," I tell Kat, taking Mom's arm.

Kat nods, relief clear in her eyes. "Thanks, Nate. She's... had a bit too much tonight."

"It's fine," I mutter, leading Mom toward the stairs.

It's not the first time and it won't be the last. She drinks to drown out the pain. I get it, better than anyone.

Every step up the stairs is a familiar dance—me steering, her leaning, both of us pretending this isn't a scene we've played out hundreds of times. I catch our reflection in the hallway mirror: her small frame against my shoulder, my hand steady at her back. We look like what we are—a son trying to hold his mother together, a mother trying to hold onto her pride.

In her room, I help her onto the bed, slipping off her shoes and tucking her in. She mumbles a slurred mess of regrets and apologies.

"Here, Mom," I offer, holding out a glass of water and some aspirin. "Drink this."

She takes a sip, her hand shaking. "Nate... I'm sorry," she slurs, her eyes wet with unshed tears. "I wish... I could've been better. Done better for you."

"Don't," I cut her off, my voice firm but tired. "Don't apologize. It's done."

"I'll do better," she promises again, a familiar refrain that doesn't sting as much as it used to.

Her hand reaches out, brushing the bruises on my face gently. "You're nothing like him." Her voice breaks, filled with a mix of pain and something like pride. "You always protect what you love. You're a good boy, Natey," she mumbles, already half-asleep. "Always taking care of everyone."

The words twist something in my chest. If she only knew how badly I've failed at that lately. But I still straighten her covers, making sure there's water within reach, check her phone is charging—all the little things Jake never had to learn because I made sure he didn't have to.

I pause in the doorway, watching her breathing even out. Tomorrow she'll be embarrassed and will try to make it up to me with pancakes or apologies. I'll brush it off like always, protect her from her own guilt the way I've been protecting her from everything else since Scott left.

It hits me then—I learned to swim carrying other people's weight. Maybe that's why I'm drowning now.

Dragging myself back to my room, a decision crystallizes in my mind. It's time to cut the bullshit, to really change. I don't want to be anything like him. Now or ever.

I head straight to the bathroom, my hands shaking as I reach for the last stash of weed and bag of pills I keep tucked away for emergencies. It's been my crutch—a pathetic escape I've clung to for far too long. With grim satisfaction, I dump it into the toilet. Watching it swirl away, I feel a part of me—the weakest part—get flushed down with it. The house falls silent as I crawl into bed, but it's a different kind of quiet now. It's not the oppressive silence that usually suffocates me.

Tonight, there's a hint of peace—a fragile thing I'm not quite used to. It's not perfect, but it's a start. My father broke me long before anyone else even had a chance. That's the truth I've avoided for too long. But acknowledging it—really facing it—is the first real step toward putting myself back together. Tonight, I start rebuilding, not just for them, but for me too.

CHAPTER 15
THE BEGINNING OF THE DOWNFALL
NATE

September 2005
Age 18

IN THE DIM GLOW OF MY DESK LAMP, MY TEXTBOOK BLURS INTO meaningless scrawls. Radiohead pounds through my headphones, but even the familiar comfort of rock can't dull the bone-deep ache from today's football practice and the fight I got involved in with Dad two nights ago.

The house stands silent around me—Mom's been gone all day and Jake's lost in whatever's been consuming his time lately. The illusion of solitude shatters when yelling pierces through my music. My heart slams against my ribs as I rip off my headphones. The voices escalate, raw and furious, bouncing off the walls like shrapnel. Mom and Dad's fights have been getting worse, but this—this is different. There's an edge of violence in their voices that turns my blood to ice.

Dad's been spiraling lately. Coming home late, clothes reeking of booze and shame. I found his stash last week—pills and cocaine tucked away in those special pockets of his suits, the ones designed for keeping ugly secrets. The discovery sits like lead in my stomach, another weight added to the burden of knowing.

Their voices tangle in the air, a brutal symphony of accusations and denials. They're fighting about her again—the other woman, the shadow that's been slowly poisoning our family. Dad's words slur together, each denial dripping with the desperation of a man caught in his own web of lies.

A crash rips through their argument—the sound of shattering glass splitting the night. My body moves before my mind can catch up, terror and rage fueling each step as I sprint downstairs. Another sound follows, heavier, more final—the sickening thud of flesh meeting floor.

The scene in the living room stops my heart. Mom is crumpled on the ground, barely moving, tears cutting paths through the blood on her face. The stench of whiskey rolls off the monster I no longer recognize in waves as he towers over her, his familiar sneer twisting his features into something monstrous.

Something inside me fractures.

The air grows thick, each breath like swallowing broken glass. A dark fury claws its way up my throat, threatening to drag me into an abyss I might never escape.

"Scott, I'm sorry," Mom whispers, her voice splintering like the fragments of glass scattered across the floor.

The walls of my restraint crumble. Every silent tear she's shed, every bruise she's hidden, they all converge into this moment, feeding a hatred that burns through my veins like acid.

He catches my eye, that cruel smirk I've grown to despise playing on his lips. "Go to your room," he spits, voice dripping with contempt.

Something inside me snaps.

Like a dam breaking, years of pent-up fear and helplessness surge through me. I lunge forward, grabbing his arm and yanking him away from her with every ounce of strength I possess.

He hits the floor hard. Before he can recover, I'm on him, hands fisted in his shirt. My vision blurs red as my fists connect with his face, each impact sending shockwaves of savage satisfaction through my body.

"Stop it, Nate! Please, stop!" Mom's voice cuts through the haze, trembling with fear—not just for herself anymore, but for me.

I freeze, chest heaving. Beneath me, that fucking smirk still plays on his face. "You better get off me," he hisses.

"Get out," I growl, the words scraping my throat raw. "Before I fucking kill you."

He hesitates, calculating. When he finally stands, I shove him back. His hands find my throat, slamming me against the wall. "You need to remember your fucking place while you're under my roof," he spits, grip tightening before he releases me.

I hold his gaze until he stumbles out, the door's slam echoing through the house like a gunshot.

The silence that follows is deafening. Mom remains crumpled on the floor, hands trembling as they ghost over her bruised throat. I drop beside her, pulling her into my arms, trying to shield her from a world that's already hurt her too much.

"Mom," I whisper, my voice cracking. "You're bleeding."

She clings to me, her silent sobs soaking through my shirt. Each tear adds another crack to my heart as I hold her on the cold floor, offering the only comfort I can—my presence.

As her breathing steadies, I loosen my grip but don't let go. Can't let go.

"Mom, you can't keep doing this," I say quietly. "You have to leave him. This isn't normal. It's not okay."

She shakes her head, pulling back to meet my eyes. "He's just stressed. Work has been rough, and the drinking—he doesn't mean it. He's just—"

"No," I cut her off. "You can't keep justifying this. It's not stress, and it's not just the drinking. It's the lying, the cheating. He's hurting you in every way, and it's getting worse."

Her face crumples. "You're not going to understand this but I'm trying to keep us together. And I'm sorry, Nate. I wish you didn't see any of this."

"Well, it's too late for that. I've seen it all. And if you think this is keeping us together, look around. We're falling apart." The words feel like shards of glass in my throat.

She twists her fingers together; a nervous habit I've watched develop over years of abuse. "I know you think I'm stupid for staying," she whispers.

"I don't think—"

"It's not as easy as you think," she interrupts. "I don't want to lose everything."

The realization hits me like a sucker punch—she's not going to leave him. No matter how bad it gets, she's trapped in this cycle of hope and despair.

"Mom, I can't watch this anymore," I say, emotion thick in my voice. "I'm supposed to go off to college soon, but I'm starting to think maybe I—"

Her head snaps up, panic flashing in her eyes. "No, Nate. You can't do that. You've worked so hard, and you deserve this. You need to focus on your future, on college and football. You need to get out of here, build your own life."

"If I leave, who's going to protect you? Who's going to look out for Jake?" The thought of leaving them unprotected tears at my insides.

"I'll be okay. He wouldn't touch Jake." Though the first part is clearly a lie, I half-believe the second. Dad adores Jake, but I don't trust him around my little brother.

She forces a smile that doesn't reach her eyes and touches my face.

"You don't need to worry about me or Jake or anything else, okay? You need to think about your future. You can't throw that away. I need you to get out of here and live your life, Nate. Okay?"

I study her face—the carefully concealed bruises, the deep stress lines, the dullness in her once-bright eyes. She's breaking, piece by piece, and nothing I say seems to matter.

"I'm not throwing anything away," I lie, trying to convince myself more than her. "But I can't leave you here with him."

"Nate," she whispers, cupping my cheek. "You've always been so strong. But don't carry this weight. Promise me you won't. Please. I can't bear the thought of you being stuck here. Please, Natey. Please, for me."

I swallow hard against the burning in my throat. She doesn't understand what she's trying to ask of me. I want to believe her, to trust that she'd be okay without me. But the truth sits like poison in my gut—she won't leave him.

If I go, who will save her next time?

Or the time after that?

"Mom," I manage, barely audible, "I can't."

She smiles through her tears.

"You can. And you will." She draws me close, our foreheads touching, before pulling me into another embrace, as if her arms could protect me from the shadows that have already claimed our family. I know it's not enough. It will never be enough. That knowledge cuts deeper than any physical wound.

The shift in Dad started around my seventh birthday. His eyes changed when they looked at me, disappointment clouding what used to be pride. I learned quickly to stay quiet around him, but as I grew older, silence became another form of betrayal—watching him destroy Mom piece by piece.

Pain comes in countless forms; the worst is watching it consume those you love. Mom is the greatest casualty in this war. If I leave now, who shields her? Who protects Jake from the monster wearing our father's face?

Sitting here in this moment, surrounded by the evidence of tonight's violence, held by the woman who loved me first, my future crystallizes with stunning clarity.

I realize, in this moment, I no longer have a father.

CHAPTER 16
LOST STORIES, FOUND WORDS
NORA

THE DAYS BLUR TOGETHER, EACH ONE INDISTINGUISHABLE FROM THE LAST. Nate's mood swings are giving me whiplash—one minute he's vulnerable and the next he's acting like I'm invisible.

As much as I try to block him out, it's become nearly impossible because we're living in the same house. My traitorous mind keeps circling back to that night. Nate in the pool, looking like some brooding, gothic prince under the moonlight. His dark hair slicked back, muscles tensed, voice low as he admitted his discomfort with Connor's touch. Then there was the way he'd thanked me for keeping his secret, like I'd given him something precious. It was unfair how good he looked, even when he was driving me crazy. But his hot-and-cold routine is exhausting. I suppose two can play at that game.

He wants space? Fine.

He can have all the space in the world.

I push back from my makeshift desk on the porch, my sanctuary away from Ollie and Jake's gaming wars and the lingering breakfast smells from the kitchen. The afternoon heat presses against my skin as I stare at my laptop's blank screen. The house is quiet with the boys out surfing and Mom at the market—perfect conditions for writing, yet the words won't come. My anger at Nate's silent treatment mingles with something deeper, something that makes my chest tight when I think about him.

"Ugh, screw you, Nate," I whisper, the words hissing between my teeth. I hate how much space he takes up in my head, and how much I miss him even though he's right here, always just out of reach.

The front door's creak breaks my reverie as Lydia steps in, arms laden with shopping bags. Her smile is warm, but concern shadows her eyes. "Hi, honey. How's your day going?"

I shrug, aiming for casualness. "It's going."

She chuckles, the sound knowing and gentle. "That good, huh?" Her eyes drift to the wine rack, lips quirking. "It's five o'clock somewhere, right?"

It's barely noon, but I won't comment. "Wait, where's Mom?"

"Your mother can't help herself when it comes to saving people. An elderly woman fell at the farmer's market. So, your mom wanted to make sure she got the right scans and tests at the hospital."

That's Mom for you—always the hero. It's one of the things I love most about her.

"So, since it's just the two of us, spill. What's up with my favorite girl?"

I shift in my chair, the words sticking in my throat. "I'm trying to write, but my brain's just... stuck."

Lydia's expression softens. "You're writing again! Oh Nora, your dad would've been thrilled."

The mention of Dad sends a familiar ache through my chest. Writing was our thing—he'd encouraged me to pursue it even more when Ms. Ryan pushed for that UK writing scholarship. After he died, the words dried up, along with so many other things.

"Everything's been tough since Dad died. Writing, staying here, just... everything," I manage to say, my voice barely above a whisper.

Lydia moves to sit opposite me, her presence steady and warm. Her hand reaches across the table to squeeze mine. "I can't imagine what you're going through, sweetheart. I'm here for you, always. Anything you need, or if you just need to talk, it stays between us. Promise."

The weight on my shoulders lightens a fraction, but the words remain trapped. How do I tell her about last summer? About the nightmares that have returned full force? Some days it feels like I'm playing a part—the Nora everyone remembers versus who I've become. The nightmares, the cold sweats, the constant fear of him appearing around any corner, ready to take more of what was never his to claim.

"Whatever it is, Nora, you can tell me. Your mom won't hear it from me."

I deflect, gesturing toward her wine glass. "What about you? Why the early start?"

Her smile shifts, accepting my evasion. "The fundraiser gala's coming up. Planning, organizing, making sure everything's perfect. Hence, a little morning wine to smooth the edges." She takes a sip. "Actually, I could use a hand if you're up for it."

The prospect of diving into something—anything—that isn't my own thoughts or Nate feels like a lifeline. "Sure, I'd love to help."

Her face brightens. "Fantastic! We're going to make this event unforgettable." She pauses, studying me. "And who knows? Maybe it'll spark some inspiration for your writing."

I laugh, the sound hollow. "Maybe."

"You know," she continues, voice earnest, "sometimes inspiration isn't something you wait for. Sometimes, you have to go out and find it. It's there—in every little thing, every event, every interaction. Maybe you just need to squint a bit harder to see it."

Her words settle in my chest, and for the first time today, something like hope stirs. "Thanks, Lydia."

She squeezes my shoulder before heading to the kitchen. I watch her go, then push my laptop away. "I think I'm going to head out for a bit," I announce, stuffing papers into my backpack.

"Sure, honey, be safe," she calls after me.

The sea breeze cools my skin as I pedal through familiar streets, each rotation of the wheels steadying my thoughts. Almost without conscious decision, I find myself at Gracie's bookstore. The moment I step inside, the scent of old books wraps around me like a hug, bittersweet with memories of Dad.

Alfie looks up from his novel, gray hair charmingly disheveled. "Ah, couldn't stay away, could we?"

"Away from you Alfie? Never."

"You flatter me."

"This place feels like... home to me."

His eyes soften as he leads me to the classics and poetry aisle, pulling out a copy of *Jane Eyre*. "This was Gracie's favorite. Well, one of them."

"Really?"

"It's a book about a woman's quest for a fulfilling life on her own terms." He gives me a knowing look. "You remind me a lot of her."

"Jane Eyre or Gracie?"

"Both," he says with a heartfelt smile.

"Because we both love books?"

"Because you're all incredibly bright women. And it's how you talk about the books you love. Like they're more real than reality itself."

I trace my fingers along the book's spine. "I guess it's easier to lose yourself in a world someone else has created than to deal with your own."

Alfie settles into a nearby chair. "You know, the first time I saw Grace, she was immersed in that exact book in the corner of this tiny little coffee shop down the street from where I lived." He points to a cozy nook by the window. "She was so engrossed, the world could have ended and she might not have noticed."

"Was it love at first sight?"

He chuckles, nostalgia warming his features. "Well, I was a shy boy back then so when I first noticed her, I memorized her coffee order, thinking one day I would buy her a coffee and that's how we would strike up our first conversation. But she only came through on a Tuesday, each time with a new book in her hand. Took me months to gather the courage to speak to her. So, it wasn't immediate, but it was inevitable. When I finally did talk to her, something just clicked. I knew I was going to fall in love with her. Like gravity pulling me in."

"Sounds like it was a slow burn."

"It was more like a recognition. Like, 'Oh, hello, it's you. Of course, it's going to be you.' I think that's the best kind of love story. It takes time, but it was worth every moment."

His words echo something in my chest, something I'm not ready to name. "Alfie, would you be willing to tell me more? Maybe over a few visits? I'm writing a story for a scholarship application—"

"Nothing would make me happier than talking about my Gracie," he interrupts, eyes bright.

"Would you maybe consider being the subject of the story? I think this could be perfect, but only if you'd be okay with—"

"I'd be honored, Nora."

For the first time in weeks, excitement sparks through me. "Thank you, Alfie. This... this could be exactly what I need to get out of my writing slump."

"Then let's make sure it's a story that does justice to my Gracie. Come in whenever you like and I'll tell you more."

The prospect of writing their love story thrills me—not just a distraction from my troubles, but something meaningful to pour myself into.

Alfie's smile carries a hint of melancholy. "This bookstore isn't just a place of business, it's a living memory— legacy of the love Gracie and I shared. Every book here, every corner, keeps that memory alive."

His words resonate with how I feel about Nate—this inexplicable pull I can't shake.

"What's on your mind?" he asks, noticing my distraction.

"Nothing," I murmur, running my fingers along the book spines.

"Oh, come on now. What's really going on?"

"I haven't figured it out if I'm being totally honest."

He chuckles, knowing glinting in his eyes. "Maybe you're trying too hard to find what's already in front of you." He starts toward the counter. "Sometimes the only way we can see what's always been there is losing it to understand its true value. It's a harsh lesson, but one that often wakes us up."

"Are you always this spot on?"

"Most of the time," he winks. "You're welcome."

Leaving the bookstore, I feel lighter, inspired. There might still be a story within me, waiting to be told. Perhaps it's not my story, but Alfie and Gracie's—one that could somehow help untangle my own.

I'm unlocking my bike when a familiar silhouette catches my eye—someone getting into a car down the street. The way they move, the set of their shoulders—too familiar. For a brief moment, my heart stops beating.

No, it can't be him. He's supposed to be in Europe, not here in Eden.

The car drives away, taking the figure with it. *It's just my mind playing tricks,* I tell myself, spurred by stress and exhaustion. *I'm just tired, that's all.*

"Nora!" Mia's voice cuts through my spiral. I turn to see her approaching, striking as ever in her perfectly coordinated outfit.

"Hey!" She waves, catching up. "I was hoping I'd run into you."

"You were?"

"Yeah, you left the bonfire before I could say goodbye. If you're free now, want to hang out?"

"Sure." I welcome the distraction. We fall into step together. "So, what did I miss at the bonfire?"

Mia rolls her eyes but grins. "Not much, honestly. Though Kelsie and Jake... they got pretty cozy. Like, close, close."

"Kelsie and Jake? Really?" The thought of Jake with the blonde who'd flirted so openly at Farrah's party isn't surprising.

"I mean, I don't know them well, but they seem like they could be good together." She grips my arm, wincing. "Oh shit, sorry. Was that weird to say?"

"Why would that be weird?"

"I just meant... you and Jake?"

"We're just friends," I clarify. "And no, you're not wrong about them."

She nods, relieved.

"What about you? Any new developments?"

Mia hesitates, a shy smile forming. "Well, I might... kinda sorta like your brother."

I stop walking. "Ollie?"

Her cheeks flush pink. "Is that weird? It's weird. I know, it sounds crazy. Oh, God, I can't believe I just said that to you."

I can't help but laugh at her nervous excitement. "Relax, it's okay."

"I barely know him, but he's just... he's different. Really sweet."

"Ollie's a big talker but he's a teddy bear. Don't tell him I said that." We resume walking. "And if we're being honest, I think he likes you too. Also don't tell him I said that."

Her eyes widen. "Really?"

"Ollie's one of the good ones. Though he might drive you insane sometimes, he'd do anything for people he cares about."

It's true.

Ollie should be worrying about typical freshman things but this year transformed him. Ollie's mind constantly races with scenarios most people his age haven't considered. Where once he shrugged off life's minor inconveniences he now meticulously analyzes every possibility. I've watched my brother closely and noticed the way his heart races at unexpected texts, how he checks his bank balance three times daily, and how he calls home every night just to make sure everyone is still breathing.

Sometimes when I look at him, I see glimpses of the carefree brother I knew before. But those moments are fleeting, like sunshine between storm clouds. At eighteen, he's carrying worries that shouldn't belong to him.

Mia's voice cuts through my spiralling thoughts.

"That means a lot coming from you. I wanted to be upfront because I don't want things to get weird between us."

"My brother deserves to be happy after the year we've had. And not that you need my approval, but if you want it, you've got it."

Her smile says more than words could.

We walk in comfortable silence before she asks, "Hey... are you okay? Like, really okay?"

For a moment, I consider telling her everything. But the words catch in my throat. "I'm fine," I lie, forcing a smile. "Just been thinking about a new story idea."

She links her arm through mine. "I'd love to hear about it whenever you're ready."

As we continue down the street, gratitude mingles with relief in my chest. Mia's presence, her genuine concern—it feels real, not fabricated. Maybe someday I could tell her everything. But for now, discussing my potential story feels like enough. I tell her about Alfie and Gracie, the scholarship, even Dad. The whole time, I can't help but think this is what friendship should feel like—being seen, being heard, feeling, even briefly, like you're normal again.

CHAPTER 17
LADS DAY OUT
NATE

SIX DAYS CLEAN. YEAH, I'M COUNTING.

Ever since that night at the beach I haven't touched a single drug. Not one. It's the longest I've been sober in... fuck. I don't even know.

The withdrawal was a special kind of hell—sweating through sheets, puking my guts out when no one was looking, hiding the shakes. But something about her eyes that night, wide with fear and disappointment, hit harder than any comedown.

This morning feels different though—there's a whisper of something I'd almost forgotten: *hope.*

My mind has been a war zone for as long as I can remember. Thoughts aren't just thoughts when they've haunted you long enough. They transform into nooses—fashioned from your own memories, woven tight with regret. They dangle in the corners of your mind, patient, always waiting for those quiet moments when you think you might be free. Then they tighten, one by one, choking out any hope of silence.

That's the thing about the noise in your head—it's not just sound. It's a physical thing, wrapped around your throat, your chest, your future. Doesn't matter how many times you've heard the accusations, felt the shame. The rope just gets stronger with every loop of the same old shit.

That's why I started popping pills in the first place. One hit and bam —blessed fucking silence.

No more voices.

No more replaying every single screwup in surround sound.

Just... nothing.

But nothing isn't living.

And Nora's face that night—Christ, I can't shake it. The way she backed away from me, like I was some stranger she'd never seen before. Like everything between us had been a lie. And maybe it had been. Maybe I'd been lying to both of us about who I really am.

So six days.

One day at a time.

The cravings still hit like a freight train sometimes, especially when the noise gets too loud. But I'm holding on. By my fingernails some days, but I'm holding.

One step, then another, then another.

Even when your mind's screaming at you to just lie down and fucking quit.

I toss off the covers and swing my legs out of bed, muscles protesting as I stretch. By the time I'm downstairs, Ollie's voice booms through the house, yanking me firmly into the present.

"Nate! Jake!" His shout cuts through any remaining fog. "Get your asses downstairs. We're leaving in ten!"

I pull on a fresh t-shirt, the fabric still warm from the dryer, and jog down to meet them. Today's about starting fresh—just skating, surfing, being the kids we used to be. The simplicity of it feels exactly like the cleanse I need. No drama, no heavy shit, just the open road and waves. Ollie's already in the kitchen, his broad frame taking up too much space as he slings a protein bar my way.

"About fucking time," he jokes, eyes crinkling at the corners. I catch the bar mid-air but drop it on the counter.

"You need it. You're looking a bit outta shape there, Natey boy." There's a familiar smirk playing on his face.

I roll my eyes but can't help laughing. We both know I still have the physical edge on him. Jake stumbles in, hair a mess, barely awake, but the energy in the room instantly lifts him.

"Lads day out, just like old times," Ollie declares, tossing another protein bar at Jake.

Just like old times.

The car buzzes with the old thrill of anticipation as we pile in, the leather seats still cool from the morning air. Jake takes the wheel while Ollie lounges in the passenger seat. It doesn't take long for Ollie to break the silence.

"Sooo, Mia," he teases. "Thoughts?"

I scoff, raising an eyebrow. "Didn't take you long, did it?"

He tries to shrug it off, but I catch the flush creeping up his neck. Jake chimes in from the driver's seat, "I saw those looks you were giving her. All puppy dog eyes and shit."

"Well you haven't met her. She's not just cute," Ollie admits, his voice softening. "She's off the charts. Fun, smart, beautiful. How many girls can you say tick all those boxes in one hit?"

I can think of only one.

"You're whipped, my guy," Jake adds, grinning at our friend.

Ollie's laughter fills the car, but there's a vulnerability in it I rarely hear. "I think I like her. A lot. She's different, you know? Not like the usual crowd."

I nod, understanding exactly what he means. Even though I haven't met her, I trust Ollie's judgment—he's always had a knack for seeing through people's facades.

"Well man, she sounds like a winner then," I say, clapping his shoulder from the backseat.

His expression shifts, becoming more serious as he turns to me. "What's up with Farrah, Nate?"

The mention of her name tightens something in my chest. My situation with Farrah is nothing but complicated—a tangled mess I'm not ready to unravel. "Nothing," I reply, the word coming out too quick, too defensive.

Ollie's gaze sharpens. "Nothing as in nothing's new, or nothing as in you two are nothing?"

Jake's trying to contain his laughter now, the car vibrating with his suppressed chuckles.

I exhale, long and heavy. "It's nothing serious. We're just... you know."

"A fling that's lasted over two summers?" Jake's voice drips with skepticism.

"She knows it's nothing serious," I insist, the words sounding hollow even to me. "It ends when summer does."

"Sure," Jake drawls, his knowing grin reflected in the rearview mirror.

"Shut up, Jake," I mutter, but there's no real heat behind it.

Ollie raises his hands in mock surrender. "Hey, man, no judgment here."

It's not their judgment I care about, anyway.

We reach the beach, and it's like stepping into a memory. The boardwalk stretches before us, less crowded than usual, giving us the freedom we crave. We skate along, morning sun warming our backs, the rhythmic crash of waves providing a constant backdrop to our laughter.

The ocean welcomes us with its brisk chill. I strap my board to my ankle, muscle memory taking over as I paddle out. For a while, every-thing else fades—just sun, surf, and the pure freedom of being on the water. Time stretches and compresses all at once, reality narrowing to this single perfect moment.

Exhausted from the morning's exertions, we eventually slow down, lounging on our boards, trading jokes and stories. It's in these moments, simple and unguarded, that I realize what I've missed most—just being with my brother and best friend, no drama, no tension. Just us, the ocean, and the endless sky above.

It's a rare kind of peace, and for now, it's enough.

As the sun climbs higher and the crowd swells, I feel the pull to stay until sunset, but I promised Jay I'd catch up with him. Reluctantly, I agree it's time to pack it in.

"I'm starving," Ollie announces, breaking through my thoughts.

I raise an eyebrow at him. "And you're telling me this because...?"

"I need you to feed me," he says, deadpan.

Jake snorts, and I shake my head, chuckling. "Are you ever not hungry?"

"You calling me fat?" Ollie shoots back, his mock scowl barely hiding his grin.

"You're an idiot," I retort.

"A hungry idiot. Seriously, what's the plan for food?" He rubs his stomach theatrically.

After loading the boards into the car and watching Jake head off to rinse, Ollie and I linger by the trunk. I've been holding back all morning, but there's one thing—one person—gnawing at me. I've been avoiding her since that night by the pool, but I can't shake the persistent sadness I saw in her eyes.

"Hey, uh, your sister," I start, the words catching in my throat like fishhooks. "Is she... is she doing okay? After the other night at the party?" The memory of her expression haunts me—there was something in it beyond typical grief, something that set off warning bells I couldn't ignore.

Ollie doesn't seem surprised by my question. "You know Nora. Resilient as hell but stubborn to a fault. She seems fine though."

"How has she been since... since your dad passed? I mean, really been?" The guilt of my absence weighs heavy in my words.

His face clouds over.

"She was the one who found him. And by the time Mom and I got home..." he trails off. "It's like she was there, but not really. She suffered in silence and didn't talk to anyone about any of it. Mom and I tried our asses off. And then those fucking friends of hers at school just dropped her like she was nothing when she needed them most."

My throat tightens and my heart aches at the thought of anyone hurting someone like Nora.

"I'm sorry," I admit, voice low. "I should have been there. For you, for her."

Ollie looks at me, his expression softer than I deserve.

"I won't lie. It sucked not having you around, man. You're one of my best friends, and Nora—she had Jake, but I know she missed you too." He claps me on the shoulder. "But I get it, you had your own hell to deal with. Life's too fucking short to hold grudges against the people you care about. So, I forgive you." A half-smile crosses his face. "Just don't miss my birthday or you're really dead to me."

I laugh, as he pulls me into a quick hug. The forgiveness lifts a weight I didn't realize I'd been carrying, but my mind keeps circling back to Nora, to those shadows in her eyes.

Jake reappears, breaking our moment.

"We gonna chat all day, or are we gonna eat?"

My phone buzzes again—Jay's fifth call today.

"You guys go ahead," I say, forcing a smile. "I need to handle something. I'll catch up later."

Ollie gives me a long look but nods.

"All right, man. Hit us up when you're free."

IT TAKES JAY FIFTEEN MINUTES TO MEET ME IN AN EMPTY PARKING LOT. He steps out of his Camaro, cigarette smoke curling from his lips, anxiety radiating off him.

"Nate, where the fuck have you been?"

"I was with my brother." I shrug, avoiding eye contact. "What's up?"

"What's up is that Monty has been on my fucking ass about you." He leans in, lowering his voice. "They want their money."

"I told you, I'll get it," I say, keeping my voice hard while clenching my jaw.

"It's not just that." He runs a hand through his hair, glancing over his shoulder. "I think Monty knows who you are, who your family is. They're going to ask for more. Way more."

Fuck my life.

"I'll get their money," I grit out, nostrils flaring. "Then I'm done with this shit. For good."

Jay looks skeptical but nods, exhaling slowly. "Fine. I'll try hold him off a couple of days. But for real," he grabs my shoulder, "be careful. These guys don't fuck around. I'm being dead ass serious."

"I know," I mutter, shaking off his grip. "Can you give me a lift home?"

I haven't even sat in the car when Farrah calls.

This day keeps getting better and fucking better.

I pick up the phone like ripping off a bandage.

"What?" I snap, slamming the car door shut.

"Where have you been?" Farrah's voice cuts like glass. "You've been avoiding my calls all day." I can practically hear her pacing.

"What do you want, Farrah?" I pinch the bridge of my nose, catching Jay rolling his eyes in the driver's seat.

"Are you coming to the carnival tonight?" Her tone shifts to something almost hopeful.

"No." I stare out the window, watching the streets blur by.

A heavy pause. "Why not?" Her voice tightens.

"Because." I tap my fingers against my knee, agitated.

"You're unbelievable," she hisses. "Two weeks ago, you were all over me and now?"

I lean my head back against the seat, "I don't think this arrangement is working out anymore."

"Are you breaking up with me over the phone?" Her voice cracks slightly.

"Farrah, listen—" I start, rubbing my temples.

"No. Fuck you, Nate."

The line goes dead.

"That girl is batshit crazy. I don't know why the fuck you're putting up with her still." Jay says, shooting me a sideways glance as he turns the corner.

The honest answer is, I have no fucking clue either. I just toss my phone onto the dashboard and sink deeper into the seat.

I'm home for less than two minutes before I grab my keys and head out. The road stretches out before me, a ribbon of asphalt cutting through the fading afternoon light. Time passes and each song ticks over into the next one before I realise I've been driving aimlessly. My mind a tangled fucking mess of thoughts about the way one girl seems to be haunting every corner of my consciousness, even when I'm trying to escape her.

Cary Brothers' *"Ride"* plays softly, its melancholic melody a perfect soundtrack to my current state of mind. The irony isn't lost on me—the song's themes of longing and uncertainty mirroring my own internal

120

chaos. I'm not even sure why I'm driving, only that movement feels like the only way to quiet the noise in my head.

And then—because life has a cruel sense of fucked up humor—there she is.

Nora, walking alongside her bike, looking both determined and vulnerable. The universe seems to be laughing, dropping her directly into my path when I'm least prepared to handle it.

I pull up beside her, rolling down the window. "What are you doing?"

She yanks out her earphones, startled. "Jesus Christ! You scared the shit out of me, Nate." Her eyes narrow. "What are you doing here?"

"I was heading home. Get in."

"No, thanks. I'm good."

"Nora, just get in the car."

"I don't need a ride. I've got my bike."

I get out of the car.

"I'm not letting you walk home alone. Just toss the bike in the back."

"Thanks, but no." She starts walking, chin lifted.

"Why do you have to make everything so difficult?"

She whirls to face me. "I'm not the one making things difficult. You're the one who refuses to listen when I say I'm fine walking."

"What's your problem?"

"My problem?" She laughs sharply. "You, Nate. You're my problem. This hot and cold game you play is getting old." She steps closer, lavender and vanilla filling the space between us. "I'm fine on my own. I don't need you saving me every five seconds, okay?"

"You're right." The words come out softer than intended. "You don't need anyone saving you. But that doesn't mean I can't look out for you. Please, just let me drive you home."

She holds my gaze for a moment before walking toward the car, bike in tow.

My knuckles whiten on the steering wheel as we drive. Nora's voice cuts through the silence, sharp with frustration.

"So why?"

"Why what?"

"Why have you been acting like a royal jackass and ignoring me?"

"I haven't been ignoring you."

"Yes, you have." She turns in her seat, eyes searching my face. "One minute we're fine, and the next, it's like I don't exist. What gives?"

Rays of dying sunlight flash across her face. She looks—I don't know —unreal. Untouchable. Fractured in that way that makes you want to look and not look at the same time. "It's not you."

"Then what is it? Because I'm sick of tip-toeing around you. It's fucking annoying."

The curse catches me off guard—Nora never swears. "I've just got... a lot on my plate right now. It's not about you." But that's a lie so big it could choke me.

It has everything to do with her.

With how close I am to imploding when I'm near her yet how natural it felt to have her in my arms the other night. And how fucking terrifying it is to want something—someone—this much when everything in my life is a house of cards waiting to collapse.

Nora shifts, folding her arms as she stares out the windshield. "Welcome to life, Nate. We've all got shit going on that other people don't know about."

As soon as the words leave her mouth, I look over and catch the flash of regret across her face, like she's said too much, revealing a card she wasn't ready to play.

"What does that mean?"

"Nothing." Her voice drops, soft and wounded. "I just... I feel like I've done something to make you this mad at me. Have I?" She asks, and fuck if those words don't sound like every sad playlist I've ever hate-listened to.

"No," I say, which is basically a lie wrapped in bullshit.

You just exist in a world where I can't have you and it's slowly killing me.

I mean, how do you tell someone: you're everywhere and nowhere, and I'm losing my mind trying to figure out which hurts more?

"Listen, you didn't do anything wrong," I rush to reassure her, guilt gnawing at my insides like acid. "It's just... everything's been a mess lately, and I'm trying to sort myself out. I shouldn't have been so hot and cold with you, okay? I'm sorry."

She sighs, the sound heavy with everything we're not saying. "I just wish you'd talk to me. I thought we were better than this." Her expression softens. "Is it even possible for things to go back to the way they were before?"

I meet her eyes, finding my own longing reflected back. "I don't know."

"Can we try?" she says quietly.

"We can try," I reply, not knowing if either of us believe me right now.

The rest of the drive is quieter, but it's different now—less like a weapon and more like a truce.

We pull into her driveway, and she pauses before getting out. "Thanks for the ride."

"Anytime," I reply, watching her walk away.

The stark realization I'm having right now is that for her, I'd try anything. Even if it means facing all the shit I've been running from.

CHAPTER 18
CARNIVALS AND CONFRONTATIONS
NORA

CALLING IT A DISTRACTION WOULD BE LIKE CALLING A HURRICANE A LIGHT breeze. For the past hour, I've been hopelessly replaying Nate's words from our earlier car ride, each syllable etching itself deeper into my consciousness.

It's not about you.

The way he wouldn't meet my eyes, the tense set of his jaw making the muscle tick beneath his skin—none of it sat right. My fingers hover over the keyboard, the blank document's cursor blinking accusingly. Nate's presence weaves through my thoughts like smoke, stubborn and persistent. We said we'd try to be okay, but what does "okay" even mean when every glance between us feels charged with a thousand unspoken words?

I force my eyes back to the screen, its harsh light burning my tired eyes. I should be focused on Alfie's story. When he talked about Gracie, something in me stirred—a flicker of inspiration that's been dead for too long.

Jake's voice cuts through the silence. "If you need a muse for your main character then I volunteer as tribute."

I look up to see him lounging against the doorway, a familiar smirk playing on his lips. The sight of him, so effortlessly casual, makes me smile—this is how simple friendship should be. I laugh, shaking my head, grateful for the momentary escape from my thoughts.

"I'll keep that in mind for the next one. I think I'm onto something. It's not fully formed yet, though."

"Oh?" A grin spreads across his face. "Do tell."

"It's actually about Alfie," I manage, tucking a strand of hair behind my ear. "I went back to the bookstore. He told me more about how him and Gracie met, and it got me thinking about a story I could write. Their story." The words feel inadequate, unable to capture the depth of what I'd witnessed in Alfie's eyes when he spoke of her.

"Well knowing Alfie and the life he's lived, I don't doubt it'll be anything short of incredible. Especially if you're writing it." He winks, his grin turning cheeky.

Jake pulls out a chair, the sound scraping against my nerves. "Are you sure you don't want to hit up the carnival tonight? Could be a good distraction. Might even help spark that idea into life."

I hesitate, then shake my head. "I'm good. I've had my fair share of drama already. Besides, I really want to dive into this story while I'm still feeling inspired."

He settles in, looking thoughtful, his blue eyes studying me in that way that makes me wonder if he sees right through my excuses.

"Fair enough. But if you change your mind, I'll come back and get you."

"How was your day, anyway?" I ask, partly to change the subject, partly to stop my mind from wandering back to Nate.

"Good, actually," Jake begins, leaning forward. "Nate was... different today. Better. Guess getting his ass kicked did him some good." There's a teasing lilt to his voice, but his eyes are serious, watching me like he's waiting for something to crack.

Just hearing Nate's name makes my heart skip a beat—a familiar stumble I've grown to hate. The car ride floods back in vivid detail—his half-apologies hanging in the air like mist, his confusing signals ricocheting off the walls I've built around myself. I feel a sharp pang of longing mixed with frustration. He had said sorry, kind of, but it wasn't enough. Memories of last summer surface unexpectedly—the night that changed everything. I'd needed him, believing with every fiber of my being that he'd be there like he always was.

But he wasn't. That absence, that silence on the other end of the phone, had shattered something inside me I hadn't realized existed until I was holding the broken pieces.

I hadn't told him about that night, how I'd cried into the silence until my throat was raw, feeling foolish and abandoned. He had always been my rock; the one person I believed would be there without judgment. But when I needed him the most, he wasn't there.

The worst part?

He doesn't remember any of it.

125

Or at least, he pretends not to.

That was the moment it hit me. Life can shatter you into pieces so small you don't recognize yourself anymore, and no one is immune to that pain. Staying open, even when you're hollowed out by hurt is a choice that feels like trying to breathe underwater.

Then, Dad passed away.

Just when I thought I couldn't break any further, the final piece of my heart cracked. I nearly let myself drown in that grief, let it pull me under like a riptide. You hold onto things, onto moments, thinking you've got forever to memorize the sound of someone's laugh or the way they say your name. But everything is temporary.

That includes Nate.

I wanted to confront him earlier today. Sitting in the car with him while his hands were clenched around the steering wheel just added to the thick tension suffocating the air between us. I wanted to scream, demand to know why he abandoned me, then proceeded to act like I didn't exist. But all I managed was to ask why he'd been ignoring me. As if it was just about the distance, the silence from the beginning of this summer. Not about the gaping void his absence had left over the past year.

I muster a small smile, murmuring, "That's good."

Jake studies me for a moment. "You sure you're okay?"

"Yeah, just tired," I lie smoothly, and he lets it slide.

After dinner, as our moms head out for their night, while the boys take off for the carnival, I settle back at the table outside, determined to immerse myself in writing. The house falls silent, filled only with the soft hum of the dishwasher and occasional creak of the floorboards.

Outside, the air is warm, thick with the scent of grass and salt from the lake. Crickets chirp softly, their sounds weaving into the night's calm. The sky stretches vast and navy above, dotted with stars, traces of sunset lingering at the horizon in stubborn strokes of purple and blue. Trees stand still, their leaves whispering secrets in the gentle breeze. Everything feels distant, simpler. Tonight, at least, the world is quiet, and I am at peace with its silence.

As I stare at the blinking cursor, trying to find words that could capture a love as deep as Alfie and Gracie's, the sudden sound of footsteps on the stairs sends a jolt through me. My heart hitches—I was sure I was alone. Looking up, I see Nate walking into the kitchen. The light falls across his strong jaw and angled features, casting subtle shadows that play up the intense look in his deep-set eyes. He's dressed casually in a black t-shirt that fits snugly across his broad shoulders, complemented by a backwards baseball cap that somehow adds to his rakish charm.

"I thought you'd gone to the carnival," he comments casually as he heads for the fridge.

"I need a break from crowds and drama," I respond, eyeing him warily. He moves with a familiarity that seems out of place after our strained talk. "Why didn't you go?"

He shrugs, leaning against the counter. "Same reasons."

I tilt my head, studying him. "Don't enjoy crowds and cotton candy?"

He lets out a laugh, then his jaw tightens. "When I was ten, yeah." He avoids eye contact, and I suspect it's because of our earlier conversation. "Where've you been hiding all day?"

"Just around, trying to find the right spot to write," I admit, aware of his intense focus. "Still haven't found it, so I'm settling for here tonight. At least the view's decent."

His eyes drift to my computer, curiosity flickering across his face. "What are you working on?"

It feels odd talking like this—almost normal, as if we're skirting around deeper issues, both of us waiting for the other to drop their guard again.

"Remember Alfie from the bookstore in town?" I say, leaning back. "He inspired something in me today."

A slow grin spreads across Nate's face, unexpectedly gentle. "You know, my favorite story you ever wrote was the one about Daisy and Archer's adventures to Illyria."

I blink, taken aback. "You remember that?"

"Yeah, well," he laughs, "it cost me six packets of Skittles to read it because you wouldn't let anyone see it."

A laugh escapes me, tinged with nostalgia. "And I only ate the yellow ones."

His eyes light up with familiar mischief. "Are they still your favorite?"

Yes, they are.

Just like that, amidst the familiar banter, a sliver of the past slips in, reminding me why it's hard to completely shut him out. Because sometimes, in moments like these, he's still the boy who traded candy for stories, who knew exactly how to make me smile—and that boy still has the power to break my heart all over again.

"It was good. Hard to believe a nine-year-old wrote it," he says, his tone laden with sincerity I haven't heard since before everything fell apart.

He steps closer, his movements careful, almost cautious. I feel the heat radiating from his body, the air between us crackling with electricity that quickens my pulse. His breath fans my cheek, warm and familiar, and though he hasn't touched me yet, it feels like he's tracing lines of fire across my skin. The scent of him—pine and soap, and something uniquely Nate—wraps around me like a memory I've tried too hard to forget.

He leans in slightly, lowering his voice. "But then again, you've always seen the world differently..." he trails off, looking away for a split second, struggling with his words. Then, like a switch being flipped, his expression shifts. He smirks—a dark, knowing smirk that makes my heart stumble even as my mind screams warnings. "It's why I'm not surprised you don't have a boyfriend."

Wait, what?

Just like that, the spell shatters. The walls slam back up—his and mine —fortified by years of practice at keeping each other at arm's length.

"Wow, you're a royal jackass," I snap, pushing past him, trying to shake off the sting of his words and the lingering warmth of his proximity.

But before I make it far, his hand gently clasps my arm, pulling me back. His touch zaps through me like lightning, my body tensing as if bracing for a storm. His eyes lock onto mine, filled with a sincerity that seems to pierce right through my armor.

"I didn't mean it like that," he murmurs, his voice low and steady, tinged with vulnerability that throws me off balance. The kitchen light catches the gold flecks in his eyes, making them appear like amber caught in sunlight.

"What I mean is you find depth where others skim the surface," he continues, his voice soft but firm. "I guess not everyone can handle that." His thumb traces an absent pattern on my arm where he's still holding me, probably unaware he's even doing it.

"Your eyes light up when you talk about what fires you up," he adds, his voice barely above a whisper, intimate as a confession. "And you're not scared to push against the grain. You just... live. And that scares people."

I stare at him blankly, unsure what to say. His words envelop me like a warm tide, threatening to sweep away my defenses.

"And that's what I admire most about you."

The moment stretches taut between us. I'm teetering on the edge of something indefinable, my emotions tangled and raw. Then, abruptly, he breaks the tension.

"Want to go to the carnival?" he suggests, his voice unexpectedly light, though something darker still lingers in his eyes.

"What?"

"The carnival," he clarifies, a casual hand slipping into his pocket. "Do you want to go?"

"Together? With you?" The question slips out before I can catch it, still reeling from the quick shift from intensity to nonchalance.

He glances around theatrically, though his eyes keep finding their way back to me. "Well, unless you see someone else lurking around here that would be better company..."

I roll my eyes, though his playful tone coaxes a reluctant smile from me. His earlier words hang in the air between us, warming me despite my reservations.

"Okay, fine," I concede, snapping my computer shut. "But I'm driving."

"Yeah, no. That's not happening."

"Yes, it is."

"No, it's not."

"Hand over the keys," I demand, arms folded as I extend my hand expectantly.

He chuckles, head shaking. The sound wraps around me like warm honey. "As reckless as I can be, I still value my life, thank you very much."

I feign outrage, though my heart skips at the way his eyes crinkle at the corners when he smiles. "You diss my non-existent love life and now doubt my driving? Seriously?"

He leans closer, a mischievous glint in his eyes that makes my breath catch. "I'm just saying, I haven't witnessed your driving firsthand. Yet."

We lock eyes, the challenge clear between us, crackling with an energy that feels dangerous and familiar all at once.

"Compromise," he finally offers, still smirking. "You can control the music tonight. And about driving, maybe later this summer I'll give you a lesson. Then you can take the Mustang for a spin."

"Deal," I relent, brushing past him with a playful nudge that sends electricity shooting through my arm. "But I will be driving that car before summer's over."

His laughter echoes behind me as we head out, rich and warm as sunshine. A lightness blossoms in my chest despite the earlier tension, despite knowing better, despite everything. Because with Nate, it's always been like this—a dangerous dance between what we say and what we mean, between what we want and what we can have.

The vintage radio of Nate's Mustang crackles with static, setting a backdrop of nostalgia. My fingers find the dial, dancing across its worn surface until the unmistakable opening riff of *"Mr. Brightside"* crashes through the speakers.

Nate lets out a low, amused chuckle that sends warmth spreading through my chest. His eyes catch mine for a split second in the dim dashboard light, and something electric passes between us. I turn the volume up until the bass thrums through my bones, and dive headfirst into the lyrics, singing with the kind of abandon that only comes when you're either completely broken or perfectly whole.

I glance over and catch Nate trying to hide a full-on grin, his usual cool demeanor melting away. The sight of him like this, guard down and genuine, makes my heart stumble over itself. His smile is contagious, spreading through me like wildfire, and suddenly my spirits are soaring higher than they have in forever.

The wind rushes through the open window, tangling my hair as I belt out the lyrics with a freedom I haven't felt in months. Nate's fingers tap rhythmically on the steering wheel, his eyes flicking between the road and me like he can't quite help himself. I catch him watching and flash a quick, carefree smile between lines, pretending not to notice how his breath catches slightly. The song dwindles into its last notes, leaving me breathless and giggling. Nate shakes his head, a lopsided grin breaking through his usual reserve, and my heart does that stupid flutter thing it always does when he looks at me like that.

"That was... something," he chuckles, the warmth in his tone wrapping around me.

I sink deeper into the cool leather, feeling its smooth embrace—trying to hold onto this moment like it might slip away if I breathe too hard. "It's my favorite song," I say, my voice riding that thin line between vulnerability and defiance.

He shoots me a look. That knowing smirk that does something ridiculous to my insides—makes my stomach twist and my heart do these stupid little somersaults.

"You don't have a favorite song," he says. Not a question. A statement.

"Uh, yeah I do."

His eyes are doing that thing. That infuriating thing where he's picking me apart, seeing right through me.

"You think you have one single favorite song?" he asks, leaning in closer. His voice drops—soft, conspiratorial—close enough that I can smell his cologne mixing with leather, close enough that my breath catches.

"I just told you it is," I retort, but we both know I'm losing whatever argument this is.

"Nora..." The way he says my name—god. "I know you. And I know you don't have a favorite song."

He's right, and we both know it. Songs aren't static for me. They're living, breathing things—snapshots of emotions, little time capsules that capture exactly how it feels to be alive in a single, perfect moment.

"You have songs for moments," he continues. "Songs that resonate with what you're feeling right then."

And shit if he isn't completely correct.

His observation hangs in the air between us, weighty as a confession, and I find myself momentarily speechless. I turn away, staring out at the passing lights that blur like shooting stars, trying to mask how his words stir something deep within me. It's ludicrous to think he might know me better than I know myself. Yet, as the engine hums beneath us, I can't shake the feeling that he might be right.

"Tell me I'm wrong," he says softly, confidence in his voice making my skin prickle.

"You're wrong," I reply, my voice weaker than I'd like.

"You're lying," he laughs softly, and I can hear the smile in his voice.

"I am not," I insist, putting on a defiant front.

"Then why did you just scrunch your nose?" he points out with a gentle tease.

I blink, taken aback. "My nose?"

"When you lie, you scrunch your nose." His tone softens, filled with an affectionate familiarity that aches. "You know how I know that?"

I remain silent, the atmosphere thickening around us. He watches me, his gaze intense, silently urging me to look at him. When our eyes meet, there's a gravity in his look that has always drawn me in.

"Because I know you," he whispers, the space between us charged with an unspoken understanding.

The words hit me harder than they should, slicing through the air with an accuracy that's almost cruel. I hate that he's right, and how he's always been able to see through me like I'm made of crystal.

And the worst part?

He knows it.

I feel my cheeks heating up, that familiar prickling of vulnerability spreading under my skin. He smirks, an infuriatingly triumphant expression painting his face as he leans in close enough that I can count his eyelashes in the passing streetlights.

"Your poker face sucks, Leni. It's what makes you such a terrible liar."

My heart skips at the way he says my nickname—it's soft, almost reverent, and it jerks me back to a time I thought I'd packed away in the dusty corners of my memory. Nobody has called me that since Dad was around. And he's used it more times in the space of three days than anyone else has in over a year. Hearing it now, from him, feels like a punch to the gut, like jumping into deep water, or falling without knowing where you'll land.

Does he even realize what that does to me?

Does he understand the weight that name carries, the flood of memories it unleashes?

I sneak a look at him, my eyes flickering up through my lashes, wondering how he sees me. Do I still look like that awkward eleven-year-old with braces and glasses, trailing behind him like a lost star in his orbit? Or does he see something more, something beyond just little Leni?

It's almost laughable this dance we do.

Here I am, trying to catch glimpses of him like stolen moments, desperately hoping he'll see me the way I see him. Yet, the moment our eyes meet, I have to look away, scared he might see too much, might read the story written in my eyes like pages from a diary I never meant to share.

It all feels too real, too raw, like a nerve exposed to open air. The truth is, to Nate, I might just be a chapter in his life—a brief story from his past, pages he's already turned.

But to me?

Nate Sullivan has always been the whole damn book.

CHAPTER 19
COTTON CANDY AND DAISY BRACELETS

NATE

As Nora flicks through the CD tracks, her finger pauses on "Mr. Brightside" by The Killers, and the intro bursts through the speakers. The spark in her eyes—those carefree, exhilarating sparks I've missed—makes my chest tighten. She cranks the volume high, belting out lyrics slightly off-key but perfect in its imperfection. Eyes closed, head thrown back, wild hair catching streetlights like copper and gold, she's completely lost in the song.

It's pure, unfiltered Nora, raw and beautiful, and devastating in ways I can't let myself think about. I catch myself staring like a man dying of thirst, and she snaps her eyes open, suddenly self-conscious. She shifts to face me, knees up, her posture radiating a vulnerability that makes my hands itch to reach for her. When our eyes lock, something electric passes between us, heavy as thunder before a storm. She bites her lip, hesitating, and there's this honesty in her expression she rarely shows anymore, not since everything went to hell.

For a moment, I forget why I need to keep my distance, why I can't let myself have this—have her. Her voice fills the car, rough and perfect and painfully beautiful. I manage a laugh as she powers through the chorus, trying to shake off the intensity before I do something monumentally stupid like tell her the truth.

Just enjoy the moment, Nate, don't fuck this up.

The car stops at the carnival, and she's laughing that infectious laugh that makes my heart stumble. We step out into a wash of neon blues, pinks, and yellows, the air filled with games, shouts, and distant laughter —a perfect cover for the chaos in my head. I scan the crowd instinctively, searching for any sign of Farrah or anyone else who could shatter this fragile peace, who could remind Nora why she shouldn't trust me.

Nostalgia hits unexpectedly as we weave through the crowd. Suddenly I'm ten and she's seven, her tiny hand pulling me toward the carousel, her favorite. Her laughter was a clear bell back then, making everything else fade. Before I learned how to break things, before I became someone who could hurt her.

Now, as she tugs my arm toward a booth, the feeling surges back like a tide. The carousel looks smaller, more weather-beaten, but still blinks rhythmically with familiar lights. The air is thick with fried dough and cotton candy, sharpening the ache of nostalgia.

"Where to first?" Nora's voice pulls me back. Her face, lit by neon, looks so untroubled it makes my chest hurt.

"I'll let you lead the way." I gesture ahead, ignoring how my fingers tingle with the urge to reach for her hand.

We drift toward the cotton candy stand, and she stops, grinning mischievously.

"Really? Cotton candy? First up?" I chuckle, affection roughening my voice.

"You said lead the way." Her smile lights up her whole face, cracking my heart wider.

I hand over money for the pink cloud of sugar, and her genuine smile makes it feel like I've given her the world. We pick at it as we wander, the familiarity of our shared past easing the tension between us.

"Remember that summer we tried to sneak into the haunted house?" Her laughter is soft, tinged with nostalgia.

"How could I forget? You freaked out and we bolted through the emergency exit," I tease, the memory of her trembling hand in mine still burning in my palm.

She bumps my shoulder, feigning indignation, the brief contact electric. "I didn't freak out."

"Nora, you screamed so loud they almost called the cops."

"They called the fire brigade instead." Her laughter rings out, clear as summer rain.

We approach the Shoot the Hoops game, and Nora's eyes light up with a dangerous spark I know all too well.

"You think you can still beat me, Nathaniel?" The challenge in her voice makes my pulse quicken.

"I don't think—I know." I take the basketball from the attendant and pass it to her, our fingers brushing briefly. "Ladies first."

She takes the shot. It bounces off the rim.

I sink my shot perfectly.

"Lucky shot," she grumbles, though her mouth twitches into a smile.

We trade shots back and forth. I make three more while she manages two but misses her final one. The competitive energy between us builds with each throw.

"Oh, did I just win?"

"You don't play fair, Nate Sullivan." She crosses her arms, her tone playful yet accusing.

"You have no idea," I smirk, watching her cheeks flush pink.

"Do you want the truth?" I lean closer. "You've always sucked at this game."

She gasps and slaps my arm. "I used to kick your ass at this when we were kids!"

"To be fair, you and Jake were both equally terrible. Ollie and I used to let you win to avoid the meltdown on the way home."

Her eyes narrow. "Has anyone ever told you you're like the human version of period cramps?"

I laugh, surprised by the genuine joy of it. She grins, knowing she's scored a point.

"Cheer up, Leni. You've got a whole year to practice."

Her head snaps up at the nickname, something tender passing through her eyes.

I used to call her that when we were kids—Little Leni, the girl who could light up my darkest days. She's still that same force of nature, equal parts chaos and magic.

"Whatever," she huffs, but her smile gives her away.

"Pick out a prize," I suggest, nodding toward the counter.

"Oh yay, a pity prize, how generous."

"It's not a—"

"I'm messing with you," she interrupts, touching my arm. The contact sends a jolt through me, and I wonder if she feels it too.

Something catches my eye.

"Shit, remember those?" I point to a collection of bracelets.

Nora pauses, recognition softening her features.

"Oh, my God, I'd completely forgotten about those."

"You spent a whole summer making them, handing them out to everyone."

"How do you remember that?" she asks softly.

Because when it comes to you, I remember everything.

I shrug, though every moment with her is carved into my memory.

"I remember a lot of things. You turned our living room into a bead factory. Said they could bring joy to someone's bad day."

She blushes.

"You know what, I want one. You pick it though."

I choose a bracelet that reads "Fearless" and slide it onto her wrist. The simple touch sets my pulse racing, but I force myself to pull away before the moment turns awkward.

"You never made one for me," I say, watching the bracelet settle against her skin.

"That's because you were too cool back then."

"I was not."

"Were you really gonna wear a bracelet with daisies and smiley faces?"

"If you made it, I'd have." The truth slips out before I can stop it.

The carnival worker cuts in. "You guys still have some tickets left. Wanna grab something else?"

"Still think you're too cool?" Nora challenges.

I glance at my all-black outfit and laugh. "Not tonight."

"Close your eyes," she commands.

I hesitate but comply. A minute passes, then two.

"Did you ditch me?"

"Just wait. Almost there."

Her hands close something around my wrist, the touch sending electricity through me. "Okay, open."

I look down to see "infinite" spelled out in beads.

"Can't say I never made you one now," she says, proud of her surprise.

"Why 'infinite'?"

"It's to remind you that magic's real, that no matter how old we get, we're surrounded by infinite possibilities. They're everywhere—you just have to be open to seeing them. Even when they're right in front of you."

Her words cut through my defenses. The bracelet becomes more than jewelry—it's a piece of her heart that I don't deserve but desperately want to keep.

"Thank you," she says after a moment.

"For what?"

"For tonight."

"Guess I'm not such a heartless prick after all."

"I never said you were a heartless prick."

"Oh, right, I believe the term was 'royal fucking jackass.'" I keep my tone light, though her words always matter more than I let on.

She blushes and laughs. "God, you really do hang on to every word I say, don't you?"

136

If she only knew how true that was.

"Well, before you retract your loving description, maybe hold off until you see what I've planned for us next." I can't help grinning at her sudden suspicion.

"No. Absolutely not. No way. No." She shakes her head, hair falling around her face.

"Come on, you know the rules. One for one, and now it's my turn to pick."

She stares me down, considering, then sighs.

"Nate," she says, my name both warning and promise, "you're a royal jackass."

Coming from her, it sounds like the highest compliment I could get.

CHAPTER 20
I GOT YOU
NORA

June, 1997
Age 7

THE CARNIVAL FILLS MY NOSE WITH SWEET PROMISES—POPCORN AND fried dough mixing with night air that sparkles like Dad's Christmas lights. I'm seven years old now, and even though I'm bigger, everything else still feels ginormous. It makes me feel like an ant in a world built for giants. Jake stands next to me, my partner for the night, while Nate and Ollie wait across from us at the Shoot the Hoops game. My stomach does this weird flippy thing that happens whenever Nate's around.

I tug at my overalls—the ones with the sparkly butterfly patch that Mommy says makes me look *"cute as a button."*

But standing here next to Nate, I feel small and babyish. I wonder if *"cute"* is just something moms have to say, like when they pretend your scribbles are masterpieces.

Jake nudges me with his elbow, passing over the ball.

"C'mon, Nora, you're the secret weapon on our team."

"Yeah, secret weapon," Ollie snickers with his annoying big brother grin. "More like a secret disaster."

"Shut up, Ol," I say, but I can't help giggling even as my cheeks burn.

They always tease me like this—not the mean kind that makes you cry, but the kind that reminds me I'm the baby of the group. I squint one eye like Daddy taught me, the hoop looking impossibly far away. I throw as hard as I can, and the ball clangs off the rim.

Ollie turns to Nate with mock seriousness. "If you make this shot, we win and become the reigning champions. Don't mess it up, Nate."

Nate does that cheeky smirk thing, catching my eye as his fingers dance across the ball's surface. He shoots... and misses! The ball bounces away and Ollie immediately starts whining, arms crossed like a toddler denied dessert.

"Dude no! Now Jake and Nora are going to be impossible to live with!"

Jake scoops me up in a victory hug that lifts my feet off the ground, then drapes his arm over my shoulder like we're NBA stars. "Champions! Has a nice ring to it, don't you think, Nor?"

I playfully push him away, sneaking another glance at Nate. He's looking right back at me with a smile that sends those weird butterflies doing cartwheels in my stomach, before stuffing his hands in his pockets and turning away.

As we walk through the carnival, Jake and Ollie fall behind, probably talking about gross boy stuff. I peek at Nate—he's all casual, like missing that shot meant nothing.

"Did you miss it on purpose?" I whisper, trying to sound grown-up and indifferent even though my heart's doing jumping jacks.

He shrugs, maintaining his cool stride. "Don't know what you're talking about, Leni. You won fair and square."

The smirk again, the one that makes my heart go all funny in ways I don't understand yet. I stick my tongue out at him, feeling my face flush. Nate always speaks in riddles, leaving my brain twisted up trying to decode his meaning.

"Guys! Ferris wheel!" Jake and Ollie suddenly shout, making me jump. "Let's go!"

My stomach drops like I've swallowed an ice cube.

Heights.

Just the thought of dangling up there with nothing but sky makes my legs wobble.

"You're not scared, are you, Nora?" Jake teases.

"She totally is," Ollie interrupts, poking my side. "You wouldn't even go on the baby swings earlier."

"Am not!" My voice betrays me, coming out squeaky.

"Liar. You squirm like a little girl on the escalators, and Dad always has to carry you up," Ollie says, grinning.

My face burns as I try to disappear into my shoes. I glance at Nate, mortified he heard about the escalator thing, but he's just watching me with gentle understanding in his dark eyes.

139

"I don't squirm," I mumble, staring at my light-up sneakers. "I'm going on the stupid Ferris wheel."

"Wooo! Let's go!" Jake bolts toward the line with Ollie, leaving me frozen with Nate.

"Are you sure you want to go?" Nate asks softly. "We could play ring toss instead?"

I shake my head despite my scrambled insides. I won't be the baby who ruins everything, even if I'm scared enough to throw up.

"Yeah... I'm sure."

"Then I'll go with you," he says, and somehow those simple words wrap around me like a warm blanket.

The Ferris wheel looks so big above us. It's like a giant metal spider, its lights painting the night in rainbow colors. My sweaty hands grip the cold, bumpy safety bar as we settle into our seats, my heart racing like I've run ten laps around the playground. The wheel creaks to life, and the ground starts shrinking away. I squeeze my eyes shut, trying to pretend I'm anywhere else.

"Hey, Leni," Nate whispers, his voice gentle as a bedtime story. "If we go down, at least we'll go down together."

He gives me that special smile that crinkles his eyes at the corners, the one that makes my insides feel warm and gooey like fresh-baked cookies. The carnival lights dance in his eyes like captured stars, and suddenly being up high doesn't feel quite so scary. My heart's still racing, but now it's more like Christmas morning excitement.

Without thinking, my hand finds his, my smaller fingers wrapping around his bigger ones. That's when I notice it—the purple-blue bruise across his knuckles. I touch it gently, feeling him tense, but he doesn't pull away.

"What happened?" I whisper.

Nate shrugs, looking away. "Nothing."

I don't believe him, but I focus instead on how safe his hand feels in mine.

"You ready?" he asks.

"To die?" I joke weakly.

Nate laughs softly, squeezing my hand.

A happy bubble grows in my chest as we reach the very top. The wind plays with my hair, and I'm not so scared anymore, not with Nate holding my hand like it's the most important job in the world.

"I got you, okay?" he says again, the words feeling like a pinky promise—the most serious kind there is.

I look at him, and suddenly everything clicks into place. He's not just my friend or my brother's best friend. He's something bigger, something that makes my heart feel too full, like a balloon about to burst.

Right here, at the top of the world with the stars sprinkled above us like magic dust, I realize something huge: I think I love Nate Sullivan.

CHAPTER 21
SEEING GHOSTS
NORA

PRESENT DAY

HE REMEMBERS. THE REALIZATION MAKES MY HEART SKIP LIKE A RECORD needle catching on vinyl. I glance down at the beaded bracelet hugging my wrist. He always throws me off balance, seeing right through the walls I've carefully constructed. The air feels charged with possibility, electric like the atmosphere before a summer storm. Each bead under my thumb brings back summers I've tried to box up and label "do not open" in my memory.

My stomach twists as I look up at the Ferris wheel, its lights spinning constellations against the ink-black sky. Heights have never been my thing, and they're not about to start being my thing tonight. But Nate catches the flicker of hesitation in my eyes—reading me like a book he's memorized cover to cover.

"Are we doing this?" he asks, his voice deceptively casual, as if he's talking about what movie to watch, not about catapulting us into the waiting arms of the sky.

I muster a grin that feels plastic on my face. "Uh... yeah. We are." My voice pitches too high, betraying me.

"Sure?" He arches an eyebrow, amusement flickering across his face. "Are you still afraid of heights?"

"Me? Pffft." I wave off the accusation with a flourish worthy of Broadway, trying to steady my quivering hand. "Let's do it."

His grin broadens and stretches out his hand, and just like that, I'm convinced I can handle this. With Nate, the impossible always seems within reach. He makes everything less terrifying, like adding color to a black and white world.

We board the ride, and as the seat lifts, only the metal bar feels real under my white-knuckled grip. Nate leans back, annoyingly at ease while I'm sitting here like it's potentially our last moment on Earth. The carnival worker drones through the safety spiel, like he's done a thousand times already tonight, his words fading into the symphony below. I can barely breathe, let alone appreciate the 'view'. But Nate's calm presence beside me anchors me to sanity. As we ascend, the view spreads beneath us—a tapestry of lights and laughter woven into the night.

Okay, this isn't so bad.

Then the Ferris wheel hoists us higher, and my stomach performs an Olympic-worthy gymnastics routine. I clutch the safety bar, knuckles bleaching white. The town shrinks into a dollhouse version of itself, and panic mounts, tightening around my chest like a python. My breathing hastens, teetering on the edge of a full-blown panic attack. Nate's head swivels toward me, his concern piercing through my spiral.

"Len," he coaxes gently, his voice a calm harbor. "Count your breaths with me, okay?"

I press my eyes shut, trying to sync my breathing with his steady cadence. It helps—a bit. But then, the Ferris wheel jerks to a halt, shuddering under us, and my heart catapults to my throat. Without thinking, I grab Nate's hand, my fingers interlacing with his like they remember exactly where they belong. His hand tightens around mine immediately, warm and steady, and my racing pulse stutters at the contact.

When was the last time we touched like this?

The familiarity of it hits me like a physical ache.

"Hey, hey," he murmurs, "I got you." The simplicity of his words, laden with an unspoken promise, anchors me. "If we go down, we go down together, remember?"

I do.

I pry my eyes open, meeting his. His expression is tender, imbued with a quiet strength that somehow, despite past hurts and broken promises, compels me to believe him. I manage a small, shaky smile, though my heart drums wildly against my ribs.

The ride eventually lowers us back to solid ground. My legs wobble like unset gelatin, nearly buckling beneath me. I stagger, and immediately, Nate's hand steadies me with a gentle grip on my elbow that sends sparks racing across my skin.

"Thanks," I mumble, embarrassed by my earlier unraveling.

"You good?" he asks, his touch lingering like a question mark.

"If by 'good' you mean still breathing, then yeah," I manage, attempting humor to mask my lingering disquiet.

His soft laugh briefly fills the air—until Farrah's sharp approach slices through it, her blonde hair a bright flag of warning in the carnival lights. Flanked by Shay and Harlow, her gaze cuts to our intertwined hands with surgical precision. I withdraw mine, the contact suddenly scalding, just as her stormy expression lands on us.

"I thought you weren't coming tonight?" Farrah's voice drips with venom disguised as honey, her eyes glinting as she looks at Nate like she's marking her territory.

Nate doesn't miss a beat, cool as winter frost. "Plans changed."

Farrah's piercing eyes shift to me, sharp and assessing. "I thought carnivals weren't your scene," she sneers, her voice laced with condescension.

"Changed my mind." He shrugs, his indifference stoking the fire in her eyes.

Feeling the tension rise like mercury, I interject, "I'm gonna grab something to drink." I edge away, hoping to escape the brewing storm. Girls like Farrah had a way of making simple nights feel like walking a tightrope over shark-infested waters.

But my retreat halts when Nate says, "I'll go with you," his words falling like a gauntlet between us and Farrah's fury.

I realize this night is about to become much more complicated than a simple fear of heights.

Farrah's arms cross over her chest like a shield. "We're not done here," she snaps, voice tight with promised retribution.

Nate's response cuts through the carnival noise. "Yeah, we are actually."

His dismissal sends a shiver racing down my spine. I've witnessed this kind of possessive drama before—it never ends well. I make my way through the crowd, the sticky night air thickening around me. Nate catches up, his footsteps falling into sync with mine.

"I'm sorry about that," he murmurs, voice tinged with concern.

I nod, forcing a smile that feels as artificial as the carnival's neon glow. "It's fine."

Another familiar voice cuts through the chaos like a firework.

"Nora!" Camilla bounds over, her energy infectious as she wraps me in a tight hug. "I saw Jake before and he said you weren't coming?"

"Plans changed," I repeat Nate's words.

We chat, but a sudden sight catches my eye—a figure in the distance, eerily familiar, partially obscured by the crowd. Everything in me freezes solid. He looks just like Evan—Evan the guy who has haunted every nightmare for the past year, whose shadow lurks in every dark corner.

No, it can't be him.

He's not here.

He can't be.

I shake my head, trying to dislodge the memory. I've tried so hard to erase that night. But what the mind tries to forget, the body always remembers, like muscle memory of a dance you never wanted to learn.

In the car, I'm silent sitting in the back seat with Jake while Ollie navigates up front for Nate. The night air whispers through my cracked window, carrying lingering scents of carnival sugar. I catch Nate's eyes in the rearview mirror more than once, dark and concerned, searching my reflection like he's reading a book written in a language only he understands.

"Everything okay?" Jake's voice cuts through my haze as we near home.

I muster a weak smile. "Yeah, just tired."

Jake frowns slightly, too knowing. "You were so set on staying home tonight. What changed?"

I glance toward Nate, who's focused on the road, his profile carved in shadows and streetlight. The muscles in his jaw work slightly—he's listening to every word.

"You were right. I needed a distraction," I admit, the truth slipping out. "Nate was heading out anyway and offered a ride."

He doesn't look too convinced, but thankfully he doesn't press me for more.

"Tomorrow, wanna hang out? Just you and me?"

I feel Nate's eyes on me through the rearview mirror. I'm too afraid to make eye contact with him in case he reads something on my face I don't want him to see.

"Sure, sounds like a plan," I say with a smile that's reciprocated by Jake.

When we finally pull into the driveway, I mumble a quick goodnight to everyone and make a beeline for the bathroom. I stand under the hot shower longer than necessary, letting the water wash away the night's tension, hoping it might also clear my head. With damp hair and skin still flushed from the heat, I slip into my pyjamas and pad down the hallway toward my bedroom. Wanting nothing more than to crawl into bed and disappear, the last thing I expect to see is Nate sitting on the edge of my bed, gently stroking my old stuffed animal Bones. The sight of him—this boy who embodies both danger and safety—cradling something so innocent from my childhood makes my chest ache with unnamed feelings.

"Sorry." Nate quickly sets Bones down, then looks up with an intensity that catches me off guard, his hazel eyes burning like amber in firelight. "I just wanted to make sure you were okay." His usual guarded demeanor has softened, leaving him looking unexpectedly vulnerable.

"I'm good," I mumble too quickly, avoiding his eyes that always see too much. "Just a long day."

"I thought we already figured out you have a terrible poker face," he says, playful but concerned. It doesn't lighten the mood. Instead, it feels like he's peeling back layers I've tightly wound around myself.

He takes my hand in his, the unexpected touch sending electricity racing up my arm. He leans in, his voice dropping to a soft whisper that wraps around me like a familiar blanket.

"Listen, I know I haven't given you many reasons to trust me lately... but you can talk to me, Nora. Whatever it is, I'll listen."

His sincerity hits me like a tidal wave, and for a moment, I consider letting it all spill out—the anger, the heartbreak, the mess I've been drowning in. But fear freezes the words in my throat. I can't let him see that part of me, still bleeding from wounds I've hidden beneath smiles and casual conversation. I want to believe him. God, I want to so badly it physically aches.

But how can I? After that night? The night I called him, desperate, my hands shaking so badly I almost dropped my phone. I needed him and he wasn't there.

Instead, he was with *her*.

Farrah.

Her voice still cuts through my memories, cool and dismissive. *"Nate's busy,"* she'd said, the words dripping with disdain. Like I was nothing. Like my whole world wasn't shattering around me.

"I appreciate you checking on me," I say instead, forcing a smile that feels like porcelain about to crack. "But I'm good, really. I just need to sleep."

He stands reluctantly, like he's surrendering a battle but not the war. At the door, he turns back, his eyes soft yet piercing as starlight.

"For what it's worth," he says, voice barely above a whisper, rough with something that sounds dangerously like longing, "I'm glad you're here."

"Me too," I manage, forcing the words out like pushing through thorns. It's not the whole truth, but it's all I can offer without crumbling.

"Goodnight, Leni." The nickname falls from his lips.

"Goodnight," I whisper back, and he closes the door softly behind him, the click of the latch sounding final as a period at the end of a sentence.

Alone again, I collapse against my pillows like a puppet with cut strings. I wonder how long I can keep pretending that the cracks in my foundation aren't spreading like spider webs across glass. Being invisible has become my shield against a world that feels too sharp, too dangerous. But invisibility can't last forever—I know that truth like I know my own reflection.

CHAPTER 22
PIECES OF A PUZZLE
NORA

IT'S BEEN A FEW DAYS SINCE THE CARNIVAL, AND THE TENSION BETWEEN Nate and me has started to dissipate. The awkward pauses are becoming rare, giving way to the easy talks we used to have. Things feel lighter now, almost hopeful.

Needing a change of scenery, I grab my laptop and head to Corrigan's Bakery. The moment I push open the door, the aroma of fresh coffee and vanilla envelops me. The comforting murmur of conversation fills the space, and the familiar tinkle of the bell above the door welcomes me in. I spot a cozy table by the window where sunlight pools on worn wood.

I've been here for hours, alternating between typing furiously and people-watching, with coffee as my steady companion. The afternoon light has shifted to gold when a familiar voice cuts through the café's gentle buzz.

"Nora?"

I turn to find Mia, effortlessly stylish as always, but there's something in her expression—a flash of genuine warmth that catches me off guard. She cradles her coffee cup like precious cargo.

"Mia, hey," I say, brightening despite myself. "Want to sit?"

She smiles, her dark hair catching the light. "Actually, I was just grabbing a quick bite before heading home. You could come over if you're free? It's a ten-minute walk. I could use the company."

There's something in her tone—a hint of vulnerability that makes the invitation feel weightier than casual plans. I pack up my laptop, intrigued by this glimpse beneath her polished exterior.

"Yeah, sure." I had no other plans except maybe drowning in more coffee at home.

Walking with Mia, the conversation flows naturally, though there's an undercurrent of something more, like looking in a mirror and seeing familiar cracks. She opens up about her life: elite boarding schools where success meant perfect scores, relentless academic pressures, and a nomadic existence following her father's business demands. Her stories scatter across continents, each city seeming to have taken a piece of her with it.

When we round the corner, I freeze. The house before us isn't just large, it's something from a luxury magazine. Marble steps gleam, leading to regal columns that stretch skyward. Expansive windows, framed by pristine shutters, reflect the late afternoon light.

"Uhh, this is your house?" I blurt out, unable to mask my astonishment.

Mia gives a small, strained smile that doesn't reach her eyes. "Yeah," she says, typing in a gate code with practiced efficiency. "I know, it's a bit... much."

"Mia, this place looks like it's straight out of *The Great Gatsby*." I laugh.

Her laugh is light, but her eyes flicker with a mix of pride and resignation as she looks back at her home. "It's beautiful, but being an only child in a house like this sometimes feels like living in a museum where you can't touch anything."

The garden feels staged, too perfect—no weathered decorations, no evidence of life being lived.

Mia's voice drops when she mentions her dad. "He's... intense. Big shot in business. Forbes 100 and all that."

"You never mentioned your dad was..."

"The CEO of one of the biggest tech companies out there?" Mia finishes, her smirk tinged with irony. "Yeah, I don't usually start with that. Makes people act weird. Like suddenly they're talking to my father's bank account instead of me."

"Forbes 100 is pretty impressive though. "

She exhales heavily. "Honestly, most days I don't even get what he does. Growing up with all this..." She gestures at our surroundings. "Everyone you meet tends to want something from you, not just friendship. It's like being a fancy store display—everyone wants to look, but nobody really sees you."

I've only known Mia for just over a week, but hearing her open up makes her more real. She's not just the girl with perfect grades and a rich family—she's been under pressure her whole life, trying to meet impossible standards.

"You know," she continues softly, "I used to just hole up in my room with my books studying till sunrise. It wasn't about loving school; it was the only thing I felt I could control."

Makes two of us.

"I'm sorry," she says suddenly, looking embarrassed. "I don't usually talk about this stuff."

"No, I'm really glad you did," I tell her, feeling the weight of my own guarded nature.

As we step inside, the house is more showcase than home—high ceilings, museum-worthy art, and furniture that looks untouched. I turn to Mia. "For what it's worth, I really don't care about any of this. I'm just happy we're friends."

Her smile then is one of the realest things I've seen in a long time. "Me too."

Walking through the house, the walls display family portraits—young Mia in each one, wearing that kind of smile that's more pose than joy. She flops onto a pristine couch, tucking her legs under her.

"I've always kind of felt like the odd one out," she admits. "Even at boarding school, I never really meshed with everyone else."

"Why not?"

She looks off into space, lost in memory. "I was always a homebody, never cared much for the party scene. And I loved riding horses. It was my escape from feeling alone."

"Well I'm glad you found something you love that much."

Her smile brightens momentarily but fades. "I think I'm finally okay with being an outsider. The girls at school just didn't understand. Eventually, I stopped trying to make them."

"I get that. After we lost my dad, trying to fit in anywhere felt... wrong somehow."

We sit in comfortable silence until she brightens with an idea.

"You know what we need? A real girls' night. Just us, and Marcus. I think he'd kill us if we didn't invite him."

I laugh, feeling lighter. "A sleepover sounds perfect."

I DON'T EXPECT ANYONE TO BE BACK AT THE HOUSE WHEN I GET HOME. Jake had texted that he and Ollie were getting pizza, and Lydia and Mom were downtown. Music drifts from the spare living room—Guns N' Roses, *"November Rain,"* filling the space with nostalgic chords.

I find Nate sprawled on the floor, focused on a jigsaw puzzle scattered across the coffee table, pieces catching the late afternoon light. His brow is furrowed in concentration, fingers moving with unexpected gentleness.

"What are you doing?" I ask, struck by the sight of him—usually so carefully composed—lost in something so simple.

He looks up, a playful smirk crossing his lips. "A puzzle," he answers, his tone suggesting deeper meanings.

"A puzzle? To 'November Rain'?"

"It's cheaper than therapy." His grin broadens into something genuine that makes my heart skip.

"Can I help?"

"Sure."

We settle into comfortable silence, the clink of puzzle pieces filling the room. The tension between us dissolves as we work, like we're rebuilding something lost, finding each missing part of a bigger picture.

"Ever feel like you're missing pieces?" Nate asks, after a minute of silence.

I study his face, wondering if he means more than just the puzzle. "Sometimes," I begin, turning a piece over in my hands. "But I think that's the thing about life—just like a puzzle, we can't force pieces to fit just because we think they should, and sometimes the picture we're trying to create isn't even the one we're meant to make. Maybe the missing pieces aren't really missing at all; they're just not part of our puzzle."

He looks up, his eyes catching mine with an intensity that steals my breath. The soft light paints his face in gold and shadow, making him look both younger and older at once.

"That's... actually profound," he says softly.

"Well, I am a writer," I smile, half-joking but serious.

"That you are." He lets silence stretch between us before asking, "How's the writing going anyway?"

I fidget with a puzzle piece, avoiding his eyes. "I really think I might have something."

"Is that what you're planning to submit for the scholarship?"

Heat rises to my cheeks. "How did you know about that?"

"I saw the application on the table. Wasn't snooping, promise."

"I... I'm not sure I'm ready."

His eyes hold mine, refusing to let go. The heat in my cheeks starts to slowly surface.

How the hell does he do that?

"Being ready is bullshit. You're never truly ready for things that scare you."

"So then how do you know when to go for it?"

"When the thrill outweighs the fear, that's your moment. If it scares you, it's probably worth it." He focuses on the puzzle. "Besides, you're an incredible writer. It's time you believed that."

My heart races. "What if they don't like what I write?"

"Then fuck 'em."

"Nate, you don't—"

He leans forward, eyes intense. "They will love it and you."

"I can't fail. Not at this," I whisper, vulnerability raw in my voice.

"You won't fail," he insists, closer now, his Armani cologne making my head spin. "You know why? Because you're the girl who, when she sets her mind to something, doesn't back down."

His confidence is both terrifying and exhilarating.

"Want to know my prediction? You're going to be a world-renowned author. Bestsellers, translations, interviews... And I'll be here, saying, 'Remember that time we were trying to do that puzzle, and I told you so?'"

I laugh, warmth spreading through me like sunrise. "What's it meant to be?" I ask, studying the scattered pieces.

"Big Ben and the River Thames." His smirk is mischievous.

I place a piece that fits perfectly.

"Maybe it's a sign. The pieces might be aligning for you in plain sight," he says, looking up through those ridiculous eyelashes, his defined jawline and dimples making my mouth go dry.

"Do you still play?" I ask suddenly, needing to shift focus.

His smile fades. "I quit football a while ago..."

"I meant music. Do you still play?"

The haunted look in his eyes makes my heart crack. "I- I haven't touched a guitar in years."

His words throw me back to summer days—his guitar singing through open windows, Def Leppard riffs and Oasis tracks painting the air gold. His playing was effortless then, natural as breathing, passion evident in every note. Seeing him let it go is like watching someone dim their own light.

"I miss it," I confess, ache vivid in my voice. "Hearing you play."

Shock and vulnerability war in his eyes. "You do?"

"Yeah, I do." Struck by sudden inspiration, I offer, "Okay, how about this. I'll submit my scholarship application... if you start playing again."

Something raw flickers across his features. "I don't have my guitar anymore."

"We'll find you one."

He studies me for a long moment before a genuine smile breaks through. "I'm not getting out of this, am I?"

I hold out my pinky finger—a childhood gesture that feels both ridiculous and profound. "Nope, especially if you pinky swear right now."

He laughs softly, rich with memory. "We only made pinky swears for promises we intended to keep."

"I know," I reply, surprising myself with my confidence. "And we're going to keep this one."

As our pinkies link—his warm and calloused, mine small and determined—it feels like more than just a childhood ritual. It feels like a bridge being rebuilt, like finding a missing puzzle piece. Surrounded by scattered jigsaw pieces and the fading notes of "November Rain," we're making a promise to stop running from the things that make us whole, to start believing in the possibility of putting broken things back together.

Some promises are made to be broken, but this one?

This one feels like the beginning of something real, something that might just save us both.

CHAPTER 23
THE THING ABOUT ODDS
NATE

Things between Nora and me are complicated. Not the bullshit *"it's complicated"* Facebook status kind of complicated.

This is deeper. *Rawer.*

The tension's shifted—not gone, just...transformed. Like some fucked-up alchemy that turns sharp edges into something that burns slower, more dangerous. I'm still trying to keep her at arm's length, but my arms keep getting shorter.

I see it in her too—those quick glances, the way she pivots conversations like she's dodging landmines. We're both walking this razor-thin line between what we want and what we think we should do. Protecting each other by staying away, which is basically the most fucked-up version of love I can imagine.

I want to dive deep with her.

Not just scratch the surface, but after everything—all the shit I've put her through—do I even have the right to want that? To hope we might find our way back to something real? The universe has a sick sense of humor, and Nora? She's the punchline I can't stop thinking about.

The house is unusually quiet when I wake earlier than normal. Throwing on a Metallica t-shirt, I head downstairs, drawn by the rich aroma of coffee. Mom's there, newspaper spread before her, surprise flickering across her face as she looks up.

"Well, this is a rare sight," she teases, her smile gentle. "Up before noon."

"Yeah, don't get used to it." I keep my tone light while pouring coffee, letting the mug's warmth distract from the familiar nausea that's plagued me these past weeks. The bitter scent both comforts and turns my stomach—a reminder of countless mornings spent hunched over the toilet, of Ollie silently leaving water and aspirin without questions.

Mom folds her newspaper with deliberate care, studying me. "You've been smiling more lately. It's good to see you happy."

Happy.

The word sits wrong, like ill-fitting clothes. If she knew about the hell of detoxing, of hiding the worst of it... "I guess I've had things to smile about," I manage, masking my struggle with a shrug.

Her eyes soften with that maternal insight that always sees too much, but she doesn't push. We're alike that way—knowing when to give space.

"So, what are you up to today?"

"Got an errand to run," I say, depositing my mug in the sink.

THE SMELL OF DUSTY PAGES AND WORN LEATHER WASHES OVER ME THE second I push through the door at Gracie's bookstore. Alfie glances up from some stack he's arranging, those ancient glasses sliding down his nose when he spots me. Something about the way the old man looks at me—like he's actually glad to see me walk in—makes my chest tight.

"Nathaniel? What a pleasant surprise to see you here."

Alfie's voice cuts through the silence, smooth as aged whiskey.

"Morning, Alfie."

His eyes—kind, knowing—study me. "Is there anything I can help you with?"

"Uhh, yeah, actually." I run a hand through my hair. "Do you have *The Secret Garden?*"

A smile spreads across his face. "An ageless classic. We've got a few special editions just in."

He pulls out a beautifully bound copy, his fingers tracing the cover.

"It's fascinating how this book is really about healing hidden spaces. Like something locked away, forgotten—but not dead. Just waiting for the right kind of care."

I feel something shift. The book isn't just a book anymore.

"You know, Grace believed all great love stories shared one thing— they beat the odds. Just like Mary in the garden, some connections need patience. You have to believe in what you can't immediately see. Restore what others might consider beyond saving."

They beat the odds.

The words hang between us. I'm thinking about Nora—about us. A

155

connection locked away, wounded. Needing careful tending. Potential hidden beneath layers of hurt and misunderstanding.

"And if the odds are constantly stacked against you?" I ask softly.

"Sometimes, love is about fighting the odds together." He pauses, eyes meeting mine.

Isn't that what it's always been with Nora? The push and pull, the way we can't seem to stay away from each other even when it feels like the world—or maybe just me—is trying to keep us apart.

"Then how do you know if it's worth it?" I ask, my voice quieter now, like I'm afraid of the answer.

Alfie chuckles softly. "You don't."

"You don't?" I raise an eyebrow, waiting for the punchline. But Alfie just keeps walking, his grin widening like he's about to drop some grenade of wisdom right into my lap.

"Sometimes you meet someone and you don't know how or why or what brought you together. But suddenly you can't imagine life without them. Everything feels lighter and brighter. It's better just because they exist. You forget who you were before them because you've never felt more like yourself than how you feel with them there."

I stare at him, absorbing every damn word about being someone's person, not just being there but fighting alongside them.

Alfie hands me a special edition of *The Secret Garden* with a gold-embossed leather cover. "This one's perfect for her," he grins.

Caught off guard, I frown.

"How'd you know it's for a girl?"

He chuckles, tapping his nose. "Seen plenty of lost boys in here, trying to fix things with someone who matters. I think you're forgetting I've been around for quite some time. Besides, she was looking at that one the other day when she was here."

Before I can reply, the door swings open, and a new face steps in.

"Ah, just in time. Nathaniel, meet Nick, he's just moved back to town."

Nick nods at me, his demeanor laid back but sharp. "Hey, nice to meet you Nathani—"

"Nate. Call me Nate."

I fucking hated Nathaniel.

"Nice to meet you, Nate." Nick holds his hand out, waiting for me to shake it.

When I do, I notice his hands are rough and calloused. Signs of a guy who works hard.

"Nick's setting up a new bar," Alfie continues. "But hit a bit of a hurdle with renovations."

Nick rubs his neck, frustration clear. "That's now two contractors who have bailed suddenly. Now I'm short on hands and don't know if we'll get to open before the summer is over."

An idea sparks in my mind.

"Need some help?"

He looks surprised. "Are you offering?"

I shrug, trying to play it cool, but honestly, the idea of having some-thing—anything—to focus on besides the mess I've made feels like a lifeline.

"I've got time, and I know how to use a hammer," I say, feeling a shift inside. Maybe it's time to start fixing more than just old mistakes.

Nick looks at me for a moment, then nods. "All right. How about you swing by the bar tomorrow and I can show you what we're working with?"

"Sounds good," I say.

"Well, that was easier than I thought it'd be trying to find someone. Maybe I should swing by bookstores to find more helping hands. I'm going to head out, Uncle. I will see you tonight, and Nate, I'll see you tomorrow."

"Don't work too hard, boy." Alfie says.

Nick gives him a gleeful smile. It's an exchange a doting father would give a son and it makes me wonder what the story is behind these two to have formed such a tight bond. I'd be lying if I said there wasn't a hint of jealousy bubbling underneath the surface.

Alfie, watching me with that knowing grin as Nick leaves, breaks the silence. "That nephew of mine works too hard. It's good he's got help now."

I nod, feeling a bit more purposeful.

Alfie wraps the book I've chosen, his hands steady and experienced. "You know what I believe?" His voice draws me in.

I lean on the counter, curious. "What's that?"

"We meet the most important people when we least expect it," he says, his tone soft yet certain. "And often, what you need isn't a thing—it's a person. A person who'll help you uncover the answers to the things you're searching for." He winks at me with a sly grin.

His words weigh heavy on me.

"What if you're too screwed up to keep them around?" The question slips out, raw and honest.

Alfie pauses, his task momentarily forgotten. "Healing doesn't mean the damage never existed, son. It means it no longer controls you." His gaze is piercing, seeing through me. "Remember that."

I nod, struggling to find my voice as he hands me the packaged book.

Handing him a fifty, my mind races with his insights. "Keep the change, please."

Alfie smiles, gratitude spread across his face.

As I head for the door, Alfie calls out, stopping me in my tracks, "Nate, those voices in your head? They're just echoes of past pains. Don't let them win."

Turning back, I manage a tight smile.

I step into the sunlight, feeling a strange mix of burden and relief.

CHAPTER 24
SUNRISES AND CINNABONS
NORA

THE MORNING AIR NIPS AT MY SKIN, SHARP ENOUGH TO PULL ME FULLY INTO wakefulness as Jake and I pedal hard up the hill. It's the magical hour just before sunrise. The world is bathed in a soft, golden glow, as if holding its breath. Jake was always the most nostalgic one out of the four of us. He loved holding onto memories, and I didn't fault him for it. But holding onto the past is like clutching a handful of water—no matter how tightly you grip, it always slips through your fingers, leaving only a lingering coolness and the wet traces of what once was.

Out of the corner of my eye, I catch Jake's relaxed profile, touched by the pink hues of the dawning sky. When he notices me looking, his grin widens, those familiar crinkles appearing by his eyes—his real smile. It's such a small thing, but right now, it's everything.

We reach the cliff just in time. I drop my bike on the soft grass and rush to the edge. The view takes my breath away: the ocean stretches out, a vast expanse of shimmering gold.

Jake settles beside me, his knee lightly brushing against mine. We sit in silence, the kind that's as comfortable and familiar as an old favorite song, filling the space between us without needing words.

After a moment, Jake's voice breaks the calm, gentle yet tentative. "You know you can talk to me, right? About your dad. About anything." His tone is soft but there's an earnestness to it, probing the waters of my grief.

I swallow hard, feeling the heaviness of his words. The grief and guilt are always there, lurking in the shadows like persistent fog, refusing to be chased away by the rising sun. Jake shifts closer, his shoulder pressing against mine, his presence a steady warmth.

"I'm here," he murmurs. "Whether you talk or not, I'm here."

His words settle deep in my chest, warming yet breaking me all at once. I tear at the blades of grass, not daring to meet his eyes—searching for the cracks I tirelessly try to seal. You don't tell people you're not okay because it's too hard to watch them struggle with what to do. You'll find yourself comforting them, even though you're the one who needs comfort.

Jake exhales a slow, deliberate breath. I feel his gaze, steady and earnest, as if he could make me believe simply through the force of his will. "You don't have to pretend with me, Nor."

I keep my eyes fixed on the ground. Looking at him would probably break me. My fingers clench around the grass, its sharp scent rising in the cool morning air. Sadness starts to well up again, swelling in my chest, thickening my throat until I can barely breathe.

He shifts beside me, his presence a silent plea for me to let him in. He doesn't have to say anything; I feel his desire to understand, to take away the pain. He's always been like that—ready to drown in my sorrows just to spare me the weight. But some burdens are mine alone. Not because he isn't willing to share them, but because some parts of grief are too personal, too raw to hand over, even to him.

"I know," I murmur, watching the sunlight spill across the cliffside, painting everything with a golden glow. "I'm just... still trying to figure out how to be okay."

I shift the focus away from my inner turmoil and divert the conversation. "Are you excited about Duke?"

He stretches out, looking thoughtful against the backdrop of the rising sun. "Yeah, I guess. I mean it's kinda terrifying. Feels surreal, like one chapter's ending without knowing what the next one holds."

"Is it what you want to be doing, for real?" I probe, needing to steer away from my own uncertain future.

He laughs, a sound tinged with unease. "I guess. There's a lot I still need to sort out."

The conversation shifts again, and suddenly, Jake's tone grows serious. "Your mom mentioned last year was tough with the kids at school. Did any of them show up at the funeral?" His question makes me uncomfortable because it brings to light things I've tried to bury.

No, not one.

By then, my tarnished reputation had driven everyone away.

"You were there. That's all that mattered," I say, managing a weak smile that doesn't quite mask the pain.

His eyes soften, filled with a mix of understanding and something else—perhaps a wish to offer more comfort. He nods, looking back toward the horizon where the sun climbs higher, igniting the sky with shades of orange and pink.

Inside, the turmoil doesn't cease. The ghosts of last summer, the whispers of Evan, the echoes of Claire who claimed to be my best friend, and the crushing weight of shame swirl around me. The worst of it is the last real conversation with my dad, that's where the guilt stems from. He had seen the signs and recognized my silent pleas for help. Now, he's gone, and with him, the last shred of understanding I had clung to.

Jake's question snaps me out of my thoughts.

"Where'd you get the bracelet? I haven't seen that one before."

I look down at the thin band Nate picked for me at the carnival.

"Nate won it for me," I say quietly. Jake's expression shifts, a flicker of something passing over his face.

"Oh, right." His voice has an edge to it now, and I can tell he's holding something back.

Jake's always been great at hiding his feelings, but I feel the tension between us about the whole Nate thing.

He doesn't say anything for a moment, just draws patterns in the dirt with his finger. Then he looks up, his eyes steady on mine.

I shift, trying to steer the conversation away from heavy stuff.

"So, what about Kelsie?"

"What about Kelsie?" he asks.

"I saw you two at the party, then the bonfire, and at the carnival too. She seems really into you."

Jake laughs, brushing off the idea. "There's nothing going on there. Besides, I'm waiting."

"For what?"

"For the right one." That makes my face heat up and I'm not entirely sure why. Something about the way he's waiting for someone he seems to already know freaks me out a bit. I force a laugh, trying to shake off the weird mood.

"What's next on the list to tackle today?" I ask, desperate to keep things light.

Jake brightens up, back to his usual self. "Eat our body weight in Cinnabons." He grins like he's just solved all the world's problems.

"That I can do," I joke, grateful for the change of topic.

We hop on our bikes, pedaling towards Corrigan's, the cool morning air and the warm rising sun painting everything like a postcard. For a moment, I let myself believe everything can be as simple as bike rides and cinnabons.

The bakery wraps us in its warm embrace of cinnamon and sugar, a haven unchanged by time's cruel march. My stomach growls appreciatively at the fresh-baked aroma, earning a smothered laugh from Jake.

"Four of your finest Cinnabons, please," he announces, sliding cash across the counter. "Actually, make it twelve."

"You really weren't kidding about eating our body weight in Cinnabons, huh?"

"You only live once," he winks.

As Jake handles the transaction, my attention drifts to the window. That's when everything shifts—my skin prickles with awareness, my heart stutters, then races. I freeze, ice replacing blood in my veins as I spot him.

Evan.

He's across the street, surrounded by Eden's elite, laughing like he's never destroyed a life. My stomach twists into origami shapes, a silent scream building behind my ribs. The bakery door might as well be a fortress wall for how impossible it feels to move. Each second that ticks by feels like an eternity. Panic floods my system, my breathing shallow and quick as my body reacts before my mind can catch up.

Breathe.

I command myself.

Just breathe.

But the air feels like broken glass in my lungs. Pressure builds in my chest, my throat closing like it's caught in a vice. Each heartbeat sends ice through my veins, crashing against my skull with brutal force.

Breathe.

My next inhale catches, too fast and too shallow, as control slips through my fingers like water. The room starts to spin, simultaneously too quick and too slow. I dig crescents into my palms, trying to force my breathing into something resembling rhythm.

I'm not dying in a bakery, I repeat silently, searching for an anchor. It's all in my head. I'm in control. But watching him stand there, carelessly destructive, the bitter truth crashes over me—I'm nowhere near in control.

This panic isn't just in my head. It's real, visceral, consuming.

He's real.

And he's here.

The bakery dissolves around me. I'm back in that room last summer, frozen, powerless. His threats echo in my ears, venomous promises that sealed my silence. Every buried fear claws its way to the surface, leaving me raw.

"Hey." Jake's voice cuts through the fog, concern bleeding through.

"Nora? You okay?" I nod mechanically.

"Yeah... yeah, I just..." My voice wavers before I steady it. "Could we get these to go? I'm feeling off."

Jake's expression tightens with worry, but he doesn't push. "Sure," he says, guiding us out quickly, reading my desperate need to escape.

I follow, eyes down, feeling Evan's gaze burn into my back. Despite Jake's protective presence, loneliness pounds through me like a second heartbeat.

As we pedal home, the world blurs into watercolor smears, indistinguishable from my churning thoughts. Jake keeps glancing over, concern etched deep, but I keep my eyes forward, not daring to meet him.

How do I admit that Evan being here has shattered my carefully reconstructed sense of safety?

The wind whips past, but it's nothing compared to the hurricane inside me. Gripping the handlebars, one thought crystallizes with terrifying clarity: I'm nowhere near ready to face him.

CHAPTER 25
A PART OF ME DIED
NORA

June, 2006

15 years old

It's Saturday night, and for once, I'm actually excited. All week, I've been looking forward to crashing at Claire's place for our usual sleepover ritual—snacks, laughter, and endless episodes of *One Tree Hill*.

Claire, with her magnetic personality, has always been the one in the spotlight, while I preferred the quiet of the shadows. She was always transforming ordinary moments into adventures while I orbit contentedly in her glow.

The moment we reach her room after saying goodnight to her mom, Claire's energy crackles with an intensity that sets my nerves on edge. The sharp snap of her bedroom door feels like a starting gun, and when she turns to me, a familiar guilty look twists her features.

"What?" My voice cracks, betraying the apprehension coiling in my stomach.

"Don't be mad," Claire starts, her voice honey-sweet but her eyes calculating. She's never truly sorry, and we both know it.

"Just spit it out," I push, steeling myself.

"Promise you won't be mad first?" She scrunches her face in practiced remorse.

I tip my head back, exhaling slowly. "Fine, I won't be mad." The words taste like surrender.

She practically vibrates with excitement. "Evan invited us to a party, and I said we'd go." Her eyes sparkle at his name.

"He invited us or just you?"

She flashes that conspiratorial grin. "C'mon, Nor. We're a package deal, everyone knows that." Her eagerness pierces me like a needle, deflating my resistance. Fresh off our freshman year, Claire's been circling Evan like a bee to honey, and I can't bring myself to clip her wings.

I narrow my eyes, feeling the familiar sting of being Claire's shadow. In her world, she's the lead actress, and I'm just the silent extra filling space in her scenes.

"Look," she coos, linking our arms in that practiced way that always manages to soften my resolve. "This will be fun. Who knows, maybe you'll even get your first kiss." She winks like she's offering me the world's greatest prize, but my stomach knots at the thought.

It's not the kiss itself that repulses me—it's the predatory attention that seems to accompany it in Evan's crowd.

"You can't keep holding out for Nate, Nor. I'm not trying to be a bitch, but he's not your type, and you're clearly not his. Time to ditch that little daydream and focus on finding someone new to pine over." Her casual dismissal slices through years of quiet moments with Nate that she never witnessed, moments that meant everything to me.

I mask the ache with a strained smile. "Yeah, maybe."

"Come on, don't be a baby," she needles, poking at my brewing emotions. "Let's just have some fun, okay? Be a good friend and come with me." She clasps her hands beneath her chin, batting her eyelashes with theatrical flair. "Pleeeease?"

My eye roll is answer enough.

Her victory laugh rings out as she crushes me in a hug, oblivious to the dread settling in my chest. "Thank you, thank you, thank you!"

The moment she steps back, her critical gaze sweeps over me. "Let's get you something to wear. You always dress like you're about to hit the skate park."

I swallow the sting of her words. My baggy, boyish style is more than fashion—it's armor, shielding parts of myself I'm not ready to share. But arguing with Claire is futile.

"Here, try this." She tosses a sweater dress at me that looks suffocatingly small.

"I can't wear this."

"Why not? It'll highlight your curves, the ones you always hide. Just trust me."

I'm not sure that I do right now.

. . .

165

THE PARTY HITS ME LIKE A WALL OF SENSATION—PULSING MUSIC, SHARP scents of alcohol and weed, an atmosphere that constricts my lungs. Claire dissolves into the crowd with practiced ease, her charisma drawing people like moths while I fade into the background—present but unseen.

"Loosen up, will you?" She throws the words over her shoulder with a smirk. "You're at a party not a funeral."

I force another smile that feels like a grimace. Everything feels wrong, her voice carrying an edge that reminds me where I don't belong.

The house throbs with frenetic energy, air thick with sweat and cheap perfume. My senses heighten in the dim chaos as guys lean too close, their gazes crawling over my skin. I tug at my sweater's sleeves, mourning my usual protective layers. Claire, blind to my discomfort, pulls me toward Evan's court of admirers. I trail behind like a forgotten shadow as she basks in the potential of her moment with him. Every cell in my body screams to retreat, but I stay frozen, trying to disappear within myself. Evan Matherson's very presence sends ice through my veins, his charm too polished, too precise. Claire giggles beside me, and I force a smile despite my thundering heart.

This isn't my world.

"There he is." Claire tugs my arm. "Evan!" Her voice carries too much hope.

He turns, his gaze lingering on me before he approaches. "Hey. Glad you could make it. Want a drink?"

"Sure!" Claire jumps at the offer. Evan's eyes fix on me, waiting.

"No, I'm good," I say quickly, but Claire's sharp elbow and whispered, "Lighten up," make me waver.

Without waiting for further protest, he thrusts a red cup into my hand. Claire's encouraging nod compels me to sip—the liquid burns, bitter and wrong.

Why do people drink this stuff?

And do they actually enjoy it when they do?

"Just relax and have fun, okay?" she insists before Evan whisks her away.

I want to leave but can't abandon Claire, not with her judgment clouded and vulnerable. I retreat to a couch, wedged beside a couple lost in each other until they sprawl over me, oblivious to my presence.

That's my breaking point. I stand, but the room spins violently. Though I've barely touched my drink, my vision blurs and my limbs feel like lead. I take another sip, hoping to steady myself, but the disorientation deepens.

Everything loses focus.

The room tilts and sways.

My legs threaten to buckle as Evan's voice cuts through the haze, too close.

"Hey, you don't look too good," he murmurs, his hand already gripping my elbow. "Here, let me help."

First mistake—letting him guide me through the crowd.

Where's Claire? Why isn't he with her?

The world blurs as he steers me, supposedly toward the bathroom. Realization hits as a door clicks behind us—we're in a bedroom. Panic spikes, but my screams stay trapped in my throat. My vision clears just enough to see Evan's triumphant smirk.

"Evan, I—" The words slur, foreign to my ears. The floor seems to vanish as I sink into the mattress.

His laugh chills me to the bone. "This will be more fun if you relax."

My attempts to push him away are useless, my arms refusing to respond.

"Mm, I do like a challenge. Especially when they start begging." His voice drips with dark anticipation.

Desperation claws at me, but I'm voiceless, powerless. His fingers trace my jaw with false gentleness against the backdrop of my terror.

Then his weight pins me down.

My body won't respond.

My mind races, screaming to fight, but I'm trapped in stillness. I'm powerless beneath him.

"Shh, shh. It'll be over soon," he whispers, his tongue trailing my jaw as I try to shake my head. His hand holds me still. "Don't make this harder for yourself."

My heart threatens to burst from my chest. Tears burn as I squeeze my eyes shut, praying for an end to this nightmare. His hands invade, cruel and claiming, each touch a brand of ownership that scorches through me. I'm fragmenting, a silent scream lodged in my throat as he takes pieces of my soul.

Inch by inch.

"You feel real fucking good." His words echo in the chaos of my mind. I wish I could dissolve, vanish into nothing and forget.

But you don't forget something like this. As much as your mind tries to, your body always remembers.

I try to detach, to convince myself this isn't real. Just a horror movie scene, not my life. I shut my eyes to escape, but the darkness only sharpens his presence—his hands roaming with terrible ownership, one

167

at my neck, the other violating. His body keeps me pinned, a constant reminder of my helplessness.

"Please st—" My voice breaks, pathetically weak.

His whisper poisons the air. "Just ride it out baby, ride it out."

A bang at the door pierces my despair. "Evan!" someone shouts.

Hope flickers, fragile and brief.

"Fuck off," he snarls, hand clamping over my mouth. I can't breathe. He leans close, threat dripping from every word. "Scream and I'll fucking ruin you. Tell anyone this wasn't what you wanted, and everyone will see this." His phone flashes, capturing my humiliation.

"This is going to stay between us. You keep that pretty little mouth of yours closed," he taunts.

I manage a weak nod, a tear escaping as reality crashes down. I tell myself if I just hold my breath, maybe this nightmare will fade to black. Maybe I can pretend none of this is real. But the darkness offers no escape; he still dominates every sense.

The door bursts open. Claire's voice cuts through everything: "Nora!?"

Evan recoils, his weight suddenly gone. Air floods my lungs as I collapse inward, shaking violently. Claire yanks at him, but her fury is aimed at me. Her words slice through the chaos, pinning me down.

"Are you fucking kidding me?" Claire's rage contorts her face, veins throbbing at her temples. "I can't believe you'd do this to me. You two-faced whore."

Her accusations hit like physical blows, twisting reality into a grotesque parody where I'm the villain. In this moment, I realize I'll never be the same. Something fundamental has shattered inside me.

I stumble past Evan, his sneer following me. "Frigid bitch." Each syllable cuts deeper than the last, exposing raw wounds I didn't know existed. They've broken me completely.

Some damages are too profound to ever fully heal.

Panic seizes control. My only thought—escape.

I push through the crowd, their faces a meaningless blur.

The cold night should feel refreshing on my face but instead it slaps me as I burst outside. It does nothing to clear the chaos in my head. My steps waver, the world distorted by alcohol and trauma. Calling Mom or my brother isn't an option—I'm too far gone. I collapse on the curb, sobs wracking my body. Fumbling with my phone, I scroll past Jake's name— he's at training camp—and land on Nate.

The phone rings.

I hold my breath, desperate for his voice, but a girl answers, her words slurred and tone cruel.

"Hello?"

"Is, uh... is Nate there?" My voice breaks, tears threaten to fall but I hold them back.

Her laugh cuts like glass. "Nate's busy." Music and voices blur in the background.

The rejection stings worse than a slap. "Oh, right... well could you—"

"I said he's busy," she snaps.

"Please, it's important. I just need to talk to him." Pride abandoned, I'm begging now.

"Don't know what to tell you, sweetheart. He couldn't talk to you even if he wanted to right now." The implication is clear—too drunk or high to function.

My composure shatters completely. "Can you please tell him to call—"

Click.

Silence swallows me whole.

In this crushing quiet, I've never felt more alone. For the first time, I truly understand what it means to have no one.

WHEN I GET HOME EVERYONE BLISSFULLY UNAWARE OF WHAT COMES BACK with me. Each step upstairs feels impossible, my body and spirit equally heavy. The bathroom light flickers harshly and unforgivingly. I barely reach the sink before retching violently, my body desperate to purge the night's poison. My throat burns, but the internal stain remains. The mirror shows a stranger—pale, hollow-eyed, tear-stained. There's an emptiness in those eyes now; something vital has been extinguished.

Tears fall, but I force them to stop.

I grip the sink until my knuckles turn white.

This didn't happen.

If I cry, it becomes real.

But it isn't real.

Nothing happened.

It isn't real.

I repeat the denial like a prayer, hoping to convince myself. If I believe hard enough, maybe this horror will fade like a nightmare at dawn. I stare one final time at who I used to be, reflected in the glass. That girl is gone now, buried beneath tonight's wreckage. With one last defiant swipe at my tears, I make my choice.

I choose to erase her.

I choose to deny reality.

In the stark bathroom light, I vow never to forget. I shut off the light, lock away the memories, and leave the girl in the mirror behind—forever.

CHAPTER 26
WHAT'S HIS NAME?
NORA

PRESENT DAY

I PUSH THROUGH THE FRONT DOOR WITH HASTE. NATE LOOKS UP FROM THE half-finished puzzle sprawled across the coffee table, concern flooding his face as his eyes meet mine. His brow furrows instantly, jaw tightening as he takes in my state. He's always been able to read me, to sense when something's wrong, and right now every cell in my body screams with wrongness.

I force myself past him, each step measured and careful, as though walking on glass. I feel his eyes tracking me, heavy with unasked questions. My lungs feel too small for my chest when I hear him ask Jake, "What the fuck happened?"

"She wasn't feeling great. Upset stomach or something," Jake replies, his casual tone a stark contrast to the storm raging inside me.

I don't stop—can't stop.

Lingering would shatter the fragile composure I'm desperately clinging to. The stairs become my escape route, each step echoing my mounting panic until I reach my room and slam the door. My back slides down against the cold wood as my breathing fractures into quick, shallow gasps. The familiar tightening in my chest signals an approaching panic attack as the edges of my vision blur and darken. I wrap my arms around my knees, trying to anchor myself as the room tilts and spins around me.

Time hasn't dulled the pain—it's only taught me to hide it better. For twelve months, I've perfected the art of burying everything so deep that

171

sometimes I almost believe my own lies. But the memories, when they surface, cut just as deep as they did that first day.

"Nora?" Nate's voice penetrates my solitude, gentle but unmistakably firm.

I squeeze my eyes shut, willing him away. I can't let him see me like this, stripped of all my carefully constructed defenses.

"Go away," I manage, my voice barely a whisper. Rising unsteadily, I begin to pace, as if movement alone could dispel the shadows closing in.

"Nora, what's—"

"Nate!" My voice cracks like thin ice. "Just leave me alone."

The door creaks open, and he stands in the threshold, concern etched deep in the lines of his face. He doesn't enter, but his presence fills the space anyway, steady as a heartbeat.

"You're shaking," he observes, his voice soft as falling snow.

I turn away, but his words follow me. "Talk to me Len—"

"I'm fine," I say, the lie tasting bitter on my tongue. My trembling hands betray me, and I curl them into fists at my sides.

His footsteps whisper across the floor as he approaches, moving with the careful precision of someone approaching a wounded animal.

"Your eyes are red," he murmurs.

I feel naked under his scrutiny, as though he can see straight through to the fractured pieces I'm trying so desperately to hold together.

My throat constricts as tears threaten to spill over. Crying now would undo everything—would tear down the walls I've spent a year building. But Nate watches me with those knowing hazel eyes, and I feel my defenses crumbling like sandcastles against the tide.

"You've been crying," he states simply, no question in his voice.

I stand frozen as heat creeps up my neck, caught in the gravity of his gaze. When he reaches out to tuck a strand of hair behind my ear, his hand lingering against my cheek, the world seems to still. The tough exterior he shows others melts away, leaving just Nate—raw and real. His touch grounds me, creating a pocket of safety in the midst of chaos.

"Who was it?" The question cuts through the silence, sharp with controlled anger.

"What?" I gasp, fear spiking through my confusion.

"Who hurt you this badly?" His eyes are soft but determined, promising retribution without words. His gaze, usually comforting, now terrifies me with its intensity.

"N-No one," I stammer, the lie hollow in my mouth.

"That's not going to fly with me, Nora. Was it Connor?"

"No," I manage as the room spins faster. "It's not Connor."

"Hey." Nate's hands frame my face, steadying me. "Look at me, Leni."

The nickname tightens something in my chest. I meet his eyes, seeing the depth of concern there, and it overwhelms me—not because of Evan, but because I dread what Nate might do if he discovers the truth.

"Nate, please," I whisper, my voice threadbare. "I don't want to talk about it. It's nothing. I'm just tired."

"Don't do that," he says, frustration flickering across his features. "Don't downplay this. Someone hurt you, and I want to know who."

"Why?" The question escapes like a breath.

"Because, Nora." His voice softens dangerously. "There's very little I wouldn't do for you. So, either you tell me, or I'll go find out myself. And it's going to be a lot worse for them if I have to find out on my own."

My attempts to deceive him are futile; he sees through every shield I raise.

"Nate," I choke out, "I just want to forget it. Please."

He exhales heavily, but his touch remains steady, anchoring me to the present.

"Okay," he concedes, though his eyes tell a different story—he's waiting patiently for my walls to crumble.

"Nora," he whispers, his gentleness pulling at the loose threads of my composure. "Can I hug you?"

The question catches me off guard, but I nod without hesitation. His arms encircle me, strong and secure, and I bury my face in his chest. For the first time in what feels like forever, I'm cocooned in safety, protected from the threats beyond this bedroom. My tears soak into his shirt as I finally let go, allowing myself to be vulnerable in this sanctuary of his embrace. The closeness is overwhelming yet soothing—both a balm and a spark that ignites something deeper, more complicated. I surrender to it, letting my guard fall. His silence speaks volumes, his presence more comforting than any words could be.

"They're not going to do this to you again," he whispers into my hair, his voice steady with conviction.

I want to believe him, to let his promise shield me from further pain. But hope feels like a precipice when you're already falling apart—beautiful, terrifying, and impossibly far away.

CHAPTER 27
LATE NIGHT DRIVES
NATE

THE SECOND I SEE NORA PUSH THROUGH THE FRONT DOOR, EVERY instinct in me goes on high alert. She's always been good at building walls, locking away her pain behind carefully constructed barriers, but I see right through them—I always have. Today, her panic is a neon sign, bleeding through her usual composed facade. Her eyes are wide, haunted, her breathing uneven and sharp. Jake claims she's just feeling sick, but that's bullshit. There's something deeper written in the tremor of her hands, the way her eyes won't settle.

I'm up the stairs after her before I can process the decision to move. Her closed door is a clear message to stay away, but I've never been good at following rules when it comes to her. I tap on the door, and her voice comes through, strained and distant, telling me to leave.

I don't.

Instead, I push the door open to find her pacing, arms wrapped around herself like she's holding her pieces together. The sight of her like this—vulnerable and scared—hits me like a physical blow. The room feels charged with her anxiety, the air thick with it.

"Nora," I start, my voice coming out soft.

She's lost in her head, trapped in whatever nightmare is playing behind those green eyes. Her shoulders shake with each ragged breath, and it kills me to see her trying to handle this alone. I step closer, careful to give her space. She attempts to brush it off, claiming exhaustion from a long day, but the lie sits heavy between us. Someone's hurt her—the thought ignites something primal and protective in my chest—and I'm determined to find out who.

Right now though, what she needs isn't my rage. She needs the comfort we've always found in each other, the same safety we shared as kids.

"Can I hold you for a minute?" Sixty seconds to show her she's not alone, that she can break apart in my arms and I'll keep her safe while she does.

She collapses against me, fitting perfectly against my chest like she always has, like she was meant to be there. Her body trembles, and I feel her heart racing against mine.

"Hey, hey, you're panicking, Nor." Her eyes are vacant, lost in some private terror. It reminds me of that night on the beach, the same raw fear etched across her features.

"If you don't slow down, you're gonna pass out. Focus on me." I run my fingers through her hair, the silky strands familiar against my skin. The gesture seems to ground her, pulling her back from whatever edge she's teetering on.

"Feel that? You're here with me." I guide her breathing, keeping my voice steady. "In for four, hold, now out for eight. Slow and easy."

Her breath steadies gradually, like waves calming after a storm.

"Nate?" Her voice is barely there, fragile as spun glass.

"I'm right here," I assure her, the words a promise I intend to keep.

"You're okay." Confusion clouds her features, as if she's trying to piece together what just happened.

Inside, I'm seething, wanting to tear apart whoever caused this, but I keep my voice gentle. "You're okay now." The contrast between my calm exterior and the inferno of protective rage burning inside me is almost painful.

"How'd you know how to help?" she asks, her voice stronger now.

"Google." I half-smirk, trying to inject some lightness into the heavy moment.

She narrows her eyes, seeing through my deflection. "Nate, be serious."

I sigh, not ready to unpack my own demons, not when hers are still so raw. "Does it happen often?" I ask instead. "The panic attacks?"

Her hesitation speaks volumes—I can almost see the internal debate playing out behind her eyes: trust or retreat. But she nods, a silent admission that cuts deep. Exhaustion is written in every line of her body.

"Do you need anything?" I ask, stepping back to give her space.

"I think I just need a nap... maybe a shower," she whispers, her voice still carrying echoes of her panic.

I plant myself on her bed while she goes to the bathroom. Something's off—and I know her too well to miss it. The way she's biting her lip, how her eyes bounce around the room like they're trying to escape my gaze. I've got a PhD in reading Lenora Wells, and right now, every nerve is screaming something's wrong.

She comes back from the bathroom, stops cold when she sees me still here. Like she can't believe I'd stay.

"You don't have to stay," she says, her voice this weird mix of surprise and something else. Resignation? Hope? "I'm okay now."

"I'm not going anywhere," I tell her. It's not a promise. It's a fact. Gravity doesn't ask permission, and neither do I.

I tap the bed. "Lay down."

She hesitates—classic Nora. Always overthinking, always calculating the risk. But she comes, curling up on her side, facing me. Her eyes are these heavy, exhausted things, like she's carrying worlds I can't see.

I watch her breathe. In, out. In, out. Counting like it's the only thing keeping her together. Time becomes this weird, liquid thing. Just her breath. Just us.

She inches closer. Her hand—fuck—her hand brushes mine, and something inside me breaks and reforms all at once.

I shift, pull her into me. She melts against my chest like she was carved to fit exactly here. It's dangerous. We're a minefield, her and me. One wrong move and we'll detonate everything we've barely held together.

But right now? I don't give a shit about consequences.

Right now, I let myself be exactly what she needs—even if it's killing me from the inside out.

I stay until her breathing evens out, until the tears dry on her cheeks and her grip on my shirt loosens. Only then do I carefully extract myself from her grasp, tucking the blanket around her shoulders. She stirs slightly, mumbling something unintelligible before burrowing deeper into her pillow. I watch her for a moment longer, memorizing the peaceful look that's finally replaced the pain on her face.

With a deep breath, I slip out of her room, easing the door closed with barely a sound. The weight of everything—Jesus, it's crushing. Like carrying a fucking universe of shit I can't begin to unpack. You'd think I'd be used to that feeling by now.

Mom is in the lounge, those all-seeing eyes locked on me the second I hit the bottom of the stairs.

"Nate?" Her voice is all soft concern. "Is Nora okay? Jake said she wasn't feeling well."

"She's okay," I throw out, shrugging like it's nothing. The lie tastes like ash in my mouth. "Just exhausted."

She gives me that look. The one that sees straight through everything. "You know, you've always been the only one she lets in."

I lean against the doorframe, wood cool against my shoulder. Feels like the only steady thing in this moment. My entire body is a live wire of fucked-up emotions.

"Yeah, but things have changed." The words come out rough.

Her smile does something dangerous—soft, knowing. "If two people can't stay away from each other, maybe they're not meant to be apart."

Maternal wisdom.

Always hitting exactly where it hurts most.

"Maybe you both need to stop running."

The words sink into me like stones, creating ripples I'm not ready to face. The hardwood blurs as I try to breathe, to hold myself together.

"I've watched you love that girl all your life," she continues. "Maybe you should give her a chance to love you too."

It lands like a punch.

Right in the chest where all my most fucked-up fears live.

I need out. Now.

I escape to the patio, but Mom's words follow me like persistent shadows. Out here, under the late afternoon sky, my feet shuffle restlessly against the weathered boards. I'm haunted by memories of my parents' tumultuous relationship, the echoes of their chaos still reverberating through my bones. The deep-seated resentment I've harbored toward my mom for not leaving Scott sooner burns in my chest—a familiar anger at how she allowed his destructive nature to tear through our lives like a hurricane.

Each night I spent as a kid, stationed outside my mom's door, making sure she was safe, left scars that run deeper than I care to admit. The weight of those memories presses down on me now, feeding into my fears about letting Nora in completely. The twisted logic I've lived by— that no one could hurt me more than I could hurt myself—feels like a prison of my own making. How do you let someone in when all you've seen of love is manipulation and pain?

I'm not just tired. I'm terrified of becoming my father, of dragging Nora into the same kind of darkness that nearly destroyed my family. The responsibility of holding it all together when I feel like I'm crumbling inside is exhausting. Every step forward feels like walking through quicksand, pulled back by the ghosts of my past.

So I run.

It's what I'm good at, what I've always done when emotions threaten to overwhelm me. But even as I try to escape, my mind drifts to possibilities I've been avoiding.

"You okay?" Mom's voice cuts through my spiral, gentle but knowing. I nod, but the gesture feels hollow, unconvincing even to myself.

"Yeah, uh..." My voice comes out rough, hesitant. "I was thinking maybe I could clean out the sunroom. Since no one's really using it." The words tumble out before I can second-guess them.

Mom raises an eyebrow, a mix of curiosity and understanding crossing her features.

"The sunroom? Why?" There's something knowing in her tone that makes me shift uncomfortably.

I run a hand through my hair, aiming for casual but probably missing by miles. Her expression shifts to something warm, almost proud, and it makes my chest tight.

"Go ahead," she says with a wink that says she sees right through me.

In my mind, I can already see it—Nora's safe haven, a space away from whatever demons are chasing her. The image solidifies something in me, a purpose taking root. After today, feeling her shake against me, seeing that raw fear in her eyes—I'd do anything to keep her safe.

But just as that thought starts to settle, my phone buzzes, the sound sharp and intrusive in the quiet night air. My stomach drops when I see Monty's name on the screen.

I stand abruptly, muttering about needing to handle something. Mom doesn't push, just nods with that infinite patience of hers, but I'm already moving, seeking refuge on the dock where the air feels cleaner, though it does little to calm the anxiety building inside me.

The message stares back at me.

Monty
Your debt just tripled, Preppy. Don't make me ask again.

I close my eyes, one hand coming up to rub the tension gathering at the back of my neck as the weight of my mess crashes down on me. Drug money, Monty, Nora, and all the things she knows nothing about. It's like walking a tightrope over a canyon, knowing one wrong step could send everything crashing down.

Then Jay's message cuts through.

Jay
Can we meet tomorrow? Freaking the fuck out here, man.

The text stirs something in me. Jay's the only one who truly gets the shit storm I'm in—the kind that tears through families like a tornado, leaving nothing but wreckage behind. I still remember the day I met him, just a kid dealing with a runaway dad and a mom drowning in her own struggles. When diabetes hit her hard and money was tight, she turned to the worst kind of help—men who paid in pills instead of cash.

The night Jay broke down and told me everything, I stepped in without hesitation, covering his mom's medical bills. He was a good kid that was dealt a fucked up hand, and even though what I did wasn't much, to him it meant everything. Now, a year later, we're still caught in each other's shit, pulling each other out of the fires I seem to keep starting. Getting him tangled in my mess with Monty was a mistake that haunts me daily. It tears me up knowing he's losing sleep over my fuck-ups, especially now that Monty knows about my family's stake in half the county.

I'm slowly starting to realise there might be no clean way out of this.

Standing here on the dock, watching the ripple across the water, I skip another stone, letting it dance across the surface. Each bounce creates perfect circles that expand outward, intersecting and fading like the memories I'm trying to process. The stone eventually sinks, disappearing beneath the darkening water, but the ripples continue their journey to the shore, touching everything in their path. Just like my choices, affecting us all, whether I want them to or not. I'm drowning in questions with no answers.

How do I claw my way out of this without dragging Jay—or anyone else—down with me?

The day offers no solutions, just the quiet sound of water lapping against wood and the weight of decisions I can't undo. After the weight of the day's revelations, I need to clear my head. I grab my old skateboard —a relic from simpler times—and lose myself in the rhythm of wheels against pavement until the sunset paints the sky in shades of amber and rose.

Coming home to the sounds of post-dinner cleanup and video games feels surreal, like walking between two worlds. Kat mentions Nora's been sleeping since the afternoon, and as I pass her closed door, concern twists in my gut. But I keep moving, retreating to my room where the darkness matches my mood.

It's 11 PM when my phone lights up the darkness with a text.

Nora
Awake?

My heart slams against my ribs, her two syllables enough to send electricity through my veins. The darkness envelops me, broken only by the soft blue glow of the screen.

Me
Yeah.

I swing my legs over the bed, sitting there in my boxers, every nerve ending alive with anticipation. Her next message makes my pulse jump.

Nora
I need to get out of this house.

Relief floods through me like a shot of pure adrenaline. Ridiculous how a few words from her can still do this to me after all these years.

Me
Wanna go for a drive?

The seconds stretch into eternities while I wait for her reply. Being alone with her is playing with fire, and I'm already burning. I'm about to back out when my phone buzzes again.

Nora
Give me five?

Well, fuck.

So much for self-preservation.

I'm out of bed before I can talk myself out of it, grabbing my keys and jacket in one fluid motion. I slip out the front door and slide into the Mustang, heart pounding in my ears as I wait.

She appears like a ghost in the darkness, quietly closing the door behind her. When she slides into the passenger seat, she brings with her the faint scent of lavender and vanilla. It drives me fucking crazy. I start the engine but keep the headlights off until we're further down the street, away from prying eyes. The air between us feels charged, alive with possibility. A mysterious smile plays on her lips as she watches me, expectant, patient. The empty streets feel like our private universe, a world where only we exist. The silence should be uncomfortable, but it's not. It's full of all the things we're not saying.

"Can I ask you something?" The light turns green, but I hesitate, caught in the gravity of her gaze.

She nods, those piercing green eyes locked on mine, making my heart stutter in my chest.

"What would you do if everything you planned just... blew up and you couldn't fix it?" The question comes out raw, honest, in a way I rarely allow myself to be.

She draws her knees up, wrapping her arms around them, thoughtful in the soft glow of passing streetlights. Her silhouette against the window is achingly familiar, a sight I've seen a thousand times but never tire of.

"The only thing you can do, I suppose," she finally says, her voice carrying quiet wisdom that's always been uniquely hers.

"And what's that?"

"Create a new future." Simple words, but they hit me like thunder.

"And if there isn't one?" I probe, hyper-aware of her presence, of how she makes the car feel too small and too vast all at once.

"There's always a future, Nate," she says softly, her fingers finding the bracelet on my wrist. Her touch sends electricity sparking through my skin, and I have to focus on breathing normally. "The world's full of endless possibilities, remember? You just need to figure out what you want your future to look like and walk toward that."

Her optimism fills the space between us—warm and infectious.

It's fucked up how easily we fall back into this—like my body remembers hers even when my brain's screaming to keep distance. A year of shit between us, and here we are, finishing each other's sentences like we never stopped. Makes zero sense that I still know exactly what she's thinking when she tilts her head that way, or how she still calls me on my bullshit with just a look.

But it also makes complete sense.

Some things just get carved into you.

For a second, I almost forget that we're supposed to be different people now—that I'm not the boy who'd do anything for her smile, and she's not the girl who knew all my secrets.

It's a lie though.

Because I still am and she still does.

Her tender voice pulls me from my own thoughts.

"Dreams matter, you know? They can turn real when you least expect it. Like stories—they start and end, but you get to shape everything in between."

She turns to the window, lost in thought, and the streetlights paint patterns across her face.

The air between us feels too damn comfortable, like slipping back into your favorite hoodie after someone else has been wearing it. Both wrong and right at the same time.

I let myself believe for a dangerous moment that maybe nothing's changed. That we could just—what? Pick up where we left off? But then reality sucker punches me back to now.

This familiarity is a mind-fuck, a reminder of what I had and what I threw away by thinking distance was the solution.

Knowing I did it to protect her, doesn't make it hurt any less.

"And sometimes," she adds, still continuing on with her thoughts. "You have to trust that the universe will surprise you, usually when you least expect it. That's where the magic happens." Her smile fades slightly, touched with melancholy. "That's what dad always said."

The mention of David tightens my throat, guilt a familiar weight. But before I can spiral, she speaks again.

"That's what you have to do. Don't lose faith in magic."

I can't respond.

Anything I say would shatter this moment, this delicate balance we've found. She's too much, too bright, too real. Looking at her is like staring into the sun—beautiful and dangerous and impossible to resist. It's not just her physical beauty, though that's undeniable. There's something wild and innocent about her—a storm always brewing behind those eyes, threatening to ignite everything in its path. She's lighting me up from the inside, and I know I'll let her burn me alive if she asks.

I'm in deep, drowning in her, and the scariest part is I don't want to surface. I'd let her destroy me completely if it meant taking away the shadows I sometimes see in her eyes.

"I hope you're right," I whisper, turning back to the road, shifting gears more to have something to do with my hands than any real need. Her hand covers mine on the gearshift, and the warmth of her skin sends shockwaves through my entire body.

I look at her hand on mine, then back at her face. She smiles, adding a playful wink that does dangerous things to my heart.

"Always am."

"How do you do it?" The question escapes before I can stop it, raw with honesty.

She tilts her head, confusion furrowing her brows. In the shifting shadows of passing streetlights, her face is a study in contrasts—soft and sharp, familiar and mysterious.

"Do what?"

"Be so sure of yourself all the time?"

Her laugh is soft, musical, and far too intoxicating for my sanity. "I'm not sure of anything. Did you not see what happened earlier?"

"Bullshit." I shake my head, feeling the weight of what I'm about to admit. "You walk around like you know exactly who you are. Meanwhile, I'm here feeling like I'm trying out a hundred different versions of myself, getting further from the truth every time."

Her expression softens as she considers this, and something in her eyes makes my chest tight.

"Well, maybe that's the problem. You're too busy trying to find who you are instead of remembering who you've always been."

Her words cut through the fog in my head, simple and sharp as a blade. The way she says it, like it's the most obvious truth in the world, gets under my skin in ways both exhilarating and terrifying. She's always had this ability to see right through my defenses, to read the parts of me I keep locked away. Sometimes I think she was made to know me better than anyone else, better than I know myself.

The rest of the drive wraps us in silence, but it's heavy with unspoken words and ghosts of conversations we're both too afraid to start.

When I park the car, the clock is nearing 2 AM and my body is exhausted but my mind races with dangerous possibilities. Each tick of the clock reminds me that this fragile peace we've found could shatter at any moment. Being near her is like standing at the edge of a cliff—the fall inevitable—but I can't seem to step back.

"Can I ask you something now?" Her voice breaks through my thoughts, light but hesitant in the darkness.

"Sure." My grip tightens on the steering wheel.

Her gaze dances away, a tell I've known since we were kids. "Have you been... you know..."

"Using again?" I cut in, my voice sharper than intended, defensive.

Color blooms across her cheeks—embarrassment mixed with genuine concern.

"I haven't since the night at the beach." The memory of her terror-stricken eyes that night still haunts me. Seeing her look at me like I was turning into my father... it was the wake-up call I needed.

Never again.

Relief floods her features, mixed with something that looks danger-ously like joy. "Oh..."

"Yeah." The word hangs between us, weighted with everything we're not saying.

"Thank you," she whispers. The melody of her voice resonates through my chest, striking chords I thought I'd buried years ago.

"For what?" My voice comes out raw, exposed.

"For being there," she answers simply, but her tone carries layers of meaning that make my heart race.

Before I can process what's happening, she leans closer, erasing the careful distance between us. Her lips brush my cheek, soft as a whisper, leaving a trail of fire in their wake. It's barely a touch, but it ignites every nerve ending in my body, sending electricity coursing through my veins. She pulls back too soon, slipping out of the car like a dream fading in the morning light. Though she's gone, the phantom sensation of her lips lingers, burning into my skin like a brand. I nod dumbly, trying to gather the scattered pieces of myself as she disappears into the night.

I slump back against the seat, the void she leaves behind almost tangi-ble. My heart thunders against my ribs, a chaotic drumbeat that echoes the turmoil she stirs in me. Something has shifted tonight, changed irrevocably, and I'm left grappling with a feeling that's both exhilarating and terrifying.

The urge to follow her, to pull her into my arms and show her how she makes me feel alive in ways nothing else can, is almost overwhelm-ing. But I stay rooted to my seat, hands white-knuckled on the steering wheel. While I'm prone to making mistakes, she's one I can't afford to risk. Not when the stakes are this high.

When I finally make it to bed, I stare at the ceiling, knowing sleep is a lost cause. Her words keep echoing in my mind like a persistent melody.

What if she's right?

What if the universe is trying to tell me something, and I'm just too fucking scared to listen?

As I start to drift off, the image of her floods my consciousness—those eyes, and a smile that could outshine the stars. Nora is etched into every part of me, a piece I can't excise no matter how hard I try. I know I should be running from this, from her. Every lesson life has taught me screams to get away before I destroy the one good thing I have left. But for the first time in years, I don't want to run.

And that terrifies me more than anything.

Because loving Nora isn't just about risking my heart anymore—it's about risking hers, too. And I'm not sure which would be worse: losing her again or watching the light in those bright green eyes dim because of me. As I lie here in the darkness, her lingering warmth still ghosting across my skin, I realize I really am in too deep.

But then again, when it comes to her, I always have been.

CHAPTER 28
YOU'RE NAKED

NORA

THE EARLY MORNING AIR CLINGS TO MY SKIN AS I PUSH THROUGH EDEN'S quiet streets. My feet pound against the pavement in a steady rhythm that keeps me grounded, each step an attempt to outrun the thoughts that have haunted me since that night last summer—since seeing Evan here again. His presence lingers like the smell of smoke in an empty house—subtle at first, then suddenly suffocating as you realize what it might mean.

Running became my salvation after Dad died. After finding him sprawled on the living room floor.

One year ago today.

The anniversary sits heavy in my chest, a weight no amount of miles can shed. I remember the way time fractured in that moment—before and after—how I stood frozen in the doorway, how the neighbors heard my screams before I even registered I was making them.

What started as an escape from grief transformed into my daily ritual, my slice of freedom when life feels unbearably heavy. On mornings like this, with dew still glistening on the grass and the world half-asleep, I can almost pretend he's waiting at home, coffee brewing, asking about my route when I return.

Almost.

Even as my muscles burn and the world blurs around me, I can't escape the pain. That's the thing about pain... it doesn't care how fast you run or how desperately you try to outpace it. It lives in your bones, travels with you, waits patiently for quiet moments to remind you it never left. The pain of what happened last summer. I can't outrun the fact that today marks twelve months since I became the girl who found her father dead, and had a piece of her soul stolen from her.

The streets are empty save for an elderly couple tending to their garden. I keep my eyes fixed on the ground, fighting the urge to take in my surroundings. The last thing I need is an early morning panic attack.

At the beach, waves lap against the shore in gentle contradiction to my racing thoughts. I pause, breath ragged, staring at the horizon painted in dawn's watercolors. The question that's been eating at me surfaces again: What would I do if I saw Evan? Would I crumble, or finally stand my ground?

My mind drifts to Nate.

The way he knew exactly how to calm me down during my panic attack, breathing with me when I couldn't remember how. There was something familiar in his understanding, like he'd had to do that hundreds of times before himself. The thought tugs at something deep within me, making me wonder what else lies beneath his stoic exterior.

That late-night drive reminded me of simpler times, when Nate first got his license and drove straight to my house just so we could listen to the new Kings Of Leon album together. We barely spoke then, just let the music fill the space between us, but I felt untouchable with him there. Last night felt the same, yet different, charged with something new and unnamed.

Back home, the house is silent when I slip inside. With headphones still in, I head upstairs, my body humming from exertion but my mind clearer, the morning fog lifting just enough to breathe. I push open the bathroom door and my breath catches. My phone clatters to the floor as I collide with a wall of muscle. Nate stands there, fresh from the shower, with only a towel slung low on his hips. Steam curls around him like something out of mythology. Water trails down his face, catching in dark strands of hair. His skin glistens, each muscle and contour sharply defined as if carved from marble. The scars mapping his skin tell stories of battles fought and won, only adding to his allure. My heart aches with a mixture of awe and something deeper, more dangerous.

I'm staring, and we both know it.

The pull between us is magnetic, impossible to resist. My breath hitches as my gaze drops to his chest, then snaps back to his eyes. My heart pounds so hard I swear he can hear it.

He catches my eye and grins. "Hi."

Words jam in my throat. He laughs, stepping closer, and the air between us crackles with electricity.

"You're naked," I blurt out.

The laugh sends shivers down my spine. I'm speechless, still unable to look away. He leans in close enough that his breath fans warm across my cheek, the scent of mint toothpaste teasing my senses.

"If you're gonna keep staring," he whispers, his voice dropping to a velvet rumble as his smirk deepens, "at least buy me dinner first." The words hang between us like a promise, an invitation in the narrowing space.

"I—I wasn't—"

"Your face says otherwise," he teases, folding his arms and flexing, making it impossible not to notice every defined muscle.

I roll my eyes, attempting deflection, but my racing heart betrays me. This isn't the Nate of my childhood anymore—he's transformed into something more, something overwhelming.

The greenish-gold of his eyes burns fierce, but there's a shift. The vulnerability I've glimpsed these past few days vanishes, replaced by raw hunger that steals my breath.

"Are you done?" My voice wavers.

"Are we done?" His tone is low, teasing, with an edge that sends electricity through my veins.

"What?" I blink, disoriented.

"Huh?" He tilts his head, clearly enjoying my struggle to keep my eyes off his ripped body.

Shit.

My body refuses to move, every nerve ignited. Nate bends down slowly, grip tightening on his towel as he retrieves my forgotten phone. He stays on one knee, looking up through those impossibly long lashes, lips curled in that infuriating smile that makes my stomach flip.

"You dropped this."

"Right. Thanks." The words sound foreign in my ears.

He stands and somehow the space between us is even smaller. I try to brush past him, his heat nearly suffocates me. When he finally lets me pass, I slam the door behind me. Only when his footsteps fade do I exhale, pressing my forehead against the cool surface. Just as I'm about to shower, a knock startles me. I reach for a towel only to realize there are none.

Perfect.

I crack the door open carefully, hiding behind it. There's Nate—fully clothed now, thank God—holding fresh towels, his smirk unchanged.

"You might need these." His eyes glint knowingly.

"Thank you," I manage, clutching the doorframe like a lifeline while keeping my naked body hidden behind it. "Wouldn't want another naked run-in, would we?" The words escape before I can stop them, hanging in the air between us like an accidental invitation.

Nate's eyes darken perceptibly, the transition so subtle yet so powerful it steals my breath. He leans against the doorframe with one arm, the defined muscles of his forearm tensing visibly beneath sun-kissed skin. His bicep flexes against the fabric of his shirt, the cotton stretching taut over the curve of muscle. His body angles closer to mine, close enough that I catch the lingering scent of his cologne and now I feel drunk off his scent alone.

Dear God.

"I wouldn't hate it," he murmurs, voice dropping to that dangerous register that seems to vibrate directly against my skin. His cocky grin spreads slowly, deliberately, revealing perfect teeth and the hint of a dimple I haven't seen in a long time. The look in his eyes is equal parts playful and hungry, as if he's imagining exactly what he'd see if the door between us disappeared.

What the hell is happening right now?

Heat floods my cheeks and cascades downward, warming places I refuse to acknowledge. I accept the towels with trembling fingers, our skin brushing again in a contact that feels anything but accidental. His thumb traces the lightest circle on my wrist before releasing me.

"Enjoy your shower, Nora," he says, my name on his lips sounding like something sinful, something sacred.

I close the door quickly, perhaps too quickly, leaning against it as steam from the running shower swirls around me. My heart hammers against my ribs—a chaotic rhythm that has nothing to do with embarrassment and everything to do with that deeper, more primal sensation I've been trying desperately to ignore since the day we met.

The bathroom mirror has begun to fog, but not before I catch a glimpse of my reflection—flushed cheeks, dilated pupils, lips slightly parted. I barely recognize myself, this woman undone by a few words and meaningful glances.

I step into the shower, letting hot water cascade over me, but it does nothing to cool the burning awareness that has taken root beneath my skin. His voice echoes in my mind: *I wouldn't hate it.*

Four simple words that have somehow rewritten everything between us.

The shower was exactly what I needed, but I'm still not sure what to make of the whole Nate situation. I thought I was confused before our little morning run in. But now, my mind feels like a mess of tangled wires, each thought connected to him. Every time I try to pull away, I get shocked.

I need air.

Fresh, un-Nate-filled air.

Lydia and Mom decide to head out for errands soon after, and I jump at the chance to join them. Lydia has a million things to do for the gala she's chairing, and it's the perfect opportunity to bury my thoughts in something that doesn't involve a broody, dark-haired guy who makes wearing a low-slung towel look like it deserves to be on a billboard.

The annual Eden Charity gala commands attention as one of the town's most prestigious events. As kids, we'd stay home with Dad while Mom supported her best friend. Now, with this year marking the twentieth anniversary, Lydia's been planning for months to make it the biggest yet. The event raises money for community housing and local projects—proof that beneath Lydia's polished exterior beats a heart of gold. She's not just about the glitz and glamor; she genuinely cares about making a difference. As we browse high-end stores, Lydia's enthusiasm bubbles over.

"We've already raised more than ever, but being the twentieth anniversary, it has to leave a mark." She dives into details about the silent auction, champagne reception, and keynote speakers, her energy infectious.

As her charity plans wind down, Lydia's expression shifts to something more personal.

"So, Nora," she says, perching on a nearby bench with the air of someone settling in for gossip, "Any special someone in your life?"

I shrug with practiced nonchalance.

"No. School's been intense this year. Haven't had time for socializing, let alone dating." I keep it brief, already steering the conversation back to safer waters. "What community projects are you supporting this year?"

She takes the bait, and I'm off the hook—at least temporarily.

After hours of shopping, my stomach protests with gremlin-like sounds, making Lydia's suggestion of brunch sound like salvation. We pass a building under renovation, windows masked with brown paper, fresh paint glistening on the exterior. Lydia halts mid-stride, recognition sparking in her eyes.

"Oh, this is the place I was telling you about, Kat!" She gestures enthusiastically. "Some big shot out of towner is turning it into a wine bar. Word around the country club is he's quite the catch, not my words, but the ladies at brunch are certainly intrigued."

As if summoned, Nick appears, juggling heavy boxes. Under the bright sunlight, his golden hair frames his well-chiseled jaw, softening his sharp edges. His face brightens at the sight of us.

"Nora, hey."

I manage an awkward wave. "Nick, hey. This is Lydia and my Mom..."

"Katherine or just Kat," mom interjects, her tone clipped.

Nick's warm smile doesn't waver as he nods respectfully, his gaze lingering curiously on Mom.

"Nice to meet you both."

"Do you need help with those?" I gesture to the boxes, though his straining biceps suggest he's more than capable.

Setting them down with a grunt, he flashes a tired grin.

"I've got it, thanks." He straightens up, his presence both commanding and welcoming. "But come in, let me show you around."

Inside, the interior stretches out, luxury waiting to be unveiled. "We're aiming for one of the East Coast's finest wine bars, but keeping it casual-elegant," he explains, enthusiasm evident in every gesture. "Renovations wrap up soon, now that I've got help coming."

I notice his subtle glances at Mom as he describes his plans, trying to draw her into conversations about décor. But Mom remains politely distant, her heart still carefully guarded since Dad's passing. While Nick fetches wine samples, Lydia leans in conspiratorially.

"I'm playing matchmaker here. Are you okay with that?"

Watching Mom's interaction with Nick, I raise a skeptical eyebrow. "I'm not sure that's going to work out."

Lydia's eyes sparkle with mischief. "That man hasn't taken his eyes off her, and she's not as indifferent as she seems."

Nick returns with drinks, offering me a specialty non-alcoholic option with a knowing wink. "Thought you'd prefer this. Still good though."

As we sample our drinks, he outlines his timeline, mentioning contractor troubles. Lydia jumps in,

"You know, my son Nate could help. He needs something to keep himself busy this summer."

Nick's surprise is evident. "Nate? Nate Sullivan?"

Lydia half-jokes, "Please don't tell me he's caused trouble."

"No trouble," Nick laughs. "He actually offered to help when he visited my uncle's bookstore. He's coming in later today actually."

The revelation startles both Lydia and me. Nate at the bookstore? Volunteering?

Mom interjects proudly, "Well, Nate's always been handy with a great eye for detail. You'll have this place fixed up in no time."

I nod, lost in thought. Mom's always seen something special in Nate—something I'm beginning to understand myself.

At Criniti's, we claim a cozy corner booth, perfect for Lydia's conspiratorial glances between Mom and Nick. The conversation inevitably turns to him.

"So...," Lydia draws out his name, eyeing Mom suggestively.

"Lydia, no," Mom cuts her off with a knowing head shake.

"I didn't say anything!"

"Your face says plenty," Mom retorts, rolling her eyes playfully.

"I'm just saying he's single. And—"

"You don't know that," Mom interrupts, crossing her arms defensively.

Lydia sips her wine with exaggerated elegance. "Please, the Country Club gossips could out-sleuth the FBI. He's definitely single. And successful. And hot. Really hot."

The tension thickens as Mom shifts uncomfortably. We've never really discussed her dating since Dad, and her reluctance is clear. It pains me to see her so closed off.

"He's really nice, Mom," I offer softly, surprising both women. Mom's expression softens as she traces her coffee cup's rim.

"I—I just don't know if I'm ready. It's been so long... since your Dad." The familiar pang in my chest sharpens. Dad was her great love—how could anyone compare?

Lydia persists, "What if we invited him to the Fourth of July party? Just as a welcome to Eden gesture?" Mom scoffs at the transparent suggestion.

Checking her watch, Lydia changes course.

"Think about it. We should go—Jake will be here soon. I'll get the bill." As she stands, she wobbles slightly, catching herself on the table. "Should've worn better shoes," she jokes, drawing a soft chuckle from Mom. I take the moment to excuse myself to the bathroom.

Threading through the narrow restaurant, the ambient chatter fades as a group of teenagers bursts in, their laughter bouncing off the walls. Their carefree energy highlights just how heavy my world has become. I keep my head down, hoping to slip past unnoticed, but something about their voices pulls at me.

They sound familiar—too familiar—and my stomach clenches with recognition.

CHAPTER 29
THE QUIET DESTRUCTION
NATE

I WAKE UP DRENCHED IN SWEAT, SHEETS TANGLED AROUND ME LIKE A VICE. My heart pounds against my ribs while the pre-dawn air sits thick and heavy in my lungs. The nightmares are always waiting, lurking just beneath my eyelids, ready to drag me back into that darkness the moment I let my guard down.

It's always him. The crack of his fist meeting bone, the thunder of my own pulse drowning out everything else. That look in his eyes right before impact—cold, detached, like I wasn't even his son.

4:48 AM glares at me from the bedside clock. I push off the sheets, but the remnants of the dream cling to my skin like tar. Without the drugs, everything's sharper, more visceral. The screams—Mom's screams—echo in my head with perfect clarity now. There's nowhere to hide anymore.

It wasn't always like this. Back when I was numbing myself with whatever I could get my hands on, the memories stayed buried, fuzzy around the edges. But now? Now they're in HD, surround sound, playing on repeat. My legs shake as I stumble to my feet, running trembling hands over my face. I've gotten good at hiding it all: the sleepless nights, the tremors, the constant gnawing need that lives in my bones. I can't afford to crack now. Not when things are finally shifting. Not when I'm starting to believe that maybe I'm capable of not destroying everything I touch.

But fuck, the withdrawals are hell.

Every nerve ending feels like a live wire, muscles seizing up like they're trying to tear free from my body. The headaches drill into my skull, and nausea rolls through me in waves. It would be so easy to make it stop. Just one pill. But I can't. I won't.

Instead, I let the nightmares remind me of who I am—still that helpless kid who couldn't fight back, who never managed to protect the people who needed him. Only now, there's nothing to dull the edges of that truth.

The bathroom mirror shows me exactly what I expect: a fucking train wreck. Dark circles carve shadows under my eyes, skin pale as a ghost. I lean against the sink, studying the stranger staring back at me. He's a mess, but at least he's trying. The cold water hits my face like needles, and I welcome the sting. It grounds me to this moment, but my mind drifts anyway—to her.

Fuck.

I wrap a towel around my waist, bare skin still damp—who the hell would be awake now?

Wrong.

She's awake.

Of course she's awake and she's pressed up against me.

My brain short-circuits. All that separates us right now is her sports bra, skin-tight shorts and my towel. Sweat from her run is making her glisten like something dangerous. Those eyes—they're wild. Hunted. I know that look. I've worn it my whole life. Running. Always running.

Nora freezes.

I freeze.

We're this weird snapshot of tension, while every breath I'm trying to take is catching in my throat. Close enough to feel her heat, to count the way her chest rises and falls.

I drop to retrieve her phone, and fuck me. Being on my knees for her changes everything. The angle. The vulnerability. All I can think is how easy it would be to press her against the wall and taste the mix of sweat and desperation on her skin. She's beautiful like this, raw and unguarded. Strength coiled tight beneath her surface.

After getting her fresh towels, we part ways, but my mind keeps circling back to one thought:

What would Nora say if she knew everything?

Would she still look at me the same way? Still trust me?

Still let me be someone she feels safe enough to turn to?

I don't know. I'm not sure I want to find out.

. . .

THE SUNROOM SMELLS OF DUST AND FORGOTTEN THINGS, MORNING LIGHT filtering through cracked blinds to illuminate years of careful avoidance. I roll up my sleeves, surveying the cluttered space. Boxes crowd every corner, each one filled with memories we tried to bury. I want to give Nora somewhere quiet to write, and this room—this shadowed corner we've long abandoned—feels destined for transformation.

My muscles protest as I start clearing boxes, exhaustion gnawing at my bones, but I welcome the distraction. This is for her. That thought alone keeps me moving.

Something catches my eye as I shift a heavy box—photo frames, hastily packed away like someone couldn't bear to look at them anymore. I pull one out, wiping away years of dust with my thumb. There we are—me, Jake, Mom, and... him. Dad. We're smiling: the perfect Sullivan family portrait.

What a fucking joke.

Every smile was a performance, every pose carefully arranged to maintain the illusion. The cracks were already there, spreading beneath the surface like spider webs, but we painted over them again and again. Broken glass held together with cheap glue and cheaper lies.

My hands shake as I stare at my father's face, his proud grin making my stomach turn. The frame slips, shattering against hardwood in a spray of glass and splintered wood. I stare at the pieces, breathing hard. The metaphor isn't lost on me—cracks everywhere, in the glass, in my family, in me. No matter how hard we try to piece things back together, the breaks are always visible.

After hours of work, the room looks different.

Still rough, but with potential. I decide to take a break and head toward the kitchen.

The note on the fridge is in Mom's neat script:

Went out with the girls for the morning.

I down a glass of orange juice, letting the cold calm the heat in my chest. A few weeks ago, this would've been mostly vodka. Progress, I guess.

Jake's call pulls me from my thoughts, waves crashing in the background of his voice.

"Can you pick up Mom and the girls from Criniti's? Ollie and I won't make it back in time."

"Sure," I answer, already grabbing my keys.

I find Mom and Kat giggling on the curb like teenagers, swaying slightly as they stumble toward the car. Seeing Mom like this—light, unburdened—stirs something hopeful in my chest. But a knot forms in my stomach at the sight of her glassy eyes, her midday intoxication another reminder of her fragility. I can't ignore the unease creeping through me, it's a contradicting tangle of relief and worry.

"Our knight in shining armor!" Kat throws her arms up dramatically as they pile in.

"Where's Nora?" I scan the street.

Kat grins from the backseat. "She went to the bathroom about five minutes ago. Must be a line. She'll be out any minute."

"Stay here," I tell them, already climbing out of the car. Something feels off.

Inside Criniti's, I spot them immediately—Connor and his crew, harassing a waitress with their usual brand of entitled bullshit. My fists clench at my sides. Then Nora appears, pale as chalk, like she's seen a ghost. She stops short when she sees me, something fragile in her expression.

"Nate?" Her voice wavers. "What are you doing here?"

"I'm your ride." I study her face. "You good?"

She nods too quickly. "Yeah. Let's just go."

But before we can leave, a voice cuts through the restaurant noise—unfamiliar to me, but Nora goes rigid at the sound.

"Lenora Wells, is that you?"

The guy who approaches screams old money—perfectly styled hair, designer polo, country club smile. Everything about him sets off warning bells in my head, especially the way Nora shrinks from his attention.

"E-Evan?" Her voice trembles on his name.

Evan.

Something dark coils in my gut as I watch him eye her like a prize he's already won.

"What are the chances of running into you here? You're looking good." His tone makes my skin crawl. "Oh, come on, Nora. Why aren't you as happy to see me as I am to see you?"

I step between them, blocking his view.

"We're having a conversation here," he clips.

"No, you were monologuing. Takes two for a conversation, Ethan."

"It's Evan."

"Don't care."

"Someone's possessive," he sneers.

The last thread of my patience snaps. "You're done talking to her. Turn around and leave."

My voice drops low, dangerous.

Connor steps in as Evan backs off. "Take it easy, Sullivan. My cousin here was just being friendly." He turns to Evan. "Let's go, before he decides to throw another cheap shot."

I scoff. Nothing cheap about that shot.

"I'll be seeing you Nora." Evan winks as he retreats, and it takes everything in me not to put him through a wall.

"Nate," Nora whispers, her heart pounding so hard I can almost hear it. "Please, can we just go?"

Outside, I study her face—the fear in her eyes cuts deeper than any knife.

"Who was that?"

The question comes out harder than I mean it to, but seeing her like this, shaken and pale, makes something dark curl in my chest. She wraps her arms around herself, a defensive gesture that makes my jaw clench.

"No one."

"Didn't look like no one." I step closer, keeping my voice low. "How do you kn—"

"Drop it. Please?"

Everything about this makes me feel uneasy, but I don't push her to talk.

"Fine, let's go." We head towards the carpark in silence until she breaks it.

"I thought you were going to hit him," she says and there's something in her tone I can't read.

I was.

The moms are too drunk to notice the tension in the car, but I see how Nora sits rigid beside me, staring out the window like she's trying to hold herself together. Her breathing comes in short bursts, and she won't look my way.

"You two are awfully quiet up there," Mom slurs.

"Long day," I shoot her a look in the rearview.

"Long day? It's not even 1 PM!"

Yeah. And look at the state you're in.

I can't get home fast enough. Right now, all I can think about is figuring out who the fuck Evan is and what he did to put that look in Nora's eyes. I've felt rage before, but this is different—deeper, darker, threatening to pull me under.

The drive passes in tense silence, Nora staring out the window while our moms chat obliviously in the front seats, the wine from lunch making them loose and giggly. I keep glancing at her profile, trying to read what's going on behind those walls she's put up.

When we finally pull into the driveway, our moms stumble out first, arms linked as they make their way to the front door, still reminiscing about something from their college days. The sound of their laughter feels jarringly out of place against the heaviness hanging between Nora and me.

As they disappear inside, I reach for Nora's wrist without thinking. She flinches away like my touch burns.

The pieces click together—her reaction to Evan, her recent edge.

"Nora, did he..." My voice drops low. "Did he hurt you?"

"No."

Her response is too quick, too defensive.

"Then how do you know him?"

"He's just someone from school, Nate. That's it." Her voice strains against something bigger. "I-I don't know why he's here."

I step closer, she steps back. Like she's afraid of me. But when our eyes meet, her expression softens.

"I notice, you know."

"Notice what?" she asks.

"How you flinch when someone touches you. The other day, when you were crying—was it because of him? You saw him that day, didn't you?"

Anger flashes in her eyes. "Stop, Nate. Just drop it."

"Nora—"

"I said stop!" She backs away, voice raw. "I don't want to talk about it. I don't want to talk to you. I just... I just need to be alone."

The words hit like a slap. And I've copped a few of those in my lifetime, but this one stung a little more than I expected it to. I watch her retreat inside, the cool breeze doing nothing to calm the noise in my head. Evan did something to her. I feel it in my bones. But I can't help her if she keeps pushing me away.

Hours pass before I decide to leave my room and head downstairs. There's only so much overthinking a person can do before they drive themselves to the point of insanity. The TV casts soft shadows across the living room as I find Mom in her usual spot—half-conscious on the couch, wine glass teetering on the coffee table's edge. For a moment, I just watch her, aching for the woman she used to be, the one who lit up rooms with her presence. But that person's long gone, buried under years of disappointment and carefully hidden addiction.

I move the glass to safety and drape a blanket over her. She stirs, blinking up at me with unfocused eyes.

"Nate?" Her voice is thick with sleep and wine. I sink down beside her, chest tight at the sight of her pale face. "You didn't have to—"

"I got it, Mom," I cut her off gently, knowing this well-worn path.

She shifts, gripping my hand with trembling fingers. "I'm sorry," she whispers, breaking. "I know I haven't been... I haven't been what you deserved."

I close my eyes against the familiar ache. It's the same guilt, same apology, same regret. But it's too late.

"It's okay," I lie, like always.

"No, it's not." She squeezes my hand, breath uneven. "You've done so much. Looked after Jake, taken care of me. You've been more of a parent than I ever was. I'm so sorry, honey. You deserved better."

The words shake something in me, unearthing memories I've tried to bury. Nights spent waiting up, only to find her stumbling through the door reeking of alcohol. Covering her with blankets when she couldn't make it upstairs. Holding my breath, praying Jake wouldn't wake to see her like this. I was just a kid, but I had to be more. I had to be the one holding everything together.

My mind drifts to that night when I was sixteen, cramming for calculus and found her in the bathroom. She'd emptied a bottle of gin, then moved on to wine. I spent hours beside her, holding her hair back, listening to slurred apologies and bitter truths.

"You're so much more than I ever could have wished for," she'd said between retches. "You're too good for this world, my sweet boy."

The story spilled out that night—her alcoholic father, her mother's parade of boyfriends.

She never stood a chance, really.

She was broken long before I was born.

She met Scott at a college party, back when she still had light in her eyes. Scott Sullivan, with his polished name and family reputation, fell hard for her. His parents hated her—she wasn't good enough for their world of wealth and status. But they married anyway, and for a while, things were good. She loved him completely, but he chipped away at her until that light went out.

She thought I didn't know about the cheating, the endless string of women, the drugs I found evidence of—empty bottles, bags of white powder. When I confronted him, I wasn't expecting an apology, but I wasn't ready for the fury either. He threw me into a wall so hard I blacked out. Woke up with a concussion that cost me two weeks of football. Our relationship died that day.

I've been stuck here since, caught between the love I wanted to feel and the hate that's consumed me. Through it all, I had to shield Jake and protect him from seeing the ugliness of our family. I became the parent, the one who carried the weight of our dysfunction.

"I should have done more. Should have protected you better," Mom says softly, breaking. "I'm so sorry, Nate. For everything."

I nod, but the words won't come. I can't tell her it's okay, that I've forgiven her for staying, because I'm not sure I ever will. But I do what I've always done—I take care of her. Pull the blanket higher, sit with her until she sleeps.

And then, like every night before, I carry the weight in silence.

CHAPTER 30
WANNA FLY?
NATE

February 2005
18 years old

THE BUZZ OF ADRENALINE IS STILL THRUMMING IN MY VEINS. THE TEAM won today, but that high comes crashing down the second I step inside the house. The living room is destroyed with furniture overturned, glass shards glinting across the floor like cruel confetti. The stench of stale booze and something burnt hits me, and my gut twists because I already know what I'll find.

"Mom?" My voice barely carries as I move toward the kitchen. The silence screams louder than any noise could.

And then I see her.

She's curled up near the counter, clutching an empty vodka bottle like a lifeline. Her shoulders shake with silent sobs, messy strands of hair hiding her face. She doesn't register my presence.

"Mom?" I try again, louder this time, stepping closer as panic sets in. My breath catches at the fresh bruise forming under her left eye—a sickly purple testament to his handiwork. Rage surges through me like electricity through a downed power line, my fists clenching until my knuckles go white.

He fucking did this.

I kneel beside her, reaching out to touch her shoulder, to bring her back to reality. The moment my fingers graze her skin, she flinches, her body recoiling like I'm the monster. Like I'm him.

"It's okay, Mom. It's me. Nate," I say softly, each word splintering my heart. "I'm not going to hurt you."

But she's lost in her own personal hell, eyes wide and terrified, seeing past me into something I can't protect her from.

"This is never going to stop is it?" I whisper, though we both know the answer.

My throat constricts as her eyes dart around, checking if he's still here, her body trembling uncontrollably.

I was supposed to leave for college. Get out of this fucking hell I'd been living in. Play football. Build a life beyond the suffocating mess my father created. I had a way out, a future. But how can I walk away knowing he'll come back, again and again, until one day he takes it too far?

"I'm not leaving," I say, the decision settling in my chest like lead. "I'm not going to college. I'm staying here."

Her head snaps up, panic flashing in her eyes as my words finally register. "No, Nate. No, you're not doing this." Her voice cracks, raw and broken. "You have to get out of here. I want that for you. Please..."

But it's too late. The choice is made. I can't leave Jake to fend for himself when he comes back next week. I can't leave her at Scott's mercy.

"I can't leave you like this. Look what happens when I'm not around. This, Mom. This."

She grabs my hand, her grip weak but desperate. "Nate, you're supposed to make something of yourself. Don't throw that away for me. Please, baby." Tears cut tracks through her mascara, but I'm already lost to the decision I can't take back.

I'm angry.

So fucking angry.

The emotion burns through me, directed at him for being the piece of shit he is, at her for staying and forcing my hand. The anger subsides into guilt when I see the fear in her eyes. I still don't understand why she puts up with this, why she won't save herself.

The next day at school, reality settles in.

Scott would never allow his son to be a dropout or not attend an Ivy League College. He might be a deadbeat, but he's still proud, in his twisted way. He has an image to maintain.

So I'll find another way.

By lunchtime, my mind's made up. I text Aaron, known for dealing more than just party drugs behind the bleachers. We've never spoken, but I've watched how he operates—he's got what I need.

The meeting happens after school, behind the gym. Aaron leans against his car, wearing a knowing smirk.

"Never thought I'd see the day the captain of the football team comes running to me." His voice carries a hint of challenge as he pulls out a small baggie. "This shit is not like what you've smoked before, you sure you wanna try it?"

"I'm sure," I say, though certainty is the last thing I feel. All I know is I need an escape, something to dull the pressure crushing my chest.

The first hit feels like fire in my veins, but then, euphoria takes over. The burn transforms into something else entirely, wrapping around me like a warm blanket, numbing everything. Every worry, every weight pressing on my chest, evaporates like smoke. I lean back, close my eyes, and for the first time in what feels like forever, I feel... light. The moon hangs above me, half-hidden like the truths I keep buried. As the euphoria of the pills Aaron gave me takes full control, I sink deeper into the ground, letting it swallow me whole. It's not Earth anymore—it's absolution, soft and endless, pulling me under. I can't tell if I'm falling or floating, but for once, I don't care. I want to disappear into this nothingness.

Her name comes to me through the haze.

The thought of her pulls me back, even just for a moment. Those big beautiful eyes that are so full of life with a smile to match. The way she laughs when she thinks no one's watching. My heart clenches because it beats for her.

Always has.

Always will.

But even as I picture her, I know it's fading. She can't know this version of me. She can't ever see me like this.

This is the beginning of something I can't control.

And I'm not sure I want to stop it.

Audioslave's *"Be Yourself"* fills the air, the opening notes haunting and slow, curling around me like an embrace. The sound penetrates deeper than just my ears—it's inside me, resonating in my bones. Each note vibrates against my skin, the music pulsing through my blood. The guitar solo hits electric, every chord sending shivers down my spine. The lead singer's voice cuts straight into my mind, and I feel the irony of every word. The highs, the lows—they're all part of me now, the drumbeat matching my heartbeat until I can't tell which is which anymore.

I open my eyes to find the stars blurring together, the night alive with an energy I can't explain. My head's swimming, but it's not unpleasant. It's freeing, like I could drift away into the notes forever.

I'll never be like him.

The thought cuts through the fog, sharp and clear. A promise I've made before but never voiced. But as the music swells, filling every empty space inside me, I realize how hollow that promise is. Because deep down, I know I'm already too far gone. This is where it starts.

The spiral.

The addiction.

And with the music pounding in my head, I almost don't care anymore.

Being myself isn't an option.

I want to be anything but.

WEEKS BLUR TOGETHER, PARTLY BECAUSE I BARELY FEEL PRESENT ANYMORE. True to my word, I'm spiraling. That much is clear. Showing up to school high becomes my new normal, and football practice?

A joke.

The bruises are too frequent now, too hard to explain away. Coach pulls me aside, looks me dead in the eyes, and asks what's going on.

I lie. I have to.

There's no way I'm telling him what happens behind closed doors, that my own father uses me like a punching bag when life gets too much for him.

So, Coach fucking calls him. Like that's going to do anything except make my life worse.

And it does.

I walk through the door that night, high and out of my mind. The tension hits me immediately, heavy like a noose tightening around my neck. Scott waits for me, seething, fists clenched at his sides. I hear Mom trying to stop him, playing peacemaker like always. But there's no peace to be found in this purgatory.

"Where the hell have you been?" Scott's voice is low, dangerous. He doesn't slur when he's like this. No, when it's not just the alcohol, he's sharp. Mean. Calculated.

"Oh, now you want to play the role of caring parent? You're ten years too fucking late, Dad."

"Nate, please—"

It happens too fast.

He backhands Mom hard enough that I hear the crack before I see it. She stumbles back, clutching her face, and something inside me finally snaps.

"Don't fucking touch her." The words tear from my throat, shaking with pure hatred. I'm not scared of him anymore. I stopped being scared years ago.

Scott turns, bloodshot eyes locking onto me. "What did you just say to me, boy?"

"Hit someone your own fucking size."

He steps closer, away from Mom, whose lip is bleeding, her eyes wide with fear.

Fear for me.

"When did you decide to grow a pair, huh?" he taunts. "Look me in the eyes and say it, like a real man."

We're nose to nose now, his sour breath washing over my face. His bloodshot eyes bore into mine, unblinking, while a muscle twitches in his jaw. I don't back away, even as his fingers curl and uncurl at his sides. The room seems to shrink around us, the air turning thick and hot.

"Burn. In. Fucking. Hell."

His fist connects with my jaw before I can brace for it. Pain explodes in my mouth, metallic taste flooding my tongue. My vision blurs, but I don't stumble. I don't back down; instead, I laugh, and this throws him. I'm running on pure adrenaline fuelled by intense rage. The only thing I know to be true right now is a person who has no fucks left to give is lethal because they don't care if they live or die.

The fight escalates quickly. Blood sprays across the floor as my fists connect with his face again and again. I'm not his son anymore, not the peacekeeper, not the protector.

I become him.

A monster.

Each hit brings a sick satisfaction. I've always known my place, always let him beat me down to save Mom. But not tonight. Tonight, I'm fucking done.

With one final surge of fury, I throw everything I have into a crushing blow that connects with his jaw. His head snaps back, eyes rolling as he crumples to the floor. He lies there, sprawled and vulnerable, and something primal takes over. I lunge forward, ready to finish what he started years ago, my fist cocked back for another strike.

"NATE! STOP!"

Mom's scream pierces through the red haze. It's not anger in her voice—it's terror. Terror of me.

I freeze, knuckles white, breath heaving.

The sudden silence is deafening.

I look down at my hands, covered in his blood, and see his hands in mine.

"Scott, get up." Her voice is barely a whisper. "You need to get up and get out. Now."

He stumbles out, leaving me standing in the wreckage. I don't breathe until I hear the front door slam shut. When it does, Mom rushes to my side, tears streaming down her face.

I can't look at her.

I don't go to school the next day; instead, I end up at the lake house in Eden, the only place that ever felt like home. It's empty now, just a hollow shell of memories. The pier down at South End beach stretches out before me, cold and silent. I sit beneath it, hidden from the world, watching the water lap against the shore, wondering how everything got so fucked up. How I got so fucked up.

That's when I meet a kid with dark hair, dark clothes, tattoos in patches, and an attitude that screams fuck it all. He introduces himself as Jayden and he's no older than Jake.

"You look like hell, bro."

"Been a week," I reply, taking another drag of my joint.

Our conversation reveals a kindred spirit—another soul running from a broken home. He introduces me to Monty, and just like that, my descent accelerates.

Most nights now I find myself at South End Beach. A different group of people each time. I don't remember names and hardly remember faces.

Tonight, the acid I took hits differently than anything before. The sand beneath me transforms into something soft and endless, pulling me under. The beach seems to breathe with me, rising and falling in gentle waves until I feel a presence beside me.

She settles onto the sand with practiced grace, her blonde hair perfectly done up. When she turns to look at me, her eyes are the bluest I've ever seen—though somewhere in my hazy mind, I register disappointment that they aren't green.

"Beautiful night, isn't it?" Her voice floats somewhere above me, golden and distant, as if she's speaking through layers of water rather than sitting right beside me. She tells me her name is Farrah, as if I'm going to remember it come morning.

When my phone rings, she answers with casual dismissal.

Through the chemical haze, my thoughts drift to a different kind of escape—one with brown hair and a smile that could light up the darkest corners of my mind. Even now, the memory of her threatens to pull me back from this edge I'm dancing on. She'd see right through me with those knowing eyes, straight to the darkness I'm letting consume me.

Part of me wants her to save me.

The rest of me knows I'm already in too deep.

I close my eyes against the night sky, letting the high carry me further from the person she once knew. It's better this way—Nora's memory of me preserved in summer days and innocent laughter, not this hollow shell I'm becoming. Every hit, every high, every bad decision pulls me further from her orbit, and maybe that's exactly where I need to be.

Because this path I'm choosing?

It's a one-way trip to somewhere she can never follow.

CHAPTER 31
FROSTED FLAKES AT 2AM
NORA

PRESENT DAY

It's 2:03 AM and my thoughts are deafening. I slip out of bed, my bare feet silent against the wooden floors as I pad downstairs to the kitchen. The familiar path to the Frosted Flakes feels like muscle memory—a comfort I can't explain. I reach for a mug instead of a bowl, an old habit that will never be broken. The faint creak of stairs breaks through my reverie, and I turn to find Nate standing in the doorway, hair tousled and shirtless. Even exhausted, he looks like he stepped out of a Greek myth—all sharp angles and perfect shadows with a body I'm struggling to keep my eyes off of.

"Late-night snack?" His trademark smirk appears, the one that still makes my heart stumble over itself after all these years.

"Old habits die hard." I shrug, grateful for the dim light hiding the heat in my cheeks. "Why are you up?"

"Couldn't sleep."

I don't push because I know the way secrets feel safer in the dark. I have my own demons I'm not ready to share—the nightmares where Evan's weight suffocates me, where Dad's final words echo endlessly.

Nate moves into the kitchen with fluid grace, retrieving a spoon before claiming my mug of cereal without asking.

"Still eating cereal out of a mug, huh? You know bowls exist, right?"

I roll my eyes, reclaiming my midnight snack. "Shut up. I like it this way. It's efficient."

"Efficient?" His laugh is low, intimate in the quiet kitchen. He leans against the counter, eyes lingering on me with an intensity that makes my skin prickle. "You're still a little weirdo."

A small laugh escapes me. "It was Dad's idea, actually. We'd eat Frosted Flakes together in mugs like it was some covert operation. Mom never knew—it was our thing."

Something unreadable crosses Nate's face as he looks down, stirring milk with his stolen spoon. "Your dad was one of the best people I knew."

The words hang heavy between us, and I know we've stumbled into a moment we've been dancing around. I try to redirect.

"I'm sorry," I say softly, setting down the mug. "For how I acted the other day. After..." His name sticks in my throat like broken glass. "You were just trying to help, and I—"

"Stop," he interrupts, voice gentler than I expect. "You don't have to apologize. If anyone should be apologizing for fucking things up, it's me."

Confusion knots in my chest. "For what?"

He exhales roughly, running a hand through his hair. "For not being there for you and Ol when I should have been. Your dad... he was more of a father to me than mine ever was. But I—" His voice catches, revealing a glimpse of the pain he's buried so deep.

"It's okay." I whisper.

We stand suspended in this moment, years of unspoken words filling the air between us. His eyes lock onto mine, and the kitchen shrinks until there's nothing but us. His fingers brush mine, sending sparks racing up my arm. The mug in my hands feels like an anchor keeping me from floating away.

"I'll never forgive myself for missing the funeral. And I don't expect you to forgive me for—"

"I do," I cut him off. "Forgive you. So how about this—a clean slate?" I manage, trying to steady my racing pulse. "I think it's time we both just move forward, with everything."

He closes the distance between us. His hand grazes my cheek as he tucks a strand of hair behind my ear, the simple gesture setting every nerve ending alight.

"I like the sound of that plan."

The air feels thin, like we're standing on a mountaintop instead of in the kitchen at 2 AM. His eyes study me with such tenderness it makes me feel raw, exposed. They're the kind of eyes you could drown in, and I always have. Something about him makes me feel more alive, less lost, and that terrifies me as much as it thrills me.

"Speaking of plans," he murmurs, gaze flickering to my lips again, lingering there just long enough to make my pulse quicken. "Want to come out on the boat with me?"

I swallow hard because the thought of being alone, with Nate, in the middle of the ocean, scares the living shit out of me. My throat is suddenly desert dry.

"I... I have plans."

"You have plans?" His smile turns teasing as he steps closer, reducing the space between us to something dangerous.

"Why is that so hard to believe?" I'm half offended, though my voice betrays me with a slight tremor.

"Well, I haven't told you when we'd go yet." His voice drops lower, more intimate. His devilish smirk makes an appearance as he crosses his arms across his broad chest, the movement pulling his shirt tighter.

My laugh comes out shaky. "Okay, maybe I don't have plans."

"Good. We'll go over the next couple of days," he says, voice barely above a whisper now, the space between us nearly nonexistent.

"Sounds like..."

"A plan," he finishes with that smirk.

Our eyes lock, and the connection jolts through me like lightning. It's as if he's reached inside and touched something I didn't know existed, something I've never felt before. His gaze holds me captive, seeing straight through me and I hate it. That desperate feeling climbs from my belly to my chest, closing my throat until I gasp, finally breaking eye contact. The heat, the proximity—it's overwhelming. If I don't leave now, I might do something I'm not ready for. Something that could change everything.

"I should, uh, go to bed." I retreat, forcing a smile.

"Yeah," he says softly, but his eyes tell me he knows exactly what I'm doing. "Goodnight, Leni."

"Goodnight, Nate."

I turn and flee the kitchen, heart thundering against my ribs, but not before stealing one final glance at him. Whatever this is between us, it's far from over.

It feels like it's only beginning.

GOLDEN LIGHT STRETCHES ACROSS THE LAKE LIKE HONEY, DAWN PAINTING the water in watercolor shades of pink and orange. Jake and I paddle out in comfortable silence, our boards cutting gentle ripples through the glass-smooth surface. There's a peace out here, watching the world wake up in silence.

Jake glances over, his paddle slicing through water with practiced ease. "I'm glad we're doing this."

"Paddle boarding?"

He laughs, the sound carrying across the water. "Well, yeah, paddle boarding, but the list too. I know it's been rough lately. I guess," he pauses, lowering himself to sit on his board, feet trailing in the water, "I just want this summer to remind you of better times."

My chest tightens at his thoughtfulness. "Jake?"

Those bright blue eyes meet mine, made even more striking by the early sun. "Thank you."

His smile could stop traffic—I've seen it happen. "So, how's the writing going?"

I sigh, tilting my face to catch the morning warmth. "It's coming together. Slowly. There's this block though, like something's stuck. It's like this paralyzing fear of failing."

Jake gives me that look, equal parts concern and understanding.

"Remember when we were kids, and you had to prove you could do whatever Ollie and I were doing? When we decided to dive off the pier, you were terrified but determined to jump." He pauses, ensuring I'm following. "You were scared, but you did it anyway."

A soft chuckle escapes me, the memory warming me despite the cool morning air. "Yeah, I remember the shocking red mark on my stomach from hitting the water wrong."

"Yeah, I don't think you're entering the Olympics anytime soon." His laugh echoes across the water. "We can work on your diving skills this summer though. But the point is, you felt the fear, leaned into it, and jumped anyway."

Silence settles between us like morning mist.

"That's one of the things I've always admired about you."

"One of the things?" I raise an eyebrow, teasing. "How many things are there?"

Jake smirks, glancing over. "How much time do we have?"

The lightness eases the constant pressure in my chest, and I shake my head, smiling.

"My favorite thing though," his voice softens. "Is the good you see in things—people, moments. You've always been that way."

"How do you mean?"

"Significant." The word carries weight. "You always find beauty every-where. You notice things other people miss." His eyes meet mine beneath dark lashes, intensity crackling between us.

Over the years, I've collected my own list of Jake-observations: the way he fidgets when nervous, his fingers tracing absent patterns on his paddle; the sadness that lurks behind his easy smile, even when he tries to hide it.

I know Jake.

I see him, truly see him, and I notice all those things.

"I wish I could see myself the way you do," I laugh, more to myself than him.

Jake's expression softens, a smile tugging at his lips. "One day you will."

We drift in comfortable silence, the sun climbing higher, the world stirring around us. But here on the water, we exist in our own bubble of time.

"Ready to head back in?" He breaks the spell after some time.

"Sure." I carefully stand, finding my balance. "Race you?"

His eyes flash with that familiar competitive spark. "You read my mind."

Before he can steady himself, I shove my paddle against his board, sending him splashing into the lake. When his dark blonde head surfaces, I know I'm in trouble.

"Ohh, you play dirty, Lenora." He lunges for my board, tipping me into the frigid water.

The cold shock makes every cell feel alive. Jake's watching me with those bright eyes and that infectious smile. "What am I going to do with you, huh?"

"Race me," I challenge, already swimming for shore.

His laugh—sweet as honey—follows me through the water.

Jake and I burst into the house like kids, trailing water and laughter. The sound bounces off the walls, lifting some of the weight I've been carrying. My clothes cling to me, but I'm too invigorated to care. The sunrise paddle session was exactly what I needed—a moment of pure escape. Mom spots us from the kitchen, eyeing the puddles we're creating.

"You two better dry off before you soak my freshly mopped floors." She points to the towels by the back door.

Jake grabs one, tossing it over his shoulder with a grin. "Yes, ma'am."

"Nora," she says, wiping her hands. "Your phone's been going off. I think Camilla texted you about eighty times."

"Shit!" I smack my forehead. "I totally forgot I'm meeting her and Mia soon."

"I'll give you a lift." Jake offers.

When Jake drops me off I sit in my usual spot and pull out my note-book. But the words won't come. My mind is a tangle of grief, fear, and the humiliation Evan left branded on my soul. No matter how hard I push against this weight, it won't budge.

The door chimes, and I look up reflexively.

My stomach drops when I see Connor walk through the door.

He approaches with that entitled swagger, wearing what he probably thinks is a sincere expression.

"Nora, listen, uh, about the other night. I was just..."

I stare him down, his half-baked apology hanging stale in the air. "You were just what, Connor?"

His face hardens. "Jesus, I'm trying to be nice here. You don't have to be such a bitch about it."

"Just leave me alone," I cut him off, ice in my voice.

The door chimes again, and my heart plummets further. Evan. His eyes lock onto mine immediately, that predatory smirk spreading across his face. My skin crawls—he can smell fear like a shark smells blood.

"Well, look who it is," he drawls. "Where's the bloodhound? Your pet not around to keep an eye on you today, huh?"

I clench my jaw, but before I can respond, his hand brushes my cheek.

The moment his fingers make contact, my stomach lurches violently. A wave of nausea hits me so hard I can taste bile rising in my throat. My skin crawls, like thousands of icy spiders racing beneath the surface. My lungs seize, breath caught somewhere between inhale and scream.

"Come on, Nora, why the cold shoulder? We got pretty friendly last summer, didn't we? Thought we were past this whole 'I don't know you' act."

Connor's eyebrows shoot up as realization dawns. "So that's why you weren't interested," he sneers. "You already fucked my cousin?"

It's no wonder they're related—poison runs in families.

Reality fractures around me, the ground beneath my feet suddenly unstable. My pulse hammers in my ears, drowning out everything except the sickening memory his touch drags to the surface. Before I can defend myself, shame burns up my neck like acid, tears threatening to spill. The humiliation, the fear—it's as fresh as yesterday. I want to run, but I'm frozen in place, my body locked in a horrifying replay I can't escape.

Then, like an avenging angel, Camilla's voice cuts through the toxic air.

"You know what we need that only you two can provide right now?" She storms over with Mia close behind, both radiating protective fury.

"Your absence," Camilla snaps. "Now get lost, both of you."

Connor scoffs, his smug grin faltering. "What's your problem, Camilla?"

"Isn't it clear?" Her eyebrow arches perfectly. "You. You're my problem." She dismisses him with a flick of her wrist.

Evan snickers, nudging Connor. "The chicks in this town are fucking insane."

Camilla's head snaps to him. "I'm sorry, but you are?" Her expression is perfectly deadpan.

"I'm—"

"Oh, that's cute. You thought I actually wanted to know." She waves him off like an annoying fly, turning back to Connor. "Did Daddy dearest not teach you how to follow orders, or do you just have a problem with your hearing because your head is shoved so far up your ass?"

Connor's smirk deepens. "I don't take orders from women like you."

"Oh, Connor. You've had your entire life to be a pretentious dick. Don't you ever get tired? Maybe take a day off once in a while, yeah?"

"No rest for the wicked, sweetheart." He winks, making my stomach revolt.

Camilla's eyes narrow to slits. "Well, if ignorance is bliss, then you must be the happiest person on the planet."

Connor's confidence cracks, but Evan steps forward, sneering. "You remind me of a little chihuahua. All bark and no bite. Maybe someone ought to put a leash on you, teach you some obedience."

Camilla's death-glare could freeze hell. "Oh, Abercrombie," she purrs, voice arctic, "you really don't want to see me bite."

Evan leans in, biting his lip in what he clearly thinks is seductive. "Actually, I think I'd quite enjoy that."

Her expression morphs from deadly to disgusted. She surveys him like something stuck to her shoe before getting dangerously close to his face, so they're nose to nose.

"I'd rather shit in my hands and clap." Her voice drips venom as she appraises him again.

Connor's smile twists into something cruel, his lips curling at the edges.

"Bitch should really be your middle name."

"It is, right after Clara and in-between Annabelle." She mocks, voice dropping to absolute zero. "While it's been so highly entertaining watching you two fit your entire vocabulary into one sentence, why don't you take your privileged, white-boy asses and kindly fuck off. Or do I need to throw a stick?"

Evan bristles, clearly trying to regain control. "Jesus, you really are a fucking chihuahua—never knowing when to quit."

"Coming from the two idiots who, at this point, are grade A stalkers." Her smile could freeze fire. "Tell me, were you born this stupid, or did you take classes?" Her voice is light, almost playful, as if she's just warming up. "I mean, everyone's entitled to act stupid once in a while, but you two? You really abuse the privilege."

Connor tries to step in again, but Camilla's already steamrolling past him.

"And for the record, Connor, if you think your daddy issues give you a free pass to walk around acting like your own shit doesn't stink, news-flash, it doesn't. Not everyone wants to kiss your ass or suck your dick." She leans in slightly, her voice turning into a deadly whisper. "Grow. Up."

Connor's face flushes red, his smirk crumbling as her words hit home.

Mia snorts beside her, barely containing her laughter, and I almost lose it too, but the knot of anxiety in my chest only tightens, making it harder to breathe.

Camilla steps closer to them, arms crossed, her eyes narrowing even more.

"Now, unless you want to embarrass yourselves further, I suggest you both exit stage left before you make bigger idiots of yourselves."

Evan glares daggers at her, but it's Connor who tugs him by the sleeve, muttering something under his breath as they retreat. I release a shaky breath, my entire body trembling from the confrontation.

Mia turns to me, concern etched across her face. "You okay?"

"God, what is it with those assholes? Why won't they just leave you alone?" Camilla's question hangs in the air, and all I can manage is a weak shrug.

"Seriously though, are you okay?" she asks again.

I nod, but we all know it's a lie. I don't think I'll ever be okay while Evan's around, lurking in the background, ready to remind me of everything I wish I could forget. I'm not sure what else to tell them or how to tell them.

"Idiocy must run in the family," Mia observes.

"Well, their family tree must be a cactus 'cause they're all a bunch of pricks," Camilla adds.

I can't help but laugh, feeling grateful for them being here. "Thank you. Both of you."

"Girl, the only thing you should be thanking me for is not clawing dumb and dumber's eyes out with my nails." She holds up her hand, freshly painted fingernails wiggling in front of us.

"They're lucky I just got them freshly done."

CHAPTER 32
YOU'RE SAFE WITH ME
NORA

June, 1998
8 years old

THERE'S A LOUD BANG AND IT WAKES ME. MY ROOM IS SUPER DARK, AND I forget where I am for a second. Then I remember I'm at the lake house, just like every summer. There's another bang and I jump out of bed really fast and run to my door. I open it a tiny bit, and see Nate and his dad Scott in the hallway. My tummy feels weird when I see that Nate's head is bleeding. He's hurt.

But why isn't his dad helping him?

Scott's holding Nate's arm so tight it looks like it hurts, but Nate just stares at the floor while his dad yells in his face. I don't like Scott—he's big and mean, like the bullies at school the teachers always tell off. I don't think Nate likes him much either, even though it's his dad.

I jump back from my door super quick, scared that maybe Scott saw me peeking. I hear Nate's door close and hear Scott talking really mean. I know I'm not supposed to spy on people—Mom always says it's not nice. My heart's going boom-boom-boom so loud in my chest, I think they might hear it. Scott's getting louder and angrier—he's yelling at Nate again. I can only hear bits and pieces, but it's about Nate doing something wrong. Scott always says Nate does things wrong, but that's not true. Nate's the best person I know.

When the door opens, I jump back and squish myself against the wall before running into the bathroom. Scott walks past, and he smells like the gross drink that makes grown-ups act weird at parties. Dad always

217

tells me to stay far away from it. Scott looks super scary right now, and even though he's never yelled at me, I don't want him to start.

As soon as he's gone, I tiptoe down the hallway like a ninja. I know exactly what to do because I've watched Mom fix Ollie's cuts and scrapes lots of times. I grab some band-aids, a washcloth, and that special cream Mom always uses. My hands are shaky, but I try to be brave. I sneak into his room—the door makes that creaky sound like in scary movies—and there he is, curled up on the floor. His shoulders are moving up and down; he's crying. Even though he tries to hide it because Nate never wants anyone to see him cry.

"Nate?" I whisper, getting down on my knees next to him.

He keeps his face hidden, but I can see the big red mark on his cheek and the cut on his head. I wish I had magic powers to make it all better. He tries to hide his face more, but I touch his arm super gentle.

"You don't have to hide from me."

He stays quiet while I clean his cut, just like Mom showed me. The blood gets a bit messy, but I'm really careful.

"How do you know how to do this?" Nate's voice sounds all scratchy, like when I get a sore throat.

"Mom taught me," I say, trying to put the band-aid on just right. "She fixes people up all the time, mostly Ollie 'cause he's always falling off his bike. She says it's important to know how to help people when they're hurt." I smile when I see Nate watching me, like he's trying to figure out a puzzle.

"Does he hurt you a lot?" I ask in my quietest whisper-voice.

Nate doesn't say anything, but his eyes get all sad and that tells me everything.

"I'm sorry," I tell him, making sure the band-aid is stuck on good. "But you know what? It's gonna be okay, you know why?"

His sad eyes look up at me. "Why?"

"'Cause one day, when we're big, we're gonna run away together. We'll find a secret place, just like in *The Secret Garden* book my dad reads us. Nobody will know where it is except us. We'll have a giant treehouse, and maybe some animals, and a huge waterfall to swim in!"

I see Nate's mouth twitch like he wants to smile but isn't ready yet.

He looks at me, taking big breaths like he's trying not to cry again. It makes my cheeks feel all warm when he looks at me like that, the way it always does.

"Promise?"

"Pinky promise." I stick out my pinky finger, trying to sound super brave even though my tummy feels full of butterflies.

218

He links his pinky with mine and we look at each other for forever.

"You know I'm right, like, one-hundred and ninety-seven percent of the time." I give him my biggest smile ever, hoping he'll laugh, and finally he gives me a tiny smile back.

There's my Nate.

I don't say it out loud, but my heart feels so big and full. I know for sure that this boy with the saddest eyes ever has my whole heart.

Nate moves a little and makes an *"ouch"* face.

"Why did he hurt you?" My voice is all wobbly now.

Nate looks up at me and his eyes get all watery again, but he's trying super hard not to cry in front of me. I want to tell him it's okay to cry. Mom always says crying helps get the sad out.

He tells me what happened. There was a big fight between his parents earlier while my family was out getting pizza. He found his dad's medicine and flushed it down the toilet, but his dad caught him. Then Scott pushed him really hard, and that's when Nate hit his head on the bathroom sink. My tummy feels sick when he talks about the blood, and how his dad slapped his face and pushed him against the wall, telling him not to tell his mom. Then Scott got even madder when Nate started crying, saying boys aren't supposed to cry.

I want to fix everything for him, like how Mom fixes my scraped knees or when Dad fixes my broken toys. But this feels bigger than band-aids can fix. I wish I could make all the hurt go away and take him to our secret garden right now.

"Come to my room," I say, holding my hand out. He looks confused, but I just say, "Come on."

In my room, I start pulling all my pillows and blankets off my bed while Nate sits there looking super tired.

"What are you doing?"

"Building a fort, silly!" I tell him like it's the most obvious thing ever.

"A fort?"

"Uh-huh!"

"Why?"

"'Cause forts protect you from bad stuff."

"Your pink fluffy pillows aren't gonna protect anyone Leni," he says, but I see he wants to smile.

"Hey, you've never seen me in a pillow fight."

His lips do that almost-smile thing again.

We crawl inside once it's done. It's super cozy with all my stuffed animals around us, and my star lights make it look like we're camping under real stars. I grab Bones, my special stuffed toy that Dad gave me when I hurt my ankle last summer. Nate carried me all the way back to the house that day when I fell out of the tree.

"Here. Bones will keep you safe," I say, giving him my most special toy.

Nate doesn't say anything, but he hugs Bones real tight. I turn off my lamp and the whole room lights up with tons of stars on the ceiling and walls. Nate's eyes finally look a little less sad.

"You know what Dad says about stars?"

He sniffles and moves his head a tiny bit. "What?" His voice is so quiet.

I take a big breath like I'm about to tell the biggest secret ever.

"He says that even when you can't see them, they're still there. They're just playing hide and seek behind the clouds."

He's quiet for a long time but then lets out this big breath like he was holding it forever.

"We're kind of like stars too." I add in my special quiet voice, "Sometimes everything gets super dark, but we're still here. And one day, you'll be the brightest star ever, Nate!"

"You really think so?" he asks. His voice sounds all hopeful.

"I know so." I say it like it's the truest thing ever, like how I know chocolate ice cream is the best flavor. "Right now, you're just playing hide and seek behind some clouds, but they'll move away. They always do."

His mouth does a tiny smile and it makes my heart feel happy.

"Want to listen to music?"

He nods, and I grab my Discman—the one Mom gave me for my birthday. We share the headphones, one ear each, and I press play on *"Iris"* by the Goo Goo Dolls.

I've told him it's my favorite song.

What I never say is that it's only my favorite because it reminds me of him.

As soon as the music starts, Nate's body relaxes, like when you let go of a big breath you've been holding. He wraps his arms around my waist and puts his head in my lap.

I lean over him and whisper, "I got you."

That's when he starts crying for real. Not the quiet kind, but the kind that shakes your whole body.

I hold him as tight as I can, like I'm trying to keep all his broken pieces together. I wish I was strong like a superhero so I could fight all his monsters away. But I'm not.

All I can do is be here and hold him.

When *"Iris"* ends, *"Name"* starts playing next, and it feels like this moment will stay frozen in time forever. Me looking down at the boy with sad eyes who deserves a whole damn sky full of stars.

I make a serious promise to myself right then—I'll never ever let him go. I'll always be there for him, just like this, holding on to him until all the bad stuff goes away.

Until nobody can hurt him ever again.

Nate falls asleep in my lap while the music plays in our ears. His head feels heavy against me, and looking at him, I know for sure that this is the boy I love. Even if he's a little bit messy and a little bit damaged, he's perfect to me.

I don't know much about fighting monsters, but loving Nate is like the first time I heard my favorite song—I knew it would be my favorite forever.

And he was my favorite. Forever.

CHAPTER 33
HAPPY BIRTHDAY JAKE
NATE

PRESENT DAY

IT'S QUIET. TOO QUIET AS I STEP THROUGH THE FRONT DOOR OF THE LAKE house. The air feels wrong—thick and suffocating, like the walls are closing in around me. My lungs struggle against the heaviness as I scan the empty living room. This place is supposed to be peaceful, but this silence? It's the kind that makes your skin crawl, the kind that warns you something's terribly wrong.

Then I see her.

Mom, lying there on the floor, her body contorted at impossible angles. Her face is ashen, eyes vacant, staring into nothingness. Blood seeps into the floorboards beneath her, spreading like dark watercolors on wet paper. My legs lock up, refusing to carry me closer, refusing to let me accept this reality. But it's real. And it's my fault.

"Mom!" The scream tears from somewhere deep inside me, my voice shattering like glass. "No, no, no, NO!"

I collapse to my knees, trembling hands reaching for her lifeless body. I pull her into my lap as if my touch alone could breathe life back into her. The panic claws up my throat, turning my vision blurry, my breaths coming in sharp, desperate gasps.

How did I let this happen?

I'm rocking back and forth, clutching her close when I hear it—a voice cutting through the chaos in my head. Soft. Familiar. Her voice.

"Nate..."

I freeze, my heart stumbling. For a moment, I think I've finally lost it completely.

Her voice pulls me up from the darkness. But this can't be real. None of this is real.

"Nate, wake up," she whispers again, closer now.

I blink, disoriented, as Mom's body slips from my grip. The floor tilts beneath me, reality shifting like sand through an hourglass. The blood fades, the walls blur, and when I look down again, it's not Mom I'm holding.

It's me. Lifeless.

My heart slams against my ribs, but her voice keeps calling, tugging me toward consciousness. The nightmare crumbles piece by piece, dissolving like smoke, and suddenly, I'm not in the living room anymore. I'm in my bed, and Nora's straddling me, her hands pressed against my chest, shaking me gently. Her face hovers above mine, brows knitted with concern, eyes searching. Her breath fans warm against my neck as she whispers,

"Nate, you're okay. It's just a nightmare."

My body reacts before my mind catches up. In one fluid motion, I flip her over, pinning her to the mattress. Panic courses through my veins, adrenaline making everything feel too fast, too raw, too real. Her eyes widen in shock, and for a split second, I'm lost between reality and dreams. All I know is the fear—the kind that chokes you, that drowns you, and follows you even in your sleep.

I see that same fear reflected in her eyes.

I never know what to do when the nightmares come like this. The lines between reality and imagination blur until I can't tell what's real anymore. They've been worse lately, with no drugs to numb them, no high to silence the noise. Just this—the crushing weight of everything I'm terrified of. Reality crashes into me like a tidal wave, and I scramble off her like her skin burns mine.

"Fuck—Nora, I'm... I'm sorry. I didn't mean to—God, I didn't mean to grab you like that."

She shakes her head, sitting up slowly. Her breathing is still quick, but the fear in her eyes has been replaced with something softer.

"It's okay," she says quietly.

"It's not okay," I snap, running a hand through my hair as guilt slices through me. "I shouldn't have—" The words die in my throat. I can't even finish the thought, can't bear to imagine what could have happened.

But then she does something unexpected. She reaches out, her fingers wrapping around my arm, pulling me back down beside her.

"What are you doing?" My voice comes out hoarse, raw with emotion I can't contain.

"Lay down," she says softly, settling beside me, her hand still resting on my arm. "You can close your eyes. It's okay."

I stare at her, trying to understand why she's still here, why she isn't running from me like she should be. "You shouldn't be here."

"Why?"

"Because I—"

Because you being this close, seeing me like this, makes me feel more out of control than anything else.

"Nate," she whispers, her eyes locking with mine. "I've got you, promise. Lay down."

Her words calm the chaos inside me like magic. It's as if someone's flipped a switch, and for the first time in a long time, I feel something other than fear. For a brief moment, there's blessed silence in my head. Nora has no idea what her voice does to me. How it's always been the thing that pulls me back to the surface when I'm drowning.

I let my head fall back as I relax into her, my heart rate slowing, just enough to let the sound of her heartbeat fill the quiet between us. We lie there, staring at each other in the darkness, neither of us willing to break this fragile peace.

"You're okay," she whispers into my hair.

I close my eyes, letting her warmth ground me in a way nothing else ever has. Minutes stretch into silence, and I think she's fallen asleep until she speaks again.

"I wish I hated you." Her lips brush against my hair, leaving behind the softest kiss. "But instead, you make me feel things I don't want to."

She thinks I'm asleep.

"I pretend to be this put-together person, but I'm just as broken and damaged as you believe you are. And the worst part is, I want you to know all the messed-up parts, but I'm scared."

I want to ask her what she's afraid of, but I don't want to stop her confessions.

"I wish I could face my demons too and maybe..."

She trails off, leaving the thought unfinished. I wait, but nothing else comes. Though I fight to stay awake, exhaustion wins. I let myself relax in her presence as my eyes drift shut, listening to her breathing as her heartbeat falls in sync with mine.

Sleep takes me, but this time it's different. This time, the nightmares don't come.

When I wake, the first thing I notice is sunlight filtering through the curtains, painting golden stripes across the bed. Morning has crept in while I slept, bringing with it an emptiness I can't ignore. The second thing I notice is the hollow space beside me where Nora should be.

For a heartbeat, panic grips me. Maybe I dreamed it all—her being here, my arms around her waist, my face buried in the curve of her neck where her pulse beats steady and sure. Her warmth. Her scent. The whispered confessions pressed into my hair like secrets.

Could my mind have conjured her, like it has a thousand times before in my restless nights?

I sit up, running a hand through my hair, trying to shake off the disorientation that clings to me. But then I see Bones, perched on the pillow next to me. Nora's favorite stuffed animal from when we were kids, left behind like a silent guardian. She always did this when we were young and I had nightmares, leaving pieces of herself behind to remind me I wasn't alone.

A faint smile tugs at my lips, but it's bittersweet, tasting of longing and regret.

I'm mad for her.

Stupidly, hopelessly, desperately mad for her.

And the worst part? I can never have her. Not in the way I want, not without destroying everything.

I rub my hands over my face and take one of those deep breaths that's supposed to steady you, but it doesn't work. I suddenly remember what today is—Jake's birthday. My not-so-little brother is seventeen, and here I am, still pretending I've got it together for him, like I've done every day for years now.

After a quick shower and a half-assed attempt to pull myself together, I head downstairs, bracing myself for whatever the day might bring. I find Jake in the kitchen, hunched over a stack of waffles—the kind Mom always makes on birthdays, their sweet scent filling the air with memories of simpler times.

"Happy birthday," I say, reaching out to clasp his shoulder. The touch is brief, awkward. Hugging isn't our thing anymore. It used to be, back when things were easy—back before everything got so fucked up. I know Jake still blames me for the dysfunction that is our family, but if he only knew how deep the rot really runs.

"Thanks," he says, his voice muffled by the waffle he's shoving into his mouth. His smile is genuine, but it's been so long since I've seen one directed at me that it stings like salt in an open wound.

"Where's Ol?" I ask, reaching for coffee, needing something to sustain me before I lose my grip entirely.

"He's out with Mia. Horseback riding on the beach or some shit," Jake answers, smirking.

I raise a brow, taking a sip of the bitter coffee. "Jesus. Ollie on a horse?"

"I know. The poor horse." Jake laughs, and for a second, I join in. But the laugh feels hollow because, even though it's light between us right now, there's still this chasm. One I dug myself, shovelful by shovelful of secrets and lies.

The silence that follows is thick, uncomfortable, pressing against my skin like humid summer air. My gut twists, this gnawing feeling growing stronger with each passing second. I want to fix this. I want to tell him everything—the real reason I've been such an asshole. I want him to understand that I did it for him, to protect him from the same shit that's been eating me alive every day for years.

But before I can speak, his phone buzzes on the counter. DAD flashes on the screen, and suddenly, my chest tightens like a vise. The air shifts, tension crackling between us like static before a storm. Jake hesitates, glancing at me before grabbing the phone.

"Dad, hey." There's a pause, and I can only imagine he'd be calling while he's on his way to his next meeting or next assistant he's fucking. "Thanks... Yeah, that sounds good. Okay, talk then."

I clench my jaw so hard it aches, my fists tight enough for nails to bite crescents into my palms.

Must be fucking nice to have a dad who remembers your birthday. The bitterness churns in my gut, a tidal wave of resentment I've been trying to suppress for years.

When Jake ends the call, I ask, my voice sharper than broken glass, "What did he want?"

He shrugs, avoiding my eyes like they burn. "To wish me a happy birthday."

There's more to it than he's letting on. He busies himself, putting away his dishes like he's trying to escape not just the conversation, but me.

"When are you seeing him?" I push, unable to keep the bitterness from seeping into my words.

Jake doesn't meet my gaze. "Not sure."

Liar.

I let out a huff, the frustration bubbling over like a pot left too long on the stove. Jake notices. His brows furrow, and he looks at me with something between confusion and frustration.

"Would it kill you to make a little effort with him? For all our sake?"

"Pass." I spit out the word like poison.

He throws his hands up in frustration. "I don't get you, Nate. I know you and Dad don't see eye to eye, but you've shut everyone out. Him, Mom, me... even Nora." His voice falters slightly when he mentions her, like her name physically pains him to say.

"You're going to end up pretty fucking alone if you keep pushing away the people who actually care about you."

His words hit me like a punch to the gut because deep down, I know he's right. But isn't that better?

Better than letting them in and failing them.

Alone means no one else gets dragged into the mess that is my life. I'm about to respond when the door swings open, and Nora walks in like a force of nature, cheeks flushed rose-pink from her morning run, hair wild and untamed. She's a whirlwind of chaos, a dangerous mix of beauty and defiance that steals the breath from my lungs. That's always been her way—whiskey in a teacup, sweet and sharp and more intoxicating than anything I've ever tasted.

"Happy birthday, Jake!" she chirps, wrapping Jake in a tight embrace. The jealousy flares up so fast it nearly chokes me, burning hot and bitter in my throat.

She looks my way, her gaze softening like morning fog.

"Hey." Her voice is barely above a whisper, testing the waters, trying to gauge if I'm still spiraling after last night.

"Hey."

Jake looks between us, his eyes narrowing slightly, picking up on the electricity crackling in the air.

"So," Nora says, casually reaching for a strawberry off Jake's plate. The way her lips close around it has my pulse racing.

Is this what it's come to? Jealous of a fucking strawberry?

I swallow hard, trying to rein in my spiraling thoughts before they betray me.

"What's the plan for the birthday boy today?" she asks, her smile faltering slightly as she looks at Jake.

He shrugs, standing to clear his plate. "Actually, I've got to help Mom out later. But maybe we can hang out tonight after dinner?"

"Sure," she says, her smile not quite reaching her eyes.

He leans down, presses a quick kiss to her head, and leaves, the front door clicking shut behind him with a finality that echoes in my chest.

And just like that, it's the two of us.

The silence stretches between us. I want to say something—about last night, about everything—but the words catch in my throat like thorns.

"Are you—" I start.

"I'm heading—" she says at the same time, both of us cutting each other off.

We pause, the moment awkward as a teenage slow dance.

"You go," I say quickly, my heart racing like a trapped thing.

"No, it's nothing. What were you going to say?" she asks, her gaze locking with mine, holding me captive.

I hesitate, rubbing the back of my neck where tension coils like a spring.

Fuck it.

"I was just thinking, while Jake's out and Ollie is with Mia... maybe today we could take the boat out?"

Her eyes soften, and for a moment, there's a flicker of hesitation that makes my stomach drop.

"Or do you have plans?" I ask, knowing she doesn't.

"Actually, you're in luck because today I do not." Her tone is causal and she's fighting back a smile.

Relief floods through me, though I can't say why. Maybe it's because we'll be alone for longer than five minutes. Or maybe it's because she wants to be alone with me. Whatever the reason, I'm just glad she said yes.

"Well, I have to head down to Sonder for a few hours to help Nick with something. But I'll be back around 4 PM. We should catch the sunset." I make a quick move toward the sink to clean up the mess Jake left behind.

"Nate."

Her voice stops me mid-step, like a hand on my chest. She's moved around the kitchen counter, now standing directly in front of me.

"Are you... okay? Last night—"

"I'm good." The lie slips out too easily but I can see she doesn't buy it.

Her eyes narrow, and her voice softens to velvet.

"Does it happen a lot?" She's careful, too careful, like she knows I'm made of glass, and one wrong touch will shatter me into pieces too small to ever put back together.

Now it's my turn to hesitate. I hate this conversation, hate that she sees this part of me, but I force out, "I'm handling it."

She frowns, not convinced. "Is that why you were using?"

Her words hit me like a punch to the gut, and for a second, I want to run. But I don't. I give her the truth. "Yes."

The way her face falters—it's like I've given her something she wasn't expecting.

"I wasn't lying when I told you I haven't touched anything since... since that night at the beach. When shit went down with Connor."

The confession sits heavy between us, like something too big to say aloud, but then she breaks the tension with a soft smile that warms me from the inside out. "That's good."

I want to tell her why I stopped. That it was because of her. That I couldn't stand the thought of her seeing me like that again, seeing me as someone to be afraid of. But the words don't come.

"I, uh, I'm gonna go take a shower and then start writing."

Her face lights up, and for a second, I'm free of everything weighing me down. She's always been happiest when she's talking about her writing. She's been doing it since we were kids, but she still doesn't know how good she is.

"How's it going?"

"I feel like I'm getting somewhere now," she says with a small grin that makes my heart skip. "I just need to sit down, no distractions, no noise—just write."

I watch her, captivated.

"What?" She looks self-conscious, like she's said too much, given away too many secrets.

"Nothing. It's just," I lean against the kitchen counter, not sure why I'm telling her this, "every memory I have of you involves books."

Her cheeks flush the perfect soft pink I love.

There's a smile she can't hide. "Just like every memory of you involves music."

"Why do you love it?" I ask, wanting to hear more, even though I'm running so fucking late right now. I want to keep her talking just to hear her voice and see her face light up when she talks about the things she loves.

"Writing?"

I nod.

"Escapism, I guess. Anything's possible in the stories you write. There's this kind of magic in believing in possibility, whether it's on paper or in real life." She flips the question back on me. "Why do you love music?"

"Same reason," I say, feeling the truth of it in my bones. "It takes you somewhere else. Or it brings back a thousand memories at once."

"Guess there's something we can finally agree on." She lets out a soft laugh, and it hits me all over again—I'm hooked on finding each new laugh she has, each one different, each one just as addictive as the last.

"Shit, I better get going or Nick will be pissed."

"I guess I'll see you later then?"

"You will."

I'm halfway out the door when Mom walks in, surprise flickering across her face like sunlight through leaves.

"Nate, where are you off to this early?"

"To Sonder, that new bar in town," I reply, already anticipating the worry that will cloud her eyes. "To help, not to—"

"I know," she cuts me off, her eyes soft as morning light. "I heard you volunteered. I'm proud of you."

I manage a smile, but inside, guilt gnaws at me like a hungry beast. Over the past year, she's seen me walk out this door too many times, always left wondering where I was going, what I was doing, or if I'd even come back. She's been a saint, enduring the shit I've added to her life on top of everything else.

"Hey, Mom, what's Jake helping you with today?" I ask, trying to keep my voice casual as I pull the door open.

Her face scrunches in confusion, lines appearing between her brows.

"Jake? He's not helping me with anything. Kat and I are heading to the markets, then lunch by the waterfront. He said he's spending time with Ollie this morning."

A prickle of something dark creeps up my spine like ice water. I force a smile as she squeezes my arm.

"You okay, honey?"

"I'm fine." I kiss the top of her head, "Nothing to worry about. I promise."

I don't know if it's true, if the buzzing in my head and the tightness in my chest will get better or worse. But I give her what she needs, and she smiles, her concern easing for now.

"We're doing dinner and cake tonight, so don't be late," she calls after me.

"Sounds good," I say, shutting the door behind me.

But all I can think about now is why Jake's lying. Why suddenly, of all people, is my brother hiding something from me?

"Sorry I'm late," I call out to Nick as I step inside the bar.

He waves it off, glancing up from where he's sketching something on a clipboard. "Actually, you're right on time. Can you help me move those planks out back?"

We get to work, moving piles of wooden planks, one by one. By the looks of it, I won't be needing to hit the gym this summer. This place is a wreck, and it's going to take a lot of heavy lifting to get it ready by the end of the season. I keep my head down, focusing on the repetitive rhythm of moving wood from one spot to another. Every plank feels like a step further away from the shit swirling in my head.

"So, what's the plan?" I ask, stacking another pile against the wall, muscles burning pleasantly from the work.

Nick grins, the kind of smile that tells me he's thought this through more than I've realized.

"The booths need reupholstering, the stage needs a complete overhaul, and I'm redoing the entire menu. Luckily the bar was in pretty decent condition so it didn't take much work to fix that."

He looks around the space like he's seeing something I can't—not what is, but what could be.

"I want this place to have a different feel. You know, a place where people want to be on any night of the week, not just weekends. Where they can experience a taste of Spain right here in Eden."

"Spain?"

I can see the flicker of excitement in his eyes, like he's already there in his mind.

"I spent a lot of time in the South of Spain when I was younger. It's a place where people stayed for hours, eating, drinking, and talking. I want to bring that vibe here. Only local produce, local wines, and we showcase local talent. Make it feel like this place belongs to the town."

"How'd you end up in Spain?" I ask, curiosity getting the better of me.

His expression shifts, becoming more contemplative. "Life at home wasn't easy growing up. So I did what any teenager would do and I ran. Only California didn't feel far enough so I ran to another country where I didn't know anyone and couldn't speak the language." He laughs, but there's an edge to it that I recognize—the kind of laugh that covers old wounds.

"I was a pretty messed up teenager and if it wasn't for my uncle giving me a way to get out, I don't know where I would have ended up."

I can sense the gratitude in his voice and the love he has for Alfie.

"It was a special place. I felt like I found some part of myself that I'd lost there. As time went on, I set myself up, got myself straight, learned more about the culture, cuisine and wines. Eventually I bought a house there and started a little business. But then Uncle Alfie got sick a few years back. He's the only family I have so instead of flying back and forth like I was, I packed up my life in Spain and here we are."

"Opening a bar," I add.

"Restaurant bar actually," he corrects with a hint of pride.

Nick continues, painting a picture of open mic nights, live bands—making this the spot everyone in town wants to play at. He's a dreamer, but he's done this before. I can tell by the way he talks, confident and decisive. I admire that about him.

"So why 'Sonder'?" I ask.

Nick's face lights up as he leans back against the counter. "When I traveled, I loved to sit in the window of cafés and watch people. Just living their lives, completely unaware of me watching. Everyone's got their own story, their own journey. And every now and then, I'd see the same person walk by, and we'd just nod, like we shared something without even speaking. Those little moments, they're meaningful even if we don't understand the full extent of them."

I let that sink in for a moment.

"That's some stoic shit," I mutter, earning a laugh from him.

"Well, that's what 'sonder' is. It's the realization that every person you see has a life as full and complicated as your own."

We keep working for a few more hours, hauling junk, clearing out old furniture, getting the place ready for its transformation. My muscles ache, but there's something satisfying about it—physical work that pulls me out of my head for a while.

Nick heads to the back, leaving me to wander until my eyes land on something. A guitar case, half-hidden in the corner of the unfinished stage, like a ghost from my past waiting to be discovered. My fingers twitch with muscle memory. Nora's question from earlier echoes in my mind: *"Why do you love music?"*

It's been so long since I've even touched a guitar. I think about that night two weeks ago, fitting puzzle pieces together listening to *November Rain*. The way she'd looked at me when she asked if I still played, her eyes lighting up with something between curiosity and challenge.

I'd linked my pinky with hers, thinking it was just another throwaway moment. But something about the way she'd smiled afterward, like she'd won something precious, had lodged itself in my chest.

Before I can talk myself out of it, I'm crossing the room and flipping open the case. An acoustic, pre-loved but well-maintained. I run my fingers along the strings, feeling the vibrations ripple through me like electricity. I strum a chord, then another. The sound fills the empty bar, soft but resonant, and before I know it, I'm playing a melody I wrote when I was sixteen.

For a moment, everything else fades—the noise in my head, the pressure in my chest, the weight of all my secrets. It's just me and the guitar, the music grounding me in a way nothing else ever could.

I made a pinky promise. And I'm starting to realize that any promise I make to Nora, I want to keep. No matter how small. Because each one feels like a step toward something real, something I can't name yet but know I've been missing. Something worth fighting for.

"Nate."

Nick's voice pulls me back to reality, and I stop, guilt flashing through me like lightning.

"Sorry, I didn't mean to touch—"

Nick shakes his head, a knowing smile playing at his lips. "That's what it's there for. Sounds like you've been playing for a while."

I set the guitar down carefully, scratching the back of my neck where tension coils.

"I used to. But I don't anymore." I take a deep breath, the memories rising like smoke from a dying fire.

"Nora's dad got me my first guitar, for my tenth birthday. I started teaching myself how to play, learning chords, and reading music. It became my escape." I pause, swallowing the bitter taste that comes with the memory. "But my dad... he hated it. Thought it was a waste of time."

The memory of Scott slamming through the door that night comes back to me, sharp as broken glass. He was drunk, rage rolling off him in waves. The sound of me playing set him off. He walked right into my room, grabbed the guitar, and smashed it to pieces like he was trying to break more than just wood and strings.

"You think strumming a fucking guitar is your future? I don't pay school fees so you can fuck around. Stop wasting your time with this shit." His words still echo in my head, sharp and cruel as the day he spat them at me.

I never picked up a guitar again after that.

"I stopped playing to focus on school and football," I add, my voice hollow as an empty promise.

Nick gives me a look, one that says he's reading more into my words than I'm letting on. "Well, I think you should try picking it up again."

I shake my head, pushing away the temptation. "I don't own a guitar anymore."

He gestures toward the one I was just playing. "That one's been sitting there, collecting dust for God knows how long."

"It's not really my thing anymore."

Nick studies me for a moment, then sets down the box he's carrying.

"Look, Nate. I don't know you all that well, but I know talent when I see it. And trust me, you've got it." He puts a hand on my shoulder, the weight of it steady and grounding. "Don't let your father's version of your life be the one you end up actually living. You owe it to yourself to choose your own path in this lifetime."

I look away, swallowing hard against the truth in his words. He's right, but it's not that simple. Nothing ever is.

"Sometimes healing means reopening old wounds, taking a good look at them so you can finally let them close for good."

"What if the wounds run too deep?" I ask before I can stop myself.

Nick pauses, turning back to me. "They might never go away completely, but that doesn't mean you can't start fresh. You've got a whole life ahead of you, Nate. And at any point, you can begin again. Trust me."

He walks away, leaving me with those words settling into my bones.

"And for someone who hasn't touched a guitar since he was fifteen, you've still got it," he shouts, without turning to face me.

I smile at the compliment, and just like that, something in me shifts. It's tiny, barely there, like the first spark of a flame—but it's there.

CHAPTER 34
EXPECT THE UNEXPECTED
NORA

THE TWO HOURS OF SLEEP I MANAGED AFTER SNEAKING OUT OF NATE'S room feel like shards of glass behind my eyelids, but I'm already lacing up my running shoes. Sometimes moving is easier than staying still with your thoughts. The house holds its breath around me, as if afraid to disturb the remnants of darkness we fought through together. I can't shake the image of Nate from my mind—his eyes wild with terror, body trembling beneath the weight of nightmares that have haunted him since childhood. But now they seem darker, more violent, as if something fundamental inside him is unraveling.

It happened like so quickly.

One minute I was dreaming, the next his scream tore through the walls—sharp and broken. I tried to snap him out of it, only to find him above me, his hands pinning mine to the bed with a desperate strength I didn't know he possessed. For a heartbeat, I didn't recognize him through the mask of fear distorting his features.

But then reality crashed in, and I knew—he was lost in one of his nightmares again.

The horror that crossed his face when he recognized me carved itself into my memory.

He scrambled away, apologies spilling from his lips. But beneath my concern, beneath the ache of watching him suffer, something else stirred —a heat that caught me off guard, desire threading through my veins. I can still feel him pressed against me, and I wanted—God, I wanted him. But I couldn't voice that need, not when he was shattered with shame. And even if I could reach for him now, the shadow of what Evan did to me last summer looms like a wall between us. The way he stripped me down to nothing, left me feeling small, powerless, broken. I haven't let anyone touch me since then—not really, not in the ways that matter.

And then last night, after Nate finally calmed and I held him like I used to when we were kids, words I never meant to speak slipped out into the darkness between us. I'm still not sure if he was awake, his breathing had evened out against my collar bone, but the confession hung in the air like smoke—how afraid I was, how weak I felt, how the thought of being touched again made me want to crawl out of my own skin.

Now, with the inevitability of seeing Evan again, my stomach turns to ice. The mere thought of pretending everything is fine makes bile rise in my throat.

My lungs burn as I push myself harder along the empty streets, trying to outrun memories that refuse to fade. With every exhale, I attempt to release the past. He's always been damaged in his own way, carrying scars that run deeper than the ones visible on his skin. When we were kids, I thought I could protect him from nightmares. Now I'm not sure who needs protecting more.

I slow to a walk as I reach the pier, brushing away sweat-dampened hair from my face. The sunrise bleeds through the clouds, painting everything in soft gold, but it feels like a beautiful lie—nature's attempt to pretend everything is okay when nothing feels right anymore.

I want Nate in ways that terrify me. But I'm more afraid of what giving in to those feelings could mean. Because once we cross that line, there's no going back. And I don't know if I'm ready for him to see all the broken pieces I've been hiding.

But losing him entirely?

That's a risk I can't bear to take.

By the time I make it back, sweat trickles down my spine and my legs feel weighted with lead. The summer heat wraps around me like a suffocating blanket, my breath still ragged from pushing too hard. I needed the burn, the distraction, something to quiet the chaos in my mind. But standing at the front door, exhaustion has replaced relief.

The moment I step inside, raised voices drift from the kitchen—Jake and Nate, their argument a familiar dance. I pause, wiping my forehead, straining to make out words spoken in tense, barely contained voices.

"Would it kill you to make a little effort with him? For all our sake?" Jake's voice cuts like a blade.

"You never had to deal with him like I did." Nate's reply carries an undercurrent of frustration.

"I'm not making excuses. I know he's not the picture-perfect family man. I know he's done shit too, but—"

"No, you don't," Nate interrupts, his voice cracking. "You've never had to—" The words shatter against silence.

I lean against the wall, my stomach knotting as I listen to them tear at old wounds. Their different childhoods always stood out like a stark line drawn between them—Jake the golden child Scott praised endlessly, while Nate could never seem to measure up. I'd watched Scott's face light up at Jake's every achievement while Nate bore the brunt of his disappointment, his anger, his bitterness.

It wasn't fair.

Their voices drop when they realize I'm here. I take my cue, stepping in to wish Jake happy birthday, even though I know Lydia will insist on the real celebration tomorrow. She's been doing this since we were kids —making a grand production of our "birthday-and-a-day" celebrations, since Jake and I were born exactly a year and a day apart.

Tomorrow will be all decorated cakes and embarrassing childhood photos, but today is just Jake's. And since he's already heading out to whatever plans he's made, that leaves me alone with Nate—something that rarely ends well. Which is why his invitation to go out on the boat later today catches me completely off guard.

"Or do you have plans?" He jokes with a sly smile, like he already knows the answer because my silence said as much.

I try to match his casual tone. "Actually, you're in luck because today I do not."

His smile grows a fraction, that small curve in his lips sending my stomach into a free fall. This is exactly why I avoid being alone with him. Too many reactions I can't control.

"Well, I have to head down to Sonder for a few hours to help Nick with something. But I'll be back around 4 PM. We should catch the sunset."

Great, a sunset. On a boat. In the middle of the ocean. With the guy I've been in love with since I was eight.

My internal sarcasm does nothing to slow my racing heart. This is exactly the kind of situation I've been carefully avoiding for years—just Nate and me, no buffers, no easy escapes. Nowhere to hide from the questions I see sometimes lingering in his eyes.

I freeze, nerves spiking with a cocktail of excitement and fear. Part of me yearns to understand what's happening with him, to finally talk about

237

the nightmares and everything he's carried for so long. But another part —the smarter, self-preserving part—trembles at the thought of being alone with him, of what truths might surface.

What's the worst that could happen?

Oh, just complete emotional devastation.

Totally fine.

The walls I've built between us have kept me safe. They've kept the fragile peace we've managed to establish.

And here I am, walking right into the fire anyway.

Once I'm freshly showered with hair still dripping, I head downstairs. Lydia is in the kitchen and she looks exhausted, but her eyes brighten when they meet mine.

"Oh, I didn't realize you were home." A smile plays at her lips.

"The boys are all out so I thought I would spend some time writing. Have you seen my computer? I thought I left it down here."

Her smile turns knowing. "It's in the sunroom."

"The sunroom?" Confusion furrows my brow.

"Go and see for yourself." There's something mischievous in her tone.

I hesitate before pushing open the sunroom door.

My breath catches.

Sunlight streams through the windows, casting a warm glow over the spotless room. Fresh flowers grace the desk beside what appears to be new pens, my laptop perfectly positioned.

Next to it sits a framed photo—the same one we have at home of all of us kids with dad on the lake. Tears prickle at my eyes as I notice a gift wrapped in simple brown paper, a note resting on top.

My hands tremble as I recognize Nate's handwriting.

This might be a more inspiring place to write a New York Times Best Seller than the kitchen table.

I swallow hard, carefully unwrapping the gift to reveal a limited-edition copy of *The Secret Garden*. My fingers trace the cover as memories of bedtime stories with Dad flood back.

It's the note on the final page that steals my breath.

The end is only a chance for another beginning.

Expect the unexpected, and that's where you'll usually find the magic. - N

My heart twists as I sink into the chair. Nate's always been kind, protective, even when hurting. But this gesture feels different—thoughtful, intimate, purely him.

There's so much I don't know about this version of Nate but the boy I knew still exists beneath the surface. I place the book down gently and open my laptop.

Something about his gesture makes me want to write, to pour everything onto the page.

Taking a deep breath, I begin.

> Stories have a beginning that defines them and an end that is inevitable.
> But in between the beginning and the end, that's up to us to determine.
> And sometimes we just have to trust that the universe will surprise us.
> Usually when we least expect it.
> Because if we expect the unexpected, that's usually where we'll find the magic.

CHAPTER 35
RIPPLES OF THE PAST
NATE

"You've known her your whole life. Why do you look like you're walking to your own funeral?"

Nick side-eyes me as I pack up to leave.

I let out a breathy laugh, raking a hand through my hair. "Is it that obvious I'm shitting bricks?"

"Pretty much." He smirks, crossing his arms. "What's the deal? Why are you so nervous?"

I pause, rubbing the back of my neck as tension settles between my shoulder blades.

"It's complicated between Nora and me. There's history there and—" The words feel heavy in my throat, like they've been sitting there for years. Because they have.

"I fucked up with her last year. I wasn't there for her when her dad died, and now every time I look at her, all I feel is guilt."

Nick narrows his eyes. "Is that all you feel when you look at her?"

The question hangs in the air. Lying isn't an option, and even if I tried, Nick would see through my bullshit. We've spent a few long days together, half them hammering nails into wood, yet somehow he's become the first person in a long time who I can trust. Who doesn't see me as some lost cause.

"How do you know she hasn't forgiven you?"

I look down, kicking at the floor like a goddamn teenager.

Because I haven't forgiven myself.

"She shouldn't forgive me. But now it's like there's this permanent wall between us, and no matter what I do, I can't break it down."

Nick shrugs, tossing a rag over his shoulder.

"Maybe you don't need to break it down. Maybe you just need to open a door. And maybe, the key to that door is forgiving yourself first."

I give him a dry look. "What self-help book is that from?"

He grins. "Actually, it was a fortune cookie."

I laugh despite myself. As much as I try to act like it's not a big deal, it is. It's not just missing the funeral. It's everything—the way I've let my own shit stop me from being and doing anything in life. She deserves more than what I can give her emotionally. I can't give her the fairytales she dreams about and writes about.

"Before you go," Nick heads towards the back and returns with a box. "Taste test these on your date and give me some feedback."

"It's not a date."

"You're whisking a girl you've known your whole life, who you clearly have feelings for away on a boat during sunset. Call me old-fashioned, but I'd say that's a date."

I don't fuel the fire with a response, instead offering a grin and thank you before walking out the door.

THE DRIVE BACK TO THE HOUSE DOES MY HEAD NO GOOD. I CAN FEEL THE nerves building again, curling tight in my gut. And then, when I finally see her standing on the front porch waiting for me, everything goes quiet and still in my mind. She opens the door, and the sweet smell of her perfume fills the car. It's like the world just pauses, and all I can see is her.

Fuck me.

She's beautiful, and it's effortless. Her presence alone makes my chest tight with a feeling I can't—won't—name.

I am so fucked. So fucking fucked.

The drive to the marina passes in comfortable silence, broken only by occasional questions and soft small talk. Her presence fills the space between us with an electric charge that makes my skin hum. Why does this girl have such a tight grip on my every emotion? How does she make me so fucking nervous with just a glance?

I help her onto Scott's boat—the one he impulsively bought Mom as an *"I'm sorry for being such a piece of shit husband"* gift, masquerading as an anniversary present months after their actual anniversary.

As I steer us out toward the ocean, the further we get from dry land, the more the tension in my shoulders begins to ease. The water has always been my sanctuary.

She's wearing loose linen shorts that show off her long, already—

241

tanned legs, and a tank top that clings to her curves in ways that make it hard to focus on anything else. Her hair's pulled back, but the salt breeze is already working its magic with the loose strands framing her face. And fuck, her smile. If I ever wanted to bottle up the feeling of sunshine, I'd just have to see that smile.

I catch myself staring, and it's only when she says my name that I snap out of it.

"Nate?"

"Huh?"

Smooth dickhead.

Real smooth.

I clear my throat, gripping the steering wheel a little too tight. She laughs softly, the sound carrying on the wind.

"I was trying to say thank you."

"For what?"

"For what you did with the sunroom. You really didn't have to."

I shrug, aiming for casual even as my heart races. Her eyes soften, and for a second, I see something in them I can't quite place—something that makes my breath catch.

"It was really thoughtful and meant a lot."

I shake my head, swallowing past the tightness in my throat.

"I'm happy you like it. And you're welcome." It was a small gesture, but more than anything, I wanted her to know that I'd always be in her corner, making sure she followed through with her dream. Even after everything, the guy she once knew was still here for her.

We fall into a comfortable silence as we sail toward the open sea. The sun hangs lower now, painting the water in shades of gold and amber.

Eventually, Nora speaks again, her voice quieter this time.

"The last time I was out on the water was with Dad... all of us, together." Her voice wavers as she looks down at the bracelet that's been on her wrist ever since the carnival. She runs her thumb over it, a ritual I've seen her perform countless times. "I can't believe it's already been a year."

Her eyes are sad and it physically causes me pain seeing so much hurt in them. One year since they laid David to rest, and I wasn't there. I wasn't standing beside her in that cemetery. I wasn't there to hold her hand or offer my shoulder when she needed it most. The guilt of that absence has been the wall between us that I've never known how to tear down.

It wasn't lost on me, the significance of today. How could it be? The date has been etched into my conscience like a scar. It was one of the reasons I wanted to get her out on the water—away from everything that would remind her of that day, the day I failed her in the worst possible way. Maybe somewhere deep down, I thought bringing her here, to a place that held good memories of her father, might begin to make up for my absence when it mattered most. But nothing could erase that failure, the first of many ways I've kept her at arm's length because I don't deserve to be any closer.

I glance at her, my heart squeezing. Her voice cracks just a little, the weight of the memory pressing down on her. But she doesn't cry. Nora's strong like that. She carries her grief differently—quiet, private. I want to reach over and hold her, tell her I'm sorry again, but the words stick in my throat like sand.

The smell of salt and sea air wraps around us, and I breathe in deep, hoping it'll steady me. The sky bleeds into the horizon in endless shades of blue, and the setting sun casts everything in a golden glow that makes the world feel bigger than we'll ever understand.

We're alone now.

No cell reception, no distractions. Just us and the ocean. And it's terrifying, because I realize I've never wanted anything more than to keep her all to myself. To freeze time and stay like this, just the two of us, away from everything that threatens to tear us apart. I grab the box Nick insisted we take, laughing under my breath.

"Nick wants us to try some new menu items for the restaurant."

She raises an eyebrow, clearly amused. "A food critic? Now that I can do."

I grin, pulling out the containers. "He did promise dessert too. But only if the feedback is good."

We sit on the deck, legs stretched out as the boat sways gently beneath us. The ocean stretches endlessly ahead, the setting sun painting everything in fire-bright hues of pink and gold. Nora sits across from me, her hair catching the last rays of sunlight, her skin glowing like it's been kissed by the dying day. Every time her eyes meet mine, my chest tightens with an ache I can't ignore. She's like the moon in the night sky —no matter where I try to run and hide, she's always there, lighting up the darkest parts of me.

"Can I ask you something?" Her voice is soft, almost hesitant, like she's treading on fragile ground. Her eyes flicker with uncertainty, but there's a quiet determination underneath that makes my throat go dry.

I nod, not trusting my voice. Something in me already knows what she's going to ask, and instinct screams at me to deflect, to run.

But I'm tired of running.

"The nightmares..." Her voice breaks through the quiet tension. "Are they always about your dad?"

She's sitting right in front of me now, her jade green eyes locked on mine, pulling at something deep inside me that I've kept buried for too long. It's like she's demanding all my attention, though she already has it. She always does.

Her hand brushes the top of mine, steady and warm.

"Nate, you can talk to me."

I look anywhere but at her. The water ripples around us in gentle waves, but inside me, it's like a storm threatening to break loose. I swallow hard, the words lodged in my throat like they've forgotten how to be spoken.

"I—"

She wants me to talk, but how do I put words to the things I've spent my whole life trying to bury? We shouldn't be talking about me. We should be talking about her. My mind races trying to find ways to divert the conversation back to her. But then she does something that nearly breaks me.

Her hand, soft and warm, cradles my face. She leans in, her eyes never leaving mine, her fingers curling gently against my skin. It's like she's holding all the broken pieces of me together, silently promising she won't let me fall apart.

"I'm not afraid of you," she whispers, her voice steady, unshaken by the storm raging inside me. "And if you're unsure about trusting me, well, too bad. Because I'm not going anywhere until I prove to you, you can trust me."

In an instant everything cracks wide open.

Her words are a lifeline thrown into the chaos. I've spent years wading through the wreckage of my life, convinced that no one could ever stick around long enough to help me sift through the ashes. But she's here. She's not afraid. And somehow, that makes all the difference. Because no matter how much everything else falls apart, she's always been my constant—even when I hadn't shown up for her.

"You're one of the few things I'm sure of," I manage to say, my voice rough with emotion.

It's the truth, and it burns to admit it. She's the only person who sees me for who I am—really sees me—and doesn't walk the other way. She knows about the scars, both the ones on my skin and the ones buried deeper, the ones that twist like barbed wire around my heart. She knows about my parents, about my failures, and somehow, she still looks at me like I'm worthy of something I can't see in myself.

I swallow hard.

"The nightmares have gotten worse over time." My voice drops low. "Sometimes I can't tell the difference between what's real and what isn't. What I dreamt happened and what actually did. The drugs helped numb and silence everything for short amounts of time."

The memories crash over me like waves, threatening to pull me under. Scott's voice, slurred and angry. My mom's crying, the kind that never really stopped. The promises he made—empty, worthless. I shut my eyes, trying to keep it all contained.

"Mom... she cried all the time. Scott blamed everyone and everything but himself—his job, the world. Never took any responsibility when things were turning to shit. Instead, he'd just lay into mom or me if I stood in his way."

I look up at her, but she doesn't flinch. She just holds the space for me to unravel.

"The older I got, it kept escalating." My voice trembles, and I hate it. "He started drinking more. Taking more pills and fuck knows what else. And every night when he'd come home from another cocaine bender, the blows got harder. It was like the more I grew, the angrier he got. He hated me for even existing."

Nora reaches out, her hand brushing against mine, and I almost flinch. Almost. But her touch is soft, grounding me in the present.

"Nate," she says softly, my name a prayer on her lips.

"He never laid a hand on Jake. Never yelled at him. Why? I don't know. But I didn't care, as long as he never touched him. That was all that mattered. I didn't want Jake to end up like me—like this." I gesture to myself, to the broken pieces I've become.

She still doesn't look away. Her eyes stay locked on me, and there's something in them—something I can't put words to. It's not pity or fear. It's like she sees all of me, even the parts I've tried to hide, and she's still looking at me like I'm something whole, not the broken mess I know I am.

"The only thing football was good for was that I naturally got stronger. When I started fighting back, it infuriated him, but some sadistic part of him loved it. And when he couldn't hurt me physically anymore, he found other ways." I pause, my throat tightening around the words I never thought I'd say aloud. "He broke mom instead."

The confession hangs in the air between us, heavy with years of guilt and pain. I hate talking about this, hate reopening wounds that never really healed. Because they come with memories I've tried to keep buried —the screams, the tears, the sickening sound of flesh on flesh or glass shattering. The way mom would sacrifice herself to save me from the brutal beatings, closing their bedroom door and telling me to go to sleep. It'd make me physically sick, knowing what she put on the line just so he wouldn't kill me with his fists.

Nora's hand tightens around mine. "Nate, I'm so sorry."

"I wanted to leave, Nora. So many times, I wanted to just pack up and run, but I couldn't leave them. If I did, he'd..." I stop myself from voicing the worst-case scenario. "I was the only thing keeping him in check."

She doesn't say anything, but she doesn't have to. The silence between us is full of understanding.

"That's why you got caught with the drugs at school? You did it on purpose, so you'd have to stay behind." She pauses, her eyes searching mine. "That's why you weren't at the funeral?"

I don't answer, but my silence is enough.

Her eyes have become more intense because she's fighting back her own tears.

"Does your mom know that's the reason you got kicked out? Does Jake?"

I laugh, but there's no humor in it.

"Mom always had this idea that football and a college scholarship could fix everything. Like it would somehow make him stop, like he'd finally love me if I succeeded." My jaw tightens. "And Jake puts our dad on a pedestal where he can do no fucking wrong. But Scott only cares about one thing. Power. That and upholding the Sullivan name. He'd prefer me gone but not without the Ivy League degree and football trophies to brag about."

Her hand slips to my cheek again, turning my face toward her.

"Your mom wanted you out because she loves you, Nate. She wanted a future for you."

A future.

That's almost laughable now. At the rate I'm going, I'd be lucky to make it to thirty-five.

"A future," I repeat. "And leave her behind? Leave Jake behind? So he could use them instead of me? I couldn't do it. I couldn't live with myself if something happened to them."

Her eyes soften, but there's a fire in them that makes my chest ache.

"You don't really think any of this was your fault, do you?"

She continues to hold my face in her hands, her palms warm against my skin, and for the first time in forever, I feel something.

Something good. Something I don't deserve, but can't help but crave.

When she looks at me like this, it's like she's reaching into the darkest parts of my soul and telling me it's going to be okay. That it's safe to be vulnerable with her. That she'll protect what remains of my heart with everything she has. And I believe her.

"Nate, if we let our nightmares define us, then we lose sight of our dreams." She glances up at me, a small smile playing at her lips. "I read that somewhere. Sounds pretty legit."

I huff out a laugh, even though my chest feels too tight to breathe. "Do you always see the silver lining in everything?"

She thinks about it, her eyes drifting up toward the sky, as if she's searching for an answer in the emerging stars.

"I guess I just choose to believe that you can find hope in the strangest places. Even in the darkest corners."

Her words stir something deep inside me, awakening feelings I've kept buried for too long.

Hope.

She talks about it like it's something that can be found, like a light hidden under layers of darkness. I've spent my whole life in that darkness, convinced there was no way out, but she—she makes me think maybe there's more.

"You really believe that?" I ask, my voice barely above a whisper.

"Well, what's the alternative?" she says, shrugging lightly, like it's the simplest thing in the world. But that's Nora—she makes the impossible seem within reach, like there's always a way through. I've never met anyone like her, never met someone who could pull me out of my own head the way she does.

"How come you can believe in everyone else's dreams except your own?" I ask. I've always noticed that about her—she's the first to stand in someone's corner, to cheer them on, but she never gives herself the same grace.

"I've always found joy in cheering others on and watching the people I love succeed and thrive."

I watch her, the way the last of the sunlight catches the edge of her hair, turning it into a halo. How does she not see it? How does she not see the way she lights up everything around her?

"Maybe it's time someone was in your corner for once," I say, my voice low, but she hears it.

The moment feels too raw, too real. I need to break this tension before I do something reckless.

"Come with me," I say, nodding toward the front of the boat.

The boat rocks beneath us as I pull her closer, leading her to the bow.

The sunset is fading behind us, casting the water in deep orange light, and I can't help but feel like the world is about to tilt on its axis.

"Do you trust me?" I ask, a smirk tugging at my lips.

She looks at me, half-smiling, half-nervous. "Do I have a choice?"

I step closer, my chest almost touching hers. "You always have a choice."

Her breath hitches, and that beautiful blush I love spreads across her cheeks—the one that appears whenever I'm too close. It drives me crazy, the way her body betrays how she feels before she even says a word.

"I trust you," she says.

"Good. Then hold onto me." My voice is rougher than I intend, laced with something I can't hide anymore.

She hesitates but still wraps her arms around my neck. Something inside me settles as my arms circle her waist like they belong there. If I could freeze a moment forever, it'd be this one—her body pressed against mine, her head tilted up just enough for me to see every inch of her face. Her lips parted, eyes locked on mine, trust radiating from her.

"Keep your eyes on me, Leni," I say, using her nickname like a tether.

Without giving her a chance to protest, I tip us both over the edge of the boat. We crash into the water, the cool shock of it wrapping around us as we plunge beneath the surface. For a second, everything is quiet—the world muted, the only thing I'm aware of is her body pressed against mine, clinging to me like I'm her lifeline. I know she's mine.

When we break the surface, she gasps, laughing through her shock.

"You're insane!" she yells, her arms still wrapped tightly around me.

"You say insane, I say fun." I grin, holding her closer. She's still gripping me, her wet hair plastered to her face, water droplets sliding down her skin. It's like God himself took the time to carve her to perfection.

The way she's looking at me right now? I'm not sure I'll be able to keep myself in check much longer. My gaze keeps drifting to her lips, to the soft curve of her mouth, and the way her breath hitches when I run my hands down her back to hold her steady in the water.

But I know better. I can't just act on this—on us—when everything is so tangled up in the past and the chaos I've created. It would be selfish. So instead of leaning in, I take a deep breath and pull back.

"It's getting dark. We should probably head back."

"Yeah. Right. Sure." She lets go, and the second she does, the distance feels like a physical ache.

I help her back to the boat, guiding her up the step ladder as she shivers, and I'm struck again by how much I want her. How much I need her.

Every inch of me is screaming to pull her back into my arms, to let everything I'm holding back pour out into one kiss, one touch.

But I keep it together.

Barely.

I hand her some dry clothes—my favorite Aerosmith t-shirt and track pants. When she steps out of the cabin wearing just the t-shirt like an oversized dress, the sight nearly knocks the wind out of me. She's doing things to me that I won't be able to hide much longer.

"How do I look?" she teases, her cheeks flushed, but there's something in her eyes that tells me she's feeling the same pull I am.

Perfect.

Fucking perfect.

"It looks better on you, than it does me," I mutter, my voice betraying more than I want it to.

Her eyes linger on me for a moment, and I know she feels it, the charge between us. It's in the air, in the space between our bodies, crackling like electricity. I see it in the way her breath quickens, the way her fingers twitch like she doesn't know what to do with her hands. I can't take this any further. Not until I sort out the dumpster fire that is my life.

I drive her home, the tension between us still thick, still palpable. When I pull up to the house, she notices I don't get out of the car.

"You're not coming?"

"I need to do something. I'll be back in an hour," I say quietly. The look of disappointment on her face twists something in my chest. For a second, I think about telling her everything. But I can't—not yet.

"Just let Mom know to start dinner without me." I hate the way she's looking at me right now, like I've just fucked up the perfect afternoon with her. But I need to do this.

She watches me for a second, her eyes searching mine, then nods, stepping out of the car without another word.

As I drive away, I make a decision. I'm going to clean up my life and end the things that don't matter. Because the only thing that matters now is standing in the driveway watching me drive off.

CHAPTER 36
DROWNING IN TRUTH
NORA

THE TRUTH ABOUT NATE'S NIGHTMARES HITS ME LIKE SHATTERED GLASS, each piece cutting deeper than the last. These things that haunt him, even in daylight, they've always been there, tucked away underneath the surface. My chest constricts as everything clicks into place, years of puzzle pieces finally forming a complete picture. The bruises he'd laugh off, the way he'd flinch when his father's name came up, how he'd pull away if anyone got too close—it wasn't indifference. It was preservation. He's been protecting everyone else—his mom, Jake, even me—while slowly disappearing piece by piece, like a photograph fading in the sun. The realization settles in my bones, heavy and suffocating.

I turn to him, ready to unleash years of bottled anger at the unfairness of it all, but the words die in my throat when our eyes meet.

What I see there steals my breath—not just pain, but exhaustion etched into the lines of his face, years of carrying burdens that were never his to bear. Yet beneath that weight, there's something else: relief, as if sharing this secret has loosened the chains around his heart, even if just for a moment.

"People don't have power over us," I whisper, my voice trembling but sure. "We give that to them."

He stares at me, his expression unreadable, and panic flares in my chest like a match struck in darkness. But then his voice breaks through, soft as a prayer.

"Thank you."

I blink, caught off guard. "For what?"

"For being you." The rawness in his words makes my heart ache.

250

A shaky laugh escapes me, filled with emotions I'm not ready to name. "I don't know how to be anyone else but me around you."

When I look up, I catch that rare smile—the one that shows his dimples, the one that's been living rent-free in my heart since we were kids. His expression remains serious, but there's something different now, something softer. Like I'm seeing a version of him that's been locked away, waiting for someone to find the right key. I've seen all his jagged edges now—the parts he's buried under years of jokes, anger, and carefully maintained distance. Instead of running, I want to stay. To understand every scar, every shadow, every story written in the spaces between his words.

"I don't think you realize how much you've been doing for everyone else," I say softly, my fingers brushing his, electricity sparking at the contact. "But you don't have to carry it all alone anymore."

He looks down at our hands, and when his eyes meet mine again, the vulnerability there takes my breath away. It's like watching a fortress's walls crumble, revealing something precious and unguarded beneath.

"I never wanted to carry it," he admits, voice barely above a whisper. "I just didn't know how to stop."

His words break my heart and heal it simultaneously. He's forgotten how to let someone else share his burden, but that changes now. I'll be here—not to fight his battles, but to help carry the weight when it threatens to crush him.

"I see you, Nate," I whisper, emotion thick in my throat. "I've always seen you."

"I know."

For the first time in years, there's a glint of light in his eyes that tells me he believes me.

There's a brief moment of silence before his lips quirk into that half-smile that still makes my heart skip. "Do you trust me?"

The question echoes in my chest.

Do I trust him?

Even when I was angry, even when his choices felt like betrayal, I've always trusted Nate Sullivan with everything that matters—including my heart, even when I tried not to.

Before doubt can creep in, I wrap my arms around his waist. His body is solid against mine, warmth seeping through his damp shirt. His heart-beat thuds against my chest, steady and strong, and the closeness makes me dizzy. I feel him react to my touch, his breathing changing, muscles tensing beneath my fingers.

"Keep your eyes on me, Leni," he says, his voice dropping low. My name on his lips sends shivers down my spine.

Then we're falling, the cold water shocking us both. I surface laughing, clinging to him like he's my anchor in a storm.

"You're insane!" I gasp through my laughter.

"You say insane, I say fun." He grins, holding me close.

His eyes drift to my lips, lingering there, and the world narrows to just us—floating in the water, bodies pressed together, breaths mingling in the narrow space between us. Heat builds despite the cool water, and I bite my lip, trying to ignore how badly I want him to close that distance.

The moment stretches, electric and fragile, until he breaks it. "It's getting dark. We should head back."

I nod, even as every cell in my body screams for something else. He lifts me back onto the boat, his hands firm on my waist, leaving ghost prints of warmth on my skin. When I emerge from changing into his old Aerosmith t-shirt, I catch him staring at me like I'm something precious and rare. For the first time in forever, I feel beautiful. Wanted.

The drive home starts in comfortable silence, the kind that hums with possibility. I steal glances at him, watching his fingers drum against the steering wheel, his dark hair still damp and curling slightly at the ends. The muscles in his forearms flex with each turn, defined and strong, reminding me of how those exact arms had wrapped around me in the water, keeping me safe as we plunged beneath the surface. When "High and Dry" by Radiohead plays, followed by "For Me This Is Heaven" by Jimmy Eat World, his jaw relaxes in that familiar way. Memories flood back: summers spent arguing about music on the dock, him teaching me piano with endless patience, those rare smiles that felt like gifts meant just for me.

It was never just a teenage crush, though I tried to convince myself otherwise. The way my heart raced when he entered a room, how time seemed to slow when he smiled—it was deeper, more intense. He's woven into the fabric of who I am, present even when I'm not looking.

"What are you thinking about?" His voice breaks through my reverie.

I smile, studying my hands before meeting his eyes. "Did you know you hum when you're relaxed or happy?"

He laughs, rich and warm. "I do?"

"Yeah," I say softly. "You've been doing it for as long as I can remember."

His brow furrows thoughtfully. "No one's ever pointed that out before."

"Well, maybe you're not relaxed and happy often enough," I tease, truth hiding behind the lightness.

His smile grows, and something in his gaze makes my heart stutter. Snow Patrol's "Open Your Eyes" plays softly in the background, its lyrics threading through the moment like fate. I reach out, brushing his arm with my fingers. When he looks at me, there's something unspoken in his eyes that makes my breath catch.

"Hey," I whisper, my voice barely audible over the music. *I love you. God, I fucking love you* burns on my tongue, but instead, I say, "I'm really proud of you."

He squeezes my hand, his smile soft and real.

"I'm sorry," I whisper. "For not understanding sooner."

"You have nothing to apologize for, Nora. You've always been there, even when you didn't know it."

Our eyes meet again, electricity crackling between us, but his phone buzzes, shattering the moment. He doesn't reach for it, though, just holds my hand tighter as we drive through the night.

Nate drops me off and hesitates, looking down before meeting my eyes. "I, uh… I've got to take care of something."

I don't ask what—I already know. The girlfriend whose texts are lighting up his phone. I swallow hard and force a smile. He gives me one last look, heavy with unspoken words, then walks back to his car.

I don't know where we stand after today, but one truth rings clear: I was eight when I first felt the flutter of love for him, and now it's carved into my bones. No matter how many walls I build or distances I create, he'll always be the person my eyes search for in every crowded room. His name is written in invisible ink across my heart, appearing only when warmed by his presence.

Some loves are choices. Others are gravity—forces of nature we can resist but never truly escape.

And mine?

Mine has always been Nate Sullivan.

As constant as the bass line in our favorite songs, as inevitable as time itself. I've been orbiting him my entire life, and I'm beginning to understand I might never stop.

Because when all the pretending falls away, when all the anger and hurt dissolve, one truth remains, simple and devastating: it has always been, and will always be, Nate.

CHAPTER 37
RECKONINGS
NATE

When I pull up to Farrah's house, the porch light casts shadows that dance across the weathered steps like warning signs I should leave. It's late—too late for this conversation. But I can't keep living this lie, can't keep pretending what Farrah and I have is anything but poison dressed up as a relationship. My hands tremble on the steering wheel, and I force them still.

The engine dies with a soft whimper, leaving me in silence, broken only by my thundering heartbeat. Each breath feels like borrowed time as I stare at that front door, knowing what waits behind it—the beginning of an end I should've initiated months ago. The walk up the steps feel like crossing a minefield. When Shay answers the door, her eyes narrow with the kind of judgment that comes from watching someone make the same mistakes on repeat. The air around her crackles with unspoken accusations.

"Is Farrah here? I need to talk to her." My voice comes out steadier than I feel, a small victory.

She shrugs, but there's tension in her shoulders as she calls out, "Farrah! It's Nate." The words echo through the house like a death knell.

The rhythmic click of heels against hardwood announces Farrah's descent. She appears at the top of the stairs in one of her signature dresses, the fabric clinging like a second skin. But where I once saw allure, I now see armor—protection against a world she's determined to conquer, no matter the cost.

"Well, look who decided to show up." Her smirk is razor-sharp, cutting through the space between us. "Didn't think I was gonna hear from you tonight. No text, no call."

She moves down the stairs with practiced grace, each step a performance. When she leans in to kiss me, I step back, my hand rising between us like a shield. The gesture feels both defensive and definitive.

"Can we talk? In private?"

Her eyes flash—a predator sensing prey slipping away. "That sounds serious." The mockery in her tone can't quite mask the venom underneath.

My silence answers for me, and I watch as playful contempt morphs into pure fury.

"You think you're breaking up with me?" Her laugh is winter frost creeping across glass—cold, spreading, destructive.

I draw in a breath that tastes like courage.

"I'm not thinking about it. It's official, we're done. Whatever this fucked-up thing between us is needs to stop."

"No." The word drops between us like a gauntlet.

"What do you mean, no?"

Her arms cross, a barrier between us that feels more symbolic than physical. "I mean, no. We're not breaking up, Nate. You don't get to walk away from me. We both decide when this ends, and guess what? It's not over."

My fingers rake through my hair, frustration building like steam in a pressure cooker. "Farrah, this isn't working. We're not good for each other. You've known that for a long time."

She steps closer, and there's something dark swimming in those eyes —something that's always been there, but I've chosen to ignore. "Don't pull that 'we're not good for each other' bullshit. You're always the one that comes crawling back."

"It's not happening," I say, my voice rising with the tide of emotions I've kept bottled up. "I'm done. I don't want this, and I don't want you calling or texting me anymore. It's over."

Her face twists into something cruel, a mask finally slipping to reveal what's always lurked beneath. "You're seriously breaking up with me for that little whore?"

The word ignites something primal inside me. My vision narrows to a tunnel of red, and before I can process the movement, I'm in her space, finger jabbing toward her face like a weapon.

"Don't," I snarl, rage making my voice unrecognizable. "Don't let her name cross your mind or leave your mouth again, do you hear me?"

Farrah doesn't flinch—she never has. Instead, her lips curl into a familiar twisted smile, the one that's always preceded pain. Her head tilts, calculating, like a snake preparing to strike. "You think you can protect her? Or worse, save her? You can't even save yourself. A junkie like you always comes back for another hit. Stop lying to yourself. It's pathetic."

Her words hit their mark with surgical precision, each one a blade sliding between my ribs. But I've spent too long letting her see me bleed. I step back, my breathing harsh in the silence, fists clenched so tight my knuckles ache.

"Not this time," I say, the words carrying the weight of a vow. "It's over, Farrah."

Her laugh follows me out like poison, seeping into my skin even as I walk away. But with each step toward my car, the air feels cleaner, lighter. Nora's image floats through my mind—her genuine smile, the way sunlight catches in her eyes—and it's like a lifeline pulling me toward something better.

THE CAR DOOR SLAMS BEHIND ME WITH A FINALITY THAT FEELS RIGHT. I sink into the seat, releasing a breath that seems to carry years of toxic weight with it. My hands shake as I pull out my phone, but there's purpose in the tremor now. Jay needs to know what's coming—he's the only one who understands the full scope of the Monty situation.

> **Me**
> I'm going to deal with Monty. Once and for all. Then I'm out. For good this time.

The response comes quickly, concern bleeding through the pixels.

> **Jay**
> Wait, what does that mean? When are you planning on executing this little plan of yours?

> **Me**
> Tonight.

> **Jay**
> I'm out of town tonight, just wait till I'm back.
>
> Don't do this alone, man. Monty's dangerous. You know that.

Jay's call lights up my screen, but I let it ring out. His voice of reason would only slow me down, and I can't afford hesitation. Not tonight. Another message flashes.

The truth in those words settles like ice in my stomach. Of course, Monty knows—he's made it his business to know everything about everyone he deals with. But I'm past caring about the risks. Living under his thumb isn't living at all.

Another message.

I toss the phone aside, ignoring its persistent buzz, and start the engine. The old car park behind the abandoned warehouse looms in my mind like a nightmare waiting to happen. I've been there too many times, each visit leaving another scar on my soul. But this time has to be different.

I step out of the car noticing Monty's already there, lounging against a beat-up Chevy like he owns the world. The cherry of his cigarette glows like a demon's eye in the darkness, and his crew lurks in the shadows, patient predators waiting for their cue.

"Preppy," he chuckles, smoke curling from his lips like morning mist. "It's about time."

I approach him with measured steps, forcing my spine straight despite the fear coiling in my gut. The envelope feels heavy in my hand, weighted with desperate hopes of freedom.

"I brought you what I owe you. Plus an extra thousand on top. I'm done, Monty. That's it."

The silence stretches like a rubber band about to snap. For one brief, foolish moment, I think he might take it—might let me walk away. Then his laughter shatters the night, echoing off concrete walls and sending chills down my spine.

257

"You think an extra grand's gonna buy you out?" He pushes off the car, closing the distance between us. His eyes glitter with malice in the dim light. "Sullivan, you've got more money than this pathetic little offering. I mean, doesn't your dad pretty much own the entire town?"

"I don't have anything to do with him." The words taste like ash. "Take the money, Monty."

I barely register the movement before pain explodes in my ribs. The first blow sends me stumbling, and the second drives the air from my lungs in a violent rush. I hit the ground hard, concrete scraping skin from my palms. Then they're on me—a pack of wolves tearing into prey —fists and boots coming from all directions.

Monty's voice cuts through the symphony of pain. "I gave you a lot more credit than you deserved, Preppy. But turns out you're a fucking idiot." His face appears inches from mine, breath hot and reeking of nicotine. "I own your ass now, Sullivan."

I try to push myself up, defiance burning through the pain, but a kick to my ribs sends me sprawling. Stars dance at the edges of my vision, but his next words come through with terrifying clarity.

"Know your place, Preppy, or next time, it'll be your girl who gets it. She's a pretty little brunette you got yourself." The threat slides between my ribs like an ice-cold blade.

How the fuck does he know about Nora?

Rage burns through the fog of pain, but my battered body won't respond. Blood fills my mouth, copper-bright and bitter.

"Stay away from her," I manage to growl, the words more wheeze than threat. "I'll do what you want, just leave her out of it."

Monty towers over me, satisfaction painted across his features.

"I'll be in touch." He pauses, savoring the moment like fine wine. "Watch yourself, kid. You never know who might get hurt. Because someone always does in the end."

It's not a threat—it's a promise.

They leave me there, broken on the concrete like discarded trash. Every breath sends daggers through my chest, but panic drives me to move. My trembling fingers fumble with my phone, muscle memory dialing the one person I trust right now.

Nick answers on the second ring. "Nate?"

"Can I come by and see you?" My voice sounds foreign, scraped raw.

"Is everything all right? Are you all right?"

"If it's too late, I understand—"

"I'll text you my address."

Relief floods through me like morphine.

"I'll be there soon. And Nick?"

"Yeah?"

"Thanks."

"Drive safe. I'll see you in a bit."

Guilt gnaws at me as I end the call. What kind of person shows up at their new boss's door, bleeding and broken? But the alternative—letting Mom see me like this, adding to the weight she already carries—isn't an option.

The stars above blur and swim as I lie there, gathering strength. The pain reminds me of those nights with Scott, taking beatings meant for Mom. It was easier then, becoming the thing they said I was. Fighting felt pointless. But now? The thought of Monty getting anywhere near Nora or Jake sets my blood on fire. I won't let them touch either of them—not ever.

THE DRIVE TO NICK'S PASSES IN A HAZE OF PAIN AND DETERMINATION. BY some miracle, I make it to his driveway without wrapping my car around a pole. He's waiting on the porch, a dark silhouette against warm light. As I step out, the world tilts violently. I hear his voice, panic-edged and distant.

"Shit, Nate! What the hell happened?"

The words dissolve on my tongue as darkness crowds the edges of my vision. The last thing I feel is the ground rushing up to meet me, then nothing but black.

Consciousness returns in fragments—the metallic tang of blood, the sharp sting of sweat in my wounds, Nick's steady hands guiding me to his couch. The TV's flickering light creates ghostly shadows that dance across the walls. Each blink feels like sandpaper against my eyes as I fight to stay awake.

"Nate?" Nick's voice cuts through the fog like a lighthouse beam. "Hey, stay with me, yeah?"

"I'm good. I'm—" The lie dies in my throat. Nothing about this situation even approaches good.

"I'm taking you to the hospital." The determination in his voice jolts me back to full awareness.

"No!" Panic surges through me, temporarily drowning out the pain. "No hospitals. Please."

Nick studies me, concern etching deep lines around his eyes. For a moment, I think he'll ignore my plea, but then he releases a heavy sigh.

"Fine. But you're gonna have to let me at least fix the gash on your head."

I manage a weak nod as I sink deeper into the couch, consciousness wavering like a candle flame in the wind.

"I need you to stay awake, especially if you're carrying a concussion." Nick hands me a bundle of clean clothes and guides me toward the bathroom. "Get cleaned up. I'll get some painkillers."

The bathroom light is merciless, highlighting every cut and bruise in stark detail. Water stings as it hits my face, washing away blood and grime in pink rivulets. When I peel off my shirt, the mirror reveals more than just tonight's damage—it shows a roadmap of old scars, faded silver lines that tell stories I've spent years trying to forget.

Nick's eyes lock onto those scars when I return to the living room, but his expression remains carefully neutral.

"Where'd you get those?" His voice is soft, almost cautious.

"Football. Fights I got into at high school." The lie tastes stale, practiced.

He hands me pills and water without comment, but his silence speaks volumes. We both know I'm full of shit, but he doesn't push. Instead, he settles into the chair across from me, his presence oddly comforting.

"Nate," he says finally. "How did you end up like this tonight?"

I swallow the pills mechanically, years of practice making the action smooth despite my trembling hands. The question hangs in the air like smoke, and I find myself staring at the floor, unable to meet his gaze. The weight in my chest feels heavier than any physical pain.

"I got mixed up with the wrong people a while back," I admit, each word scraping against my throat. "I thought I could handle it. Thought I could find a way out. I was just... trying to fix things, trying to stop letting everyone down."

Nick leans back, something raw and understanding in his expression. "You're not the first person to end up in a mess like that. I've been there. I know what it's like to want to fix things but feel like you're in too deep."

The weariness in his voice makes me look up, surprising me with its honesty.

"When I was your age," he continues, "I got caught up in my own shit too. Thought I could save my brother from the mess he got himself into with drugs and bad people. But I couldn't. He OD'd, and I couldn't do a damn thing about it."

The clock on the wall ticks steadily, marking the weight of his words. The pain behind them feels tangible, like another presence in the room.

"And after he died..." Nick swallows hard, his gaze distant. "I drank myself stupid. I didn't care what happened to me. I'd lost my brother, the only person who hadn't abandoned me, and it felt like I'd lost everything." His voice cracks, revealing the wound that's never fully healed. "He was my kid brother who made a couple of bad decisions with the wrong people, and the price he paid for it was his life."

The silence that follows feels sacred, heavy with shared understanding. I recognize the guilt in his eyes—it's the same one I see in the mirror every morning.

"I haven't touched a drink since the night I drove home drunk," Nick continues softly. "I almost killed a mother and her daughter coming home from the movies." His head drops, shoulders heavy with the memory. "Sometimes I think that I haven't allowed myself to fully move on either. Haven't let anyone close enough because I didn't think I deserved it after that."

His words hit too close to home—echoing my own reasons for keeping Nora at arm's length, for believing I don't deserve her light in my darkness.

"I'm sorry," I murmur, though the words feel inadequate.

"For what?"

"Calling you and showing up like this. I understand if—"

Nick shakes his head, a sad smile playing at his lips. "I'm glad you called and showed up here. Don't apologize."

The silence that follows feels different, lighter somehow, like we've both set down weights we've been carrying too long.

"I do wish you'd let me take you to the hospital though. Just to be safe that there aren't any serious injuries."

"No hospitals. I—" The words catch in my throat. I can't explain about the broken bones that never healed right, the scars that tell stories I'm not ready to share, the questions that would lead to truths I've buried deep.

"Could you, uh, could you drop me home?" I ask after a while. "I can pick up my car in the morning, but if I'm not home, my mom's gonna ask questions and—"

Nick's dry chuckle cuts me off. "Unless you've got a hidden talent for makeup, she's gonna take one look at your face and know something's up."

"Yeah, probably," I admit, wincing as I shift position.

He stands, grabbing his keys from the table. At the door, he pauses, looking back at me with an intensity that makes me want to shrink away.

"You're a good kid, Nate. You've got a big heart. Don't lose sight of that, no matter what."

The words settle over me, warm and unexpected. For a moment, I feel the weight of my father's shadow lift—just enough to let in light. Maybe there's a version of me that isn't destined to destroy everything he touches. Maybe there's a version that deserves her.

For the first time tonight, I feel something close to the hope Nora spoke about—fragile as a bird's wing, but there, beating against my ribs, refusing to die.

CHAPTER 38
JUST LIKE OLD TIMES
NORA

THE MOONLIGHT SPILLS ACROSS THE ROOF AS I CLIMB THROUGH THE window, each movement deliberate and familiar. I've made this climb a hundred times before, but tonight feels different, heavier somehow, as if the very air knows something's about to change.

Jake sits at the edge of the roof, a silhouette carved against the star-studded sky. His lighter brown hair catches the silvery glow, and for a moment, I see both versions of him—the boy who used to count stars with me and the man he's becoming. The moonlight traces the sharp line of his jaw, the solid breadth of his shoulders pulling against his shirt fabric. My heart stutters, caught between memory and present.

"Hi," I breathe, the word barely disturbing the night's quiet.

He doesn't turn, but I catch the slight tension in his shoulders, the way his head dips in acknowledgment.

"Want some company?" The question hangs between us, fragile as spun glass.

His sigh whispers across the space between us, heavy with unspoken words.

"Sure." It's automatic, like muscle memory, but I'm already moving toward him before he can reconsider. The roof tiles are cool beneath my palms as I settle beside him, close enough to feel his warmth but not quite touching.

"How'd you know I was out here?" The roughness in his voice matches the gravel beneath our feet.

"Hard to forget all the nights we spent up here." I smile softly, memories floating up like autumn leaves. "Plus, this is still your thinking spot."

Silence stretches between us as the lake below ripples silver-black, keeping time with our quiet breaths. Back when we were kids, this silence felt like home. Now it holds the weight of everything we're not saying.

"So, whatcha thinking about?" I nudge his shoulder gently, trying to bridge the gap.

He exhales, long and deep, like he's trying to empty himself of something heavy.

"How the nights we spent out here were some of my happiest memories as kids." The words catch slightly, snagged on something raw.

My chest tightens. "Are you okay?"

"Yeah. Fine."

"How was your day?" I try again, gentler this time.

"It was good." His jaw tightens slightly. "Yours?"

"It was nice." The truth sits on my tongue like honey, sweet but sticky with complexity.

He turns then, ocean-blue eyes catching moonlight, and something in my chest aches at how familiar and foreign he looks all at once.

"What did you get up to?"

The truth pushes against my teeth. "Nate wanted to take the boat out on the water." Heat creeps up my neck, and I swallow the almost-kiss that still burns on my lips. "What about you?"

Jake's expression shifts, shadows deepening around his mouth. "I saw my dad."

The words hit like ice water. Scott's presence in town sets off warning bells, Nate's stories echoing in my mind like ghost stories.

"Your dad?" My voice wavers, uncertain.

"He wanted to see me for my birthday." Jake's words trail off like smoke. "He, uhh... he offered me a position at the company next year."

My heart races, torn between loyalty to Nate's warnings and Jake's obvious need for connection. "Are you considering it?"

"It's a good opportunity." Defensiveness edges his voice like thorns. "I'd be stupid not to consider it."

"But what about Duke and the scholarship?" The words tumble out before I can catch them.

"I'm not aiming for an Olympic gold medal, Nor, and I was going to study business anyway. This is a chance to make something of myself." There's an edge to his voice that wasn't there before, sharp with determination or desperation—I can't tell which.

"But working for your dad... is that really what you want?"

"You sound like Nate." The words slice through the air between us. I flinch, and his expression softens immediately. "Sorry, it's just—"

"It's okay," I cut in, though the air thrums with tension. "I just want to make sure it's your choice."

His gaze softens, vulnerability bleeding through. "It's a big opportunity. I never considered it before because I thought Nate would be the first choice... but Dad thinks I'm better suited to one day take over the family business."

The weight of Nate's secrets presses against my chest, but I swallow them back. Instead, I reach behind me, pulling out my peace offering.

"I have something for you." I present the small scrapbook, our memories bound in paper and ink. "Happy birthday."

His fingers trace the pages reverently, a genuine smile breaking through like sunrise.

"This is amazing," he murmurs, voice warm with appreciation.

I rest my head against his shoulder, breathing in the familiar scent of him. "We'll always have these memories."

He leans into me, and for a moment, we're kids again, safe in our rooftop sanctuary, where the world can't touch us.

Mom's voice drifts up, breaking the spell. Jake chuckles softly, his arm brushing mine as we stand.

"Guess we'd better head down," he says, smiling gently.

"Yeah," I reply, but part of me stays behind, tangled in the space between who we were and who we're becoming.

CHAPTER 39
PARALLEL LINES
NATE

THE ENGINE'S RUMBLE FADES INTO THE NIGHT AS NICK'S CAR DISAPPEARS, leaving me alone with my thoughts and the familiar ache of fresh bruises. The walk to the front door feels endless, each step a reminder of tonight's shitshow. Farrah might be out of the picture now, but that victory tastes hollow, mixing with the copper tang of blood in my mouth and the growing dread in my gut.

The house stands silent at 1 AM, as I drag myself up the stairs, biting back groans with each step, until a soft glow catches my eye. It's coming from Nora's room. The light spills into the hallway like a beacon, and something inside me shifts, yearns. The memory of her comfort from the last night pulls at me with gravitational force, but I resist. She doesn't need to see me like this—another reminder of how I'm the black hole in her orbit, threatening to pull her into the darkness.

Just as I turn away, the bathroom door opens. Nora steps out wearing those damned pajama shorts that make my throat go dry, her legs endless in the dim light. My body responds instantly, a pavlovian reaction I can't control. Our eyes lock, and the concern that floods her expression hits harder than any punch I took tonight.

"Nate, what happened?" Her voice wraps around me like silk, soft and strong all at once.

She moves closer, and I'm frozen in place as her fingers trace the tender skin around my eye. The gentleness of her touch burns more than the bruise itself. When her hand finds mine, the air between us grows thick with unspoken words. Her thumb grazes my split knuckles, and suddenly breathing becomes a conscious effort.

"A little altercation but I'm okay." The lie tastes bitter.

"You're either completely delusional or just stupid."

Both.

"I should—" I try to pull away, though it feels like ripping open a wound. "You should get some sleep."

But she steps closer, her presence magnetic.

"Come with me." She takes my hand again, and the universe clicks back into place. I want to resist—should resist—but I never could when it comes to her. She leads me into her room like she has countless times before, her warm grip the only thing keeping me anchored to reality.

"Sit," she commands, though there's a tenderness in her tone that makes it feel like coming home.

I sink onto her bed's edge, trying to ignore how my skin burns where her fingers brushed. "Now what?" I manage, raising an eyebrow despite the ache.

Her smile lights up the room. "Stay here."

"What am I, a dog?"

She pauses at the doorway, throwing a glance over her shoulder that makes my heart stutter. "Dogs actually listen."

When she returns with the first aid kit, I force a laugh that sends pain shooting through my ribs.

"I'm fine, Len, seriously." It's another lie—the painkillers have worn off, my head wound has bled through Nick's amateur bandaging, and my ribs feel like shattered glass under my skin.

She steps between my knees, the proximity sending electricity through my veins. The heat of her body radiates against mine, and I'm drowning in everything that is her.

"I'm glad you're not being a broody asshole for once. Stay still."

I obey because denying her anything feels impossible. Her fingers work with practiced care, cleaning the gash on my temple. The antiseptic stings, but it's nothing compared to how she cradles my face.

"You know you don't have to pretend with me," she murmurs, her words carrying the weight of years of shared history. "What happened?"

I try to look away, rubbing my jaw to hide the tremor in my hands. "Nothing you need to worry about."

Her hands capture my face, forcing our eyes to meet. "Well, your face says otherwise. Now hold still so I don't get this in your eye."

Her touch holds me steady, keeping the pieces of me from scattering into the darkness. Without conscious thought, my hands find her hips, drawing her closer until our breaths synchronize. Her thighs brush against mine, and the contact sends sparks through my entire body.

"That better?" My voice comes out rough, revealing more than I intend.

Her smile holds secrets I'm afraid to decode. "You tell me."

I can't tell her anything. Can't tell her how close I am to shattering, how much I want to lose myself in her. She tends to my wounds with the same care she's always shown, and I catch her hand as she pulls away.

"This is kinda our thing, isn't it?"

"What?"

"You fixing me."

"You don't need to be fixed, Nate. Patched up every now and then, maybe."

The laugh I let out feels like knives in my chest. I meet her gaze, holding it steady. "Thank you. For always fixing me anyway."

"Nate..." The way she says my name holds a universe of questions.

"It's all good." The words taste like ash.

"That's not an answer." Her tone is gentle but leaves no room for escape, and it kills me how much she still cares after everything.

"Len, it's nothing you need to worry about. I have it handled." The lie sits heavy between us, because I'm not sure I have anything handled anymore.

"Are you okay, Nate? And I mean, are you really okay?"

The question echoes in the hollow spaces inside me.

"This really does feel like old times," I say instead, though I'm not sure which times I mean—the innocent closeness of our youth or the darker moments when she'd patch me up after Scott's rages.

She looks away, and suddenly I'm desperate for her attention. "You're changing the subject," she points out.

I manage a ghost of my usual grin. "I am, but it's true, isn't it?"

"I hate seeing you like this." I can see beyond her sad eyes that she'd hoped things would be different.

Hope.

That fucking word.

It's a luxury I never could afford. Growing up the way I did, reality became my closest companion.

My hand moves of its own accord to her neck, freeing her hair from its bun. Dark waves cascade down, framing her face like a painting I want to memorize.

"I like your hair down," I whisper, watching color bloom across her cheeks. Nothing in this world compares to her beauty in this moment. Our fingers intertwine, and I can't look away from where we're connected.

268

"Thank you," I murmur, the words carrying the weight of years.

"I'll send you the bill via email," she jokes, and I'm laughing—really laughing—despite the pain it causes.

When our eyes meet again, she's looking at me like she can see past every wall I've built.

"What?" I ask, feeling exposed.

"Nothing," she says softly. "It's just... I haven't heard you laugh like that in a long time."

Her smile breaks through the darkness surrounding my heart. The urge to kiss her, to pour every unspoken feeling into action, nearly overwhelms me. How do you explain to someone that they make your soul feel like colliding galaxies?

"Do you want to listen to music?" she offers, but I shake my head.

"Not tonight." I lean closer, my voice dropping to match the intimacy of the moment. "I just want this." I ease back onto her bed, drawing her with me. She settles against my chest, her arms around my waist, and I run my fingers through her hair, knowing it soothes us both.

"It's finally stopped," I say after a while.

"What's stopped?"

"The noise. In my head."

We lay in comfortable silence, this moment of peace worth every ache in my body. She traces gentle fingers over my face, and I stare at her like I'm seeing her for the first time all over again.

"I miss this," I confess, barely audible, half delusional from the concussion.

"Miss what?"

"Us."

The admission hangs in the air between us, but her response is immediate, sure.

"Nate, I never left."

This is intimacy in its purest form—the ability to be completely bare, showing every scar and shadow, knowing you won't be turned away. But Nora and I, we're like parallel lines, destined to run alongside each other without ever truly meeting. She softens my edges in ways I never thought possible and all it takes is just a glance from those bright green eyes.

Before her, I believed I was impossible to love. She makes it look effortless, loving me despite every attempt I make to push her away. I can't pinpoint when I fell in love with her. It happened gradually, like watching the tide come in, until suddenly I was drowning.

Being this close to her is dangerous, addictive. But addiction is a monster that lurks in darkness, waiting to strike. This girl is more potent than any drug I've known, because nothing else comes close to the high of being near her. Like any addict, I can't resist the urge to stay close, to let her touch quiet the chaos inside me.

When she tightens her hold and whispers, "Stay," I know I shouldn't.

She's an addiction I can't kick, one I'm not sure I want to. Every cell in my body craves her presence. I settle beside her, holding her close, pretending this moment won't have to end.

"I'm here, Nate," she whispers into the darkness.

For the first time in forever, I let myself believe it.

CHAPTER 40
FRONT ROW SEATS TO THE SHIT SHOW
NORA

FOR THE SECOND TIME THIS SUMMER, NATE HAS FOUND HIS WAY INTO MY bed. His muscular body curves around mine like a shield, his breathing evening out as peace finally claims him. Though I can't see his face because I'm pressed against his chest, I feel the weight of exhaustion in his limbs, the way tension bleeds from him with each breath.

"Leni?" His voice carries a rare vulnerability, almost childlike.

"Yeah?"

"You're my favorite," he breathes, arms tightening around me like I might disappear.

"Favorite what?" I whisper, smiling against his warm skin.

A low hum vibrates through his chest as sleep begins to claim him. "Everything," he murmurs, grip steady around my waist.

I tilt my head up to find his eyes closed, features softened by approaching dreams. My fingers find their way to his hair instinctively, threading through dark strands in a soothing rhythm. The intimacy should frighten me, but instead it feels like coming home.

Our shared past pulses between us as I hold onto him, protecting him like I did when we were just kids—when he was simply a boy desperate to be seen. My cheek rests against him, catching the steady rhythm of his breath as it slows, the storm inside him quieting beneath my touch.

This is my Nate.

Not the hardened shell he presents to the world, but the boy—raw, real, and recklessly beautiful in his imperfections. My heart aches with the weight of this truth: loving him isn't a choice, it's as natural as breathing.

"Don't leave me," he whispers, voice raw with a desperation he shows no one else. Each word is a plea woven with vulnerability that cuts straight to my core.

"I wasn't planning on it," I murmur back, emotion thick in my throat. Sleep finally takes him completely. I could stay suspended here forever, lost in our private infinity where need flows both ways, where we don't complete each other but elevate one another instead. But that's exactly what terrifies me most. I would walk through fire for Nate Sullivan, shield his heart with my own, regardless of how many pieces mine might shatter into. I just pray I'm strong enough to weather the breaking.

MORNING LIGHT PAINTS GOLDEN STRIPES ACROSS THE ROOM AS consciousness finds me. There's solid warmth pressed against my back—Nate, his arm still claiming my waist, his body hard and unyielding against mine. My heart stutters, panic rising swift and sharp in my chest.

How the hell am I supposed to extract myself from this?

I attempt to shift, gently working to loosen his hold, but he only draws me closer in sleep, grip tightening possessively. I freeze, trying to quiet the whirlwind of thoughts swirling through my mind. He misses us.

But which version of 'us' does he miss? His admission lingers, igniting something deep inside that I can't keep ignoring.

When he stirs slightly, I seize my chance. I wiggle free with careful movements, heart thundering as I rise from the bed as silently as possible.

I need air.

I grab my running shoes and flee into the early morning, desperate to clear my head.

The crisp morning air bites at my exposed skin as I weave through empty streets, thoughts racing faster than my feet can carry me. Last night's revelations tangle with Scott's unsettling offer to Jake, I feel complete and utter guilt gnawing at me for keeping Nate in the dark. While the guilt eats away my gut, my mind spins with unanswered questions:

Where did Nate go after Farrah's frantic texts?

Why did he come home looking like he'd just been to war?

Why would Jake be willing to throw away his hard-earned scholarship for Scott's hollow promises?

And why doesn't Nate finally tell him the truth about his dad?

My chest tightens with fierce protectiveness, especially for Nate. I saw it clearly last night—the bone-deep sadness, the raw hunger to be enough for someone. That's what breaks my heart the most: he believes he's unworthy of love.

No one seems to be awake when I get home. Upstairs, I push open my bedroom door to find Nate gone, the bed neatly made. The only trace he was ever here is Bones, perched on my pillow like a silent guardian.

A knock interrupts my thoughts. Jake stands in the doorway, wearing an unusually bright smile.

"Nice run?" He steps inside, settling onto the bed.

I manage a smile in return. "It was."

"So, I know it's not your birthday today, but I've got something for you," he announces, producing a small box from his pocket. "Thought maybe you could wear it today."

Curiosity piques as I accept the box. Inside, nestled in velvet, rests a delicate gold necklace with a charm that pulls a laugh from me—a tiny golden whale. He remembers my obsession with whales, how I've dragged him through countless National Geographic documentaries about them, always dissolving into tears when mother and calf are separated.

"I still think you're the only person who doesn't cry at 'The Notebook' but loses it during whale documentaries," he teases.

My heart swells—not from the gift's value, but because he remembers these small details about me.

"I love it," I whisper, fingers tracing the charm. "Thank you."

"Here, let me help you put it on." Jake's hands work the clasp, but linger longer than necessary at my neck. There's an odd tension as he watches me through the mirror.

"Beautiful," he whispers, too close to my ear.

"We should, um... check if the moms need help downstairs."

I hurry toward the stairs, trying to shake off the strange moment.

The house thrums with celebration, every sense awakening to Lydia's masterpiece. Fresh-cut roses and lilies perfume the air, their sweetness mingling with the warm, decadent scent of cinnamon and vanilla wafting from towers of Cinnabons—Lydia must have cleared out the entire bakery this morning. The backyard has transformed into something from a magazine spread: crystal-clear mason jars filled with fairy lights dot the perfectly manicured lawn, while delicate white string lights weave through the trees.

Even the placement of each fork and napkin feels intentional, precise. Jake and I have always shared our birthdays and Lydia always made a big deal over it. But this year, she's outdone herself. She's been up since the crack of dawn, directing her small army of helpers with military preci-sion—adjusting centerpieces, rearranging chair formations, and fussing over every detail until it's perfect.

I catch her straightening a slightly crooked place card, and can't help but smile.

"That woman is like a bullet train. Does she even have an off switch?" Ollie grumbles, snagging a muffin while dodging Lydia's eagle eye.

I laugh, leaning against the doorframe. "Not when it comes to parties. You know how she gets."

Ollie shakes his head, cramming the muffin in his mouth. His gaze drifts to where Mia, Camilla, and Marcus are arriving. I watch the awkward dance between Mia and my brother as they hug—a gesture that reveals more than words ever could. Their connection is obvious, even if they haven't made it official. Warmth blooms in my chest watching them. It's been too long since I've seen Ollie this light, this present. But with Mia, something in him has reawakened.

"Hey, birthday girl," Mia greets me with a grin and quick hug.

"Glad you could make it." I squeeze her back.

"As if we'd miss this," Camilla gestures around, wide-eyed at the fairy-tale setting.

"That's Lydia for you," I shrug.

As afternoon deepens, the party gains momentum. Laughter and conversation wrap around me like a comfortable blanket, but something feels off. Jake keeps checking his phone, distracted, waiting for some-thing—or someone. It's subtle, but I've known him my whole life. I can read the tension in his shoulders.

Then the doorbell rings.

Jake jumps up, too quickly, muttering about answering it. Lydia glances at Mom, brow furrowed.

"I thought everyone was here?"

Unease coils in my stomach as Jake disappears inside. When I see who stands on the porch, my heart plummets.

Scott Sullivan.

Jake stands beside his father, their features suddenly mirror images. I haven't seen Scott in over two years, and he was never a welcome sight even then. Horror dawns on Lydia's face—she had no idea he was coming.

Which means neither does Nate.

Shit.

"Quite the party you've thrown, Lydia." Scott gestures around before kissing his wife's cheek. Her body goes rigid, a reaction I recognize all too well, though I wish I didn't.

"Scott, I... I thought you were in London."

"Wanted to surprise my boy for his birthday. That okay with you?"

Lydia nods with a forced smile that screams 'absolutely not okay.'

"Can I speak to you inside Scott, please?"

"Sure." His smile is cold, calculated, hiding secrets. "Kat, so sorry to hear about David. He was a good man. And Lenora, happy birthday."

Mom acknowledges his condolences with quiet grace.

Jake returns to our table, and I can't help asking, "Does Nate know your dad is here?"

His expression darkens instantly. "Why does it always have to be about Nate? Can't I invite my own dad to my birthday without him acting out?"

The words sting, but I can't focus on that now. My mind races. Nate's still at Sonder with Nick—he should have been back hours ago. My pulse quickens as I dial his number. One ring, then straight to voicemail.

"You okay?" Marcus leans in, concerned.

I fight to keep my voice steady as I turn to him and Camilla. "Nate doesn't know Scott's here. This... this could be bad. Really bad."

Marcus frowns. "Why?"

"Nate and his dad—it's complicated," I struggle to explain. "Their relationship has been broken for years. Nate's been through hell because of him. If he walks into this unprepared..."

"Glad I'm not the only one with daddy issues," Camilla jokes, trying to lighten the mood.

Marcus and Mia exchange worried looks.

"Want us to try calling him?" Camilla offers gently.

Before I can answer, the front door opens. I would know Nate's voice anywhere. He enters alongside Nick, expression neutral at first, until his eyes land on Scott. The air seems to vanish from the space around us. His entire body transforms, tensing for battle. His face hardens, eyes narrowing, and the vulnerable boy from last night disappears, replaced by someone I barely recognize—someone with hatred burning in his eyes.

I stand frozen, watching the storm gather in his expression.

My heart splinters.

All I want is to grab his hand and run. Run far from here. This look in his eyes now—this is why Nate hates his father. This is the part of him I couldn't fully grasp until yesterday, when he finally let me see behind his walls. Scott paces toward where Nate and Nick stand, each step deliberate and casual, as if he hasn't just walked straight into a minefield. The tension radiating off Nate is almost visible, like heat waves distorting summer air.

"Hello, son," Scott says, his voice strained as he tests the waters, softening the blow with that word—'son'—as if it still means something between them. As if he has any right to claim it.

Nate doesn't respond.

His fists clench at his sides, knuckles turning bone white beneath tanned skin. His breathing comes shallow and quick, like he's holding onto control by the thinnest thread. I can almost see it fraying.

"Nate?" I call softly, taking a step toward him, my heart pounding so loud I can barely hear myself.

His face is etched with a pain that makes my chest ache, eyes darkening as if the shadows inside him are growing, threatening to consume everything soft and vulnerable I'd held in my arms last night. I want to throw myself between him and this moment, protect him from it, but I know that won't be enough. Nothing ever is when it comes to Scott.

"Nora, don't," Jake mutters under his breath, suddenly beside me. His voice is tight, frustration simmering beneath the surface. "He's fine. He just needs to calm down."

But Nate isn't fine. He's anything but. His whole body is wound tight, like a bomb ready to explode, and I can almost hear the fuse sizzling down.

Scott shifts his attention to Lydia, deliberately ignoring the ticking bomb in front of him. "I was just about to speak to your mother," he says, his tone too familiar, too dismissive. The audacity of it makes my skin crawl.

"You lost the fucking right to speak to her a long time ago." The icy tone in Nate's voice and the intensity of his gaze was a look that could kill. Right now, Nate was contemplating acting on his anger.

Lydia's eyes narrow, noticing too that Nate was on the brink of losing his self-control. "Scott, I think it's time for you to leave."

"What? Why?" Jake cuts in, disbelief clear in his voice, still that little boy desperate for his father's attention.

"Jake, it's fine. I have some business to attend to while I'm here. Thanks for the invite, champ," Scott says, clapping Jake's shoulder in that fake, fatherly way that makes it look well-rehearsed.

I catch the flicker of hurt in Nate's eyes—that split-second tell that says he's used to this. Used to being second-best. Used to watching his father choose Jake, over and over, while pretending it doesn't cut him to the bone.

Nate's entire body goes rigid beside me. The muscles in his jaw work beneath his skin, and I practically hear his teeth grinding. His eyes, when they flick between Jake and Scott, hold something dangerous—a mix of betrayal and dawning realization.

Jake's expression hardens.

"Today of all days, you just had to be a dick. Couldn't let me have just one fucking day. No. Because everything is about Nate. Can't we do anything anymore without you turning it into some fucking drama?"

"Jacob!" Lydia's sharp voice cuts through the tension. She steps between them, every inch the protective mother, but I see the strain around her eyes. "You should have told me you were inviting your father."

"Why wouldn't I invite my own dad to my birthday?" Jake's voice rises, anger and hurt bleeding together. "He's your husband for Christ's sake! You're always saying he's never around, and now you're kicking him out because golden boy here can't handle—"

"Fuck you, Jake." Nate's words come out as a growl, vibrating with barely contained fury.

"No, fuck you," Jake fires back, face flushed. "I'm so sick of your shit, Nate. Everything always has to revolve around your damage, your issues. God forbid anyone—"

"Boys, enough!" Lydia's voice cracks like a whip, but the damage is already done. I see it in the way Nate's shoulders bunch, in the dangerous stillness that settles over him.

I reach for his hand, desperate to calm him, to pull him back from whatever edge he's approaching. His fingers twitch against mine, and for a moment—just a heartbeat—I feel him soften. But then he lets go and storms after Scott.

I can't let him do this on his own, so I follow him.

It's Nate's voice I hear first as I round the corner to the front door.

"You've got some fucking nerve showing up here," Nate spits, voice dripping venom.

"Calm down," Scott dismisses, as if Nate's fury is merely childish rebellion.

"Don't fucking tell me to calm down," Nate snaps, barely containing his rage.

"Watch your tone, boy," Scott growls, advancing on Nate. "We both know what happens when that smart mouth runs. Don't forget whose house you're still under."

Nate's fists clench tighter, knuckles white with strain. He gestures violently toward the house. "You think I give a fuck about any of this? Your money? Your name? It means nothing to me." His voice cracks with years of accumulated pain. Scott laughs, cold and bitter, the sound like ice cracking.

"Spoon-fed your whole life, and you still don't appreciate what I've done for you. You're exactly like your mother."

I see the exact moment something fundamental breaks in Nate—a fault line finally giving way. His eyes darken to obsidian, holding years of repressed pain and rage. He's on Scott in an instant, pushing him back, every muscle coiled with barely contained violence. When he speaks, his voice is raw, stripped of everything but pure, distilled fury.

"What you've done?" The words tear from his throat like they're ripping him apart. "All you've fucking done is destroy this family. Destroyed her." His voice cracks on 'her,' and the sound splinters something in my chest.

"You're a coward, a piece of shit who can't own up to anything. So you know what? Burn it all to the ground. Or better yet, watch me do it for you."

Scott's face hardens into something brutal. "You ungrateful little cunt," he growls, grabbing Nate's shirt with a savagery that makes my blood freeze.

I move before I can think, instinct driving me between them.

"Hey!" My voice cuts through the tension like a blade.

They both turn to look at me, and the contrast is stark. Scott's expression is unreadable, a mask of cold indifference, but Nate—God, Nate's face is an open wound. Anger twists with something deeper, more vulnerable. Pain, maybe. Or shame. The kind that comes from having your deepest fears confirmed in front of everyone you love.

Scott releases Nate's shirt with deliberate slowness, smoothing the wrinkles as if this were nothing more than a minor disagreement. His eyes, when they meet Nate's, hold nothing but contempt.

"I should have given you up when I had the chance," he mutters, the words precise and purposeful, designed to draw blood.

Then he's striding to his Porsche, gravel crunching under expensive shoes. The engine roars to life, and he peels away without a backward glance, leaving nothing but dust and devastation in his wake.

"Nate," I call out, my voice catching on his name. I reach for him, but he's already retreating, building walls I can almost see materializing around him.

He shakes his head, and when he speaks, his voice is stripped raw, barely holding together.

"Nora, don't. Please... just don't. Not right now. I need... I just need to be alone."

278

The words hit me like a physical blow. I watch him turn away, each step widening the chasm between us. His shoulders are rigid with tension, but I catch the slight tremor in his hands—the only visible sign of how deeply Scott's words cut.

The space he leaves behind feels charged with hurt and shattered possibilities. The contrast between this Nate and the one who held me last night, who whispered vulnerabilities against my skin, makes my chest ache. I want to run after him, to remind him that he's more than Scott's poisonous words, more than the damage his father inflicts.

But I stay, understanding with crushing clarity that sometimes love means knowing when to let someone bleed in peace.

Even if every instinct screams to stem the flow.

CHAPTER 41
NORA'S MIXTAPE #17
NATE

SCOTT'S WORDS DETONATE LIKE GRENADES IN MY HEAD. I'M USED TO MY father's usual arsenal—useless, fuck up—but what destroys me is his final blow before Nora interrupted.

"You're exactly like your mother. I should have given you away when I had the chance."

Molten rage courses through my veins as I storm to the boat shed, each step weighted with years of accumulated pain. The world constricts around me, familiar panic clawing at my chest. My lungs forget how to work, my heart is like a wild animal trying to break free of my ribcage. The boat shed walls press in, suffocating me with memories I can't outrun.

Too tight.

Too fucking tight.

I demolish the nearest object—an old toolbox—sending bits of metal and plastic flying. Blood wells from where steel slices my hand, but even that sharp sting can't silence the war zone in my head.

I need something.

I need out.

I need release.

The bags of pills—oxycodone and opioids I'd had stashed in the boat-shed weeks ago—mock me from the table. They whisper an old truth: once an addict, always an addict. Once a fuck up, always a fuck up.

I'm dancing with the devil, both in my mind and in those small white capsules that promise oblivion. My hands tremble as I run them through my hair, desperately seeking stability in reality. The demon inside me pirouettes on the edge of my sanity, every fiber of my being craving that chemical silence.

One second is all it would take.

One moment of stillness.

One breath where my mind isn't a battlefield.

The truth cuts deeper than any blade—I don't chase these pills for pleasure anymore. It's pure survival, a desperate attempt to numb the chaos. The addiction coils around me like a serpent, promising peace.

"Don't do it, Nate."

Nora's voice slices through the storm like a lighthouse beam. My knuckles whiten against the table's edge, shame burning through me.

"I told you I needed to be alone." My voice is fragile.

"No." Her response is steel wrapped in silk.

I can't face her, but her reflection in the window haunts me—a silhouette of salvation I don't deserve.

"I need you to come back," she whispers, words threading through my madness.

"I'm not going back to that fucking house."

"No." Her presence warms my back. "I need you to come back to me, Nate."

I shut my eyes, her words hitting like a physical force. "I can't beat this fucking devil in my head, Nora," I confess, barely above a whisper. "I can't—"

"I know."

"I'm no good for you."

"I know."

Her acceptance unravels me.

"Then why won't you just walk away?" My voice cracks as I turn to face her, terrified of what I'll see. But her eyes—a mesmerizing kaleidoscope of green that words can't capture—hold only warmth.

"Because I know you believe those things, Nate," she says softly. "But I don't."

She closes the distance between us, her touch igniting every nerve ending when her hand finds my arm. My pulse thunders, electricity crackling beneath my skin where we connect.

"I'm here," she murmurs, steady as a heartbeat. "I just need you to come back and be here with me too. Can you do that?"

"Nora, I—"

"You know what I think the devil is?" she asks, surprising me.

"What?"

Her hand cups my face, her eyes pierce through my walls, seeing straight to the broken pieces I try to hide.

"I think he's just a fallen angel in pain," she whispers. "A lost boy trying to find his place in the world. His home."

The universe shifts in that moment, reality bending around her words. I realize then I would love her in every lifetime—my atoms could scatter across galaxies, and they'd still spell her name in stardust. I'd always searched for someone to look at my darkness and still choose to stay. Here she stands, seeing all of me and refusing to look away.

"Nora..." Her name catches in my throat, heavy with so many unspoken truths.

"I told you, you don't have to do this alone anymore." Our bodies press together, gravity drawing us closer. "I got you," she murmurs, cradling my face. "Every part of you."

I lean in, expecting her retreat. "I'm not strong enough to walk away right now, so if you tell me to leave, then I'll go. But if you don't, then I won't be sorry for what I'm about to do next."

Her answer comes in the form of a kiss—soft at first, then igniting.

"Stay," she breathes against my mouth.

She's my worst fucking addiction.

I recognize it in every tingling nerve ending, every fixated thought. Wanting her is pure compulsion, raw need. Guilt wars with desire as I back her onto the workbench, hands pushing her dress up to grip the soft curves of her thighs. Her whimper shoots straight through me as I explore her mouth, tasting sweetness that puts honey to shame. Her kiss is shy but electric, setting my blood on fire in ways no one else ever has. Her body presses against mine, drawing out a groan as I pull her closer, fingers threading through silken hair that smells of vanilla and summer promises.

One second.

That's all it took for everything to change.

One second to come alive again.

One second to fall even harder for the girl who's held my heart hostage since we were kids.

"Your heart is beating so fast." She smirks against my lips. "Do I make you nervous, Nate?"

"Yeah," I admit. "You do."

Her laugh is pure music, melting my defenses. I kiss her again, pouring everything I've never said into her before slowly pulling away, letting the taste of her linger on my lips.

"Sometimes I don't know how to be in the same space with you."

"Why?"

"You make me feel," I confess rawly. "Everything. All at once. You make me feel better, and I'm not sure if I'm allowed to feel better. When I find what I want, I fucking drown in it." The truth burns my throat. "I can't do that with you. I can't drown you in my shit."

Her eyes soften like morning light. "You're right. You do drown in the things you want. You always have. But you want to know what I think? Someone who gets their addictions confused with a true need to feel things. That energy, that passion, it's yours to own, not the substances around you. When you love, you love hard. That fire inside you, Nate... it's you."

She retrieves the pills from the table, and shame threatens to swallow me whole.

"This," she holds up the bags, "this isn't you. Fight me on it all you want, but your walls are useless when I've seen the parts of you the rest of the world doesn't see. So, no. I won't walk away. And no, you won't be doing this on your own anymore. And no, the devil doesn't get to win this time."

She stands close enough that I can map every shade of green in her eyes—emerald, sage, olive, moss, mint—all swirling with intensity that steals my breath. A glance becomes an intimate exchange, a peek through the keyhole of someone's world into a vault containing everything they are. Their vulnerability, pain, vitality, power.

"Your demons don't scare me, Nate."

Our hands intertwine, and the universe tips sideways. It's more than touch—it's collision, sending shockwaves through my system. Her skin against mine feels like fate, like no matter how broken the path, we were always meant to find each other.

Again and again and again.

"Want to get out of here?" My voice comes out rough with need.

She hesitates, eyes darting between me and the evidence of my almost-breakdown, before nodding. I grab the bags of pills and hand them to her.

"Thank you."

"For what?"

"For saving me from myself."

Again.

THE MUSTANG'S ENGINE RUMBLES THROUGH THE NIGHT, A STEADY

heartbeat beneath our unspoken words. The pull between us is magnetic, impossible to ignore.

"I have your birthday present," I say softly when we stop.

"Nate, you didn't have to—"

"It's nothing, really. Just... close your eyes. Hold out your hands."

She complies, trust written in every line of her body. My heart stumbles at the sight—her vulnerability is a gift I'm not sure I deserve. I place the CD in her waiting hands.

"Nora's Mixtape #17," she reads, her smile blooming like sunrise. "I can't believe you remembered."

Her fingers trace the handwritten track list. Since we were six, this has been our tradition—me capturing our summer in songs, curating melodies that preserved our moments together. More often than not, the music said what I couldn't.

"Nora, I remember everything about us."

She puts the CD in and hits play. Aerosmith's *"Angel"* fills the car with guitar riffs slow as heartbeats. While Steven Tyler's raw voice pours emotion into the space between us, each note draws us closer, binding us together in ways that feel inevitable. Her soft sigh catches in my chest.

"This," she smiles.

"Is your favorite song?"

Her smile softens, and something cracks open inside me. Every buried feeling surfaces at once, truth hitting like a thunderbolt: I'm in love with this girl.

Wholeheartedly.

We keep driving and of all the moments I've had where I've allowed myself to just be, this has to be one of my favorite moments.

All because of her.

"Do you ever think about the future, Nate?" she asks out of nowhere.

The honest answer is no. I stopped dreaming past tomorrow long ago, learning to exist in single moments, surviving one breath at a time. Hope was more dangerous than any drug—it could kill in countless ways.

"I think learning how to just be in the single fleeting second that exists is more important than stressing about a future that doesn't exist yet."

She looks up through her lashes, beautiful enough to stop time. "You're right. There's no going backwards, but maybe it's not so bad to dwell on the past, as long as it brings you closer to the truth. So you can move forward." She turns to look at me.

"I don't know how to do that. I've made a lot of mistakes."

"Well, tomorrow is a new day without any mistakes in it yet."

By the time *"Dare You to Move"* fades out, we've circled town twice, ending up back at the lake house. The silence between us crackles with electricity, every breath charged with unspoken words. Under the porch light, she's ethereal—her cheeks flushed rose-pink, eyes dark with something that makes my pulse sprint. She bites her lower lip, gaze dancing between me and the door like she's wrestling with the same magnetic pull I am.

I can't let her just walk away. Not when everything in me is screaming to hold on.

My fingers circle her wrist, tugging her back before she can reach for the door handle. She spins into me, soft curves colliding with hard muscle, and the gasp that escapes her lips shoots straight through my body. My free hand finds the small of her back, pressing her closer until I feel her heartbeat thundering against my chest—or maybe that's mine. Maybe they're the same now.

"Nate..." My name on her lips is half-whisper, half-plea.

I tilt her chin up, and time suspends. The porch light catches the gold flecks in her eyes, turning them into their own constellation. Years of wanting, of denying, of running—it all comes down to this moment. Her fingers curl into my shirt, anchoring herself, tethering me.

The first brush of my lips against hers is feather-light, a question. Her answer comes in the way she rises on her tiptoes, pressing closer, demanding more. The kiss deepens, and it's like touching a live wire— electric, dangerous, absolutely necessary. She tastes like promises I want to keep, like every fucking dream I never let myself have. My fingers thread through her hair, tilting her head to deepen the kiss, and the soft sound she makes nearly breaks me.

When we finally part, her eyes flutter open slowly, like she's waking from a dream she doesn't want to end. She's looking at me like I've rearranged her universe, and fuck if she hasn't done the same to mine.

"Happy birthday, Leni," I whisper, voice rough with everything I'm not saying. Everything I want to say.

"Goodnight, Nate." Her words ghost across my lips, one last temptation.

I watch her disappear inside, my body still humming with her touch, my lips still burning with her taste. My heart pounds with absolute certainty—it's her.

It's always been her. It will always be her.

The moment feels perfect.
Almost too perfect.
But in my world, happy endings don't exist.

CHAPTER 42
SORRY ON REPEAT
NATE

I'M STILL FLOATING, DRUNK ON THE MEMORY OF NORA'S LIPS ON MINE only minutes ago. The taste of her still lingers, sweet and electric, making my head spin in the best possible way. My fingers trace my bottom lip for the hundredth time tonight, chasing the ghost of her touch. For once in my life my chest is light, and my heart full of something that feels dangerously like hope.

I should know better by now.

The dim light spilling from the kitchen stops me cold, yanking me back to reality like a punch to the gut.

Of course.

Of fucking course.

This is how it always goes—one perfect moment before everything goes to shit. It's like the universe can't stand to see me happy, can't let me have one goddamn thing without reminding me who I am, what my life is.

The tension coils around my chest as I step through the doorway. Mom's there, perched at the counter, fingers wrapped loosely around a half-empty wine bottle. Her eyes are distant, glazed with a familiar emptiness that used to terrify me as a kid. Still does, if I'm honest. For a moment, old fears grip me: memories of finding her unconscious, checking her pulse with trembling fingers, praying this wouldn't be the time she didn't wake up. But tonight, she's upright, coherent enough to meet my gaze. After the day's events, I feel a bitter gratitude for even that small mercy.

My high from the kiss evaporates like smoke, replaced by the heavy weight of responsibility that's been crushing me since I was old enough to understand what was happening in this house. This is my reality—not stolen kisses and teenage dreams, but wine bottles and broken promises. Mom watches me, her expression a mixture of exhaustion and guilt, as if the burden of our unspoken history is finally too heavy to bear.

"Nate, I know you're angry right now, but—"

"But?" The word escapes like venom. "No shit I'm angry, Mom." Each syllable feels like it's been lodged in my chest for years, finally breaking free. "I've spent my life trying to recover from what I should've been protected from. Angry doesn't even begin to cover it."

"I didn't know he was in town, let alone coming. Jake shouldn't have—"

"Why do you think Jake invited him?" I cut her off, my words sharp as glass. "Because he has no fucking idea about anything. Because you always painted him as some kind of hero to Jake."

I can't bring myself to say 'dad'.

He's never earned that title.

My pulse thunders as years of suppressed rage boils over.

I'm done pretending.

Done being the ghost of a child who should have known joy instead of terror.

"You don't get to stand there and tell me how to feel. Not after everything I've done to protect you from him."

She flinches as if struck. Part of me wants her to feel it—the hurt, the betrayal, the endless nights of looking over my shoulder, waiting for his shadow to reappear. All because she couldn't bring herself to leave with Jake and me in tow.

"Nate, I'm not trying to tell you how to feel. I'm trying to—"

"What?" My voice cracks with raw fury. "Help me? Protect me? Save me? You're fourteen years too late for that."

Her face crumples, tears welling up even as she fights to maintain composure—the same way she had through every one of his pathetic apologies.

"I know. I'm sorry, Nate. I'm so sorry—"

"I was forced to grow up, Mom." The words tear from somewhere deep and wounded. "I didn't have a fucking choice in any of this. You did. You could've left the first time. You should've left the fifteenth time. But you didn't. You chose him over Jake and me every single time. And for the life of me, I can't understand why."

Her voice drops to a whisper. "It's complicated, Nate. None of this is that easy to—"

"Not easy?" Rage trembles through me, my fists clenched tight enough to draw blood. "You want to talk about what's not easy?"

The memories burst forth like a broken dam.

Not easy is being suffocated by the hands of a man who's supposed to be your hero when you're nine.

Not easy is having your face smashed into a wall at thirteen because you're trying to stop him from hurting your Mom.

Not easy is walking around with more broken bones by seventeen than most people will have in their entire lives.

I step closer, my voice rising with each word.

"Not easy is lying awake outside your little brother's bedroom every single night after a fight, praying to God he doesn't go after him, too. Then waking up to go to school the next morning pretending everything in life is just fucking dandy. That's not easy, Mom!"

Years of silence has finally cracked open, everything spilling out like shattered glass. My voice shakes with the intensity of memories I can't bury anymore.

"Hearing you scream every time he came home reeking of booze— that wasn't easy. So forgive me if I can't empathize with your choice to stay with someone who didn't give a fuck if you lived or died."

Her tears fall freely now, each of my words landing like physical blows. Nothing could undo the years of damage, the choices she'd made.

She takes a shaky breath, her entire frame quivering. When she speaks, her voice is barely audible. "I'm sorry."

"Sorry?" The word claws its way out, bitter as ash. "Do you have any idea how fucking useless that word is? Sorry doesn't mean shit. It doesn't fix the fact that I had to become Jake's parent when I was still a kid myself because you couldn't protect us." I lift the wine bottle, my laugh hollow. "This? And the sleeping pills? That was your solution?"

The realization hits me like a punch: no wonder I'm a fucking addict. The two people who raised me made sure I'd never stand a chance at being anything else.

I slam the bottle down.

"Sorry doesn't change anything, Mom." Every word rip something raw and jagged from inside me.

Unshed tears burn in my eyes, but I refuse to let them fall. Not after years of holding myself together while everything threatened to shatter.

"You should've left," I spit. "You should've fucking left. I would've done everything to help you get out. But instead, you stayed. Every time he came crawling back with his bullshit apologies, you let him. You chose him and then forced me to play house." My voice cracks. "And do you know what that taught me? It taught me that I didn't matter. That the person who was supposed to love me the most couldn't even choose me."

Her shoulders shake with silent sobs, but I can't stop.

"I took every punch, every scream, every broken thing he threw at us. And for what? So I could grow up hating the person I had to become just to survive?"

She tries to speak, but no sound emerges.

I laugh bitterly.

"You don't get to cry. Not now. Not after everything."

Because no amount of tears will ever undo what you let happen to us. To me.

For the first time in years, I've unleashed everything I'd buried to protect her. The air between us feels fractured beyond repair.

"Nate, I never wanted this for you. For Jake. I was scared. I thought—"

"Unbelievable. You're still trying to justify it."

Her words feel hollow as prayers in an empty room. "I'm sorry" has become her shield, a soft phrase meant to cover damage that words could never fix. Trust needs proof, and sorry needs change.

"It's not enough anymore," I say, my voice cracking. I grip the counter, knuckles white, using it to stay upright as the past threatens to pull me under. "Same shit, different day. I'm so fucking tired of this conversation. Nothing changes. It never does. I wouldn't be surprised if he was back in our lives in a week's time and we're all out here playing happy fucking family again."

I meet her tear-filled eyes.

"I'll never get my childhood back. That's gone. And right now, I don't know what's left of my future. So if my way of dealing with this doesn't look right to you, I don't care. I'm done caring about what looks right. I'm done caring, period."

It's a lie.

I'll always care, even when I don't want to.

The truth is simpler: I'm tired. Bone-deep, soul-shattering tired. Tired of the beatings—physical, emotional, and everything between. Tired of broken promises and pain that clings like a second skin.

"I'll never stop being sorry, Nate," she whispers, wiping tears with her sleeve. "I should have done more to protect you. Just... tell me what you need from me."

I stare at her—the woman who should have been my shield—and feel hollow. "I need space."

"Nate, please—"

"If you want to salvage whatever's left between us," I cut her off, my voice quiet but firm, "then stop. Now. Before I say something I really can't take back."

She starts toward the door, then stops. From a kitchen drawer, she pulls out a folder and drops it on the counter.

"I've filed for divorce." Her voice wavers. "You're right, I should've done it years ago, but... I'm doing it now. I didn't protect you when you needed me most. Even if I... I had my reasons, I should have done better for you, for Jake. For us."

I keep my face unreadable. "Then tell Jake. Don't let him find out about this on his own."

She nods, broken determination in her eyes, and leaves. In the emptiness that follows, I sink to the floor, head in my hands.

For the first time in years, I let the tears threaten to fall.

I drag myself upstairs, exhausted and strung out. At Nora's door, I hesitate, my hand hovering over the handle. It takes every ounce of control not to go in, not to kiss her again, not to lose myself in her like before. I force myself onward.

In my room, I collapse onto the bed, mind spinning.

I kissed her.

I kissed Nora.

And it was everything I've wanted, everything I've never let myself imagine. The memory overwhelms me—the warmth of her breath, her lips fitting against mine as if they were made for me. I can't stop wondering how her skin would feel under my hands, how she'd taste if I kissed her deeper, pulled her closer, made her mine. I want her in ways I don't know possible. But reality's cold weight settles in, familiar as breathing. Good things don't last in my life. They either slip away or I destroy them first.

I do what I've always done: push people away, keep them at arm's length, shield myself from inevitable hurt. It's safer that way—for me, for her.

CHAPTER 43
SEVENTEEN
NORA

SEVENTEEN FEELS DIFFERENT THAN I EXPECTED—THERE'S A STRANGE ACHE, both comforting and terrifying. Before dawn breaks, I'm pounding the pavement, each footfall echoing the rhythm of my racing thoughts. The cool morning air bites at my exposed skin, but I barely notice. I can't shake him. Thoughts of last night circle around me, pressing heavily against my chest.

I kissed Nate.

And he kissed me back.

That memory flickers like a spark in the darkness. The taste of him lingers—sharp and intoxicating—a ghost of sensation that makes my heart race even now. I crave the closeness again, that intense connection that felt like coming home and falling apart all at once.

Yesterday spiraled from disaster into something unexpectedly magical. Scott's presence cast a shadow over everything as it always does. He's not just Nate's father; he's the origin of every hidden scar, every deep-seated pain Nate endures. Watching Nate stiffen under his father's scrutinizing gaze, every part of me wanted to shield him from that familiar darkness.

I found him in the boatshed with the dim light filtering through dusty windows. He stood hunched over a table, his hands clenched as he stared down at the small bags that seemed like both escape and chains. They bound him to everything he'd been trying to flee. I'd whispered his name, barely able to breathe.

He wouldn't look at me but I saw it—the war waging inside him, the way he fought against everything he didn't want to be. I understood more than he'd ever know. It was like staring at a mirror, seeing my own broken pieces reflected in his silence, in the shadows he carried. Then he looked at me, eyes raw and wild, and I saw his pain so clearly it became my own. For a moment, all the walls we'd built around ourselves crumbled. The only thing left was our shared need to hold each other, to find something steady and real in this storm of emotions.

The kiss was wild, fierce. Every emotion we'd buried came flooding out at once—fear, frustration, longing. There was nothing gentle about it. Every nerve in my body was alive, ignited by him, by the unspoken need between us that couldn't be denied anymore. And underneath it all, there was this ache—a bittersweet tenderness. Because this was the boy I'd known forever, who carried his scars with such quiet strength. The boy who'd suffered more than anyone deserves.

But even now, I'm afraid.

Afraid to let him see all the broken parts of me I hide, and the trauma I carry in silence. There's a darkness in my story that I can't bear to share, even with him.

What if he saw me differently?

What if all he saw from that point on was damaged goods?

The beach comes into view, and I slow my pace, letting my feet sink into the sand. The ocean stretches before me, endless and gray in the early morning light. I stare out at the waves, letting them swallow my thoughts. In these moments of stillness, Dad's absence hits hardest. This is the second birthday he's missed, and it feels like it will never get easier. Grief is a hollow space in my chest, the unspent love that has nowhere to go, it's just a constant ache that reminds me of everything he's missing.

I stand with eyes closed, listening to the waves crash against the shore, letting the tears come freely. The salt air mingles with the taste of salt on my lips, and I don't bother wiping them away. Sometimes the most important lessons come in these quiet moments, like how grief is just love with no place to go, and this morning, it's more than I can hold in.

When I finally make it back to the lake house, my legs feel like I've run a half marathon at record pace. The moment I step into the living room, I'm greeted by a burst of color and sound. Balloons and streamers fill the space as Mom, Lydia, Jake, and Ollie all scream, "Happy birthday!"

This has Lydia written all over it—confirmed by her bright, excited energy that fills the room. Jake grins as he gives me a hug. I can feel the tension in his body that's still lingering from yesterday. It makes the hug feel awkward and we've never felt awkward around each other.

Ollie steps up next, ruffling my hair like he always does.

"Happy birthday, Len," he says with his trademark lopsided grin before pulling me into another bear hug and kissing the top of my head.

"Thanks, Ol," I say, playfully swatting him away, though the familiar gesture brings comfort I didn't know I needed.

Mom waits for her turn, a soft smile on her face though worry lingers in her eyes.

"Happy birthday, my love." Her hug threatens to cut off my airways, but after this morning, it's exactly what I need. "My God, I can't believe you're seventeen."

The celebrations continue, but I can't help noticing Nate's absence. I try to hide my disappointment, wondering if like me, he needed space to process everything. Or maybe he was second-guessing it all. The uncertainty sits heavy in my stomach, even as I smile and laugh with everyone else.

At breakfast, Mom notices something's off—she always does. We rarely get moments like this anymore, just the two of us. Usually, we only cross paths at Ollie's games or briefly in the mornings as we rush in opposite directions.

"You okay?" she asks, her hand resting over mine. There's so much love there, so much patience, and I feel this rush of gratitude that almost brings tears back to my eyes.

"Yeah," I whisper, but the word feels hollow.

I wish I could tell her everything. But every time I try, it's like standing on a cliff edge overlooking a dark abyss. The words burn inside, a searing mix of shame and guilt, each memory sharpened to painful clarity. My heart pounds furiously, echoing in my ears like thunder.

Mom has been healing from Dad's loss for over a year now. I tried to keep it together, not wanting to add another worry to her life, but all it's done is chip away at me, piece by piece.

"You can talk to me, Nora. I know you're getting older now, but I'm always going to be here whether you're seventeen or forty-seven."

"I know, Mom." I offer her a small smile and take a sip of orange juice, letting the darkness win again.

"So how does it feel to be another year older?"

I stare across the café table at Mom, sunlight streaming through the window catching the light strands in her hair.

"How am I feeling?" A small laugh escapes me. "Well, I'm not sure I feel any wiser now that I'm another year older."

She laughs softly, warmth in her eyes.

"You're wise beyond your years. Just like your father." A flicker of pain crosses her expression, quickly replaced with pride. "He'd be proud of the woman you are. There was never a day that went by that he wasn't proud of you."

The words hit like a physical blow. I'm not sure that's true anymore. The memory of our last interaction burns—slamming the door in his face, telling him to leave me alone, that he didn't understand. All the words I wish I could take back but know I can't. I was angry and I took it out on him.

Then he was gone.

"Nora?" Mom's voice pulls me back.

"Hmm?"

"Where did you go just now?"

I take a breath, the next question slipping out before I can stop it. "Mom, how did you know Dad was the one?"

A tender smile spreads across her face, carrying a lifetime of memories.

"It's simple, really," she says, her gaze growing distant yet soft. "He was my best friend." She speaks with the breathless enthusiasm of a teenager remembering first love, describing what it was like to fall for the person she knew would be forever.

"I think that's how you know someone's meant to be in your life forever. They're the person you feel safest with, the one who can see through every crack and still look at you like you could do no wrong." She reaches across the table, squeezing my hand. "It's about finding someone who feels like home. Your dad, he was my home."

He was my home.

A familiar pair of hazel eyes flickers in my mind, and my heart skips.

I know someone who feels a little like that.

But he's also the storm, and I'm afraid that if I let him in, he'll pull me into depths I'm not sure I can handle.

Mom squeezes my hand again, bringing me back to the present.

"Your dad understood me in a way no one else did. It was like that from the start. Maybe that's what a soulmate really is—someone who sees you, even the parts you don't fully understand yet. And instead of telling you, they simply guide you to uncover those parts yourself when you're ready."

Her words follow me through the drive home, wrapping around me like one of Dad's old sweaters—warm and comforting despite the holes.

Jake's Range Rover is parked crookedly, taking up more space than necessary—so typical of him. I make my way up the porch steps, the wood creaking beneath my feet the way it always has. Inside, I can hear the faint sound of his music pulsing behind closed doors. He's been keeping his distance, even after the half-hearted "happy birthday" this morning. That's just him though, bottling everything up until it spills over.

I pause outside his door, fist hovering before I finally knock.

"Come in," he calls, voice low.

He's sprawled out on his bed, shirtless, scrolling through his phone. His wary eyes flicker up at me for a second before dropping back down. I sit on the edge of his bed, nudging his shoulder.

"Hey," I say softly.

"Hey," he mumbles, not looking up. His tone is flat, and it stings more than I want to admit.

I take a deep breath, words tumbling out. "Are you still mad at me?"

His eyes finally meet mine, a small grin tugging at the corner of his mouth.

"Nora, I wouldn't know how to stay mad at you even if I tried." He props himself up on one elbow, and I notice how much he's changed—how much muscle he's put on since last year. He smirks, voice lighter now. "Besides, it's your birthday. I'd be a pretty shitty person to be mad at you today."

I laugh despite myself, and he squeezes my hand, expression softening.

"I'm sorry for snapping at you yesterday. That wasn't cool. It's just... hard. When Dad and Nate are at each other's throats, and I'm stuck in the middle of it all."

I nod, heart aching because I get it. I want the same thing he does—to feel like a family again. But life's not that kind, and wanting doesn't always make things better.

"So, about that list?" I say, standing up and yanking a pillow out from under him. "Let's go tick a few things off—just you and me."

His grin spreads as he catches the pillow mid-swat. "Yeah?"

"Yeah." I grab the pillow back and swat him again, laughing. "Hurry up before I change my mind."

"All right, all right," he says, chuckling as he swings his legs over the side of the bed. "Let me get dressed."

We head out together, the tension dissolving into familiar comfort. At the bookstore, I clutch my manuscript draft under my arm, nervous flutter in my stomach as I prepare to share it with Alfie. Jake's brow furrows in surprise.

"Wait, you finished it? When were you planning to tell me?"

I fumble with the pages, "I... uh, wanted Alfie's feedback first. Maybe you can read it after him?"

There's a flicker of hurt in his eyes—I used to share everything with him first. He brushes it off with a casual nod. "Sure, whenever you're ready."

At the beach with our frozen yogurt, Jake finally breaks the silence, frustration clear in his voice.

"I just don't get it. Why can't Nate and Dad be in the same room without going to war? There's Nate's side, Dad's side, and Mom, although she seems to only take Nate's side anyway. I'm stuck in the middle. It's exhausting."

The secrets Nate entrusted to me weigh heavy—secrets that could upend everything if Jake knew. I choose my words carefully. "Maybe Nate has his reasons. And your mom, too. Sometimes, people keep things to themselves because it's their way of protecting others and themselves."

Jake narrows his eyes. "Like how you didn't tell Ollie about what happened at school last summer?"

His question catches me off guard and I freeze. "How... how did you know about that?"

What he knows—or doesn't—suddenly feels like the most important mystery in the world.

He shrugs. "Your mom mentioned it. Said you were having trouble with some girls, and I noticed none of your friends came to the funeral."

The memory stings, but I push it down. "That's just your typical high school girls being girls. I don't really think about it."

It's all I think about.

Before I can suggest heading to another location, my phone buzzes with a message from Camilla.

Camilla
HAPPY FUCKING BIRTHDAY GIRLFRIEND!!!

What are you doing now?

Come to my place. We're all here swimming.

By we, I mean Marcus and Mia. Ollie's on his way (Mia invited him).

Nate's coming too.

Get your ass down here so I can squeeze you and wish you a proper happy birthday xxxx

Jake reads over my shoulder, and I feel his body tense as soon as he sees Nate's name.

He lets out a sigh. "You should go."

"You don't want to come?"

He shakes his head. "I told Mom I'd help her with something."

"You sure?"

He nods, forcing a smile. "Go. Enjoy the rest of your birthday, yeah?"

THE MOMENT I ARRIVE AT CAMILLA'S, SHE THROWS HER ARMS AROUND ME with enough force to nearly knock me backward. Her perfume surrounds me, sweet and slightly overpowering, just like her energy.

"Happy birthday!" she beams, holding my shoulders. "I am so excited you're here!"

I smile back, her enthusiasm infectious. "For such a tiny human, you have some serious strength."

"It's all the pilates I've started doing. Did Jake come with you?"

"No. He had to help his mom with something."

She waves that off. "We'll manage without him! I take it you don't have a change of clothes?"

I hesitate. "I actually didn't think about it, but I can text Ollie to bring something over from home."

"Don't be ridiculous." Camilla grabs my hand and tugs me toward the stairs. "Come raid my closet. I've got more clothes than I know what to do with."

In her bedroom, which could rival a small department store, she pulls out a yellow bikini. "Here, wear this. It's brand new, tags still on. And yellow is your color, trust me."

I hold it up, heat flashing up my neck. "Where's the rest of it?"

"It's a bikini, not a wetsuit. You cannot tell me you're self-conscious with a body that looks like a *Sports Illustrated* model."

The compliment makes me uncomfortable. Ever since my body had been exposed and exploited, I'd felt uneasy baring my skin to anyone. Sensing my discomfort, Camilla walks over to another drawer and hands me a throw-over crochet dress.

"This looks expensive," I say, holding up the dress.

"Oh it is, but it was also a 'mom trying to buy my love' gift so I don't care if you cut it up and used it as a dish cloth."

I sense the hurt beneath the joke. Camilla has a hard exterior but like most of us, there's an underlying amount of pain that she doesn't let the world see.

"Where is your family, by the way?"

"They flew back to Beijing yesterday. Some big business deal or some shit that Dad is trying to close." She shrugs, pretending it's no big deal, but I can see the faint disappointment in her expression. "So, the whole house is mine. Well now, it's ours! I don't even know when they'll be back. If they even come back this summer."

It's on the tip of my tongue to say I'm sorry, but I know Camilla wouldn't want that. She doesn't do pity or apologies. So instead, I shift the subject, clutching the swimsuit tighter under my arm.

"Thank you, Camilla. Really."

She nudges me with her shoulder, her smile warm and easy again. "Thank me after you open your present."

"What? No. I don't—"

"Nora, open the damn present," she interrupts, shoving a ridiculously large box into my hands. "Technically, it's from Marcus, Mia, and me. But I will be taking all the credit for the idea."

"This is too much," I say, shaking my head.

"You don't even know what it is yet. Could be a pair of really ugly socks in a really big box."

It weighs more than socks. I raise an eyebrow at her before tearing into the wrapping. My heart lurches when I lift the lid and see it—a brand-new laptop.

"Camilla, this is..." My voice wavers, and the words get stuck in my throat.

"The best gift ever? Yeah, I know." She grins, crossing her arms. "Now you can write your next ten books on something that doesn't belong in a museum. You're welcome."

It's not the laptop itself that gets me, it's what it means. These people —practically strangers not long ago—have somehow become a family I didn't know I needed. A family who believes in me. Tears well up, spilling over before I can stop them.

"Whoa, are those happy tears?" Camilla asks, her grin softening.

I laugh through the lump in my throat. "They're 'how did I get so lucky' tears. Thank you. I don't think I've ever had a friend like you, Camilla."

"Best friend," she corrects, pulling me into a tight hug. I let her, leaning into the comfort of it. "And same, girlfriend. I'm glad I stalked you at that café and forced my way into your life."

"Me too," I whisper, meaning it with everything in me.

Camilla pulls back, her expression shifting, more serious now. "Okay, real talk, how are you feeling? Yesterday was a lot. Are you okay after everything that happened?"

I hesitate, swallowing hard. "Kind of. I mean, things got intense after we left. Nate and I went for a drive. And well, we kissed."

Camilla gasps, then squeals, practically bouncing on the spot. "Umm, sorry what!? How and why are you only telling me this now? But also, finally!" Her hands fly to her cheeks as her grin stretches impossibly wider. "So? How do you feel about it?"

I sigh, unsure how to put it into words.

"I don't know. We haven't seen or spoken to each other since, and now I'm kind of nervous to see him. For years, we've been stuck in this weird in-between place. Friends but maybe something more? I don't know how to move forward."

Camilla tilts her head, studying me with an expression that's all-knowing and smug. "Please, you two were made for each other."

I blink, caught off guard. "Why do you say that?"

"Because," she says with a shrug, "that boy looks at you like he's memorizing every freckle on your face."

The comment sends a flutter through my chest, and she's not done.

"You don't just look at each other with butterflies and sparkles. It's deeper. It's messy and complicated, kinda like a fairytale that hasn't been written yet, but one that's going to be worth the read."

Her observation hits me harder than I expected, and I let out a slow breath.

"It's just… different with Nate. Like I said, we've always had this… connection. But I don't know how to move forward."

Camilla grips my shoulders gently.

"Nora, you can't force chemistry where it doesn't exist, but you also can't deny it when it's there. Just talk to him. Lay it out. If he is what you want, then tell him that. Boys are dumb when it comes to what's blatantly obvious and standing right in front of them."

Her confidence gives me a tiny spark of courage. Maybe she's right. Maybe Nate and I have been waiting too long in this gray area.

She nudges me toward the bathroom. "Now go try that on and let me see how it looks."

When I step out in the bikini, Camilla whistles dramatically.

"Oh, my God! You look insane. Seriously, Nate's going to physically drop dead when he sees you. Not that his opinion matters or anything. But still, he will die."

I laugh, rolling my eyes. "You're ridiculous."

We head back downstairs, Camilla chattering about the party and who's bringing what. As we step outside, she spots Nate pulling up. She leans in, her voice low but firm, "Shoot your shot, girl. Don't wait."

Her words hang in the air, more truth than advice. She's right—waiting for life to hand you the perfect moment is a trap. Because life isn't meant to be lived halfway. You can't half love, half risk, or half believe in yourself. You have to go all in, even if it terrifies you. Especially if it terrifies you. I look down at the bracelet still on my wrist, the one Nate gave me.

Fearless.

I take a deep breath, straighten my shoulders, and step forward, ready to prove I was exactly that.

CHAPTER 44
THE RENT IS FREE IN
MY HEAD
NATE

I SLIP OUT BEFORE SUNRISE, AVOIDING MOM AND NORA. LAST NIGHT HAS left enough wreckage without facing either of them, not while I'm still angry at Mom and lost about Nora. Sonder will be opening soon, and Nick could use the help, so that's where I head. The place has become my escape, and Nick has somehow become someone I trust—a rare occurrence in my life.

He looks up as I enter, surprised but not shocked. "You're early."

"Thought you might need a hand." I nod toward the paint cans.

"Or maybe a distraction," he replies, knowing but casual.

I laugh roughly. Nick never pries, and that's rare in my world. He offers what he can and asks nothing in return.

"If distractions are on the menu, I'm in," I say, grabbing a roller.

He hands me a brush in silence, letting me work in peace.

Finally, he clears his throat. "You holding up all right after... everything?" His words carry more weight than just last night. Nick has seen my scars, the ones left by battles I never chose. He understands—he's been there.

"Yeah," I reply hollowly.

"Nate," he says, voice calm but firm. "It's not my place to ask questions, especially about family. But what I will say is this: pain moves through families until someone's ready to feel it and stop it. When you're born in a burning house, you think the whole worlds on fire. But it's not."

His words cut through the fog in my head. I nod, swallowing hard.

"You're right," I mutter, unsure if he knows how much that means. Having someone in your corner without strings feels undeserved, especially after how I spoke to Mom. But I'd hit my breaking point. Seeing Scott again had unleashed every bit of suppressed anger.

My phone buzzes.

"Ol, what's up?" I answer.

"Oh look, he does know how to answer the phone."

"Now you know why I don't answer your calls, wise ass."

"I'm pretending you didn't say that to hurt my feelings. Where have you been?"

"Riding a llama in Neverland. Where do you think?"

He chokes on his drink, and I smile. Ollie's humor has always matched mine.

"Everyone's at Camilla's. Figured you could join me," he says, too casual. "And before you say no, I'm outside."

Nick smirks, nodding toward the window where Ollie waves, grinning.

"You're good here. Go hang out with your friends." Nick says, clasping a hand on my shoulder.

Outside, Ollie leans from the car like an eager puppy. "You look like hell. Lucky for you, I'm the best friend you'll ever have. Packed a bag for you."

I slide in. "You packed a bag for me?"

"Yes, Nathaniel, I did. Just don't get used to it. It's like a one time thing," he smirks.

He pulls onto the road, watching me. "So... how are things? You and your dad still at odds after yesterday?" His tone is casual, but I catch the concern. Ollie reads people better than he lets on.

"What gave it away?" I laugh sharply. Having an abusive prick for a father who acts like God's gift is a cosmic joke.

"Were we at the same party?"

I shrug, turning to the window. It's easier to lie than tell the truth.

"He's got impossible standards, and I don't meet any. I've accepted it." Part of me wants to tell everything, but where to start? It's a short drive with too much to unpack.

Instead, I reach for a safer memory.

"You know, your dad taught me to throw my first ball. Spent hours with me while you guys were at the beach."

Ollie's expression softens. "Yeah, sounds like him. He taught us all something, didn't he?"

"I'm sorry I wasn't there," I say quietly. "I should've been."

He shakes his head. "Hey, that's old news. You were forgiven ages ago."

"Maybe by you, but... I don't know about your sister."

Ollie grins. "Nora? Please. She'd never stay mad at you. She's been in love with you forever."

My chest tightens, heart stumbling. He says it so casually, like common knowledge I've somehow missed. His words rearrange my entire world.

I clear my throat. "What happened last year? With Nora at school?"

"You mean with her useless best friend bailing on her when she needed her most?"

I nod and wait for him to continue.

"She didn't talk about it. Believe me, Mom tried. I tried. But she just shut down completely. Then I heard some guy made a move at a party, and Claire, her best friend, got jealous."

Something sharp twists in my gut. "What do you mean, made a move?"

"From what I heard, he kissed her, and Claire caught the act. Claire was obsessed with this guy and dragged Nora to the party."

My fists clench at the thought of someone touching her let alone kissing her.

"But you know Nora. She's not the random hook-up type. Let alone do that to her friend."

"What was his name?"

"Uh... Eddie? Something with an E."

Cold fury builds in me, wound tight enough to snap.

"Wait, no I think it was Evan. Some lacrosse prick. Definitely not her type." He smirks. "And before you ask, no, I didn't get involved. That's not my thing, and she asked me to stay out of it. Beating people up... that's more your role in her life."

Anger rises from somewhere primal. I don't know what to do with this possessiveness clawing at my chest. The thought of her with someone who doesn't see her like I do makes my blood boil.

We pull up to Camilla's house and Ollie kills the engine.

"Coming in? Or just gonna brood?"

I laugh sharply. "Lead the way."

Even before entering, I feel her. Her laugh carries through the house, wrapping around me. She has different laughs for every emotion, just like songs for every mood. This one tugs at something deep in my core. She's everywhere, woven into every fiber of my existence. No matter how far I drift, there's always this pull drawing me back.

I'm forever ruined when it comes to her. Trying to escape her would be like tearing out a piece of myself.

"The fun has arrived!" Ollie announces, drawing every eye his way—except mine.

I only seek hers. Green and locked on me, like always.

The moment our gazes meet, everything shifts. A spark, a surge of heat straight to my chest. That's how it has always been with us. I can find her in any crowd in a heartbeat. Our eyes connect, and I feel it again—that pull, that silent confession. The kind that makes me believe, in some twisted way, we were meant to find each other. She looks away, but not before I catch the flush in her cheeks, a soft rosy hue I know I put there.

"You're staring," Marcus's voice cuts in, and I realize he's appeared beside me. I have no idea where Ollie has gone, or how long Marcus has been standing there.

"No, I'm not," I mutter, dropping into a lounge chair.

Marcus grins knowingly. "Sure. You'd have to be blind not to see the way you look at her."

"I'm not," I snap.

"Then why are you blushing?" His smirk deepens.

"I don't blush."

"For a pretty boy, you're pretty dumb sometimes."

"Ouch."

"It's cute," he adds smugly. "The way you look at her. Your face lights up. Seriously, a blind man could see it, so don't bother denying it."

"I don't know what you're talking about."

"Whatever you say, Natey boy." Marcus chuckles, pushing off toward the girls across the pool.

I sit there, feeling her pull all over again. I try to stay put, determined not to stare. But she makes it impossible. The yellow bikini showing through that barely-there cover-up. The way she leans back, and the line of her throat as she sips her drink.

Fuck me.

I'm trapped in my head, frustration clawing at me. The kind that makes you hyper-aware of yourself but clueless about how others see you. Most of my life, I haven't cared how I come across. But with her, everything is different. I've been detached for so long, an observer rather than a participant. Not in some creepy way, more like someone who stands in awe of art.

And she is art. Pure, unfiltered, breathtaking. I can't look away.

My attraction to Nora hasn't hit all at once. It has seeped into my skin, my bones, my soul over years. Slow. Calculated. Relentless.

There's no escape. She owns every piece of me and she doesn't even know it.

And now she's walking straight toward me.

Fuck. Fuck. Fuck.

Just like that, I'm seven years old again, pining after the girl who's had a hold on me my entire life.

I sit up, elbows on my knees, legs spread wide on the lounge chair. She stops in front of me, and I catch that citrusy blend of her shampoo and sunscreen. My gaze travels up, taking in every inch of her perfect body wrapped in that barely-there dress.

When our eyes finally meet, I can't tell if either of us is breathing.

"Hi."

"Hi."

I have no idea if anyone's watching.

I don't care. All I see is her.

"You left early this morning," she says.

"I did."

"Why?"

Because I don't know how to handle this.

Because being close to you tears me apart.

Because I want you in every fucking way imaginable.

"You're not going to ignore me now, are you? I thought we were past that."

"Nora—"

"Don't push me away, Nate. Not after everything."

I don't want to push her away. But I also don't want to ruin her. That's what I do—I ruin things. Break them.

"The kiss—" I start, but she cuts me off.

"Was not a mistake, and you know it. So don't bullshit me."

I smell traces of vodka on her breath.

"Have you been drinking?"

"Don't change the subject."

"Maybe you should—"

"Don't tell me what I should do, Nate. I'm perfectly fine—"

She stumbles, feet slipping beneath her. My arms move on instinct, catching her waist and steadying her before she falls. She's pressed against me now, hands on my chest, my hands gripping her hips. Heat radiates between us, her body fits against mine like it was made to be there.

Time stops. I'm about to lose my fucking mind holding her like this.

She stares up at me, wide-eyed, and something unspoken passes between us. That silent confession between us screams without words. I feel it in every point where our bodies touch, in the slight tremor of her breath against my neck. I let my hands linger longer than I should, feeling her body melt under my touch. She steps back, creating space, and I immediately regret letting go. The loss of contact feels like physical pain.

"Thanks," she murmurs, voice softer now.

These tiny, electric moments between us—brief, charged bursts that shatter the calm—come when one of us stares too long, smiles too wide, or thinks too hard. Little shocks to remind us not to slip too far. To stay safe. To keep our distance. And fuck, I crave these moments the most.

They're like matches in the dark, brief flares of light that show me everything I want but can't have.

I catch her again before she can fall. One arm loops around her elbow, the other braces her lower back. I pull her close, steadying her, and our bodies press together. Through my shorts, I feel the heat of her skin, and it takes every ounce of self-control not to pull her closer and kiss her right here in front of everyone.

Her sweet, innocent green eyes lift to mine, wide and unguarded. There's trust there I don't deserve, that I shouldn't encourage.

"I got you, Leni," I say, grinning to hide how much this affects me.

Her cheeks flush pink as she clears her throat, gaze flickering to where my hands still grip her hips. I don't move. I should, but I can't make myself let go.

"You're making this a thing," she murmurs.

I laugh softly, the sound drawing out the grin that always comes so easily when she's flustered. "You know I'll never let you fall."

I'm weak when it comes to her. Everything in me is drawn to her, this magnetic pull I can't resist. Don't want to resist, even though I know I should. We stay like that, caught in the moment. Her nails dig into my shoulders, but I don't mind. I feel it in the way her body leans into mine. It's almost primal, this need between us. It scares me how much I want her.

She's panting slightly, and it's adorable that she pretends she's unaffected when our bodies collide. The need I feel for her isn't logical; it's instinctual, coming from a place I don't recognize, a place only she can reach.

If there's one thing I know for sure, it's that Lenora Wells lives in my head rent-free. She's carved out a space in my soul no one else could ever fill.

And that terrifies me more than anything because people like me don't get to keep beautiful things.

We just break them.

CHAPTER 45
THE GEOMETRY OF ALMOST
NORA

Before I can process what's happened, Nate's arms are around me, steadying me. My heart doesn't skip, it leaps. Not from the near fall or the drinks buzzing through my system, but from him. His hands grip my waist with a sureness that makes my breath catch, and his warmth bleeds through my clothes like a brand. His touch doesn't make me flinch or hesitate—it anchors me. With him, I always feel that way, like coming up for air after being underwater too long.

"You need water," he says, his tone brooking no argument. "Come on." His arm stays wrapped around me as he guides me inside, as if afraid I might slip away again.

In the kitchen, he grabs a glass, filling it with ice and water. I hop onto the counter, letting my legs dangle, watching as his eyes trace the line of them. It's bold—something I wouldn't normally do—but today things feel different. Maybe it's the small amount of alcohol I drank when he arrived to try and take the edge off, or maybe the heat, or maybe I'm tired of pretending I don't want what I want.

He stands before me, watching as I take a sip. His gaze follows the glass to my lips with an intensity that makes my skin prickle. The water cools me down, but Nate?

He's the reason I feel light-headed.

My knees brush his legs, and he steps between them, close enough that his scent—cedar and warmth—surrounds me. God, how is it fair for someone to even smell this beautiful?

I pull in a shaky breath, and his smirk tells me he notices. His fingers flex at his sides, a tiny movement that sends my pulse racing. Then his hands slide to my thighs, fingertips grazing my skin before planting firmly on either side of my hips, caging me in. His closeness is intoxicating. I can't tell if it's my heart pounding or his, but it echoes in my ears like thunder.

"Fuck. What are you doing to me, Len?" His voice is low, sincere, like he actually cares about the answer.

I lean closer, my lips near his ear. "I could ask you the same thing."

The tension between us crackles like lightning before a storm. His eyes flutter closed for a moment, like he's fighting whatever spell binds us together. But I'm done fighting. I grab his shirt and tug him closer.

His eyes snap open, burning into mine.

Is this what it feels like to play with fire then?

"Don't play games, Leni," he warns, his voice firm but edged with something darker.

"Don't call me that," I whisper, defiant.

"Call you what?" His smirk is devastating, the kind that could pull confessions from saints.

"That," I say, my voice barely audible, but he hears it.

He chuckles softly, his gaze never leaving mine. "Then stop looking at me like that."

"Like what?" I challenge, giving his words right back to him.

His thumb glides over my thigh, a simple stroke that sends my mind spinning.

"Like you want me to—"

Before he can finish, footsteps and Camilla's unmistakable laughter echo through the house. Nate steps back, the space between us stealing the heat as quickly as it had built. I slide off the counter, trying to steady my breathing, the kitchen suddenly suffocating with the ghost of him so close.

Camilla stumbles into view, wide-eyed.

"Oh, shit, sorry!" She freezes, then gestures awkwardly toward the door. "I was just—uh, actually, never mind. I'll go check outside. For lemons," she adds, spinning on her heel and disappearing with a sheepish grin.

I take another sip of water, as if that'll put out the fire Nate just started. The glass is cool against my lips, but it does nothing to ease the burning under my skin where his fingers traced patterns of want just moments ago.

Spoiler: nothing will.

The tension between Nate and me has been building all summer, but now it's something else entirely—thicker, heavier, like tectonic plates shifting beneath the earth's surface, threatening to create an earthquake with every shared glance.

By morning, I'm raw and restless, like my skin doesn't fit quite right anymore. The house feels too small, too empty and too full all at once—every room echoing with the ghost of last night's almost-kiss. I grab my bag and practically run for the door. I go to the one place that always feels like an extension of me, Gracie's bookstore.

The familiar scent of aged paper and leather bindings wraps around me as I step inside, the little bell above the door announcing my arrival with its cheerful jingle.

Alfie is there, hunched over a worn classic, glasses perched precariously on the edge of his nose. His weathered hands cradle the book with the reverence of someone handling precious memories rather than just pages. At the sound of the bell, he looks up, and his warm smile immediately eases the knots in my chest.

"Miss Wells," he greets, setting his book aside with careful precision. "You're a sight for sore eyes."

I drop my bag at my feet and sink into the chair across from him, letting out a breath as if I'd just run the entire way here.

"Alfie, I did it. I finished the piece about you and Gracie."

His face lights up, a mixture of pride and curiosity softening his features. The afternoon light streaming through the dusty windows catches the silver in his hair, making him look almost ethereal.

"You did, did you?"

Wordlessly, I pull the pages from my bag, my hands trembling slightly as I hand them over. He takes them with the kind of reverence usually reserved for sacred things, and my heart catches in my throat.

As he reads, the room falls impossibly quiet, save for the soft rustle of paper and the distant ticking of the ancient wall clock. I watch his expression shift—eyes crinkling with warmth, lips curving into a bittersweet smile. When he finally looks up, there's a sheen of tears in his eyes that makes my own vision blur.

"Your words, young lady," he begins, his voice thick with emotion, "they're beautiful. You captured her spirit—us—perfectly. It's like you saw her the way I did."

"You really like it?" I ask, my voice small, barely above a whisper. The pressure of telling someone else's love story—especially one as precious as theirs—has been sitting heavy on my shoulders for weeks.

"No, Lenora," he says, shaking his head with a soft laugh that seems to hold decades of memories. "I absolutely love it. You've done us proud."

I exhale, relief washing over me like a warm tide.

"I was so afraid I wouldn't do you or Gracie justice."

He leans forward, resting a hand over mine. His skin is paper-thin but warm, marked with the stories of a life well-lived.

"Justice? Nora, what you've done here is a tribute. A love letter to a life well-lived. You've honored her memory more than I ever could've hoped for."

His praise makes me smile, though I can feel heat rising to my cheeks. I toy with the corner of my sleeve, gathering courage for the question that's been burning in my mind.

"Alfie, how did you know it was supposed to be Gracie?"

He chuckles softly, the kind of laugh that carries cherished memories in its echo. "The moment I saw her through that window, sitting and reading Jane Austen. She had this... quiet brilliance about her, like she belonged to the whole world but chose to sit in mine." His eyes take on a faraway look, seeing something—someone—from long ago.

"There was this sense of rightness, you see. For some, first love is just a spark, a preview of loves to come. But for others, it's the only love—the greatest love. That's why I think heartbreak exists. To remind us of the worth of what we had, even if it was just for a short while."

"Did you ever doubt it?" I ask, leaning forward, hungry for insight into a love so sure, so steadfast.

"Never," he says without hesitation, and the certainty in his voice makes my heart ache. "With the right person, it's simple. Even when it's hard, it feels simple because you never question if it's worth it. It just is. When it came to Grace, the answer was always yes."

"Was it terrifying?" I whisper, thinking of my own heart and its dangerous tendency to leap before looking. "Knowing something so big, so certain?"

"Terrifying?" He tilts his head, considering. "A little, maybe. But love, the raw and honest kind, has a way of silencing fear. No relationship is all sunshine. But two people can share one umbrella and survive the storms together." His eyes meet mine, knowing and gentle. "It's not about being perfect or easy—it's about being certain the person standing by your side is the one you want to be sharing an umbrella with."

I smile, imagining a younger version of Alfie falling for the woman he describes with such tenderness.

"You and Gracie really were soulmates."

He leans back in his chair, his gaze distant but warm.

"What we had was more than love—it was a connection that reached the deepest parts of who we were. We were better together. When you find someone who doesn't try to fix you or complete you but shows you how to be the best version of yourself, that's the person you want by your side through the depths of heaven and earth."

His words settle over me like a warm blanket, their weight and wisdom seeping into the cracks I've been trying to make sense of. I think of Nate, of the way he sees me—really sees me—even when I'm trying to hide.

"That kind of person won't pick up the pieces for you," Alfie continues, his voice gentle but firm. "They'll remind you that you're strong enough, capable enough, to do it on your own. But they'll always be there, steady and unwavering, offering a hand if you need it. They won't let you fall."

The parallels to my own situation hit so close to home that my chest tightens. I swallow hard, trying to keep my voice steady.

"But what if you're scared of losing them?"

Alfie's eyes soften with understanding. "It's the gaps in life that will teach you what's worth fighting for, Nora. The spaces between what we want and what we have—that's where we learn who we are."

I tilt my head, intrigued despite the ache in my chest.

"How do you mean?"

"Well," he says, a soft smile tugging at the corner of his lips, "think of it like this: what's the difference between a space and a room?"

The question catches me off guard. "Is there one?"

"Would you call an empty space a room? Or does a space only become a room when it holds something—when it has purpose?"

"I guess that makes sense," I say slowly, following his train of thought.

Alfie nods, settling back in his chair. "Now imagine taking the objects out of a room, one by one. The first thing you notice is the absence—you miss what you've taken away. But then, you start noticing what's left more than ever before."

I lean in, hanging onto his words, feeling like he's offering me a key to a door I've been afraid to open.

"You see, when things are taken from us, what remains takes on greater value," he continues, his voice steady. "If there's a chessboard in that nearly empty room, you're far more likely to play chess. Loss teaches us to focus on what's still here. What we lose in breadth, we gain in depth. The thing with love is, it's a risk. We open our hearts knowing they'll eventually break. But that's the paradox of it all: the very thing that makes love terrifying is what makes it extraordinary."

"Every heartbeat we share with another is both a countdown and a gift, each moment precious because it cannot last. To love is to dance on the edge of loss. But to never love? That's like keeping a bird in its cage, wings folded, never knowing the glory of flight. Better to soar and fall than to never leave the ground. Because sometimes, in the space between holding on and letting go, we find pieces of ourselves we never knew were missing."

His words settle over me like truth itself, filling the room with unspoken understanding. I nod slowly, feeling as though something deep within me has shifted.

"I hope someday I can write something that'll mean as much as her story means to you," I say, almost to myself.

Alfie's eyes soften, and he smiles—the kind of smile that feels like a blessing.

"You already have, Nora. And you will again. You have the heart for it —just don't ever stop letting it lead you." He pauses, his voice gentling. "Most of the time writing isn't about saying the right thing. It's about letting yourself say what's real. Just give yourself permission to feel and the words will come."

He's right.

When I write, I'm facing my fears—my anxieties, my feelings. I'm putting them into words, giving them life, acknowledging their exis-tence. Just like with Nate, maybe it's not about finding the perfect words, but about being brave enough to speak the truth.

I don't think Alfie realises the gift he's given me. It's more than just wisdom about writing—it's a glimpse of the kind of love and purpose I've always dreamed of. And for the first time in a long while, it feels possible. Maybe that's why, when I finally leave the bookstore, my steps are lighter despite the weight of everything unsaid between me and Nate.

The universe, it seems, has other plans for my newfound peace.

When I arrive home, I hear something unexpected—music. Not just any music, but the familiar strum of a guitar and Nate's voice humming along. The melody pulls me in like a siren song, and before I can stop myself, I'm following it down the hall.

I find him in his room, shirtless, his back to the open door. Sunlight streams through the window, painting golden stripes across his skin as his fingers dance over the strings.

"I haven't heard that song before," I say softly. My voice startles him; his fingers freeze on the strings as he turns. Something flashes in his eyes —raw and vulnerable—before he blinks it away, like shuttering a window against a storm.

"Didn't realize you were home," he mutters, fidgeting with the pick between his fingers. The casual gesture belies the tension suddenly thrumming in the air between us.

There's a flicker of something in his voice—desperation maybe, or resignation—and it catches me off guard. His eyes meet mine, searching, like he's trying to gauge whether I'll push or let this moment slip away like all the others. I step closer, drawn by whatever's crackling in the space between us.

"Nick asked me to play on opening night," he says finally, the words falling like stones in still water.

"Are you going to do it?"

He sighs, shoulders heavy with something more than just uncertainty.

"Not sure yet. Been forever since I played for anyone, let alone a crowd."

"Could've fooled me." The corner of his mouth lifts slightly—almost a thank you for noticing what he never says out loud.

"We'll see," he murmurs, trying to brush it off like it doesn't matter. But I know it does.

He's been tiptoeing around me for days, and I'm tired of this dance. My emotions are frayed, patience worn thin by his constant hot-and-cold routine. Taking a deep breath, I ignore my thundering heart and just say it.

"Can we talk about the other night?"

The question hangs between us, heavy as summer storm clouds. He doesn't answer right away. His fingers move absently over the guitar strings, the notes muted like his voice. Then he drags a hand through his hair—a gesture I know means he's wrestling with something he doesn't want to say.

"Nora, I just..." His voice drops to barely a whisper. "I can't do this." He gestures between us, his hand slicing through the air like he's trying to sever whatever thread still connects us.

"This. Us. Whatever it is, or isn't. I can't."

The words steal the air from my lungs. My mind races, replaying every moment, every look, every lingering touch that led us here. And now, just like always, we're back to square one.

I force a bitter laugh to cover the ache spreading through my chest. "Wow. Nice to see I'm that easy to throw away."

I turn for the door before tears betray me, but his hand catches my arm, sending electricity through my skin. I collide with his chest—solid, warm. His breath brushes my cheek as he holds me there like an anchor.

"Nora..." My name fractures in his throat. His eyes lock with mine, a battlefield of unreadable emotions. He brushes my hair away from my face, his fingers gentle against my temple, trailing behind my ear. The warmth of his touch is a cruel contrast to the hollowness in his stare—his hands remember what we were while his eyes have already forgotten.

"Say it," I whisper, my voice trembling with everything we've left unsaid. "Whatever it is you're so afraid to tell me, just say it."

His grip loosens slightly, his hand sliding down my arm to circle my wrist, like he's afraid to let go entirely.

"You don't get it." He whispers.

"Get what, Nate?" My voice rises, frustration spilling out as my chest heaves against his. "Because the only thing I'm getting, is that you're addicted to this back-and-forth. You pull me close then push me away, over and over, like some twisted game—"

"I'm not trying to play games," he growls, his voice low and fierce, but there's something else there—something that sounds a lot like fear.

"Then what the hell are we doing?" I snap, the heat between us charging the air like lightning before a storm.

He exhales sharply, his shoulders sagging under the weight of whatever he's carrying.

"I... I don't know."

"You don't know?" I throw my hands up, shaking my head in disbelief. "Well, you better figure it out then."

"It's not that simple," he says, his voice quiet but laced with frustration.

"Why not? Why can't it—"

Before I can finish, his hands are on face, pulling me closer until our noses touch and breaths mingle. His eyes—those eyes I've known since childhood—burn into mine with an intensity that steals my breath. He tilts my face up, forcing me to look deeper, to read what he can't say aloud. The truth is there, raw and unguarded, if I'm brave enough to see it. His voice drops to a hoarse whisper, filled with something that sounds like fear and longing twisted together.

"Because I can lose everything, every-fucking-thing. But not you. Never you. That's why."

My resolve falters.

Every part of me screams to stay, to understand, to finally break through whatever's holding him back. But he's already retreating, the wall slamming shut as quickly as it cracked open. His next words are clipped, controlled, like he's already decided our fate.

"Can we try to go back to how things were? Pretend that what happened a couple days ago didn't happen." He pulls away, putting space between us like he's done a hundred times before. "It's better this way."

Pretend?

I've practically perfected the art of pretending. With everything I've lost, it's second nature. But pretending with him feels less like a relief and more like a betrayal—of my heart, of his truth, of whatever we could be if we were brave enough to try. Still, it's what he wants, so I force a smile, nodding like it's nothing.

"Sure," I say, my voice steady even as I'm breaking inside.

"So, we're okay?"

The last thing we are is okay.

"Sure," I repeat, the word tasting like ash.

He sinks into his chair, his gaze shifting to his guitar—anywhere but me. The sting of being so easily dismissed burns more than I'd like to admit. I turn for the door, his silence heavy in the air between us. Before leaving, I glance back one last time, taking in the sight of him—this boy who's been my closest friend, my beautiful stranger, and the one who's managed to break my heart in ways he doesn't even realize.

"Do the gig," I say softly.

His head snaps up. "Why?"

"Because you sell yourself short, Nate."

He blinks, caught off guard, but says nothing. I don't wait for a response. I leave before I give him the chance to let me down again—before I can change my mind and tell him that pretending not to love him might be the hardest thing I've ever had to do.

CHAPTER 46
FRESH PAINT OVER OLD CRACKS
NATE

I'm more than an idiot—I'm the world's biggest asshole, especially after seeing the raw hurt flash across her face. It was like watching something precious shatter, knowing I'm the one who dropped it.

Pretend it didn't happen.

That's not what I want.

Not even fucking close.

But there's a gulf between desire and necessity. My life is a minefield of broken pieces barely held together by determination and denial. Yet despite everything I told her, one truth remains: I can't lose her.

Which is why, trudging toward Sonder, I finally let myself consider Nick's offer. The thought of performing on opening night makes my stomach twist like I'm facing a firing squad, but her words echo in my head, clear as day: *"You sell yourself short, Nate."*

She said it like a fundamental truth, like she could see past all my barriers. And maybe she does.

The instant I push through Sonder's doors, fresh paint fumes assault my senses. It's an oddly comforting mix—citrus cleaner mingling with the earthiness of the restored hardwood floors Nick insisted on keeping. We've been pouring ourselves into this place, every spare moment spent painting walls, hauling furniture, rewiring ancient sound systems. It's exhausting work, but it's been my lifeline. Something about the meditation of painting, the burn of moving heavy equipment, silences the chaos in my head. Right now, that silence is exactly what I need—anything to drown out the replay of Nora's hurt expression.

Nick's already here, methodically stacking chairs, and his knowing grin when he spots me sets my teeth on edge.

"Wasn't expecting you for another couple of hours."

"Thought I'd get ahead," I mutter, snagging a paint roller and beelining for the back wall.

"Yeah? Or are you working off whatever's eating you alive?" His perception is razor-sharp, but mercifully, he doesn't push.

I focus on the wall, watching fresh paint cover old scars. If only fixing myself were this simple—just keep rolling until the cracks disappear beneath a fresh coat. But I know better. Some damage runs too deep for quick fixes.

When Nick catches my eye again, his expression shifts to something lighter.

"Hey, got something for you." He produces an envelope from behind the counter, sliding it over with barely contained excitement.

Two tickets spill into my palm. Jimmy Eat World at the Summer Sounds Music Festival—a show that sold out months ago.

"You're kidding."

"Nope." His casual shrug can't hide his pleased expression. "Figured you might need an excuse to get out of town. Maybe bring a certain someone?"

My fingers trace the tickets' edges as guilt twists in my gut. "Not sure that's smart. Nora and I... we talked."

His grin falters. "And?"

"I told her we should be friends and pretend nothing happened between us."

"And is that what you actually want?" The disappointment in Nick's voice cuts deep.

"What else can I do?" The words scrape out of my throat. "I've got enough baggage to sink the Titanic, twice. She doesn't deserve that shit."

"That wasn't my question." Nick studies me with that infuriating patience of his. "What's the real fear here, Nate? What are you running from?"

My chest constricts as the truth claws its way up. I release a shaky breath. "Are you ever afraid of becoming someone you hate? Like it's written in your DNA?"

"You're afraid you'll become like your dad." He states simply, not a question.

Hearing him mention dad makes my shoulders tense. "Sometimes it feels inevitable. Like one day I'll wake up and see his face in the mirror. The anger, the destruction—it's already there, waiting."

319

Nick's expression softens. "Do you honestly believe that? That you could be him?"

My silence speaks volumes.

"Nate, you were a kid forced to be an adult, trying to protect your mom. That level of responsibility would break most people, let alone a child. Sure, it left scars. But you're not him. The fact that you're terrified of becoming him proves it."

His words crack something open inside me, letting light leak through.

"You can't keep pushing people away because you think you're broken. And you don't get to decide how other people feel toward you. That's up to them. Life's messy, Nate, but that doesn't mean you don't deserve someone who sees through the shit. Someone who accepts you as is—not as a project, but as a person."

The raw honesty makes me want to run, but I force myself to stay.

"You're running from ghosts," Nick continues, sliding the tickets back across the counter with a set of keys. "Stop hiding from what hasn't happened. Make choices the man you want to be would make. If you need a place to crash, my apartment in Brookville is yours."

I finger the keys, trying to lighten the moment. "Sure you're not a secret billionaire dressed as a hillbilly?"

He chuckles. "Nah. Just someone who believes in good people." His gaze pins me. "I see the good in you. Maybe it's time you did too."

Nora's in the kitchen when I get back, lost in a book while stirring her coffee. The domestic scene makes my heart stutter.

I clear my throat. "Free tomorrow night?"

She looks up, curiosity flickering across her face. "Why?"

I produce the tickets, aiming for casual. "Interested in Jimmy Eat World?"

Her eyes widen. "Those shows have been sold out forever! How—?"

"Nick's connections. Thought you might want to go."

She tilts her head, guard rising. "As friends?"

"Yeah." I force lightness into my tone. "We're still friends, right?"

Ollie crashes our moment, fresh from the shower. His eyes dart between us. "Where are we going?"

I smirk. "I'm taking your sister to Jimmy Eat World tomorrow."

"What!? What about me? Your best friend, remember?" His dramatic pout almost makes me laugh.

"I'm sure you can make plans with Mia. Or Jake."

"Jake's gone," Ollie mutters. "Some swim meet or some shit. Left this morning."

Something about that doesn't sit right. A swim meet during summer break? Jake never mentioned it, and he tells Ollie and Nora everything. But I file that worry away for later.

Instead, I watch Nora examine the tickets, catching her subtle tells— the way she worries her bottom lip, how her fingers fidget with her book's pages. She's weighing this, probably remembering yesterday's disaster. The doubt in her eyes makes me question everything, but Nick's words echo: *stop running from what hasn't happened yet.*

"Wait—these are VIP?" Her eyebrows shoot up as she studies the tickets.

I shrug. "Nick has got pull. So? Or should I take him?" I gesture to Ollie, who's massacring a cookie.

A smile tugs at her lips. "Fine. I'm in." She hands back the tickets and heads for the hall.

Once she's gone, Ollie turns his exaggerated disappointment on me. "For real? You're not taking me? You know I love them."

I toss him the Mustang keys. "I'll make sure your birthday gets special treatment. Don't scratch it."

His pout transforms into a grin. He points at me, suddenly serious. "Take care of my sister, yeah?"

"Always," I answer without hesitation, the word carrying more weight than he knows.

CHAPTER 47
FOUND FAMILY
NORA

The boutique's bell chimes as we enter, releasing a burst of air-conditioned air that carries the scent of new fabric and expensive perfume. Camilla, Mia, and Marcus sweep in beside me, their energy infectious enough to momentarily quiet the storm of thoughts about Nate swirling in my head—our raw conversation yesterday, the promise of tomorrow's Jimmy Eat World show hanging between us like an unspoken question.

Marcus, ever the force of nature, immediately takes command of our dress-shopping mission. His eyes light up as he prowls the racks, fingers dancing across fabrics with the precision of a surgeon.

"My girls," he declares, already pulling dresses in jewel tones and shimmer, "are going to be the absolute queens of this gala."

The next few hours blur into a kaleidoscope of silk, sequins, and Marcus's running commentary. Every time one of us emerges from behind the velvet curtain of the changing room, he's ready with a verdict that ranges from, "Girl, that dress was made for you" to "I wouldn't wear that to clean my bathroom." His dramatic flair transforms what could have been an exhausting afternoon into something that feels almost magical.

By the time Marcus whisks Mia away for her fifth round of trying on dresses, my feet are screaming for mercy. I sink into the boutique's cream-colored sofa, the plush velvet embracing me like an old friend. Camilla joins me, the cushions dipping under her weight as she settles in close enough for our shoulders to brush.

"So..." she drawls, her voice pitched low and conspiratorial. "What really happened with you and Nate in the kitchen before I walked in?"

The memory hits me with startling clarity—the warmth of his breath, the way his fingers had trembled against my skin. My neck floods with heat.

"God, I wish I knew," I admit, matching her hushed tone. "One minute he's laying his heart bare, and the next he's trying to forget it ever happened. Then earlier today, he's all casual about going to Jimmy Eat World together tomorrow. Just the two of us. As friends." The last word tastes bitter on my tongue.

Camilla's eyebrow arches skeptically. "Why are boys so dumb? Do you honestly think 'just friends' is even possible anymore?"

Before I can dive into that emotional minefield, Marcus materializes like he's been summoned, dramatically fanning himself with a wooden hanger.

"That boy," he announces, "is completely loco for you. He's just drowning in his own feelings like a cat in a bathtub. Classic man behavior—painful to watch, really."

A laugh bubbles up from my chest despite myself, but Camilla's expression remains serious, her dark eyes holding mine.

"I think he's just scared, Nora," she says, her voice gentle but firm. "But don't let his fear become your prison. If he doesn't get his act together soon, he's going to spend a long time regretting it."

Marcus breaks the moment by tossing a dress across my lap, the fabric cool and silky against my skin. "Your turn, Cinderella! Let's see if we can find something that'll make Prince Charming finally wake up and smell the obvious."

Just then, Mia emerges from the dressing room in a gold dress that transforms her into something otherworldly. The fabric catches the light like captured sunshine, making her glow from within.

"Oh, honey!" Marcus's voice carries across the store. "That's it! That's the one!"

Camilla and I nod in enthusiastic agreement, watching Mia twirl with the kind of joy that makes you forget everything else for a moment.

The afternoon continues like this, a parade of fabric and friendship. Somehow it feels like I've known these people for years, not four weeks.

"So, what's the plan with Jake?" Camilla asks.

The question hits me like a splash of cold water. "What do you mean?"

Her smile turns knowing, though there's kindness in it. "Come on, Nora. Both of them are in love with you. You've noticed, right?"

"Jake?" The laugh that escapes me sounds hollow even to my own ears. "Jake's been my best friend since we were kids. He's practically my brother."

"Are you sure he knows that?"

The words settle in my chest like stones, forcing me to examine memories I've never questioned.

We move through several more stores, the afternoon taking on a dreamlike quality. For the first time in what feels like forever, I'm surrounded by people who see me and accept every complicated piece without question. The feeling is so foreign it almost hurts. But because the universe has a twisted sense of humor, we walk into our final boutique only to find Farrah holding court with Shay and Harlow, all of them perched on display furniture like they own the place. The moment Farrah spots us, the temperature in the room seems to drop ten degrees.

"Great," Mia mutters, "way to kill the vibe."

Farrah's crew approaches like a pack of wolves, but Camilla—beautiful, fierce Camilla—straightens her spine and meets their gaze with the kind of confidence that can't be faked.

"I think you're in the wrong store," Farrah sneers, arms crossed. "The charity shop is two streets over."

Camilla's laugh is sharp and bright. "Oh, if I wanted a bargain, I'd just raid your closet." Her eyes sweep over Farrah's outfit with exaggerated precision.

The exchange escalates until Farrah crosses a line.

"You're just a charity case they keep around for diversity points."

Camilla doesn't flinch. Instead, she steps closer, her voice dripping with false sweetness. "Let me ask you something, Barbie. Do you care about the environment?"

Farrah's perfect features scrunch in confusion. "What are you even talking about?"

"Somewhere out there, there's a tree working really hard to produce oxygen so you can breathe. I think you owe it an apology."

The silence that follows is perfect, right up until Marcus snorts, setting off a chain reaction of laughter that sends Farrah and her minions fleeing the store, their faces flushed with embarrassment.

Over lunch, in a quiet corner of a café that smells of coffee and fresh-baked bread, I find myself opening up about Claire—my former best friend who stood silent when I needed her most during the Evan situation. I carefully dance around the details of that night, but the pain still leaks through my words like water through cupped hands.

Instead of offering empty platitudes, my new friends listen. Really

324

listen. And when Camilla pulls me into a fierce hug, followed quickly by the others, it feels like coming home after a long time away.

"If I ever see that son of a bitch again," Camilla says when she pulls back, her eyes flashing, "I'll break his face. I'll let karma take care of Claire."

I laugh, the sound wet but genuine. "Thanks, Cam."

She winks, her smile softening.

"You know what? I'm grateful to those bitches from your old school. It's like the universe cleared them out so you and I could find each other."

"Excuse me," Marcus interjects, draping an arm across my shoulders. "So we could all find each other."

Looking around at these faces that have become so dear to me in such a short time, I feel something shift and settle in my chest. It's like finding a piece of a puzzle you didn't know was missing—the kind of belonging that makes you realize how lonely you were before you found it.

CHAPTER 48
DEAF OR BLIND?
NATE

I HARDLY SLEPT LAST NIGHT. THE THOUGHT OF A TWO-AND-A-HALF-HOUR car ride alone with Nora made my heart race with a familiar anxiety I couldn't shake. Now, as we pass familiar streets, the silence between us feels comfortable and charged, like the calm before a storm. It's this new dance we've been doing, tiptoeing around feelings neither of us knows how to handle. Or maybe it's just me, overthinking every breath, every glance.

"Would you rather be deaf or blind?" Her question cuts through the quiet, and I feel her eyes on me like a physical touch.

I laugh, grateful for the break in tension. "That's random."

She shrugs, a gesture so quintessentially Nora it makes my chest ache. "Just curious."

"Blind," I answer after considering it.

Her brow furrows, creating that little crease I've memorized a thousand times. "Why?"

I glance at her, letting a hint of a smirk play on my lips. "You see more with your eyes closed."

She turns to the window, but I catch her reflection studying me. The space between us in this car feels impossibly vast and microscopic all at once—like we're trapped in our bubble of unspoken words and missed chances.

The irony of my answer hits me as I steal another look at her. Sunlight dances through her hair, painting it in shades of honey and gold, and I realize how cruel it would be to never see her like this again. She's been a constant presence in my mind for the past year, like a song I can't stop humming, a dream I can't shake off when morning comes.

Because that's what Lenora Wells is—a dream that feels too real, too close, too everything.

"Hey, you okay?" I ask when the silence stretches too thin.

"Yeah," she whispers, still fixed on the passing landscape.

"You sure?"

She hesitates, then turns to me with a question burning in her eyes. "Can I ask you something else?"

"Of course." I keep one hand steady on the wheel, the other gripping the gearshift like an anchor.

She takes a deep breath that seems to pull all the oxygen from the car. "Did you ever think about me? Over the past year, I mean. When we went all those months without speaking. Did you ever..."

Her voice trails off as she fidgets with her bracelet—a nervous habit I've watched her perfect since we were kids.

"You know what, forget about it," she backtracks. "It's stupid and—"

"Why?" I cut in, keeping my voice carefully neutral even as my pulse thunders.

She frowns. "Why what?"

"Why would you think it's stupid to ask?" I focus on the road ahead, but my mind replays every moment I spent trying to forget her and failing spectacularly. Just like I'm failing at this whole 'just friends' charade I foolishly thought I could maintain.

The silence thickens until it feels like we're swimming in it. She draws a shaky breath, and when she speaks, her voice carries a vulnerability that breaks something in me. "Maybe it's just... being back here with you. The other night, it made me forget about everything else that's happened —all the time we spent apart. I... never mind. Ignore me. I don't know what I'm trying to say."

Her words hang between us like suspended stars, and I grip the wheel tighter, trying to anchor myself to something solid. The confined space of the car suddenly feels electric, charged with everything we've left unsaid. She's close enough to touch, yet the distance we've carefully constructed feels like an ocean.

"There wasn't a day that went by I didn't, Leni." The confession falls from my lips before I can stop it, honest and raw.

She freezes beside me, and when I risk a glance, the look in her eyes threatens to unravel every carefully constructed wall I've built.

"Maybe we tried to forget for a reason," she whispers, but her voice wavers with uncertainty.

"Maybe," I reply, swallowing hard against the truth trying to claw its way out of my chest.

But we both know we never really tried.

THE AIR THRUMS WITH ANTICIPATION—A TANGIBLE ENERGY THAT MATCHES the rapid beating of my heart. String lights crisscross above us like fallen stars, casting warm shadows that dance across Nora's face. The scent of summer surrounds us: sunscreen, carnival sweets, and that indefinable electricity that comes before something momentous.

"Come on." I reach for her hand, and the moment our fingers intertwine, everything shifts into focus. "We can get closer."

She follows without hesitation as I guide her through the crowd. Bodies move around us like waves, the bass reverberating through the ground and into our bones. The setting sun bleeds across the sky in watercolor strokes of amber and crimson, turning the world golden.

We find our spot near the center, where the energy of the crowd feels most alive. The fading sunlight catches her features, highlighting details I've spent years trying not to memorize—the constellation of freckles across her nose, the flecks of gold in her green eyes, the way her lips curve just slightly upward even when she's lost in thought.

The band starts playing, and she moves with an effortless grace that makes my throat tight. Her body sways to the rhythm, completely lost in the music, free in a way that makes me envious and captivated all at once. She throws her head back, laughing at something, and the sound cuts through the noise straight to my core.

I tell myself to focus on the music, to let it drown out the constant awareness of her presence. Instead, I catalog every detail: how she tucks her hair behind her ear when she's concentrating, the way her shoulder brushes against mine with each movement, how her scent—something fresh and uniquely her—mingles with the summer air.

What the fuck am I doing?

I shouldn't have brought her here, shouldn't have created this moment where everything feels possible and impossible all at once. But when she turns to me, eyes bright with excitement, I can't regret it.

She leans close, her breath warm against my ear. "This is amazing!"

I manage a smile, hoping she can't see how she affects me. "Yeah, it is."

Even surrounded by thousands, she's the only person who feels real.

The band plays on, each song weaving through the crowd like electricity. When they announce their final song—*"Hear You Me"*—my heart stutters.

Jim Adkins steps up to the mic, his voice carrying over the hushed crowd. "You've been amazing tonight. We've got one last song for you. If you're here with someone special—a friend, a sibling, maybe even someone you love—hold on to them."

The opening chords float through the air, delicate and haunting. Without thinking, my hands find her hips, and she stiffens for just a moment before melting back against my chest. The contact sends electricity through my veins, and suddenly breathing becomes a conscious effort.

The song builds, guitars weaving together in a melody that feels like memory and hope tangled into one. Couples around us sway together, lost in their own worlds. Nora's head falls back against my shoulder, and I hold her like she might disappear if I don't. My fingers press gently into her sides, memorizing this moment, this feeling.

When she looks up at me, everything just fucking stops. Her eyes catch all those colored lights from the stage, turning them into something that hits me right in the chest. That smile—Jesus Christ—the smile she's giving me now isn't the guarded one she uses with everyone else. This one's real and it's aimed straight at me. My heart's slamming against my ribs like it's trying to break free. Like it knows it belongs to her. Always has.

The crowd's pressed in on all sides, bodies crushing together in the heat. Bass thumping so hard I can feel it in my teeth. But it all fades away. It's just her I see. Just us in this bubble where nothing else exists.

We've been dancing around this for so damn long. Years of almost-moments. Years of looking away when caught staring. Years of that electric current between us that we both pretended wasn't there. Years of me telling myself I'm no good for her.

Her chest rises with a sharp breath when my hand finds the small of her back. I'm waiting for her to pull away—to come to her senses and remember all the reasons this is a bad idea. Instead, she leans in. Fuck. I watch her eyes drop to my mouth and linger there. My throat goes dry. Every nerve ending in my body is on fire.

This is it.

The point of no return.

One more step and we blow everything up. Our friendship. Our families. The careful distance I've kept to protect her from the shit-show that is my life.

But I'm done fighting it.

Done pretending I don't want this—want her—more than my next breath.

"Nora," her name comes out like gravel, barely audible over the music.

The kiss happens before I can talk myself out of it—like gravity, like breathing, like finally coming home after being lost my whole fucking life. Her lips meet mine and everything explodes. Sweet and desperate and hungry all at once, not like the kiss from the other night. My hands slide to her hips, fingers digging in like I'm afraid I'll wake up from a dream I don't want to wake up from. Her fingers grip my arms, then slide up to the back of my neck, pulling me closer.

We move together like we've done this a thousand times in another life. Like our bodies remember what our minds forgot. Like we've been starving for this exact moment. When we break apart, her eyes are wide, lips parted. Something passes between us—something I don't have words for. Something that feels terrifying and perfect at the same time.

"Nate," she breathes my name like it's something sacred.

And I'm done for.

Completely fucking ruined for anyone else. Then again, I think I always have been because of her.

"Leni," I respond, the nickname falling from my lips as naturally as breathing.

She starts to speak, uncertainty dancing in her expression. "I don't think friends—"

"Len," I cut her off, unable to stop my grin. "I think we're past the just friends thing."

Her laugh is soft and full of promise. For the first time, I let myself see a future—our future—not as something fragile or fleeting, but as something real and possible.

The crowd begins to disperse as the band plays their final notes. "We should probably head out before it gets crazy," I suggest, though leaving this moment feels impossible.

She nods, and I take her hand, our fingers intertwining as we navigate the crowd. The rain starts suddenly—fat drops that quickly turn into sheets of water. By the time we reach the car, we're soaked and laughing, her giggles mixing with the sound of rain on metal.

"Since when does it rain here in July?" she asks, pushing wet hair from her face.

"It doesn't," I say, watching the windshield blur with water. Traffic ahead is at a standstill. "Traffic's not moving. Maybe we should wait it out."

She gives me a questioning look. "Wait it out where?"

I pull out Nick's spare key, offering a small grin. "Nick's got a place

330

about fifteen minutes from here. He said we could crash there if we needed to. I mean… if you're okay with it."

Her fingers brush mine as she takes the key, the contact sending sparks through my skin. After a moment's consideration, she nods. "Let's do that."

As I drive through the rain-slicked streets, the world outside feels distant and dreamlike. Inside the car, it's just us, the rhythm of rain creating our own private symphony. My hand finds hers over the console, and when she interlaces our fingers, it feels like pieces falling into place.

The rain falls harder as we drive into the night, but for once, I'm not running from anything. I'm running toward everything I've ever wanted.

Toward her.

Toward us.

Toward home.

CHAPTER 49
SIXTY SECONDS
NORA

Nate unlocks the door, and the scent of fresh paint and wood polish wraps around us like a welcome. The one-bedroom apartment is small but immaculate—a canvas painted with someone's determination to make broken things whole again. Every detail whispers of care: hardwood floors gleaming like honey in sunlight, walls dressed in soft neutrals, and baseboards crisp as new fallen snow.

The open concept living space flows seamlessly into a kitchen where stainless steel appliances mirror our reflections. Little touches betray thoughtful preparation—coasters aligned with military precision on the coffee table, fresh flowers standing sentinel on the counter. Nick's perfectionism echoes in every corner, as if leaving anything imperfect was never an option.

"You good?" Nate's voice pulls me from my spiraling thoughts.

I nod quickly, but my stomach performs its own anxious choreography.

"I don't have anything to sleep in," I blurt, hands futilely brushing at my rain-soaked clothes.

"I'll give you one of my shirts." The steady certainty in his voice holds no teasing, no smugness—just Nate, solid as earth. He adds, "And I've got sweats in the car," already moving toward the door. His gaze sweeps over me, lingering just long enough to kindle heat beneath my skin.

"You take a shower, and I'll grab my bag."

"Sure. Thanks." My voice floats unnaturally light, a poor mask for the butterflies staging a revolt in my stomach.

The door's click leaves me in sudden silence, my thoughts start racing uncontrollably.

Will we share the bed?

Does he expect to?

Do I want that?

The answer burns bright: of course I do. But does he?

The bathroom mirrors the apartment's thoughtful design—pale tiles gleaming under soft lighting, a glass-enclosed shower that belongs in a luxury hotel. When I turn the rainfall showerhead on, warm water cascades like summer rain, washing away the day's grime and the lingering cold. Steam curls around me like a protective spell, but my mind fixates on Nate—his mouth, his hands, the careful restraint behind his eyes that masks something deeper, hungrier.

What if he walked in right now?

What if he decided to stop waiting?

Heat pools low in my belly at the thought. He's always so measured with me, every action calculated. But who is he protecting—me or himself? The idea of making the first move sends my heart into overdrive.

How do you tell the boy you've loved forever that you want him to press you against wall and kiss you until the world dissolves?

I rest my forehead against the cool tile, letting the water drum against my back. The old fears surface like sharks in dark water. But then I remember the way his eyes linger, how they burn with something that mirrors my own wanting.

Maybe he's as tired of this dance as I am.

When I step out, his clothes wait on the bed—a Guns and Roses t-shirt and sweatpants with a note in his messy scrawl about getting food. The summer heat makes the decision for me. I pull on just his shirt, the fabric carrying his scent of cedar and clean skin.

The front door opens and Nate freezes, takeout bag dangling forgotten from his hand. His eyes travel over me with deliberate slow-ness, darkness bleeding into their hazel-green depths. The air thickens until breathing feels like drawing honey into my lungs. My body responds to his gaze—nipples hardening, thighs pressing together as desire coils tight in my core.

He swallows hard, voice rough as stone. "I, uh, got us food from down the road. Thought you might be hungry."

He sets the bag down and moves closer, each step measured and intent. My pulse pounds a war drum rhythm against my ribs because there's a burning look in his eyes that's filled with desire.

"Nora, I'm going to kiss you." His voice carries dangerous certainty.

"Is that a good idea?" The question is a lie, but the truth—that I'm terrified he'll regret this tomorrow—feels too raw to voice.

His thumb traces my lower lip like he's memorizing its shape. "Debatable."

"And if I think it's a bad idea?"

A smirk plays at his mouth. "You're saying if I kiss you right now, you wouldn't kiss me back?" His confidence wraps around me like smoke.

I shake my head weakly. "Yes." It's more breath than word.

His thumb follows my jawline, leaving fire in its wake. When his hand cups my neck, thumb settling over my racing pulse, my eyes flutter closed as he peppers kisses along my throat.

"Are you sure?" he murmurs, voice intimate as a secret.

I nod yes, drawing a dark chuckle.

"Liar," he whispers.

When his lips claim mine, the kiss isn't gentle. It's raw hunger and years of wanting compressed into a single point of contact. My hands find his chest, mapping the solid planes beneath cotton.

"Sixty seconds," he mutters against my mouth.

"What?"

"For sixty seconds, forget everything. It's just you and me."

"And after that?"

"We sit down and eat, then go to bed. No regrets."

I nod, knowing one minute will never satisfy this hunger, but I let him believe his own lie.

His hands frame my face as he kisses me deeper, tasting of mint and possibility. He holds me while I explore him with desperate hands, learning the man who replaced the boy I once knew. For these precious seconds, I want to know every part of him, to feel the kind of pleasure that reshapes reality. My fingers trace his arms, shoulders, stomach, drawing a sharp breath from him before his hands tangle in my damp hair. Time bends and snaps.

When he pulls back, we're both breathing hard, foreheads pressed together.

"Time's up," he whispers, stepping toward the bedroom door.

But instead of walking away, he pauses, leaning against the frame like it's all that's keeping him upright.

"Fuck this," he says softly then turns to look at me. "I'm done."

My heart stutters. "Done with what?"

"Pretending." The words rumble from his chest, heavy with frustrated desire. He crosses the space between us in measured steps. My back meets the wall as his hands cup my face, eyes locked on mine like he's committing every detail to memory.

"I'm done pretending I don't want every fucking part of you."

The kiss that follows isn't just contact—it's combustion. Slow, devastating heat that spreads through my veins. He watches me when I pull away to remove his shirt. My hands slide over his body, exploring the terrain with trembling fingers. Years of protecting those he loves has sculpted him into something beautiful and brutal—hard ridges of muscle shift under my touch, and raised scars tell stories of a childhood spent standing between a monster and the people he loved most in the world. Every mark is a testament to the way he loves—completely, fiercely, with his whole body as a shield. He was a just a boy when he received most of these scars. A boy who learnt way too young that some loves are worth bleeding for.

My fingers wind into his dark hair, silk-soft strands between my knuckles, and when I tug gently, the groan that rumbles from his chest vibrates through every point where our bodies touch. The sound shoots straight to my core, drawing an answering whimper from my throat. Every brush of his hands feels like breaking free of gravity.

We move together with an instinct deeper than memory, as if our bodies have been rehearsing this dance in dreams, just waiting for reality to catch up. His calloused fingertips trace fire up my thighs, the rough texture against my sensitive skin sending shivers cascading through me. I arch into his touch, craving more friction. When he grips the hem of his shirt that I'm wearing and slowly pulls it off, the air between us changes. His eyes darken, pupils dilating as they take in every inch of newly exposed skin. The possessive heat in his gaze is palpable, molten gold and hunger wrapped into one look that makes my knees weak.

His finger comes to rest on my bottom lip, gently tracing its outline. My breath catches as he slowly trails that finger down, over my chin, following the curve of my neck. His touch is feather-light but leaves a scorching path in its wake. He pauses at my collarbone, eyes locked with mine as his finger continues its journey downward, between my breasts, the simple contact more intimate than anything I've ever felt.

"Is this okay?" he whispers, his voice husky with restraint.

The care in his question makes my heart swell. Even now, with desire evident in every line of his body, he's checking, making sure. This is Nate —always has been. He's always been my safe space, the one person who makes me feel protected rather than controlled or used. Who asks rather than takes.

I nod, unable to form words.

"When you say stop, we stop, yeah?"

The tenderness beneath his intensity makes my heart constrict even as every nerve ending in my body hums with electric need—pleasure and anticipation twisted together so tightly I can't tell where one ends and the other begins.

"Do you want me to stop?"

I shake my head, stepping closer to him until I'm pressed up against him, my fingers tracing the muscles of his shoulders until they find their way to his jaw line and lips.

"Don't stop," I whisper against his mouth, the words more breath than sound.

His eyes don't just look at me—they *devour* me. Dark and starving and somehow still gentle. My heart kicks against my ribs when his hand slides under the soft cling of my panties, deliberate and purposeful. Fingertips graze heat and slickness and I swear, I *whimper*—a sound I didn't know I could make.

God. I *ache* for him.

The first real touch pulls matching gasps from our throats—his low and wrecked, mine sharp and wreckless. The sound hangs in the charged space between us like something holy and broken. His forehead presses to mine, and he watches me with this intense, quiet reverence, like he's learning me by feel, by breath, by every little quake under my skin.

"You're so wet for me. It's fucking beautiful," he murmurs. "*You're* fucking beautiful."

Something inside me cracks open at that. Any fear or awkwardness just burns away, gone like mist in fire. I can't speak—only feel, only *burn* —as his fingers find this perfect, torturous rhythm that scrapes the breath from my lungs.

"Do you have *any* idea how long I've wanted this?" he breathes, voice soaked in hunger and something almost... desperate. "Wanted *you?*"

And then his mouth is on mine, and it's not sweet—it's *starving*. He kisses like he means to carve himself into me, like I'm the only thing that's ever made him feel real. He starts slow, yeah—but it's the kind of slow that unravels you. That *owns* you. Like worship, but wilder. More raw.

I melt for him. And somewhere beneath the softness, something wild in me starts to stir. Starts to *howl*. Because no one's ever touched me like this before—not just my skin, but *me*. All of me.

And now I don't know if I'll ever let him stop.

I know, with bone-deep certainty, that nothing will ever be the same again.

"*Fuck*, Len... you have no idea what you do to me," he rasps, voice thick with something jagged.

His hands map every inch of me like I'm made of secrets he's been dying to uncover.

Slow. Merciless. Intentional.

Each touch sets off tremors under my skin until I'm gasping—needy, unmoored, half-feral.

"You're going to ruin me," he breathes against my mouth, and then he *takes* it—kissing me like the words alone weren't enough to bleed the truth out of him. Like he's trying to drown in me.

I let out this broken little laugh between kisses, the sound raw and tangled in everything I feel.

"You ruined me a long time ago." I grip the back of his head like I'll fall apart if I don't hold on, burying my fingers in his hair.

His eyes lock onto mine. "Lenora Kennedy Wells, you will be my greatest undoing."

And then his fingers quicken, dragging me toward the edge of something I've never stepped off before. Something that feels like dying and living all at once.

"Now let me watch you come undone for me."

I crash into him, kiss him like it's the only language I know, like I can pour years of love and ache and longing into the heat of his mouth. My body arches against him, chasing the rhythm, chasing release. His free arm slams against the wall beside my head with this raw, explosive force that makes me flinch—and *want*—in the same wild breath.

Then his eyes—fuck, those deep eyes—pin me in place.

"Eyes on me, Leni," he says, low and dark, a whisper soaked in velvet and command. My mouth gapes open while my spine turns to liquid. His thumb drags across my lower lip, slow and firm, just enough to make me freeze.

"I want to watch you let go."

And I do.

I can't tear my gaze from his even if I tried. There's something primal in him now—something untamed that calls to the wild thing waking up in me. I let it out. Let it *burn*. I meet his eyes without flinching, every wall inside me crashing down. I let him *see* me—raw, vulnerable, undone.

A silent offering. A surrender.

That smile he gives me? It's not sweet.

It's lethal.

Slow and smug and soaked in power, like he's just won a war. He presses into me, close enough that I can feel the full heat of him. His mouth brushes mine—not a kiss, but a promise.

And when his fingers blaze a line down my throat, I swear I stop breathing.

"Good girl," he whispers against my mouth.

Two simple words shatter everything and suddenly the room tilts sideways.

The gentle pressure of his fingers transforms into something else—something rough, demanding, wrong.

Evan's hands, were too harsh, taking what wasn't his to take. The sweet cedar scent of Nate's skin morphs into the sour stench of beer and cigarettes that clung to Evan that night.

Panic spreads through my chest like ice water in my veins.

No, stop.

This is Nate.

Safe, gentle Nate.

Count to three.

One...

But Evan's voice drowns out my counting.

My skin crawls with phantom touches. The soft lighting dims in my mind, replaced by suffocating darkness. The wall against my back feels like that mattress—the springs digging into my spine, the sheets tangled around my legs like restraints. The taste of mint from Nate's kiss turns metallic, like the blood in my mouth from biting my lip to keep quiet.

This isn't real.

It's Nate.

It's Nate.

But my body doesn't believe my mind.

The harder I fight the memories, the stronger they become, like quicksand pulling me under. Evan's grip on my wrists, the weight crushing my ribs, his hot breath against my neck—it all crashes back in vivid, terrible detail. When Nate's fingers ghost along my thigh, reality splinters. I'm falling through time, through space, through that trap door I thought I'd sealed shut, back into the darkness where monsters wear human faces.

My lungs forget how to work. The room spins faster. Every touch, even Nate's gentle ones, feels like burns on my skin. My throat closes, remembering the pressure of Evan's hand, the way he squeezed until stars burst behind my eyes.

"Nora?" Nate's voice cuts through the fog, and I realize I'm shaking, breath coming in panicked gasps.

He pulls back immediately, hands raised as if he's the one who's done something wrong. The hurt and confusion in his eyes guts me.

"Shit, Nora," he says softly, my nickname breaking in his mouth. "Hey, fuck, I'm so sorry. I—did I hurt you?"

"N-no," I force out, though the word scrapes my throat raw. "I...I just need—" But the words die as I'm yanked back to that dark bedroom, feeling Evan's weight crushing me, his hand suffocating me.

Be a good girl and stop screaming.

It will hurt less if you stop moving.

You wanted this, you little bitch.

The concern in Nate's eyes makes my stomach turn. Doubt shadows his features, his own demons layering over mine. We're like two broken mirrors trying to reflect something whole.

"Nora, hey, I'm sorry. I shouldn't have... I pushed you too far. Fuck. " he says, voice steady despite the pain in his eyes. "Hey, hey." His hands frame my face, grounding me. "I don't know where you've gone, but right now I need you to listen to my voice, okay? Just listen to me."

I nod, barely meeting his eyes as he takes my hand.

"Squeeze my hand," he murmurs, thumb tracing gentle circles on my knuckles. "When you can't breathe, just focus on that. Squeeze as hard as you need to, okay?"

I grip him like a lifeline, nails marking his skin as I fight the spiral.

"I'm here, Len. I got you. Now just keep breathing in and out for me." His voice anchors me, each word deliberate and sure.

Gradually, the panic recedes, leaving me hollow but steady.

Tears spill unbidden, but Nate brushes them away with tender thumbs before grabbing his Guns and Roses shirt off the ground and dressing me in it.

"Lay down," he whispers, guiding me to the bed like something precious. He cradles me against his bare chest where I fit perfectly, arms wrapping around me, lips pressing against my hair. Everything about him feels like coming home.

"I'm... I'm sorry," I choke out, but he shakes his head fiercely.

"Don't," he says firmly. "Don't ever apologize for something that makes you uncomfortable. Not to me. Not to anyone."

There's no stopping the tears from falling once they start, so I let them while he settles beside me. His fingers find my hair, stroking gently like he used to when we were kids and sleep eluded me. The familiar gesture pulls me back to simpler times, before life complicated everything.

As sleep tugs at my consciousness, I feel his fingers drawing on my back—soft, deliberate patterns. A heart, then the initials N + L inside it.

I drift between sleeping and waking, his warmth keeping the nightmares at bay. Through the haze, I hear his voice, low and aching.

"Who hurt you this badly?"

The name rises like poison to my lips.

Evan.

It slips out, a whisper I never meant to voice.

His sharp inhale follows me into darkness.

CHAPTER 50
WHERE SHADOWS MEET
NATE

I LAY IN THE DARK, NORA'S BODY CURLED INTO MINE, HER BREATH WARM against my neck. It should calm me—but it wrecks me.

She's wrapped around me like she belongs here. Her thigh slung over mine, fingers against my chest like an anchor. Every curve pressed against me brands itself into my skin.

Her mouth on mine.

Her legs trembling.

Her gasps like broken prayers.

That look in her eyes when I told her to keep them on me—*fuck*, that look.

It wasn't just lust. It was something deeper.

She looked at me like I was her only tether to earth. And briefly, I believed I could be that.

Steady. Safe. Enough.

But I'm not.

My mind loops endlessly—her mouth on my neck, her voice cracking when she said I'd ruined her long before tonight. The way she trusted me completely, falling apart in my arms without fear or shame.

I didn't deserve any of it.

She sleeps beside me now, breathing easily like we didn't just shatter every boundary. Not because she didn't want it—but because she deserves better than what I am. I stare at the ceiling while shadows dance like ghosts of all my former selves. And still, she trusts me with her silence.

With her body.

With everything.

I want to be good for her. To be the man she sees when she looks at me with her heart in her eyes. But underneath, I'm all sharp edges and smoke. I'm terrified that staying close will only burn her.

I kissed her like she was mine. Touched her like she was sacred. Loved her like it wouldn't destroy us. But in the brutal quiet of night, one question splinters through me: *Did I just fuck up the one good thing I've ever had?*

I know exactly when it happened. I saw it.

Felt it.

One moment she was clinging to me like I was worth holding—and then...

Her eyes changed first.

That flicker—impossible to miss. Not fear of me, but something deeper. A shadow I know too well. I've seen it in the mirror. On Mom's face whenever Scott entered a room. The kind of fear that bruises souls, not just skin.

Her breath hitched in panic. Her hands trembled. Her heartbeat raced against mine like she was running with nowhere to go.

She pulled back—not physically—but I felt her retreat. Curl inward like an animal cornered once too often. Her tears fell quietly, almost apologetically, as if pain was something she had to bear alone.

I wanted to tear the world apart and rebuild it so she'd never feel that way again. I held her tighter, fingers in her hair, whispering her name like a lifeline.

Then she whispered his.

"Evan."

One word.

One name—and everything inside me detonated.

That smug prick from the restaurant with our moms, looking at her like she was something to take. I should've known when Ollie mentioned him. Should've done something.

Now I know.

And I want to kill him.

I've never felt rage so blinding and feral. It rose so fast I thought I'd be sick. But I couldn't move or react. Because this moment wasn't about me.

It was about her—trusting me to hold her through her silent breaking.

So I stayed and became the wall she could lean on. My storm could wait. I prayed my touch didn't make it worse. That maybe my presence could help mend what was torn from her.

342

She deserves peace and safety. I don't know if I can give her that. But I'll try. Because even broken and haunted by whatever that bastard did, she's still the bravest, most beautiful thing I've ever known. I'm worried she'll never see herself the way I do.

"Nate?" Her voice breaks through, soft and trembling as her hand cups my face. Her thumb traces my cheek, grounding me, pulling me back from the edge. "What's wrong?"

"You're asking me what's wrong?" Of course, she is—she always puts everyone before herself. I press my forehead to hers, trying to steady the hurricane in my chest.

"You scared me last night." My voice stays low, careful, as I brush a strand of hair from her face. "I need you to tell me what happened, Nora. Please. Not knowing is killing me."

She looks up at the ceiling, her body going rigid. I worry she's about to shut down again, so I wait, drawing invisible patterns on her arm while she finds her words. She might not see it, but I hope she feels it—feels how much she means to me, even when the words stick in my throat.

"It happened last summer, right before Dad—" she swallows hard, tears pooling in her eyes. "Before he died."

I take her hand, weaving our fingers together. I want to be her anchor now, the way she's always been mine. She studies our intertwined hands like they hold answers to questions she's afraid to ask. I prop up on an elbow, cradling her face with my free hand.

"Nothing you say will change how I see you, Leni. Whatever it is, you can tell me."

Her eyes close, a shaky breath escaping her lips. Then the words that shatter my world: "Last summer, Evan... He tried to..." Her words catch in her throat and I can see how hard she's trying to fight back tears, so I squeeze her hand as a reminder that I'm here.

"He what Nora?" I regret asking as soon as the words leave my mouth.

"He forced himself on me."

Rage explodes in my chest, white-hot and violent. I'm grateful she's still focused on our hands, blind to the fury I know is written across my face.

"It happened at a party," she continues, voice distant. "One I didn't even want to go to, but my friend—" She pauses, pain flickering across her features. "Well, I thought that's what she was. She dragged me there because of some guy she was obsessed with."

"Evan." His name tastes like poison.

I thought I knew pain, thought I'd lived it every day in that house of broken promises and shattered dreams. But seeing her look so small, so vulnerable, it kills me. She was never meant to be small, and the fact that some bastard made her feel that way makes me want to tear him apart. I know he's why she looked at me with fear last night.

Why her voice trembled.

Why she couldn't breathe.

I want to kill him.

I keep perfectly still, forcing down the rage threatening to explode. She needs me steady right now, needs to feel safe in my arms where she belongs. Her voice wavers, and I squeeze her hand gently, urging her to continue.

"He spiked the drink he gave me." she says, lost in the memory. "Then... next thing, his body was on top of me. The room was dark. I couldn't scream. Couldn't breathe. Couldn't move."

Her eyes search mine, gauging my reaction. I grip my self-control with everything I have, desperate not to let her see how close I am to breaking.

Nausea rises in my throat. Every word she speaks is another knife in my gut, but I force myself to stay steady. She needs my strength now, not my rage.

"Did he...?" The words die in my throat, too terrified of the answer.

"No," she whispers, shaking her head. "He tried and got far enough before Claire walked in. She thought..." Her breath catches. "She thought I wanted it. Called me a two-faced whore. That was the end of our friendship."

Two names on my hit list now.

Her words feel like bullets. She's been carrying this alone, drowning in silence while I was blind to her pain. The rage inside me burns hotter than anything I've ever felt, even in my darkest moments at home.

"Did you tell anyone?" My voice barely holds together.

She shakes her head, tears falling freely now.

"My dad knew something was wrong," she says, breaking. "He kept asking me to talk to him, but I couldn't. I hadn't processed it myself. And the day he died... we fought. I told him to stay out of my life because I was so angry and overwhelmed." A sob tears from her throat. "Nate, the last thing I ever said to him was that I didn't need him. And then he was gone."

Her sobs rip through me like razors. I pull her close, holding her as tight as I dare without hurting her.

"Hey, no. You can't do that to yourself, Len," I whisper into her hair, pressing a kiss to her crown. "Your dad loved you more than anything. Anyone could see that."

She pulls back slightly, wiping at her tears, but I catch them with my thumb, cradling her face. Her eyes meet mine, and I see it—the shadow of something more.

"That's not all, is it?" My voice stays low, steady, though my heart threatens to break through my ribs.

Please, let me be wrong.

Her lips tremble, her voice barely a whisper. "Evan took photos. Of me in that state. He threatened to send them to everyone at school if I told anyone."

The air leaves my lungs. A cold, dark rage settles in my chest, consuming everything else. He didn't just hurt her—he stole her voice, her power, her safety.

Evan doesn't know it yet, but he's just signed his death warrant.

CHAPTER 51
THE ALCHEMY OF LETTING GO
NORA

Nate and I slip through the back door just as the sun is rising, our footsteps barely whispers against the hardwood floor. His hand in mine feels both familiar and electric—his thumb tracing lazy circles on my skin sending shivers down my spine. Everything has shifted between us, transforming what was once comfortable into something thrilling and new. Or maybe it was always there, waiting for one of us to be brave enough to acknowledge it.

In the hushed darkness of the hallway, he draws me close. The kiss is unhurried, deliberate—the kind that makes time stretch like honey, sweet and endless. My world narrows to the gentle pressure of his lips, the steady beat of his heart against my palm.

"Keep looking at me like that," he murmurs, voice rough with promise, "and sleep becomes optional."

"Maybe that's the point," I whisper back.

His smile turns dangerous as he leans in, breath warm against my ear. "Careful, Leni. Push me too far, and I might forget about being quiet."

A soft laugh escapes me as I press a finger to his lips. "Go. Before we wake everyone."

He takes my face in his hands and asks, "You sure you're okay?"

I nod and he brushes a final kiss across my forehead—tender, almost reverent—before disappearing down the hallway. I stand there, pulse racing, letting the reality of the last 24 hours settle into my bones. For the first time since Dad died, the future doesn't feel like a weight around my neck.

Hours later, I find Mom on the verandah, bathed in morning light.

She's curled into her favorite chair, lost in *The Alchemist*—Dad's dog-eared copy that she used to tease him about reading every summer. The sight of her there, peaceful and present, catches in my throat.

"Morning," I offer, settling into the chair beside her.

She looks up, warmth flooding her features. "Morning, sweetheart. How was the concert?"

Guilt flashes through me—I never texted. "It was incredible. I'm sorry I didn't—"

"Nate texted Lydia and me," she interrupts gently. "He let us know you were safe."

"He did?"

Her smile widens knowingly. "You were with Nate. I knew you'd be fine."

I study her face, noting how the shadows of loss had haunted her this past year seem less pronounced. "You seem happy," I observe. "Really happy."

She sets the book aside, meeting my gaze with an openness that makes my chest tight. "I am."

"Would that happiness involve a certain tall, handsome restaurateur with perfect blondish hair?"

A blush colors her cheeks, and I can't help but smile at how young she looks in this moment. "He does have really nice hair, doesn't he?"

I laugh at her terrible attempt at hiding her crush. I'm happy to see her smiling the way she is.

"He's a good guy, Mom," I cut in, suddenly fierce with the need to protect this fragile happiness she's found. "A really good guy. If he makes you happy, don't let Ollie or me stand in your way."

Gratitude softens her expression. "He is. You have no idea how much it means to hear you say that." She tilts her head, reading me with that uncanny maternal insight. "Now, what's going on in that beautiful mind of yours?"

"Not much."

Lie of the century.

"One day, when you're a mother, you'll understand how we always know when our children are lying straight to our faces."

I fidget with my shirt hem, avoiding her knowing gaze. The truth sits heavy on my tongue, waiting to be spoken.

Finally, the words break free.

"I feel like I'm trapped in this cycle of pain, wanting to move forward but feeling like I can't." My voice cracks around the admission.

She reaches over, tucking a strand of hair behind my ear—a gesture so achingly familiar it nearly undoes me.

"I get it. God, do I get it," she says, voice gentle but firm. "Everything is hard in one way or another. Staying stuck is hard. Letting go is hard. Loving is hard. Losing is harder. Life is hard, but you get to choose what's worth risking and fighting for."

Her words settle into the spaces between my ribs, filling the hollow places.

"No one is ever really ready to move on," she continues softly. "But when something—or someone—makes you feel alive again, it's worth risking everything to try. Love always carries the risk of loss. Always. But you can't let that fear keep you from living. I will always love your Dad, and there will be moments where I'll miss him so much it hurts. But I know your father and what would hurt him more is if he knew we all stopped living our lives because he's gone."

She's right. I hear the echo of her own journey in those words, see it written in the quiet determination of her expression.

"Pain is inevitable, but suffering is a choice. You have to choose your hard Nora."

Tears blur my vision as understanding dawns. She's right. I'm tired of being a prisoner to my grief, letting it dictate the boundaries of my world.

"I don't want to suffer anymore," I whisper.

Mom squeezes my hand, her smile tender. "Then don't. It's your life, honey. Take it back."

I might not know exactly what that looks like yet, but I know this: I'm done letting fear and guilt write my story for me.

CHAPTER 52
FATHER FIGURE
NATE

April 2004
17 years old

THE SLAMMING DOOR RIPS THROUGH THE SILENCE LIKE A GUNSHOT, jolting me awake. My heart slams against my ribs as the sound reverberates through walls so thin they might as well be paper. The familiar surge of adrenaline floods my system—a well-practiced dance with fear that leaves my fingertips tingling and my mouth desert-dry. His voice cuts through next, each word slurred and venomous, crashing together in a violent symphony of anger and something stronger than just whiskey.

Coke, maybe. Or pills.

These days, it's harder to tell what demon is riding him.

Mom's voice follows—soft, pleading, desperate. The sound makes my teeth ache. How many times have I heard this same scene play out, like some sick theatrical performance where we all know our parts but can't escape the stage?

The clock on my nightstand reads 01:58 AM, its red digits burning into my retinas like a countdown to chaos.

A wave of relief washes over me as I remember the one blessing in this nightmare: Jake isn't here.

My little brother's safe at training camp, chasing his dreams far from this hellhole. The thought gives me some form of peace, even as bile burns the back of my throat and my pulse thunders in my ears.

Jake—the kid who still believes in heroes. Who sees Scott as some kind of mythical father figure, straight out of those movies where dads teach their sons to throw perfect spirals and give sage advice about life.

Jake never saw the bruises blooming across Mom's skin, never noticed how her hands trembled while pouring his cereal, never caught the way her eyes would dart to the nearest exit whenever Scott's voice rose above a whisper.

The memory of us—the last time we felt like brothers—hits me out of nowhere. Teaching Jake to skateboard when he was ten. His determined little face scrunched up after each fall, tears threatening but never falling because he wanted to be *"tough like his big brother."* The scrapes on his knees were battle wounds, his persistence a shield against failure.

"One more time, Jake," I'd said, steadying the board beneath his feet, my hands firm on his shoulders. *"I'm right here. I won't let you fall."*

When he finally got it, the triumph in his eyes could've lit up the whole damn world. He'd jumped off the board and thrown his arms around me, grinning so wide it made my chest ache.

"You're the best big brother ever."

That moment sealed a promise I'd been keeping since the day he was born: I'd always be there to catch him. I'd never let him see how ugly the world could really be. It's why I pushed Mom so hard to send him away whenever possible—training camps, competitions, anything to keep him out of this house where monsters wear the mask of family, and love comes with a price tag of bruises and broken spirits.

A floorboard creaks outside my door, and my pulse spikes. The bruises from last week's "lesson" still burn beneath my skin, my wrist screaming with every slight movement. But I push through the pain and stand. Because this is what I do. This is who I am.

The shield. The protector. The punching bag.

It's been my role since I was eight years old, and I've played it perfectly. Back then, I thought I could be a hero too—naive enough to believe I could actually stop him. But I'm not that little kid anymore.

He made fucking sure of that.

I shove the door open, its hinges shrieking in protest. The kitchen light spills into the hallway like toxic waste, casting long shadows that feel like prison bars closing in. Scott's silhouette looms against the wall—massive and monstrous, a physical manifestation of every nightmare I've lived through.

For a heartbeat, I falter because of the sheer size of him. How the fuck am I supposed to face down a man twice my size? The rational part of my brain screams at me to retreat, to hide, to survive.

Then I hear it—the sickening thud of something hitting the wall, followed by Mom's strangled gasp.

The fear evaporates, burned away by something colder. Sharper. A rage so pure it crystallizes in my blood, turning every heartbeat into a war drum. There's no time to think, no time to plan. There's only the split-second choice I've made a thousand times before: step into the line of fire and pray I can take the hit.

My vision narrows to pinpoints of red and black, my pulse thundering in my ears. My hands clench so tight my knuckles scream, but I don't dare loosen my grip. If I give an inch, if I let go for even a second, I'll lose whatever control I have left.

"Stop!" The word rips from my throat, raw and sharp as broken glass.

He turns, bloodshot eyes locking onto mine. That glare used to freeze me solid when I was a kid, but I'm not that scared little boy anymore. I stopped being him the first time I watched Scott raise his hand to her and did nothing.

"Get your fucking hands off her." My voice comes out steady, despite what's raging inside me.

His lips curl into a sneer, his words dripping venom. "What the fuck did you just say to me, son?"

Son. The word is acid on my tongue. This man has never been a father to me—just a nightmare wearing the mask of family.

"You fucking heard me."

A smirk twists his features. "Well, would you look at that? Did you finally decide to grow a pair?" He steps away from Mom, whose trembling form is pressed against the wall. Blood trickles from her split lip, and something inside me fractures at the sight.

His bloodshot eyes bore into mine. "Look me in the eyes and say what it is you need to say. Like a real man."

"Fuck. You. *Dad.*"

The words barely leave my mouth before his fist connects with my jaw. Pain explodes across my face, the taste of blood flooding my mouth—metallic and bitter, a familiar flavor I've grown to hate.

"Scott! Stop! Please, I'm begging you!" Mom's cries echo in the background, but they're drowned out by the thundering in my skull.

Thump. Thump. Thump.

Each impact of his fist sends shockwaves through my head.

Once, twice, three times.

I don't have anything left to fight back with. Even if I did, what's the point? The punches would keep coming anyway.

One more hit.

351

Just end it.

Please.

Just fucking end it so it stops.

His attention snaps back to her, his voice pure poison. "This is all your fucking fault to begin with."

Then his hand wraps around my throat, squeezing just enough to remind me who holds the power. "And you—if you ever dare speak to me like that again, it won't end well for you. You hear me?"

"Go to Hell," I spit through blood-stained teeth.

From the corner of my eye, I catch movement—Mom, trembling but determined, a kitchen knife clutched in her white-knuckled grip.

What the fuck is she doing?

"Get away from him now, Scott." Her voice shakes, but there's steel underneath.

The sight of her standing there, weaponized desperation in her hands, sends ice through my veins. He's not in his right mind. He's going to kill her.

The instant his grip loosens on my throat, I explode into action. We crash to the ground together, and my fist finds his face. Something snaps —his nose or my hand, I'm not sure which. Pain shoots up my arm, but adrenaline drowns it out. If I don't stop him now, he'll go after her next.

"Nate, stop. Please."

Her voice cuts through the haze of violence, and something in my chest splinters. Why does she keep defending him? Why does she always choose his side? Why does she stay after every nightmare he puts us through?

"I fucking hate you." The words taste like truth and shame.

"You're just like your mother." His hand finds my throat again, and suddenly I'm on my back, the full weight of the devil himself crushing the air from my lungs. "Weak."

When he finally releases me and storms out of the room, I wait for the door to slam shut before my knees buckle, and I drop to the floor. Spitting blood onto the pristine tile, I gingerly massage my jaw, wincing at the sharp ache radiating through my skull.

Mom rushes to my side, her hands trembling as she reaches for me. "Nate, honey, are you ok—"

"Mom, don't." My voice cracks, but I don't look at her. I can't. If I see her broken like this, it'll destroy whatever piece of me is still holding on. "Just don't."

She swallows hard, her voice shaking. "He just... he had too much to drink, and he—"

"Are you fucking kidding me right now?" Anger surges, momentarily drowning out the pain. I force myself to my feet, glaring down at her. "You're seriously going to feed me that bullshit again? Look around, Mom! Look at you. Look at me!"

Her silence is deafening, her eyes shining with tears she won't let fall.

"It's not just the bruises, Mom," I continue, my voice trembling with rage and exhaustion. "It's the fucking humiliation. The way he makes you cater to his every whim like we're nothing more than props in his fucked-up play. Smiling for his friends, dressing up for his parties. It's all a sick joke to him. We're just collateral damage in his fucking game of power and control."

She opens her mouth to speak, but I cut her off.

"I'm tired, Mom. I'm tired of the lies. The excuses. The pretending. I can't do it anymore. I'm fucking done."

Her tears spill over, and she reaches for me again, but I pull myself up off the ground and step back.

"You need to send Jake away," I say, my voice breaking.

Her brows knit together in confusion. "What?"

"Send him away, for good." I repeat, firmer this time. "Get him out of here. Send him to a different fucking state. For once in your fucking life, do the right thing and protect your son from that piece of shit before he does to Jake what he's done to us. I don't care where he goes—just force him somewhere safe. Please, Mom."

Her face crumples, and she shakes her head. "Nate, I can't—"

"What do you mean you can't? Pay whoever you have to whatever stupid money. It's not like we're short on cash. Jesus fucking Christ. You have to," I snap, desperation clawing at my chest. "He doesn't deserve this. He doesn't deserve..." My voice trails off, choked by the lump in my throat and the pending concussion.

"Nate, sit. You look like—"

I don't hear the rest of what she says because the room slowly starts to fade to black.

THE HOSPITAL ROOM FEELS LIKE A PRISON CELL.

Sterile and suffocating.

The kind of quiet that wraps around your chest and squeezes until black spots dance at the edges of your vision. Every hum of fluorescent lights, every faint beep of monitors down the hall, every squeak of nurses' shoes on linoleum—it all grates against my raw nerves like sandpaper on an open wound.

I focus on the ceiling, counting uneven grooves between each tile. Anything to block out the throbbing in my wrist and the steady drumbeat of pain at the base of my skull. The smell of antiseptic burns my nostrils, mixing with the metallic taste of blood I still can't wash from my mouth.

I don't want to be here.

Mom dragged me in at 3 AM, her grip on my arm desperate, like she could hold all our broken pieces together through sheer force of will. Credit where it's due—it's the first time she's actually brought me to the ER after one of Scott's episodes. I should probably feel grateful for that small mercy. The lie she told the nurse rolled off her tongue with practiced ease: *I fell.*

Might have rebroken my wrist and obtained a concussion with additional bruises. Her voice was steady, believable—you'd think she actually bought into her own bullshit.

A fucking fall. That's the story this time.

She'd managed to clean most of the blood away before we left, even changed my shirt. Anything to hide the truth. The perfect wife, the caring mother, protecting her family's reputation like it's worth more than her son's broken bones.

I wanted to scream the truth. Wanted to tell them it wasn't a fall, that she was lying to protect the monster who did this. But the words lodged in my throat like shards of glass. Because I've been lying for Scott my entire life too. Every black eye, every fractured rib, every time I went flying into a wall—I covered for him.

Football practice. A rough tackle. A stupid accident. The lies came easier than breathing.

But hearing her tell those same lies, watching her carry on this sick performance like we're both method actors in a tragedy—it makes me feel like I'm going to explode.

I sit up too fast and the room tilts sideways, pain shooting through my skull like lightning. Swallowing back nausea, I glance at Mom. She's perched in the chair by the door, arms crossed tight like she's physically holding herself together. She hasn't looked at me once since we got here.

I'm not sure what's worse—the silence stretching between us or the way she keeps pretending this is normal. Like ending up in the ER at three in the morning is just another Wednesday night in the Sullivan household.

"Nate, sit down," she says, her voice clipped. Her eyes dart toward the hallway like she's afraid someone might overhear, might see through the cracks in our carefully constructed facade. "You look like—"

The rest of her words fade as darkness creeps in at the edges of my vision. The room spins, and for a moment, I let it all go—the pain, the lies, the weight of pretending. I collapse back onto the bed, staring at the ceiling as realization hits me like a physical blow.

This is how it's going to be.

Nothing will change.

She'll keep going back.

He'll keep tearing us apart.

And I'll keep ending up here—with broken bones, a broken spirit, and nothing but lies to stitch me back together.

Hours blur together under harsh fluorescent lights. I shift on the bed and flex my wrist experimentally. Sharp pain shoots up my arm, pulling a hiss through clenched teeth. My head throbs in time with my pulse, each beat a reminder of why I'm here. The doctor who walks in looks like he's been practicing medicine longer than I've been alive. His expression is carefully neutral as he studies his clipboard, but there's something in his eyes that makes my stomach clench.

"How are you holding up, Nathaniel?"

"Been better." My voice sounds like I gargled gravel.

"I'll bet. You took quite a fall." His tone makes it clear he's calling bullshit on that story. "Listen, Nathaniel—"

"Nate," I correct him. "Just Nate."

He nods, something softening in his expression. "Nate, I wanted to see you before your mother comes back. You're over eighteen now, so this information can be shared with just you."

He starts examining the x-rays, but I already know what's coming. I can read it in the careful way he chooses his words, in the gentle tone that speaks of years of delivering bad news.

"Your wrist is fractured, so are two of your fingers, and there's definitely a significant concussion." He pauses, eyes meeting mine. "But from your x-rays, I noticed something else."

My throat closes, the air suddenly too thick to breathe.

"You've got older injuries—breaks and contusions—that didn't heal properly. It looks like they've been re-injured multiple times. In fact, that wrist looks like it's already had fresh fractures only weeks old." The weight of his gaze feels like another bruise forming. "I need to ask this," he says, voice gentle but firm. "Is someone hurting you repeatedly?"

The question hits like a sucker punch, but I keep my face blank. Years of practice make it easy.

"No," I say, my voice steady, rehearsed. "It's from football. I'm a quarterback. I've been playing for years. Injuries happen."

He doesn't look convinced. Leaning forward slightly, his voice drops lower.

"Nate, I've been a doctor for over twenty-five years. I've seen football injuries. These don't look like that."

I open my mouth to argue, to spin another lie, but the words die in my throat.

I'm so fucking tired of lying.

Dr. Colson reads my silence, sees the truth in my inability to meet his eyes.

"If you're not comfortable talking to me right now, I understand. But I urge you to find someone you trust. If things aren't safe at home, there are people who can help."

People who can help?

The bitter laugh rises in my throat, but I swallow it down. This guy clearly has no idea who my family is. The only help that's offered in my world is to clean something up or hide something, making it disappear to keep up appearances. I nod, jaw clenched so tight it sends fresh waves of pain through my skull. He watches me for another moment before leaving a card on the side table. The door clicks shut behind him with a finality that echoes in my chest.

The room feels smaller now, the walls closing in. I grab the card—a direct line to a domestic abuse hotline. I shove it in the drawer and retrieve my phone, scrolling to Nora's name. My thumb hovers over the call button, and for a moment, I let myself imagine what it would be like to tell her everything.

But I don't press it.

Instead of calling Nora, I scroll up to David's name and hit call before I can talk myself out of it. The phone rings twice, each tone stretching like years between heartbeats.

"Nate, how are you doing, kid?" His voice comes through warm and steady, so different from the cold fury I'm used to hearing directed my way.

I can't speak.

The words are trapped in my throat and I almost hang up, but then his voice comes again, calm and patient as always.

"Nate, are you okay?"

"I… I don't know anymore." My voice cracks on the last word, and I hate myself for it. Hate how weak it makes me sound. Hate how much I need someone to ask that question and actually care about the answer.

David exhales softly, like he's been waiting for this call. "Talk to me, kid. I'm here. Whatever's going on, you can talk to me, I'll listen."

His tone doesn't demand anything. Doesn't judge. It's the opposite of everything I've known, and something in my chest starts to crack.

"Where are you?" He asks with genuine concern.

"In bed."

Not a complete lie. Hospital beds still count, right?

"Nate, what happened?"

The question hangs in the air, heavy with everything I can't say.

David's always been different.

When I was six, he bought me my first CD—Oasis. I played it until Noel Gallagher's voice was etched into my soul, until the lyrics became a shield against the chaos in my house. The next summer brought The Beatles, then Nirvana. By thirteen, music wasn't just an escape anymore —it was oxygen.

David noticed, like he always did. The day he showed up with that acoustic guitar, something inside me sparked to life. It was the first time I felt excitement that was too big to contain, too pure to hide. Of course, it pissed Scott off. He hated that David saw me, really saw me. Hated that he gave me something to look forward to that wasn't football, that wasn't violence dressed up as character building.

David saw things others missed.

The way I limped after games. How I winced when someone slapped my shoulder. The way my eyes would drop to the floor whenever he visited. He saw what football—what living in my house—was doing to me, physically and emotionally. But he never forced me to answer questions I wasn't ready to face.

Instead, he'd call randomly to talk about music, like it was the most natural thing in the world. *"Did you hear the new Foo Fighters album?"* he'd ask, or he'd drive hours just to surprise me at a game, sitting in the stands like some kind of guardian angel in disguise.

But I knew he knew.

There was something uncomfortable about that—having someone see through the cracks I worked so hard to hide.

Last summer, before he and his family headed back home, he finally said something. It was late, the kind of night where cicadas drowned out everything else. We sat on the back porch, my bruises hidden under long sleeves despite the suffocating heat.

"Nate, if you ever need to talk about anything—anything at all—you can come to me. You know that, right?"

My throat had closed up so tight I couldn't answer. I just nodded, gripping the can until my knuckles went white. He didn't push after that. Just sat with me, letting the silence say what I couldn't.

Now, on the phone, that same silence stretches between us. He waits, giving me space to find my voice, to make the next move. I wonder if he can hear the hospital monitors beeping in the background.

"Do you remember when you gave me that guitar for my birthday?" I finally manage.

"Of course I do. You played *"Time of Your Life"* for hours. I thought your dad was going to lose his mind."

He did.

A quiet laugh escapes me despite the lump in my throat. The memory carries a sharp edge now—Scott had destroyed that guitar as soon as the Well's left that summer. Shattering not just wood and strings, but the small piece of joy I'd managed to carve out for myself.

"I haven't picked up a guitar since."

"Well, maybe this summer you pick it up again and we can have a little jam session. Is that what the kids these days call them? Jam sessions? Or am I that old now?"

I laugh, trying to ignore how it makes my head pound harder.

"Son, are you really okay?"

That word—*son*—coming from his mouth feels like warmth spreading through my ice-cold heart. So different from when Scott uses it like a weapon.

"Yeah, I'll be okay. I'm not really sure why I called. I'm sorr—"

"Never apologize for calling me. I mean that. Okay?"

"Okay."

A few seconds of silence passes, heavy with everything unsaid.

"You know, you've always been more than what you think you are, Nate. You've always been special. I know parents say that all the time, but I mean it, kid. You have something inside of you just waiting to be discovered."

The tears come before I can stop them, hot and relentless. I swipe at my face, hating myself for breaking down, but I can't hold it together anymore. David gives me space, waiting until the worst of it passes before speaking again.

"You've got so much life ahead of you, Nate. Just remember that."

I close my eyes, letting that sink in, trying to believe it could be true. For a moment, I let myself imagine a different life. One where someone like David wasn't the exception. Where love didn't come with conditions, and I didn't have to wonder if I'd ever be enough.

"Thanks, Dave."

"Anytime, kid. You take care of yourself, yeah?"

"Yeah."

"I'll be seeing you, Nate."

The call ends, but his words echo in my mind, a lifeline in the sterile darkness of the hospital room.

I SPEND TWO MORE DAYS IN HOSPITAL UNTIL THEY FINALLY RELEASE ME. School's not an option right now because my face looks so fucken swollen still. I can't use my hand and this concussion is still lingering. So instead I'm sprawled on the couch, an ice pack numbing my wrist and a pillow propped behind my aching head. Mom hovers, asking every five minutes if I need anything, each question dripping with the kind of guilt that makes my teeth ache.

I finally wave her off, telling her she can go if she has things to do. She doesn't argue, but the guilt lingers in her eyes as she leaves.

Scott flew out to Minnesota this morning. No warning, no timeline—just gone. It should feel like a reprieve, but instead, it feels like a count-down. A ticking clock measuring the moments until the next explosion. At least the house is quiet. It gives me time to figure out what the hell I'm supposed to do next with my life, assuming I can piece together enough of myself to build some kind of future.

A knock at the door shatters the silence. The sound jolts through me, and I wince as pain flares in my wrist. My head feels like it's stuffed with cotton thanks to the concussion, making every step toward the door a battle against vertigo.

When I pull it open, I freeze.

David.

He's standing there in jeans and a worn casual jacket, wearing that calm, steady expression he always has—like nothing in the world could shake him. Like showing up unannounced at my door is the most natural thing in the world.

He tilts his head, a hint of a smirk playing at his lips. "What, no hello?"

"What are you doing here?" The words tumble out before I can stop them.

Panic rises in my throat.

"Is everything okay? Nora? Ollie? Kat?" My voice tightens with each name. "Did something happen?"

David laughs, resting a gentle hand on my shoulder. "Everyone's fine," he says, his tone easy and warm. "I was in town for work and thought I'd stop by."

Work? He's a lecturer at a university three states away.

What kind of "work" brings him here?

359

I narrow my eyes, but he doesn't flinch, brushing past my suspicion with practiced ease.

His eyes scan my face, taking in the bruises, the busted lip, the faint discoloration spreading across my jaw. The faint crease in his forehead deepens, and I see it—sadness. It's subtle, buried beneath his usual composure, but it's there, clear as day.

For a moment, he doesn't say anything, and I brace myself for the questions I know he wants to ask.

But instead, he shifts his weight, tilts his head slightly, and says, "Are you hungry?" like this is any other day, like I'm any other kid he's checking up on.

I blink, caught off guard by the normalcy of the question. "Uh... I guess?"

"Good," he says, clapping me on the back. "Let's grab something to eat. I'm starving."

The drive-thru burger joint is quiet, a welcome change from the chaos I've been drowning in. David orders for both of us with the kind of certainty that comes from years of family dinners and shared meals. He slides the bag onto the seat between us before driving to a nearby park. We find a picnic table under an ancient oak tree, its branches spreading out like protective arms above us. The only sounds are distant laughter from kids on the playground and the rustle of leaves in the breeze.

As we sit, I catch sight of a dad helping his little girl climb a slide. When she reaches the top, he cheers like she's just scaled Everest. She laughs, pure joy radiating from her small face as she throws her arms around his neck, and they slide down together.

My chest tightens with an ache that has nothing to do with my injuries.

I never had that.

Maybe I did once, in some distant past I can't remember, but those memories are buried so deep under years of yelling and bruises and broken promises that they might as well not exist.

David follows my gaze, his expression softening.

"I remember when Nora was that small," he says, his tone warm with nostalgia. "That little girl never feared anything."

I smile faintly at the memory of Nora as a kid—her wild hair always tangled from adventure, knees perpetually scraped from climbing too high and riding too fast.

"Yeah. Leni was always brave."

David's knowing smile makes something in my chest flutter.

"You always brought that out in her, you know. She always tried to impress you boys, to prove she was capable of keeping up with you lot." I go quiet, unsure where he's going with this, afraid to hope. "You looked out for her whenever she wanted to do something terrifying. It brought out the best in her growing up."

I stay quiet, while watching the little girl on the playground make a second attempt at climbing.

"You ever thought about having a family of your own one day?" he asks suddenly, his voice gentle but intent.

I nearly laugh, pushing a fry around in circles. "Haven't really thought about it."

That's a lie.

I have.

More than I'd ever admit.

And every time, the same image comes to mind—a home filled with love instead of fear, a family built on trust instead of terror, and *her* standing beside me, hand in mine. But it feels too far out of reach, too much of a fantasy for someone like me, someone as broken as I am.

David studies me for a moment, then leans forward slightly.

"You're a good man, Nate. You've been through hell, but it hasn't hardened your heart. One day, you're going to make an incredible husband and father because of it."

I can't respond because I don't know how. I don't know why he believes in me so much when most people don't even bother to look past the surface.

Then he says it, casual as breathing, like he's commenting on the weather: "You have my blessing, by the way."

I blink, caught completely off guard. "Your blessing?"

"With Leni," he clarifies, his smirk sharp but somehow kind. "If that's something you want one day with my daughter."

My throat tightens as I stare at him, searching for any hint of insincerity, any trace of the conditions and catches I'm so used to. But all I find is calm certainty, an offer of belonging that feels too good to be true.

David takes another fry, biting into it as if he didn't just drop the microphone and walked off stage. As if he didn't just offer me a future I've only dared to dream about in my weakest moments.

And for the first time since I can remember, possibility exists.

CHAPTER 53
A VERY UNHAPPY FOURTH
OF JULY
NATE

PRESENT DAY

THE MORNING IS A BLUR OF TABLES, CHAIRS, AND OLLIE'S NON-STOP chatter. Fourth of July at the Sullivans is always chaos, and Mom thrives on it. It's her thing. She runs the show, and the rest of us just follow orders. Ollie and I haul another set of chairs onto the lawn. The July sun beats down mercilessly, while sweat trickles down my back and humidity wrap around us like a suffocating blanket.

"So," I say, wiping my hands on my shorts, fighting for casual. "You and Mia? What happened while we were gone?"

Ollie's signature smirk appears as he adjusts the chairs. "I don't kiss and tell, pal."

"Come on," I prod, leaning against the table. "You're walking around on cloud nine right now. What's the deal?"

He straightens, and something shifts in his expression—a rare moment of genuine vulnerability that catches me off guard.

"Fine. I really like her, man. Like, wife, kids, the whole deal kind of like her."

I bark out a laugh, but his expression doesn't waver. "Shit, you're serious."

"Dead serious, asshole." He folds his arms, but there's a lightness in his eyes. "Keep giving me shit, and you can kiss that Best Man title goodbye."

"Well, fuck me. Ollie-boy is going to beat us all to the altar."

"Shut up," he replies, throwing a cloth napkin at me, but I see it in his eyes—he's already picturing that future, and honestly? It suits him.

362

"For real though," I say, my voice softening. "I'm happy for you."

"Thanks for your blessing," he says, and beneath the sarcasm, I hear genuine appreciation.

We continue pulling out chairs according to Mom's meticulous seating chart when Ollie clears his throat.

"Hey, uh, heads up about Jake," he adds, his tone shifting. "He came home late last night. Seemed pretty pissed about you and Nora at that concert. I told him it was a last-minute plan, for her birthday and all."

My muscles tense involuntarily. "Where is he?"

"Store run, I think." Ollie starts saying something else, but my attention scatters the moment I spot Nora. Everything else fades to white noise.

"I'll be back."

"You're not seriously leaving me to finish this, are you?" Ollie's voice follows me, but I'm already gone, drawn like a magnet to its pole.

Nora's in the kitchen, wearing a yellow dress that hug her curves in all the right places. It makes my blood surge hot. Her smile hits me like a physical fucking blow, threatening to knock me flat on my ass. Without thinking, I cross the room, grab her hand and pull her into the laundry room, door clicking shut behind us.

Her startled gasp mingles with my thundering pulse. Those wide eyes lock on mine, her chest rising in shallow breaths that match my own frantic rhythm.

I cradle her face, thumbs brushing velvet skin, and for one suspended heartbeat, we teeter on the edge of something inevitable. Then I break—lips crashing into hers with pent-up hunger that's been building for years. Not gentle—deep, consuming, desperate. She tastes like mint and something sweeter, something I could get drunk on forever.

"Hey," I rasp against her mouth.

She throws her arms around my shoulders, pulling me closer until there's nothing but heat and need between us.

"Hi," She says, smile growing wider.

My hands dive into her hair, wrapping those silky strands around my fingers, tugging her head back to deepen the kiss. The noise she makes nearly ends me.

I push her up against the door harder than I meant to, some animal part of me roaring to life when her body cushions against the wood. Her hands are everywhere—chest, shoulders, waist—setting fires with every touch. When I trace those curves I've fantasized about for years, her gasp breaks against my mouth and I swallow it greedily.

My lips find her jaw, her throat, her pulse racing wild beneath my tongue. I want to mark her. Mine. Fucking mine.

"Nate," she whispers, and my name in that breathless voice makes my cock throb painfully.

She pulls back slightly. "Someone could catch—"

"Let them," I growl, forehead pressed to hers, breathing her in. "I'm done pretending. I don't care what anyone thinks about us."

The blush that spreads down her neck makes me want to follow it with my tongue. Her lips—swollen from my kisses—part slightly, and I'm fighting not to take her right here with a houseful of people on the other side of this door. I find the hollow of her throat, sucking lightly, feeling her body arch into mine.

"You have no idea Nora," I rasp, barely recognizing my own voice. "The fucking power you have over me." I kiss her softly before saying into her mouth, "This dress..." My fingers dig into her hips, fighting the urge to tear the thin fabric like paper. "It's dangerous, Leni."

Her laugh vibrates against my lips, her fingers yanking my hair just enough to make my eyes roll back.

"Dangerous?" she whispers, breath hot against my ear, and I'm so hard it hurts.

"Mhm. I'm gonna ruin it later," I murmur, nipping her earlobe. "It and you." I take her mouth again, catching her bottom lip between my teeth, wanting to devour her whole. "Can't wait to rip it off... watch it fall to the floor."

The moan that tears from her throat nearly shatters my control. Her head falls back, throat exposed—trusting me completely when she shouldn't.

"Like that idea?" I whisper against her collarbone, tasting salt and sweetness. "You'd let me tear it right off you before I devour you."

"Nate," she gasps, body pressing closer as my hands slide under her dress, finding bare thighs that scorch my palms. "You can't say things like—"

I pull back, chest heaving like I've run miles. "Why not? Not pretending anymore, remember?"

The way she looks at me—fuck—like I hung the moon and stars. It peels me open, leaves me bleeding and raw and terrified and invincible all at once.

"We're not," she whispers without a trace of doubt.

"Good," I growl, eliminating every molecule of space between us. "Because, Len, you're mine."

Her gasp vanishes as I claim her mouth again, unleashing everything

I've held back. She matches me beat for beat, like she always does—the only person who's ever kept up. My hands roam everywhere, greedy for more. The fabric bunches in my fists as I pin her hips against the door, fighting the urge to grind against her like a horny teenager.

I break away, lungs burning.

My fucking undoing.

I groan. My hands grip her thighs, lifting her until her legs wrap around my waist. The heat of her core against my stomach makes my vision blur at the edges. I'm gonna embarrass myself like I'm sixteen again if she keeps looking at me like that.

"Nate..." Her fingers trail down my chest, each touch burning through my shirt.

I kiss her harder, desperate to taste more, to memorize every inch of her. My lips find her jaw, her neck, feeling her shiver against me like she's coming apart.

"I've never wanted anyone like this," I confess against her skin, truth tearing out of me before I can stop it. "You make me want to lose control and it fucking terrifies me."

Her fingers yank my head back until our eyes meet. I see everything there—vulnerability, desire, trust I don't deserve.

"Then lose it," she whispers, and those two words nearly break me.

A sound tears from my throat—half growl, half groan—as I crush my mouth to hers again. My hands slide higher, feeling the damp heat through her panties.

Fuuuuck.

Her whimper against my lips sends lightning down my spine.

Then she says it: "I am yours, Nate, and I want you to be the one to take it. All of it."

I freeze, blood roaring in my ears. Searching her face for any hesitation, any doubt. There's none—just those eyes that see right through every wall I've ever built.

"Nora," I manage, something protective and fierce clawing at my chest. "That wasn't what I meant when—"

She cuts me off with that soft laugh that makes me feel ten feet tall. "I know. But I'm asking you to. I want it to be you."

Something cracks open inside me—something raw and vulnerable I didn't know existed. I kiss her again, slower this time, trying to pour everything I can't say into it.

"We should probably go back," she whispers, not sounding convinced.

My fingers tease the edge of her panties, feeling slick heat that makes my head spin. "Just a couple more minutes. I missed you."

"You saw me this morning. In bed, no less."

The memory slams into me—her beneath me, gasping my name, nails drawing blood down my back—and I groan, adjusting myself painfully.

"Fuck, Nora. I don't know how I'm supposed to make it through this party when you do this to me."

Her giggle makes my chest ache with something I never knew I could feel.

"Tonight," she promises, eyes dark. "Just don't actually ruin the dress. It's my favorite."

I pull her against me one last time, kissing her hard before whispering, "I'll buy you a closet full if it means I can keep ruining them whenever you wear them."

She laughs. "You're crazy."

"For you? Entirely." And nothing has ever been more true.

We slip out of the laundry room, her hand brushing mine as we move back toward the chaos of party prep. The distant hum of chatter and laughter filters through the walls, grounding us back in reality. Each step feels like we're emerging from our own private world into one that's suddenly too bright, too loud.

Nora's cheeks are flushed, her hair slightly tousled, and she looks at me from under her lashes, a small, secret smile playing on her lips. Her fingertips touch her neck where my lips were moments ago, and the gesture sends heat coursing through me all over again. I catch her glance and wink, sealing our private moment between us.

"Try not to stare too much, will you?" she teases, smoothing down her dress with trembling fingers.

"I'll try, but I'm not making any promises." To her surprise, and maybe to prove a point about being done with hiding, I plant a kiss on her lips right there in the open. "Later though, I'm keeping all my promises."

"You're trouble, Nathaniel," she whispers, but her eyes spark with something that makes me want to drag her right back to that laundry room.

"Likewise, Lenora." I say with a wink.

We part ways and Ollie spots me the second I step back outside, his arms crossed, and a single eyebrow raised. "Oh, perfect timing, Nate. Really. Now that I've folded approximately forty napkins, rearranged tables twice, and listened to Lydia lecture me about floral symmetry, you've decided to grace us with your presence?"

I shrug, slapping him on the back as I pass, still riding high on the lingering taste of Nora's lips. "You're killing it, Ol. Keep up the good work."

He scoffs, leaning dramatically on the counter like he's about to pass out. "I am killing it, thanks for noticing. But you know what would be great? Some help from my brother-in-law."

I freeze mid-step, turning to glare at him. "You want to run that by me again?"

Ollie grins, waggling his eyebrows. "You think I didn't notice you slipping off with my sister? You're not exactly stealthy. And she came back looking like she just ran a marathon in a wind tunnel. I've got eyes, you know."

"Eyes and a death wish," I mutter, grabbing a tray of drinks to hide my mixed emotions. Part of me wants to deny it, another part wants to shout from the rooftops that she's mine.

"Relax," he says, throwing up his hands in mock surrender. "I'm not going to say anything. But if you disappear again, I'm telling Lydia and letting her assign you to napkin duty. And trust me, she's ruthless."

I roll my eyes, but I can't help the small laugh that escapes. "You're such a pain in the ass."

"That's what I'm here for," Ollie says cheerfully, grabbing a bowl of chips and heading toward the yard. But then he pauses, his expression shifting to something more serious. "Hey." He turns back to look at me, all traces of teasing gone. "Don't hurt her, yeah?"

The simple request hits me like a punch to the gut. There's trust in those words—trust I'm not sure I deserve but desperately want to earn. I nod, a lump forming in my throat, and watch him walk off. For all his teasing and big-brother antics, Ollie's always had Nora's back. Seeing him now, giving me a quiet warning but still trusting me with his little sister, hits differently.

I've always known Ollie as the jokester, the one who doesn't take anything too seriously, but when it comes to Nora, he's different. Protective, but not suffocating. He's letting me in, even though I know it can't be easy for him to see his little sister and his best friend together like this. I respect the hell out of him for it. For trusting me not to screw this up, for giving me a chance to prove I'm the guy who's going to take care of her heart, not break it.

Guests start trickling in not long after, filling the backyard with the familiar mix of neighbors, family friends, and the odd straggler who always manages to find their way to a Sullivan party. Laughter spills out from every corner, kids chase each other across the lawn, and the scent of barbecue wafts through the air. Mom is in her element, effortlessly charming everyone as she floats from group to group, ensuring drinks are topped off and plates are full. It's chaos, but it's her brand of chaos, the kind that makes everyone feel like they belong.

I'm hauling another bag of ice inside when I spot Nick making his way through the door. He's casual as ever, hands shoved in his pockets, that signature smirk plastered across his face like he doesn't have a care in the world. Somehow, he always manages to look like he belongs, no matter where he is.

"Your mom invited me," he says in lieu of a hello, grinning as he claps me on the shoulder.

I snort, handing him a beer from the fridge without him even asking. "Surprised it wasn't Kat."

Nick chuckles, twisting off the cap. "You're funny."

We settle into an easy rhythm of conversation, catching up on nothing and everything. When I bring up the concert, I fish the key to his apartment out of my pocket and hand it back.

"Thanks again for letting us crash," I say.

Nick waves it off like it's nothing. "Anytime. It's yours whenever you need it."

For a moment, I just look at him, taking in the casual confidence, the way he's always been there when I needed him, whether I realized it at the time or not. Nick's not just a friend; he's become something more. A mentor, maybe, or the older brother I didn't know I needed. He's steady in a way I envy, a grounding force in a life that's felt like it's been spiraling for as long as I can remember.

"So, how're things with Nora?" he asks, the question casual but weighted with more meaning than his tone lets on.

I don't have to scan the crowd to find her. I never do. She's standing near the pool, laughing at something Camilla said, her hair catching the glow of the sun overhead. She's magnetic, effortlessly drawing people in. And me? I'm utterly and hopelessly caught.

"I think things are looking up," I say, my voice softer than I intended.

Nick glances at me, his smile subtle but knowing. He claps me on the shoulder again, the gesture saying more than words ever could. Approval. Encouragement. A quiet reminder that I've got someone in my corner. He doesn't linger, leaving me with my thoughts as he wanders off to join a group by the grill. I look back toward Nora, watching the way she lights up the space around her, and I want this feeling to last forever.

That's when Jake's voice cuts through the yard, clear and loud, like he's announcing some grand prize.

"I brought an addition to the party," he calls out, and the grin in his tone is unmistakable.

The words barely register before a familiar voice follows, stopping me dead in my tracks.

"Hi, everyone!"

Farrah.

My grip on my drink falters, and for a split second, I'm sure it's going to hit the ground. Fury bubbles up hot and immediate as I glance toward the patio. There she is in her designer shoes and perfectly curated casual look, standing like she fucking owns the place. Jake, either oblivious or deliberately reckless, stands next to her, looking far too pleased with himself.

The question burns in my mind: Is this his way of getting back at me?

The air in my lungs feels sharp, like broken glass as I scan the yard. My eyes land on Nora, who's sitting with Mia and Camilla at a table. She's mid-laugh until her gaze shifts, catching sight of Farrah. Her shoulders stiffen, the light in her expression dimming as she tugs at the hem of her dress—a nervous tic I know all too well. The sight is like a knife to the gut.

The boiling anger in me shifts, sharpening into something primal and protective. Every muscle in my body coils tight as I stride across the yard. By the time I reach Farrah, I'm barely holding it together.

She turns at the sound of my footsteps, lips curving into that saccharine smile I've grown to hate.

"Nate," she coos, and I recognize the fake sweetness in her tone.

"Inside. Now," I grit out, my voice low and controlled, barely.

Her brows lift in mock surprise. "Aren't you happy to see me?" She reaches out to stroke my hair like she used to, the gesture calculated to provoke.

I jerk away from her touch, my glare cutting like a blade. She tilts her head, amusement dancing in her eyes. She's enjoying this. She always did thrive on drama.

"Inside," I repeat, my voice like steel.

Rolling her eyes with exaggerated flair, she lets me steer her toward the house. As soon as the door shuts behind us, I round on her, my hands braced on the counter as I fight to keep my voice level.

"What the actual fuck is your problem, Farrah?"

She crosses her arms, the picture of indignation. "My problem? You're the one dragging me in here like some overbearing asshole."

"We're done, remember?" I snap. "Done. What part of that didn't you get?"

"Your brother invited me, asshole," she interrupts with a smirk that sets my teeth on edge.

Her words reignite the fury burning in my chest.

"And you just had to accept, didn't you?"

Her smile widens as she steps closer, pressing against boundaries she knows damn well exist.

"Come on, Nate." She starts tracing a hand down my chest. "You and I both know we're never really done."

I grab her wrist, holding it firm enough to stop her but not hurt her. "Don't touch me."

She pulls back, her eyes narrowing as her sweet facade crumbles. "Is this seriously because of *her*?" she spits, venom dripping from every word.

"Watch your mouth, Farrah," I warn, my voice dangerously low. The thought of her even speaking Nora's name makes my blood boil.

She presses on, undeterred. "Do you love her, Nate? Or is she just another distraction from your fucked-up little life?"

Her words hit a nerve, raw and exposed, but I don't back down. I step closer, my gaze locking with hers.

"You don't get to talk about her, period. Because she's..." I pause, the truth clawing its way to the surface.

She's everything you could never be.

Her face twists in anger before she sneers, "What? A fragile little whore who needs you to fight her battles for her?"

Something snaps inside me.

Before I can stop myself, I've pinned her against the counter, my rage a barely controlled inferno.

"I told you to watch your fucking mouth," I growl, my voice shaking with intensity. "I won't say it again. Understand?"

Her eyes widen, a flash of fear flickering before she masks it with defiance. Before the tension can escalate further, the door creaks open and Mom steps in. The timing is almost too perfect, like she has a sixth sense for damage control. I step back, putting distance between us.

"Everything okay here?" she asks, her sharp gaze flicking between us.

Farrah's smile returns instantly, syrupy sweet. "Of course. I was just grabbing a salad bowl to take outside."

I watch, incredulous, as she picks up the nearest bowl and walks out, her exit as graceful as ever. The smell of her perfume lingers, cloying and artificial, so different from Nora's subtle, sweet scent.

Mom raises an eyebrow, clearly unimpressed. "Just so you know, I never liked her."

I let out a humorless laugh, running a hand through my hair. The anger is still there, simmering under my skin, but Mom's presence helps ground me.

"To be fair, I'm not sure I ever really did either."

Mom folds her arms, concern etching lines around her eyes. "Jake invited her?"

I nod, frustration bleeding into my voice. "We're not—I don't know why he did."

Her gaze softens, but there's worry there too. "Have you spoken to him yet? About—"

"No," I cut in. "You need to though. Sooner the better."

"I know, Nate. Just… not today. Please. We've got guests, and the last thing I want is a scene." The irony of saying this after what just happened with Farrah isn't lost on me.

"Fine," I say softly, though the word tastes bitter.

Kat strolls into the kitchen, her eyes bright with mischief. "What'd I miss?"

The second I step outside, I zero in on Jake.

He's leaning against the table, drink in hand, talking to Ollie, looking far too casual for someone who just lit a goddamn fuse.

"Jake," I snap, striding over to him. The sun beats down mercilessly, but the heat in my blood burns hotter.

He looks up, feigning surprise with practiced ease. "What?"

"Why did you invite her?" I demand, keeping my voice low enough not to draw attention. My fists clench at my sides, the sharp edge in my voice could cut through steel.

He shrugs, his calculated nonchalance lighting a fire under my already boiling blood. "Guess it must really suck to be out of the loop when things are happening."

"What the fuck does that even mean?" I growl, tension crackling between us like static before a storm.

"Relax, man. Jesus." He takes a slow sip of his drink, as if he's got all the time in the world. The casualness is practiced, deliberate, designed to get under my skin.

"I saw her at the store. She didn't have anything on, so I invited her. You'd think you'd be happy to see your—"

"She's not my girlfriend," I bite out, cutting him off. The words taste like acid. "She never was."

"Oh, that's right," he says, his tone laced with bitterness that runs deeper than this moment. "She's just your side piece"

What the hell is he so mad about? Mom hasn't told him about the divorce yet, but does he already know? Or is this about Nora? The questions swirl in my mind, each possibility more maddening than the last.

"I don't know what's going on with you," I say, my voice dangerously low, each word measured and precise. "But that—" I point toward where Farrah disappeared, the gesture sharp and accusatory— "was really unfucking-called for."

I turn to walk away, trying to rein in the fury simmering beneath my skin, but Jake's casual jab pushes me past my breaking point. I whirl back around, words spilling out before I can stop them.

"And honestly, consider yourself lucky for being out of the loop. Must be nice living a life with such ease."

His eyes narrow, and the easygoing façade he was wearing shatters. "What's that supposed to mean?" His voice rises, loud enough to draw eyes from across the yard.

"Okay, how about we all just take a nice, long, deep breath," Ollie interjects, stepping between us like a human barrier. The tension in his shoulders betrays his light tone—he knows this is more than just brotherly bickering.

But Jake isn't backing down. Something's shifted in him, like a dam breaking.

"You know what? I'm so tired of your cryptic bullshit, Nate." The words burst out of him, raw and accusatory. "That's half your problem. You expect everyone to just know what you're going through, but you never actually talk about any of it. Dad was right. We're all just supposed to walk around on eggshells because God forbid we say the wrong thing and send you down on another one of your—"

"Enough!" Mom's voice slices through the noise, sharp and commanding.

The word echoes in my head as I look at Jake, my little brother, still living in his bubble of ignorance. He still thinks Scott's innocent, and part of me envies that luxury. I wish I could believe that. I wish I could simmer in denial and imagine a version of our father that wasn't the monster I knew him to be. Bile burns in my throat while nausea churns in my gut. The urge to destroy something—anything—claws at my insides. I want to pound my fists against a wall until my knuckles crack and bleed. I want to scream until my throat is shredded, raw and blistered.

Until I can't speak.

If I can't speak, I can't lie.

And if I can't lie, I won't have to live in this version of purgatory, caught between protecting him and destroying his world.

The yard falls silent, every pair of eyes burns into us. I feel like most of my life I've been living in a zoo anyway, so this seems fitting. The anger that's been brewing for years boils over, impossible to contain any longer.

"Open your fucking eyes, Jake."

The words hang heavy in the humid air, and for a moment, confusion flickers across his expression. It's like he doesn't want to hear what I'm saying, doesn't want to acknowledge the cracks in the perfect picture he's painted of our father. The willful blindness in his eyes just feeds the fire in my chest.

"If you think he actually gives two fucks about you, you're setting yourself up for heartache," I continue, my voice low but firm. Each word feels like glass in my throat. "You're a pawn in his game, and the second you cross him, he'll forget you're his blood."

Jake's face hardens, his jaw tightening as anger flashes in his eyes. "Wow. You really do have your head so far up your own ass you can't hear the shit you're spitting out."

"Paint me as the villain all you want," I say, stepping closer, the weight of years of secrets pressing against my chest like a stone. "But you're making a bed with the devil, so you better be ready to sleep in it, because I'm done protecting you from him."

"I never needed you protecting me from shit!" he yells, his voice cutting through the buzz of the party like a knife.

The hardest part?

He has no idea how wrong he is. But he'll learn.

He has to.

Even if watching that realization break him breaks me, too.

CHAPTER 54
LIKE A BULL IN A
CHINA SHOP
NORA

NATE'S VOICE SLICES THROUGH THE AIR AS COLD AS EVER.

"But you're making a bed with the devil, so you better be ready to sleep in it, because I'm done protecting you from him."

Jake's response erupts, raw and jagged. "I never needed you to protect me from shit!"

My heart stutters in my chest. I've seen Jake angry before—storming off after fights with Nate—but this feels different. This anger has teeth, deep-rooted and poisonous, like something that's been festering beneath the surface for years.

I stand frozen, anxiety crawling up my throat like thorns. Every muscle in my body screams to move, to do something, but I'm paralyzed in this familiar space—the no-man's land between two brothers tearing each other apart. It's killing me watching the people I love most turn into strangers before my eyes.

"Jake, please—" My voice comes out soft, pleading, as I step toward him.

He doesn't look at me. "Not now, Nora."

The words crack like a whip before he storms into the house, leaving me standing there with Nate, the summer night suddenly cold against my skin. I glance at Nate—his expression thunderous—but Jake's retreating figure pulls me after him like gravity. I follow him into the kitchen, only to stop dead at the sound of hushed voices.

"Does Jake know about the divorce yet?" Mom asks, voice careful and low.

"No," Lydia replies, barely a whisper. "We haven't told him yet. We were waiting for the right time."

My blood turns to ice.

Jake's voice cuts through the tension like shattered glass. "You're getting a fucking divorce?"

I peek around the corner to see him standing there, color draining from his face, betrayal etched into every line of his body. Lydia reaches for him, but he recoils like her touch might burn.

"Jake," she begins, voice trembling. "We were going to tell you—"

"When?!" The word explodes from him, raw and bleeding. "Jesus Christ, does everyone in this family love keeping secrets from me?"

Lydia flinches, tears welling in her eyes. "We thought we were protecting you—"

"You and Nate just love throwing that in my face, don't you?" His laugh is hollow, echoing off the kitchen tiles. "Protecting me from what? The truth? Because apparently I'm the last person here who deserves it."

"Jake, please," she tries again, desperation threading through her words.

"Don't." The word falls flat and lifeless. "Just... don't."

"We thought we were doing what was best," Lydia pleads, tears streaming down her face.

"We?" Contempt drips from his voice. "Who's 'we'? Because the only person who actually seems honest with me anymore is Dad. He said you were good at keeping secrets."

Lydia's face drains of color, her composure shattering completely.

The silence stretches, thick and suffocating, until Jake breaks it by grabbing his keys off the counter. The metal jingles discordantly as he heads for the door, his movements sharp and jerky. My stomach drops—he's in no condition to drive.

"Jake, wait!" I chase after him, panic rising in my chest. "Please, just—wait."

I catch him on the porch, but he's already halfway down the steps. That's when I notice the sleek Mercedes idling at the end of the driveway, bass-heavy music pulsing through the night air. Farrah leans against the passenger door, her friends watching us like vultures circling prey.

"Don't do this," I plead, moving closer.

He turns, and the storm in his eyes makes me step back. "Did you know?" His voice drops low, dangerous.

I falter, heart pounding. "Know what?"

"About the divorce?" He snaps, the words cracking like thunder. "Did you know and not say anything?"

The word falls from my lips like a stone. "I—I didn't know about the divorce."

"Don't fucking lie to me, Nora. Not you." His eyes search mine, looking for deception.

"Jake, I swear, I had no idea." I reach for his arm but he pulls away.

I swallow hard, guilt turning my tongue to lead. "Look, Nate wanted to talk to you about every—"

"Un-fucking-believable." He cuts me off with a sharp laugh that holds no humor. "I thought we didn't keep secrets from each other?" His voice cracks. "You're just as bad as they are."

The accusation hits like a physical blow, stealing my breath. "Jake, I wasn't trying to take sides—"

"Of course, you weren't," he says, bitterness dripping from every word. "You never take sides. Unless Nate's involved."

"That's not fair—"

"Let me ask you something." He steps closer, his eyes boring into mine with an intensity that pins me in place. "If it were Nate in my place, would you have kept any of this from him?"

The silence stretches between us like a chasm. My hesitation speaks volumes.

Jake's bitter laugh cuts through the night air. "That's what I thought."

He turns toward Farrah's car, raising his voice. "Got room for one more?"

Farrah's triumphant grin gleams in the darkness. "For you? Of course."

Jake tosses his keys at me without looking back. "Guess I won't be needing these."

I catch them reflexively, the metal biting into my palm as I watch him climb into the car. The door slams with a finality that echoes in my chest, and seconds later, the Mercedes peels out of the driveway, taillights bleeding into the late afternoon glow like fresh wounds.

I stand frozen, clutching his keys until my knuckles turn white. This isn't just about the divorce or the secrets. It's everything—years of feeling second-best, of buried hurt and unspoken words, all erupting at once like a volcano we should have seen coming.

And I don't know how to fix it.

I don't even know if I can.

When I head back inside, I find Nate sprawled on the couch, a beer bottle dangling from his fingers like a lifeline. The party continues outside, but here, time seems suspended. He stares at the ceiling, shoulders rigid with tension, looking more defeated than I've ever seen him.

"Jake just left," I say, the keys still cutting into my palm. "He got in a car with Farrah and a group of people."

Nate barely glances at me, taking a long pull from his drink before responding. "Let him go."

"Are you serious?" My voice rises sharply, but his detached gaze remains steady. "He's angry, Nate. He's not thinking straight."

"And you think I am?" He raises the bottle in a mock toast. "He's a big boy. Let him make his own mistakes."

"That's not fair, and you know it." I step closer, anger and fear warring in my chest. "He's spiraling. I'm not just going to sit here and do nothing."

He lets out a harsh laugh that sounds more like pain than humor. "What do you want me to do? Drag him back by his ear? He doesn't want my help. He doesn't want yours. Let him go."

"No," I say, planting my feet. "Someone has to look out for him, and if you won't, then I will."

He sets the drink down with a sharp crack, leaning forward with intensity burning in his eyes. "I've spent my whole life looking out for him. Maybe he's right. Maybe it's time he sees how fucked up things really are."

"Fine." I cross my arms, steel in my spine. "Then I'll go after him myself."

He stares at me, frustration and something deeper etched into his features. Before he can argue, voices spill in from the hallway. Ollie, Mia, Camilla, and Marcus burst into the room, their laughter dying as they read the tension crackling in the air.

"Where's Jake?" Ollie asks, his grin fading as he takes in our expressions.

Nate leans back, voice flat as desert sand. "He left. Apparently, Farrah's more fun than we are."

Marcus perks up. "Shay and Harlow are throwing something tonight. I wouldn't be surprised if that's where they were heading."

"Well looks like we're going to a party then," Ollie says, already moving toward the door. "I'll drive!"

"No, you won't," Mia cuts in, planting herself in his path. "You've had too much already."

"I'm fine," Ollie protests, but Mia's stern look silences him.

"I'll drive," she declares, gesturing to Marcus and Camilla. "You three are coming with me."

"You two okay to ride together?" Camilla asks, glancing between Nate and me with knowing concern.

"I'm driving," I say quickly, before Nate can object.

He groans, rubbing his face. "Fine."

Mia shepherds her group out, and Nate pushes off the couch with deliberate slowness, like every movement costs him. At the door, he pauses and looks back. "Don't get your hopes up."

I don't reply because hope isn't what's driving me anymore. It's fear—fear of what Jake might do, fear of losing him, fear of everything falling apart.

The late afternoon air bites at my exposed skin as Nate unlocks the Range Rover and slides into the passenger seat. I start the engine, the dashboard casting an eerie glow across his face. He looks exhausted. I pull out of the driveway, the silence between us heavy with unspoken words.

What the hell are we about to walk into?

THE PARTY HITS ME LIKE A WALL OF CHAOS—PURE, UNFILTERED TEENAGE rebellion ripped straight from a movie screen. Music thunders through the walls, making my ribcage vibrate. Bodies pack every corner like sardines, the air thick with the sickly-sweet smell of spilled beer and stale smoke. Red cups litter every surface, and the kitchen's a warzone of scattered liquor bottles and sticky counters. A couple is tangled against the wall in the living room, lost in their own world. A whoop echoes from upstairs, and I force my mind away from what that might mean.

This is not my world. I feel like an imposter as I navigate through the crowd, searching for Jake's familiar face. People greet Nate like he's returned royalty, but his expression remains distant, focused. His hand hovers protectively over my lower back as he guides me through the chaos, his broad frame carving a path through the sea of bodies.

He leans down, his breath warm against my ear. "I'm gonna check out back. You good here?"

I nod quickly, trying to project confidence I don't feel. "Yeah, I'm fine."

He studies me for a moment, clearly unconvinced, but heads toward the sliding glass doors, leaving me to navigate this maze alone. I walk aimlessly around for a few minutes. The bass-heavy music pulses through my chest as I squeeze past sweating bodies, muttering apologies. The air feels thick, almost unbreathable, and my eyes dart frantically, searching for Jake.

Instead, I collide with someone else entirely.

"Sorry," I mumble, looking up, and my world stops spinning.

Time freezes, the music fading to white noise.

Evan.

His predatory eyes rake over me like hot coals, and my stomach lurches. Ice floods my veins.

"Well, well," he drawls, lips curling into that familiar, sinister smile. "Look who it is."

I want to run, to scream, to shove past him, but my body betrays me, locking up as terror coils around my throat like a snake.

"You've been avoiding me," he says, stepping closer, his voice a poisonous whisper. "Starting to think you were doing it on purpose."

"Leave me alone," I manage, my voice trembling like a leaf in a storm.

But he doesn't. He leans in, his breath hot and suffocating against my skin.

"Remember what I told you, Nora? Open your mouth and those sexy little videos go viral. You wouldn't want that, would you?"

My chest constricts painfully, bile rising in my throat. His hand brushes my waist, and memories of his touch flash through my mind like shards of broken glass.

I'm frozen, sick, helpless all over again.

"God, I missed how you tasted," he murmurs, his grip tightening as he leans closer.

And then suddenly, he's gone.

Yanked backward with such force that I stumble. Before I can process what's happening, Nate's fist connects with Evan's jaw with a sickening crack that echoes over the music. The room seems to hold its breath.

"You have some fucking nerve touching her," Nate growls, his voice like gravel dragged over steel.

Evan stumbles, laughing bitterly as blood trickles from his split lip.

Nate doesn't flinch. His hand fists in Evan's shirt, eyes blazing with murderous fury. "Touch her again," he says, voice low and lethal, "and I'll break every fucking bone in your body, twice."

"Enjoy my seconds, Sullivan," he spits venomously. "She's a little too soft for my taste, but still fun."

I see the exact moment Nate snaps—his eyes darkening to obsidian, his body coiling like a spring loaded with violence. Fear stabs through me, sharp and cold.

"Nate, don't—" I choke out, but it's too late.

In a heartbeat, Nate tackles Evan, driving him through the coffee table with a thunderous crash. The room erupts—gasps and shouts mixing with the sound of shattering glass. Nate pins Evan down, his fists flying with a brutality that turns my stomach. Evan thrashes beneath him, swinging wildly, but Nate's rage is unstoppable, a force of nature unleashed.

"Stop it!" I scream, but my voice drowns in the chaos.

Connor bursts through the crowd like a bull, grabbing Nate and wrenching him back. Before anyone can react, Connor's fist catches Nate's jaw with a sound that makes me flinch. Nate staggers but recovers instantly, the fury in his eyes burning brighter as he launches himself at Connor, turning the fight into a savage brawl.

CHAPTER 55
THE RESPONSIBLE ADULT
NATE

The music hits like a thunderclap the second we step inside Shay and Harlow's house, bass reverberating through my bones. Bodies pack the space wall-to-wall, the air heavy with sweat and cheap beer. By the keg, guys chant like they're summoning ancient spirits, while couples press against walls as if the world might end tomorrow. Some kid I half-recognize lies unconscious on the couch, fingers wrapped around an empty bottle like it's keeping him alive. A classic Eden elitist party—nothing subtle about it, nothing genuine either.

The crowd surges around me like a living creature, hungry and suffocating. People slap my back, shouting my name as if we share some deep connection, treating me like their hometown hero. It sets my teeth on edge. They're clueless about what's really at stake tonight, and I don't have patience for their manufactured friendship.

I push through the mass of bodies, a single question burning in my throat: "Have you seen Jake?"

Most just shrug, eyes glazed and distant, too far gone to care. Others can't even hear me over the music that rattles the windows like an approaching storm.

"Nate!" Jay's voice slices through the chaos. He leans against the kitchen counter, joint dangling from his fingers like a red flag, wearing that perpetual smirk that seems permanently etched on his face.

"What the hell are you doing here?" I ask, tension coiling in my muscles.

He exhales smoke in lazy spirals, unbothered as always.

"Got some buyers here. Came to make a quick deal." His eyes flick over me, calculating. "Didn't expect to see you. Thought this wasn't your scene."

"It's not." My gaze drifts to the writhing mass of bad decisions behind me. "I'm looking for my brother. Have you seen him?"

Jay takes another drag, the gesture as loose as his ethics. "By the firepit. Guy looks pretty cooked."

Of course he is.

My fingers curl into fists, knuckles whitening as familiar guilt twists in my chest. Jake drinking himself stupid with people who couldn't care less about him. Maybe I've been wrong all these years, trying to shield him from the truth like some misguided guardian angel —it's done more harm than good. Maybe the lies I told to protect him, pretending everything was fine while our world crumbled, make me no better than our parents. Just another person in his life dealing in beautiful deceptions.

"Let's go," I say, voice hard as steel as I turn toward the backyard.

Jay falls in step beside me as we navigate the human labyrinth. Outside mirrors the chaos—more bodies, more noise, weed smoke hanging thick as fog. The firepit blazes like a warning signal, surrounded by guys laughing too loud, bottles glinting dangerously in their hands.

And there he is.

Jake sways on his feet, beer clutched like armor, drunker than when he stormed out earlier. He spots me before I can speak, throwing his arms wide like he's center stage in his own tragedy.

"Well, look who it is!" His voice cuts through the night like shattered glass, sharp with something darker than alcohol. "The prodigal son! You just don't quit, do you?" He turns to the girl beside him, who clings to his waist like she's afraid he'll dissolve into smoke. "Kelsie, you know my brother Nate? I'm sure you've probably hooked up at some point, right?"

The girl shrinks away from his venomous words.

I clench my jaw until metal floods my mouth but keep my voice steady as still water. "Let's go. We're leaving."

He barks out a laugh that sounds nothing like my brother, lifting his beer in mock salute.

"Nah, I'm good right here, thanks."

He drains the bottle in one go, throat working like he's trying to swallow more than just alcohol, and someone hands him a fresh one like feeding kindling to a fire.

"Jake, I'm fucking serious. Let's go."

He stumbles closer, firelight dancing in his glassy eyes like fever dreams.

"Why are you even here, Nate? I don't need you to babysit or protect me anymore."

Frustration tangles in my chest like barbed wire. He doesn't understand—everything I've done, my whole life, has been about shielding him from the pain that's haunted our family like a curse. But I swallow the words. He wouldn't hear them anyway, not through the walls of alcohol and anger he's built around himself.

"Nora was worried about you," I offer instead, truth extended like an olive branch.

His smirk turns sharp as a blade. "Sure she was." He pauses, voice cutting deeper than any knife. "Tell me, have you fuck—"

"I'm going to stop you right now before you say something you'll really regret." My words sharpen to a razor's edge, warning wrapped in steel. "You're drunk and need to get your ass home."

"Oh, I know exactly what I'm saying." He steps closer, beer sloshing like blood as he points at me with unsteady precision. "I should have known she'd always choose you. No matter how fucked up you are, no matter what it costs, she'll always choose you. And that's what will destroy her someday. You can't be stupid enough not to see that."

Each word slices into wounds I've been trying to ignore, reopening them with surgical accuracy. Would she always choose me? And if she did, was that salvation or damnation? Was I toxic for her, dragging her into my darkness in ways I refused to acknowledge?

Before I can respond, Jake gets in my face, anger radiating off him in waves hot enough to rival the fire. But before things can escalate into something irreparable, Ollie appears with Mia and Camilla trailing behind like shadows.

"All right, that's enough," Ollie says, voice calm but solid as bedrock. His eyes move between us, assessing the situation like a bomb tech. "Nate, take Nora home. I'll look after our boy here."

Jake snorts, turning away like we're beneath his notice.

Ollie leans closer to me, voice low. "Go find my sister and make sure she's okay. I'll bring Jake back."

I hesitate, eyes lingering on Jake, who's already laughing with strangers like nothing happened, like he hasn't just torn open wounds that might never heal.

Finally, I nod, the weight of everything unsaid heavy as lead. "Thanks."

Ollie grips my shoulder, the gesture grounding. "Just get her home safe, yeah?"

I don't need to be told twice.

Some fires you can't extinguish—you can only watch them burn and try to salvage what remains.

Jay and I push back through the crowd, bass pounding like war drums in my chest. Jake's words echo in my head, but I force them down like bitter medicine. Right now, I need to find Nora and get her out of here.

"You good, man?" Jay asks, voice low as grave dirt.

Before I can answer, my entire body locks up like I've been struck by lightning.

I see her.

And I see *him*.

That motherfucker has his hands on her waist, fingers digging into her flesh like he's marking territory. He's leaning in, whispering something that makes her face go pale, eyes darting around the room like a trapped animal searching for escape. She looks terrified, and something primal inside me snaps like a steel cable under tension.

"Oh, fuck," Jay mutters beside me, voice taut as a bowstring.

I don't hear the rest. The world narrows to a tunnel, red bleeding into the edges of my vision. Pure, unfiltered rage surges through my veins like liquid fire, and before I can think, I'm moving through the crowd like a bullet finding its target.

Evan barely has time to look up before I rip him away from her. He stumbles back, expensive shoes squeaking on polished floor, and I don't give him a chance to recover. My fist connects with his face with a sickening crack that reverberates up my arm, the impact sending shockwaves through both our bodies.

"You have some fucking nerve touching her," I growl, voice low and lethal as a blade against throat. Blood drips from his split lip, staining his perfect white teeth as he staggers.

"Touch her again," my voice drops even lower, promising violence, "and I'll break every fucking bone in your body, twice."

Instead of backing down, he smirks through the blood. "Enjoy my seconds, Sullivan. She's a little too soft for my taste, but still fun."

The words barely register before everything goes red. My fist finds his jaw again, harder this time, bone meeting bone with a sound like thunder. He stumbles into a group of people, sending drinks and shouts flying, but nothing exists except him and the rage burning through my veins like acid.

"Nate, don't!" Nora's voice cuts through the chaos like a knife, desperate and shaky as autumn leaves, but I can't stop.

I tackle him through the coffee table and glass shatters beneath us. He groans as we hit the ground, shards tinkling like broken wind chimes around us. I pin him down, each punch fueled by the fear I saw in Nora's eyes and his smug expression I want to permanently erase. His hands flail uselessly against me, but I'm relentless. One punch after another, each impact sending jolts through my knuckles that I barely register.

"Stop it!" Nora's voice pierces through the red haze, but it barely reaches through the roar of blood in my ears.

A hand yanks me back and I twist, ready to swing. A punch lands on my jaw, sending me stumbling, copper flooding my mouth.

Fucking Connor.

The sight of him reignites the fire in my veins. He throws another punch that cuts through air like a blade. I duck, feeling it whistle past, then counter with a shot to his ribs. He doubles over, grunting, before charging again.

The crowd erupts around us, a chaotic blur of shouts pulsing with the music, but it's all background noise. My focus locks on Connor, everything else fading to shadows as adrenaline narrows my world to fists and fury.

"Nate!" Jay's voice cuts through the chaos like a knife through fog. He steps between us, hands against my chest like trying to hold back a storm. Connor seizes the moment, swinging past Jay's guard. The punch lands with a sickening thud, and Jay stumbles back, blood trickling from his mouth.

"Son of a—" Jay spits red onto the floor, shaking his head. His eyes darken like storm clouds. "Oh, you're fucked now, Country Club."

Jay launches forward like a spring uncoiling, fist connecting with Connor's face. The impact sounds like thunder, sending Connor reeling into the crowd.

"Nora, wait!" Camilla's voice slices through the noise, pulling me from the red haze. My fists drop instantly as I glare at Connor and Evan through sweat and blood.

"Nate, Nora's leaving!" Camilla calls again, desperation threading through her voice.

I turn just in time to see Nora pushing through the crowd like a ghost, dark hair disappearing into the sea of bodies.

Connor sneers from the wall, wiping blood from his split lip. "Get the fuck out of here, Sullivan," he spits, crimson staining his teeth.

But I'm already moving, focused on Nora, everything else falling away. The fight, the pain, the rage—none of it matters anymore. Only she does.

"Nora!" I call after her, my voice cracking in the cold night air like ice breaking.

She doesn't stop, shoulders shaking visibly as she walks faster, pushing past people like she's trying to outrun something darker than just this night. The distance between us stretches like an endless chasm, and for the first time tonight, I feel real fear—not of fists or blood, but of losing her in ways that can't be fixed with violence.

By the time I catch up, she's leaning against the car, arms wrapped tightly around herself like she's holding something broken together. The streetlamp casts harsh shadows across her face, making her look fragile. She won't look at me, but her trembling makes my heart ache like someone's carved out something vital.

"Nora," I say again, softer now, trying to steady my breath. Adrenaline still courses through me making my bloodied hands shake, but I force myself to move slowly, carefully, like approaching a wounded bird.

When I reach for her wrist, she flinches away sharply like my touch burns. It stops me cold, her reaction cutting deeper than any punch tonight, deeper than glass or bone could reach.

"Don't—" she starts, voice trembling like leaves in a storm. She finally turns, and the light illuminates her tear-streaked face like rain on glass. The sight guts me worse than any hit I've taken. Her eyes look to my face, expression twisting with something complex and painful.

Fear? Guilt? Pain? All of them tangled together like thorny vines.

"You're hurt," she whispers, the words falling between us like broken pieces of something we can't put back together.

"It's nothing," I say quickly, even as my jaw throbs like a second heartbeat and my knuckles sting. Blood dries on my skin like war paint, but none of that matters.

"Are you okay?" The question feels inadequate for what I see raging behind her eyes.

She shakes her head, tears falling faster now like stars breaking free.

"I can't do this, Nate," she says, voice breaking like glass under pressure. "I can't—"

Her words dissolve into a choked sob that sounds torn from somewhere deep and wounded. I step closer, hands hovering in the space between us.

"I'm sorry," I whisper, "I didn't want you to see that, but he—" I stop, running a hand through my hair, frustration and guilt clashing inside me. "I couldn't watch him touch you like that."

Her eyes glisten in the dim light, full of emotions I can't unravel, like looking into a kaleidoscope of pain.

"Why do you always have to fix everything?" she asks, tone raw and accusing, but there's no anger—just bone-deep exhaustion.

I step closer, careful as if approaching the edge of a cliff.

"Because even though you don't need anyone saving you, where I can, I'll always try," I say simply, words rough but honest as an open wound.

Her breath hitches and I watch her defenses crumble like a castle made of sand. Her face collapses as she lets out a shaky breath that sounds like surrender, arms still hugging herself.

"Hey," I whisper, reaching for her again. This time, she doesn't pull away when my hands cradle her face, touch gentle despite split knuckles. My thumbs brush away her tears as I lean down to catch her eyes, trying to keep her in this moment with me.

"Don't cry. Please. I'm here."

She shatters completely and falls into me, clutching my shirt in her fists. I wrap my arms around her frame, holding her tightly against me, feeling her heartbeat race against my chest as I rest my chin against her hair. She shakes in my hold and I try to be the shelter she needs.

"I found Jake," I murmur, voice low and steady as I can make it, trying to give her something solid to hold onto. "Ollie's staying back to make sure he gets home."

She nods against my chest, breaths still uneven as waves, but relaxes slightly in my arms, tension easing fraction by fraction. My hand strokes her back in slow circles, trying to ground her, to remind her she's safe now, even as my own heart thunders with everything.

"I'm taking you home," I tell her softly, lips brushing her temple.

And in this moment, with her trembling in my arms and my blood still singing with violence, I know I'd burn down the whole fucking world to keep that promise—to keep her safe, even if it means protecting her from myself.

CHAPTER 56
THE CALL
NORA

THE SOFT STRUMMING OF AN ACOUSTIC GUITAR DRIFTS THROUGH THE CAR like whispered confessions. The Goo Goo Dolls' *"Before It's Too Late"* fills the space between us, its melody rising with an urgency that mirrors the storm inside my chest. Each note feels like a plea to hold onto something precious slipping away, and I can't help but appreciate the universe's cruel poetry in this moment.

My forehead rests against the cool glass of the passenger window, seeking relief from the inferno of emotions burning beneath my skin. Outside, the world blurs as streetlights and shadows pass by. All I can focus on is the quiet hum of the engine and the way the music wraps around us like a living thing.

Nate's presence beside me is steady as a heartbeat, but the tension radiating off him charges the air like static before lightning. The fresh cut on his lip stands out angry and red—a harsh reminder of everything that's brought us here.

"I know the answer, but I'm still going to ask," he says finally, his voice low and careful. "Are you okay?"

I keep my eyes fixed on my ghostlike reflection in the window, unable to meet his eyes. After everything—not just tonight but all the moments leading here like dominoes falling—words feel impossible, trapped behind walls I've built between my heart and my tongue. Instead, I shake my head, a motion so small it's barely there, but he notices, like he always does.

The song shifts to a softer, almost pleading riff that resonates in my bones like a second heartbeat. It mirrors everything we're yet to say—all the things I can't voice and the questions he's too afraid to ask. We're like two people speaking different languages but understanding the same pain.

His fingers twitch on the wheel, and I know he's fighting the urge to reach for me, uncertain if he still has the right. I keep my eyes forward, watching the road stretch endless as my fears into the darkness ahead.

"Sometimes," I whisper, my voice barely audible over the engine's hum, "it feels like I can't move. Like everything around me is swallowing me whole and I'm drowning in air."

The words hang between us, raw and jagged as broken glass. I feel exposed, like I've peeled back a layer of myself I wasn't ready to show. Then his hand finds mine, our fingers lacing together.

"Like no matter what you do, you're stuck in this place where everything hurts, and there's no way out." It isn't a question, it's recognition—a truth I half expected he'd carry too. We're both walking through life with matching scars we try to hide.

Tears spill down my cheeks before I realize they've formed, but when I finally dare to look at him, there's no judgment in his eyes. Just that quiet intensity he always carries.

"What do you do," I ask softly, my voice trembling like autumn leaves, "when everything goes wrong?"

Nate signals and pulls the car to the side of the road, tires crunching on gravel like broken promises. When the engine cuts off, we're left in an almost sacred silence, the world outside fading until it's just us, painted in soft blues and shadows by the dashboard lights.

"What are you doing?" The words barely escape my lips.

He turns to me then, hazel eyes locking onto mine with a depth that steals my breath. In the half-light, his gaze holds something ancient and understanding, like he's carrying answers to questions I haven't learned to ask yet.

"You know what you do when the world crumbles around you, Len?" His voice is soft but unwavering, pulling me closer like gravity.

I swallow hard, searching his face like trying to read a language I once knew but have forgotten. "What?"

He lifts my hand, turning it palm-up in his own with a gentleness that makes my heart stutter. Slowly, he brushes his lips against the inside of my wrist, the gesture so tender it leaves me undone. Through that single point of contact, it feels like he's trying to pour all his strength into me.

"The only thing you can do," he whispers against my skin, before pressing another kiss to my palm. "You breathe it all in, and then you let it out. Because the more you hold onto it, the more it eats at you from the inside out, like poison in your veins. You can't let the fear, the hurt, or the pain win. You just have to learn to let it live by your side and acknowledge it when it's there, like an old scar. One that reminds you that you survived. You can't just give in when it wants to consume you like wildfire."

His words settle around us like a blanket heavy with truth. "It's not easy, but I think it's possible."

The faint glow from outside catches on his face, highlighting the bruise darkening his cheek and the split in his lip that looks like a crimson fault line. He's both breakable and unyielding in this light, a contradiction I can't look away from. His thumb traces patterns on the back of my hand that feel like secrets being written on my skin.

"You don't have to hold onto it alone anymore," he murmurs, his voice steady as bedrock but tender as dawn. "I can carry it with you. If you'll let me."

Something inside me shatters.

His words are a lifeline thrown into deep water, a promise that feels both impossible and inevitable as gravity. He sees me—every broken, messy part, all the jagged edges and dark corners—and he's still here, still holding on.

Nate Sullivan is my paradox, my calm in the chaos, the eye of a hurricane. The one person who can reach me when I feel unreachable. With his eyes on me like this, it makes me feel like I'm his whole universe condensed into flesh and bone. I know one truth that burns through me: I don't want to hide from him anymore.

We drive home in comfortable silence, his hand steady in mine like an anchor. Every gentle squeeze of his fingers says what words can't: *I'm here. I still got you.*

For the first time in what feels like forever, I believe it with every fractured piece of my heart.

The car rolls to a stop in the driveway, gravel crunching softly beneath the tires. Nate comes around to open my door, and without a word, I start walking toward the dock by the lake, my feet finding the path like muscle memory. The night air whispers cool against my skin, but it does little to quiet the tempest raging inside me.

I sink onto the edge of the dock, wrapping my arms around my knees as the wood creaks beneath me like old bones. Nate's presence hovers a few steps behind, hesitant as morning fog.

"I can leave," he offers, his voice quiet as falling snow.

"I don't want to be alone right now."

He settles beside me, careful to maintain a small distance, like I might shatter if he gets too close. The lake stretches before us, black as ink and just as willing to swallow secrets.

"What did Evan say to you at the party?" The tension beneath his steady voice rumbles like distant thunder.

"It's not worth repeating," I mutter, staring into the darkness of the water.

"Nora." My name on his lips is soft but insistent as waves against shore. "Please."

I exhale sharply, the sound like glass breaking. The determination burning in his eyes tells me he won't let this go—he's as relentless as the tide.

"He threatened me," I admit, my voice shaking. "With the photos from that night."

Nate stiffens, his hands curling into tight fists. "What?" The word comes out dangerous and low.

"He said if I opened my mouth, if I said anything to anyone, he'd leak them. To everyone back home." I look away, unable to face the fury I know is blazing in his eyes. "I have one more year until I can get out of there. I just want to make it through without any more drama."

His silence stretches longer than thunder, and when he finally speaks, his voice is raw as an open wound. "Fuck, Nora. I wish I'd known."

I flinch at his words, not because they're harsh, but because they drag up a memory I've tried desperately to bury. The reaction doesn't escape his notice—nothing ever does.

"Nora?" His head tilts with careful precision, amber eyes darkening like storm clouds gathering. "What's wrong?"

I stare at my hands, watching them twist together in my lap. The air between us thickens like smoke before fire, heavy with words that taste like ashes.

"Okay," he says, gentler now, like someone approaching a wounded animal. "You've got about twenty seconds to tell me what's on your mind. And please don't lie to me."

A weak smile tugs at my lips. "I never could."

"Then tell me." His words fall between us like stones in still water.

When I remain silent, he moves closer. His hand finds my chin, tilting it up with a gentleness that breaks something inside me. The intensity in his eyes steals my breath like a plunge into winter water.

"Hey, Leni." The nickname falls from his lips.

He searches my face like reading a map to buried treasure, and I know I can't keep this secret any longer—it burns in my throat.

"I did," I whisper, avoiding eye contact.

His brows furrow, creating valleys of concern. "You did what?"

"Call you. To tell you." The admission hangs in the air like mist over the lake. "The night it happened."

His hand drops from my chin as if burned, confusion shadowing his face like clouds across moonlight. "You... you did?"

"I didn't know who else to call," I continue, each word like glass in my mouth. "Jake was at training camp. I couldn't call my parents. Ollie would've told them. So, I called you."

Nate freezes beside me, becoming still as stone. His silence fills the space between us with unspoken regret as realization dawns in his eyes like a cruel sun.

"I don't..." He shakes his head like trying to clear fog. "I don't remember."

"I know." My laugh comes out bitter and broken. "Farrah answered."

He flinches as if struck, and I watch something break inside him like ice cracking on a frozen lake.

"She told me I should call someone who cared." I continue, unable to stop now that the dam has broken. "Because apparently you were too high to care about anyone that night."

"Nora..."

"I shouldn't have called you." My voice cracks like thin ice, betraying my weakness. "But I didn't have anyone else."

He buries his face in his hands like trying to hide from the truth, his breathing rapid and shallow. "I—I'm so sorry."

"Nate—"

"No, don't," he cuts me off, voice raw. "I should've been there for you. And I wasn't."

"There's nothing you could have done anyway. You were thousands of miles away, it's not like—"

"I should have been there for you, Nora," he interrupts, self-loathing thick in his voice. He stands abruptly, running hands through his hair like he's trying to pull the memories out by force, pacing in circles like a caged animal. "Instead, I was too busy getting fucking high."

I rise and grab his wrists, stilling his restless movement. His pulse races beneath my fingers like trapped birds. "You were dealing with your own demons. But you're here now," I say, trying to catch his eyes that seem to hold all the darkness of the lake behind us.

"That's not—"

I silence him with a kiss that tastes like forgiveness and fear mixed together. When I pull away, the look he gives me makes my heart stop—not pity or anything I feared, but a fierce pride.

"You're brave. So fucking brave, but I—" His voice breaks, and his hands begin trembling.

I see what he's thinking in the way his jaw clenches like steel, in how his eyes darken to match the night. He wants to destroy Evan. The thought terrifies me—not for Evan's sake, but for Nate's, for how violence seems to call to him like a siren song.

"Don't," I whisper, my voice steady as the north star despite the storm inside me. "Whatever you're thinking of doing, please don't."

His gaze snaps to mine, his expression torn between rage and devotion.

"I don't want anything to happen to you," I say firmly, anchored in certainty. "Please, Nate."

He looks away, chest heaving like he's running from something. He's falling apart before me, and I can't bear to watch.

I place my hands on either side of his face, feeling his warmth beneath my palms despite the cool night air. The pain in his eyes makes my chest ache like an old wound reopened.

"Listen to me. You're here now," I whisper, the words a balm against broken things. "That's what matters."

I lean in, pressing my lips to his in a kiss that's as much a plea as it is a promise. For a moment, he's frozen, but then his hands come up to cradle my face and he kisses me back with a tenderness that feels like coming home.

The world falls away, leaving just us, broken but together, finding wholeness in each other's fragments. The lake whispers secrets behind us, and the stars above bear witness to this moment where pain and healing dance like light on water, where two damaged souls find sanctuary in each other's arms.

CHAPTER 57
MAGNATA
NATE

SHE CALLED? MY MIND RACES, DESPERATELY SEARCHING FOR ANY MEMORY of that call. There's nothing but a dark void where I should've been for her. Nausea rises as I piece together the timeline, each second of silence between us sharpening the ache like broken glass.

"Farrah answered."

Every muscle in my body tenses. Her words shatter something in me. I would've taken any amount of pain—broken bones, my father's fists, anything—over this. She reached for me, and I let her fall.

"Nora, I'm so sorry," is all I can find myself saying, over and over again. My voice is barely louder than my thundering pulse. Her pain mirrors my own, a reflection of all my failures.

"I swear to God, if—" I mutter, the words slipping out like venom. My fists clench until my knuckles ache.

Her hand covers mine and her eyes lock onto mine, wide with worry —not for herself, but for me.

"Don't," she says firmly. "Please, Nate. I just got you back... I can't lose you again."

She isn't afraid of Evan. She's afraid of what I might become because of her. That thought weighs heavier than mountains.

I want to promise her I won't do anything reckless, that I'll let it go. But that would be a lie darker than the lake below us. If Evan breathes near her again, I'll make him regret every second of his miserable existence.

"You didn't deserve any of this. Not then, not now, not ever."

She searches my face like she's trying to untangle the tempest inside me. Instead of retreating, she leans in, cradling my face like I'm something precious rather than destructive. Her touch steadies my world on its axis. Then she kisses me. It's everything I didn't know I needed until this moment suspended between heartbeats. The anger, pain, and guilt fades like in an instant.

There's nothing but her.

I kiss her back, framing her face with my hands. She's been my solace, keeping me from losing myself to the darkness that's always threatened to consume me long before now. With her lips on mine and her heart against my chest, I understand that broken things can be beautiful in their healing. When we break apart, her forehead rests against mine, skin warm and damp with tears. Our breaths mingle in the cool night air, creating a sanctuary between us.

One truth I know for certain is that I would go to the ends of the earth for this girl. No length I wouldn't go to, no line I wouldn't cross, no fire I wouldn't walk through. Because she isn't just part of my world—she's the entire galaxy, and I'm caught in her orbit like a planet that's forgotten how to spin any other way.

Her sobs echo through me like thunder, each shaky breath a scream in my soul. How could she think she had to hide this from me—the one person who knows what it's like to carry darkness as a second skin?

"It's okay to cry, Len. I've got you," I whisper, my voice breaking like waves on rocks.

She crumbles completely, tears soaking through my shirt. The rage builds inside me like magma beneath the earth.

I'll kill him.

I'll make him regret ever touching her.

I rub her back in slow circles, running my fingers through her silk-soft hair, pressing kisses to her crown like each touch could erase her pain. If I could, I'd take it all and make it my burden just so she'd never hurt again.

"I'm sorry," she whispers, fragile as frost.

I pull back to see her tear-streaked face glinting in the moonlight.

"What the hell could you possibly be sorry for?"

"Your shirt," she breathes. "It's ruined."

A bitter laugh escapes me. "I hated this shirt anyway."

We stay wrapped in each other, time slipping away like water. I'd stand here forever if it meant keeping her close. She makes me feel alive —more than any high has ever given me.

"Do you know what magnata means?"

I wait, fascinated by how her mind finds beauty in strange places.

"It's the reflection of the moon on water," she says, gazing where silver light dances on black waves. "You know what it makes me wonder?"

The silence stretches between us as I continue to wait.

"Why does everyone want to be someone's sun?" she muses, watching the moon. "Why not be someone's moon? Moonlight proves there's always light in the darkness."

Her words strike deep, making me wonder if I've ever truly felt anything before this moment.

She's lost in thought, but I'm lost in her.

Entirely.

Completely.

Like the moon lost in the night sky, knowing exactly where it belongs.

"You can't stare at the sun the way you can admire the moon." Her luminous eyes meet mine, shimmering like sea glass in dawn light. "Sometimes it's nice to look at something long enough to realize how much you love it."

She doesn't realize she's describing how it feels to be looking at her right now.

"And the moon," she adds, "reminds you you're never actually alone. No matter where you end up, you can look up at night and know someone else is seeing the exact same thing." She tucks her hair behind her ear, thinking. "It's weird to think about—people who'll never meet, maybe don't even speak the same language, all connected by this one thing hanging in the sky."

She glances up.

"When everything feels like too much, I remember people have been staring at that same round rock forever. All these centuries of humans having their worst nights and best nights under it."

The thought makes her smile and it's the most beautiful thing I think I've ever seen.

"It's only visible because of the darkness. How could you ever be afraid of something that gives the stars a home?"

I want to tell her she's the light I didn't know I needed until it found me but the words tangle in my throat. Instead, I pull her closer until her heartbeat meets mine, kissing her hair that smells of lavender and night air, then her temple—gentle, reverent, like something sacred.

This beautiful, fractured but unbreakable girl doesn't just hold my heart. She owns every piece of me, even the ones I thought too dark to give, too broken for love. To love her is to surrender, to stop fighting and fall like rain meeting the ocean.

And fuck me, I'm falling—harder and deeper than possible. Her quiet smile, meant just for me, undoes me completely.

"You know, you should consider writing a book one day."

Her laugh makes my heart ache because all I want is to hear that sound every day, to be its cause.

"Maybe."

"Come on," I say softly, coaxing like trying to tame something wild. "You're tired. Let's go inside."

"I'm glad you're not ignoring me anymore." Her teasing holds a vulnerable plea that cuts through me.

My fingers slip into her dark-silk hair.

"I wasn't trying to ignore you," I admit roughly. My hands frame her face like holding something precious, tilting her chin up. "I was trying to stay away," I continue, truth burning out of me. "And I failed miserably."

There's no hiding now, just us and everything buried beneath my skin.

"Don't you get it?"

"Get what?" Her voice wavers.

"I was keeping my distance because I knew I couldn't have you." The words tighten like a noose, but she needs to know how she's become my gravity.

"What does that even mean, Nate?"

"I told you. I can lose everything and can say goodbye to everyone else, but not you, Leni. Not you. But I'm done fighting it," I surrender.

"Nate?" Her gaze drops to my lips. "Kiss me."

"If I kiss you," I murmur, "I won't want to stop."

"So don't."

I close the distance and everything dissolves into her—her sweet taste, her touch electric as lightning, her body fitting against mine like puzzle pieces completing a picture. My hands tighten in her hair, pulling her closer as she clutches my shirt, matching my need, my desire for her and only her.

Her soft moan breaks something loose as my lips part hers, claiming them. Her legs tremble, and I hold her tighter, holding us both steady. But it's not enough—it's never going to be enough.

"We should head back," I manage, though everything in me screams to keep her close.

She sighs and takes my hand.

Inside, silence wraps around us. The house is spotless, showing no signs that a party took place only hours earlier.

Nora turns with a teasing smile that makes my heart stumble. "You're actually walking me to my door?"

"I wouldn't want you to trip over the floorboards," I smirk, but catch her wrist when she playfully shoves me.

Our lips meet again, and her hands close around my neck until there's no space between us.

"I need to—" I whisper, shaking with restraint.

"Stay. You need to stay."

I rest my forehead against hers, letting her read the truth in my eyes.

"I sleep better when you're next to me," she confesses.

"Me too," I admit.

I lay beside her and her sleepy voice whispers, "You have a big heart, Nate. It's always in the right place."

I hold her tighter, breathing her in as she claims my arm around her waist.

"I'll keep the demons away if you do the same for me."

She doesn't know she already does.

As her breathing evens, something shifts inside me like tectonic plates realigning. I'm falling toward a truth I've fought too hard to ignore.

Falling for her isn't new, but this feels different. I mean she's always been the moon on some of the darkest nights, the voice pulling me from the abyss for most of my life. This has always been us. Written into the fabric of who we are like poetry carved in bone. We belong to each other in ways defying logic, always just beneath the surface.

But does she know it?

Does she feel it like I do?

Because I feel it in every bone, in every beat of my wrecked, bleeding heart that somehow still knows how to love because of her.

"For the record," she murmurs, soft as silk but certain as sunrise, "I like the dark parts of you, Nate. Almost more than the light, happy parts." She pulls me closer, eliminating even space for breath between us.

She's seen my buried skeletons, the shadows crawling through my soul like smoke through empty rooms. We've both got pasts that should've kept us apart, but now there's nothing left to hide.

The dark side of the moon—where my demons live, where I've buried my worst parts—she sees it all. Instead of running, she stays. She illuminates the darkest corners, proving light exists in shadows, like stars showing their beauty against the night sky.

In every lifetime, every universe, she's my constant.

And I'd follow her into darkness every time.

CHAPTER 58
THE AFTERMATH
NORA

I WAKE TO SUNLIGHT FILTERING THROUGH CURTAINS AND THE UNCANNY sensation of being watched. Blinking sleep from my eyes, I turn to find Bones—my well-loved, lopsided stuffed animal—propped on the pillow beside me, his crooked button eyes watching like an old friend. Beneath one worn paw lies a folded note.

HAD TO GO HELP NICK THIS MORNING AND DIDN'T WANT TO WAKE YOU.
SEE YOU LATER.
N x

A soft smile tugs at my lips as my fingers trace over his familiar scrawl like trying to read braille. Memories of last night wash over me. Nate's arms around me, his steady warmth and quiet presence lulling me to sleep like the sweetest lullaby.

I can't remember the last time I felt safe.

Held.

Wanted.

Not the fleeting, superficial kind of wanted, but the kind that feels like a secret whispered just for you.

I push myself out of bed and head downstairs, only to be greeted by the familiar chaos of my brother and Jake. The blender's angry whir fills the kitchen as Ollie's exasperated voice booms with underlying affection.

"Jake! Get your lazy ass up!"

The words echo through the house, carrying notes of warmth that only years of friendship can create.

I hesitate on the staircase, lingering like a ghost. Their bickering fills the air like morning music, and while I'm tempted to peek in, I hold back. After yesterday, I'm probably the last person Jake wants to see. Giving him space feels better than forcing a conversation he's not ready for. At least he's still talking to Ollie. That's something.

"Here, drink this," Ollie commands with military authority, shoving a glass of suspicious green sludge toward Jake, who's sprawled on the couch in a picture-perfect image of dramatic suffering. The care beneath Ollie's gruff exterior shows in the strategically placed water bottle and in the already-drawn curtains dimming harsh morning light.

Jake wrinkles his nose like a child faced with vegetables. "What's in this? Nuclear waste?"

"Avocado, banana, spinach, turmeric, and lemon," Ollie recites with pride. "It boosts cognitive function, something you clearly lack." The insult carries the fondness only best friends manage.

Jake takes a hesitant sip, his face contorting in betrayal. "Ollie, what the actual fuck is this?"

"Health. Now drink it." Ollie's tone brooks no argument, carrying the same firm kindness Mom uses when she knows what's best for us.

"I hate you."

"And yet, here we are." Ollie shoves the glass back at Jake like a life-guard throwing a rope. "Now get up. I'm not letting you wallow in whatever this is." He waves a finger in Jake's face with the authority of a conductor directing a very reluctant orchestra.

"No."

"Yes."

"No."

"Yes, shit face." Ollie yanks the blanket off Jake with practiced ease, revealing his half-dressed state. "Get up or I'm dragging your sorry ass out there myself."

Groaning like a bear woken mid-hibernation, Jake snatches the clothes Ollie tosses at him—ones clearly picked out and brought down earlier, another silent act of care.

"Do you ever stop talking?"

"Maybe if you listened, I would."

"You're the reason God invented the middle finger," Jake mutters, tugging on his shorts but leaving his chest bare.

"And you're more disappointing than a soggy pretzel, but I still tolerate you." Ollie crosses his arms, triumph softening his eyes even as

400

he maintains his stern façade. "Now drink the sludge, brush your teeth, and be ready in ten. We're hitting the waves."

Jake sighs, running a hand through his messy hair in defeat.

"Yes, Mom," he grumbles, offering a mock salute before trudging upstairs.

Ollie turns to the blender, unbothered, as if wrangling Jake is just another part of his morning routine—which, in many ways, it is. I watch as he quietly prepares another smoothie, recognizing these small gestures that reveal who my brother truly is: the guy who remembers everyone's favorite foods, notices when someone's struggling, and wraps his care in jokes because that's the language boys like them understand best.

From my hidden spot, I release a breath. Jake's mood isn't something I can handle this morning, not when my own emotions feel like glass ready to shatter.

Stepping into the kitchen, I'm greeted by Ollie's signature brightness that somehow fills every corner like summer sunshine.

"Morning, Nor," he says, sliding a glass of green sludge across the counter with showman's flourish. I eye it suspiciously before taking a sip, grimacing at the taste of liquid grass.

"Oh, my God, what is this?"

"Not you too." Ollie throws his hands up with theatrical flair. "Does anyone in this house care about their health?"

"Says the self-proclaimed King of the Keg," I counter, arching an eyebrow.

"Exactly," he grins, lifting his own glass in a mock toast that catches morning light. "The secret to my success is recovery, dear sister. Drink it." His eyes dance with mischief and something deeper, that eternal spark that makes Ollie who he is.

Despite myself, I laugh—the sound surprising me with its authenticity—and take another hesitant sip. Ollie leans against the counter, his tone softening like snow melting, seriousness slipping through his usual bravado.

"So, I'm taking Jake out today. Getting him away from the house. He wasn't in a good place last night. And you? You good?"

Ollie's always been the one who steps into roles none of us ask him to, wearing responsibility like a second skin. It's not just me he looks out for—it's all of us.

"Yeah, I'm good. Thanks, Ol," I say softly, meaning every syllable.

He clinks his glass against mine, grinning with that infectious warmth that's uniquely Ollie.

"Finish that smoothie."

I roll my eyes but comply, lifting the glass in mock toast as he brushes past Lydia entering the kitchen, their movements fluid like ships passing in familiar waters.

"Morning, Lyds!" Ollie chirps, flashing her a boyish smile that could charm birds from trees.

"Morning, sunshine," she replies, ruffling his hair affectionately as he heads down the hall, her fingers lingering like she's touching a memory.

Lydia's light laugh doesn't quite mask the weariness etched into her face—the faint circles under her eyes like bruises, the slight tremble in her hands reminiscent of autumn leaves. She crosses to the counter, pouring coffee with movements mechanical as a wind-up doll.

"What are you drinking?" she asks, confused at the dark green sludge Ollie left me with.

"An Ollie special."

"I think I'll stick to coffee in the mornings."

"You okay, Lydia?" I ask, leaning against the island, watching her carefully.

She pauses, hand hovering over the sugar jar like a hummingbird unsure where to land, before letting out a bitter laugh that sounds like breaking things.

"Honestly, I don't even know how to answer that anymore."

That is something I can relate to.

Lydia has always been the strong one but sitting across from her now, I see the fault lines she tries to hide, running deep beneath her composed surface.

"For what it's worth, I admire your strength, Lydia," I offer gently, the words falling between us like autumn leaves.

She sighs, taking a seat across from me. "Strong doesn't mean invincible." Her weary smile carries years of weight. "But sometimes, what other choice is there than to be strong?" Her voice drops as her gaze shifts toward the hall where Ollie disappeared, carrying love and worry in equal measure. "But I appreciate it, sweetheart," she adds, her faint smile not quite reaching her eyes.

I recognize that smile—I've worn it myself like armor. One that hides too much, like ocean depths beneath calm surface. Mom's late-night conversations echo in my mind, fragments of Lydia's story pieced together like a broken mirror: a childhood home that was more battlefield than sanctuary, where silence meant safety and love spoke a foreign tongue. Her mother's abandonment left her with a father who drowned his pain in bottles, inflicting wounds deeper than skin.

The memory of Mom describing young Lydia, huddled in closet with a pillow pressed to her chest, trying to muffle her father's thunderous rage, makes my heart ache. She made herself a promise then, written in tears and determination: if she ever had children, she'd never abandon them. She'd protect them at any cost, even if it meant carrying scars that never fully healed. But life has a cruel sense of irony. Lydia married a man cut from the same cloth as her father—abusive and volatile. As if she believed such treatment was her birthright, clinging to whatever scraps of love she could gather. I see it in her occasional flinch at sudden movements, how her eyes track exits in crowded spaces.

She takes another sip of coffee, her hands trembling slightly as she sets the cup down.

"Nate mentioned he'll be at Sonder all day," she says, breaking the silence. "He's really changed since the beginning of summer." Her voice carries a weight I can't quite decipher.

I nod, unsure how to respond, feeling exposed under her knowing gaze. Does she see what's happening between Nate and me?

Whatever we are?

Her expression softens as she reaches across the table, her warm hand covering mine. The touch grounds me, and for a moment, I'm transported back to childhood. The scent of her vanilla lotion mingles with coffee in the morning air.

"Those boys of mine," she says gently, her thumb brushing over my knuckles in that motherly way that makes my chest ache, "they'd do anything for you."

I swallow hard and nod, feeling the truth of her words settle in my bones. The kitchen clock ticks steadily, marking each loaded second.

"Nate especially," she adds, her voice soft as a secret. Something in her tone makes me look up, meeting eyes that hold too much understanding. "He might not want to care about anyone, but he does. And despite his track record, there's only one girl who could actually make him really smile."

Heat rises to my cheeks as I stay quiet, letting her words sink in while the morning holds its breath around us.

"Since you've been around, he smiles more." She pauses, and I hear what she's not saying—how rare it is for Nate to let anyone close enough to matter. "I know he can be distant, even difficult, especially when he's trying to figure things out. But don't give up on him."

I take a breath, her words hanging between us like something tangible.

I couldn't give up on him even if I tried.

"Actually, before I forget," Lydia says, straightening up, "Nate left his phone here this morning. It's been ringing nonstop. If you're heading to Sonder, would you mind taking it to him? It's driving me crazy."

"Of course," I say, standing. My chair scrapes against the floor, breaking our intimate moment's spell.

She hands me the phone with a grateful smile, and I tuck it into my pocket, noticing how her gaze follows the movement. There's something in her eyes, something more she wants to say.

"Thank you, love," Lydia says, her eyes lingering on me with an intensity that makes me wonder what she sees. But she doesn't elaborate, and I don't press.

Nate might not make things easy, but neither does life. And maybe that's the point—to find the people worth fighting for, even when it's hard. Even when they don't know how to ask for help, or when they push you away thinking it's for the best.

THE GUITAR'S MELODY REACHES ME BEFORE I EVEN STEP INSIDE SONDER—A soft, mournful sound that wraps around my heart and squeezes. My pulse quickens because I know exactly who's playing. I'd recognize his music anywhere.

I slip inside quietly, letting the door click shut behind me. The place is unrecognizable from my last visit. Leather booths stretch along the walls, tabletops gleam with newness, and the bar stands fully stocked, rows of bottles catching light like captured stars. But my eyes are drawn to the stage, where a single spotlight creates an island of warmth in the dim room.

And there he is.

Nate sits perched on a battered water cooler, guitar cradled against his chest like something precious. His head bows over it in complete absorption, dark hair falling across his forehead, creating shadows that dance across his face. His fingers move across the strings with a reverence I've never seen him show anyone else, plucking each note with precision and care, as if he's speaking a language only he understands.

There's something achingly vulnerable about the way he plays, how completely he gives himself to the music. It's not just a performance—it's confession. Each chord seems to pull something from deep within him, revealing layers I rarely get to see. Here, he's not Nate Sullivan, the captain of the football team, the guy everyone leans on, the one carrying burdens too heavy for his shoulders.

He's just... Nate.

Raw and real and breathtakingly honest.

The connection between him and the instrument feels visceral—they breathe together, move together, speak together in a language of wood and wire and want.

For a moment, I feel like I'm witnessing something sacred, something not meant for anyone else's eyes. He's completely lost in the music, his face softening, as if every note releases another piece of armor he usually wears. The burdens he carries seem to slip away, leaving only the boy who found salvation in six strings because music was the one thing that couldn't betray him. Every movement flows naturally, as if the guitar isn't just an instrument but a part of him. He's not playing it; he's bearing his soul through it.

"What song was that?" I interrupt softly, almost afraid to break the spell.

His head snaps up, eyes finding mine with startling intensity. There's no embarrassment at being caught in this vulnerable moment; instead, something almost relieved flickers across his expression.

"It's uhh… something I wrote," he says, flashing me a smile that makes my knees weak with its authenticity.

"Really?" My voice wavers slightly as our eyes lock, electricity crackling in the space between us.

"Do you like it?"

"I… I love it. It's really beautiful, Nate." The words feel inadequate for what I've just witnessed.

"Good," he says, his fingers pausing on the strings while his eyes hold mine, soft and intense all at once, as if he's trying to tell me something words can't express. "You inspired it."

The confession hits me square in the chest, stealing my breath. "Me?"

"I always wanted a muse." His lips curve into a gentle smile that holds too many emotions to name.

I stand there, rooted to the spot as he resumes playing. I see it then— the moment he truly loses himself in the music. He's just a boy with a guitar, free from the weight of expectations and past mistakes.

No baggage, no pain.

The boy I fell in love with all those years ago, before life taught us both how to build walls.

I shake myself out of the trance as the last chord fades and pull his phone from my pocket. I walk toward him, trying to ignore how each step closer makes my heart beat faster.

"You forgot your phone at home," I say, holding it out.

When he takes it, his fingers brush mine, sending sparks across my skin. He stares at the screen momentarily, and something dark passes across his face like storm clouds gathering. He does a good job hiding whatever has him ticked, but I've known him too long not to notice.

"Thanks," he mutters, setting the guitar aside with gentle reverence. His presence fills the space around me, making the air feel thick.

"Is it just you here?" I ask, my voice barely above a whisper in the hushed atmosphere.

"Yeah. Nick ran to the hardware store. He'll be back in twenty minutes or so."

"Twenty minutes, huh?" I step closer, sliding myself between his legs until there's nothing but heat and electric tension between us.

My hands find their way to his shoulders, feeling the ripple of taut muscles beneath my palms, still warm from playing. His calloused hands —rough from years of football and hard work—instinctively find their way to my hips. His eyes darken to amber in the dim light, a lazy smirk tugging at the corner of his mouth that makes my heart stumble.

"What are you doing?"

"What two people who want each other do." My voice carries more suggestion than I intended, my lips brushing dangerously close to his, close enough to share breath.

"You want me?"

I nod.

"How do you want me Nora?" His smirk deepens, his hands tightening slightly on my hips, fingers pressing into soft flesh through denim.

"In all the ways that matter, Nathaniel." I draw out his full name deliberately, savoring how his jaw twitches.

"Nathaniel?" He looks up at me from underneath dark eyelashes, those hazel eyes turning liquid amber in the fading light. There's a question in them, mingled with something darker, hungrier.

"People only call me that when I'm in trouble." Slowly, with aching deliberation, he leans forward. His warm breath fans across my stomach as he presses a kiss just above my navel. Then another, slightly higher. A third, just below my ribs. Each touch of his lips burns through the thin fabric of my shirt.

"Am I in trouble, Nora?" he murmurs against my skin, his voice low and rough around the edges, sending shivers racing down my spine.

"Maybe," I whisper.

My breath catches when his fingers graze the sensitive skin just above my jeans. In one fluid motion, he stands, closing the distance between us until we're sharing the same air. My hands find the waistband of his shorts, fingers hooking through the belt loops, pulling him closer still.

The hard planes of his body press against mine, and I can feel his heart hammering in perfect rhythm with my own. A low groan rumbles from deep in his chest. He catches my hands in his, halting my exploration. My heart stutters, expecting rejection, preparing for him to pull away.

"I don't want to rush this—or you," he says, his voice low and steady as bedrock, laced with a tenderness that makes my chest ache. "I don't ever want you to feel like you have to. We've got time. I just want you to be sure. Of this. Of me. Of... us."

Us.

The word hangs in the air between us, heavy with promise, wrapping itself around my heart like ivy. My throat tightens under the weight of his sincerity. I lean in, resting my forehead lightly against his.

"I've been sure about you since I was eight years old," I whisper, my voice trembling with raw honesty.

His hands slide up my back, pulling me closer until there's no space left for doubt between us.

"You are the only thing I'm sure of right now," I continue, conviction threading through my voice like steel. "I can't think of anything else I want more than this."

In one swift movement, his arms encircle my waist, lifting me effortlessly onto the edge of the nearby table. My legs part instinctively, and his hips press firmly against mine, grounding me with an intensity that sets every nerve ending alight. His hands cradle my face with a gentleness that contradicts his usual strength, the pads of his thumbs grazing my cheeks as if memorizing my features. When his lips find mine, the world dissolves into sensation.

It's not just a kiss—it's confession and claim wrapped into one. Every suppressed longing, every stolen glance, every unspoken word between us pours into it, igniting something primal and profound within me.

When he leans back slightly, his dark hair falls messily across his forehead. His eyes catch mine, no longer empty but alive with emotion, their flecks of amber burning in them.

"Fuck Nora. You have no idea how much I've wanted this," he murmurs, his voice rough with honesty. His lips curve into a smile, one so devastatingly wicked yet achingly soft that it makes my breath catch. "How much I've wanted you."

His hands slide lower, fingers grazing the curve of my waist before gripping my hips with a possessiveness that sends heat rushing to my core. Every touch feels deliberate and careful.

"I've wanted to touch you like this," he says against my neck, his lips trailing fire along my skin. "Kiss you like this." His teeth graze the delicate spot beneath my ear, and I gasp, my hands instinctively gripping his shoulders.

His shoulders—broad and powerful—tense beneath my fingers, and I feel the strength coiled in him, barely restrained. My hands wander down his arms, brushing over the hard lines of his biceps, memorizing every curve, every ridge of his physique like a map I want to trace forever. His muscles flex under my touch, and the heat pooling in my stomach intensifies.

When I breathe his name, soft and desperate, his entire body stiffens. His grip on my hips tightens.

"Do you have any idea hearing you say my name like that does to me?" His voice is raw, almost tortured, and his eyes darken with something primal. "It drives me fucking crazy, Nora."

The way he looks at me—like I'm his salvation and destruction all at once—makes my heart stutter. His gaze drops to my lips, and before I can respond, his mouth crashes against mine again, stealing every coherent thought. It's overwhelming, intoxicating, the way he takes me apart piece by piece. I arch into him, needing more, craving the way his touch sets me on fire and soothes me at the same time. He pulls back just enough for his eyes to lock onto mine. There's something raw in the way he looks at me—primal and unrestrained—like I'm the only thing he's ever wanted.

He moves, and the next thing I feel is his hand sliding down, warm and deliberate, as if he's savoring every second. When his finger enters me, my breath leaves my lungs in a sharp gasp and the sheer sensation has me clutching onto him like he's the only thing keeping me grounded.

"Nate," I manage, his name breaking on a moan.

"I've dreamt of you like this," he whispers into my ear, his breath hot against my skin, sending shivers cascading down my spine. "For so fucking long. Come for me."

The word falls from my lips before I can think, a breathless whisper that's equal parts surrender and certainty. "Yes."

A devilish grin tugs at the corner of his mouth, wicked and devastatingly beautiful.

"Good."

My body arches against him, desperate and willing as he moves with an intimacy so devastatingly raw it feels like he's branding himself onto my soul.

"Nate..."

"What is it, Nora?" His tone is teasing, but there's an edge to it, a hunger that matches mine.

"I..."

"You what?" His smirk grows, dark and knowing as his pace quickens. Every time he moves, my body screams for more. It's like nothing will ever be enough with him. He's unrelenting, driving me to the brink of madness, and I barely form the words, but I force them out.

"More."

"More what, Len? Tell me."

"I need more," I whisper, the plea cracking through the tension.

Another low, devilish laugh escapes his lips, and his eyes—those dark, amber-flecked eyes—grow impossibly darker, pulling me into their depths like a vortex.

"You want me to take you right here?"

I nod, but it's not enough for him.

"Words. I need your words."

It's possessive and tender, and it sets my pulse racing like a drumbeat.

"Yes, Nate. Yes, I want you to fuck me right here," I say, the words tumbling out, raw and unfiltered. "Please."

An animalistic groan escapes him, low and primal, and I feel it reverberate through his chest, straight into mine. His hands tighten on my hips, and his lips crash against mine with a ferocity that's intoxicating. He devours me like he's starved, his movements deliberate and intense, his body pressing against mine with the kind of need that makes me feel like I'm the only thing keeping him alive.

His free hand roams my body, his touch leaving trails of fire in its wake. His fingers press into my hips, his palms exploring the curve of my waist, and I memorize the way he feels—strong, unyielding, yet impossibly tender. My hands run across the hard planes of his chest, his shoulders, and down his arms, marveling at the strength in his muscles. Every ridge and curve of his body is burned into my memory, and I can't stop myself from tracing them, wanting to know him in every way possible.

But it's not just a yes to this moment.

It's a yes to him—to everything he is and everything he's asking of me.

Because I know as I look into his wild, amber eyes, that I'd do anything for Nate Sullivan.

All he'd have to do is ask.

And I know how dangerous that is.

CHAPTER 59
HE WON'T HURT YOU ANYMORE
NATE

I can't believe what's unfolding right now. Here, against this worn oak table, stands the girl who's been etched into every atom of my existence. Not just in my thoughts—in my fucking bloodstream. Everything about right now feels primal and possessive, her hands digging into my shoulders like she's afraid I'll vanish. Each brush of her lips against mine rewrites everything I thought I knew about desire. It's like someone set off fireworks under my skin, electric currents racing through every nerve ending.

Kissing her feels like coming up for air after drowning for years, and I'm gulping her in desperately. The distant hum of street traffic filters through the windows, but it might as well be on another planet. All that exists is this moment, this girl, this consuming need that's burning me alive from the inside out.

She pulls back just enough to look up at me, and fuck, the sight nearly brings me to my knees. Her eyes are wild, glassy with desire, pupils blown wide in the dim light. A strand of hair clings to her flushed cheek, and my fingers itch to brush it away, to feel more of that silky skin that's making me lose my goddamn mind.

My heart hammers against my ribs so hard I swear she must hear it.

"More." She whispers.

"More what, Len? Tell me."

"I need more,"

The words send electricity racing down my spine, pooling hot and urgent until I'm rock hard and aching for her. Her tongue darts out to wet her lips, and I track the movement, mesmerized by how something so simple can make me feel like I'm being torn apart.

A laugh rumbles from my throat, dark and heavy with promise. The paradox of her drives me wild—the innocent curve of her cheek against the bold heat in her eyes, the soft sweetness of her smile masking the fierce want beneath. It's like watching an angel decide to fall, and knowing I'm the reason.

My eyes lock onto hers, and I know mine are wild—hungry and desperate, and probably terrifying in their intensity. But she doesn't look away. She meets that intensity head-on, challenging me, inviting me deeper.

She wants me to fuck her. Right here, right now.

Fuck.

My hand slides up to cup her face, thumb brushing over her bottom lip, feeling it tremble beneath my touch. The softness there makes my chest constrict painfully.

She nods, but it's not enough. Not nearly enough. I need to hear her voice, need the words to solidify what's unfolding between us, need to know she's as lost in this as I am.

"Words. I need your words." I demand, and feel her whole body tremble against mine, the vibration passing into my own chest like we're sharing one nervous system.

"Yes, Nate," she breathes, her voice unsteady and full of need. Her fingers dig into my shoulders, anchoring us both in this moment that feels too good to be real. "Yes, I want you to fuck me right here. Please."

It's the please that forces my control to shatter like glass.

A growl rips from my chest, primal and unrestrained, as I crash my lips against hers again. The taste of her—sweet and addictive—floods my senses. She's every dream I've ever had coming true at once, every wish granted, every prayer answered, and the intensity of it threatens to tear me apart.

My hands explore her body like I'm trying to memorize every curve, every dip, every reaction. The way she arches into my touch, her body responding instantly like it was made for my hands, the soft gasp when my fingers trail down her spine sending goosebumps racing over her skin, and the way she whispers my name like a prayer against my lips—it's almost too much to bear.

I press her against the table, feeling the solid wood beneath us, grounding us in this moment that feels too surreal to be happening. Her hands are everywhere—in my hair, tugging just enough to send sparks shooting down my spine; clawing at my back, her nails leaving trails of fire that make me hiss through my teeth; pulling me closer until there's no space left between us, her soft curves molding perfectly against the hard planes of my body.

"Fuck," I rasp, barely recognizing my own voice, hoarse with desire and something deeper, something that scares the shit out of me. "You are going to fucking ruin me Len."

The words trail off as I bury my face in the curve of her neck, my lips tracing a burning path down to her collarbone, tongue tasting the salt of her skin, feeling her pulse hammering wildly beneath my mouth. The knowledge that I affect her this way—that she wants me as desperately as I want her—is fucking intoxicating.

She moans my name over and over again, the sound shooting straight through me like a bullet, her body arching into mine like she can't get close enough. It's everything—she's everything. A fierce protectiveness surges through me, mixing with the desire until I can't separate them. I want to wreck her and shield her, consume her and cherish her. The contradiction is fucking maddening.

My hand slides lower, fingers tracing the waistband of her shorts, hesitating for just a moment—giving her one last chance to back out before we cross this line. Her hips rock forward impatiently, answering my unspoken question. But just as I slip my hand lower, reality crashes back in with the sound of my name.

"Nate." Nick's voice, clear and unrelenting, cuts through the thick fog of desire like ice water down my spine. "You still here?"

My forehead presses against hers, both of us breathing hard, hearts racing in tandem. Her pupils are blown wide as she looks up at me, lips swollen from my kisses, cheeks flushed pink, hair mussed from my fingers. The sight nearly breaks my resolve—I want to tell the whole world to go to hell just to stay in this moment with her.

I hear the back door slam, and the real world comes rushing back in all its unwanted clarity.

"Shit," I mutter under my breath, forcing myself to step back just enough to put space between us, though every cell in my body screams in protest at the distance.

Nora looks utterly wrecked in the best possible way—hair mussed from my fingers, shirt slightly askew, chest rising and falling rapidly. It takes everything in me not to kiss her again. She fidgets adorably, smoothing her hair and tugging at her clothes, movements awkward and endearing. The way she won't meet my eyes sends a surge of tenderness through my chest.

"You okay?" I say softly, reaching out to tip her chin up until those green eyes, still clouded with desire, lock onto mine. I can't help but smile.

She nods quickly, but her blush deepens, spreading down her neck, and I laugh softly.

"What?"

"Nothing. You're just cute when you're flustered."

"Shut up," she laughs, swatting at my chest without any real force behind it. The sound wraps around my heart like a caress. I never knew love had a sound until I heard her laugh.

I step back reluctantly, my hands aching to pull her close again.

"We'll finish this later," I murmur, voice low enough for only her to hear.

The way her breath catches tells me everything I need to know.

Later. We both know it's inevitable.

My phone buzzes against my thigh, the vibration jarring in the charged air between us. Jay's name flashes across the screen, but I ignore it. I can't look away from her yet—the flush still painting her cheeks, lips swollen because of me.

God, she's stunning, and I'm completely fucked up because of her.

"I'll see you at home," I manage, my voice still rough with need. "I need to check if Nick needs me to stick around for a bit."

She smiles softly, tucking a strand of hair behind her ear. My hand finds her jaw as I lean in, kissing her one last time, slowly. Her lips part beneath mine, hands gripping my waist, pulling me closer like she can't help herself.

Fuck me. Literally and figuratively because I'm about to implode.

It takes everything in me to pull back, my lips lingering a second too long. She exhales shakily, those green eyes meeting mine.

"Go," she whispers with a small laugh, the sound soft and warm. "Nick's waiting for you."

I nod, dragging a hand through my hair in an attempt to steady myself. As she heads for the door, I catch one last glimpse of her smile.

Nick is stacking boxes, his knowing smirk already in place.

"You're not exactly subtle, you know that?" he teases, his tone light but genuine.

I huff out a laugh, shaking my head as I grab a towel to busy my restless hands. The familiar motion helps ground me, even as my mind keeps drifting back to Nora.

"Yeah, yeah. You done?"

Nick nods toward a bouquet sitting on the bar—roses and something purple I can't name, wrapped in brown paper. "Just about. Got a date tonight."

"Kat?" I ask, already knowing the answer. The slight flush creeping up his neck says everything his words won't.

"I don't kiss and tell," he shoots back, though his grin betrays him. The happiness radiating off him is almost tangible. It's good to see him like this, letting someone in.

"Good luck, Romeo." I toss the towel onto the counter, my phone heavy in my pocket as Jay's missed call nags at my conscience.

"Don't need it," he says, but his smile gives away the nerves beneath his confidence.

"You need me for anything else?" I ask, already reaching for my phone. The weight of what I need to do tonight settles in my chest like lead.

Nick waves me off. "Nah, I'm good. Head out."

The mid-afternoon air hits me as I step outside. I pull out my phone to a screen of missed calls and text messages. I'm dialing Jay's number and my knuckles are already itching for what's coming. The phone rings once before he picks up.

"Well, well. He lives," Jay says dryly. "I was about to send a search party."

"I need you to meet me at the pier at six," I cut in, my voice clipped. The warmth from my moment with Nora drains away, replaced by cold purpose.

There's a pause, and Jay's voice drops, cautious. "The pier?"

"I need a favor," I say, my grip tightening on the phone until my knuckles turn white. Images of Evan's phone, of what he did, flash through my mind. "Setting an asshole straight."

The line goes quiet for a beat, then Jay exhales, his voice hardening with understanding. "I'll drive."

WHEN WE PULL UP TO CONNOR'S HOUSE LATER THAT NIGHT, THE THRUM OF bass bleeds into the night air, light strobing against windows and spilling across the manicured lawn. It's the same scene it always is—loud music, too much booze, and people pretending their lives are more interesting than they are. But none of that matters. My focus narrows to one target: Evan.

Jay moves through the crowd like a ghost, a wolf in sheep's clothing. He doesn't need instructions—we've done this dance before. Five minutes is all it takes for him to corner Evan, flashing that fake smile that never reaches his eyes. The baggie of pills he holds up might as well be a golden ticket. I hang back by the bar, lighting a cigarette to steady the adrenaline clawing at my chest. The ember glows bright then dims with each drag as I watch Jay work. He leans in close, dropping his voice like he's sharing some precious secret.

Even from here, I can read his lips: *"Not here, though. Too many people. Next door in the backyard. The neighbors are out."*

Evan, the stupid fuck, grins and downs his drink before heading for the side gate. Jay catches my eye on his way out and gives a barely perceptible nod.

We're on.

I wait in the shadows of the massive oak tree, cigarette burning low between my fingers. I really need to quit this shit too.

Evan stumbles into view, his movements clumsy and erratic. He freezes when he sees me, recognition flashing in his bloodshot eyes, followed closely by fear.

"Shit," he mutters, taking a shaky step back. But Jay's already there, blocking his escape.

Jay lifts the gun—a prop, unloaded, but Evan doesn't need to know that. The panic that washes over his face is almost satisfying. Almost.

"Relax," I say, keeping my voice deliberately calm, razor-sharp. "We're just gonna have a little chat."

"You're fucking insane," Evan spits, but his voice trembles, betraying his fear.

I let out a low, humorless laugh. The sound echoes in the dark space between us. "Maybe. But at least I'm not a piece of shit who preys on underage girls."

His mouth opens, but no sound comes out. He's frozen now, trapped in the snare he's been setting for others.

"You think you're untouchable," I continue, taking a slow, deliberate step forward. The gravel crunches under my feet. "Rich boy, smooth talker. You get off on it, don't you? The power it gives you, the control you feel when you're terrorizing girls, degrading them. Boys like you grow up to be men who think they can do whatever the fuck they want to whoever they want."

Before he can muster a reply, I drive my fist into his stomach. The force knocks the wind out of him, and he collapses to the ground, gasping like a fucking fish out of water. The sound of his pain is music to my ears.

"Get up," I bark, grabbing the front of his shirt and yanking him to his feet. His glazed-over eyes meet mine, and I shake him hard enough to

415

rattle what little sense he has left before slamming my fist into his jaw. His head snaps back, and he stumbles, blood dripping from the corner of his mouth onto his pristine white collar.

I crouch down to his level, leaning in close to make sure he sees my face when I tell him, "You come near Nora again—you even think about her—and I'll make fucking sure the last thing you ever see is my face before you find out what Hell really looks like. Do you understand me?"

He groans weakly, nodding, but it's not enough. It'll never be enough for what he's done.

"I said, do you understand me?" I growl, grabbing a fistful of his shirt and pulling him so close our noses almost touch. The metallic scent of his blood mingles with expensive cologne.

"Y—yes," he croaks, his voice barely audible over the distant thrum of bass from the house.

I release him, and he crumples back onto the grass, limp and pathetic. Reaching into his pocket, I pull out his phone, holding it up for him to see.

"This? I'm keeping it," I say coldly, slipping it into my pocket.

I head back inside to find Jay who'd walked away after I sent Evan to the ground. The bass reverberates through the floorboards, the music a dull roar in my ears. Instead of finding Jay, I spot Farrah almost immediately. Her body is practically glued to Connor's as they fuck each other's mouths in the corner. She sees me and horror flashes across her face, like I'm some ghost that has come back to haunt her.

She pushes past Connor, who looks pissed—probably nursing a hard-on and wounded pride. I'm about to walk away when she calls my name, her voice cutting through the chaos of the party.

For fuck's sake.

"Get out of my way." My voice comes out flat, emotionless.

She looks up at me, lips swollen and expression annoyed, like I'm the one interrupting her night. "What are you doing here?"

"Came to see a friend." I keep it short because I don't have time for her bullshit tonight.

Her eyes narrow, venom dripping from every word. "Your little whore not with you?"

"There's only one of those around here, and she's standing right in front of me." I step closer, my voice deadly calm.

She scoffs, stepping back like I'm something contagious before her palm connects with my chest, shoving me back a step. The touch feels wrong, tainted.

"Better go and finish off your deadbeat fuckboy over there before he finishes himself off in the bathroom." The words come out cold, precise.

The slap comes out of nowhere, sharp and stinging. My head snaps to the side, and for a moment, I stand there, staring at the ground. The party around us goes quiet, dozens of eyes watching the drama unfold. For once, I'm glad they're here to witness this.

"How was that, Farrah?" I say quietly, finally turning my head back to her. My jaw throbs, but I manage a smile that isn't really a smile at all.

"Fuck you, Nate," she spits, her chest heaving with anger.

I laugh, watching how it aggravates her even more that I find this entire thing comical. I step closer so that only she can hear me whisper, "I really hope you enjoyed that, because it's the last time you'll ever touch me."

Her eyes widen, uncertainty flickering across her face. I catch the faint tremble in her hands, and for one fleeting moment, I almost feel sorry for her. But then I remember what she said about Nora, and every ounce of pity vanishes like smoke.

I sink into the passenger seat of Jay's Camaro, releasing a long breath. My head falls back against the headrest as the faint buzz of adrenaline lingers in my veins like static electricity. Jay looks over at me, fiddling with the ignition, trying to find the right words. The dashboard lights cast shadows across his face.

"You all right? Or do we need to have an 'I'll help you move the body' conversation?"

A rough laugh escapes me before I can stop it. Somehow, the idea of Jay casually offering to commit a felony on my behalf is oddly comforting. That's just who he is—the guy who'd help you bury a body and crack jokes while digging the hole. And isn't that what makes a good friend?

"Relax, Norman Bates," I say, running a hand over my face. "No bodies. Yet."

He shifts into gear but keeps darting concerned glances my way. The streetlights paint stripes across his face as we drive, each flash revealing the concern he's trying to hide.

I stare ahead, my voice quieter now. "Thanks."

"For what?" he asks, his tone casual but curious.

"For always having my back." The words feel heavy with everything we've been through together.

Jay laughs, easy and familiar, but there's something warm beneath it. "Careful, Nate. You keep talking like that, you might catch feelings for me."

417

I smirk, leaning over to shove his shoulder. "Shut the fuck up and drive."

The Camaro roars onto the street, the tires gripping the pavement as the tension in my chest starts to ease.

"You know it's not just me who's got your back, right?"

I glance at him, frowning. "What are you talking about?"

He hesitates, drumming his fingers on the steering wheel because he's nervous. "Look, I wasn't supposed to say anything, but you'd kill me if you found out later."

"Jay…"

He exhales, keeping his eyes fixed on the road. "The dude you're working for, Nick. He paid off Monty's debt and then some. I don't know how much, but it was enough to get them to back off."

The words hit me like a gut punch. Nick, who's already done more for me than anyone has a right to, went out of his way. Again.

"When?" I ask, my voice tight.

"A couple of days ago," Jay replies, his voice soft with understanding.

Nick never said a word. Not a hint. No expectation of gratitude or payback. Just quiet support, like always. I chew on the thought for a moment before I speak again.

"Hey, I need one last favor."

Jay cuts a look at me, raising an eyebrow. "Need me to take out a life insurance policy for you or something?"

I finally turn my head to look at him, meeting his eyes. "Take me to the police station."

Jay's hand freezes on the gear shift, his eyes narrowing. "Wait, what?"

"Please." It might be the first time I've ever used that word with Jay.

"Do I want to ask why?"

"To finally try doing the right thing," I say in a low voice, thinking of Nora, of Nick.

Jay mutters something under his breath about my tendency to act on impulse, but he doesn't argue. With a resigned sigh, he flicks on the blinker and makes a U-turn, heading for the station. The neon signs blur past us, each one bringing us closer to whatever comes next.

As the glowing sign of the police station comes into view, Jay pulls into a spot and cuts the engine. For the first time tonight, he looks directly at me, his usual smirk replaced with something softer, more serious.

"You sure about this?" he asks.

I nod. The only thing I'm sure of is I'm trying to do better. Be better.

He nods and reaches out, squeezing my shoulder briefly. He doesn't need to say anything else. That one gesture says it all: *Call me if you need.*

The Camaro's taillights fade into the night as Jay speeds off, leaving me standing alone under the flickering streetlight. I pull Evan's phone from my pocket, its screen lighting up like a window into his twisted world. The idiot didn't even have a passcode, like he wanted to get caught.

As I scroll through his photos, my stomach churns. It's worse than I imagined—photo after photo of girls who can't be older than sixteen, their faces etched with fear and vulnerability. My grip tightens around the device, and for a moment, I want to smash it against the pavement.

But I don't.

He deserves what's coming, and this is evidence that will bury him. I'll make sure of it.

Before stepping inside, I find the photos and video of Nora. The sight of them makes my blood boil all over again, but I don't hesitate. One by one, I delete them, my thumb pressing harder with each swipe. I probably shouldn't be doing this from some legal point of view, but at least she'll be able to sleep easy knowing they're gone. When they're deleted, I exhale sharply, my chest loosening ever so slightly.

I square my shoulders, trying to shake off the lingering adrenaline, and push through the station doors. The cool, sterile air inside smells of coffee, cleaning products, and faint regret. A middle-aged officer behind the desk glances up. His uniform is crisp, badge polished, and his nameplate reads Deputy Officer Stanton.

"Can I help you?" he asks, his tone casual but his gaze sharp. His eyes narrow slightly, scanning me with a mix of curiosity and wariness that I've grown used to over the years.

"I'm here to report something," I say, my voice steady despite the knot in my stomach. "And to turn myself in."

Stanton raises an eyebrow, his interest clearly piqued. "You're reporting something and turning yourself in?"

"Yes, sir."

There's a pause as he leans back in his chair, arms crossing over his chest. "You're Sullivan's boy, right?"

I fucking hate that question, but I don't flinch. Instead, I straighten my posture, meeting his gaze. I hate that I even have to own up to it.

"Yes, sir."

Stanton studies me for a moment longer, his expression unreadable. "I've heard things about you."

Great.

Here it comes—the judgments, the assumptions, the shadow of my father's reputation looming over me yet again. But then Stanton surprises me.

"Nick has mentioned you a couple of times," he says, leaning forward slightly. "Says you've been helping him out over the summer."

His words catch me off guard, and I clear my throat, trying to cover the brief flicker of surprise. The last thing I expected is Nick talking about me here, of all places.

"Well, he needed help, so." I shrug, keeping my tone casual.

Stanton gives a small, almost approving nod and motions toward a chair. "Sit tight. I'll be back."

"Wait," I say quickly, pulling the phone from my pocket. "The thing I wanted to report—it has to do with this."

I hand him the phone, already unlocked. Stanton's face hardens as he scrolls through the images, his brows furrowing in disgust. The ticking of the wall clock fills the silence between us.

"Is this your phone?" he asks, his voice clipped.

"What? No," I reply quickly, bile rising in my throat at the thought. "It belongs to the guy I... well, the guy I beat the shit out of at a party. That'll probably get reported tomorrow, so I figured I'd come forward first. Save them the hassle of involving my mom."

Stanton's lips twitch, as if he's trying not to smirk. "So, let me get this straight—you beat up a guy, took his phone, and then came straight here?"

"Yes, sir."

"And how did you know there'd be photos like this on his phone?"

Because he's a twisted bastard who hurt the girl I love.

Because monsters don't always look like monsters.

Because sometimes the worst predators hide behind familiar faces.

"Call it intuition," I say instead, keeping my tone measured.

Stanton's brow rises skeptically. "Intuition, huh?"

"Yes, sir," I repeat, my gaze dropping to my hands. The dried blood on my knuckles tells its own story.

He doesn't buy it. I can tell by the way his eyes linger on me, unblinking and assessing. But he doesn't press further. Instead, he exhales sharply and stands, the chair scraping against the linoleum floor.

"All right. Don't move. I'll be right back."

As he disappears down the hallway, I exhale slowly, rubbing my palms against my thighs. My knee bounces involuntarily while I look at the clock on the wall, each second dragging painfully slowly. The buzz of the fluorescent lights mixes with distant phone rings and radio chatter, a symphony of late-night law enforcement.

I am so, so fucked.

I'm still sitting in the same spot twenty minutes later, my leg bouncing impatiently, when the sound of my name snaps my head up.

"Nate."

Nick strides into the station, his presence commanding as ever. His dark eyes find mine immediately, filled with what looks like relief rather than disappointment. Stanton follows close behind, still holding Evan's phone.

"Nick?" I ask, standing, confusion and gratitude warring in my chest.

He stops in front of me, nodding once before turning to Stanton. "Thanks for calling me, Danny."

Danny? How close are these two?

Stanton looks between us, his voice calm. "Your boy here did the right thing coming in. If this Evan kid tries to press charges, he's going to have a hell of a time explaining what's on this." He holds up the phone for emphasis, disgust flickering across his features.

Nick's eyes narrow as he takes the phone from Stanton, a muscle jumping in his jaw. "Good. And Nate? Is he free to go?"

Stanton grins, something knowing in his expression. "He's good to go."

Nick claps him on the shoulder, like old friends do. "Appreciate it, Danny. Really."

Stanton nods, then lowers his voice. "By the way, did you sort out that issue with—" He stops himself, trying not to look in my direction as if he'd give something away.

Nick's jaw tightens briefly before he nods. "Yeah. It's handled. Thanks again, Danny."

THE RIDE HOME IS QUIET, THE HUM OF NICK'S TRUCK FILLING THE SPACE like white noise against my thoughts. Streetlights pass overhead in rhythmic flashes, each one marking another moment of silence between us. Finally, I break it.

"I'm trying, you know," I say, my voice low as I watch the shadows play across the dashboard. "To be better. Better than my dad ever was."

Nick doesn't respond right away, and I feel him weighing his words. When he does speak, his voice is calm, steady.

"Nate, listen. We don't get to choose our parents or the way we come into this world. But we do get to choose what we do with it. We can

421

decide to accept who they are, let go of what they've done, and become everything they weren't."

His words settle in my chest, heavy and solid like truth. After a moment, I exhale.

"I'm sorry," I say quietly, my gaze still fixed out the window at the passing night. "For being a burd—"

"Don't," Nick cuts me off, his voice firm but not harsh. "You're not finishing that sentence. The people who made you feel like you were? They were dead wrong."

I don't know how to respond to that—to the unwavering certainty in his voice, to the fact that someone sees me as worth something.

Instead, I pivot.

"I know about Monty," I say after a pause. "I'll pay you back. Every cent."

Nick looks over at me briefly, his expression unreadable in the dim light, before turning back to the road.

"You call me when you're in trouble—that's the deal. Always has been." His jaw tightens. "As for Monty, guys like him who prey on kids need to be put in their place." He shifts in his seat, the tension in his expression softening as a smirk tugs at his lips.

"But if you're serious about paying me back, I've got a deal for you."

I arch a brow, grateful for the lighter turn. "What kind of deal?"

"You say yes to playing on opening night."

I laugh, shaking my head. The sound feels foreign after everything tonight.

"You know playing one gig doesn't even come close to covering what you probably paid."

"Maybe not," he admits with a grin. "But it's a start."

I stare at him for a moment, my chest tightening with the question that's been gnawing at me since I found out what he did.

"Why?"

"Why what?" he asks, glancing over.

"Why do you keep helping me when I keep screwing up?"

Nick pulls into the driveway, kills the engine, and turns to face me fully. His usual teasing expression softens, something raw flickering in his eyes under the porch light.

"Because I don't see a screw-up," he says quietly. "I see a guy who got dealt a shitty hand but keeps fighting anyway. Someone who loves hard, even when it'd be easier to give up."

He pauses, his jaw tightening with old pain. "I wasn't there for my brother when he needed me most. That's a regret I'll carry forever. But I'm here now—for you. Got it?"

I nod, his words hitting harder than any punch I've ever taken. For once, I don't have anything to say.

As I step out of the truck, guilt twists in my stomach as I remember his plans for the night.

"Shit—didn't you have a date with Kat tonight?"

Nick grins, the tension easing from his shoulders. "Worked in my favor. Got myself a second date."

Before I can shut the door, he calls out, "Nate, what you did tonight— for Nora—already makes you a better man than your father ever was."

The house is dead silent when I push open the front door. My knuckles throb with every heartbeat, the blood dried and cracked across them, but I barely notice. I take the stairs two at a time, the creak of wood under my feet the only sound in the darkness. Nora's room is at the end of the hall, a soft glow spilling out from beneath her door. I stop there, my hand resting on the doorknob, hesitating. I shouldn't go in. I should leave her alone, let her sleep in peace.

But I can't. I need to see her.

To remind myself why tonight had to happen.

The door opens with a quiet creak, and the sight of her steals my breath. She's curled on the bed, her laptop casting a faint blue glow across her face. Her lashes rest against her cheeks, her breathing slow and steady. The tension in my chest loosens, just a fraction.

She's safe.

I step inside, careful not to wake her. The laptop screen blinks off as I close it, leaving the room bathed in the warm light of her bedside lamp. I grab the blanket folded at the foot of the bed, draping it over her and tucking it gently around her shoulders. Bones, her stuffed toy, is on the nightstand, his lopsided eyes staring back at me. I set him beside her, exactly where he belongs.

The mattress dips slightly as I sit on the edge of the bed. For a long moment, I just watch her. She's so soft, so serene, and it feels like I'm looking at something I'll never deserve. My gaze drops to my hands— bloodied, bruised, and calloused. Her world and mine couldn't be more different.

But God help me, I'd burn for her.

I'd set this whole world on fire if it meant keeping her safe. I'd destroy myself to save her.

Is that healthy? Probably not, but I don't care.

I reach out, my fingers brushing back a strand of hair from her face. The touch is featherlight, yet it makes my chest ache. She stirs slightly, her face turning toward my hand, and my throat tightens. She's an angel, pure and whole, and I'm the devil clawing at the edges of her light. I lean down, pressing my lips to her forehead, letting the warmth of her skin seep into me.

"He won't hurt you ever again." I whisper, my voice barely audible. "I promise."

I pull back, my eyes tracing every line of her face. She's too good for me, and it's not just her beauty—it's everything else. The way she always adds two sugars to her coffee, even though she hates the bitterness, because tea feels like giving up.

She smells like lavender, not because she loves it, but because she'd read somewhere that it made people feel happy and calm.

She has this quiet need to brighten the world, always saying hello to anyone who smiles at her first, like she can't let kindness go unanswered.

She laughs too hard at stupid movies and cries at ones she's seen a hundred times.

And she spent hours making those beaded bracelets for strangers, just to make their day a little brighter. I never understood how someone so effortlessly extraordinary could look in the mirror and not see what everyone else did.

That's been the theme all along, hasn't it? From the moment she walked into my life, everything shifted. I knew it was too late to turn back.

She isn't just someone I love—she is it.

The endgame.

The one I've been searching for in this lifetime, and probably every one before and after.

She became a part of me in ways I'll never fully understand, but I don't need to.

Some things aren't meant to be questioned.

Some things just are.

And she's always been my answer to most things.

CHAPTER 60
I KNOW WHAT YOU DID
LAST SUMMER
NORA

THE SOFT HUM OF THE DESK LAMP MINGLES WITH THE RHYTHMIC TAPPING of my fingers on the keyboard, creating a soothing symphony in my cozy corner. I inhale the familiar scent of paper and coffee, letting my eyes drift over the organized chaos Nate created for me—scattered notebooks, loose papers, and an empty mug that's more decorative than functional now. The space feels lived-in, like it was always meant to be an extension of my soul.

Leaning back, I rub my tired eyes and glance at the notebook beside me. Its pages overflow with scribbled notes about Alfie and Gracie. There's something magical about this room, as if the walls themselves coax the story from my fingertips.

I'm halfway through the final edits, and for the first time since Dad died, pride replaces the constant whisper of self-doubt.

The door's gentle creak breaks my reverie. Mom stands in the doorway, arms crossed, and head tilted in that knowing way only mothers can perfect. Her smile holds equal parts amusement and affection, warming the room.

"Hey, Mom," I say, quickly saving my work on the new laptop before spinning to face her.

She steps inside, her keen eyes taking in every detail of the space.

"Nate did a nice job here," she observes, nodding approvingly. "Looks like it's working for you."

"It is." A small smile tugs at my lips as warmth blooms in my chest. "I've written more in the last couple of weeks than I have in months."

"Speaking of progress… have you applied for that scholarship yet?"

"How do you even know about the scholarship?"

"Nothing gets past me, you should know that by now," she says, her smugness tempered by maternal warmth.

I laugh softly, but guilt coils in my chest like a thorny vine. "I was going to bring it up," I rush to explain. "But... I guess I was worried about how you'd feel. With everything going on and Ollie leaving for college soon..."

She pulls out the chair across from me and sits, her posture open, expression gentle.

"Nora, sweetheart, you don't have to worry about me. I'll be fine. This scholarship? It's your dream. And if your dad were here, he'd be the first to tell you to take every opportunity you can."

I look down at my hands, focusing on the beaded bracelet that's become more talisman than accessory—a reminder to take the risk or lose the chance.

"It's just... hard to think about leaving," I admit, my voice barely above a whisper. "Things feel fragile sometimes."

Mom reaches across the desk, her hand covering mine. It's warm and steady, just as it's always been.

"Honey, I'm tougher than you think. And besides," she adds, her voice lifting playfully, "I know how to keep myself busy."

I smirk, grateful for the shift in mood. "Speaking of keeping busy, how did your date go last night?"

She laughs softly, leaning back. "It was going great until Nick got a call about a family emergency."

I arch an eyebrow, suspicion prickling at my skin. "Family emergency? Like, Alfie?"

She shakes her head, but something flickers across her face—a hesitation that makes my heart stutter.

"Actually, I saw Nick dropping Nate off late last night."

Her words hang heavy in the air, and my stomach knots. I search her face for clues, for anything that might explain what she's not saying. A cold wave washes through me as I remember Nate's text from last night claiming he was with Jay. The lie sits bitter on my tongue. Nate and his secrets—they're as much a part of him as his crooked smile or the scar above his eyebrow. Could I live with that? Could I make peace with the parts of him I'd never know?

"Nora?" Mom's voice pulls me back.

"Hmm?"

"Your phone's ringing."

I glance at the screen to see Camilla's name flashing.

"Shit," I mutter, grabbing it. "I totally forgot about the polo match today."

Mom laughs. "Lydia is dragging me to a luncheon with a few ladies this afternoon."

We share a laugh at the absurdity of our new lives—polo matches and upper-class gatherings so far removed from our old reality. For a moment, the weight of my thoughts about Nate lifts, replaced by the simple joy of sharing this moment with Mom.

She kisses the top of my head before turning to leave.

"Your dad would be really proud of both you and Ollie. I know I am."

Her words follow her out the door, settling into my heart like a warm embrace.

I SMOOTH THE PALE BLUE FABRIC OF MY DRESS ONE FINAL TIME, STUDYING my reflection. Marcus outdid himself—the cut hugs my curves perfectly, the neckline striking a delicate balance between daring and elegant. My hair falls in soft waves, and for the first time in what feels like forever, I feel beautiful without having to convince myself.

"You've got this," I whisper to my reflection, forcing a smile that almost reaches my eyes.

My phone buzzes, Camilla's text lighting up the screen with her characteristic enthusiasm.

Camilla:
We're out front!!!

I grab my bag and head for the door, but as I step into the hallway, I collide with a solid chest, one that sends electricity through my veins before I even look up. The scent hits me first—clean and woodsy with that hint of mint. My breath catches as his arms steady me. A slow, dangerous grin spreads across his face as his gaze sweeps over me, igniting heat beneath my skin.

"You're beautiful," he says, as if it's not an observation but an undeniable truth.

My stomach flips, his words settling over me like a caress. I study him carefully, relieved to see no fresh cuts or bruises on his face. But then I notice his hands—knuckles raw and angry—and Mom's words echo in my mind about Nick dropping him off last night.

"Where were you last night?" I ask, keeping my voice soft despite the anxiety churning in my gut.

He shrugs, too casual. "Sorry, I should've called. Jay and I hung out, lost track of time."

"What'd you guys do?"

"Nothing exciting," he says, but his tone is measured, careful—a red flag I'm learning to recognize.

I narrow my eyes, sensing the wall going up, but a car horn blares outside, shattering the moment.

"I have to go," I say reluctantly, motioning toward the stairs. "Will I see you at the polo match?"

He snorts. "I'd rather stick a fork in my eye."

I laugh despite myself. "Figured as much."

"Besides," he continues, "I should probably practice."

"Practice?" I blink, caught off guard. "Wait—you're playing?"

He shrugs, downplaying it in the way he does when something matters too much. "It's just a couple of cover songs. Nick helped me out a lot this summer. It was his one ask—"

Before he can finish, I throw my arms around him.

"Nate! That's amazing!"

He chuckles, wrapping me in a hug. "It's not a big deal," he mutters, but the sparkle in his eyes betrays him.

I pull back just enough to cup his chin, making him meet my gaze. "It is a big deal. I'm proud of you."

A faint blush creeps up his neck—a rare sight that makes my heart skip.

"I'll see you later, okay?" I turn to head downstairs, but before I can take a step, Nate catches my wrist and pulls me back.

I gasp as I'm spun into him, my chest pressed against his. One hand cups my face, his thumb tracing my cheekbone while the other rests low at my waist. The bruises on his knuckles catch my eye again, concern flickering through me.

"Nate—"

He silences me with a kiss that consumes everything—thought, breath, doubt. It's electric and demanding, setting every nerve ending alive. My hands find his chiseled jaw, and in moments like this, the world beyond us ceases to exist. When he finally pulls back, his forehead rests against mine, both of us breathless.

"I'll see you later," he murmurs, his lips curving into that devastatingly familiar grin.

I nod, my cheeks flushed and heart racing. And just like that, Nate Sullivan has turned my entire world on its axis.

Again.

The distant honk of a car horn and my buzzing phone drag us back to reality.

"Call me if you need to bail early," he says, his voice rough but serious.

I kiss him one last time, still marveling at how we got here, before heading toward the stairs. Just as I reach the top, his voice follows me.

"Stay out of trouble, Leni."

I glance back with a grin. "I'll try."

The cool air outside feels sharp against my flushed cheeks as I slide into the waiting G-Wagon. Marcus sits at the wheel, and Camilla greets me with a knowing smile that makes me want to sink into the leather seats.

"What took you so long?" she teases, eyes dancing. "I thought you fell down the stairs or something. I was this close to calling an ambulance, or maybe the fire brigade."

I roll my eyes, but her gaze flicks to my lips, making me self-conscious of how swollen they must be from Nate's kiss.

"Ohhh," Camilla draws out the word like honey. "Guess it wasn't the stairs after all." She winks.

Heat floods my cheeks.

Marcus's grin is visible in the rearview mirror. "So, how are the boys getting there?"

"Nate's not coming," I say, focusing on the passing scenery to hide my disappointment. "Ollie and Jake left about twenty minutes ago."

Camilla's playful smile dims. "Jake still giving you the cold shoulder?"

I nod, a familiar ache settling in my chest. "He's been avoiding me like the plague."

Marcus hums thoughtfully. "He'll come around. Just give him time."

But the wall Jake's built between us feels more permanent than temporary, like a fortress I don't have the key to breach. The guilt of hurting him mingles with frustration. How do you fix something when the other person won't even look at you?

Camilla reaches over and squeezes my hand, her touch grounding. "Let's just have some drama-free fun today, okay?"

I nod, grateful for her optimism even as unease lingers beneath my skin. Taking a deep breath, I try to focus on the day ahead and hopefully no more surprises.

THE BUZZ OF THE POLO GROUNDS SNAPS ME BACK TO REALITY. SUMMER-warmed air carries the mingled scents of freshly cut grass and expensive perfume, while excitement ripples through the crowd like electricity. The grounds stretch out before us like a scene from another world—pristine white tents gleaming under the golden afternoon sun, their peaks reaching toward a cloudless sky.

Luxury cars line up like soldiers on parade—Rolls-Royces, Aston Martins, and Bentleys reflecting the day's opulence in their polished surfaces. Men in tailored linen suits and women in flowing designer dresses drift across the manicured grass, champagne flutes catching the light like stars.

"God, it's like a Ralph Lauren catalog exploded in here," Camilla mutters, her gaze sweeping the scene with amused disdain.

My attention catches on Mia, already warming up on her horse. She's grace personified, her focus unshakable as she guides her mount through practice movements. The sight of her so in her element, so purely herself, brings a smile to my face. Whatever today holds, Mia deserves this moment to shine.

As we weave through the buzzing crowd, I spot Ollie standing off to the side, arms crossed, and attention fixed on Mia like she's gravity itself. There's a softness in his expression I rarely see anymore—a glimpse of the brother I knew before grief hardened his edges.

"I'll catch up with you later," I tell Camilla and Marcus, already moving toward him.

"Sure, we'll be by the bar trying to snatch the overpriced champagne," Camilla says with a wave before turning back to Marcus.

I make my way to Ollie, nudging his arm when I reach him. "Hey, Ol."

He glances down, his face breaking into that easy grin that makes him look so much like Dad.

"Well shit, you actually scrub up all right, Len."

"Shut up," I reply with another playful nudge. "Where's Jake?" I scan the crowd despite knowing it's probably futile.

"He decided to bail," Ollie replies, his tone casual but laden with unspoken concern. "I don't think crowds are his thing right now after, well, everything."

My stomach twists with familiar guilt. I want to press, to ask if he's okay, but Ollie's pressed lips tell me he's already walked that road and found it blocked. I swallow the questions burning my tongue—for now. We both turn back to watch Mia, who guides her horse across the field with the kind of effortless grace that comes from years of dedication.

"She's really good," I say softly.

"She's amazing," he replies, voice rich with quiet admiration.

I glance up at him, unable to resist teasing. "You like her."

He doesn't deny it. Instead, he lets out a small sigh, running a hand through his hair in a gesture so familiar it aches.

"I think I love her."

The vulnerability in his voice tugs at my heart. My tough big brother, finally letting someone past his walls.

"She's head over heels for you too, you know," I say gently. "Don't tell her I said that."

He smiles faintly, nudging my shoulder in our old familiar way. The moment feels frozen in amber—precious and perfect.

We stand in comfortable silence until Ollie speaks again.

"I know about you and Nate."

My head snaps up, startled. "What?"

He shrugs with deliberate casualness. "Relax, I already had the big brother talk with him. I gave him the green light."

The words leave me speechless. Nate talked to Ollie—about us. About whatever this electric, terrifying thing is between us. Heat crawls up my neck as I struggle to find words.

"Just don't let me catch you hooking up and shit because you're still my little sister and he's still my best friend. And also, eww."

If my face wasn't burning before, now it's on fire.

"Nate's always looked out for you," Ollie adds, his tone easy but weighted with meaning. "Even when you didn't know it."

I blink, thrown. "What do you mean?"

Ollie shifts his stance, crossing his arms in that protective way he picked up after Dad died. "Remember when Jackson Dalton made fun of your self-cut bangs that summer when you were eleven?"

"I try not to." The memory still makes me cringe—those uneven bangs I'd chopped off in a moment of misguided inspiration.

"Nate beat the living shit out of him and told him if he ever said anything about you again, he'd spill Jackson's secret."

"What secret?" Curiosity pricks at my skin.

Ollie's lips quirk into a knowing smirk. "Doesn't matter. Jackson never said another word about you."

I stare at him, mind racing through years of memories, searching for signs I might have missed. "He didn't have to do that."

"Nate was the only one allowed to pick on you," Ollie says with a laugh. "Remember Justin Kemp?"

The name sounds familiar, but I can't recall. "The guy from Nate's football team?"

"One summer, during a scrimmage, Justin saw a photo of you and said something. Something I, as your brother, refuse to repeat."

Heat creeps up my neck. "It was about my boobs, wasn't it?"

"Gross. Don't say that," Ollie groans, shuddering like the twelve-year-old boy he used to be. "Nate ripped off Justin's helmet and pretty much rammed him to the ground. Told him if he ever said another word about you—or any part of you—he'd cut his you know what off and make him swallow it."

I gape at him, my heart doing a complicated dance in my chest. "He really said that?"

Ollie nods, grinning. "Pretty sure Justin still has his you-know-what, so he never tested Nate again."

The revelation settles over me and something in my chest tightens.

"I hate that you all feel like you need to stick up for me."

Ollie steps closer, resting one arm around my shoulders. His expression mirrors Dad's so perfectly it steals my breath—the same intense focus when he needed me to really listen.

"Whether you like it or not, you're always going to have people looking out for you. That's what family does."

"Yeah but—" I mutter.

"That's what older brothers are for," he says, pulling me into a hug that smells like his cologne and childhood memories.

I wrap my arms around his waist, holding tight. "Dad would be proud of you, Ol."

He pulls back just enough to meet my eyes, and for a moment, I see the boy he was and the man he's becoming.

"He'd be proud of us both."

The horses are magnificent in the afternoon sun—sleek, powerful creatures with coats that gleam like silk. Players in crisp white polos guide them with practiced ease, their mallets swinging in graceful arcs as the game unfolds. The thudding of hooves against turf mingles with polite applause, creating a rhythm that feels surreal after the weight of Ollie's revelations about Nate.

"Go you fucking absolute queen!" Camilla screams from beside me, making several well-dressed spectators jump.

Marcus and I share an amused look at our friend's complete disregard for polo etiquette.

"Great," Camilla drawls suddenly, tipping her glass toward the far tent. "Look who decided to grace us with their obnoxious presence."

Following her gaze, I spot Connor, Farrah, and their usual entourage lounging like they own the place. Farrah's draped in a slinky white dress, laughing at something Connor is saying while he basks in the attention. But it's not them that makes my stomach turn.

It's Evan.

He's lingering at the edge of their group, taking periodic pulls from a flask he's not bothering to hide. The sight of him sends ice through my veins, but it's not just his presence, it's his condition. His lip is split and swollen, dark sunglasses failing to hide the violent purple bruising under his left eye. There's a stiffness in his movements that suggests bruised or broken ribs.

My breath catches as my mind immediately goes to Nate.

Those raw knuckles from this morning flash in my memory like a warning signal—fresh, angry bruises he'd barely tried to hide when we'd spoken. The cold dread pooling in my stomach deepens.

Camilla follows my gaze and lets out a sharp laugh. "Looks like Abercrombie got what was coming to him."

"What do you mean?" I try to keep my voice casual, but it comes out tight.

"Apparently," she draws out the word with relish, "there was some kind of drug deal that went sideways at Connor's party. Rumor has it, Evan tried to screw someone over and got his head kicked in for his trouble."

Marcus raises an eyebrow but doesn't comment, sipping his champagne with practiced indifference.

My heart hammers against my ribs.

A drug deal gone wrong.

Someone kicked Evan's head in.

That someone could only be one person, and the thought makes me dizzy.

"Do they know who did it?" I ask, not sure I want to know the answer.

Camilla shrugs, a wicked smile playing on her lips. "I'm guessing whoever it was sent a pretty clear message, considering the state of him." She glances at me, her smile fading slightly. "You okay? You look like you've seen a ghost."

I force a weak smile. "Yeah, I'm fine. I just... I need to use the bathroom."

The world feels like it's tilting as I make my way across the grounds. This has Nate written all over it—the bruised knuckles, the vague explanations, the tension in his shoulders this morning when I'd asked where he was.

A drug deal gone wrong?

No. This feels personal. And Nate doesn't get involved unless it's personal.

The bathroom is a stark contrast to the bustling polo grounds—all marble surfaces and echoing silence, perfumed air heavy with whispered conversations and the click of designer heels. I let out a shaky breath as I wash my hands, studying my reflection. My cheeks are flushed from earlier, lipstick slightly faded like a secret I can't quite hide.

Keep it together

The air shifts, growing thick and suffocating. Through the mirror, Farrah appears behind me like a perfectly coiffed demon, her red lips curved in a smirk that doesn't reach her cold eyes.

"Well, if it isn't Eden's little train wrecker," she sneers, her voice bouncing off the marble walls.

My spine stiffens.

"Farrah." I keep my voice steady despite my racing heart.

She moves closer, claiming space like it's her birthright. Her manicured nails tap against the counter—click, click, click—each sound a tiny needle under my skin.

"You've been getting around quite a bit since you got here. Haven't you?" Her voice drips sweet poison.

I turn to face her, hands clenched to hide their trembling. "I don't know what you're talking about."

Her laugh cuts like broken glass. "Don't play dumb. It doesn't suit you." She pulls out her phone like drawing a weapon. "First Evan, then Jake, now Nate. Have you fucked both brothers yet?"

The words hit like a physical blow, stealing my breath.

"I know what you did last summer." Her eyes glitter with malice. "I didn't think you had it in you to put out like that."

She turns her phone around and there they are—the photos that have haunted my nightmares for a year, now weaponized in the hands of my worst enemy.

My stomach lurches.

She steps closer, the scent of her expensive perfume choking me. "Has Nate seen them too? Or maybe he doesn't know about how easily you spread your legs for strangers." Another step forward, then a sharp shove that makes me stumble.

Her voice turns to ice. "You're so pathetic."

Tears burn behind my eyes, and her smile grows sharper.

"You going to cry?" she mocks. "You going to run and hide behind Nate every time things get tough?"

"Farrah, stop," I manage, hating how my voice trembles.

"Stop? Why?" Her laugh echoes off the walls. "You think Nate is yours to claim? He's not. And deep down, you know it. You've been nothing but a problem since you got here. And now? Now I'm going to fix it." She jabs a perfectly manicured finger into my chest, forcing me back. "You think this little damsel in distress act isn't going to get tiresome? As if Nate needs more drama in his already fucked up life. You're nothing but a little slut who can't handle reality."

The words slice through old wounds, dredging up Evan's cruel voice, the way he'd sneered those same words before everything shattered.

My breath catches on a sob.

Farrah's grin turns feral.

"Poor little Nora, so fragile." She leans in close, her breath hot against my ear. "Pa-thetic."

Then comes the final blow—she spits in my face.

I freeze, humiliation and fury warring in my chest. Before I can move, a voice cuts through the tension like a blade.

"Back the fuck away." Camilla's voice rings with steel.

Farrah barely turns before Camilla strides in, her heels striking the floor like war drums. Her eyes blaze with protective fury, her smile promising violence.

"Unless you want me to rip out each one of your fake eyelashes and those bargain-bin Barbie extensions, I suggest you turn around and get the fuck out of here," Camilla says, voice low and dangerous.

Farrah's confidence cracks, her smirk slipping. "Stay out of this, Camilla. This doesn't concern you."

"When it comes to my friends, everything concerns me." Camilla's arms cross, her stance ready for battle. "But then again, you wouldn't know what it's like to have actual friends now, would you? Fuck off before I show you how far my foot can travel up your ass."

Farrah glares, but after a tense moment, she backs down.

"Slut," she mutters as she storms out.

The second she's gone, my legs give out. I sink to the cold floor as the walls close in, each breath a struggle. The world feels distant, underwater, everything muffled except the roar of blood in my ears. Camilla kneels beside me, her hands steady on my shoulders.

"Nora, it's okay," she says firmly. "You're okay."

But I can't focus. Can't breathe. Can't think past Farrah's words echoing in my head.

"Nora," Camilla says again, softer now. "Do you want me to call Nate?"

I nod weakly, unable to form words. Through the fog, I hear her on the phone, her voice sharp and commanding as she tells Nate what happened. But all I can think about is Farrah's truth—the one I've been trying to deny.

Maybe she's right. Maybe I am the problem.

Tears spill over as the weight of everything crashes down, and for once, I don't try to hold them back.

CHAPTER 61
RESTORING WHAT'S BROKEN
NATE

SONDER IS FINALLY COMING TOGETHER. THE BAR STANDS LIKE A COPPER-wrapped beacon, its surface catching the amber glow of overhead lights until it seems to pulse with its own heartbeat. Above, a canopy of carefully strung greenery transforms the space into something alive and breathing. Lanterns nestle in the leaves like fireflies caught in mid-dance, their light painting stories across the walls.

Nick's woodwork grounds the space—dark, polished mahogany that begs to be touched, to have fingers trace the stories carved in its grain. Modern meets timeless here, sleek edges softened by lived-in comfort. His vision breathes through every corner, but my fingerprints are here too, subtle signatures in the details that make this place ours.

Standing here now, pride mingles with something deeper—a recognition of what transformation really means. We didn't just build a restaurant bar; we wrote a testament to second chances. Every crack we filled, every surface we restored, whispers the same truth: broken things don't have to stay broken. They can become something new, something that holds both their history and their hope.

The work should be a welcome distraction like it usually is, but today every task feels heavy while I'm trying not to think about Nora in that blue dress, the way her hair caught the light like liquid copper, or how she smiled before heading to the Polo event. It's all I can see, playing on repeat behind my eyes. The broom in my hands moves mechanically while my mind races toward all the things I wanted to do to her before she left.

Nick's hand on my shoulder startles me back to reality. "You've swept the same spot for fifteen minutes, I don't think it's getting any cleaner. If you want to hang around and practice, go for it."

My eyes drift to the guitar waiting against the wall, patient as an old friend. "Yeah, maybe I will."

The moment I pick it up, something in my chest unclenches. The guitar feels more like home than any place I've ever lived. My fingers find their place on the strings without thought, muscle memory deeper than conscious choice. The first notes vibrate through wood and bone, and suddenly, I'm breathing easier than I have all day.

Music fills the empty bar like water filling cracks, seeping into every shadow and corner. Each chord pulls me deeper into myself, into that quiet place where everything makes sense. Time loses its grip here—there's only the rhythm, the melody, the conversation between strings and silence.

Until my phone shatters the peace with Nora's ringtone.

"Hey, you," I answer, voice rough with unspoken words.

"Nate?" Camilla's voice crackles through, sharp with panic. "Nora needs you. She's freaking out—you need to come and get her, like right fucking now."

I'm on my feet before she finishes speaking, adrenaline flooding my system like ice water. "What happened?"

"Fucking Farrah happened," she spits, a story in those three words that makes my stomach drop.

The guitar finds its resting place as I snatch my keys. "I'm on my way."

I end the call, and my feet carry me toward the door, every heartbeat hammering out Nora's name.

Nick appears in my path, concern etched across his features. "Everything okay?"

"I don't know." The words taste like fear. "I need to go. Nora—"

He steps aside without hesitation. "Go."

The engine roars to life under my hands, a reflection of the storm building in my chest. As I tear out of the lot, memories of the last time Nora needed me—and I wasn't there—claw at the edges of my mind. I made a promise then, written in the scars of regret: *never again.*

This time would be different.

This time, I'd be there.

Even if I'm rushing blindly into whatever chaos awaits.

CHAPTER 62
THREE WORDS, NONE OF THEM I LOVE YOU
NORA

THE AIR CLAWS AT MY LUNGS, EACH BREATH SHALLOWER THAN THE LAST. The fluorescent bathroom lights slice through my vision, too bright, too harsh against the growing darkness at the edges. My hands grip the sink like it's the only thing keeping me from drowning in the tide of panic rising in my chest.

Through the chaos of my thoughts, I hear his voice—the one sound that's always been able to reach me.

"Where is she?"

Nate's frantic tone cuts through the static in my head, and for a heartbeat, the suffocating feeling lifts. The door flies open, and there he is, filling the door frame with a presence that's both familiar and commanding. He crosses the space between us in three long strides, his eyes never leaving mine.

"Nora." His voice is steel wrapped in velvet.

The warmth of his hands on my shoulders sends electricity through my veins, a current strong enough to quiet the storm raging in my mind. He tilts my chin up, and I'm caught in his gaze.

"Hey, hey... look at me." His voice softens but holds firm. "Breathe with me."

"I... I can't—" The words scratch against my throat, brittle and broken.

"Yes, you can." His hands frame my face, leaving me nowhere to hide. "Look at me. I'm here."

My chest constricts tighter, and my knees threaten to buckle. Beyond our bubble, I hear the bathroom door open, voices murmuring, Camilla

439

shooing people away. But Nate moves instinctively, pressing me against the wall, shielding me from prying eyes with his body.

"Listen to me," he murmurs, his voice low and steady. "We're going to do this together, okay? I need you to find three things to ground yourself. Start with my voice. Hear me?"

"Y-yes." The word is barely a whisper, but it's something.

"Good. Now feel my hands. You feel them on your shoulders?"

I nod, focusing on the steady pressure of his touch, the warmth that seeps through my skin.

"Last one," he says, leaning closer until his face fills my vision. "Keep your eyes on me. Don't look away, Leni."

The nickname hits me like a wave of nostalgia—summer days and secret hideouts, skinned knees and shared ice cream. Memories. Happy ones. My breath catches, but it's different now. Less panic, more recognition.

"Good," he whispers, and the pride in his voice wraps around me like a blanket. "You're doing good. Just keep going. Breathe."

Slowly, the world stops spinning. My vision clears, the dizziness ebbs, and my lungs remember their rhythm.

"Tell me what you need."

"I-I need to scream," I confess, the words ripping from somewhere deep and raw inside me.

His eyes soften, and he pulls me into his chest like he's trying to absorb my pain through osmosis.

"Okay," he murmurs, cradling my head against his heart. "Then scream. I've got you. Let it out."

Those three words—I've got you—echo through my bones. Not 'I love you', not empty promises or hollow comfort. This is Nate, showing me what he's proven all summer: he's here, he's real, and he won't let me fall.

The scream tears from my throat, years of buried pain finally finding release. It's muffled against his shirt, but it shakes through both of us. He doesn't flinch, just holds me tighter like he's daring my personal demons to try getting past him. His arms are an unbreakable fortress, steady even as I pour out everything I've been holding back. When the scream fractures into sobs, he keeps me upright, one hand threading through my hair while the other traces circles on my back. He creates a cocoon around us, just like the blanket forts of our childhood, where nothing bad could touch us.

"I got you," he whispers against my hair, his heartbeat steady under my ear. "Always."

I feel the truth of it in every touch, every breath we share. The tightness in my chest unravels, the sharp edges of my pain gradually smoothing under his careful hands. When my sobs quiet to hiccups, I pull back just enough to meet his gaze. His thumb brushes away a tear, so gentle it cracks open something new inside me—not destruction, but possibility.

"Hi," he whispers, tucking a strand of hair behind my ear, his hand lingering on my cheek.

"Hi," I breathe.

His eyes search mine, seeing past the mascara tracks and tear-stained cheeks to the truth I can't hide anymore. "Len, what happened?"

"She... she has them, Nate," I whisper, my voice raw.

"Who?" His brows furrow, but I see the storm gathering in his eyes.

"Farrah. She has the photos."

His body goes rigid, the tenderness in his expression hardening to steel.

"Stay here," he says, his voice careful but brooking no argument.

"Where are you going?" Panic flutters in my chest as he steps away.

"I'll be right back," he promises, his touch lingering on my cheek before he strides past Camilla and through the door.

Camilla catches my eye and shrugs. We both know there's no stopping Nate when he's like this.

I slide down to the floor, exhaustion tugging at my bones. But even as the weight of everything threatens to pull me under again, I hold onto the one truth I know: Nate has me. In every way that matters, in all the ways that count, he has me.

CHAPTER 63
HE CAN'T, BUT I WILL
NATE

RAGE SURGES THROUGH ME, RAW AND UNRELENTING. MY CHEST constricts and my throat burns as my vision narrows to Farrah's smug smirk, her casual cruelty a knife twisting in my gut. The moment Nora's trembling voice told me what Farrah did—that she somehow got those photos I thought were destroyed—everything else faded away.

That fucker must've sent them to her before I got to him. My fists clench until my knuckles ache, but the pain is distant, meaningless compared to the fury coursing through my veins.

I cut through the crowd like a storm front. Farrah stands with Shay and Harlow and a crew of elite assholes, their laughter grating against my eardrums as she positions her phone for a selfie. Without hesitation, I snatch it mid-pose and slam it to the ground. The screen shatters with a satisfying crack that silences nearby conversations. I grind my heel into the pieces, reducing them to glittering dust.

"What the hell is wrong with you?" Farrah's shriek pierces the air.

"What's wrong with me?" My voice emerges as a dangerous growl as I step closer, the scent of her expensive perfume turning my stomach.

"What the fuck is wrong with you, Farrah? You threatened her? Do you have any idea—"

"Don't try to make me the bad guy!" She steps forward, privilege and entitlement radiating from every pore. Her chin lifts in challenge, venom flashing in her eyes. "Maybe if your little charity case kept her legs closed, none of this would've happened."

The room plunges into suffocating silence, the air crackling with tension as every eye fix on us. My jaw clenches so tight it aches, cold fury crystallizing in my chest as I lean in closer, my voice cutting through the stillness like a blade.

"That? Coming from you?" A dark laugh escapes me, loud enough for our audience to hear. Then I lower my voice to a lethal whisper meant only for her. "Take a good, hard look in the mirror, Farrah. You might not like what you see, and trust me, none of us fucking do either."

Her face contorts with rage, and before I can react, her hand flies toward my face. I catch her wrist mid-swing, my grip iron clad. The contact sends a jolt of revulsion through me, but I hold firm.

"I told you last time," I say, my tone deadly calm, "that was the last time you'd ever lay a hand on me. You don't get another chance."

Farrah's lips curl into a venomous smirk, her eyes glinting with calculated malice.

She leans in close enough that I can smell the mint on her breath. "Bet you'd love to hit me, huh? To even the score? We both know you want to." Her smirk deepens as she delivers the killing blow in the form of a whisper. "Just like Daddy does."

The words hit like a physical blow, knocking the air from my lungs. My grip falters, hand trembling as rage and restraint wage war inside me.

Before I can do something I'll regret, a blur of motion cuts between us. The crack of Camilla's fist connecting with Farrah's face splits the air like lightning. The sound is sharp, electric, followed by a collective gasp that ripples through the crowd. Farrah stumbles back screaming, manicured hand flying to her face, eyes wide with disbelief as they lock onto Camilla.

"He can't," Camilla drawls, shaking out her hand with lethal grace, her voice dripping honeyed venom. "But I will. And trust me, I won't hesitate to do it again." She smirks, flipping her dark hair over her shoulder with effortless defiance. "Try photoshopping that out Barbie."

I make a mental note to never cross Camilla while watching Farrah's fury morph into helpless rage. When she opens her mouth, Camilla steps forward, each word razor-sharp with warning.

"Go ahead. Say something. Give me one more reason to shut you up again. I dare you."

Farrah's mouth snaps shut, her gaze darting around the room as whispers ripple through the crowd like wind through grass. The shift in power is palpable—she's lost, and everyone knows it. Camilla stands tall, fierce and unapologetic, every inch the warrior she's always been.

Ollie's grip on Camilla's shoulders loosens slightly as she raises her hand in mock solemnity. "And just so we're clear, if you come for my friends again just know, I'm not afraid to cut a bitch."

"Oh, we know, Rocky," Ollie chuckles, patting her shoulder with exaggerated care. "Trust me, we know."

"Please don't encourage her," Marcus adds with a long-suffering sigh, but I catch the pride flickering in his eyes.

The tent falls into charged silence, tension humming like a live wire. Every gaze flicks between us, waiting. Farrah stands frozen, her face a mask of barely contained fury, but the fight has drained from her. Her confidence crumbles, leaving nothing but a bruised ego and sharp humiliation. Her eyes dart around the room—taking in Camilla, Ollie, Marcus, the crowd—and realization dawns on her face. She's outmatched, out of moves, and rapidly losing what little ground she has left.

I step forward, my voice cutting through the silence. "Get a fucking life, Farrah," I say, each word heavy with finality. "Stop fucking everyone else's up."

Farrah's glare wavers for a heartbeat before she snatches up the remains of her phone. She storms out of the tent, muttering curses. Shay and Harlow trail in her wake like lost satellites. I watch her go, letting out a slow breath. The tension in my chest loosens slightly but doesn't disappear.

Camilla twists free of Ollie's grip, rolling her shoulders like she's just finished sparring.

"I'm good, I'm good," she mutters, though the satisfied smirk playing on her lips says otherwise.

"Jesus," Ollie runs a hand through his hair, exasperation warring with admiration. "What are you, an underground street fighter or something?"

Camilla's grin turns wicked, her eyes flashing. "I don't like entitled bitches who think they can bully anyone they want."

"Noted," Ollie replies, hands raised in mock surrender.

Camilla turns to me, her expression softening just enough to remind me why she's one of the few people I trust completely. "Go," she says, jerking her head toward the tents. "Take our girl home."

I nod, pausing beside her. "Thank you. For calling me."

"She wanted me to," Camilla says simply, the words settling like a balm over my frayed nerves.

CHAPTER 64
A WRINKLE IN TIME
NORA

The day that's turned into night feels both endless and too short, hours spent in Nate's Mustang watching streetlights blur past. He knew exactly what I needed after the disaster at the polo event—no words, just miles of road and a carefully curated playlist that spoke volumes about how well he knows me.

We drove until the sun disappeared, Radiohead's *"High and Dry"* bleeding into Fuel's *"Bad Day"*, then Feeder's *"Feel A Moment"*—each song a thread stitching my frayed edges back together. Nate's fingers drummed against the steering wheel, his presence steady and sure beside me. He didn't push me to talk, didn't try to fix what was broken. He just let the music fill the space between us until the shadows started feeling less heavy.

The opening synthesizer notes of *"Bette Davis Eyes"* drift through the speakers, that haunting melody filling the confined space. Kim Carnes' raspy voice follows. Nate's been trying to lift my mood all night, and when I catch him glancing at me with that gentle half-smile of his, I can tell he's not done trying.

He starts singing along, purposefully off-key and dramatic, his head bobbing with exaggerated enthusiasm. The usually composed Nate Sullivan is full-on performing now to Kim Carnes. There's something so carelessly happy about him in this moment—one hand draped over the steering wheel, polo drama forgotten in favor of making me laugh.

It's working.

Watching him like this, sometimes it hits me all at once—how much of himself he keeps hidden from the world, and how easily he lets those walls down for me. Even on my worst days, even when I'm pulling away from everyone else, he knows exactly how to slip past my defenses without making it feel like an invasion.

"Did you know this is my favorite song?" he asks, drumming his fingers against the steering wheel in time with the beat.

I turn to look at him, surprised. "'Bette Davis Eyes'? Why?"

His smile grows wider, streetlights catching the warmth in his eyes.

"Because thirty seconds ago, I started singing it completely off-key, and you finally smiled." He shrugs, but I can hear the tenderness beneath his casual tone. "It made it my new favorite song."

The simple honesty of it catches me off guard, making my heart beat hard and fast despite everything. He turns up the volume, and we both start singing along—me, tragically off-key, and him in perfect pitch. I tend to forget how beautiful his singing voice is until moments like this when he lets his guard down completely. Watching him now, head tilted back slightly as he hits the high notes, I feel like I'm witnessing something sacred. The way music flows through him isn't just talent or practice, it's like watching someone's soul take flight. In these rare, unguarded moments, when his voice wraps around each note like a confession, I understand why music is more than his passion. It's the language his heart speaks when words aren't enough.

It's these little things about Nate people don't see—the way he uses music to say the things he can't put into words, how he remembers every song that's ever made me smile, and the quiet way he carries my heart in his hands without making a show of it. These are the moments that remind me why he's had my heart since we were kids, why he still does. I'm glad he's finally letting himself explore music more. His whole face lights up when he sings, like he's finally letting himself be seen.

When we're finally home, my mind is a tangled mess. The emotions swirl, bleeding into one another until I can't tell where one ends and another begins.

I feel Nate's hesitation as we reach the porch, see the worry etched across his features as he glances toward the kitchen window. I know what he's thinking without him having to say a word. The way his shoulders tense, how his eyes dart between me and the house—his silent battle is written in every line of his body.

"Go check on her," I tell him, my voice steadier than I feel.

I watch the conflict play across his face, the responsibility he carries like a physical weight. I step closer, raising my hand to his cheek, feeling the warmth of his skin beneath my thumb.

"It's okay," I whisper before pressing my lips to his. I pour everything I can't say into that kiss—reassurance, understanding, a promise. When I pull back, his eyes search mine, and I see gratitude mingled with reluctance.

"I'll be fine," I tell him softly. "She needs you."

He nods, and I slip through the door alone, feeling his gaze on my back until I'm inside.

The wooden stairs creak beneath my bare feet, each cool step both soothing and accusatory. I stop when I see a warm glow spilling from Mom's bedroom door, left slightly ajar like an invitation. Part of me wants to retreat to my room, to let the darkness swallow my thoughts whole. But that light pulls at something deep inside me, like a thread connecting me to every time she's ever made things okay.

I push the door open, and there she is, a snapshot of comfort in human form. Her legs are tucked beneath her in that impossible way she's always managed, making the king-sized bed look like a cozy reading nook. Her worn copy of *Wuthering Heights* rests in her hands like an old friend, its spine bearing the battle scars of countless readings. For a moment, I see myself twenty years from now, hoping I've inherited even half of her grace.

"Nora," she says, marking her place with practiced care. Her eyes find mine and I can already tell she knows something is off.

The weight of my heels suddenly feel unbearable. I set them down by her bed, the clunk against the floor oddly final, before crawling into the space beside her. She opens her arms without hesitation, and I fold into them like I'm still small enough to believe a mother's hug can fix anything.

The familiar scent of her cardigan—vanilla and sandalwood, the perfume she's worn since before I can remember—wraps around me like a security blanket. It's amazing how some things never change. How the smallest of things can make the biggest impact when it feels like the world is burning around you.

"Do you want to talk about it?" Her fingers weave through my hair, each stroke untangling more than just the physical knots.

I shake my head against her shoulder.

"Are you and Nate okay?"

The nod comes automatically.

"What's on your mind?"

"How do you do it?" The question slips out before I can catch it, small and uncertain.

Her hand stills. "How do I do what?"

"Everything." The word feels inadequate. "How do you hold everyone else together without falling apart yourself?"

She presses a kiss to my crown, and I feel her smile. "You mean, where do I find the strength to keep going?"

When I nod, she's quiet for a moment, thoughtful in that way that always preceded her best advice. "Do you remember *A Wrinkle in Time?*"

"Of course." The memory rises like warmth in my chest. "It's one of my favorites."

"Why is it one of your favorites?"

"Because Dad..." My voice catches. "Because Dad used to read it to me every night. He loved it too."

Her smile reaches her eyes now, soft with memory. "Did you know your grandmother used to read it to him when he was little?"

The revelation hits me like a gentle wave, washing away some of the night's heaviness. This simple thread of story and love, weaving through generations of our family, feels like a gift I never knew I had.

She continues, her voice taking on that storyteller quality I remember from childhood. "Remember when Charles Wallace was possessed by IT? What did Meg have that IT didn't?"

"Love," I whisper.

"That's right. Love saved him—fierce, unconditional love. That's what restores order in chaos." Her arms tighten around me. "Your father's love, my love for you and Ollie, it's what keeps me going. When I look at you both, I see him. He lives in the way you twist your lips when you're thinking, in how Ollie laughs with his whole body. Love doesn't end, it transforms."

The tears come without warning, hot and urgent. She holds me closer, and I let myself break a little, knowing she'll help me put myself back together.

"You have to love fiercely," she murmurs, her hand tracing circles on my back. "Love with intention, even when—especially when—it would be easier to close yourself off. That's when your heart needs to stay open the most."

Looking up at her through blurred vision, I see the strength that's carried us through everything—every scraped knee, every broken heart, every impossible goodbye.

"Mom? Can I sleep here tonight?"

Her smile is warm enough to chase away the last shadows of doubt. "Of course, honey."

I settle against her, letting the steady drum of her heartbeat become my lullaby. Mom's right. The trick isn't to avoid the pain; it's to keep your heart open wide enough to let the light back in.

CHAPTER 65
A FLICKER OF HOPE
NATE

"Go check on her," Nora says softly, her voice steady and sure, as if she's already traced the path of my inner conflict.

I hesitate, torn between following her upstairs and checking on Mom. The weight of responsibility pulls me in opposite directions, threatening to split me in two. Nora steps closer, her hand rising to cradle my cheek. Her thumb traces my skin with butterfly-light pressure.

"It's okay," she whispers, leaning in to press her lips to mine. The kiss is soft, meaningful—a promise wrapped in warmth. Her hand lingers, heat seeping into my skin, and for a precious moment, I let myself believe in the possibility of okay.

"I'll be fine," she murmurs, pulling back just enough to meet my gaze. "She needs you."

I nod, grateful for her understanding even as reluctance weighs heavy in my chest. She slips inside, the porch light casting her in a warm glow before she disappears. The space between us suddenly feels sharp and electric, like a live wire exposed. I stare at the closed door, gathering courage, before heading to the kitchen.

The quiet clink of glass leads me forward. Mom stands at the counter, dark liquid swirling in her glass, shoulders curved inward like wilting petals. She looks small. Fragile. The sight twists something deep in my gut.

"Mom?" My voice barely disturbs the air.

She startles, quickly wiping tears from her eyes as if erasing evidence.

"Nate," she says, voice thick with emotion. "I didn't hear you come in."

Ignoring the wine glass, I step closer, studying her face. "You okay?"

She releases a shaky breath, avoiding my gaze as she pushes a stack of papers toward me. "I, um…" Her voice catches, and she forces herself to meet my eyes. "They're officially signed."

The weight of those words hits me slowly. The divorce. After years of being chained to Dad's toxic presence, she's finally broken free. Pride and relief war with a complicated knot of emotions I can't name. I pull out a chair, the wood scraping against tile as I lean forward.

"Mom… I'm sorry about what I said—"

"No, you had every right to be mad, Nate. I should have done more. You were just a little boy and—"

I reach over to grab her trembling hand. "Mom, I love you," I say, keeping my voice steady but gentle, even as my heart thunders against my ribs. "And I'm proud of you. It's a step forward. You did the right thing."

Her lips tremble, composure cracking like thin ice.

"I should've done it sooner," she whispers, voice splintering. "For you and Jake. For me. But I didn't, Nate. I didn't, and I'm so sorry. For all of it."

She drops her gaze to her trembling hands, and something shifts beneath my feet—like the ground I've been standing on isn't as solid as I thought. I lower my head so I'm at eye level with her. When she tries to look away, I take her hands in mine, holding them tight enough to stop their shaking.

"Stop," I say firmly, though my chest constricts with each word. "You did the best you could with what you had. You gave us everything you had to give."

Tears well in her eyes, and she opens her mouth to argue, but I press on, my voice softening like a wave reaching shore.

"You weren't a shitty wife. He was a shitty husband. That's on him—not you. You didn't deserve any of the things he put you through."

Her face crumples, and the tears come—quiet but heavy, like rain on windowpanes. I pull her into my arms, holding her as years of guilt and pain pour out. She clings to me, her sobs muffled against my shoulder. This shirt has absorbed more tears than a November rain, but I hold her tighter, becoming the shelter she's always tried to be for me.

The sobs gradually quiet, her breathing steadying though grief still hangs thick in the air. She pulls back slightly, wiping her tear-streaked face with unsteady hands.

"I waited so long because… I was scared, Nate," she confesses, voice barely above a whisper, fragile as moth wings. "I had nothing growing up —no one, until Kat. My biggest fear was losing the only thing that mattered to me. You and Jake. He threatened to take you both away, and I knew I couldn't fight him. You know him better than anyone. You've seen what he's capable of. I—"

"Mom, stop." Her words knock the air from my lungs, and I grip her shoulders, steadying us both. My jaw clenches, rage simmering beneath my skin at the thought of what that bastard put her through. "You didn't lose us. And you won't. Ever. Do you hear me?"

She nods, drawing a shaky breath that seems to rattle in her chest.

"I need to ask you something," she says after a moment, her eyes searching mine like she's trying to read a story written in water. "And I want you to be honest with me."

Tension coils in my muscles, my heart drumming a warning beat. "Okay."

"The drugs," she says carefully, each word carrying the weight of sleepless nights and unanswered prayers. "Have you really stopped?"

I exhale slowly, fingers raking through my hair as memories of darker days flash through my mind like lightning in a storm.

"I haven't touched anything in weeks," I admit, the truth both bitter and sweet on my tongue. "Since the beginning of summer."

Her shoulders sink with relief, but the words aren't finished clawing their way out of my chest. That night flashes through my mind with brutal clarity—the fear in Nora's eyes when she saw what I'd become. That look, like I was a stranger wearing familiar skin. It gutted me. Left a wound I never want to reopen.

"I almost slipped up after Dad showed up here," I confess, my voice dropping to match the heaviness in my chest. "Nora stopped me."

The memory floods back. That first night at the beach party, when Nora looked at me like I was someone else entirely. Someone dangerous. Someone she couldn't trust. And in that moment, I knew I couldn't be that person anymore.

Not for her. Not for Mom. Not for myself.

Mom's hand reaches out, trembling as she cradles my face. The touch is so gentle it aches.

"You've come so far," she whispers, voice breaking with emotion that mirrors my own. "I see you trying, Nate. And I'm so proud of you."

Her words wash over me, soothing the wound I've been carrying so long I forgot it was there. Her eyes find mine, and I watch something shift behind them, like hope breaking through storm clouds, tentative but determined.

"It's in the past now, all of it," I say, my voice soft. "I'm more focused on the future. And you should be too."

She nods, the motion starting hesitant before gaining strength, like she's letting the words take root somewhere deep inside.

"You're right," she says, her voice finding its footing. "And... I am. I'm trying."

Then she does the thing I've been silently praying she'd find the strength to do for years. She reaches for the bottle of red wine on the counter, fingers wrapping around its neck like she's confronting an old enemy. My heart clenches, caught between wanting to take this battle from her and knowing this has to be her choice. With a breath that sounds like courage, she tips the bottle over the sink. The wine spirals down the drain in a crimson rush, taking years of pain with it. The glass follows, emptying itself like a final confession. The smile that touches her lips isn't triumphant—it's fragile as a new leaf in spring—but her eyes, though red-rimmed, hold something I haven't seen in years. Resolve.

I realize I've been holding my breath only when she looks at me and says, "We're both going to do better."

"We are," I agree, the words feeling like a promise I finally believe I can keep.

"Are you nervous about tomorrow night?" she asks, her voice lighter now. In this moment, she's not the broken version of herself I've grown used to seeing. She's the woman who used to sing while making pancakes, the one who taught me about strength even when life was crumbling around us.

Pride swells in my chest, warm and unexpected.

A soft laugh escapes me, easing some of the tension that's been hanging in the air like smoke.

"Maybe a little," I admit, lowering my voice as if speaking the fear too loudly might make it more real. "Okay, maybe more than a little. It's been a long time since I've played, let alone played for a room full of people."

Her hand finds mine, warm and steady—an anchor I didn't know I was searching for.

"I'm so proud of you," she says, voice trembling just slightly, like a leaf caught in a gentle breeze. "For so many things." There's warmth in her words, but also something heavier. "I've made more mistakes than I can count in my life. Some of them haunt me, but if every single one had to happen to bring you and your brother into this world, then I forgive myself for them all. And I think it's time you forgive yourself too, so you can start to embrace every opportunity life gives you."

Forgiveness.

A word that feels too big to hold yet too important to ignore. I've carried guilt like armor, kept it close because being burned so many times has taught me to expect the worst. Maybe because somewhere along the way, I started believing forgiveness was something I didn't deserve. Or maybe because I never thought I was worthy of it in the first place.

But hearing her say it now—seeing the love and sincerity shining in her eyes—something shifts. A crack forms in the walls I've spent years building. Small, but enough to let light seep through.

THE MORNING SUN STREAMS THROUGH SONDER'S WINDOWS, PAINTING everything in shades of gold and possibility. The place still carries the crisp scent of fresh paint and polished wood, an electric anticipation humming in the air as final touches are made for tonight's opening.

Nick's already here—probably has been since dawn broke, knowing him. The guy treats sleep like a suggestion rather than a necessity. He's adjusting bar stools with surgical precision, fussing over a vase of flowers like they hold the secret to perfection. But I get it—this place isn't just a business to him, it's a dream given form.

"Morning," I call out, my voice carrying through the quiet space. The mingled scents of wood polish and fresh espresso hang in the air like a held breath before tonight's storm.

Nick looks up from behind the bar, his grin easy but eyes sharp as ever. "Morning."

"Figured I'd get a head start, make sure everything's set for tonight." My words carry more nerves than I let on—this isn't just another gig, it's a chance at something I'm only beginning to understand.

He waves me toward the small stage tucked in the corner, already moving with his characteristic efficiency. I set the guitar case down, the familiar motions of unpacking grounding me as my fingers instinctively check the strings.

"Hey," Nick says after a moment, his tone shifting to something softer, more deliberate. "I got you a little something. To say thanks for helping with this place and—"

"Nick," I cut him off, shaking my head as I straighten up. "I can't keep taking from you. You've saved my ass more times than I can count. Me helping out this summer? That was because I wanted to."

"And I wanted to do this," he counters, amusement sparking in his eyes like flint striking steel. "So don't fight me on it, just say thank you and make sure you use it religiously."

Before I can form another protest, he disappears to the far corner of the stage, returning with a sleek black guitar case. The kind that makes my heart skip a beat just looking at it.

"Nick, I—"

"Nate," he cuts me off, mock sternness failing to hide the warmth in his voice. "Just open it."

I flip the latches with hands that suddenly feel clumsy, my heart drumming an irregular beat against my ribs. Inside, cradled in deep velvet like a sleeping dream, lies a guitar worth more than I'd like to think about.

"Nick, this is..." My voice catches as I trace the ornate detailing with my eyes. "A Martin D-45? Are you fucking kidding me?"

His grin spreads wider, pride radiating from him like heat. "Actually, it's an authentic aged 1936 Martin D-45. Only a handful exist, and now one of them is yours."

My fingers hover over the polished wood, almost afraid to touch it, like it might dissolve under my fingers like morning mist. The question burns in my throat: Why would he give me something like this? After everything this poor guy has had to do for me this summer, after every mess he's helped clean up...

"Why?" I finally manage, my throat tight as a fist. "Why all of it? This. The job. Bailing me out of jail..."

The blind faith in me when I'd given him every reason not to believe.

Nick's hand finds my shoulder, his gaze steady as a lighthouse beam. "Because maybe you don't see it in yourself yet, but I do. I see a guy with a good heart and a hell of a lot of raw talent. And I want to make sure you never forget that there will always be someone in your corner, rooting for you to win."

The lump in my throat threatens to choke me, and all I can manage is a quiet, "Thank you. For everything."

Nick's smirk cuts through the weight of the moment like a blade through butter. "I also did it because I wanted my guitar back. It was passed down to me by a special friend."

A laugh bursts from me, unexpected and genuine, my head falling back as I shake it in disbelief.

"You know you could of just asked for it back?" I say, grinning at the simple truth of it.

"Come on, let's hear something," the teasing edge in his voice making the moment lighter.

Nick smiles before turning to fiddle with the soundboard, his movements precise and practiced. The strings hum under my fingers as I tune, each familiar motion keeping me present to this moment.

"You know," Nick says, his tone casual but carrying weight like storm clouds heavy with rain, "I really do mean it when I say you've got real talent, Nate. Ever thought about making music more than just a side thing?"

I pause, glancing up at him, fingers stilling on the strings. "Never seemed like an option to be honest."

"Why not?" he asks, leaning against the table, his posture relaxed but eyes sharp as broken glass.

I shrug, avoiding his gaze. "I guess my dad always saying music's a hobby, not a real man's job, made me believe it." Saying *my Dad* leaves a bitter taste in my mouth.

Nick's face hardens, something dangerous flickering behind his eyes. "Your dad is a real piece of work."

I let out a laugh that's more scar tissue than sound.

"You have no idea."

"But do you believe him?"

The question hangs in the air like smoke, making me think harder than I want to.

"I don't know," I admit, running my thumb along the guitar's smooth neck. "I guess I never gave it enough thought. I mean, I've only just started playing and writing again."

"Gotta start somewhere." Nick straightens, crossing his arms as something shifts in his expression. "He came by a few weeks ago. I want to be honest with you. Scott tried to throw his weight around and offered to buy the place out because he thought a wine bar was a 'waste of real estate.'"

Familiar heat rises in my chest, anger burning like acid.

Of course he did. Typical Scott Sullivan thinking money is a skeleton key that can unlock any door, fix any problem, or better yet, control anyone who dares stand in his way.

"Sorry," I mutter, jaw clenched tight enough to crack teeth.

"Don't apologize for him, ever. Especially not to me. Guys like that? They'll never be happy. Always chasing something they'll never catch because nothing will ever be enough for them. Don't let that be you, Nate. You're not him. You never were."

I pluck at a string, the note ringing sharp and clear as truth. "Sometimes it feels like it's in my blood, though. Like poison running through my veins."

"You know what you have to do? Rewrite the narrative," Nick says simply, his tone leaving no room for argument. "You don't need to live in his shadow. Father or not, you need to trust your gut and follow your own heart, even if it leads you down paths he'd never understand."

I look up at him, caught off guard by the quiet strength in his voice. "You're full of advice today."

Nick's smirk returns, a flash of light in darkness. "I call it as I see it. And lately, I've noticed you seem… different. Lighter, even. Like you're finally letting yourself breathe."

I can't help but smile, thoughts drifting to Nora like a compass finding true north.

"Maybe I've got more reasons to smile than I used to."

Nick chuckles, shaking his head like he's reading a book he's seen before. "When it's real love, you know."

"How?" I ask, curiosity warring with lingering skepticism.

His grin spreads slow as sunset, too knowing for my comfort. "Because you'll suddenly start believing in destiny. And on bad days, hope will see you through it."

I raise an eyebrow, seizing my chance. "Is that how you feel about Kat?"

The question catches him like a hook, but he doesn't try to hide the smile that creeps across his face like dawn breaking.

"Shut up and finish your sound check, will you?"

I laugh, shaking my head as my fingers find their place on the strings. "You should consider taking your own advice when it comes to her, you know?"

Nick shrugs, but there's a glint in his eyes. "Wise ass." He steps closer, his tone shifting to something more serious. "If and when you start to figure out what you might want to do with music, I've got a good friend in Spain who runs a studio. You could always go for a summer to write, play, and get a tan."

The idea floats in my mind. It feels so far removed from the chaos of my life here that it's almost impossible to grasp. But maybe that's exactly the point.

"Think about it," Nick adds, clapping me on the shoulder. "Sometimes getting away isn't about running—it's about finding your way back to who you were always meant to be."

I nod, letting his words settle into the spaces between my thoughts.

A summer away.

Just music.

No ghosts, no shadows, no expectations.

It sounds like an escape, but maybe it's the beginning of something I've been too afraid to dream about.

CHAPTER 66
NAME
NORA

I'M STILL ON THE PHONE WITH CAMILLA WHEN I HEAR FOOTSTEPS IN THE kitchen.

"So, are you and Marcus coming tonight?" I twirl a strand of hair around my finger, the familiar nervous habit grounding me.

"Are you kidding?" Camilla's laugh crackles through the line, warm and bright. "Of course we are. There's no way we'd miss it. Let's just hope it's our first drama-free event of the summer."

"That we can both pray for." I step into the kitchen, my breath catching at the sight of Jake. "I'll see you there."

I hang up and pause, taking in Jake's presence by the counter. Steam rises from the mug in his hand, but his eyes are distant, lost in thought. The air between us feels thick with unspoken words, weeks of tension crystallized in this single moment. It's the first time we've been alone since the Fourth of July blow-up, and my heart pounds against my ribs like it's trying to escape.

"Hey," I say softly, the word barely more than a whisper.

Jake looks up, and the shadows in his blue eyes make my chest ache. There's something different, something darker in them I haven't seen before. The Jake I knew—the one who could light up a room with his smile—seems buried beneath layers of hurt and uncertainty.

"Hey," he replies, his voice low and rough, like he's been carrying these words for too long.

The silence stretches between us, heavier than any argument we've ever had. I take a hesitant step closer, my fingers finding the back of a chair, needing something solid to hold onto.

"Jake, I hate this," I say, my voice cracking. "This... isn't us. When did things get so weird between us?"

He drops his gaze to the floor. "I don't know, Nora," he murmurs. The sadness in his voice cuts deeper than anger ever could.

I swallow hard, forcing myself to bridge the gap between us.

"Look, I'm sorry. About what happened the other day."

Jake exhales deeply, running a hand through his already messy hair. The gesture is so familiar it makes my heart hurt.

"I know. And I'm sorry, too. I shouldn't have said what I did. I was angry, and I took it out on you. That wasn't fair."

"No more secrets," I say firmly, stepping closer. I hold out my pinky like we used to do as kids, the gesture both a peace offering and a promise. Something shifts in his expression, and for the first time in what feels like forever, a faint smile tugs at his lips.

"No more secrets," he echoes, his voice softer now.

He hooks his pinky with mine, and for a moment, the tension eases. Relief washes over me. But Jake doesn't let go. His eyes stay fixed on our intertwined fingers, his voice barely above a whisper when he speaks again.

"Mom officially signed the papers. For the divorce."

My breath catches. "She did?"

"Yeah." He releases our pinkies and leans back slightly. His expression is heavy but calmer than I expected. "She actually sat me down and told me when it was done. I guess I thought... I don't know, maybe I thought this summer would feel like it used to. The four of us all together, my family could feel like a family again, you know? But it's been anything but that. Maybe we're not supposed to go back."

His words make me realize how much we've all been clinging to ghosts of the past. For Jake, it's been more than nostalgia—it's been a lifeline, something to hold onto when everything else feels uncertain.

"Maybe," I watch Jake's face carefully, "it's not about trying to recreate what was. Ever since Dad died, all I feel like I've been doing is chasing the ghost of him. Thinking if I could just do the same things, go to the same places, somehow, I'd feel closer to him. But all it did was remind me of what I'd lost." I pause, the truth of my own words hitting me. "The past is like a photo, it captures a moment perfectly, but you can't step back into it. Maybe healing isn't about trying to rebuild what broke. Maybe it's about taking those broken pieces and creating something new, something different but just as beautiful."

The words surprise me even as they leave my lips. I've been struggling

459

so much with my own past, with the idea of moving forward. Maybe I needed to hear these words as much as Jake did.

He looks at me, and for the first time in weeks, the sadness in his eyes lifts just enough for hope to peek through.

"Yeah," he says quietly. "It just sucks that things are so fucked up."

"It's just a blip in time," I offer with a small, tentative smile. "Things won't stay like this forever."

But even as I say it, I know believing those words is a whole different challenge. For now, though, I hope they're enough.

SONDER PULSES WITH LIFE TONIGHT. THE CROWD'S CHATTER HUMS LIKE electricity, glasses clinking a delicate symphony against the backdrop of laughter. Amber lighting bathes everything in a warm glow, catching on the polished wood and twinkling fairy lights that Nick and Nate have carefully curated. Every detail speaks of intention, of the heart they've poured into making this place feel like home.

My eyes find Nate immediately.

He stands to the side of the stage, guitar balanced against his hip as he tunes it with meditative focus. There's something different about him tonight—a quiet confidence that seems to radiate from within. His fitted black t-shirt follows the lines of his body like a shadow, and his dark hair falls in that perfectly imperfect way that makes my fingers itch to run through it. But it's more than his appearance that catches my breath, it's the way he holds himself, like he's finally stepping into who he's meant to be.

The real Nate.

The one who's always been there, just beneath the surface, waiting to be seen. This is the boy who, despite his scars, stands steady and true, with a heart so vast it seems infinite. He's been the constant thread woven through every chapter of my life, teaching me how to find light in the darkest moments. He's held pieces of me I didn't even know were missing, never trying to fix me because he never saw me as broken.

I've caught him playing before—stolen moments in his room or on the back porch when he thought he was alone. It always felt like witnessing something sacred, watching him unfold parts of himself usually kept hidden. Music isn't just something Nate does—it's the language his soul speaks in.

Standing here now, watching him, the feeling hits me so hard it steals my breath.

I love him.

Completely, inevitably, like we were always meant to exist together.

He adjusts the mic stand, his fingers moving with the same gentle precision I've felt in every touch. When his eyes lift, scanning the room before finding mine, I realize I'm completely lost in him.

I slide into a booth near the stage, finding the perfect vantage point. Across the room, I catch sight of my mom and Nick. She's laughing, head tilted back in genuine joy, while Nick watches her with undisguised adoration. It's been so long since I've seen her this light, this free.

"She looks happy, huh?" Ollie slides in beside me, following my gaze.

"She does," I say softly, unable to suppress my smile.

Ollie shifts, studying me with that perceptive look he's mastered. "What about you? Are you happy?"

I glance back at Nate as he settles onto the stool center stage, guitar balanced with easy grace across his knee. He looks like he belongs there, as if the spotlight has been waiting for him all along. The crowd hushes as he leans into the mic, fingers poised to play.

"I think I am, Ol," I whisper.

Then Nate starts to play, and time stops.

The opening chords of *"Name"* by The Goo Goo Dolls ripple through the room. Each note falls with deliberate precision, creating something hauntingly beautiful. It's a confession wrapped in melody, truth dressed in sound.

Memories flood in, vivid and overwhelming. Us in our pillow fort, safe in our own world. The night he fell asleep with his head in my lap, music playing softly through my old Discman, his face peaceful in sleep. Now, with each note, I'm transported back there. Just us, in our sanctuary built of blankets and trust.

His fingers dance across the strings with fluid grace, like the guitar is simply an extension of his soul. When his voice joins in, low and rich with emotion, the air itself seems to hold its breath. His voice carries something raw and honest, the kind of sound that reaches past your ears and straight into your heart.

The lyrics take on new meaning as I truly hear them for the first time —each word sinking deep into my bones. They speak of hidden truths and the yearning to be understood completely. That's what we've always been—an unspoken truth, a bond that defies explanation.

The fort, the late-night drives and conversations, the moments no one else witnessed—they existed in our own private universe.

This isn't just a cover of a song—it's a declaration.

It speaks of searching for connection in a world that often feels too big, too empty. Of being truly seen by someone who knows every shadow of your soul. And as he sings, I understand with startling clarity that he isn't performing for the room.

He's singing for me.

For us.

Nate's expression shifts as he loses himself in the music, brow furrowed in concentration, eyes closed as if he's diving deep into something only he can see. Every word feels purposeful, like he's offering pieces of his soul to the room, but in my heart, I know this is ours.

The song builds, his voice rising with it, and I feel every note resonating in my chest, tightening my throat and sending shivers down my spine. The room fades away until there's nothing left but him—just a boy brave enough to pour his heart into sound.

Suddenly, it's too much.

The intensity of the moment, of him and the memories, start crashing over me. My chest constricts as the song reaches its crescendo, and I can't seem to catch my breath.

I need air.

"I'll be back," I mumble to Ollie, not waiting for his response as I push myself out of the booth.

With the bathroom line stretching halfway across the room, I duck into a small utility closet instead, pressing my back against the cool wall. I close my eyes, trying to steady my breathing. My hands tremble as echoes of his voice linger in my mind, and I press my palm against my chest, willing my racing heart to slow before I pass out. A minute or two passes by and I hear the crowd clapping and cheering uncontrollably.

It's interrupted by the door creaking open, forcing me forward. Nate fills the doorframe, his presence making the small space feel even smaller. The scent of his cologne wraps around me, making my head spin.

"Well, this is cozy," he says, leaning against the door as he closes it. His grin is pure mischief, but there's something softer in his eyes. "Why are you hiding in a broom closet?"

"I just needed a second," I mumble, crossing my arms. The air feels electric with him here, and I'm already regretting my ridiculous choice of hiding spot.

He tilts his head, those bold hazel eyes reading me like a book he's memorized.

"Are we playing hide-and-seek now?"

I hesitate, thoughts tumbling over each other, before blurting out, "Why didn't you tell me about Jackson?"

Nate frowns, confusion crossing his features. "Jackson? Who's—"
Understanding dawns in his eyes.

"Ollie told me you... beat the shit out of him back when we were kids.
Because he teased me about my bangs." The words sound absurd now
that I'm saying them out loud. My cheeks burn as I realize how nonsen-
sical I sound.

Nate's low chuckle fills the small space, warm and teasing.

"Wait, are you seriously mad because I beat up some kid for making
fun of your bangs—what—ten years ago?"

"I'm not mad!" I throw my hands up, flustered. "I'm... I don't know
what I am! It's frustrating and confusing... I feel everything all at once,
and I don't know what to do about any of it!"

His grin widens into that infuriatingly charming smirk only he can
pull off. He steps closer, eliminating what little space remained
between us.

"If I kiss you right now, will it make things better or worse?" His tone
walks the line between daring and tender, his eyes dancing with both
amusement and something deeper.

My breath catches, my mind going blank. "I... I don't know."

"Well," he murmurs, leaning closer until I can feel his breath on my
skin, "can I test the theory?"

The intensity in his gaze is devastating—raw and unguarded, like he's
finally letting me see everything he's been holding back.

"All this time?" I whisper, the words barely audible.

"Yes, Leni. All this time," he says softly, the words carrying the weight
of years. "All this time, it's been you and only you for me."

The space between us hums with tension, an invisible pull impossible
to resist. His lips curve into another smirk as he adds, "You're real cute
when you're flustered, you know."

"And you're infuriating when you think you're being charming," I
retort, but my voice wavers despite my attempted glare.

I turn to step past him, but his hand catches my wrist, gently spinning
me back. He leans in, his eyes darkening with an intensity that sends heat
coursing through me.

"The last time we were in a closet together," he murmurs, voice rough,
"it was our first kiss."

I blink, confused, then laugh.

"I'd hardly call the spin the bottle kiss a kiss. We were twelve and you
missed my mouth. And we weren't even in a closet."

He laughs, the sound rich and knowing, like he's holding onto a
secret. "I'm not talking about that one."

His expression softens, and the change steals my breath. "I'm talking about the one on my seventh birthday. When you kissed me."

My heart stumbles, a long-buried memory crashing into me. "You... you remember that?"

His lips curve into a softer, more intimate smile as his thumb traces gentle circles on my wrist. The touch sends electricity through my veins, igniting something primal in the space between us.

"I told you," he murmurs, his voice deep and deliberate. "I remember everything when it comes to you."

He leans closer, and that intoxicating scent of his fills my lungs, simultaneously dizzying and grounding. His face hovers inches from mine, his breath warm against my lips, and when he speaks again, his voice is a low rasp that makes my stomach flip.

"And from now on, I'll make sure I never miss."

Then his lips find mine.

The kiss starts gentle, like he's asking permission. But within seconds, it transforms into something raw and consuming. His mouth claims mine with years of pent-up longing, and I'm lost to it—the taste of him, the feel of his hands sliding around my waist, pulling me closer until there's nothing between us but heat. Every nerve ending comes alive as his fingers trail up my back, his touch certain and reverent, like he's mapping territory he's dreamed of exploring.

My hands find their way into his hair, tugging slightly, and the sound that rumbles from his chest is pure satisfaction. We're seconds away from crossing a line there's no coming back from in this tiny, airless utility closet.

And then there's a knock on the door.

"Uh, sorry to interrupt." Nick's voice cuts through the fog of desire, and I jerk away from Nate, my heart thundering against my ribs. "But the crowd's asking for more, Nate."

Nate steps back reluctantly, his lips curving into a knowing, almost smug smile.

"One day, we're not going to be getting interrupted. But right now, duty calls," he says, throwing me a wink before turning toward the door.

I lean against the wall, trying to catch my breath, my cheeks burning, but the door doesn't close. When I look up, Nate's walking back to me with purposeful strides, his eyes dark and intense. Before I can speak, his hands cup my face, touch firm but tender, and his lips crash into mine once more.

This kiss is different. It's not just desire—it's everything. It's every unspoken word, every lingering look, every moment we've held back

464

suddenly breaking free. His lips move against mine like they've been waiting lifetimes for this moment, and I feel myself unraveling, melting into him.

A soft laugh vibrates through his chest, and he presses the lightest kiss to the tip of my nose.

"I'm glad I found you again."

I blink up at him, still dazed. "What do you mean again?"

His thumb strokes the curve of my cheek, and though his expression is unreadable, his voice—his voice is low and certain, sending shivers down my spine.

"I don't just mean in this lifetime, Leni."

My breath catches in my throat. He looks at me like he sees beyond skin and bone, like he's glimpsing something eternal.

"I mean in every single one before this one."

It's in these unguarded moments, the ones he doesn't even realize he's giving me, that I fall deeper than I ever thought possible.

He pulls me into his arms, holding me against his chest, and the world beyond this closet ceases to exist. Warmth blooms in my chest, steady and sure, like a truth I've always known but am only now understanding. I know with bone-deep certainty, we are two souls who have been finding each other through time and space, lifetime after lifetime.

"I never want to forget this moment," I whisper, my fingers tracing the sharp line of his jaw, the rough scratch of his stubble keeping me tethered to reality.

He stares at me, his perfect lips curving into the kind of smile that will haunt my dreams.

God, I am so in love with you.

It's as if he hears the unspoken thought, because he leans in, his lips brushing mine, our breath mingling, his voice barely above a whisper— raw and reverent.

"I could never forget the second time I fell in love with the first girl I ever loved."

CHAPTER 67
DID WE JUST BECOME BEST FRIENDS?

NATE

I'VE BEEN BUZZING ALL DAY FROM LAST NIGHT'S GRAND OPENING OF Sonder. Things are slowly starting to feel as if they're looking up. That brief surge of optimism fades when I spot Jake at the dock, his back to me, looking out onto the water just like when we were kids. Back then, we'd sit for hours watching the sunset while the sky changed colour, sharing secrets and plans for impossible adventures. Now the ten feet between us might as well be miles.

The dock creaks under my feet. Each step I take now feels like crossing a minefield of memories. His silhouette cuts against the water like shattered glass, all rigid angles in the golden afternoon light. He doesn't turn when I call his name, but I catch the tension rippling through him—shoulders locking, hands curling into fists at his sides. My chest aches with the wrongness of it.

"Jake." I keep my voice steady even as the air between us crackles with unspoken accusations. "Can we talk?"

He turns just enough to show his profile, jaw clenched like he's fighting back venom. I search for traces of my little brother in that hardened face—the kid who used to climb into my bed during thunderstorms, who wore my old football jersey's like badges of honor.

"What's there to talk about?" His words slice through the space between us.

I close the distance between us, shoving my hands deep in my pockets. There's nothing but ice in his tone where warmth used to live.

"A lot, actually."

A bitter laugh tears from his throat. "Fine. Let's talk, Nate."

The way he spits my name—the same name he once shouted across football fields with pride, the name he'd call when nightmares woke him —makes it clear this conversation is already derailed, but I have to try. I settle beside him, hoping the calm water might steady us both. The proximity is physically close but emotionally distant, like sitting next to a stranger wearing my brother's face.

I need to tell him about Nora, about these feelings I've been suffocating. I know my little brother better than he thinks. I've seen the way he looks at her, even if he hasn't figured it out himself yet. And it's killing me that the person I would have once trusted with every secret is now the one person I can't confide in about the heaviest thing on my heart.

"Look, I'm sorry about everything that's happened lately—"

"Fuck your sorry." Jake whips around, face contorted with a rage that feels too familiar, too much like our father's. "My entire fucking life, I've lived in your shadow. At school, at home, everywhere I went, I was just 'Nate's little brother'. Then you go and fuck up your life, and somehow I'm left scrubbing clean the mess you made of our family name."

Anger pulses hot in my veins. I dig my nails into my palms until the pain numbs the anger in me, anything to keep from saying something I can't take back. Jake springs to his feet, pacing like a caged animal, like he's got poison he needs to spit out.

Go ahead.

I can take it.

I'm the one who always takes the hits—verbal, physical.

They all leave the same scars now.

"And the one goddamn time I finally feel like I'm finding my feet, when everything's finally falling into place, you show up and wreck it all. Like you always do."

His words slice straight for the throat, but I force myself to stay calm.

"Jake, that's not what this is about—"

"Isn't it?" He spins to face me, and the hatred in his eyes hits harder than any physical blow. "I'm done cleaning up after you, done with your self-destructive bullshit. You're nothing but a selfish prick who—"

I'm on my feet before I register moving, going toe-to-toe with him. His venom catches me off guard, but the fury in my voice makes him flinch.

"No one's stopping you from doing whatever you want. You created this rivalry in your head. Not me. You're the one living in a fucking fantasy world, pointing fingers when shit doesn't go your way. Welcome to reality, little brother." The words taste bitter on my tongue. "But while

467

you're busy letting everyone else poison your mind, you're missing what's right in front of you. I'm not your enemy."

Maybe someday you'll understand why I did everything I did.

Maybe someday you'll know what it cost me to keep you safe.

He takes a step closer, his jaw set like stone. "And what you keep failing to see is I'm not a fucking child anymore. Something both you and Mom can't seem to understand."

Not a child anymore.

If you only knew what that means in this family.

I snap.

"This is what you've been keeping pent up inside all this time?"

His voice rises like a storm. "Dad never noticed anything I did because he was too busy watching you. The golden boy. Nate and his football career. Nate and his scholarships. Then you go and blow that up, and suddenly both Mom and Dad are focusing on trying to keep you out of jail and off the fucking streets."

Watching me.

Yeah, he was always watching me.

Waiting for me to slip up, to give him a reason.

My hands start to shake, and I shove them deeper into my pockets. "That's not—"

"What? Not fair?" He barks out a laugh that sounds like broken glass. "You wanna talk about 'fair'? Let's talk about how when you started losing your shit—quitting football, partying, spiraling—Mom stayed up all night worrying about you. You! Dad was pissed at the world because of you! And me? I'm the one getting shipped off to fucking camps for months at a time to stay out of the way. Because God forbid I add to their stress, right?"

Mom wasn't up worrying about me. She was worrying about you.

She was up hiding bruises, while I was planning escapes we'd never take.

And those camps... they were the only nights we could sleep knowing you were safe.

I clench my fists so hard my nails break skin, copper-scent mixing with the salt air. There's nothing I can say right now to make him see the bigger picture. Anything I do say, he won't believe anyway. I stay silent, letting him drain his poison.

"Doesn't matter anyway in the end," he snaps, voice raw. "Because just when I think maybe things can't get worse, you and Mom start keeping your own secrets. Did you ever think I deserved to know that our parents were getting a divorce? Or was that on a need-to-know basis, and I didn't fucking qualify?"

My breath catches like barbed wire in my throat.

Tell him.

Tell him why Mom finally left.

Tell him about the hospital visits that never happened, the police reports that were never filed, the nights I stood guard outside his door.

"It wasn't like that—"

"It wasn't like what? Like I didn't deserve to know the truth about what goes on in my own fucking family? Do you know what that was like for me? Hearing it in front of an entire audience at a fucking party?"

The truth would break you, little brother.

"Jake—"

"No, Nate. You don't get to talk your way out of this. Not this time." His voice trembles, anger spilling into something rawer, deeper. "You've been screwing up for years, and the rest of us are the ones paying the price. Mom's breaking her back trying to keep you afloat, and Dad's been bailing your ass out of shit left right and center."

Every muscle in my body goes rigid. The mention of our father sends bile rising in my throat.

Bailing me out? Is that what he told you?

What about the night he put me through the mirror in the bathroom?

About the time he "helped" me down the stairs?

Of all the things he's said, the way he defends our father like he's some kind of hero burns me the most. My hands tremble with the effort of holding back fifteen years of truth.

I take a shaky breath, trying to push back the rage rising in my chest. "Jake, listen to me. Whatever Dad's feeding you, it's not the truth. He's manipulating you. That's what he does. He makes you think you need him, but you don't. You don't."

Just like he did with Mom.

Just like he did with me.

Until we were nothing but shells of ourselves.

Jake's laugh is hollow, his shoulders stiffening like armor.

"You think I don't know that? You think I don't see what he's doing? But here's the thing, Nate, at least he's paying attention to me now. At least I'm not invisible anymore."

No, no, *no.* This is exactly what I tried to prevent.

"That's not attention, Jake. That's fucking control," I snap, my voice sharp enough to cut. "This is what he does. He uses you, manipulates you, and slowly takes away everything you love until you're under his thumb. If you paid attention, you might start to see things a lot clearer. But you don't. You just blame the world for everything that happens to you."

Jake's eyes flash with something dangerous, his voice a low growl. "Fuck you, Nate. Seriously, fuck you."

"You need to demonize me to fit your narrative, fine." I take a step forward, chest heaving. "You want to make me the villain in your story so you feel better? To justify running off and saying fuck you to me, to Mom? Okay. But don't you ever say I didn't care about you. My entire fucking life, all I've ever done is care about you. About Mom."

He opens his mouth to respond, but it's my turn to cut him off, my voice rising with years of buried truth fighting to break free.

"Every single fucking decision I've made over the last four years has been so you and Mom could—"

Don't.

Don't break.

Don't tell him how Dad used to wait until he was asleep.

Don't tell him about the sound-proofed basement.

Don't tell him why you really quit the team and school.

I stop myself, jaw clenching as I look away. The morning sun catches on the water, blinding. When I open my mouth again, my voice is quieter, almost broken.

"Forget it. Hate me. Villainize me. Do whatever you want. I don't care anymore."

I'm about to walk away when his voice hardens again, cutting through the air like a blade.

"You'll break her heart, and you know it. It's not a matter of if, but when."

His words hit me like a physical blow to the chest. I know exactly who he's talking about. I open my mouth to argue, but no sound comes out. He shakes his head, his anger simmering just below the surface, and turns to leave.

And just like that, I'm left standing on the dock, the gravity of his words dragging me down like an anchor. The morning sun feels too bright, too exposing, highlighting every crack in the armor I've spent years building.

Maybe one day you'll understand, little brother.

Maybe one day you'll forgive me for keeping you in the dark.

But I'd rather have you hate me than know the truth about the monster you call Dad.

The fight with Jake leaves ash in my mouth.

My knuckles ache from holding back, and his words pound against my skull like a hammer. His face haunts me—twisted with anger, hurt, betrayal. I thought I could save him, pull him back before Dad dragged

470

him under completely. But to Jake, I'm not his protector anymore. I'm the villain, the convenient target for everything wrong in his life.

I need a drink.

And I need the one person who's seen me at my worst and stayed anyway.

Jay picks up on the second ring, his voice casual but threaded with that familiar concern that always steadies something inside me. "To what do I owe the pleasure this time, Nathaniel?"

The use of my full name almost makes me laugh. Almost.

"Want to hang out?" My voice sounds hollow even to me.

"Does this version of hanging out involve kidnapping or stealing a car?"

"You're funny."

"Well, the last time we hung out, you beat the shit out of a guy right before I dropped you off at the police station, so I just need to know what I'm in for this time." There's no judgment in his tone, just that unwavering acceptance he's always shown me.

Jay's silent for a moment, and I can practically see him weighing his next words. "You good man?"

"No." The honesty surprises even me. "I just… I don't want to be alone right now."

"Where are we going?"

"Meet me at Furlo's? That bar just outside town?"

"The sketchy one by the old gas station?" There's no judgment in his voice, just that unwavering acceptance he's always shown me. "See you there."

HOURS LATER, I PUSH THROUGH THE HEAVY DOOR OF FURLO'S. THE BAR IS A study in shadows and secrets, dimly lit and heavy with the kind of silence that swallows confessions whole. A jukebox in the corner bleeds old country songs into the stale air. It's the kind of place where people come to disappear, and tonight, that suits me just fine.

I slide onto a stool, nodding at the bartender. The worn wood beneath my fingers feels like every bad decision I've ever made.

"What can I get for ya?"

Any other time, I would've drowned the anxiety with whatever I could get my hands on. Cocaine would've been my first choice—that familiar rush, the way it made everything sharper, brighter, more manageable. The craving hits me like phantom pain, my fingers drumming against the bar in a rhythm my body remembers too well.

471

One call. That's all it would take.

The numbers are still carved into my brain like scars.

But I can't do everything right now.

Jay has helped me keep that unspoken promise through countless late-night calls and impromptu drives. Through the shakes, the cravings, the moments when the walls of my bedroom felt like they were closing in and the only escape I could think of was chemical. He'd let me show up without question, sometimes just to sit in silence, sometimes to drive aimlessly until the sun came up and the need subsided.

But it's Nora's eyes that haunt me the most.

Every time the craving hits hard enough to make me consider breaking, I see them. I remember the fear that lived in them the night on the beach when she saw me high, fueled with anger. I hit thirty days clean last week and didn't tell a soul, too afraid that speaking it might break whatever fragile progress I've made. Of all the uncertainties in my life right now, there's one thing I know for certain: I never want to see that fear in her eyes again.

"Scotch," I tell the bartender, even as every nerve ending in my body screams for something stronger.

The bartender places the glass in front of me, then leans forward slightly, his voice dropping. "You just missed your old man."

My hand freezes mid-reach, ice sliding down my spine. "What?"

"You're Sullivan's kid, right?" In a town like Eden, there's no escaping who you are.

"Yeah, he was here with his lady friend." The bartender smirks like we're sharing some private joke.

The divorce papers aren't even cold and he's already found his next victim. My throat tightens as I think about Mom, how many *"lady friends"* there must have been while she was at home, trying to hold our family together with bloody hands and broken bones.

"Wait, does he come here often?"

The bartender shrugs, his rag making lazy circles on the polished wood. "Lately, yeah. Been in here a fair bit the past week. Tips well, too."

Of course he fucking does.

It's hush money, just like everything else with Scott—buying silence, crafting his image, making sure everyone sees exactly what he wants them to see. But what eats at me more is why he's still in Eden.

Then the pieces click into place like a gun being loaded. Jake's whereabouts during the day. The way he's been disappearing for hours, giving vague answers about where he's been. The subtle changes in his behavior, the new edge to his anger, the way he's started parroting Scott's words like they're gospel.

Fuck.

Every time Jake went M.I.A., every time we couldn't reach him, every time Mom's calls went straight to voicemail—he was with Scott.

My grip tightens on the glass until I'm afraid it might shatter. While I've been trying to keep Jake away from Scott's influence, the bastard's been working his way in through the back door, poisoning my little brother's mind one "*father-son*" moment at a time. The same way he did with me, before I learned the truth about what kind of man he really was. Before I understood that his attention always came with a price. That his love was just another weapon in his arsenal.

I'm halfway through contemplating whether smashing the glass against the bar would be cathartic or just messy when Jay walks in—hood up despite the heat, hands shoved in his pockets. His eyes sweep the room once before locking on mine, and he heads over with that easy, no-nonsense stride.

"You look like shit," he says, sliding onto the stool next to me. No preamble, no bullshit—just Jay being Jay.

"I look better than I feel," I mutter, taking another sip of my drink, wishing it was strong enough to dull the frustration gnawing at my chest.

He gestures to the bartender for a Coke, then leans back. His body language is casual, but his eyes scan me the way they did that night. He found me bloody-knuckled in a parking lot—the night everything changed between us.

"All right, you gonna tell me what's going on, or are we playing twenty questions?"

I huff out a laugh, low and humorless.

"Same shit, different day. Jake blew up at me before I came here. Scott is pulling his strings like a pro all while fucking around with any woman under twenty-five. Guess the only good thing that's happened as of late is Mom finally signed the divorce papers." I swirl the liquid in my glass, watching it dance.

Jay lets out a slow whistle. "Hell of a week."

"That was just today."

He takes a long pull of his beer, his expression unreadable. Then, with a tilt of his head, he says, "For someone who acts like he doesn't give a shit, you've got a real talent for helping people who don't deserve it."

I glance at him, brow furrowing.

Jay shifts in his seat, setting his bottle down with a soft clink. His eyes hold mine, heavy with a sincerity that makes my chest tight.

"Like me and my mom. That time we couldn't afford her meds, and you showed up outta nowhere with a solution. You didn't have to do that."

The memory hits, uninvited but clear. The desperation in his voice when he called at 3 AM, the way his hands shook as he tried to count out change at the pharmacy. The look in his eyes when I handed over the cash, like he couldn't decide whether to punch me or hug me.

I shrug, the gesture feeling heavier than it should. "You would've done the same for me."

Jay snorts, the sound almost bitter. "Doesn't change the fact that you did it when you hardly knew me."

I wave him off, uncomfortable under the weight of his gratitude. Some debts don't need to be acknowledged between brothers, and that's what we are, even if neither of us says it out loud.

"You deserve someone looking out for you."

His lips twitch into a smirk, breaking the tension. "Glad we're such good acquaintances or whatever the fuck we are."

The laugh that escapes me is genuine this time, if only for a second. It's the first real one I've had since everything went to shit with Jake.

"No one's had my back like you have. I'd say we're better than just acquaintances."

He quirks an eyebrow, his smirk widening. "Wait, did we just become best friends?"

"Shut the fuck up."

"It's a lie anyway. Your girl has had your back longer than I ever have."

The mention of Nora as *"my girl"* makes my chest tighten, a pang of something raw threading through me. I keep my face neutral, even though Jay can probably see right through it.

"She's not my girl," I say, but it's not entirely a lie.

A girl like Nora doesn't belong to anyone. But if anyone tried to claim her as theirs, I'd probably gauge their eyes out.

"You keep telling yourself that, pal," Jay drawls, his grin morphing into something knowing. "You'd have to be blind to not see the way you two are around each other. It's cute and shit." He pauses, then adds with practiced casualness, "Speaking of girls, what's the deal with Camilla? She seeing anyone?"

A real grin spreads across my face, grateful for the change in subject. "Why?"

"Do you always answer a question with a question?"

"Yes."

"Yes, you always answer with a question or yes she's single?"

"Yes to both."

"Well in that case, I think you should put in a good word for me, friend."

My brow arches. "You do realize she could kick your ass in a heartbeat, right?"

He laughs, raising his beer in a mock toast. "That's what I like about her."

Shaking my head, I smirk. It feels good to talk about something normal for once, to pretend for a moment that we're just two guys shooting the shit about girls, not two broken kids trying to piece themselves back together.

"I'll see what I can do, but no promises."

"Good lad." Jay's expression softens, his tone dipping. "You good, though? For real?"

I pause, the words sticking in my throat. Even if I'm not right now, I don't need him to know it.

"I will be." I say it with more confidence than I feel, but the truth lingers unspoken between us like smoke.

Jay watches me carefully before nodding. "All right. Well, just know I'm here. Anytime." He stands, clapping a hand on my shoulder. "Should we, like, hug or some shit now?"

I snort, shoving his arm away. "Get the fuck out of here."

He chuckles, stepping back. "Gotta check on my mom anyway."

"How's she doing?"

Jay hesitates, his hand resting on the edge of the bar.

"Not getting better. But not getting worse. It's like she's got one foot in and one foot out. Some days she fights, other days..." He trails off, shaking his head. "Anyway, don't forget about Camilla."

"Got it."

When he's gone, I stare at my drink, the condensation dripping down the sides like slow-moving tears. Jay's right. I do have people who have had my back even when I didn't deserve it. But Nora—she's different. She's never stopped believing in me, even in moments when I couldn't believe in myself. Even when I gave her every reason to walk away, she stayed and fought for me.

Happiness isn't something I trust—not fully. Every time I let it in, it slips through my fingers, leaving behind nothing but regret. My phone feels heavy as I pull it from my pocket. My thumb hovers over her name before I shove it away again. The truth is, I don't want to be half in, half out with her anymore. I'm done waiting, done letting fear hold me back, done pretending she isn't everything I've ever wanted but never thought I deserved.

If she goes to London, I'll wait for her. She won't want me to, but secretly, I will. If she stays, I'll stay by her side. Either way, I'm hers— completely, irrevocably, with every broken piece of myself that she somehow makes feel whole.

I'm about to take a sip of my untouched drink, then decide against it. It's time to stop running from the best thing that's ever happened to me and start running toward it instead. It's time to tell Nora exactly what she means to me—that she's not just the reason I'm still breathing, but the reason I want to keep breathing.

That loving her isn't just a choice anymore—it's as natural as my heartbeat, as necessary as air.

The parking lot unfolds before me like a concrete wasteland, empty except for the electric hum of streetlights that paint everything in sickly yellow. My car sits in the shadows where the light doesn't reach, and that's when I see them. Monty and his crew, their Harleys gleaming dull under the fluorescents, passing a cigarette between them like some twisted communion.

Monty looks like hell—eyes bloodshot and hollow, face gaunt with days of sleeplessness, movements jerky like a puppet with cut strings. His entire being radiates the kind of dangerous desperation that makes my muscles tense for a fight. But I walk toward them anyway. There's no point in running. Nora's voice echoes in my head, pleading with me to be careful. The memory of her fingers brushing against my cheek this morning sends a knife through my chest. I should have told her then.

"Nice night isn't it, Preppy?" Monty's voice drips with mockery as he crushes his cigarette under his boot. "Noticed your daddy's been busy."

I stop just out of swinging distance, face blank. "You got your money, Monty. I'm out."

Monty steps closer, and I catch the faint stench of whiskey and desperation on him.

"You're out when I say you're out. See, now my fucking problem is your old man. He's been throwing around all these threats. Running his mouth, trying to drive out my business and take over this part of town." His voice slows to a taunting drawl. "But Scott Sullivan owes me some money too. And instead, he's spending it on cheap hookers. What's with you rich folk anyway? You have all the money in the fucking world and you settle for cheap trash?"

I don't flinch, don't let my surprise show.

Of course my father would choose the one dealer in the whole fucking state who I'm trying to get out of my life. The inevitability of it would be laughable if it wasn't so goddamn tragic.

"Not my problem," I say evenly.

Monty's laugh cuts through the night air like broken glass. "Not your problem? No kid, see if he screws up, you're going to pay the price. An eye for an eye."

A bitter laugh escapes me. "You think he cares what you do to me?"

His grin turns cold, predatory. "Oh, I know him well enough. Your old man has been sniffing around my turf, waving cops and lawsuits in my face. Thought he could scare me off." He steps closer, breath hot with bourbon. "But I don't scare easily."

"So what do you want me to do about it?"

The words hang in the air for a heartbeat before his fist slams into my stomach. Pain erupts like a bomb inside my ribs, and I stagger back, lungs desperate for air that won't come. Before I can straighten, a boot crashes into my side, sending me sprawling onto the gravel. I curl in on myself instinctively, arms shielding my face, but it doesn't stop them.

Fists and boots rain down—sharp, brutal, unrelenting. A kick catches my ribs, and I swear I feel something crack. The pain is blinding, but through it all, I see her face, like every other time I've danced along the edge of death.

God, I need to make it through this.

There's so much I haven't told her.

Gravel bites into my palms and cheek as I try to roll away, but it's useless. They're everywhere, surrounding me like wolves on a kill. Each impact sends shockwaves of agony through my body, but I cling to thoughts of her like a lifeline.

The warmth of her laugh. The way she curls into me in the mornings when I wake up next to her.

"Stay down, Preppy," Monty growls, his voice dark with venom. Another kick lands square in my stomach.

I convulse, dry heaving as I gasp for air that won't come. Blood fills my mouth, copper-bright and sickeningly warm.

"Fucking hell," one of them mutters somewhere above me. "He's still moving."

A sharp blow to my back makes my vision blur, and a boot slams into the back of my knee, forcing me flat. I squeeze my eyes shut, trying to block out the agony and humiliation. It's like being broken down piece by piece, every kick driving home what I am—just another pawn in Scott Sullivan's endless games.

477

But through the pain, through the darkness creeping at the edges of my consciousness, I hold onto her. My anchor. My reason.

I love you, I think, as another blow lands.

I love you, I love you, I love you.

When the hits finally stop, I don't move. I can't.

Blood trickles down my lip, warm and metallic, pooling on the gravel beneath me. The coppery taste fills my mouth, but I let out a low, ragged laugh anyway. It's harsh and broken, but it's all I have left.

Monty crouches next to me, grabbing a fistful of my shirt and yanking me up. His breath stinks of whiskey and smoke, and his eyes burn with an anger that's been simmering too long. My head spins, and for a moment, I see Nora's face instead—the way she looked at me this morning, worry creasing her forehead as she traced the dark circles under my eyes.

"You think he cares about this being a message?" I rasp, my voice barely audible through the pain. "This is exactly what he wanted. Scott never gets his hands dirty. He leaves that to scum like you."

Monty's expression darkens, and his fist crashes into my jaw. Stars explode behind my eyes, and I taste more blood as my cheek hits gravel. The world tilts dangerously, but I stay conscious—barely. Monty grabs me again, hauling me up like a rag doll. My legs dangle uselessly, my body too wrecked to resist.

His sneer is inches from my face, his voice low and lethal. "One way or another, he's going to get a message." His grip tightens, fingers digging into bruised flesh. "And you're going to deliver it. You get me my money, or I'll take away everything."

His eyes glint with malicious understanding. "Come to think of it, maybe I went after the wrong son. Maybe your kid brother should be next." He leans in closer, bourbon-soaked breath hot against my face. "Or maybe I just go straight for that pretty little brunette with the nice legs you've been spending time with. She looks like she'd be a fun time."

Something inside me—something I didn't even know existed—snaps.

A surge of protective fury burns through me, stronger than the pain, stronger than fear. Despite the agony shooting through my battered body, I force myself to lift my head. My voice comes out low and deadly, each word carved from ice and steel.

"You go anywhere near my brother or dare to fucking touch her," I say, "and I'll kill you myself."

It's not a threat—it's a promise.

Monty's grin widens, cruel and amused. "Struck a nerve, huh? Rule number one, kid: don't fall for tits and an ass. They'll get you killed. And family doesn't mean shit. They're only good for stabbing you in the back anyway. But I think you've learned that lesson by now."

He shoves me back down, letting me crumple to the gravel. His crew laughs as they mount their bikes, the roar of their engines slicing through the night like thunder. The sound of their departure echoes off the buildings, matching the pounding in my head.

I lie there, bloodied and broken, staring up at the stars. They seem too peaceful, too distant from this hell. My chest burns with each breath, every inhale a sharp reminder of my fractured ribs.

Monty knows about Nora now.

That thought alone twists deeper than any blow they landed. She's no longer just my secret, my safe harbor—she's become a target. The realization sits like lead in my stomach, heavier than all my injuries combined. I try to move, but my body screams in protest. Blood drips steadily from my split lip, marking the gravel like morse code—a desperate message to no one.

The night air grows colder, or maybe it's just the blood loss. Either way, I know with absolute certainty that everything has changed. This isn't just about surviving anymore—it's about protecting what matters. The only pure thing left in my dark, twisted world.

I close my eyes, seeing Nora's face behind my eyelids. The way she looks when she's reading, completely lost in another world. The small crease between her eyebrows when she's worried. The sound of her laugh, how it makes everything else fade away. I have to keep her safe, even if it means pushing her away.

Even if it means breaking both our hearts.

Whatever it takes.

I love you.

I love you.

I love you.

CHAPTER 68
DANCING IN THE DARK
NORA

THE AIR HANGS THICK WITH HUMIDITY, SALTWATER LAPPING AGAINST THE dock that stretches into the lake like a wooden finger reaching for infinity. The familiar creak of weathered planks beneath me feels like home as I dangle my legs over the edge, letting the cool night air kiss my skin.

"Wonderwall" plays softly from my iPod, its familiar melody wrapping around me like muscle memory. Above, stars scatter across the vast darkness—nature's own light show against velvet black. I close my eyes and tilt my face toward the night air, and that's when I feel it—the shift in the atmosphere that always signals his presence.

My body knows before my mind does, responding to him like a compass finding true north. The air itself seems to rearrange around him, molecules dancing to accommodate his presence. It sends my heart into a familiar spiral of beats I can't control.

He's always felt like this—both known and new, like a song I've had memorized since before I first heard it. His absence leaves me hollow, an echo chamber waiting for sound. His presence lights up every nerve ending until I'm almost dizzy with awareness. Sometimes I think it's dangerous to need someone this much, to love with an intensity that borders on physical pain.

"Sorry," he says, voice rough. "Didn't mean to creep up on you."

When he steps closer, my stomach drops. His lip is swollen, his cheekbone painted in violent shades of purple and blue. He's favoring his left side, one arm wrapped protectively around his ribs. The sight of him —broken but still standing—fractures something inside me.

"Oh, my God, Nate," I whisper, scrambling to my feet as my heart pounds against my ribcage. "What happened to you?"

He shakes his head and eases himself down beside me, swallowing back a groan that makes my chest ache. I sink down next to him, fighting the urge to reach out, to try to piece him back together with my bare hands.

"Nothing you need to worry about," he mutters, staring out at the lake where moonlight plays across the water like scattered diamonds.

"Do you need—" The word 'hospital' dies on my tongue as he cuts me off.

"What I need is to just be here with you right now. Please, Nor." His voice is a plea wrapped in pain and something darker that makes my soul ache.

I've learned not to push when he's like this. Sometimes love means being still while someone weathers their own storm, offering shelter rather than solutions. But my heart rebels against the helplessness, thundering so hard I swear he must hear it echoing across the water. My fingers itch to trace his wounds, to heal more than just the physical damage.

His eyes meet mine, they're guarded, but there's a vulnerability in them that pulls at something deep in my chest. Before I can stop myself, I lean in. When my lips meet his, I taste copper and pain—sharp and raw. The metallic tang of his blood lingers between us, but it only makes me hold him tighter, as if I could absorb his hurt through touch alone.

His hand slides to my neck, grip desperate like I might dissolve into thin air. The intensity of his need mirrors my own, making my pulse race beneath his fingers.

I shift onto his lap, straddling him, feeling heat radiate between us like a living thing. His hands find my waist, fingers pressing into the fabric of my dress as if memorizing the shape of me. Our heartbeats sync and still it's not enough. I want to crawl inside his soul and wash away years of hurt with nothing but love.

When his eyes lock with mine, they're raw amber, flecked with gold. There's something unguarded there that steals my breath—pure, unfiltered truth that makes my heart stutter in my chest.

"This has to stop, Nate," I whisper, my voice trembling but certain. "I know you think you deserve this pain, but you don't."

His forehead rests against mine, breath warm and ragged against my skin.

"I don't know anymore, Nora," he argues, but hope bleeds through his words.

"Nate," I brush my lips over his again, "I'm here. I'm not going anywhere."

I press closer, wishing I could pour every ounce of warmth I possess into his wounded soul. His grip tightens, pulling me in until there's nothing between us but shared breath and need. The world beyond the dock fades away—no pain, no past, no bruises or scars. Just us, two souls holding onto each other like we're the only real thing in this vast universe.

"If you won't go to the hospital, at least tell me what happened," I plead, fingers ghosting over his bruises. "Please don't lie to me."

He exhales sharply, running a hand through his hair before meeting my gaze. His eyes are dark wells of exhaustion, heavy with secrets that weigh on his shoulders like concrete.

"I don't want to lie to you. Ever," he says quietly.

"So don't."

A sigh escapes him, and I watch the internal battle play across his features.

"Scott owes money to a dealer I used to run with. They wanted to send a message." His jaw tightens. "Well, you're looking at the message."

My hand flies to my mouth, chest constricting until breathing becomes a conscious effort.

"Nate, please, you need to go to a hospital—"

"No," he cuts me off, firm but gentle. His fingers find mine in the darkness. "I just... I can't deal with any of that right now. I just want to be here. With you."

Moonlight shapes him from shadow, carving out broad shoulders and wild dark hair. His eyes are like windows to a universe he rarely lets anyone see, offering glimpses of his soul in fragments and flashes.

"Where do you go when you do that?" I ask.

"Do what?"

"That faraway stare, like you're here but somewhere else entirely." I watch him the way he's studied me all summer—with curiosity and something deeper, like trying to decode a mystery.

He tilts his head skyward, a small smile playing at his lips that makes my heart flutter.

"Did you know some of the greatest philosophers had this theory that music wasn't just sound, but something celestial? That it traveled through the cosmos, carried by stars and planets, connecting us in ways we'd never be able to even comprehend?" His voice drops, almost reverent.

"There's geometry in the humming of the strings; there's music in the spacing of the spheres." The words settle between us. "Pythagoras said that," he adds with a soft smile.

"Do you secretly study astronomy in your spare time?" I tease.

His laugh rumbles through his chest, rich and warm where I'm pressed against him.

"I think about things most people don't notice. Like how small we are in the grand scheme." His gaze drifts to the lake, where moonlight dances on rippling water. "Sometimes it makes existing easier. To think, in a hundred years, no one will remember us."

"Unless you make it matter," I counter, conviction burning in my chest.

His smile reaches his eyes this time, making my pulse skip. "It's freeing, either way. Just depends on how you choose to see it."

Silence stretches between us, alive with possibility—like gravity itself holds its breath in the space between heartbeats. These stolen moments feel infinite, as if the universe pauses just for us.

"Have you ever heard of Pluto Square?"

I shake my head no.

"It's a reckoning, a time for breaking patterns and choosing new paths." His fingers trace abstract patterns on the weathered wood. "That's why I wanted to play music. Maybe if I leave something that matters, even to one person, it'll feel worth it."

His laugh is gentle—the same one I remember from childhood, when he'd lose himself at the piano and the world couldn't touch him.

I fidget with my iPod, switching songs. *"Stop Crying Your Heart Out"* by Oasis weaves through the night air like incense.

"What about you?" he asks.

"What about me?"

"What's on your mind?"

"Just thinking." I shrug, trying to make light of the storm in my head.

"Sounds dangerous."

"You don't want to be up here." I tap my temple, forcing a smile. "Trust me. It's chaos."

Nate watches me with those eyes that see too much. He shifts, wincing, and I try to move off his lap, but his hands keep me still.

"I like you here," he smirks, making my heart somersault. "Seriously, though. What were you thinking about before I showed up?"

I hesitate, twisting my sleeve between my fingers like I'm wringing out the words.

"It's nothing," I whisper. "You've had such a horrible night, and my problems feel small now—"

"Tell me, please." He interrupts, cradling my face like I'm made of stardust.

My gaze drifts to the stars that watch us with ancient eyes.

"I was thinking about Dad," I say softly, words catching like thorns. "When I look at the stars, I talk to them. It feels... it's the closest I can get to him now."

Nate's jaw tightens, his gaze dropping to the dark water below.

"You know, your dad came to see me," he says finally. "After everything with the scholarship and expulsion. I was in a bad place, so I called him after Scott..." His voice breaks on memories too sharp to touch. "He flew in the next day and sat with me in the park eating burgers."

My breath catches, pieces of the past clicking into place.

"He said it was a teaching conference," I whisper, truth unspooling in my chest. "What did you talk about?"

His eyes drift away, heavy with unspoken words. "He told me I wasn't my mistakes. That I could choose better if I wanted better."

"And do you?" The question slips out before I can catch it. "Want better?"

"Yeah, I think I do." He nods, eyes glassy in the moonlight. "Your dad was more of a father to me than Scott ever was." His voice breaks like waves on rocks.

I cup his face, thumb brushing the bruise on his cheek with reverence. "Dad loved you like his own, Nate," I murmur, pouring truth into every syllable. "He was so proud of you. I know he still is."

His lips part, stunned silent. I press on, needing him to understand.

"He kept every newspaper clipping about you, even made your mom send him your school newsletters. He was proud of the boy you were and the man you're becoming, despite everything. Maybe even because of everything."

Nate's gaze dips to the iPod beside me, and I follow his line of sight.

"You know, this song..." I begin saying, lifting it.

A smirk tugs at his lips. "Let me guess, it's your favorite?"

"How'd you know?" I tease, tilting my head.

"Because I know you." His quiet certainty sends ripples through my soul. When his hand covers mine, warmth radiates from the touch, and my heart stumbles to keep pace with the shifting air between us.

"You know what this song reminds me of?" he asks, voice intimate as a secret.

"What?"

"That time we danced on the dock under the night sky."

Before I can question him, Nate shifts beneath me. With careful grace, he pushes himself up, bracing against his bruised ribs. Even injured, there's a fluid strength to him that makes my pulse flutter. He reaches for the iPod, but I snatch it first. Rising slowly, he masks his pain with determination that tugs at something deep inside me. Standing tall, he extends his hand—a silent invitation that speaks volumes.

"Dance with me."

I laugh softly. "This is becoming a thing now."

"Yeah, but it's our thing." His smile unfolds slowly, the kind that makes time pause, that turns everything else to background noise.

The opening notes of *"You and Me"* by Lifehouse drift from the earbuds. Nate places one in my ear, the other in his—an intimate gesture that sends butterflies through my chest. He tucks the iPod into his pocket and pulls me close, his grip steady against my back. Cool evening air mingles with the warmth of his body as we move together, finding our rhythm in the space between heartbeats. The world quiets, holding its breath as we dance in the dark.

His forehead touches mine, breath soft on my face as I rest my cheek against his chest. His heartbeat drums beneath my ear, steady and strong —a rhythm I could lose myself in forever. When he sings the chorus, low and gravelly, my lips curl into an involuntary smile, the kind that breaks through like sunshine after rain. I look up, and the light in his eyes steals my breath.

"You know what's messed up?" he murmurs, thumb tracing circles on my back.

"What?"

"There are over a billion words in hundreds of languages, and none of them could describe how you make me feel," he says, each word weighted with truth.

I swallow past the tightness in my throat.

"Maybe that's because some feelings aren't meant for words. They're just meant to be felt."

His fingers tighten around mine, gaze burning into me like he's committing every detail to memory.

"I want this," he says, voice thick with emotion. "I want us. You and me. But..." He closes his eyes briefly before meeting mine again, raw vulnerability in his expression. "I'm scared I'll fuck it up because... because my life is such a wreck."

"Right now," I whisper, touching his bruised face, "I just want this moment."

He pulls me closer, and we look at each other like this cosmic dance we've been doing all along was finally bringing us home. And so, we hold on to this fragment of time, fleeting and infinite all at once.

The universe began in a single moment.

A cosmic explosion that birthed stars, planets, and the very matter that makes us who we are. Before it, there was nothing. Then everything. Moments like this remind me of that—a blip in the vastness of existence, but no less profound. Like stars being born, some moments burn so bright they leave their mark on eternity.

But moments are always destined to become memories, precious and fragile, even as they shape who we become.

CHAPTER 69
NO MORE HIDING
NATE

A FEW DAYS HAVE PASSED SINCE MONTY TURNED ME INTO HIS PERSONAL canvas. The bruises are fading from purple-black to sickly yellows and greens, like a twisted watercolor painting. My ribs still protest with each breath, but they're healing. Hospitals aren't an option—too many X-rays would map out years of Scott's handiwork in broken bones and hairline fractures.

So, I do what I've always done: *survive.*

Nora's become my morning ritual, her small hands gentle as she covers the worst of the damage. Each brush of her fingers against my jaw is both salvation and torment—a reminder that she sees all of me, even the parts I try to bury.

That night after Furlo's haunts me. Every breath felt like swallowing shattered glass, blood seeping into my clothes from places I couldn't count. The lake stretched before me like black silk under the moonlight, and there she was—a beacon in the darkness, perched on the dock just like when we were kids, feet skimming the water's surface. Everything in me screamed to walk away. Monty's threats echoed in my head like a death sentence. Knowing about her—it's painted a target on her back.

Each step toward the dock felt like wading through molasses, weighted with equal parts longing and dread. She turned, her expression softening at the sight of me before hardening with concern as I stepped closer, revealing Monty's handiwork.

She reached for my hand, and I let her. Her touch was warmth in the cold, a reminder that not everything in my world was violence and shadows. But looking at her—God, all I could hear was Monty's voice, his threats about her playing on repeat. I couldn't drag her into this darkness. Not her. Not my one pure thing.

Her green eyes searched mine, questions swimming in their depths. The kiss that followed tasted of blood and desperation, and she didn't pull away. She tightened her fingers in my ruined shirt, drawing out my darkness with each press of her lips. Her fingers in my hair felt like absolution. I didn't want to open my eyes, scared it would be another pain-induced hallucination.

Or worse, she'd finally see what Jake already knew—that I'm not good enough for her. Never have been, never will be.

But I'm selfish, and I'm addicted to how she makes me feel. She's the closest thing to heaven I'll ever know, and I'll burn in Hell for wanting her this much.

Nora's fingers ghost over my jaw, dabbing concealer on the worst of the bruises pulling me from the memory. She's precise, methodical—like she's done this a thousand times before.

"You're thinking too loud," she murmurs, tilting my chin to catch better light. Her touch is feather-light, but it burns straight through me.

I try to smile, but it pulls at my split lip. "Just remembering."

THE REST OF THE MORNING IS SPENT AT SONDER WITH NICK, USING THE space to rehearse. Music has always been my escape hatch, the one place where I feel untouchable, where the noise in my head transforms into something beautiful. Summer's winding down, and if I've got no plans, I could take Nick up on his offer to go to Spain to write and maybe record an album. I don't know how, but Nick seems to have connections within the industry.

The ping of a message yanks me back to earth.

> **Mom**
> Your tux is ready—left it in your room. You're driving
> Nora and Camilla, they're getting ready at the house.
> And please don't be late for the gala. Love you x

When I get home, the house is silent as a graveyard. Jake and Ollie must've left with the moms already.

"Hello? Anyone here?" My voice echoes off empty walls, returning lonely and hollow.

I'm halfway up the stairs when Camilla bursts out of Nora's room, practically vibrating with excitement. She's got that look—the one that means she's sitting on information that could start or end wars. Her dark curls are wild from what I assume was an intense styling session, and there's a smudge of mascara above her left eye that she hasn't noticed yet.

"Wait until you see her," she stage-whispers, bouncing on her toes. "She looks like an absolute fucking queen."

I don't doubt it. Nora could wear a trash bag and still outshine anyone in any room. I try to keep my face neutral, but Camilla reads me like a billboard. She pokes my chest with one perfectly manicured finger.

"It's actually painful watching you try to play it cool right now."

"I need to talk to you about something, or someone..." She freezes mid-bounce. "Jay—"

"Oh God," she groans, but the flush creeping up her neck betrays her. "Not this again."

"Why not?" I dodge her swat, grinning. "The guy is crazy about you, Camilla, give him a chance."

"He is not!" She lands a hit this time, her rings catching my arm.

I rub my arm, still smirking. "It's actually painful watching you try to play it cool right now," I mimic her earlier remark.

"Oh, shut up," she mutters, but her lips are twitching. "We're polar opposites. He's all..." she waves her hands vaguely, "broody and dark, and I'm—"

"A hurricane in a party dress?" She swats my arm again, harder. "It's why it works. Opposites attract."

"It's not going to happen." She's fighting a smile now, tucking her hair behind her ear—her tell when she's flustered. "Besides, we'd kill each other within a week."

"At least you'll never get bored." I wink, knowing I'm pushing her buttons. But she can't deny what's there. I've seen it, Nora has seen it, and Jay isn't someone who gives up easily when he decides he cares about something.

"I will end you, Sullivan." But she's grinning, her eyes bright with possibility she won't admit to. "And if you breathe a word of this to him—"

"Your secret is safe." I raise my hands in surrender. "Though it's hardly a secret when you stare at his arms every time he wears a t-shirt."

"Jesus, you're insufferable," she groans, already heading for the stairs. At the top, she pauses, throwing me a look that's pure mischief. "And speaking of insufferable pining, wait till you see what your girl is wearing. Try not to swallow your tongue, Sullivan."

She disappears down the stairs before I can respond, her laughter trailing behind her like perfume, her heels clicking against hardwood fades replacing the thundering of my own heart.

489

Downstairs, I adjust my bow tie again, the fabric suddenly too confining. Then I hear her footsteps trailing down the stairs, each one making my pulse skip like a needle finding that perfect scratch in a vinyl record. The sound resonates through my bones, through spaces I didn't know existed inside me.

There's a feeling when you're waiting for that one person to enter a room—something beyond mere anticipation. It's like standing on an edge, but it's not like the jagged precipice of addiction I know too well. This edge is different—diamond-sharp, splitting me between who I was before this moment and who I'll be after.

My eyes catch her feet first, bare against the hardwood. My gaze trails upward, and when our eyes lock, it's like magnets finding their match. I've had the shit kicked out of me multiple times, but I've never had the breath stolen from my lungs quite like this. Nora descends the stairs like a dream walking into reality. Her emerald dress clings to her frame, the slit high enough to make my pulse forget its rhythm. The color makes her eyes more vibrant than I've ever seen them, and her hair cascades in waves, catching the light as she moves with so much grace. Every step is deliberate, unhurried, as if she knows exactly what she's doing to my sanity.

She's not just beautiful—she's blinding.

The kind of sight that makes everything else blur around the edges until there's nothing left but her. Lenora Wells is the song I've been trying to write my whole life, the melody that's always been stuck in my head, but I could never quite catch.

She reaches the bottom of the stairs, barefoot, holding her heels with a dramatic sigh.

"I hate these things. If I could, I'd wear my Converse instead."

I chuckle, because of course she would. She was always the girl who preferred the Stones over The Backstreet Boys, who'd rather play football than with dolls. She was always different, and that's what I loved about her.

"I think Marcus would have a meltdown if you showed up in Cons."

We both laugh and she rolls her eyes, but there's a hint of a smile there—the same smile that used to make my teenage heart skip beats, now doing dangerous things to my adult one. As she leans against the railing, struggling with one heel, the fabric of her dress makes it impossible for her to bend.

"Ugh, stupid dress. I can't—"

"Here, I've got it," I offer, kneeling without thinking.

Her foot rests lightly against my knee as I slide the shoe on and do up the buckle. Her dress shifts slightly, the slit parting just enough to reveal the curve of her leg. My fingertips brush against her ankle, and that small contact sends electricity through my veins. I glance up at her, and the world narrows to just this: her catching her lower lip between her teeth, the pulse visible at the hollow of her throat, and the way her hands grip the railing tighter. A faint blush creeps up her neck.

She's mesmerizing—I notice things I've spent my whole life learning to read about her, each freckle and smile, and gesture a thing I know by heart now. I secure the other shoe, my fingers ghosting over her ankle.

"There," I manage, my voice rough. "You're good to go."

"Thanks," she breathes, the word falling from her lips like a secret.

Camilla's entrance shatters the moment. "Let's go! We're going to be late!"

As Nora passes, her perfume—vanilla and something darker, something that reminds me of midnight promises—wraps around me like a noose. Her lips curve in that knowing smile that's haunted my dreams for years.

The car ride is exquisite torture. Not because of Camilla's chatter, but because Nora's bare thigh catches my eye with every streetlight we pass. The emerald silk flows like water over curves I shouldn't memorize. She stares out the window, either unaware or too aware of how she's unraveling me thread by careful thread.

At the country club, Camilla vanishes in search of Marcus, leaving us alone under lights that paint Nora in gold and shadow. The gala's music pulses behind us like a heartbeat.

I catch her wrist, pulling her close enough to count her eyelashes, close enough to feel the hitch in her breath. She stumbles slightly, steadying herself against my chest, and suddenly breathing becomes optional. Her eyes catch the light like diamonds, turning my thoughts to static.

"You're…" The word dies in my throat, inadequate.

She tilts her head, lips curving into that devastating smirk that's both invitation and challenge.

"Do I make you nervous, Nate?" The words drip like honey, sweet and dangerous.

My laugh comes out strangled.

"Speechless," I confess, letting my gaze trace her like an artist memorizing his masterpiece. "You make me speechless. You're the most beautiful woman I've ever seen."

"Liar," she whispers, trying to turn away, but my hand slides from her wrist to her waist, claiming this space between heartbeats as ours.

"I wouldn't lie to you. Not about this. Not about anything."

Then I'm kissing her, soft but deep. Her lips part beneath mine with a surrender that makes my heart stutter—she's been waiting for this, too. When she presses closer, fingers clutching my jacket like a lifeline, I groan into her mouth, losing myself in the taste of her. I pull back only when breathing becomes necessary, taking in her flushed cheeks and swollen lips with a satisfaction that burns through my veins.

"Tell me, Nate," she breathes, voice teasing but eyes ablaze, "how are you going to stop yourself from doing that tonight?"

I meet her gaze, letting her see the raw truth of what she does to me. "Who says I'm going to stop?"

A blush paints her cheeks, and when a strand of hair falls across her face, I brush it back, my fingers lingering on her skin. I take her hand, pressing a deliberate kiss to her knuckles.

"I don't want to hide anymore." Her eyes search mine, waiting, so I continue, words spilling out like a confession, "I want everyone to know you're mine, Nora. The future, the distance—we'll figure it out. I'll do whatever it takes. I just need this to be real."

"Nate," she whispers, "this has always been real."

I capture her lips again, desperate now, pouring everything I can't say into the kiss. She tastes like promises, like homecoming, and when her arms wind around my neck, I'm lost.

"I'd love nothing more than to take you home right now."

She laughs softly against my mouth. "Your mom would murder us if we bailed."

"Fine," I sigh, resting my forehead against hers. "I'll behave. Torture myself with admiring you from afar."

Her grin turns wicked. "Let's see about that."

"I've had eleven years of practice," I smirk. "What's one more night?"

Then she gives me that smile—the one that stops time, that makes my chest ache with possibility. The smile I'd spend a lifetime chasing.

"Ready for this?" she asks softly. "Everyone's going to be staring."

I squeeze her hand. "Let them."

We step inside together, and the room hushes. I catch Jake's gaze—his jaw tight, eyes dark—before he looks away. The guilt twists briefly in my chest, but I made my choice. It's her. It's always been her.

I press my lips to her temple.

"No more hiding. It's you and me."

Her fingers tighten in mine, and we move forward, together at last.

CHAPTER 70
MIC DROPS AND BOMBSHELLS
NORA

The hall unfolds like a fever dream, each detail shimmering with Gatsby-esque grandeur. Art deco archways soar overhead, draped in cascading gold and black, while crystal chandeliers scatter light like falling stars. Lydia has transformed every inch into a glittering testament to excess that makes reality feel paper-thin.

The polished marble reflects hundreds of golden votives, their flames dancing across mirrored tables adorned with white orchids and gold-dusted roses. A jazz band plays from their velvet-draped platform, brass instruments gleaming like liquid gold against an enormous art deco mural that creates the illusion of a metallic cityscape reaching toward heaven.

The air is thick with champagne and designer perfume as wait staff in immaculate tuxedos weave through the crowd. The guests themselves are living art—women in gowns that ripple like precious metals, diamonds catching light at their throats, feathered headpieces blurring the line between vintage and couture. Men stand like dark pillars in perfectly tailored suits, every detail from their cufflinks to their shoes whispering old money and influence.

Nate's hand in mine is the only thing keeping me from freaking out as my eyes sweep the room, each familiar face hitting like a wave. Farrah and Connor's group notices us first, their expressions shifting into something carefully crafted. Relief flickers through me when I don't spot Evan, but it's short-lived. My mom and Lydia beam with unmistakable pride from across the room, their joy reaching through the crowd like sunlight. It should comfort me, but instead, my chest tightens as I spot Camilla and Marcus.

And then there's Jake.

The air abandons my lungs when I see him with Ollie, his signature smirk replaced by raw devastation. His fingers strangle an empty glass as he signals for another, jaw clenched tight enough to shatter. Ollie watches him with worried eyes, and guilt crashes through me. I'm holding the weapon that broke him.

Nate feels my grip tighten, leaning close with quiet certainty. "I'll talk to him."

"No," I whisper, the word catching like thorns. "Let me."

He hesitates before nodding, his hand lingering in mine for one more heartbeat before letting go.

The night stretches endlessly, conversations swirling around me like smoke, but Jake haunts the edges of my awareness. His absence feels more present than his being here. I should have told him before tonight, should have explained before he had to watch me walk in with Nate's hand in mine.

When I finally can't bear it anymore, I find him at the bar, his eyes sharp enough to draw blood despite their glassy sheen.

"Dance with me," I offer softly, hand extended like a white flag. He looks ready to refuse until I whisper, "Please." The word hangs between us like the last thread of something precious breaking.

On the dance floor, the space between us feels dense with everything unsaid. Before I can find the right words, he breaks the silence, his voice laced with bitter wine and harder truths.

"So. You and Nate. You're a thing now?"

"I should've told you—"

"Why?" His laugh holds no warmth. "Keeping Jake in the dark seems to be the running theme around here." He pulls me closer, my chin resting on his shoulder, a move I realize is so he doesn't have to look at me. Over his shoulder, I catch Nate watching us, his expression mirroring my guilt.

"I just..." Jake's voice drops to something raw and honest that breaks my heart. "I wish you'd chosen me for once."

The words shatter against my skin.

"Jake... you'll always be my best friend. You—"

"No, Nora." He steps back, severing our connection like a blade through silk. "I can't do that. I can't just play the role of your best friend, especially when he breaks your heart. Because he will."

494

His eyes bore into mine, hard as steel. "And when he does, I can't be the guy who picks up the pieces. I won't be your second choice."

The song ends, but the finality in his voice echoes long after the music fades. He steps away, leaving me stranded as my chest caves in around the hollow space he used to fill. When his eyes find mine again, they're cold enough to burn.

"The worst part is you kept this secret," he says, each word precise as a surgeon's cut. "When you were the one who said no more secrets, remember? Maybe you both do deserve each other. You're both good at fucking lying."

Jake's jaw sets like marble as he delivers his parting shot.

"I'm glad we never finished the summer list," he says as music swells around us."Because you just made sure number seventeen on my list never happens."

The harshness of his words sinks into me like poison. I reach for him, desperate, but he pulls away with a finality that breaks something inside my chest.

"I need to go get ready."

"Jake, please—" My voice splinters, but he's already vanishing into the crowd, leaving me stranded in a sea of whispers and stares.

Before I can follow, the microphone crackles to life, an older man's voice commanding attention. I stand frozen, legs too heavy to move, when designer perfume announces trouble in six-inch heels.

Farrah materializes like a shark scenting blood, her smile carved from glass and malice.

"Well, well," she purrs, voice pitched to carry. "If it isn't the prodigal princess." Her eyes glitter with cruel amusement. The concealer she's wearing doesn't do a good enough job covering the dark shadow under her eyes after Camilla's assault at the Polo. "How adorable, you and Nate. Though I should warn you, he's not as pristine as you might think. Trust me, I would know."

My blood simmers, but I keep my expression neutral. She's hunting for a reaction, and I refuse to give her the satisfaction. "Farrah," I say, voice steady despite the storm in my chest. "Not now."

"Oh, not now?" She laughs, the sound like breaking crystal. Her sequined dress catches light as she steps closer, turning her into something sharp and dangerous. "You lost the right to dictate terms when you decided to play the small-town saint who fucks her best friend's brother." Her smile twists, dripping venom.

They're just words.

But Farrah's always known exactly where to slide the knife.

Camilla steps in, her Louboutins clicking against marble as she positions herself like a shield. Her expression is lethal, red lips curling into something between a smile and a snarl. "Oh look, if it isn't Satan's apprentice. Are you back for another round?"

Farrah's perfectly lined eyes narrow, her French manicure catching light as her fingers twitch. "I should have you deported back to your own country." Her voice drips with venom, but there's a tremor beneath the bravado.

Camilla laughs, a sound like breaking glass that sends chills down spine. She adjusts her designer clutch with practiced dominance.

"God, it must be exhausting being this bitter all the time. Let alone trying to act like you actually have somewhat of a personality."

The crowd around us pretends to be engrossed in their champagne, but their attention is magnetic.

Farrah steps closer, her voice dropping to a dangerous whisper. "Careful, Camilla. You don't know who you're fucking with."

Camilla moves forward, her presence electric and unyielding.

"Oh, I know exactly who I'm fucking with," she fires back, each word precisely aimed. "A desperate girl clinging to relevance because she knows it's slipping through her fingers. Question is, when are you going to realize *you're* the one who's fucking with the wrong person?"

I step between them, heart thundering. "Camilla, let's just go. She's not worth it."

Camilla's expression softens as she meets my eyes, looping her arm through mine with practiced grace. She turns back to Farrah, sugarcoating her voice. "Nice face. That new eyeshadow really suits you."

Farrah's words chase us like poison darts. "Enjoy your little moment while it lasts, Nora. We both know it won't."

Camilla's middle finger rises with elegant defiance as we stride toward Marcus and Mia's table, where they've been watching with barely concealed fascination.

"Do we even want to know?" Marcus asks, already pulling out a chair.

Camilla leans close, her Chanel No. 5 a comforting shield. "I swear, if she comes at you again tonight, I'll have Marcus dump his champagne on her dress and claim it was an accident." Her eyes sparkle with mischief and fierce loyalty.

A laugh bubbles up from my chest, unexpected but welcome.

"Oh shit." Marcus' words force us to turn, and my heart stops.

The air doesn't just shift when Scott Sullivan enters, it fractures like ice moments before it shatters. He moves through the crowd, his presence electric and suffocating, commanding space with the confidence that comes from decades of crushing others beneath Italian leather shoes.

Lydia's gasp from nearby is barely audible, but it reverberates through my bones. Nate transforms beside her, his spine snapping straight as though replaced with steel. His expression settles into something carved from marble—beautiful, cold, and utterly lifeless. It's a mask I've seen before, the one he wears when burying emotions six feet deep.

But Jake—Jake is different.

Where others ripple with tension, he remains still waters. There's an unsettling serenity in his demeanor, like he can finally exhale. When he meets his father's gaze across the room, their subtle nod feels like a secret handshake to a club I never knew existed.

"This is not good," I whisper, turning back toward our table like a moth seeking flame.

Camilla's perfectly arched brows knit together, her crimson lips pressing thin as she tracks the Sullivans. "No kidding. Who invited that walking midlife crisis?"

Marcus swirls his champagne with practiced nonchalance. "Forget reality TV. You can't script this shit if you tried." His attempt at levity dissolves into the thickness of the air.

My eyes magnetically pull back to Nate. The sight makes my heart fold in on itself—his jaw works like he's grinding glass, hands clenched into fists so tight I hear his knuckles protest. The usual fire in his eyes has been replaced by something worse: a vacuum-sealed emptiness that swallows light whole as he watches his father work the room like a master puppeteer.

The council head's voice cuts through tension like a dull blade.

"Ladies and gentlemen, tonight we honor a legacy that runs as deep as Eden's foundations themselves. Please welcome to the stage, one of the founding family members of this town, Mr. Scott Sullivan."

The room's applause swells like an approaching tide, but Nate stands immobile. Lydia's fingers dig into his arm like she's afraid one of them might shatter. Scott takes the stage like a king claiming his throne, his smile as practiced as a surgeon's hands and twice as cutting.

"Thank you, Joe." Scott's voice fills the room with practiced authority. "When my grandfather first came to Eden, this was nothing but untamed coastline and big dreams. He saw potential where others saw wilderness. My father expanded that vision, turning those dreams into reality, brick by brick." He pauses, words settling like seeds in fertile soil. His eyes sweep the crowd with calculated warmth.

"Tonight, as I accept this recognition, I'm reminded that the Sullivan

497

name isn't just a family legacy—it's Eden's legacy. We've shaped this town, its economy, and its very identity. But legacies aren't meant to be preserved in amber. They're meant to evolve, to grow stronger with each generation."

The way he looks at Nate feels less like a father's gaze and more like a predator marking territory. Each word about legacy drips with honey-coated venom.

"Which is why I'm proud to announce that our five-year plan for this town is to expand. And I'm especially proud to announce that my brilliant son, Jacob, will be joining The Sullivan Group this year." He gestures to Jake, who rises with practiced grace. "Come up here, son."

Jake joins him on stage like a prince being crowned, and the air grows thick as concrete.

"Jacob understands what it means to be a Sullivan. He knows that our name carries not just privilege, but responsibility. Under my guidance, he'll learn to shoulder the weight of this legacy, to carry Eden into a future worthy of its past."

Scott's words about Jake's future leadership detonate across Nate's features in microscopic flinches that only someone who knows him would catch.

"Legacy is everything," Scott continues, words slithering like smoke. "It's about making the right choices. Some of us know how to honor that, and for others—" His lips twist into something that resembles a smile the way a knife resembles a spoon. "Well, let's just say not everyone is suited to the responsibility."

The barb finds its mark with surgical precision. Nate's mask fractures for a heartbeat, revealing raw devastation before walls slam back into place.

"This is bad," I breathe.

The applause that follows feels like the nail in the coffin. Scott's gaze, when it finds Nate and Lydia, carries all the warmth of a snake sizing up prey. Jake follows as Scott descends, but my attention is locked on Nate. He's a statue carved from tension and spite, every muscle wound so tight he might shatter at a touch.

This isn't just a celebration anymore—it's ground zero, and the Sullivans are nuclear.

The moment Scott exits, Lydia transforms—her gentle demeanor crystallizing into something dangerous. She tracks him like a lioness stalking wounded prey, each step carrying the weight of twenty years of buried rage. Nate stands motionless, as if movement might detonate him. His fists are clenched white-knuckled, tendons straining beneath skin.

Ten eternal seconds pass before he follows, trailing storm clouds in his wake.

"I need to go," I say quickly, chair scraping marble like a warning bell.

"Call if you need backup!" Camilla's worried voice chases after me.

The hallway beyond swallows the ballroom's noise into plush carpeting. Nate stands ahead like a sentinel, staring at patio doors, shoulders rigid with barely contained fury. I approach cautiously, taking his hand between mine like something precious and volatile.

"They're fighting," he says, voice rumbling like thunder before lightning. Rage radiates from him in waves hot enough to burn, his body coiled tight as a spring. This isn't just anger, it's muscle memory—the response of a boy forced to become a warrior in his own home.

"You should go." His words are sharp edges wrapped in velvet.

"I'm not leaving you, Nate."

"Nora, please." His hazel eyes are battlefields of pain and pride.

"No." My voice rings with unexpected steel. His gaze cuts into mine like a blade seeking purchase. "I'm with you. No more hiding."

Something in him softens for a fraction of a second and his fingers tighten around mine.

Then Lydia's voice shatters everything.

"You're unbelievable, Scott!"

The sound ignites Nate like a match to gasoline. He bolts toward the patio, his hand tearing from mine.

"Nate!" My heart lurches after him as he crosses the threshold into gathering tempest.

I follow to find Scott advancing on Lydia like a shark scenting blood, his smirk a crown of thorns.

"A congratulations would have been nice, or is that asking too much?"

"Congratulations?" Lydia's voice quivers like a bowstring pulled too tight, each word poisoned with twenty years of venom. "You promised, Scott. You promised to leave Jake out of this."

Scott's expression remains unchanged, but his eyes gleam with something darker than triumph—the satisfied glitter of a puppet master watching his strings dance.

"Jake made his own decision, Lydia. He's a grown man. Or are you forgetting that? You already babied your first born, you're not tarnishing Jake."

"You twisted him into this! Manipulated him!" Her voice rises like gathering thunder. "You're poisoning him, just like you've poisoned everything else you've touched."

The night air crackles with electricity, every word another step toward an explosion that feels as inevitable as gravity. We're all just waiting for the match to hit the powder keg, and judging by the darkness gathering in Nate's eyes, we won't have to wait long.

Scott's smile warps into something feral, a predator baring its teeth. "Watch your tone, Lydia. You're lucky I didn't take him away for good when I had the chance."

The slap shatters the night like lightning striking glass. The sound reverberates across the patio, sharp and final, Lydia's hand suspended in the aftermath like a flag in a dying wind. Her fingers tremble, but her eyes blaze with two decades of swallowed silence finally finding voice.

"You bastard," she breathes, the words splintering like ice.

Scott's composure evaporates like morning dew in hell. His hand strikes like a cobra, pinning Lydia against the wall with bone-crushing force. Horror spreads through my body like frost, each cell screaming in protest as he looms over her, his cologne-laced breath hot with malice.

"This is all your fault. You couldn't keep your legs closed. Couldn't keep your mouth shut. And now look where we are."

My blood crystallizes in my veins.

This isn't happening.

This can't be happening.

But then Nate moves—a blur of contained violence, eighteen years of rage compressed into a single moment. He crosses the patio like an avenging angel, hands fisting in Scott's expensive lapels before slamming him against brick. The impact is a symphony of violence—flesh meeting stone, startled wheeze of expelled air, Lydia's sharp intake of breath slicing through chaos like a blade.

"Don't fucking touch her." Nate's voice is barely human, a guttural snarl ripped from somewhere primal and dark. His words vibrate with the force of an earthquake about to level cities. "Does it make you feel powerful every time you lay a hand on her?"

Scott's laugh crawls through the air like poisonous gas, thick with condescension. He doesn't resist, doesn't even flinch—a snake comfortable in its own venom.

"Still fighting your mom's battles." His eyes narrow to reptilian slits, targeting Nate's core with surgical precision. "I'm glad I only have one son."

I watch the words detonate across Nate's face. They fracture him in slow motion—his jaw grinding like tectonic plates about to split, hands trembling with the herculean effort of not becoming the monster before him.

"Stop!" My voice slices through the chaos like a desperate prayer.

Lydia's eyes find mine, heavy with secrets finally dragged into light, shame and defiance warring in their depths.

Scott adjusts his suit with theatrical precision, brushing off violence like lint.

"My one regret is letting her keep you." He turns with military sharpness, each step away a calculated insult, as if he's won not just this battle but every war yet to come.

The silence that follows feels radioactive, contaminating everything it touches.

Nate remains frozen, his breathing ragged like a wounded animal's, each exhale weighted with years of suppressed rage. His fists are still clenched, knuckles bleached white with restraint that's rapidly unraveling.

"Nate, leave it. Please." Lydia's voice is soft but urgent, like trying to talk down an approaching tornado.

But he's beyond words now, lost in a red mist of fury and old wounds torn fresh. His body vibrates with barely contained violence, a bomb with a rapidly burning fuse.

"Nate," I plead, my voice cracking like thin ice. "Whatever you're thinking right now, just breathe. Don't let him win."

He doesn't acknowledge me. His focus is laser-locked on the door Scott disappeared through, every muscle coiled for pursuit. Then he moves, and it's like watching destiny unfold in slow motion.

Lydia turns to me, her face a roadmap of desperate fear.

"Stop him. Please. Don't let him do something he'll regret."

I nod, already running.

"Nate!" My voice chases him down the hallway, but it feels futile, like trying to stop an avalanche with whispers.

Because deep in my gut, I know this isn't something anyone can stop. This is Nate's Rubicon, his point of no return, and all I can do is pray I'm fast enough to prevent the impending catastrophe. Or at least be there to gather what remains when the dust settles.

CHAPTER 71
THE SINS WE INHERIT
NATE

I'M SITTING IN THE CAR, KNUCKLES WHITE AGAINST BLACK LEATHER, watching the neon sign above Furlo's flicker like a dying heartbeat. Each breath feels like swallowing glass, sharp and cold against my throat. The parking lot stretches before me, a canvas of shadows and regret.

My phone illuminates the darkness again—Nora. The voicemail notification blinks accusingly, her words from earlier echoing in my mind: *"I'm with you, Nate. No more hiding."*

The truth sits heavy in my chest.

I can't drag her into this anymore.

She deserves better than someone who carries destruction in their DNA. She broke through every wall I built, only to find herself in the middle of my personal hell. That's my specialty—corrupting everything pure that dares to touch my life. Maybe it's the universe's twisted way of saying I don't get the fairytale ending. No girl, no dreams, no shot at redemption. Just my father's legacy of rage wrapped in designer suits and trust fund guilt.

Another call lights up the screen. I throw the phone onto the passenger seat, watching her name fade to black. It feels like watching my last chance at happiness slip through my fingers. The night air hits me as I step out. There's a sick irony in heading into another bar, choosing another fight—becoming everything I swore I'd never be. But this—this familiar dance of anger and self-destruction—is the only home I've ever known.

The bar door creaks open, and the thick wall of stale beer and cigarette smoke wraps around me like an old friend. That's when I see

502

him—Scott Sullivan himself, hunched over the bar like some regular working man drowning his sorrows. A woman leans close, her laughter carrying across the room, her manicured hand resting on his arm like she can't feel the poison beneath his skin. Something primordial awakens in my chest. This bastard, playing an eligible bachelor while systematically destroying everyone who shares his blood. Mom, me, and now Jake —we're all just collateral damage in his grand performance of life.

I move toward them, each step weighted with two decades of fury.

"You look like a smart girl," I say, my voice slicing through the ambient noise. The woman startles; Scott doesn't even flinch. Just sits there, tumbler in hand, waiting for the show. "The guy you're thinking about fucking is a piece of shit with a wife and two sons he pretends don't exist. Isn't that right, *Dad*?"

She gathers her dignity along with her purse and disappears into the crowd. Scott's pathetic, "Kelly, wait!" follows her retreat.

"Are you fucking serious?" The rage burns familiar paths through my veins. "You've got some serious nerve sitting here while your real life's a fucking train wreck."

"Lower your voice," he slurs, bloodshot eyes struggling to focus. "I don't need a scene."

Of course. Drunk and high in his thousand-dollar suit, straight from his moment of triumph at Eden's gala to this dive bar. And I'm supposedly the family disappointment.

"A scene?" I lean close enough to taste the whiskey on his breath. "You haven't seen one yet. You've already destroyed Mom's life. Mine. And now Jake? Was that part of the master plan? I told you to walk away and never come near us again. But you just couldn't help yourself, could you?"

His jaw tightens, eyes going glacial. "And what are you going to do, son?" The last word drips with contempt.

"You only have one son, remember? And it sure as hell isn't me. You're a fucking disgrace," I spit, hating how my voice betrays me, hating how after all these years, he can still reduce me to that terrified nine-year-old boy.

"And you're my biggest disappointment." The words slide off his tongue like a practiced script.

"Your insults don't cut like they used to." But even as I say it, an old wound throbs—that desperate need for approval I've never managed to excise. "Nothing you say hurts me anymore."

His smirk is surgical in its cruelty. "You know what your problem is, Nate? You think I'm the villain while your mother's some kind of saint."

He leans closer, words burning like acid. "You might want to fact-check that story."

Confusion slices through my anger. "Don't talk about her to me. You lost that right years ago."

He responds by downing his drink, wielding silence like another weapon. The fury builds in my chest, drowning out everything good, everything I've fought to become. All of it eclipsed by his toxic shadow.

"You hate me," my voice cracks, and I despise myself for letting him hear it. "You've always hated me. What the fuck did I do to you that was so bad?"

His only answer is another swallow of whiskey, and somehow that cuts deeper than any insult. Because even now, some broken part of me still wants answers. Still needs to understand why I wasn't enough.

The silence stretches dangerous and thin, until something ancient and dark breaks loose inside me.

"I wish it had been you instead of David. At least he knew how to be an actual father." The words tear free like barbed wire, carrying years of accumulated poison.

Scott's face twists into something inhuman. "Then maybe your mother should've fucked him instead." His laugh scrapes against my nerves. "Who knows, she probably already did."

The words detonate in my chest, and suddenly my hands are moving on pure instinct, fingers curling into his expensive collar. I slam him against the bar with a sound that echoes through my bones.

"Every ounce of hate you have for me? It's doubled when I think about how much I despise you," I roar, voice shattering. Each word is a bullet I've been saving, each syllable weighted with memories of broken furniture and my mother's tears. "Every time you hurt her, every time you tore us apart, did it feel good? Was the control worth your one-way ticket to hell?"

Scott laughs, and I see myself through the years—at eight, hiding in closets; at twelve, standing between him and mom; at sixteen, nursing split knuckles and a broken heart. Every version of myself that he created pulses beneath my skin.

"I should have never let her keep you." He spits the words like venom, and for a moment, I'm that little boy again, desperate for love that would never come.

I raise my fist, years of rage compressed into five knuckles, but suddenly there are hands pulling me back.

"Nate!" Jay's voice cuts through the red haze. He drags me away with surprising strength, and I let him because some small part of me knows

—this isn't who I am. This isn't who I fought to become. "You don't need to go to jail right now, man. Walk it off."

Scott stumbles up, adjusting his suit like armor, his sneer a perfect mirror of my childhood nightmares.

The bartender's voice cuts through. "Get out, Sullivan, before I call the cops."

I watch him leave, chest heaving, body vibrating with aftershocks of rage and something deeper—grief for the father I never had. Jay's hand on my shoulder pulls me back to reality.

"How'd you find me?" The words scrape past my lips.

"Nora called," Jay says simply. "Said you were in a bad way after seeing your dad. I figured you'd follow him here." Jay squeezes my shoulder, grounding me. "For what it's worth," he says, voice low and sincere, "I've always thought your dad was a piece of shit. And you've never been anything like him."

I nod mechanically, but the words can't compete with the voice in my head—his voice—telling me I'll never be enough. Never be worthy. And now he's got Jake too, molding my brother into his image while I stand here, drowning in the same old rage that's been my only constant companion.

"Come on," Jay says. "Let's get you back to your girl."

The words slice fresh wounds.

My girl.

The truth settles like lead—she's not mine. She never will be. Not with this anger inside me, this curse running through my veins. I've spent so long trying to be anything but him, and tonight proves what I've always feared: I'm my father's son after all.

And that's exactly why I have to let her go.

CHAPTER 72
BLINK AND GONE
NORA

MY HANDS TREMBLE AS I STARE AT MY PHONE. SEVEN MISSED CALLS ECHO like heartbeats in the void.

Each message sits there untouched, a timeline of mounting desperation:

> **Nora**
> Where are you?
>
> Please just let me know you're safe.
>
> Nate, you're scaring me.
>
> I'm not letting you do this alone.
>
> Please just answer.
>
> I need to know you're okay.

The phone weighs like grief in my hands as I pace the balcony, fighting tears that threaten to break the dam of my composure. Each step feels like wading through memories of every time I've watched him walk away, my heart a desperate metronome counting seconds of silence. Camilla's approach registers in soft heel-clicks against stone, her presence cutting through the static of my panic.

"Hey," she says, voice gentle as morning light. "What's going on?"

My head shake sends the world tilting. "Nate's gone. He followed Scott out, and I can't—" The words fracture in my throat. "He's not in a good place."

"What happened?" Camilla moves closer, her usual sharp edges softened by concern.

"Scott and Lydia had a fight. Scott lunged at Lydia and—God, you should have seen Nate's face, Camilla." Another call hits voicemail, another crack in my resolve. "He won't answer, he won't—"

"What about Jay?" Camilla's voice cuts through my spiral, practical as always. "He might know where Nate went."

"I don't have his number."

A hint of a smile plays at her lips as she pulls out her phone. "Lucky for you, I do."

I grab her phone, questions about that particular connection filed away for a less urgent moment. Each ring makes my pulse spike.

"Didn't think you'd call so soon," Jay answers, playful tone a jarring contrast to my racing heart.

"Jay, it's Nora." My words tumble out like scattered puzzle pieces. "I need your help. It's Nate."

His voice shifts instantly to steel. "What happened?"

I explain in fragments—the gala, Scott's ambush, the aftermath that hangs in the air like smoke. Jay's curse cuts through the static of my fear.

"I think I know where he went," he says, and relief floods my system. "If he followed Scott, he's probably at Furlo's. Meet me there."

"Thank you," I breathe, inadequate for the weight of my gratitude.

Camilla squeezes my arm. "Want company?"

I shake my head, already moving. "No. The fewer people, the better." I leave unspoken the ways this night could spiral into chaos.

Inside, I spot Ollie laughing with Mia, their joy a stark reminder of how quickly happiness can shatter. I snatch the Jeep keys, mind racing ahead to every possible scenario, each one darker than the last.

Please, I think as I run, let me reach him before the damage becomes irreparable.

"Nora!"

Jake's voice freezes me mid-stride. I turn to find him approaching, his expression a battlefield of frustration and raw need.

"Where are you going?" His tone is sharp but refined.

The keys bite into my palm. "I need to go."

"Where?" Each word lands like an accusation.

"To find Nate." His name hangs between us like smoke signals.

Jake steps closer, taking my hand. His palm is warm but wrong. "You don't need to follow him every time he goes rogue. Stay," he pleads, voice honey-sweet. "Stay here. With me."

I close my eyes, because some truths are easier to deliver in darkness. "Jake, I can't. I can't let him do this alone."

His jaw works beneath perfect skin. "Number seventeen on my list... it was to tell you how I feel." He looks up through those unfairly long lashes, the perfect Sullivan son with his perfectly wrong timing. "About you."

My chest aches with the familiar pain of inevitable heartbreak. "Jake, stop."

His fingers dig into my shoulders with desperate intensity. "Nora, I love you."

The words hit like shrapnel, and I feel the moment everything changes. "Jake, I... I can't do this with you now."

"Because you have feelings for him?"

"Because I love him." The truth explodes between us like fireworks. "And I have for a long time."

"You don't have a future with him. But you could have one with me. That's why I said yes to the position with Dad."

The words land like a slap. "You what?"

"I said yes because I wanted to build something for myself, for you—"

"No." Rage erupts in my chest, volcanic and violent. "Don't you dare use me as a reason. You knew this would happen and you went along with it anyway." Seventeen years of protected silence shatters like fine china. "You're delusional if you think Scott cares about you, Jake. He wants pawns he can manipulate, and you fell right into his hands like the perfect little soldier you've always been."

"Why do you let Nate get in your head like this?" His voice rises with frustration.

I laugh, the sound sharp enough to draw blood. "You still don't see it. All Nate has ever done is protect you. Every time you were sent away, it was to protect you. From seeing your dad abuse your mom. Abuse him. Your brother gave up everything so you could have a childhood he never got."

The color drains from Jake's face, his perfect world cracking like thin ice. "You're lying."

"I wish I was." My voice softens despite my anger, because watching someone's reality implode isn't something you can do without feeling it. "Nate sacrificed himself so you could have what was stolen from him. And now, I have to go before we lose him completely."

I push past him, chest burning with fury and regret. In my rearview, Jake stands alone in the dark, shoulders curved inward like a wounded child discovering his castle was built on quicksand, and the brother he resented was his shield all along.

The highway stretches before me like an obsidian river, empty except for distant taillights burning like dying stars. My knuckles bleach white against the steering wheel as I hit redial again, each unanswered ring another nail in my chest.

My phone chimes, sharp as breaking glass.

Nate
I'm coming back now. I'm sorry.

Relief floods my system—and then.

Twin suns explode in my vision.

Headlights blazing on the wrong side of the road, bearing down like the eyes of a metallic beast. They say your life flashes before your eyes, but that's not quite right. Time fractures instead, each millisecond crystallizing with perfect clarity:

Blink.

Mom's perfume as she hugs me goodbye.

Blink.

Ollie teaching me to ride a bike, promising not to let go.

Blink.

Nate's smile across a crowded room when his eyes find mine.

Blink.

All the firsts I'll never have.

Blink.

All the moments that were supposed to be mine.

They don't tell you it's not the big moments you see, it's the small ones—the quiet ones you didn't know were precious until they're about to be gone. It's the future you thought was guaranteed, slipping away like sand through an hourglass suddenly turned on its side.

The impact happens in slow motion.

My world implodes in a symphony of destruction. The hood crumples like paper, the sound of buckling metal so loud it becomes a physical thing, rattling my bones and rupturing the quiet night. The windshield splinters in slow motion—a spiderweb of cracks blooming outward before the whole thing dissolves into a thousand glittering daggers. They catch the streetlight as they hurtle toward me, beautiful and lethal, slicing skin and embedding themselves in my flesh.

The seatbelt locks, crushing into my ribcage with such force I swear I hear bones crack. My teeth clack together, the impact sending shockwaves through my skull as my head whips forward then back. The airbag explodes in my face like a bomb mixing with the taste of my own blood. The Jeep pirouettes, each rotation bringing new waves of agony as my body ragdolls against the constraints.

Blood pools hot and thick in my mouth. Each swallow brings the copper-salt tang of mortality. But underneath it all is the primal scent of fear—sharp and terrifying. It radiates from my pores, mingles with the blood and smoke, marking this moment as the line between before and after.

Consciousness slips away in pieces as voices pierce the fog.

"Oh, my God! Are they dead?" A woman's voice, brittle with terror.

"No. Fuck, it's you."

Male.

Familiar.

That cologne cutting through the wreckage—something expensive, tainted with guilty panic.

"Should we call an ambulance?"

"No. We need to go. Now."

"Do you know her?"

"Get in the car."

"We can't just leave her! She's still breathing."

"I said get in the fucking car now."

Footsteps crunch away on broken glass. I try to scream, to move, but my body has become a prison of twisted metal and shattered bone. The darkness creeps in, soft and seductive.

Through the kaleidoscope of broken glass and rising smoke, I see him. He's running towards me in a halo of impossible warmth, wearing a smile that made monsters retreat and storms seem less scary.

"Dad?" The word escapes like a dying breath.

His voice cuts through clear as morning bells: *It's okay, Leni. I've got you. I always got you. Hold on, a little longer okay? I love you.*

His image dissolves like watercolors in rain, replaced by different eyes—hazel ones that contain entire universes. Nate's eyes, memorized like favorite poems, stare back at me.

The realization hits harder than the crash—this isn't how our story was supposed to end.

Not with unspoken words and half-finished promises.

Seconds.

That's all it takes.

One choice.

One cosmic blink, and certainty dissolves into smoke.

Time doesn't just break—it fractures completely.

Before stands forever separated from after, the boundary marked not by a gentle line but by a jagged barrier of broken glass and scattered memories.

When death arrives, it brings no patience for bargaining. It watches the raw, animal desperation of someone seeing their future burn.

Death only laughs—cold and ancient—reminding that each heartbeat was merely borrowed, asking with cruel interest: *What did you do with my generous loan?*

It's where the realization hits you: life isn't possessed but temporarily held, like a library book with its due date written in vanishing ink. No one belongs to another forever. The universe simply allows brief custody, its permission already fading as it's granted.

These are the moments that transform.

That demolish and reconstruct something entirely different—something permanently marked by the knowledge that everything changes between inhale and exhale.

Seconds.

That's all it takes.

Blink.

Gone.

Only darkness remains, with echoes of words forever unspoken.

CHAPTER 73
GOD, CAN YOU HEAR ME?
NATE

THE CAR IS TOO QUIET, JUST THE LOW HUM OF THE ENGINE AND JAY drumming his fingers on the steering wheel. I shoot a quick text to Nora, telling her I'm on my way back. To her.

I rub my hands over my face and exhale sharply. Scott's words, his sneer, still cling to me like oil on water. I wanted to tear him apart, but I couldn't let him win by dragging me down to his level.

Jay glances at me, his voice slicing through the silence. "You good, man?"

I nod stiffly. "Yeah. Just—keep driving."

The road stretches dark and endless ahead of us, headlights painting yellow ghosts on the asphalt. I stare out the window, watching the trees blur past, until something catches my eye—a flash of white off the side of the road that feels wrong, like a bone jutting through skin. It's nothing at first, just a car pulled over. Then reality fractures: the mangled front end, glass scattered like diamonds in the dirt, and the unmistakable curve of the Jeep's fender twisted into something grotesque. My chest constricts as recognition hits—I know that car. I know who drives that car.

"Jay—pull over."

"What? Why?"

"Pull the fuck over! Right now!"

Jay slams on the brakes as I fling the door open, the car still rolling. I'm running before my feet hit the ground, gravel crunching beneath my boots as I race toward the wreckage. The smell hits me first—gasoline sharp enough to burn my nostrils, mixed with something metallic and sweet that turns my stomach. Then I see the flames, hungry orange tongues licking at the hood, reaching for the night sky.

"Nora!" My voice shatters like the windshield I'm staring through, my hands trembling as I yank at the door handle until my muscles scream. It doesn't budge.

Jay appears beside me, his face ghostly in the firelight. "Shit. Is that gas?"

"Help me get her out!" The words tear from my throat.

We pull at the door until our arms shake, but it's sealed shut. My fists pound against the glass, each impact a desperate prayer. Jay disappears and returns with a rock.

"Stand back!" He hesitates for a heartbeat, his eyes locked on Nora's still form. "Sorry, Nora," he whispers before bringing the rock down.

The glass splinters, then explodes inward. I tear off my suit jacket and drape it over the jagged edges. Even now, with flames licking at the hood and time slipping away, I can't bear the thought of the glass cutting into her skin. I reach through the makeshift barrier, barely registering the shards that slice into my own arms. The heat from the fire crawls over my flesh, but pain is irrelevant. Nothing matters except getting her out.

Her seatbelt is jammed, the metal around her legs twisted like modern art. I hear myself whispering, voice cracking, "Leni, it's me. I'm here. I'm gonna get you out, okay? Just stay with me. Please, stay with me." Each word is a promise I'm terrified I won't be able to keep.

Jay's already at the other side, muscles straining against the crushed metal pinning her down. "On three!" he shouts over the growing roar of flames.

We heave together, and I feel the weight shift just enough. I slip my arms under her, and for one heart-stopping moment, she's nothing but dead weight against me. But then I have her, and I'm stumbling back, cradling her. The asphalt is cold and unforgiving as I lay her down, my hands shaking as they brush her face. Blood paints abstract patterns on her skin, her hair a dark halo matted with crimson. Her dress—the one she wore when she smiled at me across the ballroom just hours ago—is now a canvas of violence.

"It's okay, Leni," I whisper, every word a desperate prayer. My throat closes around the words, but I force them out anyway. "Hold on a little longer, please."

Jay crouches beside us, his voice urgent. "Nate, we have to go. She's not gonna make it if we don't move now."

I can't stop the tears that fall as I kiss her forehead. "I love you," I repeat, like if I say it enough times it'll be strong enough to keep her here. "Don't leave me. Please. Please, not you."

"Nate!" Jay's hand clamps down on my shoulder, reality crashing back in. "Pick her up. Let's go!"

His voice breaks through the fog of terror, and I lift her as gently as possible. As Jay peels out, tires screaming against asphalt, I hold her close in the backseat, whispering promises into her hair. I cradle her in my lap, my trembling hands pressing against wounds that won't stop bleeding. The crimson seeps between my fingers, warm and relentless. Behind my eyes, memories flash in rapid succession. Little Leni in pigtails and that worn Mickey Mouse shirt, twirling until she's dizzy. Her voice filling the house with off-key Guns N' Roses at fourteen. The way her nose still scrunches when she's angry. How her green eyes catch the light when she's creating something beautiful.

"Stay with me, Len. Please."

Jay's voice cuts through the fog, stretched tight with panic but holding steady. "We're almost there. Hold on."

I press my lips to her forehead, tasting copper and salt, my tears mixing with her blood. "It's okay Leni." The words ghost against her skin.

"I've got you. I always got you. Hold on a little longer, okay? I love you."

The hospital doors part like gates to purgatory, flooding us with harsh fluorescent light. The antiseptic smell burns my nostrils, mixing with the metallic tang of blood that's soaked through my shirt. Everything moves in slow motion and too fast at once—a herd of squeaking shoes on linoleum, metal instruments clattering, voices overlapping in urgent tones.

"Help!" The word tears from my throat. "Somebody help her!"

A nurse emerges followed by doctors. When they take Nora from my arms, the void left behind is physical, an amputation of something vital. I stumble backward, my vision tunneling to my hands—red, so red, like I've been finger-painting in nightmares.

"What happened?" The question floats somewhere above my head.

It's Jay's voice that cuts through. "Car accident—she was trapped, unconscious. We broke the window to get her out—there was fire, gas everywhere. I don't know how long she was there. It was a hit and run. She's lost a lot of blood and she's not breathing right—please, just help her!"

They disappear behind swinging doors, taking Nora with them. I'm left staring at my hands, at the abstract art of her life force drying on my skin. The room tilts like a carnival ride gone wrong.

She's not breathing right.

No, she isn't breathing at all.

My knees give out and a sound escapes me—something primal and broken that I barely recognize as human. The truth hits me in waves: nobody knows. Her mom is still laughing at some joke, Ollie's probably rolling his eyes at another of Marcus's stories, all of them existing in a world where Nora is still whole and safe.

"Nate." Jay's voice anchors me as his hands grip my shoulders. He crouches before me like a shield against the fluorescent glare. "She's a fucking warrior, okay? She's gonna pull through this. That girl is stronger than you think."

The words bounce off me like rain on glass. Even if she survives— even if by some miracle she opens those green eyes again—will I ever forgive myself for being the reason they almost closed forever?

Jay helps me to a row of cold, plastic chairs. My legs won't stop shaking, hands twitching in my lap like dying birds.

"I need your phone," I manage, my voice hollow and cracked.

Jay hands it over. My fingers tremble as I dial Mom's number, each ring echoing in my skull like a death knell.

"Nate! Thank God!" Kat's voice bursts through, bright as sunshine. "Your mom has been worried sick. Where are you? Is Nora with you?"

I try to swallow past the razor blades in my throat. "Kat." The words splinter, and I have to squeeze my eyes shut against the burning. "We're at the hospital. Nora… she's hurt."

The silence that follows is deafening. When Kat's voice returns, it's sharp with fear. "What? What do you mean she's hurt? Nate, what happened?"

I can't do it.

Can't form the words that will shatter their world like mine. My throat closes completely, and I just hand the phone back to Jay, pushing to my feet. I need to move, need to escape the fluorescent interrogation lights and the nurses' pitying stares. Jay's voice fades behind me as I stumble away, explaining what I can't.

The waiting room erupts when they arrive, a tsunami of fear and desperation crashing through the sterile calm. Kat charges toward the nurses' station, her voice razor-sharp as she demands answers. Mom appears before me, her face drained of color, and wraps her arms around me. Everything shatters. My knees give out, and I fold into her embrace, my body wracked with tremors I can't control. The weight of tonight— the blood, the flames, Nora's lifeless form in my arms—crushes me beneath its magnitude.

But Jake stands like a statue carved from fury, his fists clenched at his sides. His eyes burn into me with an intensity that could melt steel, holding none of the brotherly warmth I once knew. Only raw, unfiltered hatred.

And I welcome it.

The doctor's entrance splits the tension like lightning.

"She's in surgery and we have her in a stable condition for now, but it's touch and go," he announces, and oxygen floods my lungs for the first time in hours. "Multiple fractured ribs, severe head trauma from the impact. We're running additional scans for internal bleeding and checking organ function, but she's incredibly lucky. If she hadn't arrived when she did..." His eyes find mine, softening. "You may have just saved her life. Any later, and we might have lost her."

The words should feel like absolution, but they taste like ash in my mouth. Saving her isn't redemption, not when I'm the reason she needed saving in the first place.

Jake steps forward, his face contorted with fury I've never seen before.

"This is your fault."

The words slice through me, finding every vulnerable spot. I meet his gaze, but there's nothing left in me to fight back. Instead, I feel myself sinking into the familiar darkness that's always lurked at the edges of my consciousness.

He's right.

This is your fault.

If you'd just answered her call, like you promised.

You did this.

You fuck up everything you touch, remember?

"She wouldn't have been out there if it wasn't for you," Jake spits, each word a bullet. "She was looking for you, Nate. You! But you didn't answer your fucking phone."

The darkness whispers, *you know what you need to do to make this pain go away.*

"Jake," Lydia starts, but he steamrolls over her, voice rising like thunder.

It'll be quick and easy. Like old times.

"How are you gonna handle this one, huh?" His laugh is a knife across glass. "You gonna run off, get high and forget about all the collateral damage you've caused? Like every other time before?"

Without a word, I stand, the demon's whispers drowning out Mom's pleas. My feet carry me toward the exit, toward the familiar path I swore I'd never walk again.

Like father, like son.

Some cravings never die.

I re-enter the general waiting area at the front of the hospital to find Jay still here, sitting in the corner, watching me with eyes that have seen this look spread across my face before.

His arms are crossed, jaw set like he's bracing for impact. Even after I told him to go, he stayed.

The fluorescent lights suddenly feel like searchlights, the walls pressing in like a vice. I can't stay here, can't keep seeing her blood on my hands, can't stop replaying the way her body looked so small and broken. The rise and fall of her chest was so faint I had to convince myself she was still breathing.

Because of me.

All because of me.

My fingers rake through my hair, trembling with need and guilt and something darker. "Jay, go home," I mutter, voice scraping like gravel.

"I'm not going anywhere." He leans forward, elbows on knees, eyes never leaving mine. "You're not okay, Nate. And I know exactly what you're thinking of doing."

"Don't psycho-fucking-analyze me," I snap, but the words come out desperate rather than angry. "You don't know what's going on in my head."

"You're right—I don't. But I know you." His voice softens with a decade of friendship. "You think you can carry all this shit alone, but you can't, and when shit gets too heavy, you implode."

A laugh tears from my throat, sharp and bitter as battery acid.

"Implode? Jay, I destroy. That's what I do." The truth spills out like poison.

Jay stands, closing the distance between us, his face hardening.

"Don't you dare spin that bullshit," he growls. "That's a fucking cop out and you're not using it as an excuse to throw everything away. You're not him, Nate. Never once have you resembled Scott. So don't start now."

"You saw her, Jay." The words explode from somewhere deep and broken. "She's here because of me. Because I couldn't do the one thing I promised her."

Keep her safe.

"You didn't put her in that car." Jay holds his ground, voice steady like he's talking someone off a ledge.

Maybe he is.

517

"Don't go down this path, Nate. You know where it leads."

It's too late. I'm already there.

The silence stretches between us like a tightrope. My fists clench and unclench, fighting the itch under my skin, the voice in my head getting louder with each passing second.

"I need to get out of here," I say finally, each word carefully controlled. "Give me your keys."

Jay's eyes narrow. "Where are you going?"

"Doesn't matter."

"It does to me."

"Just give me the fucking keys!" My voice splinters, revealing the desperation beneath.

He studies me for a long moment, and I see the exact second he realizes he can't save me from myself. Not tonight. With a heavy sigh that carries the weight of every time he's watched me self-destruct, he pulls out his keys.

"Nate, please," he says softly, holding them just out of reach. "Don't do anything stupid. She needs you."

I snatch the keys, unable to meet his eyes because we both know where I'm heading.

What I'm about to do.

The demons I'm about to welcome back with open arms.

The drive is a fever dream. My knuckles are white against the steering wheel as memories assault me:

The bar.

Scott's smirk.

Like father, like son.

The accident.

Fire blazing.

Glass shattering.

Nora's blood painting the asphalt.

Her eyes fluttering close as I begged her to stay.

The Bait Shop's neon sign cuts through the darkness like a beacon to the damned. The familiar purple glow bathes the street, promising relief in all the wrong places. My feet move on autopilot, carrying me down the path I swore I'd never walk again. He's waiting on that threadbare couch, cigarette smoke curling around him like a snake's welcome. Monty's always waiting. Like a spider that knows the fly will eventually tire of fighting the web.

"Well, well," he drawls, lips curling into that knowing smirk. "The prodigal son returns. What brings you to my humble abode this late at night, Preppy?"

The words stick in my throat like glass. Everything in me screams to turn around, to run, to be better than this.

But I'm so fucking tired of trying to be better.

"I need something."

Monty leans forward, eyes glinting like a predator scenting blood. "Rough night, huh?"

"I need to make it all stop." The confession tastes like surrender.

His grin widens, shark-like in the neon glow. "I thought you were out?"

"I'll give you whatever you want. You want money, fine. You want dirt on Scott Sullivan, whatever. I just need to make it fucking stop."

It's music to Monty's ears, I can see it in his eyes.

"Tell me, kid, how high do you want to fly?"

I hesitate, one last thread of resistance pulling taut. Then Nora's broken body flashes behind my eyes, and the thread snaps.

"As high as I can go," I whisper, each word a nail in my own coffin.

Monty nods, disappearing into the back room. The door creaks like Hell's gates opening, waiting for me to follow. I close my eyes and step through, letting the darkness swallow me whole. Some demons you can't outrun forever.

Sometimes you just have to lie down and let them take you home.

CHAPTER 74
BLUR
NORA

Pain pulses through my skull like a heartbeat, each throb bringing consciousness in angry flashes. I taste ash and copper on my tongue, while fragments of memory crash against the shores of my mind—pieces of a puzzle I'm not ready to solve.

Hospital machines create their own heartbeat—monitors keeping time with my struggling pulse, IV drips counting moments I can't recall. Faces drift through my vision like ghosts in the fluorescent haze, while antiseptic burns my nose, marking this space between breathing and not.

And then—*him*.

Those eyes I've memorized since childhood, now darkened to forest shadows with raw fear. Tears carve rivers through the grime on his face, each track telling a story of terror I wasn't conscious to witness. Gasoline and smoke cling to his skin, a reminder of whatever nightmare brought us here. Even now, his devastation is beautiful—that carefully controlled mask shattered to reveal the boy I've always known lives beneath.

I want to reach for him, to smooth away the worry etched between his brows, to whisper that I'm still here. But darkness pulls me under like a riptide, and I carry only the echo of his face into the void.

Consciousness returns in waves, each one carrying Jake's voice— warm honey cutting through static. His words float just beyond reach, but his presence anchors me: the gentle press of his palm against my forehead, fingers woven through mine. I try to squeeze back, to signal I'm here, but my body feels disconnected from my mind.

Sleep claims me again, soft as a lullaby.

. . .

WHEN I FINALLY SURFACE FOR MORE THAN A COUPLE OF MINUTES, A NURSE moves beside my bed, her motions a practiced dance with the machines. I take inventory like counting war wounds: ribs screaming with each breath, head stuffed with fog, pain hovering at the edges where morphine can't quite reach. Trying to sit up feels like swimming through concrete, and I collapse with a sound I barely recognize as mine.

"Whoa, easy there, Miss Wells." The voice chimes soft as wind through leaves. A woman appears beside me, dark hair in a messy bun, lips painted sunset pink.

"I'm Stella, one of your nurses." Her smile carries warmth, but there's something careful in how she adjusts my blankets—the gentleness reserved for broken things.

"What happened?" My voice scrapes past cracked lips, foreign to my own ears.

She offers water through a straw, patience incarnate as I sip. "You're in the hospital. Do you remember anything?"

I close my eyes, diving into the fog. Memories surface slowly.

The gala.

My phone heavy with his unanswered calls.

Jake's frustrated face outside.

Then—blinding light.

Metal screaming.

Rubber burning.

A voice calling my name like a prayer in Hell.

My eyes snap open, heart thundering against broken ribs. "An accident," I whisper, fear coating my tongue. "Another car came towards me and…"

Stella nods, something dark flickering behind her gentle expression. "It was a pretty serious accident, but you're stable now. Fractured ribs, concussion, bruising—we're monitoring everything closely."

I catch her hesitation, the slight fidget of her hands. "What aren't you telling me?"

"You've been here a while. Do you remember anything after the accident?"

I search the murk. Headlights. Glass everywhere. A man and woman's voices, then nothing but void.

"No," I admit.

"That's okay. Memory takes its time returning. Don't force it—healing comes first."

"How long?" The question feels like tempting fate.

Her eyes flood with sympathy. "Three weeks."

The words hit like another crash. Three weeks of life continued without me, of memories I may never recover. Time becomes physical, crushing my chest with all I've lost.

Stella's hand finds my shoulder. "The doctor will be in shortly. You're lucky your boyfriend found you when he did. He saved your life."

"My... boyfriend?" The words feel wrong, like trying to speak a forgotten language.

"Tall, dark, tortured but handsome."

Nate.

"How is he?"

"He was pretty inconsolable when he brought you in. I haven't seen much of him lately though." Her pen gestures toward Jake, rooted to the chair like an ancient tree.

"But this one? Hasn't left except for coffee. We're limiting visitors for now. Last time you woke, you were so agitated we had to sedate you. Your body's been through a lot of trauma—we need to be careful."

I nod mechanically, but two phrases echo in my mind: *Three weeks. He saved your life.*

Tears burn trails down my cheeks as tremors take hold. "M-my mom... is she here?"

"In the waiting room with your brother. They've been here every day." She pauses carefully.

My heart races against broken ribs. If Nate pulled me from death's door, why isn't he here?

The monitors pick up my panic, their rhythm sharp and urgent.

"Hey, hey, deep breaths," Stella soothes. "I know this is overwhelming. But you're okay, Lenora. You're okay."

"Nora," I whisper. "Please, just Nora."

Her smile softens. "Nora, the doctor will explain everything when you wake. For now, rest."

Before darkness claims me again, my eyes catch the bedside table—a shrine of love: defiant flowers, hopeful cards, and there—my 'fearless' bracelet, the one Nate won at the carnival.

"I got you," his voice echoes between memory and dream. I reach for him, and he smiles—that real smile, with crinkled eyes and dimples that make the world feel right.

"Nate," I whisper as consciousness slips away like sand through fingers.

The darkness is warmer now, filled with echoes of carnival lights and guitar strings and a boy who tasted like summer nights and kept all his promises he said he would.

Except one.

To stay.

CHAPTER 75
DANCING WITH THE DEVIL
NATE

Consciousness melts like ice under a blowtorch. My brain's a warzone of fractured thoughts. The needle burns cold fire in my arm, but I'm gone—floating somewhere between the ceiling and space, between pain and peace.

Through the haze, *"Angel"* by Aerosmith bleeds through crackling speakers. The sound's warped and distant, like a memory trying to resurface from the bottom of a lake.

It's her favorite song.

The one that played the night we chased the sunrise in the Mustang—windows down, her bare feet on the dash, wind tangling in her hair.

Steven Tyler wails about salvation, all grit and desperation, and it slices straight through the fog in my head.

For the first time, I finally get it.

I finally understand why she always said this song was about more than love. She said it was about finding the one person who saw all your cracks and didn't flinch.

Nora told me I didn't need fixing. It was true, though not in the way she meant it.

What I needed was saving, a hand reaching into the darkness to pull me back from the edge I've been walking since I was old enough to understand what destruction looked like.

Fucking tragic, I know. The kind of melodramatic shit I'd mock someone else for saying. But with her blood still under my fingernails and her life hanging by threads I can't see or control, I'm beyond caring how pathetic it sounds.

It was her love, always her love, that tethered me to this world when everything else turned to shit—when the reflection in the mirror started looking too much like the man I swore I'd never become.

Now, with this poison numbing the ache and dragging me under, the sound of that song and her voice, it's the only thing keeping me from slipping all the way.

My muscles twitch and spasm, a desperate dance beneath my skin. Each heartbeat stretches longer than the last, time losing meaning as the high claims me. The needle offers oblivion, but her memory offers something I've never deserved but always craved—forgiveness.

The song loops, and with each rotation, the line between Heaven and Hell blurs further. Angels and demons trade places in the lyrics until I can't tell which one I'm begging to save me. She appears in the darkness behind my eyelids, a ghost made of regret and unspoken words. Those green eyes that always saw straight through my bullshit are swimming with tears now.

Don't look at me like that, Leni.

You knew what I was from the start.

But the thought slips away before I can hold onto it, just another piece of me scattered to the wind.

The euphoria hits like a tidal wave of liquid gold, burning away every scar, every mistake, every moment I've spent trying to outrun my father's shadow. The void opens beneath me, beautiful and endless, promising the peace I've never found in sobriety.

The devil sits beside me in the darkness, patient as an old friend. We don't need words anymore—we both know this dance by heart.

They say silence is where demons come to play, but they never tell you how seductive the darkness can be. How it wraps around you like a lover's arms, promising to keep all your secrets.

The rush floods my veins, offering to erase it all—the way her blood felt on my hands, Jake's last words echoing in my skull, the poison legacy running through my veins. When you've waltzed with the devil this long, you forget there was ever any other partner to choose.

Some angels can't save what doesn't want saving.

The void swallows me whole, and for the first time since that night everything went wrong, I don't fight it.

I just fall.

CHAPTER 76
BECOMING THROUGH BREAKING
NORA

"Dad?"

He appears like a photograph in reverse development, his edges bleeding into reality with the same gentle grace he carried in life.

"Hi Leni."

That smile—the one that could chase away nightmares and mend broken hearts—hasn't aged a day. If anything, he looks younger, as if time decided to unwind itself just for this moment.

"Where are we?"

The front room materializes around us, our Sunday sanctuary where classic literature became life lessons. The walls pulse with living memories—not just frozen snapshots, but moments suspended in time. But there's a wrongness here, like a piano key struck half a step off.

"This isn't where I'm supposed to be, is it?"

Dad's smile turns knowing, tinged with the wisdom that only comes from the other side of forever.

"No, sweetheart, it's not."

A mechanical beeping slices through the dream-haze, as steady and insistent as a heartbeat. I clamp my hands over my ears, desperate to hold onto this moment like water cupped in trembling palms.

"What is that noise?"

"That's life calling you back, Leni." His eyes shimmer with something deeper than mere tears.

"But I don't want to leave you." The truth spills from my lips as my chest constricts. "Everything hurts out there."

"Feeling pain means you're still alive. Still fighting." His presence wraps around me like summer sunshine. "And you've always been a fighter, Leni."

"What if I'm not strong enough this time?"

"Look around you." He gestures to where our memories play like intimate home movies. "Every moment here is proof of your strength. Every smile, every tear, every time you got back up when life knocked you down."

"I don't want to lose you. Not again."

"Oh, sweetheart." His laugh is warm honey and childhood summers. "I never left you. I'm in every book you read, every story you write, every moment you choose to be brave."

"Dad—"

"Nora, sometimes we get second chances not just for ourselves, but for all the people who need us in their story."

The beeping grows more insistent, pulling at the edges of this dreamworld.

"It's time, isn't it?" I ask, my heart swelling in my chest while beating fast at the same time.

He nods, reaching out to almost touch my cheek.

"Don't wait for the storm to pass."

"Learn to dance in the rain." I add with a smile. "You always said that."

"And you always listened." His smile brightens. "Go. Live. Choose happiness even when it's hard. Your story isn't over yet my littlest love— it's just beginning."

The room dissolves, but his final words follow me back to consciousness:

Sometimes we get second chances not just for ourselves, but for all the people who need us in their story.

Reality rushes back like the tide returning to shore, but this time I'm ready for it. Ready to write the next chapter, ready to discover what second chances taste like.

Ready to live.

THE SHUFFLE OF PAPERS DRAWS ME FROM DARKNESS. A MAN STANDS IN MY room, his white coat catching the harsh fluorescent light that's replaced the earlier sunlight. Night has fallen, though time has become fluid— days and nights bleeding together until I've lost count. Every movement sends lightning bolts of pain through my body, and the hospital blanket feels like sandpaper against my raw nerves.

"Hi Nora, I'm Dr. Aldridge, the neurologist overseeing your care." He hovers at my bedside, clipboard in hand, studying me with eyes that have witnessed both miracles and tragedies.

"I'm sure you have questions. If you're comfortable, I can walk you through your injuries and the treatment you've received over these past three weeks. Would that work for you?"

I manage a silent nod.

I've been drifting through consciousness like a boat without anchor, reality and dreams tangling together until they're indistinguishable. Sometimes Dad visits, bringing croissants from our favorite bakery back home. In those moments, I almost believe he's still alive, until logic whispers that no one drives three hours for pastries. Then darkness claims me again, and I wake to an empty room and the hollow echo of loss.

My fingers find the 'fearless' bracelet, twisting it like a lifeline.

"Sure," I whisper.

Dr. Aldridge watches my eyes track across the room, his gaze clinical but kind.

"You've been through quite an ordeal, young lady." His words land like pebbles in still water. "When you arrived, you had sustained severe traumatic injuries—four broken ribs, a broken pelvic bone, and significant brain swelling from the impact."

He monitors the machines as he speaks, watching for signs of distress. I feel frozen, each word settling like frost on already numb skin.

"The swelling required an emergency occipital craniotomy. We had to remove a portion of your skull to allow your brain room to heal without causing further damage. The piece was replaced once the swelling subsided."

Wait, what?

My eyes stretch wide until they burn, panic rising like flood water in my chest. The thought of my skull being opened, my brain exposed—it's too much. I try to maintain composure, but my bottom lip betrays me with its trembling. In this moment, I yearn for Mom's arms around me, her voice promising everything will be okay. Instead, I grip the 'fearless' bracelet tighter, letting its familiar edges ground me in a world that's suddenly too sharp, too real, too full of truths I'm not ready to face.

The machines beside me maintain their steady rhythm, counting heartbeats I almost lost, marking time in a life I nearly left behind. Dr. Aldridge offers a reassuring smile, his hand gentle on my forearm.

"Nora, you responded remarkably well to the surgical intervention. Your cranial integrity is fully restored. We've been monitoring your progress through serial CT scans, and you're showing excellent signs of recovery."

Well, at least there's that, I guess.

"Regarding your other injuries," he continues, consulting his tablet, "while the rib fractures and pelvic injury were severe, we can find some positivity in the fact that you avoided any pleural penetration or pneumothorax." His warm brown eyes scan my face carefully.

"The medically induced coma was initially necessary to manage the cerebral edema. Your body then maintained a natural comatose state, essentially creating its own healing environment."

A tear escapes, trailing down my cheek like a silent confession. Dr. Aldridge notices but continues with gentle precision.

"There's considerable good news too. Your recovery is progressing better than our initial prognosis suggested. In a few days, we'll transition you to a specialized rehabilitation facility for comprehensive physical therapy and recovery support."

I draw in a shaky breath that feels like inhaling broken glass.

"So I'm...I'm going to be fine? I'll be able to walk again and get on with my life like normal?" The words catch in my throat, panic rising despite the fact I've been moving my toes during moments of consciousness.

"Of course, in due time. Recovery is different for everyone, but we'll make a plan, and as long as you trust the process, you're going to be fine," he assures me. "Your spinal column remained remarkably intact. Credit goes to whoever extracted you from the vehicle—they showed exceptional care."

He pauses, studying my reaction.

"Regarding your prognosis, traumatic brain injuries are highly individualized. Memory recovery can be unpredictable in both timing and extent. However, given your current neurological indicators, we're cautiously optimistic about a substantial recovery, though challenges will arise, you just need to take things day by day."

Challenges I can handle. Even if they suck, because I'm a fighter.

"You may experience various cognitive and emotional changes—memory deficits, mood lability, difficulties with concentration and executive function are common post-TBI symptoms. But let's not get ahead of ourselves. Now I know I just spewed a whole heap of medical jargon on you but things are good, you're doing extremely well all things considered. How are you feeling right now?"

Physically, it feels like I've been hit with a sledgehammer and then tossed into a cement mixer. And mentally...

"I'm confused," I murmur. "I'm tired." And terrified, I add silently.

"That's perfectly normal," he says with a gentle laugh. "You've endured significant trauma. If you're willing, I'd like to perform a brief cognitive assessment. Would that be okay?"

The anxiety churns in my stomach like a living thing, but I nod.

"Can you state your full name?"

"Lenora Kennedy Wells."

"And your mother's name?"

"Katherine Wells."

"Good. What's the last date you can recall?"

Panic floods my system.

Flashes of emerald green silk. Music. Dancing. The gala.

"July 27th. The Annual Eden Charity Fundraising Gala."

He makes a note in my chart.

"Do you remember anything else from that night? Your intended destination?"

The space between then and now yawns like an abyss, dark and full of questions I'm not sure I want answered. I hesitate, drawing in a breath that feels like inhaling shattered glass. The memories of my fight with Jake surface first—harsh words echoing in my mind before I stormed away to my car.

"I remember driving on the M80." My voice wavers like a candle flame in wind.

"I was heading to a bar just outside of town to pick up a friend but then a car was swerving on the opposite side of the road and before I could—"

The words die in my throat as the memories crash over me like a tidal wave.

The headlights exploding in my vision like supernovas. The horrific symphony of metal screaming against metal, glass bursting around me like deadly rain. The impact that felt like the world itself had stopped spinning. Then the acrid cocktail of smoke and gasoline burning my nostrils, and a voice—that voice—calling my name, sending ice through my veins despite the heat of the wreckage.

"Your blood results showed no alcohol or drugs in your system."

I nod, fingers twisting in the scratchy hospital blanket until my knuckles turn white.

"Did you see the other driver?"

My eyes slam shut, heart hammering against broken ribs as the final pieces of that night crystallize in my mind.

The voices float back, clear as day:

"No. Fuck, it's you."

"Should we call an ambulance?"

"No. We need to go. Now."

"Do you know her?"

"Get in the car."

"We can't just leave her! She's still breathing."

"No," I whisper, the lie tasting like copper on my tongue. "I didn't see anyone."

"That's okay. With rest, you might start to remember more details. Just don't push too hard," he assures me. "We can revisit this when your mind is clearer."

"No." The word comes out sharper than intended. "That's all I can remember. I was alone and blacked out before I woke up here."

The lie comes easily, born from years of protecting others before myself. Maybe it was just another hallucination, another trick of my trauma-addled brain. But deep down, beneath the fog of medication and fear, I know—I know that voice, and the thought of what Nate would do if he knew terrifies me more than any lie.

Dr. Aldridge studies me, his clipboard hanging loosely at his side.

"This is classified as a hit and run, Nora. A serious one—you could have died on that road if you hadn't been found. The police will follow up as protocol, so note down anything you remember."

He gestures to the notepad on my bedside table, pristine and waiting for truths I'm not ready to tell. "I'm here if you need to talk."

"Thank you," I manage, words feeling hollow and inadequate.

His smile is gentle but strained.

"Ready for visitors? Your mother and brother are waiting, but we can hold off if you need rest."

I think of Mom, haunting waiting room chairs for three weeks, living the same nightmare she endured with Dad. My fingers find the 'fearless' bracelet again, its familiar edges grounding me in this new reality where truth and lies dance on a knife's edge.

"You can send them in."

"Sure, I'll check in a little later."

As he leaves, I wonder how many more lies I'll have to tell before this is over, and whether the truth might destroy more than just me.

The blue curtain whispers aside, and Mom and Ollie rush in. The sight of them makes my heart ache with a different kind of pain—one that no amount of morphine can touch.

"Hey sweetie." Mom freezes, her hand flying to her mouth to cage a sob. "My god. I thought I—"

"Mom, I'm okay. I'm here." The words feel both true and false on my tongue, like trying to speak two languages at once.

531

Ollie doesn't hesitate—he surges forward, wrapping me in an embrace so careful it breaks my heart.

"Fuck, Nor. Please don't scare me like that." His voice cracks and he's fighting back tears that seem to be welling in his eyes.

"I'm sorry," I whisper, ignoring how my broken body screams at his touch. This moment isn't about my pain—it's about his relief, about the four weeks of fear finally releasing its grip on his heart.

When he steps back, Mom approaches like I might disappear if she moves too quickly, as if I'm made of morning mist that could evaporate in direct sunlight.

"My baby girl," she chokes out, pressing her forehead to our clasped hands, her tears warm against my skin like summer rain.

We cry together quietly, letting four weeks of uncertainty wash away in salt and relief.

Ollie fills the silence with updates about the world I missed, while Mom gently probes my memory, each question a pebble dropped in still water, creating ripples I'm not ready to face.

I lie to them both.

The truth sits heavy in my chest like a stone, but I've always been the keeper of secrets, the bearer of burdens. How can I add to their weight when they've already carried so much? But my mind screams the truth I'm denying: *I know that voice, know that cologne that mixed with gasoline, that's now ingrained in my memory like a scar.*

He left me there to die, drove away like I was nothing more than roadkill. My hatred burns hotter than my injuries.

His silence was an attempted murder.

Mine is just another scar.

Mom runs trembling fingers through her dark hair, her eyes mapping the room before settling back on me.

"Jake's been so worried. He's been sitting in that waiting room every day since you arrived."

His name sends my heart into arrhythmia, memories of our last conversation flooding back like high tide. I'd chosen Nate, again, and yet Jake was the one constant. Ollie reads my face like a book he knows by heart, squeezing my hand.

"He really wants to see you. But he'll wait if you're not ready."

Tears bloom hot and fast. I nod, unable to trust my voice. My throat burns as they leave, Mom's worried smile following me like a ghost.

Left for dead.

The thought circles like a vulture.

One choice, one moment, nearly ended everything.

The curtain parts again a short time later and my heart stumbles over itself. I hear him before I see him—a sound somewhere between agony and relief. I close my eyes, breathe deep, then look up. My gaze travels from casual shorts to white cotton before finding his face. Dark circles shadow his eyes like bruises, and his hair has grown wild with worry.

Our eyes lock, and time stops breathing.

Jake stands at my bed's foot, devastation painted across his features as he clutches Bones in his hands. He places the stuffed toy beside me with the gentleness one might use to handle a butterfly's wings, before looking up, swaying slightly as he fights tears.

"I went to get you Cinnabon's," he says, voice soft as a confession.

I should apologize. Should say I'm sorry for leaving. But the lies stop here—I'm not sorry I followed my heart, even if it nearly stopped beating.

My cracked lips manage a smile.

"Thank you."

If he's hoping for more, he doesn't show it. That single phrase draws him closer, emotion tightening his jaw. He takes my hand, squeezing gently.

"I thought you were gone for good."

The machines keep beeping, counting heartbeats in a life I almost lost, while guilt and gratitude wage war in my chest. Each beep feels like an accusation: alive, alive, alive—but at what cost?

"Nora," he whispers, his fingers trailing my palm with a touch so gentle it makes my soul ache. "You scared me."

I drop my gaze, unable to bear the weight of his concern. Tears burn behind my eyes like acid.

"I'm so sorry, for everything I said right before—" His thumb traces the wet path on my cheekbone, collecting my grief like precious stones.

"Hey... look at me. It's okay. You're going to be okay."

It's not okay.

None of this is okay.

Life had spun full circle, dropping me exactly where I was a year ago —living a carefully constructed lie, pretending wholeness while feeling shattered. Convincing everyone else of my okay-ness until maybe I'd believe it too.

Knowing now how he feels, it would be so easy to fall into his warmth and security. But my heart sits elsewhere, beating for someone who hasn't even come to see if it's still beating at all.

"You're safe with me, Nor." His voice carries the weight of promises I know he'd never break. The kind of promises that should make a girl's heart soar, not sink with the gravity of what she can't return.

I nod, because lies of omission are still lies, but they hurt less to tell.

"It's all just a lot," I manage through sniffles, fresh tears glazing my vision.

"I know it is. And you're doing one hell of a job keeping it together. You're going to get through this. I'll be there, carrying you if I have to. Both figuratively and literally."

My lips tremble with an earthquake of emotions—grief, fear, and guilt fighting for dominance.

"Jake..."

"I should have fought harder." His voice hardens with self-recrimination. "I shouldn't have let you walk away that easily. I should—"

"Jake, don't."

"This is all his fault. If he didn't run off like he always does to prove a fucking point..."

Anger flares hot and sudden in my chest, a wildfire in a field of guilt. I pull away, the movement sharp as broken glass.

"Where is he?"

Pain and frustration shadow Jake's eyes.

"I don't know. I haven't spoken to him since that night. Since you were admitted."

Almost four weeks of silence.

Nausea rises like a tide.

Had anyone checked on him? Made sure he was okay?

The questions circle chaotically, but I swallow them down with the bitter taste of abandonment.

I grasp Jake's hand, squeezing what little strength I have into it.

"Thank you."

"For what?"

"For always being by my side, even when I don't deserve it."

"You do deserve it, and I'll always be by your side." He pauses, weight gathering in the silence like storm clouds. "I meant it when I said I love you."

My breath catches because I know what he wants to hear, but saying 'I love you too' would mean something entirely different from what he needs it to mean.

Some silences are kinder than words.

And some truths are better left in the wreckage of a car on the side of the road, buried beneath twisted metal and broken glass, where they can't hurt anyone but me.

CHAPTER 77
BROKEN PROMISES
NATE

THE WORLD DISSOLVES INTO LIQUID, REALITY BLEEDING AT THE EDGES LIKE watercolor on wet paper. My body's dead weight against Monty's half-deflated mattress, but my mind—my mind fragments like shattered glass, each shard reflecting a different version of my personal hell.

When Monty pushed the needle in, his words evaporated before they could reach me through the chemical haze. Whatever poison cocktail he's given me this time burns through my veins like liquid fire. Too much, maybe. Or finally enough to drown out her screams that have been echoing in my skull for weeks. I'm weightless yet chained to earth, suspended in that razor-thin space between sweet oblivion and raw agony.

My limbs feel foreign, like borrowed parts that don't quite fit. My chest is hollow, a void consuming everything except the pain that refuses to die.

The room spins in slow motion—or maybe I'm the one rotating, caught in orbit around memories I can't escape. Colors pulse with my sluggish heartbeat, while bass vibrations rattle through my bones. Monty's laughter cuts through it all, sharp and jarring against the chemical quiet in my head.

Reality comes in disconnected snapshots now. My head falls back and fireworks explode behind my eyelids—her face, her blood, her body broken on blood-slick asphalt. Everything blurs together until I can't tell what's memory and what's nightmare. I've lost track of time on this filthy floor that's become my home. Days blur into weeks when you're trying to dissolve yourself into nothing.

Through the fog, voices pierce the veil—familiar, urgent, disappointed. Jay and Nick materialize like judgmental ghosts through my chemical haze. I try to focus on their faces, but my body's already surrendered to whatever darkness Monty pumped into my veins.

"Jesus Christ, Nate." The words reach me like they're traveling through deep water, warped and distant.

Fragments of sensation assault me: rough hands gripping my arms, feet dragging across carpet that reeks of stale cigarettes, the world tilting sideways. Then cool leather against my back—a car seat becoming my new reality as voices float above me like storm clouds.

"Keep this quiet." Nick's voice cuts sharper than any needle. "People don't need to know."

Jay says something lost to the void while the engine's vibration hums through my bones like a lullaby for the damned.

I'm sorry, Leni.

I'm sorry I couldn't save you.

I'm sorry I became everything I swore I wouldn't.

The darkness swallows the rest.

Time melts like wax, dripping and pooling at the edges of consciousness. I'm somewhere else now—Nick's house, I think. The air here is clean wood and expensive cologne, jarring after weeks of breathing Monty's cocktail of stale smoke and desperation. They lay me down, and the leather couch swallows me whole. I squeeze my eyes shut against the spinning room, but darkness brings no peace. Instead, she materializes like a ghost I can't outrun.

Nora.

She's five, a snapshot of innocence in that purple dress scattered with daisies. Pigtails bounce as she moves, bright eyes sparkling with the kind of hope I'd forgotten existed. Her tiny hands clutch a crayon and paper like they're precious treasures.

"Nate, you have to sign this."

"What is it?"

"It's a forever friends promise."

The memory burns bright enough to scar as she hands me a piece of paper. Her backwards S's swimming across the page, each misspelling perfect in its imperfection.

NORA AND NATE2
FOREVER FRIEND2
PROMI2E

1. We will have five puppie2 and a pony.

2. Live in a big hou2e with big window2 and no 2tair2, ju2t a 2lide.

3. And a big library room with lot2 of book2

Leni !!

Her signature sits at the bottom, waiting for mine like she never doubted I'd sign. Like she knew, even then, that I'd promise her anything.

"The pony's name is going to be called Dolly. And we can rescue all the puppies and give them Avenger names like Superman!"

I don't tell her Superman isn't an Avenger.

Instead, little-me says, *"I like the name Dolly."*

"Do you promise, Natey?" She offers the green crayon like an olive branch and a lifeline all in one. *"Do you promise we'll live happily ever after?"*

"I promise, Leni. I'll be your forever friend and we'll live happily ever after."

I sign my name, sealing a future I'd destroy years later.

Her laugh ripples through my consciousness, but the memory fractures, reality bleeding through like acid rain.

The image warps—she's not five anymore.

She's seventeen and dying, her body limp in my arms. Blood paints her lips like those cherry popsicles she loved so much. Those trust-filled green eyes flutter closed as I scream her name into the indifferent night.

I jolt upward, lungs burning for air that tastes like guilt. But I can't escape her—she's woven into my DNA, etched into every scar, living in every needle mark I've added since that night.

She's everywhere.

In every heartbeat.

In every hit.

In every broken promise.

I'm still falling, chasing oblivion but finding only memories. The drugs that were supposed to numb everything have only made her clearer, sharper, more real.

I'm sorry, Leni.

I'm so fucking sorry.

But I know better than anyone, sorry doesn't undo promises.

Sorry doesn't wash blood from asphalt.

Sorry doesn't bring back five-year-olds with backward S's and dreams of a pony named Dolly.

I keep falling, hoping the bottom will hurt less than remembering.

CONSCIOUSNESS RETURNS IN WAVES, EACH ONE BRINGING FRESH AGONY. My skull feels like it's being split from the inside, brain matter pulsing against bone. The quiet of Nick's house is deafening after weeks of Monty's chaos. Coffee scents the air, a stark contrast to the toxic mix of sweat and smoke I've been drowning in. Sunlight assaults my eyes like shards of broken glass.

"Afternoon." Nick's voice cuts through the fog. He's a shadow in the doorway, tension coiled in his frame like a spring ready to snap.

I try to sit up, but gravity shifts and tilts. Bile rises in my throat as the room carousels around me. I reach for the bucket beside the sofa and empty whatever poison is left in my system. My face feels foreign under my palms, weeks of stubble rough against raw skin. Every cell in my body screams with the memory of what I've done to it.

"I don't—" The words scrape out like they're lined with barbed wire.

Nick inches closer, reality flickering like bad television reception.

"You got high out of your mind. We were trying to give you space over the past few weeks but then hadn't heard from you in days, until Jay called and said he knew where you were. Found you at Monty's, more dead than alive."

Memories surface: Monty's serpentine smile, the sweet rush of oblivion, voices dragging me back to a world I tried to escape.

"Fuck."

"Yeah, pretty much."

I heave myself upright, legs as steady as matchsticks in an earthquake.

I need to move. Need to get out. Need to—

"And where do you think you're heading?" Nick's question cuts like a knife.

My head pounds with each heartbeat. "I can't stay here."

"What's the plan, Nate? After you walk out that door?"

My hand finds the doorknob, cold metal grounding me in reality. But there is no plan. Just more chasing oblivion. Nick moves like he's approaching a wounded animal, slamming his palm against the wooden door.

"I can't let you leave without a plan."

"There's no saving me, Nick." The truth tastes like copper and defeat. "Just let it go."

"I made the mistake of letting someone walk out once. Never again."

Something snaps inside me.

"I'm not him. Not your brother. Not your responsibility."

The second the words slip out, regret floods my system. This guy has been the only steady support in my life, the only one who saw past my walls. He doesn't deserve my venom. Which is exactly why I wish he'd just let me go before I disappoint him again.

"No, you're not him." Nick's voice hardens. "And you're not Scott either." Scott's name hits like electricity, jolting through my drug-addled system. "But you're someone I care about. Let me help you figure this out, Nate."

"Something inside me is broken." The confession feels ripped from somewhere vital, leaving me bleeding.

"Scott shattered you, left you with the pieces. I see how tired you are. But this—" His grip finds my forearm, forcing it into the light. I try to jerk away but he holds firm, twisting my arm so I have to look.

Really look.

Track marks dot the crook of my elbow like a stamp of shame, purple-black bruises blooming around each point of entry. My stomach rolls at the sight. These are my choices mapped out in broken vessels and damaged skin.

Nick's eyes burn into me. "This isn't the answer. People need you here. People love you, Nate."

People love you.

The words echo like a gunshot in an empty room.

"I love you. And I'm not letting you destroy yourself."

I can't remember the last time someone told me they loved me and meant it. My knees hit hardwood, and tears I've been holding back for years finally break free. Nick's arms find me, wrapping around me like a shelter as I shake apart. For the first time since I watched Nora bleed out on that highway, I let someone else carry the weight of my broken pieces.

"You're not doing this alone anymore, Nate," he says softly. "We'll figure this out."

His words chip away at the wall I've spent years building—the same wall Nick has been patiently trying to scale since that first day in the bookstore, when he offered me a job instead of writing me off like everyone else.

"You deserved better," Nick continues, his voice heavy with the weight of all the times he's watched me struggle, all the times he's tried to be the father figure Scott never was.

"No kid should have to grow up the way you did. And just because someone is family doesn't mean you have to tolerate their lies and manipulation. You deserve more than that. You deserve a shot at a fresh start and a life that's entirely your own."

I can't meet his eyes, but his words hit home like they always do. Nick has this way of cutting through the bullshit, of seeing the scared kid beneath all the anger and self-destruction.

"You can't keep thinking about how you've hurt people or how you've let them down. It's about you now, Nate. You need to find a way to be happy. For you."

His hand clasps my shoulder, and something in his voice changes, becomes raw with memory.

"When my brother died, I drowned myself in booze and pills. Thought it would numb the pain. It didn't. It just made everything worse because the pain never went away. It just waited until I was sober enough to start paying attention to it again. That's why I left in the first place. I needed to get away to figure out who I was and what I wanted." He squeezes my shoulder. "I think that's what you need. A fresh start. Somewhere far from here. Somewhere you can breathe and figure out what you want and who you want to be without anyone else telling you so."

His words settle over me, heavy with the understanding of someone who's walked this path before.

How many times has he tried to guide me away from making his same mistakes?

How many times have I ignored him, thinking my pain was somehow different, somehow special?

"Think about it," Nick says. "Say the word and I'll take care of every-thing and get you out." The corner of his mouth lifts in that familiar half-smile that's seen me through countless rough patches. "But I need you to want this for yourself. You need to want to help yourself. Give yourself a chance at a different life. Clear your head. Write music. Pick flowers and chase butterflies for all I care. But you can't keep living like this. It's going to kill you."

I nod, barely registering the movement. My mind is fucked right now, but Nick's words are holding me steady and keeping me from drifting too far.

"I'm not going to lie and tell you it's going to be easy. I won't pretend like it won't suck every living fiber out of you either. But I will tell you that it's still possible to find the light. Loss may be permanent but suffering isn't."

I look at him for the first time—really look at him—and see the lines of worry etched around his eyes.

How much of that is because of me?

His words hang in the air, heavy with truth. I let out a slow, uneven breath, my chest tightening, my head pounding, my body screaming for another hit, but my heart—it's caught.

"Is Nora..." The words scrape my throat raw. I can barely force them past the fear. "Is she..."

"She's okay." Nick's voice is steady, an anchor in the storm. "She has a long road ahead of her too, but she's doing okay."

Relief floods through me, quickly followed by a tidal wave of guilt that threatens to drown me. I see her again—lying with a faint beating heart in my arms. The memory twists the knife deeper.

"She deserves better than me," I mutter, shame burning my throat like bile.

Nick's grip on my shoulder tightens, his fingers digging into muscle, reminding me of all the times he's refused to let me fall. "Maybe she does. But she's not asking for better. She's asking for you. And if you can't see why, maybe it's time to stop looking at her and start looking at yourself."

I laugh bitterly, the sound like broken glass in my chest. "Everything I touch, I ruin. My family. My friends. Her." The words taste like truth, familiar and bitter on my tongue. "All I do is take and destroy."

Like father, like son—the mantra I've been running from since I was old enough to understand what Scott's fists could do.

Nick shifts to sit in front of me, slinging his arms around his knees, leveling his eyes with mine. His gaze isn't soft—it's sharp with the same tough love that's kept me alive this long. I want to look away, but I can't.

"I've been exactly where you are. Telling myself the same bullshit to justify not trying. But you know what? It's cowardly."

I flinch at the word. It cuts deeper than I expect it to.

"Yeah, cowardly. You think you're protecting her by shutting down and keeping her at bay? By pretending you don't care? All you're doing is running. And the longer you run, the harder it's gonna be to find your way back. To her. To yourself."

I hate how much his words sting because they're true. Each one strikes like a match against my raw nerves, illuminating truths I've been trying to keep in darkness.

I hate that he's looking at me like I'm worth saving when I've done nothing to deserve it.

I hate that when he says, *"find your way back,"* I think of her face—her smile and her laugh that sounds like every good memory I've ever had—it feels like hope.

And I hate hope.

Hope is the cruelest trick of all—a light that only makes the darkness deeper when it fades.

Hope is what kept Mom coming back to Dad, thinking this time would be different.

Hope is what left Jake with scars he thinks I don't see.

Hope is what put Nora in that hospital bed while I sit here, destroying my own life in the process.

"Isn't this running though? Just to another country?" My voice sounds hollow, even to my own ears.

"No." Nick's response carries the weight of experience. "It's distancing, so you can start facing yourself away from distractions. Away from old habits and familiar demons."

"What if I can't?" My voice cracks, splintering like glass under pressure, vulnerability seeping through the fissures before I can patch them. "What if I try and it's not enough?"

Nick stands, his hand dropping from my shoulder, but his presence looms larger, filling the room with an authority earned through years of his own battles.

"That's the risk, Nate. That's life. But here's the thing: losing something because you tried and failed? That's a pain you can live with. It's clean, honest—something you can learn from. Losing something because you were too scared to even try? That's the kind of regret that'll eat you alive. It'll hollow you out until there's nothing left but 'what ifs' and empty promises."

I bury my face in my hands, fingers pressing against my temples like I'm trying to hold my skull together. My chest feels like it's caving in, every breath a struggle against the hurricane of fear and want and need all tangled together inside me.

"And if I'm too far gone?" I whisper, the words barely a breath, carrying the weight of every needle mark, every broken promise, every midnight confession I've made to empty rooms.

"I don't believe you are," Nick says with a firmness that brooks no argument, the same tone he used when he came to pick me up the first time I was bleeding out. "You're here. You're still breathing. And as long as you're breathing, there's a chance. A chance to be better and be the man she sees in you. The man I've always seen in you, even when you couldn't see it yourself."

I don't know if I believe him.

Nick pulls a card from his back pocket and places it on the table beside me. The sound of cardstock against wood cuts sharp through the quiet room.

"When you're ready, call this number. Javier is a good friend of mine. Tell him I sent you and he'll take care of everything from his end. Then just say when and I'll book your flight and drive you to the airport myself."

I pick up the card, its edges fraying under my trembling fingers like my resolve. It's simple—a name, a number, and nothing else.

No promises, no guarantees. Just a choice.

Maybe the first real choice I've made in years.

"You can't outrun the pain or the darkness, Nate." Nick's voice carries the weight of someone who's tried. "But you can fight it until it knows its place in your life. And you don't have to do it alone."

His voice softens, gentles like he's talking to that scared kid he first met, and for the first time, I let his words settle into the cracks I've been too afraid to show. Maybe I'm not beyond saving. Maybe there's still something worth fighting for in the wreckage I've made of my life.

I look up at him, the card clutched in my hand like a lifeline, like a ticket to somewhere better than here.

"I don't know if I can do this."

Nick smiles faintly, a glimmer of understanding in his eyes that speaks of his own battles won and lost. "You don't have to know, Nate. You just have to try. Sometimes trying is the bravest thing we can do."

CHAPTER 78
CHOICES
NORA

EVERYTHING IS TOO LOUD AND TOO QUIET ALL AT ONCE, LIKE SOMEONE'S turned up the volume on reality while muting everything that matters. Mom and Lydia hover as they help me from the car, their touches gentle but somehow amplifying the hollow space inside me. I've come back to a life that feels like watching my favorite movie with all the scenes scrambled—familiar but fundamentally wrong.

Jake and Ollie wait on the porch, and the sight twists something raw beneath my ribs. Behind them, Mia, Camilla, and Marcus clutch an oversized teddy bear and balloons declaring 'Welcome Home' in mockingly cheerful letters.

It's overwhelming, but I force my lips into what I hope passes for a smile and let them welcome me back to a home that doesn't feel like mine anymore.

Camilla reaches me first, arms outstretched. When she hugs me, pain radiates through my side like lightning, drawing a sharp flinch. Her face drains of color as she pulls back.

"Oh, my God, I'm so sorry! Are you okay?"

"It's fine," I lie, because that's what you do when people are trying so hard to make things normal. You pretend. You smile. You swallow the pain until it settles somewhere deep inside where no one can see it.

She studies my face for a moment, tears glistening in her usually bright eyes, before pulling me into another hug, this one gentle as a whisper.

"I'm so glad you're okay. Please, for the love of God, don't you ever scare me like that again. I just got you in this life." Her voice cracks on the last words, and for the first time since I've known her, I hear Camilla cry.

Marcus steps forward, dramatically shaking his head. "Yeah, seriously. Between worrying about you and worrying about her worrying about you, I'm about to have a stress-induced cardiac arrest."

A small laugh escapes despite everything.

"For real though," he says, wrapping me in a careful hug. "We missed you."

"Stop hogging her, Marcus," Mia interrupts, stepping up for her turn. "I'm so happy you're home."

"Me too." I smile, but it feels like wearing someone else's clothes—not quite right, not quite mine.

The laughter fades quickly, and is replaced by that gnawing emptiness that follows me like a second shadow as I glance around at their relieved faces. But there's one face missing—the one that haunts my dreams and fills the spaces between my heartbeats. The one I need more than air.

"Where's Nick?" I ask, trying to mask the tremor in my voice.

Mom exchanges a quick look with Lydia that makes my stomach turn. "He had a family emergency to take care of."

"Oh. Is Alfie okay?" Dread curls through my veins like poison.

Mom's reply comes too quick, too rehearsed. "Alfie's fine, honey."

My heart pounds against my ribs as realization hits. Nick doesn't have any other family. There's only one person he'd drop everything for.

Nate.

The thought of his name alone makes my chest constrict until breathing becomes a conscious effort. I've tried calling him. Texting him. Begging the universe to make my phone light up with his name. Nothing but silence.

I force myself to stay calm, to keep my voice steady as I turn to Camilla. "Have you or Jay heard from Nate?"

She hesitates, choosing her words with surgical precision. "Jay mentioned he was going away for a while."

The words hit like shattered glass.

"He's going away?" My voice splinters. "What do you mean? Where's he going?"

Panic flashes across Camilla's face as she stumbles over her words. "I —I don't know. Jay's been really hush-hush about it. He just said Nate needed to get out of town for a while."

The ground shifts beneath me, my legs threatening to give out. The truth crashes over me like a wave of ice water. Nate is gone. He left without a word. Without answering my calls. Without giving me a reason why.

I feel their eyes on me—Jake, Camilla, Marcus, all of them—watching, waiting for me to say something, but I can't find words in the wreckage of my heart. My chest feels hollow, like someone has carved out everything inside me and left nothing but echoes.

He left. He left *me*.

And somehow, that hurts worse than any of my injuries.

The dim light in my room does little to soften the storm of emotions swirling around me. I sit cross-legged on my bed, fingers absently stroking Bones' worn fur. Each breath feels like learning how to exist in a world that's shifted three degrees sideways. A soft knock breaks through my thoughts. Lydia appears in the doorway, her presence gentle but steady.

"Hey, sweetie," she says softly. "Are you doing okay?"

We both know I'm not, but I manage a small nod. She steps inside, holding a white envelope.

"This came for you last week. I was waiting for the right time."

Curiosity flickers through the fog in my mind. The bold, official-looking logo catches my eye as I take it from her. My heart stumbles over its own rhythm as I pull out the crisp letter.

The words blur as I read and re-read them.

Congratulations! You have been accepted.

It's an acceptance into the writing scholarship program I hadn't applied for.

"I don't understand," I whisper, my voice trembling like autumn leaves. "How did they—"

"He submitted it for you before he left. Made the deadline by a day before applications closed." Lydia's voice is gentle but weighted with understanding.

"Nate did this?"

Lydia nods, her smile bittersweet.

It shouldn't surprise me—even drowning in his own darkness, he's always been my biggest champion, seeing potential in me when I couldn't see it myself. That thought breaks something loose inside my chest, sending fresh pain cascading through me.

"He asked me to tell you he's sorry he wasn't here to tell you himself. And..." She pauses, weighing her next words carefully. "Nora, he wasn't in a good place while you were in the hospital. I've seen my son in bad places over the years, but this was different. It was terrifying, I honestly thought we were going to—" The words catch in her throat and I'm glad she doesn't finish the sentence.

Tears start falling before I can stop them. Lydia moves closer, wrapping me in her arms like only a mother can, as if she could hold all my broken pieces together.

"Oh, sweetheart," she murmurs. "No one could ever come close to the love my son has for you. You've always been his way back home. I think he needs to do this for himself, so he can find his way back to you."

Her words both soothe and shatter me, because home isn't supposed to feel this empty. I cling to her for a moment longer before she pulls away, squeezing my shoulder.

"Get some rest. If you need anything, just yell out," she says, giving my hand one final squeeze before leaving.

As soon as the door closes, I lay back, staring up at the ceiling like I'm looking up from the bottom of an ocean. One tear escapes, and I let it fall, carrying with it all the words I wish I could say to him.

When I turn my head, something crinkles beneath my pillow. My heart stops when I see the yellow envelope with my name written in Nate's messy scrawl. My fingers tremble as I open it, revealing a folded piece of paper. The handwriting is unmistakably his—rushed, like the words were burning to get out.

LEN,

I'VE BEEN STARING AT THIS BLANK PAGE FOR HOURS, TRYING TO FIND THE RIGHT WORDS.
I'M NOT GOOD AT THIS LIKE YOU ARE.
MY THOUGHTS COME OUT MESSY AND TANGLED, BUT I'M GOING TO TRY ANYWAY. I KNOW YOU'RE PROBABLY READING THIS FEELING CONFUSED, HURT—MAYBE ALL OF IT AT ONCE.
I DON'T BLAME YOU.

BUT STAY WITH ME, OKAY?

THERE WAS ONE SUMMER WAY BACK, I WAS FIFTEEN AND YOU WERE ELEVEN. DO YOU REMEMBER WHEN I WAS TRYING TO LEARN "IRIS" AND YOU WERE SITTING CROSS-LEGGED ON MY BED, PRETENDING TO READ.
I KEPT MESSING UP THE CHORDS BECAUSE I WAS NERVOUS, BUT YOU JUST SAT THERE, PATIENTLY, SMILING. AFTER THAT NIGHT, I SPENT

WEEKS PRACTICING WHEN YOU WEREN'T AROUND, FUMBLING THROUGH THOSE CHORDS UNTIL MY FINGERS BLED.

I WANTED TO LEARN IT BECAUSE IT WAS YOUR FAVORITE. BUT ALSO BECAUSE AT FIFTEEN, THAT SONG SAID EVERYTHING I COULDN'T.

I DIDN'T KNOW HOW TO TELL YOU WHAT YOU MEANT TO ME. HOW YOU SAW ALL THE PARTS OF ME I TRIED TO HIDE. HOW YOU MADE ME WANT TO BE SEEN.

BUT THE SONG COULD.

MUSIC IS SUPPOSED TO MAKE SENSE. IT'S MATH AND PATTERNS, STRUCTURE AND RULES. BUT THEN THERE ARE THESE MOMENTS— THESE PERFECT, UNEXPLAINABLE MOMENTS—WHEN TWO NOTES SHOULDN'T WORK TOGETHER, BUT THEY DO. THEY CREATE SOME- THING THAT BREAKS ALL THE RULES BUT SOUNDS EXACTLY RIGHT. THAT'S WHAT WE ARE. WE'RE THAT IMPOSSIBLE HARMONY.

LOOK UNDER YOUR BED.

THERE'S A BOX AND INSIDE IS A CD I MADE YOU—TRACK 18 SAYS EVERYTHING I WISH I COULD TELL YOU FACE TO FACE.

I GUESS SOME THINGS ARE EASIER TO SAY THROUGH MUSIC. AT LEAST THAT'S HOW IT'S ALWAYS BEEN FOR US.

NORA, YOU'VE ALWAYS BEEN THE SONG I CAN'T GET OUT OF MY HEAD. BECAUSE YOU'VE BEEN MY FAVORITE EVERYTHING FOR AS LONG AS I CAN REMEMBER. WHEN EVERYTHING IN MY HEAD GETS TOO LOUD, WHEN ALL I HEAR IS NOISE, YOU'RE THE MELODY THAT CUTS THROUGH IT ALL. YOU HEAR THE MUSIC IN ME EVEN WHEN I'M OUT OF TUNE. YOU MAKE ME WANT TO BE BETTER. TO BE THE PERSON YOU SOMEHOW BELIEVE I AM.

YOU'RE MY MUSE, LENI.

NOT JUST FOR THE SONGS I'LL ONE DAY WRITE—THOUGH EVERY SINGLE ONE WILL PROBABLY BE ABOUT YOU IN SOME WAY—BUT FOR WHO I WANT TO BE. YOU INSPIRE THE BEST PARTS OF ME, THE PARTS I DIDN'T EVEN KNOW EXISTED.

GO TO LONDON.

CHASE THOSE DREAMS YOU'VE HAD SINCE YOU WERE A KID. WRITE THOSE STORIES THAT LIVE IN YOUR HEAD. SHOW THE WORLD WHAT I'VE ALWAYS SEEN IN YOU. DO IT ALL SO ONE DAY I CAN SAY 'TOLD YOU SO.'

I'LL FIND MY WAY BACK TO YOU WHEN I'M SOMEONE WHO DESERVES THE WAY YOU LOOK AT ME.

I KNOW I HAVE NO RIGHT TO ASK ANYTHING OF YOU. BUT MAYBE THINK OF THIS LIKE ONE OF THOSE LONG INSTRUMENTAL BREAKS IN YOUR FAVORITE SONGS—THE ONES THAT FEEL LIKE THEY'RE TAKING YOU SOMEWHERE NEW, BUT ALWAYS LEAD YOU BACK TO THE MELODY YOU KNOW BY HEART.

PLEASE DON'T HATE ME. (THOUGH I WOULDN'T BLAME YOU IF YOU DID.)

N.

P.S. THAT FIRST STORY YOU EVER WROTE, ABOUT DAISY AND ARCHER? IT'S STILL MY FAVORITE. ALWAYS WILL BE.

TEARS STREAM DOWN MY CHEEKS, HOT AND RELENTLESS, CARVING PATHS OF grief across my skin.

How could he ask that of me?

How could he think, after everything, that hate could ever touch what I feel for him?

Even now, with his absence burning a hole in my chest, hate is the furthest thing from what I feel.

If anything, I love him more—love him with the kind of desperation that makes stars collide and universes bend.

This isn't just a goodbye letter—it's Nate laying his soul bare on paper, showing me all the pieces of his heart that belong to me, even as he walks away.

My hands tremble as I reach under the bed, finding a blue box. Fresh tears blur my vision when I open it and find my first discman covered in stickers—the one I thought I'd lost years ago. Next to it lies a CD labeled *"Nora's Mixtape #17 V2"*.

But what breaks me completely is what remains in the box: *"Daisy and Archer's Adventures."*

This whole time, he kept it.

A teardrop falls onto the worn cover.

On the first page, there's a post-it note in his messy scrawl:

STILL MY FAVORITE.

Three words that somehow hold the weight of our entire history.

I set aside the box and take the CD and discman onto my bed, hands shaking as I put on the headphones. My heart races as I hit play.

"Take Me Away" by Lifehouse fills my ears, followed by *"Wish You Were Here"* by Pink Floyd, then *"Never Let You Go"* by Evermore, *"Chasing Cars"* by Snow Patrol and *"Iris"* by The Goo Goo Dolls.

As each song finishes and I inch toward track number eighteen, my pulse quickens with anticipation and fear. Every part of me aches to hear the song, to let his voice—or the memory of it—wash over me one more time.

My hand falls limp in my lap as the familiar warmth of him seeps into me. It's always there, that warmth. It's the part of him I can never quite let go of, the part that makes me want to hold on just a little longer.

I take a deep breath when the melody starts softly, piano keys falling like gentle rain, each note carrying the hollowness of everything left unsaid. Then his voice comes in, raw and honest and achingly beautiful.

> "The echoes of who we are,
> Were right there from the start.
> Hidden in ashes of the past
> In the darkest parts, there you are..."

His voice wraps around me like a familiar embrace, and I almost feel his presence beside me, singing these words that feel like they've been pulled straight from his soul. The piano builds as he continues.

> "So hear me when I say,
> I know your soul I'll be your home.
> Until you can breathe on your own..."

Each word feels like it's being carved directly into my heart. This isn't just a song—it's every moment we've shared, every silent understanding, every time he looked at me like I was his entire world.

And yet, it's not enough to drown out the ache, the hollow, gnawing pain of his absence. The memory of him is both a comfort and a curse—a reminder of what we had and what we've lost. He might love me, maybe even more than I'll ever fully understand. The evidence is right here, in every carefully chosen song, in every word he's written, in this melody that feels like it's been orchestrated straight from his heart.

The conflict claws at me, my heart pulling me toward him even as my mind warns me to let go. I close my eyes, exhaling shakily as the question I've been avoiding rises to the surface, bitter and unavoidable.

How long am I supposed to keep waiting for someone who might never come back?

Even if he's written our love into the stars themselves, even if he's left pieces of his heart scattered around me like breadcrumbs leading home.

Morning sun filters through the trees as Jake and I glide down the familiar stretch of road, the rhythmic hum of bike tires on asphalt filling the space between us. It feels like a lifetime since I felt this alive, since I let my legs push against the pedals with purpose.

Jake rides beside me, his protective gaze catching every bump in the road before I do. I insisted on this ride. I needed something to remind me of who I was before life got so complicated. And Jake, as always, didn't argue. He never does when it's something I need.

Corrigan's Bakery appears ahead, the smell of cinnamon and sugar wrapping around us like a warm hug from the past. The sign above the door still reads, "*Best Cinnabons in Town*" in bold cursive letters, though they're probably the only cinnabons within fifty miles.

Inside, the air is thick with the scent of fresh pastries, the cozy café humming with low chatter and clinking mugs. Jake orders without asking—two cinnabons and two vanilla lattes, our usual. The cashier's smile holds recognition, like she's missed seeing us together in this familiar dance.

We settle at our corner table by the window. Jake takes an exaggerated bite of his cinnabon, making his typical face of pure bliss, trying to coax a smile from me like he always has. It works, and for a second, everything feels like it used to—before Nate, before the accident, before everything got so beautifully and terribly complicated.

But then his expression shifts. Something heavy settles in his eye, looking at me like he's been carrying these words for too long.

"Stay in Boston," he pleads, his voice soft but insistent. His fingers twitch before reaching across the table for mine. The touch is familiar yet foreign, comfort tangled with guilt. "We can figure this out together if you're willing to give this," he gestures between us, "a real shot. I'll start working for Dad, and you can keep writing, keep going to school."

His eyes search mine, filled with an earnestness that makes my chest ache.

"Nora, we could be something fucking amazing." The weight of his next words settles over us like snow. "You're still my person, even if I'm not yours. I just want a chance to love you the way you deserve to be loved."

The light catches his face just right, highlighting all the features that make him Jake—the kindness in his eyes, the hopeful curve of his smile, the steadfast devotion that's never wavered.

For a moment, I let myself imagine it: a life with Jake, safe and sure and uncomplicated. But then Nate's face flashes in my mind, and my heart twists with the kind of longing that feels like the last note of a song hanging in the air, desperate to keep playing.

I stare at him, trying to make myself feel what he wants me to. I try to picture the future he's describing—the ease, the comfort, the predictability. A life mapped out in careful pencil strokes, each detail considered, each step planned. It's safe, steady, and so perfectly Jake. But the harder I try to make it fit, the more suffocating it feels, like trying to force myself into a shape that was never meant for me.

His words hang in the air between us, and suddenly, the truth hits me like a cold wave. He doesn't see the girl who's been clawing her way back from the edge, who's still figuring out how to exist in a world that nearly swallowed her whole. He sees what he wants to fix, not what makes me whole.

"Jake..." My voice is quiet but firm. I shake my head slowly, then with more conviction. "I can't."

His face falls, and guilt surges through me, sharp and unrelenting.

"Why?" he asks, his voice tight. "Why won't you give me a shot, Nora? We could have everything. I have it all figured out."

"I know you mean that," I say, my throat tightening. "And I love you for wanting this. But I can't give you what you're asking for. I'm not ready to commit to something—or someone—when I don't even know who I am right now."

It's the honest truth.

His jaw tightens, hurt flickering across his face. He leans forward, his words sharp and low. "If it was him sitting here, asking you for all of this, you wouldn't hesitate."

The air leaves my lungs. My silence hangs heavy between us, and Jake exhales sharply, defeat written in every line of his body.

"I hope he's worth it," he says finally, voice soft but bitter.

Something snaps inside me.

"That's the difference between you and Nate," I say, my voice shaking. "Nate would never ask me to stay. What you see is something to hold onto or fit into your life. I don't want to fit into anyone's life."

Jake flinches and without another word, I push back my chair and walk out, leaving him behind with his carefully constructed plans that never had room for who I really am.

The cool breeze hits my face, but it does little to cool the fire burning inside me. Because this isn't about choosing between brothers. This is about choosing myself, about acknowledging that love shouldn't feel like fitting yourself into someone else's puzzle.

This is about me.

My life, my choices, my future.

That's what I keep telling myself, and it's true—mostly. But deep down, I know that's not the whole story. Because even when Nate isn't here, even when he's broken my heart in ways I didn't think were possible, he's still the one who sees clearly enough to know that sometimes love means stepping aside so the other person can soar.

Staring at my packed bags, I feel the weight of every memory this room holds. The bare walls and empty drawers whisper of a life I'm leaving behind, but it doesn't ache the way I thought it would. Bones sits on my pillow, my childhood confidant, his fur worn velvet-soft from years of catching my tears and muffling my secrets. I trace my fingers over his floppy ears one last time, considering whether to take him with me. But with a soft smile—not sad, but knowing—I place him back where he belongs. Sometimes the bravest part of moving forward is choosing what to leave behind.

The discman catches my eye on my nightstand, Nate's letter safely tucked inside my journal. His words echo in my mind: *You've always been the song I can't get out of my head.*

For so long, I've been harmonizing with someone else's song, matching my rhythm to theirs. I think that's what Nate realized when he wrote his letter. In order for two people to find their way back to one another, to be good for one another, they first have to be good for themselves.

Love—real love—isn't about possession.

It's about freedom.

It's about understanding that sometimes the bravest thing you can do is choose yourself. If you can't show up for someone in the way they need—or if they can't love you the way you need to be loved—then the most honest thing you can do is let go. It's not easy, but nothing worth having ever is.

There's a forever kind of magic in some moments, just like there's a forever kind of feeling for the dark-haired, amber-eyed boy who will always be a part of my story, even if he's not my ending. I don't think Nate was ever meant to be my ending, but rather the catalyst that helped me find my own beginning. Some people come into your life not to stay, but to show you who you're meant to become. Like seasons changing, life moves in both directions—forward and backward—and the choices we make ripple through both.

This past year has taught me that nothing is permanent.

Not moments, not feelings, not people.

Everything is fleeting.

But maybe that's the point.

"Sometimes we get second chances not just for ourselves, but for all the people who need us in their story."

Standing in this empty room that holds so many memories, I finally understand what Dad meant.

London isn't just a destination—it's a declaration.

A second chance, a statement that says: I choose me.

I choose my dreams, my growth, my happiness. I choose to no longer be defined by the pain I've endured and suffering I've chosen. Grief is really just love with nowhere to go. All of that unspent love gathers in the corners of your eyes, the lump in your throat, and the hollow part of your chest. It builds until you think you might shatter from the weight of it. But you don't.

You learn to carry it, to let it shape you into someone stronger, someone deeper, someone more real. Because maybe that's the point of second chances—they're not about erasing what was, but about becoming who you need to be for all the chapters yet to come.

As I zip up my last bag, I feel it—that flutter of excitement mixed with fear, that electric current of possibility running through my veins. This is what it feels like to choose yourself. To step into the unknown not because someone else pushed you, but because you're finally ready to fly.

Will things ever be the same? No.

But they're not meant to be.

Maybe the cracks are meant to serve as reminders of what you survived, what you overcame to become this new version of yourself. The healing lies in the cracks, in the glue that fills them, making them beautiful in their brokenness.

I glance around one last time before closing the bedroom door shut.

Camilla waits downstairs, buzzing with excitement about our London adventure. We're starting something new, something big, and for the first time in a long time, I feel ready.

Not just ready—eager.

Hungry for life in a way I'd forgotten I could be.

I slip the discman and CD into my bag, their weight a quiet reminder of the boy who will always hold a piece of my heart. But I'm not staying here, frozen in the past, waiting for someone to come back to start living my life.

I'm moving forward—toward the future I've chosen for myself, toward the person I'm becoming.

Life goes on.

And so will I.

Not just surviving, but thriving.

Not just existing, but living.

Not just accepting what life gives me, but choosing what I want from it.

For myself, and for all the people who need me in their story.

This isn't an ending.

It's my beginning.

TO BE CONTINUED...

EPILOGUE
NICK

2 months later

THE WORLD FEELS QUIETER NOW, THOUGH THE ECHOES OF THE LAST FEW months still hum in the back of my mind. It's been two months since the accident—since the night I had to pull Nate out of that pit at Monty's.

Two months since everything came to a head, and in some ways, it feels like years have passed between then and now.

I'm standing on the porch of Kat's place, the same one that's started to feel like home in a way few places ever have. She's inside, likely rearranging the kitchen for the third time this week, humming to herself like nothing in the world could shake her. And for once, maybe nothing can. We're in a good place, her and me. A steady rhythm that feels like it could go the distance.

Kat has decided to stick around Eden for a while longer, and I'm not sure I've ever been so grateful for someone staying put. She mentioned opening up a private practice here for the disadvantaged who don't have health care. That woman's heart could light up the darkest corners of this town.

But even with her here and the storm finally feeling like it's passed, my thoughts still drift. Back to the night it all changed. The smell of sweat and stale desperation in that drug den haunts me—metallic and sour, like hope left to spoil. Nate slumped on a half inflated mattress, barely recognizable as the brilliant kid whose music could make time stand still. His fingers, usually dancing across guitar strings or piano keys, lay limp and blue-tinged against the filthy floor. Remembering what it was like dragging him out of that hellhole, my chest constricts with a familiar ache.

Not again.

The words pulse through me like a second heartbeat.

Not him.

Not when I know what he could become if he just gave himself the chance.

Nate and I have been through a lot these past few months. It started slow—conversations that lingered past closing time at Sonder, his eyes always restless, always watching the door like he was waiting for someone who never arrives. Working side by side, I watched his mind constantly creating, constantly worrying about everyone but himself.

Then it turned into something deeper—not as a replacement father figure even though his was never much of a father in the first place. But as someone who refuses to walk away when things get hard.

I saw a kid trying so hard to hold everything together, protecting everyone else while drowning in his own pain. He reminds me of my brother, not in the superficial ways people might assume. It's not about replacing what I've lost. It's about recognizing that same raw talent, that same fire that could either illuminate the world or reduce it to ashes.

I did what I had to do.

I got him out of Eden.

Away from the noise and the shadows that kept trying to pull him under. Because sometimes the only way to find yourself is to get lost somewhere new and face the demons without the familiar distractions, or in his case, the influences slowly poisoning him from the inside out.

I pulled every string I could, set him up with a job at one of my wineries in Europe. Something quiet and steady in a small Spanish town where sunlight spills over ancient stone walls and the air smells of salt and possibility.

A place where he could breathe. I told him to take time, figure himself out, and start living for himself instead of surviving for everyone else. I even nudged him toward the music. Hell, I all but pushed him. Because I've heard what that kid can do with a guitar and a pen. I saw the way people stopped mid-conversation when he played on opening night, like he was tapping into something universal and true. That kind of talent doesn't come along often, and I refuse to let it get buried under this town and his family's expectations.

And for once, he didn't argue. He just nodded, eyes glassy but determined, and I knew then that maybe, just maybe, he'd finally seen himself through someone else's eyes. Seen what I'd been trying to tell him all along.

Now he's over there, somewhere in the rolling hills of the town that changed my life many years ago, working the vineyards during the day and playing gigs at night in little bars where nobody knows his name or his story.

I get the occasional update—a text here, a grainy photo or sound bite of a melody he's playing around with—and each one feels like proof that sometimes, faith in someone pays off. He's still got a long road ahead, but he's walking it, one step at a time, finding his way back to himself.

As for Nora, she's thriving in London. She boarded the plane with a spark in her eye I haven't seen since before the accident. She's chasing her dreams, the ones Nate secretly believed in enough to submit that scholarship application behind her back. The irony isn't lost on me— Nate, drowning in his own mess, still managed to throw her a lifeline. It's just who he is, even when he's breaking apart. Always thinking of others first.

Always seeing the best in everyone but himself.

I look out over the quiet Eden street, the late afternoon sun casting long shadows across the lawn. This town has been a lot of things to a lot of people.

A sanctuary, a prison, a turning point.

For me, it's been all three. But as I stand here, the warm breeze carrying the scent of impending summer, I know it's also been something else.

It's been home.

For better or worse, Eden has a way of leaving its mark on you. Of getting under your skin and staying there. And while part of me wonders if Nate will ever find his way back here, another part knows that, no matter where he goes, this place—these people—will always be with him. Because that's the thing about family. It's not just blood or proximity. It's the people you fight for, the ones you refuse to give up on, even when they've given up on themselves. It's about seeing the best in someone even when they're at their worst.

I won't ever give up on Nate.

I couldn't then, and I won't now. Not when I see so much of myself in his struggles, not when I know what he could become if he just gives himself the chance.

Kat steps out onto the porch, her smile warm and familiar, pulling me back to the present. She's been my rock through all of this, understanding without judgment, supporting without pushing. The sunlight catches in her hair, turning ordinary brown into a tapestry of amber and gold.

"You okay?" she asks, her voice soft but grounded. Her eyes—those eyes that see through every wall I've ever built—search mine with quiet concern.

I nod, sliding an arm around her waist, drawing strength from the solid warmth of her.

"Yeah," I say, and for the first time in a long time, I mean it.

Life doesn't always go the way we plan. It's messy, unpredictable, and downright unfair at times. But it's also beautiful in its chaos. And if there's one thing I've learned, it's that sometimes, the hardest roads lead to the most unexpected places.

I'm lost in these thoughts when my phone buzzes on the counter. I glance at the screen, and my stomach tightens, a familiar knot of dread and anticipation.

It's from Danny, the one guy I trust with my life and probably one of the only cops who refuses to be bought in this town.

Danny
Dead end.

I reread the message like it might change if I stare long enough, like the truth I'm looking for might suddenly appear between the lines.

A hit-and-run. That's all we know officially.

No license plate, no witnesses, just the aftermath. It's been months, and still no answers. Danny's been keeping tabs on it for me—or maybe for himself, since he hates loose ends almost as much as I do. But every lead we've chased has fizzled out like smoke in the wind. And yet, something doesn't sit right.

Call it instinct or experience, but I can't shake the feeling that this wasn't random. The timing, the location—it all fits too neatly for coincidence, but the evidence doesn't connect. Not yet, anyway.

But I've got time.

And if there's one thing I'm good at, it's being patient. Because some truths take time to surface, and some secrets need to be dragged into the light.

And I plan to do exactly that.

For Nate. For Nora.

It's what family does.

Kat steps closer to me, her smile lighting up every fiber of my being.

She leans in and kisses me with the kind of familiarity that still makes my heart skip.

"You sure you're okay?" she asks, her voice laced with that gentle concern that's become her trademark.

"I definitely am now," I say, placing a soft kiss atop her head. "Have you heard from Nora and Ol? They both settled?"

Kat beams, her eyes bright with maternal pride.

"Nora sent me pictures yesterday of her and Camilla on the London Eye. She looks happy." Her voice softens with wonder. "And Ol and Mia may have found an apartment together. God, when did my babies become full grown adults?"

"They'll forever be babies in your eyes, even when they're forty and have kids of their own," I smile, watching the emotions play across her face.

"Oh don't say that. I'm not ready to be a grandma yet." She laughs, but there's a wistfulness there that makes me want to hold her tighter.

Kat leans against the railing, her expression softening.

"So," she begins, tucking a strand of hair behind her ear, a gesture I've come to recognize as her way of preparing to share news, "I need to head back to Boston for a day or two. Ollie needs help packing up the house. I'm flying out this afternoon. Lydia's picking me up in fifteen minutes and dropping me at the airport."

I arch a brow, already missing her. "You sure you don't need backup?"

She smirks, that playful glint in her eye that first made me fall for her. "I think I can handle a few boxes, Nick." Then, her tone shifts, a little more tentative. "But, I do need a favor."

"Name it." No hesitation. Never with her.

"The wreckers called," she says, a shadow crossing her face so quickly I almost miss it. "They still have a few items from the car they managed to salvage. Not sure what, but they called before. Can you swing by and pick it up?"

"Of course." My response is immediate, though my mind flickers back to the twisted metal of Nora's car, to the night that changed everything.

"Thank you." She leans in for another kiss, this one softer, full of gratitude. "I don't know what I'd do without you."

"Well," I tease as she tries to pull away, wrapping another arm around her waist, feeling the curve of her against me, "you'll never have to wonder." I kiss her deeply, trying to memorize the moment. "Have a safe flight. Call me when you get there."

She throws me a wink before heading out the door, leaving the scent of her perfume lingering in the air like a promise.

Before I can dwell too much on what the wreckers might have found, my phone rings and Jay's name lights up the screen.

"Hey, boss."

Jay's been working for me at Sonder for a month or so now, ever since Nate left for Europe. I offered him the job partly because I needed someone to fill the gap, but mostly because I saw a kid who needed an opportunity and a second chance.

Credit to the kid, he's been looking and sounding more put together than I've ever seen him. Like he's finally finding his footing in the world. I think the night of Nate's overdose scared Jay straight. He doesn't talk about it much, but I've noticed the changes: showing up on time, staying out of trouble, even offering to take extra shifts. Sometimes the wake-up calls we need come in the hardest ways.

"How's it going?" I ask, already hearing the nervous energy in his voice.

"Good. Kinda," he says, voice pitching higher in that way it does when he's about to confess something.

Before I can worry, Jay starts rambling in that endearing way of his.

"But, uh, I think I broke the dishwasher. Just thought I'd let you know. I'm happy to pay for the damages. I think I used the wrong detergent or some shit. It's leaking and making weird ass noises. Shit. Fuck. I didn't know—"

"Jay, relax," I cut him off gently. "It's fine. I'll swing by tomorrow and check it out. It's probably just a loose valve. Don't worry about it." I've learned sometimes the best way to help someone grow is to show them that mistakes aren't the end of the world.

Jay lets out a breath, as if he's been holding it the entire time. "Thank fuck. I did not want to wash these glasses by hand for the next month."

I laugh, surprised by how fond I've grown of the kid. "Anything else you're concerned about?"

"That's all boss."

"Jay, you know you can just call me Nick, yeah?"

"Boss sounds more badass. Not that your name sucks or anything. It's just—You know what, you're a busy man, so I'm just going to shut up and go finish polishing glasses. See ya round, boss."

He hangs up, and I shake my head with a smile. Some things never change, and maybe they shouldn't. Sometimes it's the small moments—a nervous phone call, a kid trying his best—that remind you why you do what you do.

And maybe that's what it's all about: being there, staying steady, giving people the chance to become who they're meant to be. Even if sometimes that means letting them go find themselves first. A sense of pride settles in my chest.

People can change.

It just takes the right moment—or the right push.

THE YARD SMELLS LIKE MOTOR OIL AND RUST, THE KIND OF HEAVY industrial scent that seeps into your clothes and lingers for days. As I step into the main office of the wreckers, the overhead fluorescent lights buzz faintly, casting everything in a sickly pale glow. Mikey's behind the counter, talking to another guy I don't recognize—a blonde kid with a crooked name tag that reads Dillon.

Their conversation dies mid-sentence when the door creaks open, but before I can step fully inside, an older woman brushes past me with enough force to make me step back.

"Sorry, ma'am," I say reflexively, but she doesn't acknowledge my existence.

She's dressed like she walked straight out of some high-end department store catalog—designer everything, from her perfectly coiffed hair to her imported leather shoes. She carries herself with that particular kind of entitled grace that comes from old money and older secrets. Her face might've been stunning thirty years ago, but now it's all harsh angles and expensive makeup trying to mask the march of time. She spares me a sideways glance that could freeze hell over before sweeping past me through the door.

"Good day to you too," I mutter under my breath, stepping fully inside. The tension in the room is thick enough to cut with a knife.

Mikey and Dillon exchange a look that sets off every alarm bell in my head. Mikey looks startled, like someone just caught him in a lie. The other guy—Dillon—leans in close to Mikey and mutters something I can't quite catch, but I don't miss the sharp glance he shoots at the door the woman just left through.

"She paid how much to get rid of it?" Mikey whispers, his voice low but still carrying in the quiet office.

I freeze, my hand hovering over the counter as my ears prick up. Twenty years of reading people tells me something's off here.

"Shut up, man," Dillon hisses, his eyes darting to me like a guilty conscience.

I pretend I didn't hear a thing, carefully arranging my face into something neutral as I approach the counter. Years of business negotiations have taught me when to play dumb.

"Mikey," I say, nodding in greeting. "I'm here to pick up some belongings from the Jeep you guys towed in." The words taste bitter in my mouth, remembering why I'm here.

Mikey straightens up, visibly relieved to focus on something else.

"Yo, Nick. Yeah, yeah, I heard about that. Is she—uh, the girl, I mean—is she okay?"

"She's recovering," I say simply, keeping my tone even while something darker stirs in my gut.

Dillon mutters something about grabbing the box and heads toward the back, his shoulders tense. As he disappears, I lean casually against the counter, watching Mikey fidget like a man with too many secrets.

"What was a lady like that doing in a place like this?" I ask, my voice deliberately light but pointed.

Mikey glances toward the door, then back at me, hesitating. He knows me well enough to know I don't ask questions without a reason. Finally, he lets out a breath, leaning in like he's about to share something he shouldn't.

"She's been in here a few times this week," he says, his voice low and conspiratorial. "A couple of banged-up cars came through, but none of 'em were like the one she wanted to buy back."

My eyebrows lift slightly, interest piqued. "Why'd she want to buy it back if it's at the wreckers?"

Mikey starts scratching the back of his neck nervously. "Don't know. Woman has got enough money to buy a fleet of 'em if she wanted, but instead, she had Dillon get rid of it."

I feel the air shift, tension crackling like static electricity before a storm.

"She wanted to get rid of it, even though it's ended up here?"

"Dude, I don't know. You know the people here, their money does the talking so you just shut up and don't ask questions," Mikey replies, shrugging. "But she paid enough to make it disappear, so Dillon handled it."

My heart starts to hammer as the pieces start sliding into place like tumblers in a lock.

"What kind of car was it?"

"A black Porsche," Mikey says without hesitation. "Looked damn near new, too. These people don't have any concept of money."

A black Porsche.

A wealthy woman trying to erase its existence.

Recent damage.

My stomach churns as the threads of logic twist tighter, forming a picture I've been trying to see for months. Sometimes the truth doesn't hit you all at once—it creeps up slowly, piece by piece, until you can't ignore it anymore.

And this truth?

It's been hiding in plain sight all along.

Before I can press further, Dillon returns, dropping a dusty cardboard box on the counter with a dull thud.

"Here you go," he says, avoiding eye contact like a man with too many secrets.

I glance at the box but don't move to touch it. My mind's already racing ahead, connecting dots I've been staring at for months.

"Thanks," I say, sliding Dillon a twenty-dollar bill. He pockets it and disappears into the shadows of the yard, the gravel crunching under his boots.

I'm about to walk out the door myself when something makes me stop. Some instinct that's saved my skin more times than I can count. I turn to Mikey one last time.

"Do you know what that woman's name was?"

Mikey looks up from the paperwork on the counter, his expression flickering with uncertainty.

"Uhh… it starts with M. Mary? Mara? The address she put down was for the Cottswold, you know that flashy manor they rent out for the summer?" His words hang in the air like smoke.

I know the one.

I also have a feeling I know exactly who the woman is now.

Back in my car, I pull out my phone to do a quick search. The results load, and my blood runs cold as the name hits me like a physical blow. The pieces slot together with a terrible clarity that makes my stomach turn.

Moira Sullivan.

In that moment, everything crystallizes. The black Porsche. The hit-and-run. The desperate cover-up. It all leads back to one person—Scott Sullivan. The coward who left Nora bleeding out on that road, and if it hadn't been for Nate finding her when he did… The thought alone makes my hands shake with rage.

And now his mother's here, doing what she's probably done his entire life—cleaning up his messes, erasing his mistakes, making sure her precious son never has to face the consequences of his actions.

The pieces fit together like a jigsaw puzzle from hell: Scott behind the wheel, probably drunk or high. And instead of calling for help, he ran. Like the worthless coward he's always been.

Now here's his mother, carefully erasing the evidence with the same precision she's probably used his whole life.

Make it disappear.

Let money solve the problem, like always.

I grip the steering wheel until my knuckles turn white, memories flooding back. Nate blamed himself for all of this. But it was his father. Just like in every instance in Nate's life, Scott was at the helm of the pain and suffering.

My phone feels heavy in my hand as I dial Danny's number, rage burning cold and steady in my chest.

"I think I've got something." I watch Mikey and Dillon through the office window, their heads bent close in another hushed conversation. "And Danny? I think this goes deeper than we thought. Much deeper."

I start the engine, my mind already racing ahead. The truth about that night is finally surfacing, and when it does, Scott Sullivan is going to learn that some accidents have consequences that even his family's money can't make disappear.

I pull out onto the main road, the setting sun painting the sky blood red. In my rearview mirror, the wrecking yard disappears into shadows, taking its secrets with it.

But not for long.

Because here's the thing about secrets in a town like Eden: they never stay buried forever.

And when this one comes to light, it's going to burn everything in its path.

Starting with the Sullivans.

ACKNOWLEDGMENTS

They say stories find their storytellers. Mine found me at five, scribbling against blank sheets of paper in the backyard. Dad would ask Mum what the hell a five-year-old could be writing about for hours, and she'd just shrug and say, "*Who knows? But let her go.*"

That was probably the first time anyone acknowledged I was a story-teller at heart, without actually realizing it.

Fast forward to twenty-nine-year-old me, squished in the backseat of a car in rural India, heading to the airport with my ancient playlist pumping through my headphones—the same playlist that's existed since I was fifteen, just like Nate and Nora's story. I started typing away in my Notes app like a woman possessed. When my best friend Elisha, leaned over and asked what I was up to, I blurted out, "*I think I'm going to write my first book by the end of the year.*"

She just smiled and said, "*Of course you are. That doesn't surprise me one bit.*" In that moment, something clicked—like a small, familiar voice inside me (the same one that had been with me since I was five) whis-pered *"finally!"* with the excitement of a child who'd been waiting far too long for the grown-up to catch up.

Music has always been my creative catalyst—as it is for Nate. A song hits, and boom, my brain explodes with possibilities. The right melody can crack me open, revealing stories that have been patiently waiting in the darkness. Each chord progression unlocks something deep within, revealing the soundtrack to life itself—our lives, fictional lives, lives I've only dreamed of living. It's in these moments that five-year-old Mon takes the wheel, dancing through my thoughts with unbridled imagina-tion, reminding me how to see the world through her eyes again. With an open sense of curiosity and wonder.

My mum waited over fifteen years for this book to exist, checking in every so often with that knowing look in her eyes. But fate choreographs to its own rhythm, doesn't it? Somewhere in my twenties, between heartbreaks and triumphs, I learned to surrender to life's perfect timing. To trust that stories reveal themselves exactly when they're meant to. To listen when little Mon would tug at my consciousness, reminding me of the promises I'd made to her about the stories we would tell.

At thirty, writing this book became a love letter to existence itself—to every messy, beautiful, chaotic moment that led me here. It became a conversation between my adult self and little Mon, who has always been my most honest critic and fiercest champion.

To my parents—who never once doubted me, even when my dreams seemed absolutely ludicrous—who never once said "get a real job" when I was chasing the impossible. Thank you for letting me navigate my own path while silently standing guard, ready whenever I needed a hand to hold. Your quiet faith in me has been my greatest inheritance.

To Elisha—for listening to my voice notes at ungodly hours and reading drafts so rough they'd give you paper cuts. You're the friend who says *"hell yeah you can"* when I'm sure I can't. You've been more than a cheerleader; you've been the one to always remind me who I am and what I'm capable of doing whenever I felt like I was drifting.

To Mez—my morning coffee buddy for nearly a decade, watching me type away while the caffeine kicked in. You witnessed the daily grind, the moments of doubt, the breakthroughs that had me bouncing in my seat. Thanks for telling me to chase the high of doing what makes me feel alive, even when it meant I was talking about fictional people like they were real. Because to me, they were.

To Ange and Jake—you creative geniuses took the mess in my head and made it visually beautiful. From the stunning front cover to those impromptu content photoshoots where we laughed until we cried. How fortunate I am that my best friends could help me see what lived only in my mind, giving shape and color to my wildest imaginings.

To Ana—who spent Sunday mornings going for walks, listening to me rant about plot twists and fictional characters. Those rants helped spark new ideas from time to time. Your silent support in the background means more to me than you'll ever know.

To my Booktok family—you breathed life into Nate and Nora's world and created the tidal wave that carried their story forward when I was too afraid to believe in it myself. Your comments, messages, and unwavering enthusiasm turned my private daydream into something real. Whatever heights this reaches, the foundation was built by your belief in these characters and their story.

And to everyone else who put up with my *"sorry, can't make it, I'm writing"* texts and my spaced-out expressions at dinner or events because I was mentally rewriting a scene—thank you for not giving up on me. Being friends with a writer when they're in the zone is like having a friend who's dating someone you never get to meet. You shared me with characters who demanded all my attention, and you did it with grace. While loving a creative spirit requires a special kind of understanding, know that your support never went unnoticed—it was the safety net that let me fly.

And finally to five-year-old Mon—we did it, kid. Those words scribbled against blank pieces of paper became chapters bound between covers. All those hours spent daydreaming weren't wasted after all. Thank you for never leaving my side, for being that persistent voice in my head that wouldn't let me forget our promise. For all the times you whispered *"remember me"* when adult life threatened to drown out your voice. I hope the story we've told makes you proud.

This one's for you—the little girl who never stopped believing in magic, even when the world tried to tell her otherwise. I hear you now, louder than ever.

ABOUT THE AUTHOR

Monique Medved is an Australian emerging author who's busy making her mark on the contemporary romance scene—one swoony meet-cute at a time. She writes stories with emotional depth about following your gut and figuring life out along the way (spoiler alert: she's still very much figuring it out herself). Her books will more than likely have you crying on public transport, so consider yourself warned.

If you don't want to miss her next book drop, follow her on socials.

Printed in Great Britain
by Amazon

63331562R00333